Cle SF-SS v.2
Clement, Hal,
The essential Hal Clement
$ 25.00

1st ed.

THE ESSENTIAL HAL CLEMENT

Volume 2

MUSIC OF MANY SPHERES

THE ESSENTIAL HAL CLEMENT

Volume 2
MUSIC OF MANY SPHERES

Hal Clement

edited by Mark L. Olson and Anthony R. Lewis

The NESFA Press
Post Office Box 809
Framingham, MA 01701
2000

FIRST EDITION, February 2000

International Standard Book Number:
1-886778-07-8

Acknowledgments

The introduction by Ben Bova is original to this volume.

"Cold Front" *Astounding Science Fiction,* July 1946

"Proof" *Astounding Science Fiction,* June 1942

"Raindrop" *Worlds of IF,* May 1965

"Longline" *Faster Than Light,* ed by Jack Dann, Harper & Row, 1976

"Planetfall" as "Planet for Plunder," *Satellite Science Fiction,* February 1957

"Sun Spot" *Astounding Science Fiction,* November 1960

"The Mechanic" *Analog,* September 1966

"Attitude" *Astounding Science Fiction,* September 1943

"Halo" *Galaxy Science Fiction,* October 1952

"Impediment" *Astounding Science Fiction,* August 1942

"Technical Error" *Astounding Science Fiction,* January 1944

"Bulge" *Worlds of IF,* September 1968

"Probability Zero: Avenue of Escape" *Astounding Science Fiction,* November 1942

"Status Symbol" *Intuit,* NESFA Press, 1987

"The Logical Life" *Stellar 1,* ed by Judy-Lynn del Rey, Ballantine Books, 1974

"Stuck with It" *Stellar 2,* ed by Judy-Lynn del Rey, Ballantine Books, 1976

"Uncommon Sense" *Astounding Science Fiction,* September 1945

All stories appear by permission of the author.

Contents

HAL CLEMENT
by Ben Bova

Multiple-choice question:
Hal Clement is:
(a) The dean of "hard" science fiction writers.
(b) A great teacher.
(c) One of the finest gentlemen of our time.
(d) An enthusiastic convention-goer.

And the answer is...(e) all of the above.

Those who know Hal Clement only through the stories he's written would undoubtedly pick (a); the really observant ones would add (b) as well, because virtually every one of the stories and novels that Hal has written offers wonderful lessons in planetary physics, chemistry, astronomy, and exobiology.

Anyone who's had the pleasure of attending one of the many science fiction conventions that Hal Clement frequents would certainly answer (c) and (d), even without knowing anything else about him. He is a cheerful and helpful guest at many cons, and always an asset to a panel discussion.

At heart Hal Clement is a teacher—the kind of teacher that you wish you had been favored with in high school. His real name is Harry Clement Stubbs, and he actually spent much of his adult life teaching science at Milton Academy, a private secondary school in Massachusetts. Lucky students! With his easy smile and pleasant demeanor, Hal puts you at ease even when he's discussing arcane subjects such as orbital dynamics or the high-pressure chemistry of volatile compounds. He has the gift for making science come alive, the knack for showing how truly variegated and wonder-full this universe can be.

11

I'm not saying that Hal writes his stories for the purpose of teaching science; the teaching (and learning, on the part of the reader) are just wonderful bonuses to the enjoyment of his work. Since his first short story, "Proof," was published in *Astounding Science Fiction* magazine in 1942, Hal has continuously amazed and enlightened us with good, strong, solid stories that deal with real science in strange, exotic and alien settings. His novels, such as *Needle, Iceworld, Mission of Gravity,* and *Close to Critical* have become classics in the science fiction field.

It's not strange that writing science fiction and teaching science are so intertwined in him. After all, Hugo Gernsback, the founder of the world's first science fiction magazine, *Amazing Stories,* saw science fiction as a way of teaching science to youngsters in an era where most teenagers did not finish grade school. Today, of course, almost every American youngster graduates high school and most go on to college—but they can still learn more about science from Hal Clement's stories than they are taught in their classrooms. And enjoy it far more!

I remember my own first readings of his early novels, and how they opened my eyes to the strange and beautiful possibilities of other worlds in space. To me, science fiction was a far better "classroom" than regular school classes, particularly because good science fiction stories—such as Hal Clement's—skipped all the boring fundamentals and showed how exhilarating science can be when you're out in the wild and wonderful universe. With that kind of excitement for a spur, going back and learning the fundamentals was easy. Motivation is the key.

Today, "hard" science fiction has fallen somewhat out of popular favor. There is the mistaken idea that science-based stories can't be interesting or exciting. Undoubtedly such a wrong-headed notion was born in the impoverished minds of people who never had the benefit of attending any of Hal's classes or reading his marvelous stories.

Einstein once said that the most incredible thing about the universe is that it is understandable. Hal Clement's fiction is a monument to that fundamental idea: the human mind can understand strange alien worlds and even strange alien creatures. That is the underlying message of Hal Clement's work. It is the same rock-bottom optimistic faith that makes science work: we can understand anything, given enough time and effort.

Hal Clement's fiction is usually based on a "thought experiment": that is, he creates stories to dramatize scientific ideas. What would it be like to be on a truly massive planet, where the gravity is ten or a hundred times heavier than here on Earth? How can you navigate by the stars when you're on the Moon, when the Moon's north pole does not point to the

North Star? How can an alien from a world that is literally hotter than hell survive on an "Iceworld" such as Earth?

The word "gentleman" might have been coined for Hal. He is a truly kind and gentle person who gives unsparingly of his time and energy at science fiction conventions—when he's not writing or painting. Oh yes, he is a gifted painter, as well. For his artwork he uses still another name, George Richard. He could illustrate his own stories, and who better?

I was enjoying Hal Clement's fiction years before I met him, and found myself entranced at his depictions of strange and exotic creatures and even stranger and more exotic worlds—all carefully based on known physics and chemistry. I was captivated by his work. This is what science fiction is all about! Today, nearly six decades after his first stories saw print, he is still producing quality work, still showing how accurate science and an insightful imagination can combine to yield stories that stir that ol' sense of wonder.

Although his first fiction was published while he was still an undergraduate student at Harvard, World War II interrupted Hal's career. During the war years Hal flew a B-24 bomber as the U.S. Eighth Air Force battled Nazi Germany's Luftwaffe for control of the skies over Europe. He once told me, though, that his most hazardous duty came at the end of the war, when his squadron flew a low-level, tight-formation mission over the Netherlands to drop food supplies to the starving Dutch civilian population. His main job on that flight was to watch the wingtip of the plane flying beside his, to make sure they didn't collide.

Years later, when the German city of Heidelberg hosted the World Science Fiction Convention, Hal was recognized and immediately swamped by eager German fans. "Have you ever been to Heidelberg before?" a student asked. Ever the gentleman, Hal replied honestly, "No, but I've been within a few miles of here." In a B-24 loaded with bombs, of course.

A gentleman and a scholar, that's Hal Clement. He is also one of the best science-fiction writers ever to spin a tale of faraway worlds and exotic creatures. Hal Clement is to "hard" science fiction as John Glenn is to space flight, or Fred Astaire is to tap dancing, or John Philip Sousa is to march music, or...well, you get the picture.

To put it another way, "Science fiction 'R Hal Clement." And we're all better off for it.

Cold Front

Astounding, July 1946

Master salesman Alf Vickers walked slowly along the beach behind his companion, and pondered. He was never quite sure how to begin his talks. If it had been a question of selling, alone, he would have had no worries, even though it was necessary to employ careful reasoning rather than emotional high pressure when one was not too well acquainted with the emotional build up of an alien race; but when the selling had to be done to an entire people, and there was a moral certainty of reprimand and perhaps of disrating if the Federation Government caught him, he began to think of the consequences of his errors, before he made them.

The people, at least, were a peaceful seeming lot for such a rugged planet; that was some relief. The frowning, almost sheer six thousand feet of Observatory Hill, at whose foot he now stood, had made him think uncomfortably of the wilder mountain tribes of history and legend on Earth. Big as they were, he reflected, gazing at the specimen walking ahead of him, the few he had met were almost painfully polite. It had made easy the task of revealing nothing of himself or his mission until he had acquired a good control of their language; but courteous or not, Vickers felt that the explanation could not be put off much longer.

Serrnak Deg, who had devoted so much time to teaching his speech to the Earthman, was plainly curious; and there was only one plausible reason for his insisting that morning that they drive alone to the beach at the foot of the mountain. Plainly, he was willing to keep Vickers' secrets from his compatriots if Vickers so wished; but he had definite intentions of learning them himself.

Vickers braced himself as Deg stopped walking and turned to face him. As the man stopped beside him, the Heklan began to talk.

"I have asked you no questions since you first intimated a desire not to answer them. I have taken you on trust, on what seemed to me a thin excuse—that you feared the results of possible misunderstanding caused

15

by your ignorance of our language. I think my expenditure of time and effort merits some reward in the shape of satisfied curiosity."

"The excuse was not thin," replied Vickers in the Heklan language. "More than one man in my position has suffered injury or death as a result of just such misunderstandings. It is important that you get no false ideas from me about my people, the world from which I come, and the other races and worlds which are depending on my success. It is my intention to tell not only you, but eventually all your people, my full story; but I am depending on you for assurance that I can make myself clear, and I also want to hear your impression of what I say before it is transmitted to the rest of the planet or to that part of it with which you are on friendly terms."

He stopped to gather his thoughts. The surroundings were not quite what he would have chosen—a rocky beach at the foot of a nearly perpendicular cliff, pounded by breakers from an ocean that was tinted a curiously disconcerting pink. The sky was a slightly deeper shade, and suspended in it was the hardly visible disk of a giant red sun.

The audience would have been more disconcerting than the environment, to one less accustomed than Vickers to nonhuman beings. Serrnak Deg had no need of the heavy jacket with which Vickers warded off the stiff breeze. He was protected by a layer of fat which must have accounted for half of his weight; and the fur that covered his body was thick enough to hide the straps supporting his only garment—a pair of trunks whose primary function was to contain pockets. His face, with its enormous eyeballs and almost nonexistent nose, reminded Vickers of a spectral tarsier; but the well-developed skull behind the grotesque features had already shown itself to contain a keen brain.

"One of our mapping vessels noted some time ago that this planet was inhabited by intelligent creatures," Vickers went on. "There is a standard procedure in such cases. We learned long ago not to make immediate, open contact with the bulk of the world's population. It is a mathematical certainty that there will be enough objection to contact with aliens, to result in violence."

"I find that hard to believe," interjected Serrnak. "Why should there be objection?"

The Earthman creased his brows and tried to remember Deg's word for "superstition," but the concept had never arisen in their conversation.

"There have been many reasons," he finally answered. "The one that leaps to my mind I am still unable to express in your language. I am afraid you will have to be content with my assurance that it is so. For that reason, a single agent is always sent to contact the smallest practicable group of individuals, to become acquainted with them and through them with their people, and with their help to accustom the race gradually to the existence, appearance, and company of natives of other worlds. Make no mistake; it is a delicate task, and an error can have really ghastly results. I hope you don't find that out first hand."

"I don't know about your business, but errors can be pretty serious in mine," said Deg. "What consequence, other than this planet's failure to join the organization you refer to as 'We,' can arise from mistakes of yours? I take it that you are the agent responsible for us."

"I am; I'm sorry if I am not giving my explanations in proper order. It is my business to convince you and your fellows at this place that the Federation can do your people untold good, and to enlist your help in persuading your race, or at least your nation, to the same effect."

"Why should persuasion be necessary?" asked Serrnak. "It seems obvious that good would result from such an action. Contact between groups living on different parts of this one world has always produced beneficial exchanges of ideas and natural products, and I should imagine that this would be even more true of interplanetary commerce. Some planets, I suppose, would have more than enough metals, for example— that occurred to me because that is one of our most serious lacks; and certainly, if you have solved the secret of interstellar travel, there is much we can learn from you. Do you really mean to imply that some races have actually refused to benefit by such a chance?"

Vickers nodded solemnly.

"Too many," he said. "A certain suspicion of strangers, a doubt as to our intentions, is natural of course. We expect and allow for it; our work is to allay it, and prove that we have no intention of dealing unfairly with anybody. Your attitude is encouraging; I hope a majority of your people share it. Do you suppose they will, Deg?"

The answer was slow and hesitant.

"I can't be sure—naturally. I have already given you my feelings on the matter, but I cannot answer for everyone. I will test my coworkers here, as I suppose you want me to, bearing your warnings carefully in mind. Will that be satisfactory?"

"That will be excellent. I can't find the words to thank you, but I'll try to give any help in my power if you have undesirable reactions. I admit I have worried a good deal about the outcome of this meeting; one can never be sure of having chosen the right person for the first advances."

Deg nodded.

"I understand why you wanted privacy as much as possible for our conversations. You chose a good place to land on this world; we are about as isolated a group as you could have found, except perhaps for the stations in the far interior of this continent. The cities are mostly located in the larger islands of the equatorial zone—I suppose you observed that, before landing. If I may ask, how did you find this station? It is not particularly easy to mark from the air, according to my experience."

"It was found by accident, on a photograph," replied Vickers. "We decided that, if it were not deserted, it should prove a good place to start operations. We were not sure of its purpose; I still don't know what you do here, but it had the desired isolation, and the presence of someone with authority seemed probable. Are you in very close touch with any of the cities?"

"We have to be. This is a weather station, and is tied into a tight communication network linking all the observatories on this continent with one of the cities. The constant flow of reports is received there, and integrated into a master weather map of the continent; and an intercity net further combines these maps into a world map in one of the largest population centers. The information and world forecasts are there made available to any who have need of them—including the original stations; we require the total picture for long-range local forecasting. All the exact sciences have a similar network for co-ordination and exchange of information."

"That sounds efficient," remarked Vickers. "We have similar organization on and between the worlds of the Union. There is a great deal of written information on such matters in my ship; I shall be glad to translate for you, any time you care to come aboard. The more you understand about our civilization, the better."

"I shall take advantage of that offer presently," returned Deg. "At the moment, I fear I have ignored my duties too long. There will be several hours' observation records in my office, and one of the computing machines has been behaving suspiciously. If it goes out altogether it may be more than our technician can handle, and I'd hate the thought of doing much of that computation manually. Would you care to visit my office? I can show you something of the station on the way, and you can return the favor when I visit your ship."

Vickers had been hoping for such an offer. He had not wanted to make the suggestion himself, but up to now he had acquired very little idea of the state of technical advancement of these people. A look at any sort of laboratory would give him a good idea of their science in general, for no field of knowledge progresses far without corresponding development in the others. He gladly accepted Serrnak's offer.

They had been walking as they conversed, toward the point where the giant breakers flung themselves against the stone rampart of the lowest terrace. Now the meteorologist turned back toward the hill, the Earthman following. Parked against the face of the cliff was Deg's car, a four-wheeled vehicle with enormous balloon tires. Its owner vaulted easily over the side into the driver's seat; Vickers clambered in more slowly, hampered by the sixty pounds that Hekla's gravity added to his normal weight.

Deg set the car in motion, picking his way between rockfalls. Vickers constantly expected to see the tires cut through by the sharp-edged fragments of slate littering the way, but the tough treads remained intact; and presently the stones disappeared, as the mountain was left behind. After a quarter of an hour, Deg was able to turn inland, and a little later there began to be signs of a narrow road, which led in a rather steep climb back toward the hill. Here they were able to put on more speed, although Deg was bothered part of the time by the sun shining in his eyes. Vickers was able to look directly at the hazy, mottled crimson disk without much discomfort.

About a quarter of the way up, the road skirted a small pocket in the hillside, covering perhaps a quarter of an acre. It was covered with regular rows of purplish vegetation, and a small, low-roofed stone building stood between it and the road. Deg stopped the car and entered the building, indicating that Vickers should wait. The Earthman heard conversation through the open door, but was unable to distinguish any words. The Heklan emerged after a moment, and the ride continued. Vickers had seen several of the little gardens on the way down the mountain, but Deg did not offer to explain them on either trip.

The rest of the drive was uneventful, and the car presently emerged from the road—now almost a tunnel—onto a nearly flat space two or three hundred yards across, beyond which the hill rose sharply to its real summit two hundred feet above. At the base of this final peak, an opening fifty yards across and half as high led into the hill; and from the opening, and equally wide, a paved, level strip ran across the flat space to its very edge. Vickers had assumed this to be a landing runway for aircraft; and the silvery hull of his own little ship lay now to one side of it.

The car drove straight on into the cavern, through it, and into a smaller chamber beyond, in which a number of the vehicles were parked. Leaving the vehicle here, the men proceeded through two narrow hallways. Along both sides of the second were a number of doors; Deg opened one of these, to reveal an elevator, into which he motioned the Earthman. It was similar to the terrestrial elevator, controlled by the passenger. Vickers counted the buttons, trying to get some idea of the extent of the station. There were forty-five of them, indicating that there were at least that many levels to the observatory.

Deg touched one of the highest buttons with the horny tip of a finger, and they were carried smoothly upwards. Vickers could not tell the number of levels they passed, but the ride was comparatively short. They emerged directly into a large room, which Deg described as the local integration and prediction laboratory.

It was about one hundred feet square. Its most prominent feature was a set of six five-foot globes, spaced equally along one wall, and representing the first maps Vickers had seen of Hekla. Each was covered with a complicated network of lines and symbols; the Earthman assumed that these were the equivalents of the isobars, fronts, cloud symbols and other data with which meteorologists habitually decorate their work. They meant little to Vickers. He was able to tell, from his recollection of the planet's surface as viewed from space, that the deep purple areas represented water, while land was white. The globes were evidently of some translucent material like frosted glass, and were lighted from within.

At the base of each globe was a desk, at which an operator sat. Some were working small computing machines; others were busy with the incomprehensible diagrams and graphs of their profession. On the rest of the floor space were a number of larger computers, some manned and active, others deserted. Across the room from the globes four more of the machines, far larger and more complex than their fellows, were set at the four sides of a large table whose top was a map, evidently of the region centering about the observatory, set up and lighted in similar fashion to the world maps. The operators of these calculators were grouped about the keyboard nearest to Vickers and Deg; and with a word of apology, the Heklan stepped over to them, to listen to their conversation.

Vickers waited for him, gazing around at the ordered efficiency represented in the activity of the laboratory. It pleased him; everything he saw bespoke a high culture, considerable progress in the physical sciences, mechanical skill, and an apparent tendency toward international co-operation—a smoothly working planet-wide weather system could scarcely be maintained in the face of strained international relationships. He also noted an apparent lack of metal; it was used only where necessary, as in electric conductors. Wood and synthetics were used almost entirely.

He was not too surprised; he had known of the low density of the planet before leaving the big interstellar flyer which had brought him and his smaller ship to the neighborhood of R Coronae. Hekla had nearly twice the diameter of Earth, but its surface gravity was only forty percent higher. The forty percent, he reflected, was plenty; his legs were aching perpetually, and he had been getting—and needing—twelve hours' sleep out of twenty-four. Hekla's thirty-two-hour day complicated his schedule; day or night, he had to sleep after twelve or fourteen hours of activity. The Heklans, even when the proportionate length of their day was considered, got along with unbelievably little rest; Deg, Vickers had learned, counted on four to five hours of sleep, which he got as soon after sunset as his work permitted.

Vickers' reflections were interrupted by Serrnak's return.

"I am very sorry," the Heklan said, "but I cannot show you more of our station at the moment. The main integrator is definitely making mistakes, and I shall have to help carry out alternate procedure with the smaller machines until the technical section can correct the trouble. I shall send someone to show you the way back to your ship, unless you wish to do something else until I can rejoin you."

"I will return to the ship, for a while at least," replied Vickers. "I can find my own way, if you will tell me the level at which I should stop the elevator. I saw no means of telling the number of the floor from which we started."

"The flight ramp and road exit are on the thirtieth level," Deg informed him. "The control buttons in the cage are in order. I regret being so abrupt, but there is nothing else to be done. I will come to your ship when I am again free."

Vickers nodded, touched Serrnak's hand in the standard Heklan gesture of farewell, and entered the elevator. It was lit by a source which would have reminded the Earthman of an old carbon filament bulb, if he had ever seen such a thing, but the reddish glow was sufficient to enable him to count off thirty buttons. He pressed the thirtieth, and felt the cage sink slowly downwards. The ride, as before, was brief, and the door opened automatically at its termination.

He stepped into the corridor, turned right—and stopped short. The hallway should have extended for twenty yards and been crossed by another at that point. Instead, only a few paces from the elevator it opened directly into a room almost as large as the integration laboratory above. Electrical equipment, as unfamiliar as any other scientific apparatus to Vickers, crowded the floor; and among the installations sat or stood fully a score of Heklans, all apparently busily occupied. Vickers stood gazing into the chamber for several moments, until one of the workers chanced to glance up. His big eyes blinked once; then he took a pair of earphones from his head, rose from his seat, and approached the Earthman.

"Your ship is out on the landing ramp, which is on the thirtieth level," he said. "Can I help you in locating it?"

"I thought I had reached the thirtieth level," replied Vickers. "Serrnak Deg told me that the elevator buttons were in order, and I certainly pressed the thirtieth." The Heklan looked steadily at him for several seconds, and blinked once more. Then he nodded his head violently.

"I think I see what must have happened," he said. "You counted upward from the bottom of the panel. You are now on the sixteenth of the forty-five levels. The station was dug downwards from the top of the mountain, and it was natural to number in that direction. Do your people normally number from the ground up?"

"Yes, we do, on buildings above ground level; but if I had stopped to recall that this place is underground I should at least have asked Deg whether you counted up or down. It is a silly error on my part. Now that I am here, however, do you mind my seeing your department? I will try to keep out of the way of any activity."

The big eyes blinked again, as their owner hesitated. Vickers decided that the expression on the grotesque face denoted discomfort.

"I dislike to appear discourteous," the answer finally came, "but the trouble in the computing department has thrown a heavy load on us. We are all extremely busy, so that I can neither guide you around our section myself, nor provide another to do so. Some of the equipment is too dangerous to permit your examining it unattended. I am extremely sorry, but there is nothing I can do to grant your request. Do you think you can find the way back to your ship from here? If not, I can show you to the landing stage."

He started to move toward the elevator before Vickers could answer him; but the Earthman declined the offer of guidance. The Heklan pointed out the proper button—they were labeled in Heklan characters, but the numbers happened not to stand out very clearly to blue-sensitive eyes—and returned to the chamber of electrical devices, leaving an elevator with a decidedly thoughtful occupant.

Vickers retraced his original way from the ship without further misadventure, passed through the air lock, still pondering. Until the time he had left Serrnak in his laboratory, everything had appeared to be proceeding favorably. The meteorologist had evidently been convinced of his sincerity—Vickers chalked up another point in favor of the policy of sticking to the truth as much as possible; but the technician on the sixteenth level had been patently anxious to get rid of him. The creature had said the entire force was too busy to show him around the department, and in the same breath had offered to guide him back to the spaceship. A personal dislike, or actual physical repugnance to a member of an alien race might be responsible, of course; but the apparently genuine effort at courtesy suggested some other cause.

Vickers settled down in a well padded chair—his ship was a converted lifeboat, and he had personally fitted it with items of luxury seldom found on such a craft—and gave his mind to the problem. In the first place, no Heklan except Serrnak Deg had had opportunity to become acquainted with him; during the three months in which he had learned the language of this race, Vickers had confined his attention to that one individual, and had caught no more than fleeting glimpses of the other inhabitants of the station. It seemed, therefore, that the Heklan on the sixteenth level either had formed an instantaneous dislike of the Earthman, had acquired one from Deg, or had been ordered by the same individual not to permit Vickers to examine that level. The first possibility the man had already dismissed as unlikely; and the other two posed the same question—to wit, what had he done or said to arouse the Heklan's suspicion or dislike? Deg must be a fine actor, if Vickers' opinion of his own ability to judge the expression of the Heklan face was not overrated; for no suggestion of any emotion save friendly interest had been apparent to the man in Serrnak's attitude.

The conversation of the last hour or two was the most probable source of trouble. Vickers reviewed his words, with the aid of a nearly eidetic memory. He had, in the first place, adhered strictly to the truth in describing the Federation and its method of establishing contact with "new" races. He had described himself as an agent of the Federation, which was his only serious departure from scrupulous verity; but the lie should not have been obvious to Deg. He had answered the Heklan's questions plausibly—and truthfully, as he recalled. He had known more than one Federation ambassador, and knew their usual troubles.

It was at this point that a recollection of the nature of Deg's questions suddenly stood out in Vickers' mind. There had been only one of importance, though he had asked it more than once, and in a variety of ways. The Heklan had been unable to understand why membership in or dealings with the Federation had been refused by some races; and—had he been entirely unmoved by Vickers' speech, "A certain suspicion of strangers is natural"? A moment later he had said that "naturally" he could not answer for the attitude of the rest of his people; had the inflection of his voice as he uttered that word denoted sarcasm, or some other emotion—or was Vickers' imagination adding to the picture painted by memory?

The man had not learned so much as he had meant to of the living conditions on Hekla. If the population were small and conditions hard, an instinct of co-operation rather than competition might be dominant; such cases were not unknown. If this were true of Hekia, Deg and his people would not be merely reluctant to have dealings with outsiders; they would be terrified at the mere thought, after the impression the meteorologist must have gained from what Vickers had considered "natural."

The theory made Vickers extremely uncomfortable, but long cogitation produced no other. He berated himself for giving so much information without obtaining any in return; but there was no use reviving a dead issue. He determined to return to the observatory, both to check his theory and to obtain some of the missing information. He arose, opened the air lock, and walked across the small plateau toward the great entry way.

Twenty minutes later, a very thoughtful man, he was sitting in his control room. He had met four Heklans inside the entrance; they had been extremely polite; but he had not reached the elevator. Something was decidedly wrong. He had learned nothing new or helpful on the second trip, but it seemed pretty certain that action was required.

Action was not Vickers' strong point, and none knew the fact better than he. Where a good personality and a working knowledge of practical persuasion were required, he shone; but if there were need of a more specialized field of knowledge, he knew when to call for help.

He turned to the panel below the outer vision screens, and pulled a small section out and down to form a shelf. On this was mounted a small medium-crystal unit. Such a transmitter was standard lifeboat equipment, but this set's crystal had been recharged, removing it from the universal distress medium, and matched to only one other unit, which was in the interstellar ship now resting on Hekla's innermost satellite. The set was keyed, as the high-frequency interrupter which permitted voice and, later, vision to be sent and received even by a ship in second-order flight had not at that time been developed.

Vickers checked the tiny green light which assured him that heat or stray static charges had not altered the crystal's medium; then, at a very fair speed, he began rapping out a message. He had to wait several minutes for an acknowledgment, but finally a brief series of long and short flashes blinked from a second bulb above the key, and he closed the unit, satisfied.

There was nothing more he could do at the moment. He had been active since mid-morning, and it was now well after noon; he suddenly realized that his legs and back were aching fiercely from the unaccustomed walking under Heklan gravity. Vickers rose, closed and secured the inner air lock door, and dropped thankfully onto his bunk.

When he awoke, the sun was quite low in the west. Its enormous disk, ill-defined at the best of times, was nearly hidden in haze; the western half of the sky was tinted a deep blood-red never approached by a terrestrial sunset. The daily cumulus cloud was still above the mountain, its top streaming away inland and forming a crimson-lit finger pointing at Observatory Hill. Vickers, looking at it, was reminded to turn on the homing transmitter in his ship, in case his help should have difficulty in locating him.

He spent more than an hour at the board, using all his radio equipment in every combination and on every band he could reach, in an effort to pick up Heklan communications. On the entire electromagnetic spectrum, except the bands of too high frequency for communication beyond the horizon, static was strong and constant; frequency modulation did little to help, and brought nothing that might have been an intelligent message. He considered charging a spare crystal, but realized that no unit so far energized on any Federation world had chanced on the medium of a widely separated crystal, and the chances against doing so had been computed as something like the number of electrons in the universe. Two crystals had to be charged in physical contact to respond to each other across what, for want of a better name, was called a "medium." Even if Heklan science had reached such a point, there was no hope of discovering the fact by searching the legions of possible media. Vickers took that for granted, and after some time at the radios was prepared to state that they had no other means of long-range communication.

He had given up the search and was eating, when a second lifeboat settled down beside his own. Vickers failed to notice it for several minutes; when he did, he immediately snapped on the standard communicator and tuned to the frequency his crew normally used on such occasions. He gave the set a moment to warm, and then called.

"Hello, Dave! Is everything all right?" The answer came back at once.

"This is Macklin. Rodin is here, all right. He's in the air lock, compressing; I'm afraid he's a little annoyed at you. Why in the name of common sense didn't you let us know that you had an atmospheric pressure of forty pounds on this blasted hilltop? He could have ridden all the way in the lock, building up gradually. He'll be over there as soon as possible; as soon as he opens the lock, you'd better trot over and help him. He had enough stuff to set up in business for himself. All right?"

"All serene. Can you stay with us, or do they want the boat back in a hurry?"

"I have to go back. I don't know what they want with this can, and I'm much too modest to suppose they'd need me, but them's the orders. You'd better watch for Dave; the lock pressure is nearly forty now."

"All right. Don't get lost."

Vickers snapped off the set, and opened the inner lock door. A glance through the control room port showed that the other ship was still sealed, but he strolled out onto the landing stage and waited there for Rodin to emerge. He noted with a shiver that the temperature at the top of the hill had not increased perceptibly since morning.

He had only a few moments to wait; the lock of the visiting ship opened silently, and its occupant hailed him.

"Hello, Alf! What have you messed up this time?"

"Don't take so much for granted, cloud-chaser," returned Vickers. "As a matter of fact, I'm not quite sure what, if anything, has been botched. I'm just a little doubtful of the attitude I aroused in the lad who runs this place. It's a weather station, and he's a member of your honored and ancient profession, so I called on you to stand by and assist in further negotiations."

"You would. I'd just gotten back on a more or less human eating and sleeping schedule. Will you help me get my stuff over to your ship? Mack is probably getting tired of waiting." Vickers nodded and they set to work; Rodin continued to talk, commenting unfavorably on Hekla's atmospheric pressure, gravity—this as he tried to lift a piece of apparatus normally well within his strength—temperature, and various other characteristics. He did not mention its weather, except to say that it looked interesting from an academic viewpoint.

The equipment had been transferred, and the men were settled in the warmth of Vickers' ship before Rodin asked for details of the situation. Vickers gave a report of the last three months, pointing out that he had refused either to give an explanation of himself or request information of his hosts until he was sure of his ability to use their language; that Serrnak Deg, the only Heklan with whom he had come into more than momentary contact during this time, had seemed both friendly and interested until exchange of information had begun; and that Vickers had given much more information than he had received. He stressed the fact that the Heklan's behavior had not become openly hostile; they were carefully keeping him away from anything in the observatory that might do him good, but they were being very polite about it. Rodin asked a question at this point.

"If they don't want you, who aren't a scientist, wandering around the place, what good will I do? Don't you want them to know I'm a meteorologist?"

"I don't want to wander. Deg said he'd call for me as soon as his emergency had passed—which may merely mean when he's made the place safe for inspection by a suspicious alien. I'll introduce you to him as a fellow meteorologist. Your inability to speak his language will take care of any risk there might be of your saying the wrong thing. I don't know how advanced their metro is—the lab I saw looked quite imposing, but they may not be up to us. That's one thing I'd like you to pass judgment on. If they're behind us, we'll try to make you helpful to them in as many ways as possible—generally produce a good impression. If they know more than you, we'll decide on some other course of action."

"You're the boss. You must have learned something about these folks, and formed some plans, so I'll follow your lead. I don't suppose you noticed anything pertinent about the climate and local weather, did you? I know it's summer, of course; but is this a representative temperature? How's the lapse rate? Did you notice anything of the prevailing winds and general cloud forms? Don't answer—I can tell by your expression. I have my work cut out for me. Can you get hold of any locally produced weather maps, or even a decent relief map either of the continent or the whole planet?" Vickers pursed his lips doubtfully.

"The only weather maps I've seen are those big globes in the integration laboratory, unless the screens of those computing machines could be called maps. I think they put out their answers in terms of the squiggles you fellows deface paper with. If Deg will let us into that laboratory again, you can judge that for yourself; but I wouldn't count on that happening. I don't know about printed maps or charts; I've seen books, bound like ours, but I haven't even tried to read their language, and haven't seen how their books are illustrated. They undoubtedly have relief maps; if you need them in meteorology, I suppose they do too, and should have them around; but getting hold of one is something you'll just have to pray for."

Rodin nodded, and dropped the subject. They discussed the physical appearance of the Heklans, speculating on their probable evolutionary history; the doings on Hekla's satellite during Vickers' three-month absence from the interstellar ship; and every subject that occurred to them. They had plenty of time, for two of Hekla's long days had rolled by and the sun was again in the west before Serrnak Deg appeared outside the air lock.

Vickers heard him slap the outer door with the flat of his hand, and immediately opened the lock. The pudgy being walked—in spite of his build, his motion was nothing like a fat man's waddle—into the control room, where Rodin was waiting. The tarsierlike face showed no surprise as the big eyes took in the two Earthmen. Vickers forestalled any remarks by speaking himself.

"This is David Rodin, a meteorologist from the crew of the ship that brought me to this planetary system," he said. "I called for him after I left you two days ago. If I had known the nature of this place, I would have arranged to have him accompany me when I came, and learn your language at the same time. I imagine you would find a member of your own profession a more interesting conversationalist than I. I shall do my best to make up for my failure by acting as interpreter—I shall have to learn more of your meteorological terms, as well as our own, if you start to talk shop. Rodin would like to see your observatory with us, if you are ready to show the rest of it to me."

"We noticed your friend's arrival," replied Deg. "I regret being kept busy for so long. I will gladly show him the integration room if you wish it—perhaps he will understand our simple installations without explanation. I should be grateful for any improvements he might suggest. Do you wish to come now, or would you rather show me some of the photographic material you promised to let me see the next time I visited you?"

Vickers felt slightly nonplussed, and admitted to himself that Deg, if he were trying to be an unobtrusive hindrance to further human exploration of his observatory, could scarcely have done better. He gave the only possible answer.

"By all means stay and see the material. Dave's arrival had driven it from my mind. The pictures are accompanied by much printed information which you won't be able to read; but we can probably make up for that. Rodin has traveled even more than I, and can give first-hand explanations of much that you will see. The atlases are in the library to the rear of the ship."

Vickers took care to hide his annoyance as the two men and the Heklan examined and discussed the records of the dozens of worlds that made up the Federation and the human, near-human, and completely unhuman beings that peopled them. Deg expressed surprise that his own world, so comparatively close to Earth and Thanno, the principal Federation planets, had remained overlooked while Federation sway had reached across the Galaxy and beyond to its sprawling satellites, the Magellanic Clouds. The men pointed out the vast number of stars, which rendered surveys either cursory in nature or prohibitively long in duration. A sun was likely to be investigated closely enough to detect its planets, if any, only if there were something intrinsically peculiar about the star itself, as was the case with R Coronae. Privately, Vickers wondered how soon the Federation actually would become interested enough in the giant variable to give it a close looking over.

Deg remained until sunset. By that time both the human beings were again badly in need of sleep, and the Heklan had gathered about as much knowledge of other races of the Galaxy as any one could without first-hand experience.

Vickers watched his guest through the control room port as he vanished into the still faintly crimson-lit gloom. A general glumness permeated the atmosphere of the room. Rodin waited for his companion to make some remark, but Vickers remained silent for several minutes. To the meteorologist's disappointment, he finally retired without saying anything about the problem in hand.

Sunrise, after the five and a half hours of darkness which prevailed at this season, found both men awake, though not entirely refreshed. Rodin, owing to his brief residence on Hekla, was in rather better condition than Vickers, but even he was beginning to feel and show the effects of the excess gravity. Both men ate an enormous breakfast—Vickers' stores were far from exhausted—and then the "diplomat" led the way out of the ship, turning purposefully toward the great entrance in the rock.

"If I don't get in this time, I think I'll give it up as a bad job," he remarked as they approached the opening. "I'm beginning to think Deg is a little too smooth for me. I wish I were more certain of what cooled him so toward us; my present idea is just a working hypothesis, and goodness knows when it may stop working."

The men passed into the shadowy hangar, in which Vickers had never yet seen an aircraft. No one was there; the tunnels opening into the great cavern yawned dimly lighted and empty. Vickers led the way toward the elevator, without stopping to wonder where the Heklans might be. He knew the natives would meet them before they got far.

He was right. As they turned the last corner, bringing them in sight of the elevator, a Heklan stepped from the cage. Vickers was not sure whether or not it was one of the individuals whom he had already encountered—his comparative isolation with Deg while he was learning the Heklan language had given him no opportunity to study facial or other differences between members of that race—but this specimen was far too tall to be Deg himself. His eyes were almost on a level with those of the Earthmen, while his general build was in normal Heklan proportion. He must have weighed, on Hekla, between four and five hundred pounds.

The tremendous native listened politely to Vickers' request to see Serrnak Deg, and nodded when the man finished speaking.

"I was coming to see you," he said. "Deg has asked me to act as your guide. He will be glad to see you whenever you particularly wish it, but routine duties of his position, which he has been rather neglecting for the past few months, prevent him from spending all his time with you from now on. He asks me to apologize for any seeming discourtesy, but I am sure you understand his difficulties. In what way can I help you now?"

"My friend is a meteorologist, and would be interested in seeing the integration laboratory Deg showed me, as well as your observing apparatus. I understand perfectly why Deg cannot be with us, and I thank you for granting your time. Perhaps if we went first to the integration laboratory, and you explained your weather maps and their symbols to Rodin, he could comprehend the rest of your system more easily. He has been eager to see that laboratory ever since I described it to him. Does that meet with your approval?" Vickers had ideas of his own about the assignment of this enormous individual as their host, but determined to make the best of the situation.

"Whatever you wish," returned the guide. "My name, by the way, is Marn Trangero—either name is acceptable as a form of address, as you probably gathered from Deg. We will go up to the integration room, then, if you are ready; as a matter of fact, Deg is probably there himself, just now, so if there is something you particularly wished to discuss with him, you will have a chance to do so."

Vickers nodded understanding as they entered the dimly lit elevator. The Heklan pressed the button—Vickers examined carefully the faint character beside it as he did so—and they slid gently upward.

The laboratory was as Vickers remembered it; the globes, the computing machines, the operating personnel. The big central machine was active this time, with the four operators in their seats on each side. Marn pointed out one of these individuals.

"Deg is here, as I thought," he said. "Did you particularly wish to speak to him?"

"Not if he is busy," replied Vickers. "Could you explain these devices to us? I will translate to Rodin as well as I can, though you will probably have to explain most of your scientific terms with simpler words. What is the connection between those globes and the computers beneath them?"

"The globes are weather maps. The computers handle observed values of air pressure, temperature, humidity, and similar factors, setting them up as isopleths on the globes and calculating their individual trends. Each of the machines handles one such variable and its individual characteristics. The results of these computations are fed to the intermediate machines, and finally to the master computer, which is supposed to give a complete weather picture. All the factors at once could be shown on the main screen, but it would make a very confusing picture. The trouble, of course, is that each factor is dependent on all the others, and the integration has to be fed back to the individual machines to correct their values for each few minutes of a prediction. It is really a very clumsy system; a single computer capable of tracking all the variables at once would be far speedier and more convenient. Such a machine is being designed at one of our research centers, but it is so far much too bulky, complex, and tricky for an outpost such as this. I should like a chance at it myself, as you can well imagine."

Vickers could imagine; he recalled scientist friends of his own who would give ten years of their lives for six months' time at some particular laboratory, or machine, or in some fellow worker's company. He relayed the explanation to Rodin, who nodded in understanding and examined very closely each of the globes in turn. The meteorologist then spent several minutes carefully observing the operation of the keyboards of several of the machines. He finally asked for an illustration of the system's accuracy; Vickers relayed the question to Marn.

"Since I am not acquainted with your own progress in this field, I hesitate to call our work accurate," was the reply. "In meteorology, it is difficult to define accuracy, in any case. If you like, however, I can translate the machine's prediction of the next few hours' weather. From a cursory glance, it seems to me that it will be different enough from the local norm to afford you a fair check on our methods. If you will wait a few moments, I will interpret the records from the machine."

He left them, while Vickers explained his proposition to Rodin. The meteorologist approved strongly, and they waited expectantly for the Heklan's return. He was gone only a few minutes.

"You know," he began as he approached the men, "that this station is at the coast of a large continental area. You have undoubtedly noticed the stiff sea breeze which forms a normal part of our weather at this season. It is a direct cause of the cumulus cloud which builds up above this hill each day.

"Since your arrival, Vickers, the weather has departed only very slightly from the norm. Now, however, a weak warm front has developed to the southwest, and is moving in this direction. Its first symptoms, high thin clouds, will arrive about midday. They will lower rapidly, reaching the level of the station three and a half hours later, and precipitation will occur almost immediately after that. Winds will continue rising until the rain starts; thereafter they will decrease, and shift from south to west. I could give you numerical values for wind velocity, air pressure, temperature, and so forth; but they would have to be translated into your units, and I don't believe either of us can do that. All clouds should disappear before sunset, including the cumulus head one usually sees over this point. Deg has just warned the gardeners on the lower slopes of the front, I see. It might be a good idea to move your ship into the hangar—though you know the strength of your own creations better than I; use your judgment. Winds sometimes become rather violent here at the hilltop."

"The ship is a pretty solid piece of machinery, and we can anchor to the mountain if necessary," replied Vickers. "Why do you warn the gardeners, if this is to be a weak front? And what is the nature of the gardens I saw on my drive with Deg a few days ago?"

"The plants nourish a fermenting protozoan in their roots, and store alcohol in their stems and spore pods. The longer they grow, the higher the alcoholic content; but a strong wind ruptures the pods and frees the alcohol. Consequently, we try to harvest just before a wind. The local gardens are small; we simply produce enough to power the station. I believe there are efforts under way to modify the protozoans to produce better fuels, but if they have met with success we have yet to receive the benefits. Your arrival, of course, may obviate the need for further work along such lines; you certainly didn't cross interstellar space on combustion engines."

Vickers nodded absently at this remark, as he translated the gist of the forecast to Rodin. The latter listened carefully, making certain of details that seemed unimportant to his companion, and finally asked to see the observing portions of the station.

Trangero agreed instantly to this request, and turned back to the elevator. Once again they traveled upward, emerging this time into a small chamber from which half a dozen doors opened. The Heklan led them through one of these.

They found themselves on a flat area, only a few yards square, and obviously artificial, located only a dozen yards below the actual peak of Observatory Hill. A metal ladder led to the peak itself, which was topped by a slender but solid-looking tower. Part of the platform was walled with stone, and the rest guarded by a metal rail. Several instruments were mounted on the rail itself, and some larger devices on the rock just outside. The tower was topped by a tiny vane. Marn showed the men each of the instruments in turn, vaulting the rail easily to demonstrate those beyond it. Neither of the human beings enjoyed going outside its protection; the rock was smooth, and after the first few feet sloped very steeply toward the landing ramp sixty yards below. The ship was just visible from the safe side of the railing.

The instruments seemed normal enough to Vickers, and even Rodin had little to say about them. There were thermometers, precipitation gauges, and hygrometers, all connected electrically to recorders in the laboratories below. The vane on the tower was similarly connected to record wind direction, and it contained a pitot head to measure velocity.

The few other devices were slight variants of standard—to Rodin— equipment; and the meteorologist felt rather let down at the end of the tour. He felt fairly surely that the Heklans, in spite of their efficient world net, were no further advanced in meteorology than any Federation planet; but he decided not to voice the opinion until after checking a fair number of their predictions. He awaited the approaching storm with interest.

He glanced occasionally to the southwest while they were at the summit, but the omnipresent haze of Hekla's dense atmosphere hid the horizon; and no signs of the approaching weather appeared before Marn shepherded the men back to the elevator. The other parts of the station, which the Heklan insisted on showing them, were connected with the maintenance of the place rather than with its primary function. The power plant was on the same level as the hangar; it consisted of six surprisingly small electric generators driven by equally diminutive internal-combustion engines, which, according to Marn, burned the alcohol produced by the gardens on the slopes of the hill. These units powered the elevator, supplied heat and light sufficient for the Heklans' small needs, and operated the numerous items of electrical equipment.

They spent fully three hours inspecting the station; if Marn had been ordered to tire the men out on nonessential details, he was doing splendidly. Rodin lost interest after leaving the roof. Vickers kept up a good front, but eventually even he had to call a halt for rest. Perhaps his fatigue can be blamed for causing him to forget an issue he had planned to force—the roomfull of electric equipment from which he had been diverted two days before, and which Marn had skipped by accident or design. Vickers did forget it, made his excuses to the Heklan, and was back in the ship before he recalled the matter. By that time he was nearly asleep, settled back in one of the chairs in the ship's library.

He slept four or five hours. Rodin remained awake for some time, but was asleep when Vickers awoke; by the time both had finished sleeping, eating, and talking over the morning's events, the sun was well up in the sky. So far the weather appeared normal, though Vickers, who had been around long enough to be used to it, thought the breeze was less strong and the cumulus banner less well developed than usual. Marn's weather was not jumping the gun, at any rate.

It was not late, either. A few minutes before noon—as nearly as they could judge the time—Rodin detected the first wisps of cirrus, high above. They must have been above the horizon for some time, invisible in the haze. As the men were on the landward—and consequently the leeward—side of the hill, the change in wind direction was not noticeable for some time; but its strength mounted rapidly as the clouds thickened and dropped closer to the hilltop. Rodin, stepping outside the ship for a moment, was taken by surprise and knocked over by a gust that eddied around the rock shoulder. He got to his feet immediately, bracing himself against the metal hull, and looked around. Toward the west, the haze had thickened so that it was now impossible to make out details on the plateau inland. Two or three thousand feet overhead, the scud raced along parallel to the coast. On Earth, under similar circumstances, the cloud layers would have been gray; but the fainter, red light of R Coronae here gave them an indescribably eerie pinkish color. All traces of the sky had by now disappeared. Rodin could actually feel in his ears the change in air pressure as other eddies swirled by him. It was still cold; the frontal surface, of course, had not yet come down to his level.

He returned to the control room, thinking. If Vickers had translated correctly, Marn had forecast a weak front; and this outside weather could already be called violent without stretching facts. Either the Heklan prediction was inaccurate, or Rodin would have to revise his ideas of what constituted a violent storm. In three months of residence, Vickers had noticed nothing extraordinary about the weather; and it seemed probable that if Heklan atmospheric phenomena were built to a different scale, the fact would have become apparent in that time. Rodin, thinking the matter over, adopted his usual course of withholding an opinion.

The wind increased, and as the clouds thickened the pinkish light faded into total darkness. Rain began to beat against the metal hull, and the light from the control room window penetrated only a few feet into the murk. The clouds had reached the level of the hilltop. Rodin cautiously opened the outer air lock door again; fortunately it was power-operated, or he would have been unable to close it. Several times the ship shuddered from end to end under the blast. Vickers charged the anchoring fields along the keel after the first tremor, but evidently the rock itself was quivering; an occasional vibration could still be felt during the heaviest gusts of wind. There would be more shattered rock on the terraces when the weather cleared.

The time passed slowly. Rodin kept watching the clock, trying to figure the time of Heklan day on the twenty-four-hour dial in order to keep check on Marn's prediction. Vickers read and thought, while the storm reached and passed its height. Twice the men were disturbed by an odd, crackling sound, and looked up to see ghostly fingers of fire crawling about the transparent ports. The meteorologist blinked at the sight; he was accustomed to electrical activity in storms with strong vertical development, but to get it with strictly horizontal winds somewhat surprised him. He wondered what velocity the wind must have reached to ionize the raindrops. Vickers felt thankful for the metallic construction of the ship.

Slowly the shuddering diminished, the howling of the wind died, and the dense fog grew once more pinkly luminous. The men ventured outside again, finding that the wind was still strong, but no longer savage. The fog was thinning, and the wind, true to prediction, was blowing from inland, bringing even to this height odors from the vast plains and hills of the great continent.

Rodin stood looking, as the view cleared, at the reappearing sun and the vaguely visible landscape, sniffing the odd smells, and gradually acquiring a puzzled expression. Vickers noted it, and started to ask the nature of the trouble; but he changed his mind, knowing that he was unlikely to get an answer, and went into the ship instead. He found himself shivering, as usual on Hekla, so he picked up the jacket he had discarded after the morning's inspection tour. Attired in this, he went outside again.

Rodin was waiting for him, the expression of puzzlement still on his face. He caught sight of Vickers, and beckoned to him. "Let's go back to the station," he said. "I want to pick a bone with Marn, or with Deg, if necessary. There are one or two things going on that I don't fully understand. These friends of yours don't have to sleep half the day like a couple of poor Earthmen, do they?"

"They should still be active," Vickers replied, looking at the sun. "It's a couple of hours till sundown, if what I can see of the sun and what I can guess of the horizon's position aren't combining to fool me. These fellows sleep for a few hours each night from habit, and I guess they can do without that for quite a time. There should be no trouble in finding Marn, if he's supposed to be looking after us."

There was no trouble. They did not meet Trangero the moment they entered the station, but the first Heklan who saw them made it his business to deliver them into the proper custody, and led them to an office on a floor two or three levels below the integration room. Marn raised his enormous bulk from behind a desk as they entered. Vickers thought fleetingly of the curious similarity between human and Heklan forms of courtesy; then he turned his attention to the task of interpreting for the two weather men. Rodin opened the conversation with a question.

"Did I understand correctly that you were basing the prediction for the last few hours upon the passage of a warm front?"

"That is correct. I was several minutes off on the time of passage; but that is not included explicitly in the machine solutions that are recorded, and I did not occupy a machine with the detailed problem."

"Then a front actually did pass? Why is it that there is no perceptible temperature change? I expected it to be a good deal warmer, from the amount of water vapor that was condensed at the frontal surface."

"I can only suppose that you are working from acquaintance with a different set of conditions. The temperature change was slight, I agree—I said the front was weak. I should have given you numerical values if we had had any measuring system in common. We must remedy that situation as soon as possible, by the way. The condensation and precipitation which seems abnormal to you agreed as usual with the predictions, as did the winds."

Rodin pondered for several moments before replying to this. "There's a good deal I don't understand even yet," he finally said. "I'd better start from the beginning and learn your units. Then I might try following some of your computations manually. If that doesn't clear me up, nothing will. Can you spare the time?"

Vickers hesitated before translating this. He hated the thought of using so much time as Rodin's proposal would require; the months he had spent on the alien language seemed more than enough. There seemed, however, no alternative; so he transmitted the meteorologist's request. Marn agreed, as he had expected; and what was worse, the energetic giant plunged immediately into the task, and kept at it for nearly four hours. The translation of units of distance, temperature, weight, angle, and so forth was not in itself a difficult problem; but it was complicated enormously by Vickers' lack of scientific vocabulary. By the time Rodin had acquired a table of Heklan numerals and a series of conversion graphs, both Earthmen were in a sadly irritated frame of mind.

Vickers was more than willing to call it a day when they returned to the ship, but the meteorologist seemed to partake of the determination displayed by his Heklan fellow. He settled down with his written material, which included one of the maps made during the recent frontal passage, and began working. Vickers wanted to remain awake to hear his conclusions, and settled into a chair in the cramped library; but sheets of used paper began to litter the place, and Rodin, whenever he had to probe among them to check some previous figures, plainly considered his friend to be rather in the way. Vickers finally gave up and went to bed—a habit into which he was falling more and more deeply. The weather man labored on.

He was a red-eyed scarecrow, hunched over the little desk, as he expounded his results the next morning. His words were slow and careful; he had evidently spent a long time on Vickers' problem after obtaining a satisfactory solution of his own.

"There is one fact that I think will help you greatly," he said. "This planet is in an ice age—we could tell that from space. In this hemisphere, where it is now two Earth years past midsummer, the ice cap extends more than thirty degrees from the pole. In the other, the large island and continental masses possess glacial sheets scores of feet in thickness to within forty degrees of the equator; and heavy snow fields reach to less than twenty degrees south latitude in spots. On smaller islands, whose temperatures should be fairly well stabilized by the ocean, there appears to be much snow at very low latitudes.

"I suppose, though that's outside my line, that these people developed their civilization as a result of the period of glaciation, just as the races of Earth, Thanno, and a lot of the other Federation planets seem to have. Now, however, they have the situation of a growing race cramped into the equatorial regions of a planet—admittedly a large one, but with most of its land area in the middle latitudes.

"On Earth we pushed the isotherms fifteen degrees further from the equator, and benefited greatly thereby. How about selling the same idea to the Heklans, if you really want a convincing example of what we can do for them?"

"Two questions, please," returned Vickers. "First, what's this about changing the Earth's weather? I don't recall ever having heard of such a thing. In the second place, I'm afraid we'll have to sell the Heklans a little more than possible advantages. Our working theory, remember, is that I inadvertently got them leery of the combative and competitive elements of Federation culture. How would curbing their ice age, if you can do it, help that? Also, and most important, how does it help us to get a corner on the metal trade here before a real Federation agent steps in and opens the place up? Once that happens, every company from Regulus to Vega will have trading ships on Hekla; and we want Belt Metals to be solidly established here by that time. How about that?"

"To answer your first point, we didn't change Earth's weather, but its climate. There'd be no point in trying to explain the difference to you, I guess. They stepped up the CO_2 content of the atmosphere, producing an increased blanketing effect. At first the equatorial regions were uncomfortably hot as a result; but when the thing stabilized again a lot of the polar caps had melted, and a lot of formerly desert land in the torrid zones, which had been canalized for the purpose, had flooded in consequence. The net result was an increased evaporation surface and, through a lot of steps a little too technical for the present discussion, a shallower temperature drop toward the poles. The general public has forgotten it, I know, but I thought it was still taught in history. Surely you heard of it sometime during your formative years."

"Perhaps I did. However, that doesn't answer the other question."

"That's your problem, at least for the details. I should say, however, that their acceptance of that proposition would entail the purchase of a lot of machinery by the Heklans. A genius like you can probably take the idea on from there."

Vickers pursed his lips silently, and thought. There seemed to be some elements of value in Rodin's idea; elements from which, with a little cerebration, something might be built.

"If they were to accept such a proposition, how long would it take to get the thing under way?" he asked finally.

"The general plans could be obtained directly from the records, and apparatus set up in a few months, I imagine," was the answer. "It would depend to some extent on the nature and location of Hekla's volcanic areas—they are the best source of carbon dioxide, I believe; they were used on Earth. I imagine the *Alula* would require quite a few round trips to Sol to transport enough apparatus for this planet."

"How soon could we promise results to the Heklans? Remember, we want to establish ourselves solidly with them before competition gets too heavy. If a Federation agent gets here before any agreements are reached, trade of any sort will be frozen until the diplomats finish shaking hands. Until one does arrive, they can't touch us legally for entering into contracts with the Heklans, though they may frown slightly at the company's failure to report the discovery of civilization here."

"I'm afraid it would be a couple of decades—half a year or so, here— before the change in climate would be really noticeable. However, the theory would be clear enough to people like Deg; and they would begin to notice results on their maps almost immediately."

"How much increase in CO_2, would be needed to produce a useful result? And would that much be harmful to the Heklans? I imagine we would have to show Deg some solid figures to overcome his suspicions enough even to consider the proposal."

"I've done a little figuring in that direction, but I can't give you a precise answer to the first question until I have more accurate and detailed knowledge of the present composition of Hekla's atmosphere. You'll have to do some investigating of your own for the second; I have no idea of the physical limitations of these people. That fellow Trangero looks rugged enough to take an awful beating from almost anything."

"The question is not whether they can stand it, but whether it will cause them discomfort. That would be plenty to squash the whole idea, unless they have a collective personality appallingly different from ours. In any case, the proposition will have to be presented delicately. We shall hold more discussions with Marn or Deg or any one else who will listen to us, provided he is a meteorologist; and I think it will be possible to build up to the subject, while describing our mechanical abilities and history and so on, in such a way as to make him think it's his own idea. The plan certainly has possibilities, Dave. We'll eat, and you'd better sleep, and then we'll have another session in the observatory. Sound all right?"

Rodin agreed that it sounded all right. It was just bad luck that Marn Trangero didn't.

The conversations seemed to steer themselves in the way Vickers desired, for several hours. They ran from subject to subject, dealing with matters connected with the Federation whenever Trangero held the conversational initiative, and veering back to things Heklan when Vickers could get control. The Earthmen learned of the lives of the half billion Heklans scattered among the equatorial islands of their planet; of their commerce, their science, their arts—but nothing of their wars, except against their environment. Casual references to feats of physical strength and resistance to cold, heat, and hunger made the human beings blink, but partly reassured them of the creatures' ability to stand slight modifications of their atmosphere.

The Heklan learned of the doings of the natives of the scores of worlds whose co-operating governments called themselves the Federation. Vickers censored carefully the more drastic references to strife, though he did try to make clear the more harmless aspects of a competitive culture. If he had known the mechanics of atomic converters and second-order drive units, Marn would probably have wormed the information from him; the creature was at least as acute a questioner as Vickers. The man was slowly realizing this fact, though he had originally believed that the giant had been chosen as their companion principally for his physical qualities. He wondered, as he strove to lead the talk to climate and the possibility of Federation science's improving it for Hekla, whether the bulky being were not laughing silently at his attempts. It was a demoralizing suspicion, which success did nothing to allay; for the "success" came with suspicious rapidity after he set to work in earnest.

He had introduced the story Rodin had told him of the undertaking to modify the climate of their home planet; and Marn had appeared extremely interested, asking for a description of the results. Then he asked for a comparison of the normal climates of Earth and Hekla. It was this request that Vickers misconstrued as success for his efforts. With rather good salesmanship, he decided to break off the discussion at this point, pleading the usual fatigue—they had been talking for several hours. Marn, he felt, had conceived the desired idea and should grow more enthusiastic if allowed to mull it over for a few hours. Vickers had become enthusiastic himself, which was a pity.

When they next met, Vickers felt happier than ever; for Main's first words were a request for the method the Earthmen had employed to modify their climate. He asked, politely enough not to give offense, that Vickers translate Rodin's explanation rather than attempt to give one of his own; evidently he wanted precision. Vickers assented gladly. Rodin had found some details of the operation in Vickers' library, and was able to add much more from his own memory; so for half an hour he and Vickers alternated relation and translation, while the absorbed Heklan listened silently, his round face showing no expression that Vickers could interpret.

"An absorbing tale," Trangero said when the Earthmen had finished. "I applaud the ingenuity of your meteorologists and astronomers. I have seen no maps of your planet, but I gathered that much of its land area is in the middle latitudes, as is the case with Hekla. An operation such as you have described would open to us millions of square miles of land areas which at present we can use only in summer and autumn, if at all. It is a pity that it would not be effective on this planet."

For a moment Vickers sat, stunned by the Heklan's matter-of-fact remark.

"Why would it not work here?" he finally asked. "I have gathered that carbon dioxide is no more dangerous to you than to us; and it should be as effective a blanketing agent here. I realize the enormous thickness and extent of your ice caps, but even they would eventually yield to a general increase in temperature."

"Undoubtedly they would," replied Marn. "Unfortunately, your plan remains unworkable. In the first place, the atmosphere of this planet already contains approximately one and a half percent of carbon dioxide. More would not harm us, but neither would it help. You have forgotten something, which Rodin should have remembered if he knows as much of astronomy as our science requires. Our sun is much redder than yours; and an increase in the atmospheric content of any infrared opaque gas such as carbon dioxide, ozone, or water vapor would cut out nearly as much additional incident radiation as it would retain the natural heat. I admit there would be some gain, but to make it enough to be a real help would demand a radical change in our atmosphere. You are working under different conditions here than you met on your own world, and your meteorology will not help us."

Vickers thought furiously as the Heklan fell silent. Rodin, who had not understood a word of the last conversation, realized from his friend's expression that something had gone seriously wrong. He tapped Vickers' shoulder to gain his attention, and asked for an explanation. It was given to him.

"Is he right, Dave?" asked Vickers, at the end. "Surely there is some modification of that trick that would work for this world. I hate to give up that idea."

"I can't, on the spur of the moment, think of anything that would serve," replied Rodin, "but it seems to me that there must be some fairly simple solution. If necessary, we can call in one of the physics or chemistry boys, though I don't like to do that. I'd advise you not to appear too perturbed about the matter—after all, this was supposed to be one of Marn's suggestions. Just let the conversation ride on for an hour or two, and we can talk it over at dinner."

Vickers recognized the soundness of this bit of advice, and endeavored to abide by it. He was never sure that Marn had not noticed and interpreted the symptoms of annoyance the Earthman must have shown; but the creature never gave any indication of realizing what had occurred.

The rest of the morning was spent in answering his questions about beings and events beyond the R Coronae system.

In spite of his promise, Rodin said practically nothing at dinner; and immediately after the meal he repaired to the library. Vickers followed, and occupied a seat well out of the meteorologist's way. Silence ensued, broken only by the rustling of paper and the occasional scratch of a stylus in Rodin's hand. Vickers neither wrote nor read; he sat and thought, while his friend worked. In his own way, he also was working.

Presently Rodin looked up. "Marn is a bright specimen, no doubt," he said, "but he went a little too far when he implied that our knowledge of meteorology would not be helpful here. There are plenty of ways to alter climate in any direction you please, and some of them must be applicable to this planet. Of course, we want methods which will require the use of plenty of heavy machinery, so that we can sell them the equipment; but that doesn't narrow the field much, when one is working on a world-wide scale.

"The problem works down to a reasonably simple root. With a given solar constant, there are a number of things that can happen to the incoming energy. A certain percentage is reflected, and a certain percentage absorbed. Modification of that ratio offers one means of climate control; that, in effect, is what we suggested to Marn. It may yet be possible, but the nature of R Coronae's radiation makes it difficult.

"If you take the absorbed energy as it is, the next point is distribution. Currents in the atmosphere and hydrosphere normally take care of that business; and both of those are subject to interference and consequently to control. Ocean currents, of course, are easier to direct; and it might be worth while to examine more closely the distribution of land and water areas of this planet, with that thought in mind. Distribution by air currents is modified by the height, friction values, existing temperature, and Heaven knows what other characteristics of the land over which they flow; that's the sad fact that makes meteorology more of a nightmare than a science, at times.

"I should say that redirection of ocean currents offered your best bet; we can try it on Marn, anyway. It will depend a lot on Hekla's geography, but he will realize that as well as I and will be able to pass judgment. That's the best I have to offer at the moment."

At least, Vickers realized, there was still hope even from his point of view. The construction work that would be required by such a plan meant plenty of heavy machinery. He agreed with Rodin on the subject of working the plan into the next conversation with Marn.

The Heklan readily agreed to show Rodin something of the geography of his world, when the meteorologist put the question up to him. He left the Earthmen for a moment, and returned with a heavy book, which proved to be an atlas. Inside its front cover was a folded leaf which opened into a map, several feet square, of the planet. It was on a projection similar to Goode's homolosine and showed the entire surface of the world; but only a few scattered areas in the arctic and antarctic regions showed anything like the detail displayed on the settled, tropical islands. The Heklans had done little exploring of their own polar caps; Marn said that such regions as the maps showed in detail were in the neighborhood of meteorological stations similar to the one on Observatory Hill.

Rodin, however, was not particularly interested in the polar caps. He examined closely the sea which extended entirely around the globe in the equatorial regions, broken only by the large islands and archipelagos on which most of Main's race dwelt. In both the northern and southern hemispheres there lay enormous continental masses divided by relatively narrow arms of sea; and the more the meteorologist looked at these, the more confidence he felt in the practicability of diverting warm currents up those arms.

"I see that you have settlements near the .equatorial coasts of these land masses," he finally said to Marn. "Why is it not possible to spread further inland?"

"The extremes of temperature in the continental interiors not only make settled life there impossible, but cause violent and uncomfortable weather at the coast settlements and on the nearer islands," was the answer, as Rodin had expected. "The polar caps never melt entirely down to the ground over more than a tiny fraction of their area. They are too thick; and any gains made in the warm seasons are lost in the cold ones—quite evenly; the planet has reached a state of near equilibrium in that respect. It is unfortunate from the point of view of living space requirements; but I hate to picture the results of a major change which would interfere with that stability."

"Why should that be serious?" asked Rodin. "I had been considering that angle ever since our last talk; and it seems to me that sea walls could be designed to deflect the currents which now run around the planet in the equatorial ocean, into these arms of the sea which reach up between the continents. If this were done, it should result in an earlier melting of the ice to the east of the water, permitting the bare ground to absorb more radiant heat. That should gradually operate to get you ahead of the melting-freezing cycle, and the new equilibrium point should give you a good deal of livable land space."

Marn appeared interested.

"Could you go into a little more detail on that plan? I should like to hear how completely you have been able to handle the situation."

Rodin bent over the map, and began to indicate what he considered the best location and design for the sea walls, working as well as he could from a memory of the current-control installations on Vega V. Marn was unable to give him much data on ocean depth, but that was not too important. The coasts of the continents involved had a more direct bearing on the situation, and Marn was well informed on their nature. Rodin once more began to feel hopeful. He finished his exposition with the words, "If you feel that the undertaking is practical, any or all of the peoples of the Federation will be glad to help you with experience and equipment."

Marn did not answer for several moments, and the expectations of the Earthmen mounted with each second of delay. They should have known better by this time.

"It is a well thought out program; better planned, I think, than your first," the Heklan finally said. "Of course, you are under a handicap in that you are so completely ignorant of Heklan conditions. Your ingenuity and evident experience, however, have started me hoping that perhaps some of your Federation scientists could perform this feat, which seems to me impossible. I hope you will present the problem to your colleagues of the Federation, and that some of them will see fit to give their attention to the matter." He paused, as though to give Vickers a chance to translate this speech; but before the man could do so, he appeared to have a further idea. "I think it would do no harm to let my people know of your presence, Vickers," he said. "I am sure they would be fascinated by the possibilities you have unfolded to me; and I don't believe your reason for wanting secrecy is valid any longer."

Vickers found himself in the hot part of a pincer movement, and thought furiously as he translated Trangero's speech to Rodin. "I guess we can let him broadcast if he wants to," he concluded, "but please do some fast talking on this weather business. He hasn't told me why your sea walls won't work; just takes it for granted."

"I don't believe he would tell me; and I believe it would work," answered the meteorologist. "He's keeping something up his sleeve, and we'll never worm it out of him. I think we'd better get out of here, and take a little trip. That would give us a chance to check my idea for ourselves—he's quite right in saying that I don't know enough about this planet. It might also present us with a better opportunity to do our work than this weather station seems to offer. Why not let these fellows announce our presence, and use the occasion to make a tour of the planet?"

Vickers could think of nothing better, and Marn seemed agreeable. So did Serrnak Deg, when the matter was broached to him. And so it was that the little lifeboat rose from Observatory Hill on what proved to be one of the most trying journeys either man had ever made. Serrnak Deg and Marn Trangero watched the sliver of metal vanish to the south; then they looked at each other, with almost human grins wrinkling their grotesque features. They left the tiny platform from which they had been watching, and entered the elevator. Marn got off at the level on which his office was situated, but Deg went on down; and Vickers would have been interested to note that the Heklan proceeded directly to the room from which the Earthman had been so carefully kept.

But Vickers had no opportunity to note this fact. He watched the cumulus banner above the hill fade into the haze astern; and when it was out of sight, he gave his attention to the landscape unfolding below them. It seemed a sufficiently pleasant country, of forested hills and open plains; but a close inspection of the forests showed great tree-ferns and fungi rather than normal trees, and Vickers knew that in Hekla's ten or twelve years of winter even this coastal strip was a howling, blizzard-racked desert of snow and ice; and just out of sight to the right as they followed the seacoast southward was the remnant of a giant ice cap where the heights were still snow-capped even at this season.

Rodin was only moderately interested in the view, until the coast began to curve gently westward. Then he began to make careful checks, using one of the maps he had obtained at the weather station. Several times he lowered the ship to the water, checking its depth and temperature; frequently he cruised as low as was safe among the hills and above the trees, examining Vickers knew not what characteristic of the planet's surface. The meteorologist's pile of notes and computations grew in thickness, while Vickers did little save look on and enjoy himself.

Southward they drove, breaking away from the coast and moving far out over a broad stretch of sea, until the geodet told them they were nearly above the equator; then westward, still dropping occasionally for Rodin's perpetual measurements, over more water, interrupted at times by islands. Twice they saw what were evidently Heklan communities; each time they were small, but each boasted a landing strip similar to, but much longer than, the one on Observatory Hill. Several winged aircraft were parked in the open near each strip, and a single machine, similar in exterior design to the terrestrian lifeboat. Vickers was curious about its method of propulsion, since the Heklans were without atomic power, but he did not bother to descend to investigate.

For ninety hours they chased the sun, veering far enough to right and left to examine the near shores of most of the continental masses.

Each time they did so, Rodin expressed greater confidence in his plan; and as the geodet told them that they were again approaching the longitude of Observatory Hill, he swung the ship northward, prepared to argue its merits to the limit.

Vickers took over the controls for a time, to let the meteorologist straighten out the last of his paper work. It was a token job, since the automatic controls were holding the craft on course and at a constant pressure altitude. They were cruising at a very moderate speed, since Rodin wanted time for his work; they were, Vickers calculated, about an hour and a half from the observatory. The usual layer of haze was overhead— thicker than normal, Vickers decided; the red sunlight pouring through the upper ports seemed less intense than usual.

He did not see the clouds until they were less than twenty miles ahead. It was the first extensive cumulus development he had seen on Hekla, and he debated calling Rodin; but he decided such clouds could not be too unusual, and failed to do so. He simply sat and watched the wall of vapor grow more distinct as the little ship approached it. It extended as far as he could see on either side and—up. An airplane pilot of an earlier century would not have come within miles of that angry black barrier; Rodin might have decided to go over it, but Vickers let the automatic controls carry the tiny machine straight into its heart. Even then, if the altitude control had been connected to the radio altimeter, no harm might have been done; unfortunately, Vickers had tied it in to the atmospheric pressure gauge, in anticipation of reaching land.

The initial turbulence made no impression on ship or occupants; but five seconds after the sun had faded from sight the ship stuck its nose into the low pressure of an updraft, and Vickers left his seat. For several seconds he was dazed by the force with which his head struck the ceiling. In those few seconds the ship lost six thousand feet of altitude as the automatic controls sought a level of pressure equal to that at which they had been set. Before they succeeded, and before Vickers could regain his feet and the manual controls, the updraft was passed; and he was pressed helplessly against the deck as the ship plunged upward again. As it slowed, he seized the back of his chair and tried to brace himself against the sickening motion. For a moment he was partially successful, and he dared to let go with one hand in order to reach once more for the controls. As he touched them, there was a violent sideward lurch; and his hand, instead of striking the toggle controlling the altitude mechanism, opened the bar switch handling the sensation currents from the attitude gyros on the automatic pilot.

The ship could not have been out of control more than three or four minutes altogether; but those minutes were more than enough. Without the gyros, she no longer held an even keel, but pitched, yawed, rolled completely over again and again, still striving to follow the dictates of the altitude control. That barometer was sensitive enough for control in the upper stratosphere of planets like Earth and Thanno; and in the tremendous pressure changes accompanying turbulence in Hekla's dense atmosphere the little device went mad. Vickers, dazed and bleeding, bouncing from floor to ceiling and wall to wall of the control room, finally managed to hold on to the board long enough and firmly enough to set the selector at zero pressure. Still bucking and rolling, the ship went shooting upwards, and at last broke out into the crimson sunlight—more than thirty kilometers above the ocean, if the radio altimeter could be believed. The air was calmer here, and the ship quieted down enough for Vickers to level it by manual control, reset the toppled attitude gyros, and cut them in again.

With a steady deck once more under his feet, he staggered back to the library where Rodin had been working. The meteorologist had taken a beating, but had suffered less damage than Vickers, owing chiefly to the fact that the library furniture was for the most part heavily upholstered. He made acrid inquiry into the cause of the disturbance, and was not particularly sympathetic with Vickers' injuries. They went forward to the control room together, and Vickers gazed through the port at the innocent-looking, fluffy pink mass below them while Rodin applied antiseptic and dressings to his contusions. When he had finished this job, the meteorologist began to observe, too.

Vickers had halted the ship when he had regained control, and they were hanging motionless above the wall of vapor. They were still in sight of the edge where they had entered it; and when Rodin set the ship in motion again, they ran within a few minutes into an almost equally sharp termination on the other side. The front was only thirty or forty miles wide; and this, together with the altitude of the cumulus barrier, indicated a frontal slope that made Rodin whistle. Then he stopped to think; and the more he thought the less he was able to understand how a mass of cold air of such size and, apparently, extreme low temperature could have wandered so far from the pole in midsummer. Then he remembered the violence which had resulted from a very slight temperature change, during the warm front he had watched at Observatory Hill; and he took the ship down on the cold side of the front to the altitude at which they had been flying when they ran into trouble, and compared temperatures. The difference was not great, but it was far greater than had been the case on the other occasion; and considering the density and other peculiarities of Hekla's atmosphere, it could account for such a violent front. It remained to account for the air mass. Rodin began to think out loud, as he considered this problem.

"This stuff appears to be of polar continental origin, judging by its temperature and dryness," he said. "It's not extremely cold, but in Hekla's atmosphere it could still have formed over the polar ice cap, and probably did. On Earth, such a mass couldn't come anything like this far south in summer. The normal surface circulation is too strong for it, and remains too strong as long as the ground is receiving much solar energy. However, it could be forced down like this if we supposed another, still colder, mass to the east of its source region, against which it was carried by the normal trade circulation and thence deflected southward. Also, a general cooling of the continental areas to the south of the source region might permit it to be carried down here around a normal cyclone.

"Either supposition demands a decrease in ground surface temperature comparable to that experienced at the onset of winter. I can't imagine any large area waiting until this late in the summer to become covered by snow; but I can't see any other means of dropping the temperature of a large area to any great extent, unless the axis of the planet shifts enough to decrease insolation in this hemisphere." He grinned wryly as he made that remark; he realized perfectly well that the application of sufficient force to shift the axis of a major planet would buckle its crust at the very least, and more probably disrupt the world.

"How about night cooling?" asked Vickers. "This planet rotates more slowly than Earth."

"Not enough; in summer the nights are short anyway; and why would it wait until now, fully two Earth years after midsummer, to take effect?"

"Then how about this mist that seems to have been cutting off some of the sunlight of the last day or two? You must have noticed it—it appears to be above any level at which we've flown, so it can't be very dense; but it seems to be practically planet-wide, and cuts off enough light for me to notice without instruments."

"I hadn't noticed it particularly," said Rodin thoughtfully. "A high layer of water vapor or dust would have a blanketing effect, and would actually increase surface temperature, even though it cut off some visible light. However, there's something to the idea; the stuff might just possibly have a high reflecting power, I suppose. It won't hurt us to go up and find this layer, anyway."

Rodin went back to the controls, and started the ship climbing slowly. Then he started the recorder of the radiograph he had set up at one of the portholes when he had first arrived, and waited while they rose through the thinning atmosphere to a level at which the outside pressure was no longer detectable. There he stopped ship and recorder, and removed the graph from the latter. The haze layer, if it existed, should have betrayed its presence by a more or less sharp break in the curve—or rather, a change in its slope—at the proper level; but Rodin, to his disgust, was unable to find anything of the sort by visual inspection. He was beginning to check the instrument for flaws that would affect its sensitivity, when Vickers remarked that the sun seemed still to be rather weaker than usual—rather as Sol would appear from Earth during a partial eclipse, allowing for the difference in their intrinsic luminosities.

"An eclipse?" queried Rodin. "Hekla has only two satellites big enough and near enough to produce a respectable eclipse; and even the partial phase would last only a few hours. You noticed this dimness a couple of days ago."

He went to the port and looked up at the sun. From Hekla's surface the human eye could bear to look directly at R Coronae's immense disk, but here above the atmosphere it was a little too bright for comfort. He rummaged in a drawer under the control panel, found a pair of shielded goggles; with these he approached the port again, and looked long and earnestly at the fuzzy crimson blot hanging in the blackness of space. At last he called Vickers, gave him the goggles, and asked him to look, describe, and if possible explain what he saw. Vickers obediently donned the eye shields and went to the port.

He had seen red giant suns before—who hadn't? He was familiar with the brilliant crimson or orange disks, with brightness fading rapidly toward the ill-defined edges, bordered by a faintly luminous rim of atmosphere that faded rapidly outward against the star-shot background of the Galaxy. R Coronae should have been the same.

Perhaps it was, he thought at last. Perhaps it did have a normal disk; but he couldn't see it—at least, not all of it. The lower quarter was visible, fading as it should and equipped with a normal atmosphere rim. A short distance up from this lower edge, however, a black line was etched across the crimson, projecting on each side. Where it appeared against the background of space, it glowed very faintly red. Above the line the stellar disk was hidden almost completely, as though by a cloud whose edge was represented by the border of black. The cloud, if it was a cloud, apparently grew thinner toward the top; for the upper side of the disk was faintly visible through it. Vickers slid the goggles up on his forehead and took a quick look at the sun without them. He could see the foggy disk, and was just able to make out the dark line. Evidently the "cloud" actually cut off less light than the view through the shields indicated; but if, as it appeared, the appendage were attached to the star rather than to Hekla itself, a drop in temperature was not very surprising. He turned away from the port and addressed Rodin, who was waiting impatiently.

"If clouds are possible in a star's atmosphere, I'd say you had something on R Coronae quite similar to this cold front of yours right below us," he said. "If it happens very often, I suppose it's the explanation of the star's variability." He made this statement, so staggering to the meteorologist, in such a matter-of-fact tone that it was several seconds before Rodin could find voice. Finally he half-spoke, half-choked:

"You...you mean you have known all along that this star is a variable, and didn't think it worth while to tell me? You mean—" he sputtered, and lost voice again; and Vickers realized that the color of his face was not entirely due to the sunlight.

"Of course I knew it was a variable; didn't you? Most of the red giants are, to a slight extent, but it doesn't particularly bother the planets of Betelgeuse and Antares. I remembered that, and looked up this star in the type index before we arrived. It gave a C.I. and size about the same as the giants I mentioned, and was marked 'V' as they were, so I supposed it was the same sort of business here."

Rodin did not answer, but turned on his heel and strode back to the library, Vickers close behind. He found the index Vickers had used, checked its source of information, and located the indicated volume on the shelves. He thumbed through this for a moment, stopped, and read silently for a minute or two; then he handed the tome to Vickers and indicated the proper section. Vickers read, and slowly understood.

" 'R Coronae Borealis is the name-star of a group of suns characterized photometrically by a light-curve of the form shown, and spectroscopically by the presence of strong carbon indications. It was suggested long before interstellar travel was achieved that the light variations were caused by temporary condensations of carbon vapor in the stellar atmospheres; and the correctness of this assumption was shown in the excellent series of photographs made by the Galactic Survey ship *Zenith*, which follow the formation of masses of carbon clouds through a full cycle from the beginning of condensation to complete dispersal. The actual mechanism and processes involved have not been closely studied, but it has been suggested that such a study should be conducted by a composite board of astrophysicists and meteorologists, as the phenomena seem to bear strong resemblance to those of planetary weather.

" 'The *Zenith* noted the presence of two planets in a cursory photographic sweep of the R Coronae system, but they were not closely examined, nor was the possibility of the presence of others eliminated.' "

Rodin nodded slowly as Vickers finished his reading.

"You called the shot very nicely a few minutes ago," he said, "when you called that black line a cold front. I should say that you were one hundred percent right. Blast it, to be a meteorologist in this system I'd have to know more astrophysics than a lot of Federation professors. You've certainly let me make an awful idiot of myself in front of those Heklans."

"Do you really think so?" asked Vickers seriously. "I don't see how they could expect you to know any better. You're a meteorologist, not an astronomer, as you said."

"On this planet, the distinction is probably narrow to the point of invisibility. Their weather men would *have* to be first-rate solar physicists. I must have seemed to them like a self-opinionated, bungling incompetent—insisting time after time on the feasibility of a plan whose greatest flaw would have been obvious to a Heklan layman. I don't want to go back to that station, Alf—I couldn't face one of those people now."

"I'm afraid you'll have to," replied Vickers. "I sympathize with you, and am extremely sorry for your sake that it turned out this way; but from my point of view it's the best thing that could have happened. I hoped for something good to eventuate from your visit, but I didn't dare hope for this much."

Rodin's interjection at this point was of an interrogative and profane nature. Vickers smiled slightly, set the ship in motion once again toward Observatory Hill, and began to explain.

"I told you at the time of your arrival," he said, "that I feared I had unwittingly aroused in our hosts a fear of the competitive aspects of our Federation culture. That was quite true and correct, so far as it went. There was a little more than that to the situation, however. The Heklans had appreciated a still more fundamental fact about us. With interplanetary and interstellar travel, an already existing and working form of interworld government, with our knowledge of space and time and matter which cropped up occasionally and inevitably in my conversations with Serrnak Deg, it was glaringly obvious to them that our civilization was materially far in advance of theirs; that their achievements, compared to ours, were childish. As that realization sank in, they began to react in a fashion too painfully human not to be recognized.

"If something weren't done about that reaction, Hekla would not only refuse the minor dealing with us such as our attempt to sell them metal and machines represents—they would, for their own protection, refuse to have anything whatever to do with the Federation and its component races. You know what has happened on other planets when a culturally and mentally inferior race was forced into contact with their betters. They died out, rapidly, and the cause was not deliberate extermination. In many cases, strenuous efforts were made to preserve them. Such things happened on Earth long before man left the planet; and it has happened all over the Galaxy since then.

"The Heklans are not our mental inferiors; they are intelligent enough to recognize a danger which must have been completely new to them, and to act on it in the only possible way—although that way is not a very good one, even from their own viewpoint. They may get rid of us, but they would have a hard time forgetting us."

"Are you sure they recognize the danger?" interjected Rodin.

"Reasonably sure; and even if they don't, it is none the less real—*and our making fools of ourselves is just as good a cure.* We showed them a field— probably not the only one, but certainly the most obvious—in which they are not merely our equals but have advanced far beyond us. We showed them in a way that will penetrate—their sense of humor seems to be as well developed as ours; and we showed them at the relatively minor price of your reputation—and mine, of course." The last phrase was an after-thought inspired by Rodin's attitude. The meteorologist calmed himself again with an effort, and asked a question.

"When did you realize what was happening to them, and what led you to that belief?"

"After my first long conversation with Serrnak Deg, I started to re-turn to the ship alone. By an error, I stopped the elevator at the wrong level, and saw a room full of electrical machinery. I am not a scientist, but I think I know a teletype keyboard when I see it. Before I could see more, I was hustled out of the room. When I got back to the ship, I spent quite a while searching the frequency bands we have found practical for com-munication. I heard nothing, and yet the station was obviously in con-stant contact with the rest of the planet—even I know that a weather map can't be kept up to date otherwise. Disregarding the remote chance that they had either medium transmitters or a means of radiant communica-tion undreamed of by us, it seemed obvious that the station was actually connected by metallic cables with other centers of communication. The method is primitive, as even you will admit; why should they conceal the installation from me, if they were not ashamed of its simplicity?

"Later, when they showed us around the station, and failed to hide any of the other primitive equipment such as internal combustion en-gines, I was sure they had decided to give up the attempt to conceal the inferiority they felt in the face of our apparatus. Deg had visited the life-boat by then, remember. They were planning then, and must have been planning until we started this trip, to break with us completely.

"You can see why I didn't tell you this before. I'm not sure I should have told you now, because it will be necessary for you to go back to that station and not only admit your ignorance to Marn and Deg, but put the capping stone on the business by asking for enlightenment. I hope you have the intestinal fortitude to do it."

Rodin smiled wryly.

"I guess I can't let you down, since you've gone this far. Perhaps I can make up the face I've lost here by staying a while, learning some Heklan meteorology, and publishing a few papers for the benefit of the rest of the Galaxy. I can be the first *non*-Heklan stellar meteorologist, anyway, which ought to have some weight with my beloved colleagues. All right, Alf, I'll try it."

Vickers nodded and smiled slightly, as he altered the course slightly to bear toward the cloud banner of Observatory Hill, now vaguely visible in the distance.

"I was sure you would. After all, reputation or no scientific reputation, you have a job for which you get paid, same as I. Just don't lose any chance of building up to the Heklans the importance of their contributions to the meteorological knowledge of the Federation races."

"I won't," answered Rodin, "and it won't need much of my help. They really have something that will drive some of my friends wild, and will probably rock the astronomers slightly in their seats.

"But speaking of jobs, you also have one; and how does your proving to all concerned that it is impractical to work on Hekla's climate fit in with a program supposed to sell large quantities of metal?"

Vickers set the ship gently down on the ramp before turning to face his friend.

"That was solved some time ago. My motives in assuring successful relations with this race were not entirely humanitarian, though of course I don't regret the good I'm doing. My personal problem, of sales, was solved long ago, as I say; but without any Heklans the solution would be somewhat impractical. Hence the call for your invaluable assistance. Tell me, Dave, what you do if the landlord won't repair the air conditioner in your apartment?" He smiled at the look of comprehension on the other's face. "Of course. Granting the availability of other quarters, you move.

"There are certainly other quarters available for the Heklans, even if they are restricted to the systems of red giant stars; and the Federation can undoubtedly find a number of suitable worlds in a very few years, even if they are not already known.

"Any race that goes in for colonization in a big way, Dave, is going to need spaceships in considerable numbers; and I am sure that Belt Metals will be only too glad to provide them. In fact, I think we might both draw a very comfortable bonus on such a transaction; and I plan, at the first opportune moment, to put the proposition to Serrnak Deg."

Vickers rose from the control seat, touching as he did so the switch that opened the inner air lock door.

"I think that covers all the problems of the moment," he said, as he struggled into a jacket. "Now come on into that station with me, Dave. I want to see you eat humble pie!"

PROOF

Astounding, June 1942

Kron held his huge freighter motionless, feeling forward for outside contact. The tremendous interplay of magnetic and electrostatic fields just beyond the city's edge was as clearly perceptible to his senses as the city itself—a mile-wide disk ringed with conical field towers, stretching away behind and to each side. The ship was poised between two of the towers; immediately behind it was the field from which Kron had just taken off. The area was covered with cradles of various forms—cup-shaped receptacles which held city craft like Kron's own; long, boat-shaped hollows wherein reposed the cigarlike vessels which plied between the cities; and towering skeleton frameworks which held upright the slender double cones that hurtled across the dark, lifeless regions between stars.

Beyond the landing field was the city proper; the surface of the disk was covered with geometrically shaped buildings—cones, cylinders, prisms, and hemispheres, jumbled together.

Kron could "see" all this as easily as a human being in an airplane can see New York; but no human eyes could have perceived this city, even if a man could have existed anywhere near it. The city, buildings and all, glowed a savage, white heat; and about and beyond it—a part of it, to human eyes—raged the equally dazzling, incandescent gases of the solar photosphere.

The freighter was preparing to launch itself into that fiery ocean; Kron was watching the play of the artificial reaction fields that supported the city, preparatory to plunging through them at a safe moment.

There was considerable risk of being flattened against the edge of the disk if an inauspicious choice was made, but Kron was an experienced flier, and slipped past the barrier with a sudden, hurtling acceleration that would have pulped any body of flesh and bone. The outer fringe of the field flung the globe sharply downward; then it was free, and the city was dwindling above them.

Kron and four others remained at their posts; the rest of the crew of thirty relaxed, their spherical bodies lying passive in the cuplike rests distributed through the ship, bathing in the fierce radiance on which those bodies fed, and which was continually streaming from a three-inch spheroid at the center of the craft. That an artificial source of energy should be needed in such an environment may seem strange, but to these creatures the outer layers of the Sun were far more inhospitable to life than is the stratosphere of Earth to human beings.

They had evolved far down near the solar core, where pressures and temperatures were such that matter existed in the "collapsed" state characteristic of the entire mass of white dwarf stars. Their bodies were simply constructed: a matrix of close-packed electrons—really an unimaginably dense electrostatic field, possessing quasi-solid properties—surrounded a core of neutrons, compacted to the ultimate degree. Radiation of sufficient energy, falling on the "skin," was stabilized, altered to the pattern and structure of neutrons; the tiny particles of neutronium which resulted were borne along a circulatory system—of magnetic fields, instead of blood—to the nucleus, where it was stored.

The race had evolved to the point where no material appendages were needed. Projected beams and fields of force were their limbs, powered by the annihilation of some of their own neutron substance. Their strange senses gave them awareness not only of electromagnetic radiation, permitting them to "see" in a more or less normal fashion, but also of energies still undreamed of by human scientists. Kron, hundreds of miles below the city now, was still dimly aware of its location, though radio waves, light and gamma rays were all hopelessly fogged in the clouds of free electrons. At his goal, far down in the solar interior, "seeing" conditions would be worse—anything more than a few hundred yards distant would be quite indetectable even to him.

Poised beside Kron, near the center of the spheroidal sunship, was another being. Its body was ovoid in shape, like that of the Solarian, but longer and narrower, while the ends were tipped with pyramidal structures of neutronium, which projected through the "skin." A second, fainter static aura enveloped the creature outside the principal surface; and as the crew relaxed in their cups, a beam of energy from this envelope impinged on Kron's body. It carried a meaning, transmitting a clear thought from one being to the other.

"I still find difficulty in believing my senses," stated the stranger. "My own worlds revolve about another which is somewhat similar to this; but such a vast and tenuous atmosphere is most unlike conditions at home. Have you ever been away from Sol?"

"Yes," replied Kron, "I was once on the crew of an interstellar projectile. I have never seen your star, however; my acquaintance with it is entirely through hearsay. I am told it consists almost entirely of collapsed matter, like the core of our own; but there is practically no atmosphere. Can this be so? I should think, at the temperature necessary for life, gases would break free of the core and form an envelope."

"They tend to do so, of course," returned the other, "but our surface gravity is immeasurably greater than anything you have here; even your core pull is less, since it is much less dense than our star. Only the fact that our worlds are small, thus causing a rapid diminution of gravity as one leaves them, makes it possible to get a ship away from them at all; atoms, with only their original velocities, remain within a few miles of the surface.

"But you remind me of my purpose on this world—to check certain points of a new theory concerning the possible behavior of aggregations of normal atoms. That was why I arranged a trip on your flier; I have to make density, pressure, temperature, and a dozen other kinds of measurements at a couple of thousand different levels, in your atmosphere. While I'm doing it, would you mind telling me why you make these regular trips—and why, for that matter, you live so far above your natural level? I should think you would find life easier below, since there would be no need to remain in sealed buildings, or to expend such a terrific amount of power in supporting your cities."

Kron's answer was slow.

"We make the journeys to obtain neutronium. It is impossible to convert enough power from the immediate neighborhood of the cities to support them; we must descend periodically for more, even though our converters take so much as to lower the solar temperature considerably for thousands of miles around each city.

"The trips are dangerous—you should have been told that. We carry a crew of thirty, when two would be enough to man this ship, for we must fight, as well as fly. You spoke truly when you said that the lower regions of Sol are our natural home; but for aeons we have not dared to make more than fleeting visits, to steal the power which is life to us.

"Your little worlds have been almost completely subjugated by your people, Sirian; they never had life forms sufficiently powerful to threaten seriously your domination. But Sol, whose core alone is far larger than the Sirius B pair, did develop such creatures. Some are vast, stupid, slow-moving, or immobile; others are semi-intelligent, and rapid movers; all are more than willing to ingest the ready-compacted neutronium of another living being."

Kron's tale was interrupted for a moment, as the Sirian sent a ray probing out through the ship's wall, testing the physical state of the inferno beyond. A record was made, and the Solarian resumed.

"We, according to logical theory, were once just such a race—of small intelligence, seeking the needs of life among a horde of competing organisms. Our greatest enemy was a being much like ourselves in size and power—just slightly superior in both ways. We were somewhat ahead in intelligence, and I suppose we owe them some thanks—without the competition they provided, we should not have been forced to develop our minds to their present level. We learned to cooperate in fighting them, and from that came the discovery that many of us together could handle natural forces that a single individual could not even approach, and survive. The creation of force effects that had no counterpart in nature was the next step; and, with the understanding of them, our science grew.

"The first cities were of neutronium, like those of today, but it was necessary to stabilize the neutrons with fields of energy; at core temperature, as you know, neutronium is a gas. The cities were spherical and much smaller than our present ones. For a long time, we managed to defend them.

"But our enemies evolved, too; not in intelligence, but in power and fecundity. With overspecialization of their physical powers, their mentalities actually degenerated; they became little more than highly organized machines, driven, by an age-old enmity toward our race, to seek us out and destroy us. Their new powers at last enabled them to neutralize, by brute force, the fields which held our cities in shape; and then it was that, from necessity, we fled to the wild, inhospitable upper regions of Sol's atmosphere. Many cities were destroyed by the enemy before a means of supporting them was devised; many more fell victims to forces which we generated, without being able to control, in the effort. The dangers of our present-day trips seem trivial beside those our ancestors braved, in spite of the fact that ships not infrequently fail to return from their flights. Does that answer your question?"

The Sirian's reply was hesitant. "I guess it does. You of Sol must have developed far more rapidly than we, under that drive; your science, I know, is superior to ours in certain ways, although it was my race which first developed space flight."

"You had greater opportunities in that line," returned Kron. "Two small stars, less than a diameter apart, circling a larger one at a distance incomparably smaller than the usual interstellar interval, provided perfect ground for experimental flights; between your world and mine, even radiation requires some one hundred and thirty rotations to make the journey, and even the nearest other star is almost half as far.

"But enough of this—history is considered by too many to be a dry subject. What brings you on a trip with a power flier? You certainly have not learned anything yet which you could not have been told in the city."

During the conversation, the Sirian had periodically tested the atmosphere beyond the hull. He spoke, rather absently, as though concentrating on something other than his words.

"I would not be too sure of that, Solarian. My measurements are of greater delicacy than we have ever before achieved. I am looking for a very special effect, to substantiate or disprove an hypothesis which I have recently advanced—much to the detriment of my prestige. If you are interested, I might explain: laugh afterward if you care to—you will not be the first.

"The theory is simplicity itself. It has occurred to me that matter—ordinary substances like iron and calcium—might actually take on solid form, like neutronium, under the proper conditions. The normal gas, you know, consists of minute particles traveling with considerable speed in all directions. There seems to be no way of telling whether or not these atoms exert appreciable forces on each other; but it seems to me that if they were brought closely enough together, or slowed down sufficiently, some such effects might be detected."

"How, and why?" asked Kron. "If the forces are there, why should they not be detectable under ordinary conditions?"

"Tiny changes in velocity due to mutual attraction or repulsion would scarcely be noticed when the atomic speeds are of the order of hundreds of kilometers per second," returned the Sirian. "The effects I seek to detect are of a different nature. Consider, please. We know the sizes of the various atoms, from their radiations. We also know that, under normal conditions, a given mass of any particular gas fills a certain volume. If, however, we surround this gas with an impenetrable container and exert pressure, that volume decreases. We would expect that decrease to be proportional to the pressure, except for an easily determined constant due to the size of the atoms, if no interatomic forces existed; to detect such forces, I am making a complete series of pressure-density tests, more delicate than any heretofore, from the level of your cities down to the neutron core of your world.

"If we could reduce the kinetic energy of the atoms—slow down their motions of translation—the task would probably be simpler; but I see no way to accomplish that. Perhaps, if we could negate nearly all of that energy, the interatomic forces would actually hold the atoms in definite relative positions, approximating the solid state. It was that somewhat injudicious and perhaps too imaginative suggestion which caused my whole idea to be ridiculed on Sirius."

The ship dropped several hundred miles in the few seconds before Kron answered; since gaseous friction is independent of change in density, the high pressures of the regions being penetrated would be no bar to high speed of flight. Unfortunately, the viscosity of a gas does increase directly as the square root of its temperature; and at the lower levels of the sun, travel would be slow.

"Whether or not our scientists will listen to you, I cannot say," said Kron finally. "Some of them are a rather imaginative crowd, I guess, and none of them will ignore any data you may produce.

"I do not laugh, either. My reason will certainly interest you, as your theory intrigues me. It is the first time anyone has accounted even partly for the things that happened to us on one of my flights."

The other members of the crew shifted slightly on their cradles; a ripple of interest passed through them, for all had heard rumors and vague tales of Kron's time in the space carrier fleets. The Sirian settled himself more comfortably; Kron dimmed the central globe of radiance a trifle, for the outside temperature was now considerably higher, and began the tale.

"This happened toward the end of my career in space. I had made many voyages with the merchant and passenger vessels, had been promoted from the lowest ranks, through many rotations, to the post of independent captain. I had my own cruiser—a special long-period explorer, owned by the Solarian government. She was shaped like our modern interstellar carriers, consisting of two cones, bases together, with the field ring just forward of their meeting point. She was larger than most, being designed to carry fuel for exceptionally long flights,

"Another cruiser, similar in every respect, was under the command of a comrade of mine, named Akro; and the two of us were commissioned to transport a party of scientists and explorers to the then newly discovered Fourth System, which lies, as you know, nearly in the plane of the solar equator, but about half again as distant as Sirius.

"We made good time, averaging nearly half the speed of radiation, and reached the star with a good portion of our hulls still unconsumed. We need not have worried about that, in any case; the star was denser even than the Sirius B twins, and neutronium was very plentiful. I restocked at once, plating my inner walls with the stuff until they had reached their original thickness, although experience indicated that the original supply was ample to carry us either back to Sol, to Sirius, or to Procyon B.

"Akro, at the request of the scientists, did not refuel. Life was present on the star, as it seems to be on all stars where the atomic velocities and the density are high enough; and the biologists wanted to bring back specimens. That meant that room would be needed, and if Akro replated his walls to normal thickness that room would be lacking—as I have mentioned, these were special long-range craft, and a large portion of their volume consisted of available neutronium.

"So it happened that the other ship left the Fourth System with a low, but theoretically sufficient, stock of fuel, and half a dozen compartments filled with specimens of alien life. I kept within detection distance at all times, in case of trouble, for some of those life forms were as dangerous as those of Sol, and, like them, all consumed neutronium. They had to be kept well under control to safeguard the very walls of the ship, and it is surprisingly difficult to make a wild beast, surrounded by food, stay on short rations.

"Some of the creatures proved absolutely unmanageable; they had to be destroyed. Others were calmed by lowering the atomic excitation of their compartments, sending them into a stupor; but the scientists were reluctant to try that in most cases, since not all of the beings could stand such treatment.

"So, for nearly four hundred Solar rotations, Akro practically fought his vessel across space—fought successfully. He managed on his own power until we were within a few hundred diameters of Sol; but I had to help him with the landing—or try to, for the landing was never made.

"It may seem strange, but there is a large volume of space in the neighborhood of this sun which is hardly ever traversed. The normal landing orbit arches high over one of the poles of rotation, enters atmosphere almost tangentially somewhere between that pole and the equator, and kills as much as remains of the ship's velocity in the outer atmospheric layers. There is a minimum of magnetic interference that way, since the flier practically coasts along the lines of force of the Solar magnetic field.

"As a result, few ships pass through the space near the plane of the Solar equator. One or two may have done so before us, and I know of several that searched the region later; but none encountered the thing which we found.

"About the time we would normally have started correcting our orbits for a tangential landing, Akro radiated me the information that he could not possibly control his ship any farther with the power still available to him. His walls were already so thin that radiation loss, ordinarily negligible, was becoming a definite menace to his vessel. All his remaining energy would have to be employed in keeping the interior of his ship habitable.

"The only thing I could do was to attach our ships together with an attractor beam, and make a nearly perpendicular drop to Sol. We would have to take our chances with magnetic and electrostatic disturbances in the city-supporting fields which cover so much of the near-equatorial zones, and try to graze the nucleus of the Sun instead of its outer atmosphere, so that Akro could replenish his rapidly failing power.

"Akro's hull was radiating quite perceptibly now; it made an easy target for an attractor. We connected without difficulty, and our slightly different linear velocities caused us to revolve slowly about each other, pivoting on the center of mass of our two ships. I cut off my driving fields, and we fell spinning toward Sol.

"I was becoming seriously worried about Akro's chances of survival. The now-alarming energy loss through his almost consumed hull threatened to exhaust his supply long before we reached the core; and we were still more than a hundred diameters out. I could not give him any power; we were revolving about each other at a distance of about one-tenth of a Solar diameter. To lessen that distance materially would increase our speed of revolution to a point where the attractor could not overcome centrifugal force; and I had neither power nor time to perform the delicate job of exactly neutralizing our rotary momentum without throwing us entirely off course. All we could do was hope.

"We were somewhere between one hundred and one hundred and fifty diameters out when there occurred the most peculiar phenomenon I have ever encountered. The plane of revolution of our two ships passed near Sol, but was nearly perpendicular to the Solar equator; at the time of which I speak, Akro's ship was almost directly between my flier and the Sun. Observations had just shown that we were accelerating Sunward at an unexpectedly high pace, when a call came from Akro.

" 'Kron! I am being pulled away from your attractor! There is a large mass somewhere near, for the pull is gravitational, but it emits no radiation that I can detect. Increase your pull, if you can; I cannot possibly free myself alone.'

"I did what I could, which was very little. Since we did not know the location of the disturbing dark body, it was impossible to tell just what I should do to avoid bringing my own or Akro's vessel too close. I think now that if I had released him immediately he would have swung clear, for the body was not large, I believe. Unfortunately, I did the opposite, and nearly lost my own ship as well. Two of my crew were throwing as much power as they could convert and handle into the attractor, and trying to hold it on the still easily visible hull of Akro's ship; but the motions of the latter were so peculiar that aiming was a difficult task. They held the ship as long as we could see it; but quite suddenly the radiations by means of which we perceived the vessel faded out, and before we could find a band which would get through, the sudden cessation of our centripetal acceleration told us that the beam had slipped from its target.

"We found that electromagnetic radiations of wave lengths in the octave above H-alpha would penetrate the interference, and Akro's hull was leaking energy enough to radiate in that band. When we found him, however, we could scarcely believe our senses; his velocity was now nearly at right angles to his former course, and his hull radiation had become far weaker. What terrific force had caused this acceleration, and what strange field was blanketing the radiation, were questions none of us could answer.

"Strain as we might, not one of us could pick up an erg of radiant energy that might emanate from the thing that had trapped Akro. We could only watch, and endeavor to plot his course relative to our own, at first. Our ships were nearing each other rapidly, and we were attempting to determine the time and distance of closest approach, when we were startled by the impact of a communicator beam. Akro was alive! The beam was weak, very weak, showing what an infinitesimal amount of power he felt he could spare. His words were nor encouraging.

" 'Kron! You may as well cut your attractor, if you are still trying to catch me. No power that I dare apply seems to move me perceptibly in any direction from this course. We are all badly shocked, for we hit something that felt almost solid. The walls, even, are strained, and may go at any time.'

" 'Can you perceive anything around you?' I returned. 'You seem to us to be alone in space, though something is absorbing most of your radiated energy. There must be energies in the cosmos of which we have never dreamed, simply because they did not affect our senses. What do your scientists say?'

" 'Very little,' was the answer. 'They have made a few tests, but they say that anything they project is absorbed without reradiating anything useful. We seem to be in a sort of energy vacuum—it takes everything and returns nothing.'

"This was the most alarming item yet. Even in free space, we had been doubtful of Akro's chances of survival; now they seemed reduced to the ultimate zero.

"Meanwhile, our ships were rapidly approaching each other. As nearly as my navigators could tell, both vessels were pursuing almost straight lines in space. The lines were nearly perpendicular but did not lie in a common plane; their minimum distance apart was about one one-thousandth of a Solar diameter. His velocity seemed nearly constant, while I was accelerating Sunward. It seemed that we would reach the near-intersection point almost simultaneously, which meant that my ship was certain to approach the energy vacuum much too closely. I did not dare to try to pull Akro free with an attractor; it was only too obvious that such an attempt could only end in disaster for both vessels. If he could not free himself, he was lost.

"We could only watch helplessly as the point of light marking the position of Akro's flier swept closer and closer. At first, as I have said, it seemed perfectly free in space; but as we looked, the region around it began to radiate feebly. There was nothing recognizable about the vibrations, simply a continuous spectrum, cut off by some interference just below the H-alpha wave length and, at the other end, some three octaves higher. As the emission grew stronger, the visible region around the stranded ship grew larger, fading into nothingness at the edges. Brighter and broader the patch of radiance grew, as we swept toward it."

That same radiance was seriously inconveniencing Gordon Aller, who was supposed to be surveying for a geological map of northern Australia. He was camped by the only waterhole in many miles, and had stayed up long after dark preparing his cameras, barometer, soil kit, and other equipment for the morrow's work.

The arrangement of instruments completed, he did not at once retire to his blankets. With his back against a smooth rock, and a short, blackened pipe clenched in his teeth, he sat for some time, pondering. The object of his musing does not matter to us; though his eyes were directed heavenward, he was sufficiently accustomed to the southern sky to render it improbable that he was paying much attention to its beauties.

However that may be, his gaze was suddenly attracted to the zenith. He had often seen stars which appeared to move when near the edge of his field of vision—it is a common illusion; but this one continued to shift as he turned his eyes upward.

Not far from Achernar was a brilliant white point, which brightened as Aller watched it. It was moving slowly northward, it seemed; but only a moment was needed for the man to realize that the slowness was illusory. The thing was slashing almost vertically downward at an enormous speed, and must strike Earth not far from his camp.

Aller was not an astronomer, and had no idea of astronomical distances or speeds. He may be forgiven for thinking of the object as traveling perhaps as fast as a modern fighting plane, and first appearing at a height of two or three miles. The natural conclusion from this belief was that the crash would occur within a few hundred feet of the camp. Aller paled; he had seen pictures of the Devil's Pit in Arizona.

Actually, of course, the meteor first presented itself to his gaze at a height of some eighty miles, and was then traveling at a rate of many miles per second relative to Earth. At that speed, the air presented a practically solid obstacle to its flight, and the object was forced to a fairly constant velocity of ten or twelve hundred yards a second while still nearly ten miles from Earth's surface. It was at that point that Aller's eyes caught up with and succeeded in focusing upon the celestial visitor.

That first burst of light had been radiated by the frightfully compressed and heated air in front of the thing; as the original velocity departed, so did the dazzling light. Aller got a clear view of the meteor at a range of less than five miles, for perhaps ten seconds before the impact. It was still incandescent, radiating a bright cherry-red; this must have been due to the loss from within, for so brief a contact even with such highly heated air could not have warmed the sunship's neutronium walls a measurable fraction of a degree.

Aller felt the ground tremble as the vessel struck. A geyser of earth, barely visible in the reddish light of the hull, spouted skyward, to fall back seconds later with a long drawn-out rumble. The man stared at the spot, two miles away, which was still giving off a faint glow. Were "shooting stars" as regularly shaped as that? He had seen a smooth, slender body, more than a hundred feet in length, apparently composed of two cones of unequal length, joined together at the bases. Around the longer cone, not far from the point of juncture, was a thick bulging ring; no further details were visible at the distance from which he had observed. Aller's vague recollections of meteorites, seen in various museums, brought images of irregular, clinkerlike objects before his mind's eye. What, then, could this thing be?

He was not imaginative enough to think for a moment of any possible extraterrestrial source for an aircraft; when it did occur to him that the object was of artificial origin, he thought more of some experimental machine produced by one of the more progressive Earth nations.

At the thought, Aller strapped a first-aid kit to his side and set out toward the crater, in the face of the obvious fact that nothing human could possibly have survived such a crash. He stumbled over the uneven terrain for a quarter of a mile, and then stopped on a small rise of ground to examine more closely the site of the wreck.

The glow should have died by this time, for Aller had taken all of ten minutes to pick his way those few hundred yards; but the dull-red light ahead had changed to a brilliant-orange radiance against which the serrated edges of the pit were clearly silhouetted. No flames were visible; whence came the increasing heat? Aller attempted to get closer, but a wave of frightfully hot air blistered his face and hands, and drove him back. He took up a station near his former camp, and watched.

If the hull of the flier had been anywhere near its normal thickness, the tremendous mass of neutronium would have sunk through the hardest of rocks as though they were liquid. There was, however, scarcely more than a paper thickness of the substance at any part of the walls; and an upthrust of adamantine volcanic rock not far beneath the surface of the desert proved thick enough to absorb the sunship's momentum and to support its still enormous weight. Consequently, the ship was covered only by a thin layer of powdered rock which had fallen back into the crater. The disturbances arising from the now extremely rapid loss of energy from Akro's ship were, as a result, decidedly visible from the surface.

The hull, though thin, was still intact; but its temperature was now far above the melting point of the surrounding rocks. The thin layer of pulverized material above the ship melted and flowed away almost instantly, permitting free radiation to the air above; and so enormous is the specific heat of neutronium that no perceptible lowering of hull temperature occurred.

Aller, from his point of observation, saw the brilliant fan of light that sprang from the pit as the flier's hull was exposed—the vessel itself was invisible to him, since he was only slightly above the level of the crater's mouth. He wondered if the impact of the "meteor" had released some pent-up volcanic energy, and began to doubt, quite justifiably, if he was at a safe distance. His doubts vanished and were replaced by certainty as the edges of the crater began to glow dull-red, then bright-orange, and slowly subsided out of sight. He began packing the most valuable items of his equipment, while a muted, continuous roaring and occasional heavy thuds from the direction of the pit admonished him to hasten.

When he straightened up, with the seventy-pound pack settled on his shoulders, there was simply a lake of lava where the crater had been. The fiery area spread even as he watched; and without further delay he set off on his own back trail. He could see easily, by the light diffused from the inferno behind him; and he made fairly good time, considering his burden and the fact that he had not slept since the preceding night.

The rock beneath Akro's craft was, as we have said, extremely hard. Since there was relatively free escape upward for the constantly liberated energy, this stratum melted very slowly, gradually letting the vessel sink deeper into the earth. What would have happened if Akro's power supply had been greater is problematical; Aller can tell us only that some five hours after the landing, as he was resting for a few moments near the top of a rocky hillock, the phenomenon came to a cataclysmic end.

A quivering of the earth beneath him caused the surveyor to look back toward his erstwhile camp. The lake of lava, which by this time was the better part of a mile in breadth, seemed curiously agitated. Aller, from his rather poor vantage point, could see huge bubbles of pasty lava hump themselves up and burst, releasing brilliant clouds of vapor. Each cloud illuminated earth and sky before cooling to invisibility, so that the effect was somewhat similar to a series of lightning flashes.

For a short time—certainly no longer than a quarter of a minute—Aller was able to watch as the activity increased. Then a particularly violent shock almost flung him from the hilltop, and at nearly the same instant the entire volume of molten rock fountained skyward. For an instant it seemed to hang there, a white, raging pillar of liquid and gas; then it dissolved, giving way before the savage thrust of the suddenly released energy below. A tongue of radiance, of an intensity indescribable in mere words, stabbed upward, into and through the lava, volatilizing it instantly. A dozen square miles of desert glowed white, then an almost invisible violet, and disappeared in superheated gas. Around the edges of this region, great gouts of lava and immense fragments of solid rock were hurled to all points of the compass.

Radiation exerts pressure; at the temperature found in the cores of stars, that pressure must be measured in thousands of tons per square inch. It was this thrust, rather than the by no means negligible gas pressure of the boiling lava, which wrought most of the destruction.

Aller saw little of what occurred. When the lava was hurled upward, he had flung an arm across his face to protect his eyes from the glare. That act unquestionably saved his eyesight, as the real flash followed; as it was, his body was seared and blistered through his clothing. The second, heavier shock knocked his feet from under him, and he half crawled, half rolled down to the comparative shelter of the little hill. Even here, gusts of hot air almost cooked him; only the speed with which the phenomenon ended saved his life.

Within minutes, both the temblors and the hot winds had ceased; and he crawled painfully to the hilltop again to gaze wonderingly at the five-mile-wide crater, ringed by a pile of tumbled, still-glowing rock fragments.

Far beneath that pit, shards of neutronium, no more able to remain near the surface than the steel pieces of a wrecked ocean vessel can float on water, were sinking through rock and metal to a final resting place at Earth's heart.

"The glow spread as we watched, still giving no clue to the nature of the substance radiating it," continued Kron. "Most of it seemed to originate between us and Akro's ship; Akro himself said that but little energy was being lost on the far side. His messages, during that last brief period as we swept by our point of closest approach, were clear—so clear that we could almost see as he did the tenuous light beyond the ever-thinning walls of his ship; the light that represented but a tiny percentage of the energy being sucked from the hull surface.

"We saw, as though with his own senses, the tiny perforation appear near one end of the ship; saw it extend, with the speed of thought, from one end of the hull to the other, permitting the free escape of all the energy in a single instant; and, from our point of vantage, saw the glowing area where the ship had been suddenly brightened, blazing for a moment almost as brightly as a piece of Sun matter.

"In that moment, every one of us saw the identifying frequencies as the heat from Akro's disrupted ship raised the substance which had trapped him to an energy level which permitted atomic radiation. Every one of us recognized the spectra of iron, of calcium, of carbon and silicon and a score of the other elements—Sirian, I tell you that that 'trapping field' was *matter*—matter in such a state that it could not radiate, and could offer resistance to other bodies in exactly the fashion of a solid. I thought, and have always thought, that some strange field of force held the atoms in their 'solid' positions; you have convinced me that I was wrong. The 'field' was the sum of the interacting atomic forces which you are trying to detect. The energy level of that material body was so low that those forces were able to act without interference. The condition you could not conceive of reaching artificially actually exists in Nature!"

"You go too fast, Kron," responded the Sirian. "Your first idea is far more likely to be the true one. The idea of unknown radiant or static force fields is easy to grasp; the one you propose in its place defies common sense. My theories called for some such conditions as you described, granted the one premise of a sufficiently low energy level; but a place in the real universe so devoid of energy as to absorb that of a well-insulated interstellar flier is utterly inconceivable. I have assumed your tale to be true as to details, though you offer neither witnesses nor records to support it; but I seem to have heard that you have somewhat of a reputation as an entertainer, and you seem quick-witted enough to have woven such a tale on the spot, purely from the ideas I suggested. I compliment you on the tale, Kron; it was entrancing; but I seriously advise you not to make anything more out of it. Shall we leave it at that, my friend?"

"As you will," replied Kron.

RAINDROP

Worlds of IF, May 1965

1

"It's not very comfortable footing, but at least you can't fall off."

Even through the helmet phones, Silbert's voice carried an edge that Bresnahan felt sure was amused contempt. The younger man saw no point in trying to hide his fear; he was no veteran of space and knew that it would be silly to pretend otherwise.

"My mind admits that, but my stomach isn't so sure," he replied. "It can't decide whether things will be better when I can't see so far, or whether I should just give up and take a running dive back there."

His metal-clad arm gestured toward the station and its comfortable spin hanging half a mile away. Technically the wheel-shaped structure in its synchronous orbit was above the two men, but it took careful observing to decide which way was really "up."

"You wouldn't make it," Silbert replied. "If you had solid footing for a jump you might get that far, since twenty feet a second would take you away from here permanently. But speed and velocity are two different animals. I wouldn't trust even myself to make such a jump in the right direction—and I know the vectors better than you do by a long shot. Which way would you jump? Right at the station? Or ahead of it, or behind it? And which is ahead and which is behind? Do you know?"

"I know which is ahead, since I can see it move against the star background, but I wouldn't know which way to jump. I *think* it should be ahead, since the rotation of this overgrown raindrop gives us less linear speed than the station's orbit; but I wouldn't know how far ahead," Silbert said.

"Good for you." Bresnahan noted what he hoped was approval in the spaceman's tone as well as in his words. "You're right as far as you committed yourself, and I wouldn't dare go any farther myself. In any case, jumping off this stuff is a losing game."

"I can believe that. Just walking on it makes me feel as though I were usurping a Biblical prerogative."

The computerman's arm waved again, this time at the surface underfoot, and he tried to stamp on it at the same moment. The latter gesture produced odd results. The material, which looked a little like clear jelly, gave under the boot but bulged upward all around it. The bulge moved outward very slowly in all directions, the star patterns reflected in the surface writhing as it passed. As the bulge's radius increased its height lessened, as with a ripple spreading on a pond. It might have been an ultra-slow motion picture of such a ripple, except that it did not travel far enough. It died out less than two yards from Bresnahan's foot, though it took well over a minute to get that far.

"Yeah, I know what you mean. Walking on water was kind of a divine gift, wasn't it? Well, you can always remember we're not right on the water. There's the pressure film, even if you can't see it."

"That's so. Well, let's get on to the lock. Being inside this thing can't be much worse than walking around on its surface, and I have a report to make up." Silbert started walking again at this request, though the jelly-like response of the water to his footfalls made the resulting gait rather odd. He kept talking as he led the way.

"How come that friend of yours can't come down from the station and look things over for himself? Why should you have to give the dope to him second-hand? Can't he take weightlessness?"

"Better than I can, I suspect," replied Bresnahan, "but he's not my friend. He's my boss, and pays the bills. Mine not to reason why, mine but to act or fry. He already knows as much as most people do about Raindrop, here. What more he expects to get from me I'm not sure. I just hope that what I can find to tell him makes him happy. I take it this is the lock."

They had reached a disk of metal some thirty feet in diameter, projecting about two feet from the surface of the satellite. It continued below the surface for a distance which refraction made hard to estimate.

Its water line was marked by a ring of black, rubbery-looking material where the pressure film adhered to it. The men had been quite close to it when they landed on Raindrop's surface a few minutes before, but it is hard to make out landscape details on a water surface under a black, star-filled sky; the reflection underfoot is not very different from the original above. A five-mile radius of curvature puts the reflected images far enough down so that human depth perception is no help.

Waves betrayed themselves, of course, and might have shown the lock's location—but under a gravitational acceleration of about a tenth of an inch per second squared, the surface waves raised by spacesuit boots traveled much more slowly than the men who wore them. And with their high internal energy losses they didn't get far enough to be useful.

As a result, Bresnahan had not realized that the lock was at hand until they were almost upon it. Even Silbert, who had known about where they would land and could orient himself with Raindrop's rotation axis by celestial reference features, did not actually see it until it was only a few yards away.

"This is the place, all right," he acknowledged. "That little plate near the edge is the control panel. We'll use the manhole; no need to open the main hatch as we do when it's a matter of cargo."

He bent over—slowly enough to keep his feet on the metal—and punched one of the buttons on the panel he had pointed out. A tiny light promptly flashed green, and he punched a second button.

A yard-square trap opened inward, revealing the top of a ladder. Silbert seized the highest rung and pulled himself through the opening head first—when a man weighs less than an ounce in full space panoply it makes little real difference when he elects to traverse a ladder head downward. Bresnahan followed and found himself in a cylindrical chamber which took up most of the inside of the lock structure. It could now be seen that this must extend some forty feet into the body of Raindrop.

At the inner end of the compartment, where curved and flat walls met, a smaller chamber was partitioned off. Silbert dove in this direction.

"This is a personnel lock," he remarked. "We'll use it; it saves flooding the whole chamber."

"We can use ordinary spacesuits?"

"Might as well. If we were going to stay long enough for real work, we'd change—there is local equipment in those cabinets along the wall. Spacesuits are safe enough, but pretty clumsy when it comes to fine manipulation."

"For me, they're clumsy for anything at all."

"Well, we can change if you want; but I understood that this was to be a fairly quick visit, and that you were to get a report back pronto. Or did I misread the tone your friend Weisanen was using?"

"I guess you didn't, at that. We'll go as we are. It still sounds queer to go swimming in a spacesuit."

"No queerer than walking on water. Come on, the little lock will hold both of us."

The spaceman opened the door manually—there seemed to be no power controls involved—and the two entered a room some five feet square and seven high. Operation of the lock seemed simple; Silbert closed the door they had just used and turned a latch to secure it, then opened another manual valve on the other side of the chamber. A jet of water squirted in and filled the space in half a minute. Then he simply opened a door in the same wall with the valve, and the spacesuited figures swam out.

This was not as bad as walking on what had seemed like nothingness. Bresnahan was a good swimmer and experienced free diver, and was used to being suspended in a medium where one couldn't see very far.

The water was clear, though not as clear as that sometimes found in Earth's tropical seas. There was no easy way to tell just how far vision could reach, since nothing familiar and of known size was in view except for the lock they had just quitted. There were no fishes—Raindrop's owners were still debating the advisability of establishing them there—and none of the plant life was familiar, at least to Bresnahan. He knew that the big sphere of water had been seeded by "artificial" life forms—algae and bacteria whose genetic patterns had been altered to let them live in a "sea" so different from Earth's.

2

Raindrop was composed of the nuclei of several small comets, or rather what was left of those nuclei after some of their mass had been used in reaction motors to put them into orbit about the Earth. They had been encased in a polymer film sprayed on to form a pressure seal, and then melted by solar energy, concentrated by giant foil mirrors.

Traces of the original wrapping were still around, but its function had been replaced by one of the first tailored life forms to be established after the mass was liquid. This was a modification of one of the gelatin-capsule algae, which now encased all of Raindrop in a microscopically thin film able to heal itself after small meteoroid punctures, and strong enough to maintain about a quarter of an atmosphere's pressure on the contents. The biological engineer who had done that tailoring job still regarded it as his professional masterpiece.

The methane present in the original comet material had been oxidized by other bacteria to water and carbon dioxide, the oxygen of course coming from normal photosynthesis. A good deal of the ammonia was still present, and furnished the principal reason why genetic tailoring was still necessary on life forms being transplanted to the weightless aquarium.

The men were drifting very slowly away from the lock, though they had stopped swimming, and the younger one asked, "How do we find our way back here if we get out of sight?"

"The best trick is not to get out of sight. Unless you want to examine the core, which I've never done, you'll see everything there is to see right here. There is sonic and magnetic gear—homing equipment—in your suit if you need it, though I haven't checked you out on its use. You'd better stay with me. I can probably show you what's needed. Just what points do you think Weisanen wants covered?"

"Well, he knows the general physical setup—temperature, rotation, general current pattern, the nature of the skin. He knows what's been planted here at various times; but it's hard to keep up to date on what's evolved since. These tailored life forms aren't very stable toward mutation influences, and a new-stocked aquarium isn't a very stable ecological environment. He'll want to know what's here now in the way of usable plants, I suppose. You know the Agency sold Raindrop to a private concern after the last election. The new owners seem willing to grant the importance of basic research, but they would sort of like a profit to report to the stockholders as well."

"Amen. I'm a stockholder."

"Oh? Well, it does cost something to keep supply ships coming up here, and—"

"True enough. Then this Weisanen character represents the new owners? I wonder if I should think of him as my boss or my employee."

"I think he is one of them."

"Hmph. No wonder."

"No wonder what?"

"He and his wife are the first people I ever knew to treat a space flight like a run in a private yacht. I suppose that someone who could buy Raindrop wouldn't be bothered by a little expense like a private Phoenix rocket."

"I suppose not. Of course, it isn't as bad as it was in the days of chemical motors, when it took a big commercial concern or a fair-sized government to launch a manned spaceship."

"Maybe not; but with fourteen billion people living on Earth, it's a little unusual to find a really rich individual, in the old Ford-Carnegie tradition. Most big concerns are owned by several million people like me."

"Well, I guess Weisanen owns a bigger piece of Raindrop than you do. Anyway, he's my boss, whether he's yours or not, and he wants a report from me, and I can't see much to report on. What life is there in this place besides the stuff forming the surface skin?"

"Oh, lots. You just aren't looking carefully enough. A lot of it is microscopic, of course; there are fairly ordinary varieties of pond-scum drifting all around us. They're the main reason we can see only a couple of hundred yards, and they carry on most of the photosynthesis. There are lots of non-photosynthetic organisms—bacteria—producing carbon dioxide just as in any balanced ecology on Earth, though this place is a long way from being balanced. Sometimes the algae get so thick you can't see twenty feet, sometimes the bacteria get the upper hand. The balance keeps hunting around even when no new forms are appearing or being introduced. We probably brought a few new bacteria in with us on our suits just now; whether any of them can survive with the ammonia content of Raindrop this high I don't know, but if so the ecology will get another nudge.

"There are lots of larger plants, too—mostly modifications of the big seaweeds of Earth's oceans. The lock behind us is overgrown with them, as you can see—you can look more closely as we go back—and a lot of them grow in contact with the outer skin, where the light is best. Quite a few are free-floating, but of course selection works fast on those. There are slow convection currents, because of Raindrop's size and rotation, which exchange water between the illuminated outer regions and the darkness inside. Free-floating weeds either adapt to long periods of darkness or die out fast. Since there is a good deal of hard radiation near the surface, there is also quite a lot of unplanned mutation over and above the regular gene-tailoring products we are constantly adding to the pot. And since most of the organisms here have short life spans, evolution goes on rapidly."

"Weisanen knows all that perfectly well," replied Bresnahan. "What he seems to want is a snapshot—a report on just what the present spectrum of life forms is like."

"I've summed it up. Anything more detailed would be wrong next week. You can look at the stuff around us—there. Those filaments which just tangled themselves on your equipment clip are a good example, and there are some bigger ones if you want *there*—just in reach. It would take microscopic study to show how they differ from the ones you'd have gotten a week ago or a year ago, but they're different. There will be no spectacular change unless so much growth builds up inside the surface film that the sunlight is cut down seriously. Then the selection factors will change and a radically new batch—probably of scavenger fungi—will develop and spread. It's happened before. We've gone through at least four cycles of that sort in the three years I've worked here."

Bresnahan frowned thoughtfully, though the facial gesture was not very meaningful inside a space helmet.

"I can see where this isn't going to be much of a report," he remarked.

"It would have made more sense if you'd brought a plankton net and some vacuum jars and brought up specimens for him to look over himself," replied Silbert. "Or wouldn't they mean anything to him? Is he a biologist or just a manager?"

"I couldn't say."

"How come? How can you work for him and not know that much?"

"Working for him is something new. I've worked for Raindrop ever since I started working, but I didn't meet Weisanen until three weeks ago.

I haven't been with him more than two or three hours' total time since. I haven't talked with him during those hours; I've listened while he told me what to do."

"You mean he's one of those high-handed types? What's your job, anyway?"

"There's nothing tough or unpleasant about him; he's just the boss. I'm a computer specialist—programming and maintenance, or was until he picked me to come up here to Raindrop with him and his wife. What my job here will be, you'll have to get from him. There are computers in the station, I noticed, but nothing calling for full-time work from anyone. Why he picked me I can't guess. I should think, though, that he'd have asked you rather than me to make this report, since whatever I am I'm no biologist."

"Well, neither am I. I just work here."

Bresnahan stared in astonishment.

"Not a biologist? But aren't you in charge of this place? Haven't you been the local director for three years, in charge of planting the new life forms that were sent up, and reporting what happened to them, and how Raindrop was holding together, and all—?"

"All is right. I'm the bo's'un tight and the midshipmite and the crew of the captain's gig. I'm the boss because I'm the only one here full time; but that doesn't make me a biologist. I got this job because I have a decently high zero-gee tolerance and had had experience in space. I was a space-station handyman before I came here."

"Then what sort of flumdiddle is going on? Isn't there a professional anywhere in this organization? I've heard stories of the army using biochemists for painters and bricklayers for clerks, but I never really believed them. Besides, Raindrop doesn't belong to an army—it isn't even a government outfit any more. It's being run by a private outfit which I assumed was hoping to make a profit out of it. Why in blazes is there no biologist at what has always been supposed to be a biological research station, devoted to finding new ways of making fourteen billion people like what little there is to eat?"

Silbert's shrug was just discernible from outside his suit.

"No one ever confided in me," he replied. "I was given a pretty good briefing on the job when I first took it over, but that didn't include an extension course in biology or biophysics. As far as I can tell they've been satisfied with what I've done. Whatever they wanted out of Raindrop doesn't seem to call for high-caliber professionals on the spot. I inspect to make sure no leaks too big for the algae to handle show up, I plant any new life forms they send up to be established here, and I collect regularly and send back to Earth the samples of what life there is. The last general sampling was nearly a month ago, and another is due in a few days. Maybe your boss could make do with that data—or if you like I can offer to make the regular sampling run right away instead of at the scheduled time. After all, he may be my boss too instead of the other way around, so I should be reporting to him."

Bresnahan thought for a moment.

"All right," he said. "I'm in no position to make either a decent collection or a decent report, as things stand. Let's go back to the station, tell him what's what, and let him decide what he does want. Maybe it's just a case of a new boss not knowing the ropes and trying to find out."

"I'd question that, somehow, but can't think of anything better to do. Come on."

Silbert swam back toward the lock from which they had emerged only a few minutes before. They had drifted far enough from it in that time so that its details had faded to a greenish blur, but there was no trouble locating the big cylinder. The door they had used was still open.

Silbert pulled himself through, lent Bresnahan a hand in doing likewise, closed the portal, and started a small pump. The pressure head was only the quarter atmosphere maintained by the tension of the alga skin, and emptying the chamber of water did not take long. The principal delay was caused by Bresnahan's failure to stand perfectly still; with gravity only a little over one five-thousandths Earth normal, it didn't take much disturbance to slosh some water away from the bottom of the lock where the pump intake was located.

Silbert waited for some of it to settle, but lacked the patience to wait for it all. When he opened the door into the larger lock chamber the men were accompanied through it by several large globules of boiling liquid.

"Wasteful, but helps a bit," remarked the spaceman as he opened the outside portal and the two were wafted through it by the escaping vapor. "Watch out—hang on there. You don't have escape velocity, but you'd be quite a while getting back to the surface if you let yourself blow away." He seized a convenient limb of Bresnahan's space armor as the younger man drifted by, and since he was well anchored himself to the top rung of the ladder was able to arrest the other's flight. Carefully they stepped away from the hatch, Silbert touching the closing button with one toe as he passed it, and looked for the orbiting station.

This, of course, was directly overhead. The same temptation which Bresnahan had felt earlier to make a jump for it came back with some force; but Silbert had a safer technique.

He took a small tube equipped with peep-sights from the equipment clip at his side and aimed it very carefully at the projecting hub of the wheel-shaped station—the only part of the hub visible, since the station's equator was parallel to that of Raindrop and the structure was therefore edge-on to them. A bright yellow glow from the target produced a grunt of satisfaction from Silbert, and he fingered a button on the tube. The laser beam, invisible in the surrounding vacuum, flicked on and off in a precisely timed signal pattern which was reported faithfully by the source-return mirror at the target. Another response was almost as quick.

3

A faintly glowing object emerged from the hub and drifted rapidly toward Raindrop, though not quite toward the men. Its details were not clear at first, but as it approached it began to look more and more like a luminous cobweb.

"Just a lattice of thin rods, doped with luminous paint for spotting and launched from the station by a spring gun," explained Silbert. "The line connecting it with the station isn't painted, and is just long enough to stop the grid about fifty feet from the water. It's launched with a small backward component relative to the station's orbit, and when the line stops it it will drift toward us. Jump for it when I give the word; you can't miss."

Bresnahan was not as certain about the last statement as his companion seemed to be, but braced himself anyway. As the glowing spiderweb approached, however, he saw it was over a hundred feet across and realized that even he could jump straight enough to make contact. When Silbert gave the word, he sprang without hesitation.

He had the usual moment of nausea and disorientation as he crossed the few yards to his target. Lacking experience, he had not "balanced" his jump perfectly and as a result made a couple of somersaults en route. This caused him to lose track of his visual reference points, and with gravity already lacking he suffered the moment of near-panic which so many student pilots had experienced before him. Contact with one of the thin rods restored him, however; he gripped it frantically and was himself again.

Silbert arrived a split second later and took charge of the remaining maneuvers. These consisted of collapsing the "spiderweb"—a matter of half a minute, in spite of its apparent complexity, because of the ingenuity of its jointing—and then starting his companion hand-over-hand along the nearly invisible cord leading back to the station. The climb called for more coordination than was at first evident; the spaceman had to catch his less experienced companion twice as the latter missed his grip for the line.

Had Silbert been going first the situation might have been serious. As it was, an extra tug on the rope enabled him to catch up each time with the helpless victim of basic physics. After the second accident, the guide spoke.

"All right, don't climb any more. We're going a little too fast as it is. Just hold onto the rope now and to me when I give the word. The closing maneuver is a bit tricky, and it wouldn't be practical to try to teach you the tricks on the spot and first time around."

Silbert did have quite a problem. The initial velocities of the two men in their jumps for the spiderweb had not, of course, been the correct ones to intercept the station—if it had been practical to count on their being so, the web would have been superfluous. The web's own mass was less than fifty pounds, which had not done much to the sum of those vectors as it absorbed its share of the men's momentum. Consequently, the men had an angular velocity with respect to the station, and they were *approaching* the latter.

To a seventeenth century mathematician, conservation of angular momentum may have been an abstract concept, but to Silbert it was an item of very real, practical, everyday experience—just as the orbit of a comet is little more than a set of numbers to an astronomer while the orbit of a baseball is something quite different to an outfielder. The problem this time was even worse than usual, partly because of Bresnahan's mass and still more because of his inexperience.

As the two approached the station their sidewise motion became evident even to Bresnahan. He judged that they would strike near the rim of the spinning structure, if they hit it at all, but Silbert had other ideas.

Changing the direction of the spin axis by landing at the hub was one thing—a very minor one. Changing the *rate* of spin by meeting the edge could be a major nuisance, since much of the apparatus inside was built on and for Earth and had Earth's gravity taken for granted in its operation. Silbert therefore had no intention of making contact anywhere but at one of the "poles" of the station. He was rather in the situation of a yo-yo whose string is winding up on the operator's finger; but he could exercise a little control by climbing as rapidly as possible "up" the cord toward the structure or allowing himself to slide "down" away from it.

He had had plenty of experience, but he was several minutes playing them into a final collision with the entry valve, so close to the center of mass of the station that the impact could produce only a tiny precession effect. Most of its result was a change in the wheel's orbit about Raindrop, and the whole maneuver had taken such a small fraction of an orbital period that this effect nearly offset that produced when they had started up the rope.

"Every so often," remarked the spaceman as he opened the air lock, "we have to make a small correction in the station orbit; the disturbances set up by entering and leaving get it out of step with Raindrop's rotation. Sometimes I wonder whether it's worth the trouble to keep the two synchronized."

"If the station drifted very far from the lock below, you'd have to jump from the liquid surface, which might be awkward," pointed out the younger man as the closing hatch cut off the starlight.

"That's true," admitted the other as he snapped a switch and air started hissing into the small lock chamber. "I suppose there's something to be said for tradition at that. There's the safety light"—as a green spot suddenly glowed on the wall— "so you can open up your suit whenever you like. Lockers are in the next room. But you arrived through this lock, didn't you?"

"Right. I know my way from here."

Five minutes later the two men, divested of spacesuits, had "descended" to the rim of the station where weight was normal. Most of this part of the structure was devoted to living space which had never been used, though there were laboratory and communication rooms as well. The living space had been explained to Bresnahan, when he first saw it, as why Silbert was willing to spend three quarters of his time alone at a rather boring job a hundred thousand miles from the nearest company. Earth was badly crowded; not one man in a million had either as much space or as much privacy.

Weisanen and his wife had taken over a set of equally sumptuous rooms on the opposite side of the rim, and had been in the process of setting up housekeeping when the two employees had descended to Raindrop's surface a short time before. This had been less than an hour after their arrival with Bresnahan on the shuttle from Earth; Weisanen had wasted no time in issuing his first orders. The two men were prepared to find every sign of disorder when the door to the "headquarters" section opened in response to Silbert's touch on the annunciator, but they had reckoned without Mrs. Weisanen.

At their employer's invitation, they entered a room which might have been lived in for a year instead of an hour. The furniture was good, comfortable, well arranged, and present in quantity which would have meant a visible bulge in a nation's space research budget just for the fuel to lift it away from the earth in the chemical fuel days.

Either the Weisanens felt strongly about maintaining the home atmosphere even when visiting, or they planned to stay on the station for quite a while.

The official himself was surprisingly young, according to both Bresnahan's and Silbert's preconceived notions of a magnate. He could hardly have been thirty, and might have been five years younger. He matched Bresnahan's five feet ten of height and looked about the same weight; but while the computerman regarded himself as being in good physical shape, he had to admit the other was far more muscular. Even Silbert's six feet five of height and far from insignificant frame seemed somehow inadequate beside Weisanen's.

"Come in, gentlemen. We felt your return a few minutes ago! I take it you have something to report, Mr. Bresnahan. We did not expect you back quite so soon." Weisanen drew further back from the door and waved the others past him. "What can you tell us?" He closed the door and indicated armchairs. Bresnahan remained on his feet, uneasy at the incompleteness of his report; Silbert sank into the nearest chair. The official also remained standing. "Well, Mr. Bresnahan?"

"I have little—practically nothing—to report, as far as detailed, quantitative information is concerned," the computer man took the plunge.

"We stayed inside the Raindrop only a few minutes, and it was evident that most of the detailed search for life specimens would have to be made with a microscope. I hadn't planned the trip at all effectively. I now understand that there is plankton-collecting apparatus here which Mr. Silbert uses regularly and which should have been taken along if I were to get anything worth showing to you."

Weisanen's face showed no change in its expression of courteous interest. "That is quite all right," he said. "I should have made clear that I wanted, not a detailed biological report, but a physical description by a non-specialist of what it is like subjectively down there. I should imagine that you received an adequate impression even during your short stay. Can you give such a description?"

Bresnahan's worried expression disappeared, and he nodded affirmatively.

"Yes, sir. I'm not a literary expert, but I can tell what I saw."

"Good. One moment, please." Weisanen turned toward another door and raised his voice. "Brenda, will you come in here, please? You should hear this."

Silbert got to his feet just as the woman entered, and both men acknowledged her greeting.

Brenda Weisanen was a full head shorter than her husband. She was wearing a robe of the sort which might have been seen on any housewife expecting company; neither man was competent to guess whether it was worth fifty dollars or ten times that. The garment tended to focus attention on her face, which would have received it anyway. Her hair and eyebrows were jet black, the eyes themselves gray, and rounded cheeks and chin made the features look almost childish, though she was actually little younger than her husband. She seated herself promptly, saying no more than convention demanded, and the men followed suit.

"Please go on, Mr. Bresnahan," Weisanen said. "My wife and I are both greatly interested, for reasons which will be clear shortly."

Bresnahan had a good visual memory, and it was easy for him to comply. He gave a good verbal picture of the greenish, sunlit haze that had surrounded him—sunlight differing from that seen under an Earthly lake, which ripples and dances as the waves above refract it. He spoke of the silence, which had moved him to keep talking because it was the "quietest" silence he had known, and "didn't sound right."

He was interrupted by Silbert at this point; the spaceman explained that Raindrop was not always that quiet. Even a grain-of-dust meteoroid striking the skin set up a shock wave audible throughout the great sphere; and if one were close enough to the site of collision, the hiss of water boiling out through the hole for the minute or two needed for the skin to heal could also be heard. It was rather unusual to be able to spend even the short time they had just had inside the satellite without hearing either of these sounds.

Bresnahan nodded thanks as the other fell silent, and took up the thread of his own description once more. He closed with the only real feature he had seen to describe—the weed-grown cylinder of the water-to-space lock, hanging in greenish emptiness above the dead-black void which reached down to Raindrop's core. He was almost poetical in spots.

The Weisanens listened in flattering silence until he had done, and remained silent for some seconds thereafter. Then the man spoke.

"Thank you, Mr. Bresnahan. That was just what we wanted." He turned to his wife. "How does that sound to you, dear?"

The dark head nodded slowly, its gray eyes fastened on some point far beyond the metal walls.

"It's fascinating," she said slowly. "Not just the way we pictured it, of course, and there will be changes anyway, but certainly worth seeing. Of course they didn't go down to the core, and wouldn't have seen much if they had. I suppose there is no life, and certainly no natural light, down there."

"There is life," replied Silbert. "Non-photosynthetic, of course, but bacteria and larger fungi which live on organic matter swept there from the sunlit parts. I don't know whether anything is actually growing *on* the core, since I've never gone in that far, but free-floating varieties get carried up to my nets. A good many of those have gone to Earth, along with their descriptions, in my regular reports."

"I know. I've read those reports very carefully, Mr. Silbert," replied Weisanen.

"Just the same, one of our first jobs must be to survey that core," his wife said thoughtfully. "Much of what has to be done will depend on conditions down there."

"Right." Her husband stood up. "We thank you gentlemen for your word pictures; they have helped a lot. I'm not yet sure of the relation between your station time and that of the Terrestrial time zones, but I have the impression that it's quite late in the working day. Tomorrow we will all visit Raindrop and make a very thorough and more technical examination—my wife and I doing the work, Mr. Bresnahan assisting us, and Mr. Silbert guiding. Until then—it has been a pleasure, gentlemen."

Bresnahan took the hint and got to his feet, but Silbert hesitated. There was a troubled expression on his face, but he seemed unable or unwilling to speak. Weisanen noticed it.

"What's the matter, Mr. Silbert? Is there some reason why Raindrop's owners, or their representatives, shouldn't look it over closely? I realize that you are virtually the only person to visit it in the last three years, but I assure you that your job is in no danger."

Silbert's face cleared a trifle.

"It isn't that," he said slowly. "I know you're the boss, and I wasn't worried about my job anyway. There's just one point—of course you may know all about it, but I'd rather be safe, and embarrassed, than responsible for something unfortunate later on. I don't mean to butt into anyone's private business, but Raindrop is essentially weightless."

"I know that."

"Do you also know that unless you are quite certain that Mrs. Weisanen is not pregnant, she should not expose herself to weightlessness for more than a few minutes at a time?"

Both Weisanens smiled.

"We know, thank you, Mr. Silbert. We will see you tomorrow, in spacesuits, at the big cargo lock. There is much equipment to be taken down to Raindrop."

4

That closing remark proved to be no exaggeration.

As the four began moving articles through the lock the next morning, Silbert decided at first that the Weisanens' furniture had been a very minor item in the load brought up from Earth the day before, and wondered why it had been brought into the station at all if it were to be transferred to Raindrop so soon. Then he began to realize that most of the material he was moving had been around much longer. It had come up bit by bit on the regular supply shuttle over a period of several months. Evidently whatever was going on represented long and careful planning—and furthermore, whatever was going on represented a major change from the original plans for Raindrop.

This worried him, since Silbert had become firmly attached to the notion that the Raindrop plan was an essential step to keeping the human race fed, and he had as good an appetite as anyone.

He knew, as did any reasonably objective and well-read adult, how barely the advent of fusion power and gene tailoring had bypassed the first critical point in the human population explosion, by making it literally possible to use the entire surface of the planet for either living space or the production of food. As might have been expected, mankind had expanded to fill even that fairly generous limit in a few generations.

A second critical point was now coming up, obviously enough to those willing to face the fact. Most of Earth's fourteen billion people lived on floating islands of gene-tailored vegetation scattered over the planet's seas, and the number of these islands was reaching the point where the total sunlight reaching the surface was low enough to threaten collapse of the entire food chain. Theoretically, fusion power was adequate to provide synthetic food for all; but it had been learned the hard way that man's selfishness could be raised to the violence point almost as easily by a threat to his "right" to eat natural—and tasty—food as by a threat to his "right" to reproduce without limit. As a matter of fact, the people whom Silbert regarded as more civilized tended to react more strongly to the first danger.

Raindrop had been the proposed answer. As soon as useful, edible life forms could be tailored to live in its environment it was to be broken up into a million or so smaller units which could receive sunlight throughout their bulks, and use these as "farms."

But power units, lights, and what looked like prefabricated living quarters sufficient for many families did not fit with the idea of breaking Raindrop up. In fact, they did not fit with any sensible idea at all.

No one could live on Raindrop, or in it, permanently; there was not enough weight to keep human metabolism balanced. Silbert was very conscious of that factor. He never spent more than a day at a time on his sampling trips, and after each of these he always remained in the normal-weight part of the station for the full number of days specified on the AGT tables.

It was all very puzzling.

And as the day wore on, and more and more material was taken from the low-weight storage section of the station and netted together for the trip to Raindrop, the spaceman grew more puzzled still. He said nothing, however, since he didn't feel quite ready to question the Weisanens on the subject and it was impossible to speak privately to Bresnahan with all the spacesuit radios on the same frequency.

All the items moved were, of course, marked with their masses, but Silbert made no great effort to keep track of the total tonnage. It was not necessary, since each cargo net was loaded as nearly as possible to an even one thousand pounds and it was easy enough to count the nets when the job was done. There were twenty-two nets.

A more ticklish task was installing on each bundle a five hundred pound-second solid-fuel thrust cartridge, which had to be set so that its axis pointed reasonably close to the center of mass of the loaded net and firmly enough fastened to maintain its orientation during firing. It was not advisable to get rid of the orbital speed of the loads by "pushing off" from the station; the latter's orbit would have been too greatly altered by absorbing the momentum of eleven tons of material. The rockets had to be used.

Silbert, in loading the nets, had made sure that each was spinning slowly on an axis parallel to that of Raindrop. He had also attached each cartridge at the "equator" of its net. As a result, when the time came to fire it was only necessary to wait beside each load until its rocket was pointing "forward" along the station's orbit, and touch off the fuel.

The resulting velocity change did not, in general, exactly offset the orbital speed, but it came close enough for the purpose. The new orbit of each bundle now intersected the surface of Raindrop—a target which was, after all, ten miles in diameter and only half a mile away. It made no great difference if the luggage were scattered along sixty degrees of the satellite's equatorial zone; moving the bundles to the lock by hand would be no great problem where each one weighed about three and a half ounces.

With the last net drifting toward the glistening surface of Raindrop, Weisanen turned to the spaceman.

"What's the best technique to send us after them? Just jump off?"

Silbert frowned, though the expression was not obvious through his face plate.

"The best technique, according to the AGT Safety Tables, is to go back to the rim of the station and spend a couple of days getting our personal chemistry back in balance. We've been weightless for nearly ten hours, with only one short break when we ate."

Weisanen made a gesture of impatience which was much more visible than Silbert's frown.

"Nonsense!" he exclaimed. "People have remained weightless for a couple of weeks at a time without permanent damage."

"Without having their bones actually turn to rubber, I grant. I don't concede there was no more subtle damage done. I'm no biophysicist, I just believe the tables; they were worked out on the basis of knowledge gained the hard way. I admit they have a big safety factor, and if you consider it really necessary I won't object to staying out for four or five days. But you haven't given us any idea so far why this should be considered an emergency situation."

"Hmmm. So I haven't. All right, will you stay out long enough to show Brenda and me how to work the locks below, so we can get the stuff inside?"

"Why—of course—if it's that important we'll stay and do the work too. But I didn't—" Silbert fell silent as it dawned on him that Weisanen's choice of words meant that he had no intention of explaining just yet what the "emergency" was. Both newcomers must have read the spaceman's mind quite accurately at that point, since even Bresnahan was able to, but neither of them said anything.

Conversation for the next few minutes consisted entirely of Silbert's instructions for shoving off in the proper direction to reach Raindrop, and how to walk on its not-quite-zero-gravity, jelly-like surface after they reached it. The trip itself was made without incident.

Because fast movement on the surface was impossible, several hours were spent collecting the scattered bundles and stacking them by the lock. The material could not be placed inside, as most of it had to be assembled before it could go under water; so for the moment the lesson in lock management was postponed. Weisanen, after some hesitation, agreed to Silbert's second request that they return to the station for food and rest. He and his wife watched with interest the technique of getting back to it.

With four people instead of two, the velocity-matching problem might have been worse, but this turned out not to be the case. Silbert wondered whether it were strictly luck, or whether the Weisanens actually had the skill to plan their jumps properly. He was beginning to suspect that both of them had had previous space experience, and both were certainly well-coordinated physical specimens.

According to the tables which had been guiding Silbert's life, the party should have remained in the high-weight part of the station for at least eighty hours after their session of zero-gee, but his life was now being run by Weisanen rather than the tables. The group was back on the water twelve hours after leaving it.

Bresnahan still had his feeling of discomfort, with star-studded emptiness on one side and its reflection on the other, but he was given little time to brood about it.

The first material to go into the lock consisted of half a dozen yard-wide plastic bubbles of water. Silbert noted with interest that all contained animal life, ranging from barely visible crustacea to herring-sized fish.

"So we're starting animal life here at last," remarked the spaceman. "I thought it was a major bone of contention whether we ever would."

"The question was settled at the first meeting of the new board," replied Weisanen. "Life forms able to live here—or presumably able to live here—have been ready for several years. Please be careful in putting those in the lock—just the odd-numbered ones first, please. The evens contain predators, and the others should be given a few hours to scatter before they are turned loose."

"Right. Any special techniques for opening? Or just get the bubbles through the second lock and cut them open?"

"That will do. I assume that a few hours in the currents inside, plus their own swimming abilities, will scatter them through a good part of the drop."

"It should. I suppose they'll tend to stay pretty close to the skin because of the light; I trust they can take a certain amount of hard radiation."

"That matter has been considered. There will be some loss, damage, and genetic change, of course, but we think the cultures will gain in spite of that. If they change, it is no great matter. We expect rapid evolution in an environment like this, of course. It's certainly been happening so far."

Bresnahan helped push the proper spheres into the lock at the vacuum end and out of it at the other, and watched with interest as each was punctured with a knife and squeezed to expel the contents.

"I should have asked about waiting for temperatures to match," remarked Silbert as the cloud of barely visible, jerkily moving specks spread from the last of the containers, "but it doesn't seem to be bothering them."

"The containers were lying on Raindrop's surface all night, and the satellite is in radiative equilibrium," pointed out Bresnahan. "The temperatures shouldn't be very different anyway. Let's get back outside and see what's going on next. Either these water-bugs are all right, or they're beyond our help."

"Right." Silbert followed the suggestion, and the newly released animals were left to their own devices.

Outside, another job was under way. The largest single items of cargo had been a set of curved segments of metal, apparently blue-anodized aluminum. In the few minutes that Silbert and Bresnahan had been inside, the Weisanens had sorted these out from the rest of the material and were now fitting them together.

Each section attached to its neighbor by a set of positive-acting snap fasteners which could be set almost instantly, and within a very few minutes it became evident that they formed a sphere some twenty feet in diameter. A transparent dome of smaller radius was set in one pole, and a cylindrical structure with trap doors in the flat ends marked the other. With the assembly complete, the Weisanens carefully sprayed everything, inside and out, from cylinders which Silbert recognized as containing one of the standard fluorocarbon polymers used for sealing unfindable leaks in space ships.

Then both Weisanens went inside.

Either the metallic appearance of the sphere was deceptive or there were antennae concealed in its structure, because orders came through the wall on the suit-radio frequency without noticeable loss. In response to these, Bresnahan and the spaceman began handing the rest of the equipment in through the cylindrical structure, which had now revealed itself as a minute air lock. As each item was received it was snapped down on a spot evidently prepared to receive it, and in less than two hours almost all the loose gear had vanished from the vicinity of Raindrop's entry lock. The little that was left also found a home as Weisanen emerged once more and fastened it to racks on the sphere's outer surface, clustered around the air lock.

The official went back inside, and, at his orders, Silbert and the computerman lifted the whole sphere onto the top of the cylindrical cargo lock of the satellite. Either could have handled the three-pound weight alone, but its shape and size made it awkward to handle and both men felt that it would be inadvisable to roll it.

"Good. Now open this big hatch and let us settle into the lock chamber," directed Weisanen. "Then close up, and let in the water."

It was the first time Silbert had caught his boss in a slip, and he was disproportionately pleased. The hatch opened outward, and it was necessary to lift the sphere off again before the order could be obeyed.

Once it was open, the two men had no trouble tossing the big globe into the yawning, nearly dark hole—the sun was just rising locally and did not shine into the chamber—but they had to wait over a minute for Raindrop's feeble gravity to drag the machine entirely inside. They could not push it any faster, because it was not possible to get a good grip on sphere and lock edge simultaneously; and pushing down on the sphere without good anchorage would have done much more to the pusher than to the sphere.

However, it was finally possible to close the big trap. After making sure that it was tightly latched—it was seldom used, and Silbert did not trust its mechanism unreservedly—he and Bresnahan entered the lock through the smaller portal.

"Aren't there special suits for use inside Raindrop, a lot more comfortable than this space armor?" asked Weisanen.

"Yes, sir," replied the spaceman, "though the relative comfort is a matter of opinion. There are only three, and two of them haven't been used since I came. They'll need a careful checkout."

"All right. Bring them in here, and then let the water into this lock." Silbert found the suits and handed them to Bresnahan to carry out the first part of the order, while he went to the controls to execute the second.

"All ready?" he asked.

"All set. Both lock doors here are shut, and the three of us are inside. Let the flood descend."

"Wrong verb," muttered Silbert to himself.

He very cautiously cracked the main inner hatch; opening it would have been asking for disaster. Even at a mere quarter atmosphere's pressure the wall of water would have slammed into the evacuated lock violently enough to tear the outer portal away and eject sphere and occupants at a speed well above Raindrop's escape value. There was a small Phoenix rocket in the station for emergency use, but Silbert had no wish to create a genuine excuse for using it. Also, since he was in the lock himself, he would probably be in no condition to get or pilot it.

5

The water sprayed in violently enough through the narrow opening he permitted, bouncing the sphere against the outer hatch and making a deafening clamor even for the space-suited trio inside. However, nothing gave way, and in a minute it was safe to open the main hatch completely.

Silbert did so. Through the clear dome which formed the sphere's only observation window he could see Weisanen fingering controls inside. Water jets from almost invisible ports in the outer surface came into action, and for the first time it became evident that the sphere was actually a vehicle. It was certainly not built for speed, but showed signs of being one of the most maneuverable ever built.

After watching for a moment as it worked its way out of the lock, Silbert decided that Weisanen had had little chance to practice handling it. But no catastrophe occurred, and finally the globe was hanging in the greenish void outside the weed-grown bulk of the lock. The spaceman closed the big hatch, emerged through the personnel lock himself, and swam over to the vehicle's entrance.

The outer door of the tiny air lock opened manually. Thirty seconds later he was inside the rather crowded sphere removing his helmet—some time during the last few minutes Weisanen had filled the vehicle with air.

The others had already unhelmeted and were examining the "diving" suits which Bresnahan had brought inside. These were simple enough affairs; plastic form-fitting coveralls with an air-cycler on the chest and an outsized, transparent helmet which permitted far more freedom of head movement than most similar gear. Since there was no buoyance in this virtually weight-free environment, the helmet's volume did not create the problem it would have on Earth. Silbert was able to explain everything necessary about the equipment in a minute or two.

Neither of the Weisanens needed to have any point repeated, and if Bresnahan was unsure about anything he failed to admit it.

"All right." Raindrop's owner nodded briskly as the lesson ended. "We seem to be ready. I started us down as soon as Mr. Silbert came aboard, but it will take the best part of an hour to reach the core. When we get there a regular ecological sampling run will be made. You can do that, Mr. Silbert, using your regular equipment and techniques; the former is aboard, whether you noticed it being loaded or not. Brenda and I will make a physical, and physiographical, examination of the core itself, with a view to finding just what will have to be done to set up living quarters there and where will be the best place to build them."

Silbert's reaction to this remark may have been expected; both Weisanens had been watching him with slight smiles on their faces. He did not disappoint them.

"*Living* quarters? That's ridiculous! There's no weight to speak of even at Raindrop's surface, and even less at the core. A person would lose the calcium from his skeleton in a few weeks, and go unbalanced in I don't know how many other chemical ways—"

"Fourteen known so far, Mr. Silbert. We know all about that, or as much as anyone does. It was a shame to tease you, but my husband and I couldn't resist. Also, some of the factors involved are not yet public knowledge, and we have reasons for not wanting them too widely circulated for a while yet." Brenda Weisanen's interruption was saved from rudeness by the smile on her face. "I would invite you to sit down to listen, but sitting means nothing here—I'll get used to that eventually, no doubt.

"The fact you just mentioned about people leaching calcium out of their skeletons after a few days or weeks of weightlessness was learned long ago—even before long manned space flights had been made; the information was gained from flotation experiments. Strictly speaking, it is not an effect of weightlessness *per se,* but a feedback phenomenon involving relative muscular effort—something which might have been predicted, and for all I know may actually have been predicted, from the fact that the ankle bones in a growing child ossify much more rapidly than the wrist bones. A very minor genetic factor is involved; after all, animals as similar to us as dolphins which *do* spend all their time afloat grow perfectly adequate skeletons.

"A much more subtle set of chemical problems were noticed the hard way when manned space stations were set up, as you well know. A lot of work was done on these, as you might expect, and we now are quite sure that all which will produce detectable results in less than five years of continuous weightlessness are known. There are fourteen specific factors—chemical and genetic keys to the log jam, if you like to think of it that way.

"You have the ordinary educated adult's knowledge of gene tailoring, Mr. Silbert. What was the logical thing to do?"

"Since gene tailoring on human beings is flagrantly illegal, for good and sufficient reasons, the logical thing to do was and is to avoid weightlessness," Silbert replied. "With Phoenix rockets, we can make interplanetary flight at a continuous one-gravity acceleration, while space stations can be and are centrifuged."

Brenda Weisanen's smile did not change, but her husband looked annoyed. He took up the discussion.

"Illegal or not, for good or bad reasons, it was perfectly reasonable to consider modifying human genetic patterns so that some people at least could live and work normally and indefinitely in a weightless environment. Whether it shocks you or not, the thing was tried over seventy years ago, and over five hundred people now alive have this modification— and are not, as I suppose you would put it, fully human."

Bresnahan interrupted. "I would *not* put it that way!" he snapped. "As anyone who has taken work in permutation and combination knows perfectly well, there is no such thing as a fully human being if you define the term relative to some precise, specific idealized gene pattern. Mutations are occurring all the time from radiation, thermal effects, and just plain quantum jumping of protons in the genetic molecules. This sort of phenomenon is used as example material in elementary programming courses, and one of the first things you learn when you run such a problem is that no one is completely without such modifications. If, as I suppose you are about to say, you and Mrs. Weisanen are genetically different enough to take weightlessness, I can't see why it makes you less human. I happen to be immune to four varieties of leukemia virus and sixteen of the organisms usually responsible for the common cold, according to one analysis of my own gene pattern. If Bert's had ever been checked we'd find at least as many peculiarities about his—and I refuse to admit that either of us is less human than anyone else we've ever met."

"Thank you, Mr. Bresnahan," Brenda Weisanen took up the thread of the discussion once more. "The usual prejudice against people who are known to be significantly different tends to make some of us a little self-conscious. In any case, my husband and I can stand weightlessness indefinitely, as far as it is now possible to tell, and we plan to stay here permanently. More of us will be coming up later for the same purpose."

"But why? Not that it's any of my business. I like Raindrop, but it's not the most stimulating environment, and in any case I'm known to be the sort of oddball who prefers being alone with a collection of books to most other activities."

The woman glanced at her husband before answering. He shrugged.

"You have already touched on the point, Mr. Silbert. Modifying the human genetic pattern involves the same complication which plagued medicine when hormones became available for use in treatment. Any one action is likely to produce several others as an unplanned, and commonly unwanted, byproduct. Our own modification is not without its disadvantages. What our various defects may be I would not presume to list in toto—any more than Mr. Bresnahan would care to list his—but one of them strikes very close to home just now. Aino and I are expecting a child, and about nine times out of ten when a woman of our type remains in normal gravity any child she conceives is lost during the fifth or sixth month. The precise cause is not known; it involves the mother's physique rather than the child's, but that leaves a lot still to be learned. Therefore, I am staying here until my baby is born, at the very least. We expect to live here. We did not ask to be modified to fit space, but if it turns out that we can live better here—so be it."

"Then Raindrop is going to be turned into a—a—maternity hospital?"

"I think a fairer term would be 'colony,' Mr. Silbert," interjected Weisanen. "There are a good many of us, and most if not all of us are considering making this place our permanent home."

"Which means that breaking it up according to the original plan to supply farming volume is no longer on the books."

"Precisely."

"How do you expect to get away with that? This whole project was planned and paid for as a new source of food."

"That was when it was a government project. As you know, it became a private concern recently; the government was paid full value for Raindrop, the station, and the shuttle which keeps it supplied. As of course you do not know, over eighty per cent of the stock of that corporation is owned by people like myself. What we propose to do is perfectly legal, however unpopular it may make us with a few people."

"More than a few, I would say. And how can you afford to be really unpopular, living in something as fragile as Raindrop?" queried Bresnahan. "There are lots of spaceships available. Even if no official action were or could be taken, anyone who happened to have access to one and disliked you sufficiently could wreck the skin of this tank so thoroughly in five minutes that you'd have to start all over again even if you yourselves lived through it. All the life you'd established would freeze before repairs could be made complete enough to stop the water from boiling away."

"That is true, and is a problem we haven't entirely solved," admitted the other. "Of course, the nasty laws against the publication of possible mob-rousing statements which were found necessary as Earth's population grew should operate to help us. Nowadays many people react so negatively to any unsupported statement that the word would have trouble getting around. In any case, we don't intend to broadcast the details, and comparatively few people know much about the Raindrop project at all. I don't think that many will feel cheated."

Silbert's reaction to the last sentence was the urge to cry out, "But they *are* being cheated!" However, it was beginning to dawn on him that he was not in the best possible position to argue with Weisanen.

He subsided. He himself had been living with the Raindrop project for three years, had become closely identified with it, and the change of policy bothered him for deeper reasons than his intelligence alone could recognize.

Bresnahan was also bothered, though he was not as deeply in love with the project as the spaceman. He was less impressed by Weisanen's conviction that there would be no trouble; but he had nothing useful to say about the matter. He was developing ideas, but they ran along the line of wondering when he could get to a computer keyboard to set the whole situation up as a problem. His background and training had left him with some doubt of any human being's ability—including his own—to handle all facets of a complex problem.

Neither of the Weisanens seemed to have any more to say, either, so the sphere drifted downward in silence.

6

They had quickly passed the limit which sunlight could reach, and were surrounded by blackness, which the sphere's own interior lights seemed only to accentuate.

With neither gravity nor outside reference points, the sphere was of course being navigated by instrument. Sonar equipment kept the pilot informed of the distance to the nearest point of the skin, the distance and direction of the lock through which they had entered, and the distance and direction of the core. Interpretation of the echoes was complicated by the fact that Raindrop's outer skin was so sharply curved, but Weisanen seemed to have that problem well in hand as he drove the vehicle downward.

Pressure, of course, did not change significantly with depth. The thirty per cent increase from skin to core meant nothing to healthy people. There was not even an instrument to register this factor, as far as Silbert could see. He was not too happy about that; his spaceman's prejudices made him feel that there should be independent instrumentation to back up the sonar gear.

As they neared the core, however, instruments proved less necessary than expected.

To the mild surprise of the Weisanens and the blank astonishment of Silbert—Bresnahan knew too little to expect anything, either way—the central region of the satellite was not completely dark. The light was so faint that it would not have been noticed if they had not been turning off the sphere's lamps every few minutes, but it was quite bright enough to be seen, when they were a hundred yards or so from the core, without waiting for eyes to become dark-adapted.

"None of your samples ever included luminous bacteria," remarked the official. "I wonder why none of them ever got close enough to the skin for you to pick up."

"I certainly don't know," replied Silbert. "Are you sure it's caused by bacteria?"

"Not exactly by a long shot; it just seems the best starting guess. I'm certain it's not heat or radioactivity, and offhand I can't think of any other possibilities. Can you?"

"No, I can't. But maybe whatever is producing the light is attached to the core—growing on it, if it's alive. So it wouldn't have reached the surface."

"That's possible, though I hope you didn't think I was criticizing your sampling techniques. It was one of my friends who planned them, not you. We'll go on down; we're almost in contact with the core now, according to the fathometer."

Weisanen left the lights off, except for the tiny fluorescent sparks on the controls themselves, so the other three crowded against the bulge of the viewing port to see what was coming. Weightlessness made this easier than it might have been; they didn't have to "stand" at the same spot to have their heads close together.

For a minute or so, nothing was perceptible in the way of motion. There was just the clear, faintly luminous water outside the port. Then a set of slender, tentacular filaments as big around as a human thumb seemed to writhe past the port as the sphere sank by them; and the eyes which followed their length could suddenly see their point of attachment.

"There!" muttered Brenda Weisanen softly. "Slowly, dear—only a few yards."

"There's no other way this thing can travel," pointed out her husband. "Don't worry about our hitting anything too hard."

"I'm not—but look! It's beautiful! Let's get anchored and go outside."

"In good time. It will stay there, and anyway I'm going out before you do—long enough before to, at least, make reasonably certain it's safe."

The wife looked for a moment as though she were about to argue this point, if her facial expression could be read accurately in the faint light, but she said nothing. Bresnahan and Silbert had the intelligence to keep quiet as well; more could be learned by looking than by getting into the middle of a husband-wife disagreement, and now there was plenty to look at.

The core was visible for at least two hundred yards in all directions, as the sphere spun slowly under Weisanen's control. The light definitely came from the life forms which matted its surface.

Presumably these were fungi, since photosynthetic forms could hardly have grown in such an environment, but they were fungi which bore little resemblance to their Terrestrial ancestors. Some were ribbon-like, some feather-like, some snaky—even patches of what looked like smoothly mown lawn were visible. The greenish light was evidently not pure color, since other shades were visible; red, purple, and yellow forms stood out here and there in eye-catching contrast to grays and browns. Some forms were even green, though it seemed unlikely that this was due to chlorophyll. Practically all seemed to emit the vague light which bathed the entire scene—so uniformly that outlines would have been hard to distinguish were it not for a few specimens which were much brighter than the others. These types bore what might have been spore pods; brilliantly luminous knobs ranging from fist to grapefruit size, raised "above" the rest of the surface as much as eight or ten feet on slender stalks. These cast shadows which helped distinguish relief.

The woman was right; weird it might be, but the scene was beautiful.

Weisanen cut off the water jets and waited for a minute or two. The vehicle drifted slowly but perceptibly away from the surface; evidently there was some current.

"We'll have to anchor," he remarked. "Bren, stay inside until we've checked. I'll go out to see what we can fasten ourselves to; there's no information at all on what sort of surface there may be. A fair-sized stony meteoroid—really an asteroid—was used as the original core, but the solids from the comets would be very fine dust. There could be yards of mud too fine to hold any sort of anchor surrounding the solid part. You gentlemen will please get into the other suits and come with me. If nothing has happened to any of us in half an hour, Bren, you may join us."

"There are only three suits," his wife pointed out.

"True. Well, your spacesuit will do; or if you prefer, one of us will use his and let you have the diving gear. In any case, that problem is low-priority. If you gentlemen are ready we'll go. I'll start; this is strictly a one-man air lock."

All three had been climbing out of their spacesuits as Weisanen was talking. The other garments were easy enough to get into, though Bresnahan found the huge helmet unwieldy even with no weight. Weisanen was through the lock before either of the others was ready to follow; Silbert was slowed by his space-born habit of double-checking every bit of the breathing apparatus, and Bresnahan by his inexperience. They could see their employer through the window as they finished, swimming slowly and carefully toward the weedy boundary of Raindrop's core.

Both men stayed where they were for the moment, to see what would happen when he reached it. Brenda Weisanen watched even more closely; there was no obvious reason to be afraid, but her breath was coming unevenly and her fists tightly clenched as her husband approached the plants and reached out to touch the nearest.

Nothing spectacular happened. It yielded to his touch; when he seized it and pulled, it broke.

"Either the plants are awfully fragile or there is fairly firm ground anchoring them," remarked Silbert. "Let's go outside. You're checked out on the controls of this thing, aren't you, Mrs. Weisanen?"

"Not in great detail," was the reply, "I know which switches handle lights and main power for the lock pump, and which control bank deals with the jets; but I've had no practice in actually handling it. Aino hadn't, either, until we started this trip an hour ago. Go ahead, though; I won't have to do anything anyway. Aino is anchoring us now."

She gestured toward the port. Her husband could now be seen through it carrying something, maybe a harpoon, with a length of fine line attached to it. A couple of yards from the surface he poised himself and hurled the object, javelin style—or as nearly to that style as anyone can manage in water—into the mass of vegetation.

The shaft buried itself completely. Weisanen gave a tug on the line, whose far end was attached to the sphere. He seemed satisfied and turned to look at the vehicle. Seeing the men still inside, he gestured impatiently. Bresnahan followed Silbert through the tiny air lock as rapidly as its cycling time would permit, leaving the woman alone in the sphere.

Outside, Weisanen was several yards away, still beckoning imperiously.

"You can talk, sir," remarked Silbert in ordinary tones. "There's no need for sign language."

"Oh. Thanks; I didn't see any radio equipment in these helmets."

"There isn't any. The helmets themselves aren't just molded plastic; they're a multi-layered arrangement that acts as an impedance matcher between the air inside and the water outside. Sound goes through water well enough; it's the air-water interface that makes conversation difficult. This stuff gets the sound across the boundary."

"All right; good. Let's get to work. If the figures for the size of the original nucleus still mean anything, we have nearly twenty million square feet to check up on. Right now we won't try to do it all; stay in sight of the sphere. Get test rods and plankton gear from that rack by the air lock. Mr. Silbert, use the nets and collectors as you usually do. Mr. Bresnahan, you and I will use the rods; simply poke them into the surface every few yards. The idea is to get general knowledge of the firmness of the underlying surface, and to find the best places to build—or attach—permanent structures. If you should happen to notice any connection between the type of vegetation and the kind of ground it grows on, so much the better; surveying by eye will be a lot faster than by touch. If any sort of trouble comes up, yell. I don't see why there should be any, but I don't want Brenda out here until we're a little more certain."

The men fell to their rather monotonous tasks. The plant cover, it developed, ranged from an inch or two to over a yard in thickness, not counting the scattered forms which extended their tendrils scores of feet out toward the darkness. At no point was the underlying "ground" visible.

Where the growing cover was pushed or dug away, the core seemed to be made of a stiff, brownish clay, which reached at least as deep as the test prods could be pushed by hand. This rather surprised Silbert, who had expected either solid rock or oozy mud. He was not geochemist enough to guess at the reactions which might have formed what they actually found, and was too sensible to worry about it before actual analyses had been made.

If Weisanen had any opinions, he kept them to himself.

Bresnahan was not worried about the scientific aspect of the situation at all. He simply poked away with his test bar because he had been told to, devoting only a fraction of his attention to the task. His thoughts were elsewhere.

Specifically, he was following through the implications of the information the Weisanens had furnished during the trip down. He admitted to himself that in the others' position he would probably be doing the same thing; but it seemed as though some compromise should be possible which would salvage the original purpose of Raindrop.

Bresnahan did not, of course, expect to eat as well as the average man of mid-twentieth century. He never had, and didn't know what he was missing. He did know, however, that at his present age of twenty-five there was a smaller variety of foodstuffs available than he could remember from his childhood, and he didn't want that process to go any farther. Breaking up Raindrop according to the original plan seemed to him the obvious thing to do. If land and sea farming areas were disappearing under the population flood, the logical answer was farming areas in the sky. This should be as important to the Weisanens as to anyone else.

He felt a little uneasy about bringing the matter up again, however. Somehow, he had a certain awe of Weisanen which he didn't think was entirely due to the fact that the latter was his employer.

Several times their paths came close together as the two plied their test bars, but Bresnahan was unable to wind his courage up to the necessary pitch for some time—not, in fact, until they had been exploring the region uneventfully for over half an hour and Weisanen had finally, with some hesitation, decided that it was safe for his wife to join them.

There was some slight rivalry between Silbert and Bresnahan over who should give up his diving gear to the woman and resume his spacesuit. If Bresnahan had won, a good deal of subsequent trouble might have been avoided; but when all four were finally outside, Silbert was wearing space armor. He had pointed out quite logically that he was the most used to it and would work better than any of the others in its restrictions.

7

The key to the subsequent trouble was that one of the restrictions involved communication. If Silbert had been able to hear clearly, he might have understood what was developing before it had gone too far; but he couldn't. His space helmet lacked the impedance-matching feature of the diving gear, and the latter equipment had no radios.

Some sound did get through his helmet both from and into the water, but not much; for real conversation he had to bring the helmet into physical contact with that of the other party. He therefore knew little of what went on during the next few minutes. He spent them continuing his ecology sample, and paid little attention to anything else.

With Mrs. Weisanen present, some of Bresnahan's unease in her husband's presence left him, and he brought up at last the point which had occurred to him.

"I've been wondering, sir," he opened, "why it wouldn't be possible to break up Raindrop just as was planned, and still use the smaller drops as homes for people like yourselves. I can't see that it would be very different from your present plan."

Weisanen did not seem annoyed, but answered in a straightforward fashion. "Aside from the fact that we would prefer to be in a single city rather than a lot of detached houses which would require us to visit our neighbors by spaceship, the smaller drops will have the radiation problem. Here we have nearly five miles of water shielding us."

"Hmph. I never thought of that."

"No reason why you should have. It was never your problem."

"But still—what do we do about food? Conditions on Earth are getting worse all the time. Starting another Raindrop project would take years. Couldn't you at least compromise? Permit the small drops to be skimmed off the surface of this one while you are living here, and while another Raindrop is set up?"

"I don't like the idea. Can you imagine what it will be like here with shock waves from exploding steam bubbles echoing all through the globe every time the skin is opened for a new farm lot?"

"Why should they break the skin? I should think they'd want to draw off the water through the lock, or other locks which might be built, anyway; otherwise there'd be a lot of waste from boiling. I should think—"

Weisanen's annoyance suddenly boiled over, though no sign of it had been visible before.

"Mr. Bresnahan, it matters very little what you think when you forget that Raindrop is now, legally and properly, private property. I dislike to sound selfish and misanthropic, but I belong to a group which has gone to a great deal of thought and labor to get for itself, legally and without violence, an environment which it needs and which no one else—including the people responsible for our existence—was willing to provide. In addition, if you would think with your brain instead of your stomach you'd realize that the whole original project was pure nonsense. The only possible way mankind can keep himself adequately fed is to limit his population. If you'll pardon the pun, the whole idiotic project was a drop in the bucket. It might have put the day of reckoning back five years, conceivably ten or fifteen, but then we'd have been right back where we started. Even with fusion energy there's a limit to the number of space farms which could be built in a given time, and the way Earth's population grows it would soon be impossible just to make new farms fast enough, let alone operate them. Cheating people? Nonsense! We're doing the rest of mankind a favor by forcing them to face facts while there are a few billion less of them to argue with each other. One group has had to exercise the same sort of control the rest of mankind should be using for a good half century. We didn't *dare* have children except when it was practicable to keep the mother in orbit for the best part of a year. Why should we be particularly sympathetic with the rest of you?"

"I see your point," admitted Bresnahan, "but you've forgotten one other thing. The food problem is yours, too. What will you do as *your* food supply shrinks like everyone else's? Or worse, when people decide not to send any food at all up here, since you won't send any down? Raindrop is a long way yet from being self-supporting, you know."

A grin, clearly visible in the light from a nearby plant knob, appeared on Weisanen's face; but his irritation remained.

"Slight mistake, my young friend. There is another minor modification in our structure; our saliva glands produce an enzyme you lack. We can digest cellulose." He waved his hand at the plants around them.

"How do you know these plants contain cellulose?"

"All plants do; but that's a side issue. The weeds near the surface were analyzed long ago, and proved to contain all the essentials for human life—in a form which we can extract with our own digestive apparatus. Raindrop, as it now is, could support all of us there are now and there are likely to be for a couple of generations. Now, please get back to checking this little world of ours. Brenda and I want to decide where to build our house."

Bresnahan was silent, but made no move to get back to work. He floated for a minute or so, thinking furiously; Weisanen made no effort to repeat or enforce his order.

At last the computerman spoke slowly—and made his worst mistake.

"You may be right in your legal standing. You may be right in your opinion about the value of Raindrop and what the rest of the human race should do—personally, I want a family some day. You may even be right about your safety from general attack because the communication laws will keep down the number of people who know about the business. But, right or wrong, if even a single person with access to a spaceship *does* find out, then you—and your wife—and your baby—are all in danger. Doesn't that suggest to you that some sort of compromise is in order?"

Weisanen's expression darkened and his muscles tensed. His wife, looking at him, opened her mouth and made a little gesture of protest even before he started to speak; but if she made a sound it was drowned out.

"It certainly suggests something, young fellow," snapped the official. "I was hoping the matter wouldn't descend to this level, but remember that while we can live here indefinitely, you cannot. A few weeks of weightlessness will do damage which your bodies can never repair. There is no regular food down here. And we control the transportation back to the station and weight."

"Aino—no!" His wife laid a hand on his arm and spoke urgently. "Wait, dear. If you threaten at all, it's too close to a threat of death. I don't want to kill anyone, and don't want to think of your doing so. It wouldn't be worth it."

"You and the little one *are* worth it. Worth anything! I won't listen to argument on that."

"But argument isn't needed. There is time. Mr. Bresnahan and his friend will certainly wait and think before risking the consequences of a mob-raising rumor. He wants a compromise, not—"

"His compromise endangers you and the others. I won't have it. Mr. Bresnahan, I will not ask you for a promise to keep quiet; you might be the idealistic type which can justify breaking its word for what it considers a good cause. Also, I will not endanger your life and health more than I can help. Brenda is right to some extent; I don't want a killing on my conscience either, regardless of the cause. Therefore, you and Mr. Silbert will remain here at the core until Brenda and I have returned to the station and made sure that no communication gear will function without our knowledge and consent. That may be a few days, which may be more than your health should risk. I'm sorry, but I'm balancing that risk to you against one to us."

"Why should it take days? An hour to the surface, a few minutes to the station—"

"And Heaven knows how long to find and take care of all the radios. Neither of us is an expert in that field, and we'll be a long time making sure we have left no loopholes."

"Will you at least stop to find out whether the air renewers in these diving suits are indefinite-time ones, like the spacesuit equipment? And if they aren't, let me change back into my spacesuit?"

"Of course. Change anyway. It will save my trying to get the substance of this conversation across to Mr. Silbert. You can tell him on radio while we are on the way. Come with me back to the sphere and change. Brenda, stay here."

"But, dearest—this isn't right. You know—"

"I know what I'm doing and why I'm doing it. I'm willing to follow your lead in a lot of things, Bren, but this is not one of them."

"But—"

"No buts. Come, Mr. Bresnahan. Follow me."

The wife fell silent, but her gaze was troubled as she watched the two men vanish through the tiny lock. Bresnahan wondered what she would do. It was because he felt sure she would do something that he hadn't simply defied Weisanen.

The woman's face was no happier when the computerman emerged alone and swam back to a point beside her. Her husband was visible through the port, outsized helmet removed, beckoning to her.

For a moment Bresnahan had the hope that she would refuse to go. This faded as she swam slowly toward the sphere, occasionally looking back, removed the anchor in response to a gesture from the man inside, and disappeared through the lock. The vehicle began to drift upward, vegetation near it swirling in the water jets. Within a minute it had faded from view into the darkness.

"Just what's going on here?" Silbert's voice was clear enough; the suit radios carried for a short distance through water. "Where are they going, and why?"

"You didn't hear any of my talk with Weisanen?"

"No. I was busy, and it's hard to get sound through this helmet anyway. What happened? Did you argue with him?"

"In a way." Bresnahan gave the story as concisely as he could. His friend's whistle sounded eerily in the confines of his helmet.

"This—is—really—something. Just for the record, young pal, we are in a serious jam, I hope you realize."

"I don't think so. His wife is against the idea, and he'll let himself get talked out of it—he's a little afraid of the results already."

"Not the point. It doesn't matter if the whole thing was a practical joke on his part. They're out of sight, in a medium where no current charts exist and the only navigation aids are that sphere's own sonar units. He could find his way back to the core, but how could he find *us?*"

"Aren't we right under the lock and the station? We came straight down."

"Don't bet on that. I told you—there are currents. If we made a straight track on the trip down here I'll be the most surprised man inside Luna's orbit. There are twenty million square feet on this mudball. We'd be visible from a radius of maybe two hundred—visible and recognizable, that is, with our lights on. That means they have something like two hundred search blocks, if my mental arithmetic is right, without even a means of knowing when they cover a given one a second time. There is a chance they'd find us, but not a good one—not a good enough one so that we should bet your chance of dodging a couple of weeks of weightlessness on it. When that nut went out of sight, he disposed of us once and for all."

"I wouldn't call him a nut," Bresnahan said.

"Why not? Anyone who would leave a couple of people to starve or get loaded with zero-gee symptoms on the odd chance that they might blab his favorite scheme to the public—"

"He's a little unbalanced at the moment, but not a real nut. I'm sure he didn't realize he'd passed the point of no return. Make allowances, Bert; I can. Some of my best friends are married, and I've seen 'em when they first learned a kid was on the way. It's just that they don't usually have this good a chance to get other people in trouble; they're all off the beam for a little while."

"You're the most tolerant and civilized character I've met, and you've just convinced me that there can be too much of even the best of things. For my money the guy is a raving nut. More to the point, unless we can get ourselves out of the jam he's dropped us into, we're worse than nuts. We're dead."

"Maybe he'll realize the situation and go back to the station and call for help."

"There can be such a thing as too much optimism, too. My young friend, he's not going to get to the station."

"What? Why not?"

"Because the only laser tube not already in the station able to trigger the cobweb launchers is right here on my equipment clip. That's another reason I think he's a nut. He should have thought of that and pried it away from me somehow."

"Maybe it just means he wasn't serious about the whole thing."

"Never mind what it means about him. Whatever his intentions, I'd be willing to wait for him to come back to us with his tail between his legs if I thought he could find us. Since I don't think he can, we'd better get going ourselves."

"Huh? How?"

"Swim. How else?"

"But how do we navigate? Once we're out of sight of the core we'd be there in the dark with absolutely nothing to guide us. These little lights on our suits aren't—"

"I know they aren't. That wasn't the idea. Don't worry; I may not be able to swim in a straight line, but I can get us to the surface eventually. Come on; five miles is a long swim."

Silbert started away from the glow, and Bresnahan followed uneasily. He was not happy at the prospect of weightlessness and darkness combined; the doses on the trip down, when at least the sphere had been present for some sort of orientation, had been more than sufficient.

The glow of the core faded slowly behind them, but before it was too difficult to see Silbert stopped.

"All right, put your light on. I'll do the same; stay close to me." Bresnahan obeyed both orders gladly. "Now, watch."

The spaceman manipulated valves on his suit, and carefully ejected a bubble of air about two feet in diameter. "You noticed that waste gas from the electrolyzers in the diving suits didn't stay with us to be a nuisance. The bubbles drifted away, even when we were at the core," he pointed out. Bresnahan hadn't noticed, since he wasn't used to paying attention to the fate of the air he exhaled, but was able to remember the fact once it was mentioned.

"That of course, was not due to buoyancy, so close to the core. The regular convection currents started by solar heat at the skin must be responsible. Therefore, those currents must extend all the way between skin and core. We'll follow this bubble."

"If the current goes all the way, why not just drift?"

"For two reasons. One is that the currents are slow—judging by their speed near the skin, the cycle must take over a day. Once we get away from the core, the buoyancy of this bubble will help; we can swim after it.

"The other reason is that if we simply drift we might start down again with the current before we got close enough to the skin to see daylight.

"Another trick we might try if this takes too long is to have one of us drift while the other follows the bubble to the limit of vision. That would establish the up-down line, and we could swim in that direction for a while and then repeat. I'm afraid we probably couldn't hold swimming direction for long enough to be useful, though, and it would be hard on the reserve air supply. We'd have to make a new bubble each time we checked. These suits have recyclers, but a spacesuit isn't built to get its oxygen from the surrounding water the way that diving gear is."

"Let's just follow this bubble," Bresnahan said fervently.

At first, of course, the two merely drifted. There simply was no detectable buoyancy near the core. However, in a surprisingly short time the shimmering globule of gas began to show a tendency to drift away from them.

The direction of drift was seldom the one which Bresnahan was thinking of as "up" at the moment, but the spaceman nodded approval and carefully followed their only guide. Bresnahan wished that his training had given him more confidence in instrument readings as opposed to his own senses, but followed Silbert hopefully.

8

The fourteen hours he spent drifting weightless in the dark made an experience Bresnahan was never to forget, and his friends were never to ignore. He always liked crowds afterward, and preferred to be in cities or at least buildings where straight, clearly outlined walls, windows, and doors marked an unequivocal up-and-down direction.

Even Silbert was bothered. He was more used to weightlessness, but the darkness he was used to seeing around him at such times was normally pocked with stars which provided orientation. The depths of Raindrop provided *nothing*. Both men were almost too far gone to believe their senses when they finally realized that the bubble they were still following could be seen by a glow not from their suits' lights.

It was a faintly blue-green illumination, still impossible to define as to source, but unmistakably sunlight filtered through hundreds of feet of water. Only minutes later their helmets met the tough, elastic skin of the satellite.

It took Silbert only a few moments to orient himself. The sun and the station were both visible—at least they had not come out on the opposite side of the satellite—and he knew the time. The first and last factors were merely checks; all that was really necessary to find the lock was to swim toward the point under the orbiting station.

"I don't want to use the sonar locator unless I have to," he pointed out. "There is sonar gear on the sphere. I should be able to get us close enough by sighting on the station so that the magnetic compass will work.

Judging by where the station seems to be, we have four or five miles to swim. Let's get going."

"And let's follow the great circle course," added Bresnahan. "Never mind cutting across inside just because it's shorter. I've had all I ever want of swimming in the dark."

"My feeling exactly. Come on."

The distance was considerably greater than Silbert had estimated, since he was not used to doing his sighting from under water and had not allowed for refraction; but finally the needle of the gimballed compass showed signs of making up its mind, and with nothing wrong that food and sleep would not repair the two men came at last in sight of the big lock cylinder.

For a moment, Silbert wondered whether they should try to make their approach secretly. Then he decided that if the Weisanens were there waiting for them the effort would be impractical, and if they weren't it would be futile.

He simply swam up to the small hatch followed by Bresnahan, and they entered the big chamber together. It proved to be full of water, but the sphere was nowhere in sight. With no words they headed for the outer personnel lock, entered it, pumped back the water, and emerged on Raindrop's surface. Silbert used his laser, and ten minutes later they were inside the station. Bresnahan's jump had been a little more skillful than before.

"Now let's get on the radio!" snapped Silbert as he shed his space helmet.

"Why? Whom would you call, and what would you tell them? Remember that our normal Earth-end contacts are part of the same group the Weisanens belong to, and you can't issue a general broadcast to the universe at large screaming about a plot against mankind in the hope that someone will take you seriously. Someone might."

"But—"

"My turn, Bert. You've turned what I still think was just a potentially tragic mistake of Weisanen's into something almost funny, and incidentally saved both our lives. Now will you follow my lead? Things could still be serious if we don't follow up properly."

"But what are you going to do?"

"You'll see. Take it from me, compromise is still possible. It will take a little time; Aino Weisanen will have to learn something I can't teach him myself. Tell me, is there any way to monitor what goes on in Raindrop? For example, can you tell from here when the lock down there is opened, so we would know when they come back?"

"No."

"Then we'll just have to watch for them. I assume that if we see them, we can call them from here on regular radio."

"Of course."

"Then let's eat, sleep, and wait. They'll be back after a while, and when they come Aino will listen to reason, believe me. But we can sleep right now, I'm sure; it will be a while yet before they show up. They should still be looking for us—getting more worried by the minute."

"Why should they appear at all? They must have found out long ago that they can't get back to the station on their own. They obviously haven't found us, and won't. Maybe they've simply decided they're already fugitive murderers and have settled down to a permanent life in Raindrop."

"That's possible, I suppose. Well, if we don't see them in a couple of weeks, we can go back down and give them a call in some fashion. I'd rather they came to us, though, and not too soon."

"But let's forget that; I'm starved. What's in your culture tanks besides liver?"

<h1 style="text-align:center">9</h1>

It did not take two weeks. Nine days and eight hours after the men had returned to the station, Silbert saw two spacesuited figures standing on the lock half a mile away, and called his companion's attention to them.

"They must be desperate by this time," remarked Bresnahan. "We'd better call them before they decide to risk the jump anyway." He activated the transmitter which Silbert indicated, and spoke.

"Hello, Mr. and Mrs. Weisanen. Do you want us to send the cobweb down?"

The voice that answered was female.

"Thank God you're there! Yes, please. We'd like to come up for a while." Silbert expected some qualifying remarks from her husband, but none were forthcoming. At Bresnahan's gesture, he activated the spring gun which launched the web toward the satellite.

"Maybe you'd better suit up and go meet them," suggested the computerman. "I don't suppose either of them is very good at folding the web, to say nothing of killing angular speed."

"I'm not sure I care whether they go off on their own orbit anyway," growled the spaceman, rising with some reluctance to his feet.

"Still bitter? And both of them?" queried Bresnahan.

"Well—I suppose not. And it would take forever to repair the web if it hit the station unfolded. I'll be back." Silbert vanished toward the hub, and the younger man turned back to watch his employers make the leap from Raindrop. He was not too surprised to see them hold hands as they did so, with the natural result that they spun madly on the way to the web and came close to missing it altogether.

When his own stomach had stopped whirling in sympathy, he decided that maybe the incident was for the best. Anything which tended to cut down Weisanen's self-assurance should be helpful, even though there was good reason to suspect that the battle was already won. He wondered whether he should summon the pair to his and Silbert's quarters for the interview which was about to ensue, but decided that there was such a thing as going too far.

He awaited the invitation to the Weisanens' rooms with eagerness.

It came within minutes of the couple's arrival at the air lock. When Bresnahan arrived he found Silbert already in the room where they had first reported on their brief visit to Raindrop. All three were still in spacesuits; they had removed only the helmets.

"We're going back down as soon as possible, Mr. Bresnahan," Weisanen began without preliminary. "I have a rather lengthy set of messages here which I would like you and Mr. Silbert to transmit as soon as possible. You will note that they contain my urgent recommendation for a policy change. Your suggestion of starting construction of smaller farms from Raindrop's outer layers is sound, and I think the Company will follow it. I am also advising that material be collected from the vicinity of the giant planets—Saturn's rings seem a likely source—for constructing additional satellites like Raindrop as private undertakings. Financing can be worked out. There should be enough profit from the farms, and that's the logical direction for some of it to flow.

"Once other sources of farm material are available, Raindrop will not be used further for the purpose. It will serve as Company headquarters—it will be more convenient to have that in orbit anyway. The closest possible commercial relations are to be maintained with Earth."

"I'm glad you feel that way, sir," replied Bresnahan. "We'll get the messages off as soon as possible. I take it that more of the Company's officials will be coming up here to live, then?"

"Probably all of them, within the next two years or so. Brenda and I will go back and resume surveying now, as soon as we stock up with some food. I'll be back occasionally, but I'd rather she kept away from high weight for the next few months, as you know."

"Yes, sir." Bresnahan managed, by a heroic effort, to control his smile—almost. Weisanen saw the flicker of his lip, and froze for a moment. Then his own sober features loosened into a broad grin.

"Maybe another hour won't hurt Brenda," he remarked. "Let's have a meal together before we go back."

He paused, and added almost diffidently, "Sorry about what happened. We're human, you know."

"I know," replied Bresnahan. "That's what I was counting on."

"And that," remarked Silbert as he shed his helmet, "is that. They're aboard and bound for the core again, happy as clams. And speaking of clams, if you don't tell me why that stubborn Finn changed his mind, and why you were so sure he'd do it, there'll be mayhem around here. Don't try to make me believe that he got scared about what he'd nearly done to us. I know his wife was on our side, basically, but she wasn't about to wage open war for us. She was as worried about their kid as he was. Come on; make with the words, chum."

"Simple enough. Didn't you notice what he wanted before going back to Raindrop?"

"Not particularly—oh; food. So what? He could live on the food down there—or couldn't he? Don't you believe what he said?"

"Sure I believe him. He and his wife can digest cellulose, Heaven help them, and they can live off Raindrop's seaweed. As I remarked to him, though—you heard me, and he understood me—they're human. I can digest kale and cauliflower, too, and could probably live off them as well as that pair could live off the weeds. But did you ever stop to think what the stuff must taste like? Neither did they. I knew they'd be back with open mouths—and open minds. Let's eat—anything but liver!"

LONGLINE

Faster than Light, Harper & Row, 1976

"We must have missed it! You could see we were going to miss it! What happened? Where are we?" Wattimlan's voice carried more than a tinge of panic. Feroxtant did not exactly nod, since this implies not only a head but a shape, but he made a reassuring gesture in his own way.

"We did miss it. We also missed the fact that it was double—two stars so close together that we sensed only one. We missed the first, and are in the other—a perfectly good landing. If you can calm down enough to do reliable work, we'd better go through post-flight check. I'd like to be able to go home again even if this star turns out to be as nice as it seems, and I won't fly a ship on guesswork. Are you all right now?"

"I—I think so." Wattimlan was young, and unavoidably short in both experience and self-confidence. This, the longest flight ever made through the void between stars where energy became so nearly meaningless, had been his first. He had done his routine work competently, but routine adds little to maturity. "Yes. I can do it, sir."

"All right. It's all yours." Feroxtant knew better than to put the youngster through any more of an inquisition; neither of the explorers was even remotely human, but some qualities are common to all intelligence. They set carefully to work. The mechanism which permitted them to exist in and to travel through a medium almost devoid of quantum-exchange niches had to be complex and delicate, and was almost alive in its occasional perversity. Until they were certain that it was in perfect order, ready to carry them back over the incredibly long line they had just traced, they could feel little interest in anything else, even their new environment.

Just how long the check required is impossible to say, but eventually the *Longline* floated, stable and ready for flight, in an equally stable pattern of potential niches, and her crew was satisfied.

"Now what?" Wattimlan's question, the captain suspected, was rhetorical; the youngster probably had already made up his mind about what to do next. "I've never seen any star but home before, and I suppose we should learn enough about this one to permit a useful report when we announce our arrival—at least, we should have seen more than just the boundary film. On the other spin, though, there's the other star you say must be close to this one—should we start casting for it right away? If it's really close, maybe we'd hit it without too many tries."

"You really want to get back into space so quickly?"

"Well—I thought you'd prefer to make the casts, at least at first, but we can take turns if you prefer. Frankly, I'd rather look over the landscape first."

"I agree," Feroxtant replied rather dryly. "Let's reinforce our identities and get to it."

Landscape is of course a hopelessly crude translation of Wattimlan's communication symbol. Inside a neutron star there is no close analogy to hills and valleys, rivers and forests, sky, sunlight, or clouds. It is a virtually infinite complex of potential levels—some unoccupied, others occupied by one or more of the fundamental particles which made up the universe known to the two explorers, some in flux among the various possible states. This is equally true, of course, of the matter universe, and just as a man groups the patterns of electrons and other force fields around him into perceived objects, so did Wattimlan and Feroxtant. A pattern capable of identity maintenance, growth, and duplication, which maintained its existence by ingesting and restructuring other such patterns, might be called a lion or a shark by a human being; such an entity would also possess an identification symbol in the minds of the explorers, but translating that symbol into any human word would be unwise, since the hearer could probably not help clothing the central skeleton of abstraction with very misleading flesh.

It is therefore not correct to say that Wattimlan was charged by a lion and saved himself by climbing a tree during their preliminary examination of the new star. It would be even less accurate, however, to say that the exploration was uneventful. It would be most accurate, but still very incomplete, to say that when he got back to the *Longline* the younger traveller held a much more tolerant attitude toward the boring aspects of space-casting than had been the case earlier.

They had learned enough for an acceptable report. They had named their discovery Brother, intending to add the prefix of Big or Little when they reached the companion star and found out which word applied. They had amused themselves, each in his own way—they were individuals, as different from each other as any two human beings. As a natural consequence, they had even perceived Brother differently, and had already developed different attitudes toward it.

The length of time all this had taken is impossible to state, since their time is not really commensurable with that in the Einstein-matter universe. Eventually they made their call to their home star, along the incomprehensibly extended line of uniform potential which their ship had marked in space. They reported their finds, and received acknowledgment. They received assurance that other ships would follow. They spent more time at their equivalents of working, eating, drinking, and merrymaking; and finally they faced the question of trying to reach Big or Little Brother, as it might turn out to be—the companion star which Feroxtant had identified in the instant of their landing.

I feel a little funny about this," Wattimlan admitted as they began the *Longline's* preflight check. "I've heard of stars which were close companions of each other, but there was always one difference. You could see one from the other just about anywhere, as long as you hadn't gone below the surface film, but you could see it only half the time. This one you can see all the time if you're in the right place in the film, but not at all if you're anywhere else. It scares me. Can it be a real star?"

"I'm not sure." Feroxtant would not admit to fear, but he was admittedly as puzzled as his junior. "At least, we don't have to worry about starting time. Since we can always see it from here, we can lift any time we choose."

"That's just what bothers me. Of course, no one minds flying when he knows where he's going—when there's a steady-pot line to follow. I didn't mind the blind start we made on this trip, since we'd either hit another star sooner or later or be able to reverse and go home. Now I don't know what we may hit. This constant-visibility situation bothers me. Could this other thing actually be a *part* of the star we're in now, separated by some strange potential pattern instead of ordinary space?"

"I hadn't thought of that," Feroxtant replied. "It's a bit wild an idea. I had thought there might be some connection between this situation and a lecture I once heard on something called *direction*."

"Never heard of it."

"I'm not surprised. It's as abstract a notion as I've ever heard of, and I can't put it into ordinary words."

"Does it suggest any special risks?"

"It makes no suggestions at all on the personal level. You knew when you volunteered for exploration that it involved the unknown, and therefore meant some risk. Now you're worrying, apparently without even considering all the peculiarities we are facing."

"What? What haven't I considered?"

"You've said nothing about the neutrino source which must also be in this neighborhood, since it is bright enough to see, but which *is* behaving normally—visible half the time, out of sight the other half."

Wattimlan was silent for a time, checking his own sensory impressions, his memories, and the *Longline*'s instrument recordings. Finally he switched attention back to his commander. and asked another question.

"Can that possibly be a star?"

"I doubt it. More probably it's a protostar—one of the neutrino sources which we think finally condenses to an ordinary star. Presumably the neutrinos carry off whatever energy manifestations prevent the formation of a normal star. In any case, it's harmless—people have probably flown through them without any effect. There's no way to tell whether this one is nearer or farther than the star we're casting for, but it's nothing to worry about. Now—do you want to make the first few casts, or shall I?"

The youngster hesitated only a moment. "I'll do it, if you trust me to make an open-space reversal."

"Sure. You know the routine. I'm not worrying, and you shouldn't be. Take her out."

"You can't make a guess at strike probability, I suppose?"

"No. It depends on target distance, and apparently on target size, though no one knows why—maybe it's another of those direction phenomena. Anyway, we know only that the distance is small—which makes the chances fairly high—and I'm not suggesting that there's any way to guess at something's size just by looking at it. Ready for final checkout?"

"Ready."

"Pressor lens?"

"Open."

"Film field one?"

"In synch."

"Line track power…"

The *Longline* emerged from the surface film of the neutron star and hurtled away from the tiny body, leaving far behind the burst of neutrino emission which accompanied the lift. The explorers had only a rough idea of the possible distance to their target, and none at all of their vessel's speed in open space. It had been discovered by experience that slowing down sufficiently to let neutrinos overtake them was apparently impossible. The more advanced theories in fundamental mechanics implied that substance as they understood it became mathematically unreal below neutrino speed; what this implied in terms of observable properties was anyone's guess. It was generally believed that stars in galaxies—that is, the neutron stars which were all they could sense of such bodies—were separated by a few hundred to a few thousand of their own diameters. Space travel had given them, in addition, the concept of galaxies separated by a dozen or two times their own size, on the average.

Wattimlan and Feroxtant, therefore, could only guess at the distance needed for their casts. They had set up an arbitrary travel time; if the pilot failed to make a landing before that was up, he would reverse and return to the starting point along the new constant-pot line his trip would have established. The time was short enough so that even the youngster, Feroxtant hoped, could hardly get either bored or nervous.

The chance of landing on any one cast was presumably very small, though there was no way of calculating just how small. Feroxtant's suggestion that this might become possible when the concept of direction was finally clarified by the advanced mathematicians was not really a serious prediction, since he had no real idea of what the theory was all about; it was more like the suggestions in Earth's early twentieth century that radium might prove a cure for cancer and old age.

Wattimlan, therefore, gave no serious thought to what he would do if and when the *Longline* made starfall. It would be routine, anyway. He flew. He readied himself for his first open-space reversal with some uneasiness, but missed its time only slightly. The miss annoyed him as a reflection on his professional skill, but it was in no way dangerous; the *Longline* was suddenly retracing its outward path. There was none of the deceleration which a human pilot would have had to plan and experience; the concept of inertia was even stranger and more abstract to Wattimlan than that of direction—or would have been if anyone had ever suggested it to him. The only observable phenomenon marking the reversal was another burst of neutrinos, vaguely analogous to the squeal of tires from a clumsily handled ground vehicle but—unlike the time error or a tire squeal—not indicative of poor piloting.

In the sub-light universe, a simple direction reversal does not involve change in kinetic energy, except for whatever entropy alteration may be involved; equal speed means equal kinetic energy. In the tachyon universe, momentum is naturally as meaningless as direction, kinetic energy almost equally so, and the interactions between forces and the various fundamental particles follow very different rules. However, the rules were the ones Wattimlan knew, and the time interval between the reversal and reentry into the neutron star's surface film was for him boringly uneventful. He landed.

Feroxtant was nowhere to be seen; he had apparently gone off either working or playing. Wattimlan decided to be pleased at the implied compliment to his competence rather than hurt at the suggested indifference to his welfare, and went through post-flight and pre-flight checks without waiting for his commander and instructor to appear. He made another cast, and another, and another...

"So pay up!" Sforza leaned back from the display tank which dominated the *Manzara's* maneuvering console, and just barely managed to refrain from smirking.

Jeb Garabed, a quarter century younger and correspondingly less restrained, glared first into the tank and then at the two-liter silvery cube beside it. He didn't quite snarl—the captain was also present—but there was a distinct edge to his voice.

"I should know better than to let myself get fooled by that old line about mechanical brains. I know that thing is made of doped diamond, but I didn't realize how much weight the first word carried!"

Sforza lifted an eyebrow. "I don't seem to appreciate your humor as much as I used to."

"Don't bother to put that eyebrow on top of your head. It would be conspicuous. I wasn't trying to be funny."

"That's just as well. You—" Sforza cut himself off with an effort, and fell silent. For a moment each of the men wondered if he had said too much, as Garabed's face and Sforza's scalp both flushed.

Captain Migna Sarjuk listened to the exchange without too much concern; she knew both men well, and could tell that the jibes were not serious. When arguments became too frequent, of course, it was a temptation to separate the disputants for a few months by judicious watch-shifting; but it was possible to be too hasty with this solution. One could break up good working teams, and even run out of possible combinations. With over eighty people on the *Manzara* the latter seemed mathematically improbable, but since most of the possible combinations were in fact eliminated by conditions of specialty training it was not entirely impossible. The ship had spent eighteen months—subjective time—en route, would be at least that long going back, and might remain several years at this end of the flight line; the captain had no intention of running out of solutions to the most likely personnel problems any sooner than she could help. She waited silently, paying close attention to Sforza's reactions; the younger man, she knew, would not lose his temper in her presence.

He didn't. The young radiometrist caught himself in turn, grinned, and tossed a couple of time-slugs onto the console. Sforza gathered them up. Garabed half-apologized as he continued to stare into the display.

It was not a picture in the conventional sense. The three-dimensional presentation did show images of a number of celestial bodies, but they were festooned with numbers, vector arrows in various colors, and other symbols. To Sforza, it was a completely informative description of all the detectable objects within a light-day of the ship. Garabed would have felt happier with the images alone, stripped of the extra symbols. He could then have thought of it as a simple bead-and-wire model.

He greatly preferred the direct view of space from the *Manzara*'s observation dome, even though human perception was not really adequate for its analysis. For most of the trip it had been an unchanging Milky Way—unchanging, that is, except as his own intellect changed it. He had found he could change its appearance from a flat spray-paint job on a screen a few yards outside the dome to a more nearly correct, but far from complete, impression of infinite star-powdered depths. His home star had been fading throughout the journey, of course, though the change in a single day had been imperceptible except at the very beginning. It was now an unimpressive object about as bright as Polaris.

The *Manzara*'s target star was now overwhelmingly bright, and the human mind had no trouble accepting that it was far closer than Sol; but its white dwarf companion had only recently grown brighter than the sun the explorers had left some ten objective years before.

But Garabed could read the display symbols even if he preferred to visualize differently, and now one of them caught his attention. It was typical of him that he did not call immediate attention to it; his first reaction was to recoup his betting losses. At this distance, a few minutes' delay in reporting a discovery would not be of importance to the ship's safety—or, more important, to the captain. He continued the conversation, and even Sarjuk failed to catch any change in his manner.

"So I was wrong. It just means we'll have to spend a year and a half of our personal time flying back—unless I turn right while we're here."

"I'll cover another bet on that, if you like."

Garabed shook his head. "I guess not. Now that real work is starting, I don't need so much distraction—and probably can't afford it. It was different on the way, when I needed amusement. Conning my way out of boring jobs by smart bets provided that—even when I lost, the jobs themselves made a change. Now it's time to be serious, though, if you'll pardon the pun. How do things look to you?"

The ballistician gestured toward the display into which Garabed was still staring. "There you are. Cutting drive didn't make much difference. It adds up to what we've known for a couple of centuries, plus what we've picked up in the last few months. One type A main sequence sun, known since before human history began—with an unexplained, not to mention unproved, charge of having been red instead of white a couple of millennia ago. One white dwarf in a fifty-year orbit with it, known since the nineteenth century. Four high-density planets discovered by us in the last few weeks. No gas giants, which would be out where the white dwarf would perturb them hopelessly anyway. And no trace of the faster-than-light ship you were betting would be here from Earth waiting for us."

Garabed shrugged. "It was still a reasonable bet. We have artificial gravity, and a field drive system which can be described as a space warp without lying too grossly. It still seems to me that those should ease us into FTL flight before I'm very much older."

"In spite of the fact that both the gadgets you mention were developed on the assumption that Einstein was right? And that even the warp which makes a portable fusion engine practical is an Einstein application? I seem to be missing a rung or two in your ladder of logic."

Garabed glanced at the captain before answering. "Yes," he said after a moment. "In spite of that."

"And in spite of the fact that this trip was only a political gesture to quiet the people who don't think Earth is home enough? And that there were long, loud screams about the better things which could be done with the resources which went into the *Manzara* and her equipment? Why-should-we-explore-the-stars, practically-no-chance-of-life, a-waste-of-resources, we've-solved-all-our-real-problems, let's-sit-back-and-live? You've heard it all."

"Sure I have." Garabed did not look at the captain this time. "But people are still curious—that's what makes them people. Once we were on the way some of them were bound to want to find out what we'd see—first. It's being human. You have the same drive, whether you want to admit it or not; I'll show you." He reached across and flicked off the display in the computer's tank. "How sure are you that there's nothing really unexpected to be found in the Sirius system? And would you bet there isn't a clue to it in your data banks right now?"

The older man looked into the blank display unit, and thought. The kid might have seen something, though Sforza himself should have noticed anything important; it was certainly possible. On the other hand, Sforza had known the young con artist to bluff his way out of one or another of the ship's less popular jobs on at least four occasions during the trip, three of them at Sforza's own expense. Had there been anything surprising on the display? Something he should, of course, have seen himself?

The captain had come over to the ballistics console to look for herself, though she of course said nothing. She knew, far better than Sforza, that Garabed might not be bluffing.

The ballistician hesitated a moment longer, straining his memory with no useful result, and decided to take a chance.

"All right. Two hours' worth." He put the slugs he had just won on the panel before him. Garabed covered them with two more, and turned the display back on. For a moment there was silence.

"What was the time limit on this?" the older man finally asked. The captain, unseen behind him, smiled and slipped back to her own station, where she busied herself at the intercom. The instrument specialist paid no obvious attention to her; the smile on his face might have been simply one of triumph.

"No time needed. Look at the white dwarf's radial velocity."

"I see it. So what? You wouldn't expect it to match A's. Even a fifty-year orbit means a few kilos per second—"

"Changing how fast?" asked Garabed pointedly.

"Not very—" Sforza fell silent again, glued his eyes to the display, and within a minute the eyebrows were climbing toward the desert above.

"It's changing!"

"How right you are. Do you pay now, or calculate first?"

Sforza waved the slugs away with an impatient gesture of his head; his fingers were already busy. He didn't stop to wonder why the velocity variation had not been spotted sooner; it was obvious enough. The axis of the previously unknown orbit must point almost exactly at the Solar system. The *Manzara* was now so close to the Sirius group that the A star and the white dwarf appeared fully forty degrees apart, and the ship was well off the line between Sol and the dwarf. Hence, there was a radial velocity component not previously detectable.

This clue to the line of the orbit axis permitted an assumption which would otherwise have been a wide-open guess in Sforza's computation. He plugged it in, let the spectral sensors which Garabed kept in such good condition feed their readings and the *Manzara*'s clock signals in after it, and waited until the display steadied. Then, and only then, did he speak.

"Take your pirated money, and call Physics and Policy—"

"They're coming," the captain interjected quietly. Sforza continued.

"The white dwarf is in a nearly perfect-circle orbit with something too small to see, but of comparable mass. The period is seven hundred seventy-two seconds. The dwarf is thirty-two thousand miles from the barycenter, orbital speed two hundred seventy-seven miles per second—"

"Miles?" queried Sarjuk. "I can sympathize with the Creative Anachronism urge, but—"

"Fifty-one thousand five hundred, four hundred forty-six. The invisible body's radius vector is open until we can get a mass ratio, but can hardly be more than a few tens of thousands of kilometers. We have a dividend. It's either a neutron star or—"

"Or nothing," pointed out the captain. "It can't be more massive than the total previously measured for Sirius B—point nine suns. Too little for a black hole."

Garabed was nodding slowly, his face nearly expressionless, but both his companions could tell he was containing strong excitement. His only words, however, formed a terse question.

"New flight plan, Captain?"

The *Manzara* had been free-falling in an orbit intended to make a close swing past Sirius B, enter a slingshot transfer to A with a periastron distance from the latter of only a fifth of an astronomical unit, and a second sling to interception with the largest, outermost, and probably most Earthlike of A's four planets.

Sarjuk was by training an engineer specializing in safety extrapolation, which naturally included administrative psychology and hence qualified her for her present command status. She was certainly no ballistician, but she knew what a change in orbit meant in terms of fuel reserve—which after all was a major safety factor for the *Manzara*. In this case, of course, a good secondary-school student could have performed the appropriate calculations.

"New flight plan, of course," she agreed quietly. "But let's hear what Physics wants before Mr. Sforza does any number work." She swung her seat about as a dozen excited researchers entered the bridge, motioned them to the seats which ringed the chamber, and turned back to Garabed.

"Jeb," she asked, "can you possibly get anything with real resolving power to cover this object? I know it must be small, but until we know just how small and just where it is we're going to be crippled in any planning. Sforza can give you the direction from the dwarf to the orbit center, and you can search along the projection of that line with whatever seems likely to work best. Build something if you have to."

Without waiting for the two men to get to work, she turned back to the newcomers and gave them a summary of the new information. They listened in near silence, their eyes never leaving her face until she had finished.

"How close can we get?" Tikaki and Distoienko spoke almost in unison.

"Will it take too much fuel to park beside it?" was the more thoughtful question from Dini Aymara, a warp theoretician. Tikaki answered instantly.

"Of course not! Look—it's a binary, with the two bodies similar in mass. All we'll need is maneuvering power; we can use an orbit which will transfer our energy to one of the bodies instead of slinging us away. When we do want to leave, we can slingshot out in the same fashion. We can get as close to the neutron star as you want—meters, if your experiments need it—"

"Three objections, Mr. Tikaki," the captain spoke quietly still. "First, at a distance even of kilos, to say nothing of meters, not even our best cameras could get clear images—figure the orbital speed at such a distance. Second, neutron stars are likely to have strong magnetic fields, and there are plenty of conductors in this ship, starting with the main hull stringers. Finally, there is such a thing as tidal force. I will not permit this ship into a gee-gradient of more than five inverse-seconds squared, and only then if all main and backup artificial gravity units are in perfect condition. Mr. Sforza, what distance would that tidal limit mean from the two bodies?"

The ballistician had finished providing Garabed's needed figures, and was able to answer the captain's question almost instantly.

"For the white dwarf it would be somewhere inside; you'll be worrying about other things first. For the neutron star, it of course depends on the mass, which we don't—"

"I have it—at least, I have a respectable mass on the line you gave me, affecting the gravity-wave unit," cut in Garabed.

"Line?" responded Sforza. The instrument technician supplied a set of numbers which the ballistician's fingers fed into his computer as they came; a set of luminous symbols appeared in the display tank, and were translated at once. "Mass is point three eight suns. The tidal limit distance you want is a hair under five thousand kilometers—about three quarters of an Earth radius."

The captain nodded, and glanced around the group. "I thought so. Gentlemen and ladies, the *Manzara* is half a kilometer long—*not* a point." If she expected Tikaki to look properly sheepish or disgruntled she was disappointed. He simply nodded, and after a moment she went on. "Very well. If Mr. Sforza can warp us into a capture orbit without exceeding tidal and radiation limits, and without using more than five hundred kilograms of hydrogen, I approve a pass. If you can all work from the mass center of the pair, I set no time limit; those who want to stay will have to make their peace with those who want to get on to A and the planets. Engineers, let's get the umbrella out. Mr. Sforza, report if we can't conform to the restrictions I've set. Meeting adjourned."

The "umbrella" was a thin sheet of highly reflective, highly conducting alloy which could be mounted on the bow of the *Manzara,* giving her rather the appearance of a fat-stemmed mushroom. Like the hull itself, it could be cooled by Thompson-effect units whose radiators were ordinary incandescent searchlights, able to send the waste energy in any convenient direction. The whole unit was something of a makeshift, a late addition to the mission plan intended to permit a brief but very close pass by each of the stars being studied. It had to be set up manually, since it had not been included in the ship's original specifications—and even a fusion-powered giant like the *Manzara* was rationed in the mass she could devote to automatic machinery. Once again, the versatility of the human researcher was being utilized.

Space-suit work, still called EVA, was still taken seriously by those who had to perform it. There is a human tendency to ignore the dangers in a given action if they become familiar enough—people who cannot bring themselves to look down from a twelfth-story window are often quite casual about the equivalent energy exposure of driving a ground vehicle at sixty miles per hour. On the other hand, the high steel worker seems as casual about walking a twelve-inch beam five hundred feet above the street.

There is, however, a difference. The professional high steel worker, or submarine engineer, or for that matter racing driver, has his apparent unconcern underlain by a solid foundation of hard-won safety habits which in turn grow from a fully conscious awareness of the dangers of his calling. Also, the professional does not like to be distracted by amateurs, though he will usually admit the necessity of devoting some time to the training of new professionals.

Space workers are professionals—normally. Some two thirds of the *Manzara's* personnel, however, were researchers whose space-suit and free-fall experience were strictly for the occasion. This would not by itself have been serious, since the ship's space professionals could have put out the umbrella without their aid—and would have been glad to do so. Unfortunately, the makeshift aspect of the umbrella included the assumption that it could serve more than one purpose. It was basically protection for the ship, of course; but the ship was a research instrument, and it had been taken for granted that the umbrella would also serve the researchers directly. They would mount instruments on it. They would study, and alter, its own activity as it absorbed and converted the radiation flux.

And during the year-and-a-half flight from the Solar system most of the scientists had improved their time developing new plans and projects to supplement the original programs and to replace them if unexpected conditions made them impractical. Consequently, the researchers expected to be on hand during the assembling and fitting of the umbrella.

"How can I possibly wait until it's set up?" Tikaki was hurt and indignant. "Look—four of these leads have to go through the mirror. I can't possibly drill holes after the segments are assembled—I'll have to groove the joints, and after they're butted put in the interferometer units—"

"Look—I obviously have to run impedance checks on every intersection junction as they're put together." Crandell was being patient. "Every stage of assembly will make changes in electrical and thermal properties of the whole unit. I *can't* just use one term for the assembled unit— different segments will be getting their irradiation at different angles; it's not a plane surface—"

"Certainly these heat-flow meters have to be installed and calibrated during the assembly—" Cetsewayo was matter-of-fact. Captain Migna Sarjuk did not debate any of the issues. She did not point out that if any imperfections developed in the umbrella, all the proposed experiments would have to be cancelled because the *Manzara* would not be able to get close enough to either star to perform them. She assumed that the scientists knew this, just as an alcoholic knows what a cocktail will do to him. She was politely firm.

"Nothing is attached to the umbrella until it is installed and its refrigeration system tested. After that, any installations will be done by engineers, engineers who know the umbrella systems and circuitry."

"But, Captain!" The howl was almost universal. "How can they—?" The details of the question varied, but the basis was constant and not very original. Scientific training does not always prevent a human being from falling in love with his own ideas and inventions; it does not always even let him recognize when he has done so. They *had* to install their own equipment—they had built it themselves, they had adjusted and calibrated it themselves, and no one else could be trusted to set it up properly for its intended use. Sarjuk was not even tempted, however, mission-conscious though she was.

On the other hand, she was not one to argue when it was not necessary. She used a technique which would not have been available to a ship's captain on the oceans of Earth a century before: she made herself unavailable for policy discussion by going outside to oversee the work on the umbrella. At least, that was her declared purpose, and in view of her responsibilities and personality it was taken for granted by those inside that she was too busy to be interrupted by radioed arguments.

She did, of course, oversee; she also relaxed. Space lacks the change, the sound, and the scents which impress human senses and combine to give planetary landscapes that subjective quality called beauty; but space, too, is beautiful, and the captain appreciated it. Between examinations of newly made connections she simply floated, drinking in her surroundings through the only sense available and reinforcing the visual images of the Milky Way, distant Sol, and blazing Sirius from the body of knowledge which was part of her heritage as a civilized, cultured being. She "saw" the four planets which the *Manzara's* instruments had detected, just as she saw the more numerous and varied worlds of the Solar system and the frozen attendants of Proxima Centauri—she could look where she knew them to be, and let memory and imagination fill the gaps left by human sensory limitations.

She spent more hours, perhaps, than she should have done at this combination of duty and pleasure. She was physically very tired, though emotionally refreshed, when she finally floated back to an air lock to face more argument from her scientists. She was met inside by Tikaki, who perhaps had been refreshed himself in some fashion during the past few hours; at least, he was changing tactics from pressure to compromise.

"Captain, if we can't do our own installing outside," he suggested, "can we choose, or at least brief, the engineer who does it? Preferably the former, of course."

Sarjuk had known something of the sort was coming, of course; as her fatigue had mounted, out there in the blissful darkness, she had delayed her return out of reluctance to face it.

But tired or not, Sarjuk was a professional. She was quite able to balance the overall safety of the *Manzara* against the reasons why the ship and crew were here at all. She was incapable of making a compromise which would be likely to cause total failure of the mission, but the idea of compromise itself did not bother her. She racked the helmet she had just removed, but made no move to get out of the rest of her vacuum armor as she considered the physicist's proposal.

"Whom would you select for your own installation job?" she asked after a moment.

"Garabed, of course. He's the best instrument specialist we have." A shade of expression flickered across Sarjuk's face.

"That's not because—" She cut off the remark, but Tikaki finished for her.

"No, it's not because he's your husband. I wouldn't budge an angstrom from my insistence on doing the job myself if I weren't willing to admit how good he is—and you should know it!"

She nodded. "Sorry. I do know it. Very well, I agree to the suggestion in principle, provided that Jeb—"

"Provided that Jeb agrees? Who's captain here?"

"I am, Dr. Tikaki. Provided that Jeb has time enough after doing his routine work *and* the favors which three out of four of the so-ingenious researchers we have here keep asking of him when they can't make their own improvisations work. I am quite aware that he is the best instrument specialist we have—and that everyone aboard this ship knows it. If you wish to put your suggestion to him, you may do so—when he comes in. Please be brief, however. He has been in a space suit for sixteen of the last twenty-four hours, and has just been delayed by another circuit problem in a Thompson unit. I don't know when he will finish, but he is considerably more overdue for sleep than I am—and if you will excuse me, I am going off watch now."

She turned away and quickly doffed the rest of her space armor, while Tikaki tried vainly to think of the right thing to say. He failed, and wisely said nothing.

However, he left the lock bay at the same time the captain did. Even appearing to stay around to wait for Garabed seemed tactless at the moment.

Nothing more was said directly—Tikaki reported the gist of the conversation to several of his fellows, and the word spread rapidly enough to the other researchers. However, twelve hours later a watch reassignment was published, putting the two other instrument workers alternately on outside duty and assigning Garabed to liaison with the researchers who had equipment to be mounted on the finished umbrella. It occurred to Tikaki that his pressure might actually have been a favor for Sarjuk, giving her an excuse to do something she had wanted to do anyway, but he decided that any experimental check of this hypothesis would be too much like trying to find the taste of monofluoroacetic acid.

Over four days were spent outside by the space-suited engineers, with Sarjuk watching them closely two thirds of the time and sleeping most of the rest. Then, the umbrella assembled, attached, and electrically proven, a tiny change was made in the *Manzara's* velocity. The result was obvious only to people like Sforza, who could read the vector symbols in the ballistics tank as readily as a novel. Sirius B had already become a dazzlingly brilliant point of light, while A was blazing well to one side; but it would be days yet before unaided human senses could convince their owners that the ship was in a B-centered orbit.

The velocity change as such was no more apparent to the *Longline's* pilot than to the human beings on the *Manzara,* but the neutrino flux from the Solar vessel's hydrogen fusers was another matter. It was tiny in amount compared to the flood from Sirius A, even after inverse square decrement, but it was well above the noise level of the *Longline's* instruments, and Wattimlan, still casting outward from the neutron star with completely unhuman patience, detected it and was properly confused.

Another pseudo-star? Did they come this small? Or was it really small—perhaps the feebleness meant distance. But did stars suddenly wink into existence like that? He had never heard of such a thing. Maybe Feroxtant would know...

So the *Longline* paused in her endless casting, and the young pilot searched the neutron star calling rather frantically for his chief. Feroxtant was amusing himself in a fashion quite beyond the possibility of describing to a human being, and did not particularly wish to be found at the moment. Consequently, even though the *Manzara's* acceleration lasted a very long time by tachyon standards, it had ended by the time Wattimlan found him, convinced him that something was strange, and got him back to the ship to see for himself. The peculiar neutrino flux had ceased—the *Manzara's* general operations were powered by chemical accumulators, since operating fusers at what amounted to trickle power was inherently wasteful. Feroxtant saw nothing, and Wattimlan had to admit that there was now nothing to see. The net result was that Feroxtant, deciding that his assistant needed a rest, took over at piloting the *Longline's* casts. Neither he nor Wattimlan gave any thought whatever to the fact that the neutrino bursts from their own vessel's acceleration would have appeared similar in intensity, though far briefer in duration, to any nearby ship.

Jeb Garabed was kept very, very busy. Neither the captain nor anyone else had mentioned a word about the Tikaki argument to him; he had, indeed, taken the reassignment almost for granted. He was not offensively conceited, but had a perfectly realistic awareness of his own competence. If the change had given him and the captain any more time together off-watch than before, he might have been slightly suspicious of an ulterior motive; but it had no such effect.

All three of the instrument workers were now occupied every waking moment. Everything the *Manzara* carried whose analytical range much exceeded that of a chemist's test tube was now in use, probing the white dwarf itself and groping for the still invisibly small neutron star whipping around it. The name of Garabed or one of his colleagues echoed over the intercom whenever something failed to operate properly—and, as he complained occasionally, whenever an unexpected reading was recorded and the researcher involved was *afraid* his machine was working improperly.

Consequently, while Garabed was not actually the first to detect impulses from the *Longline,* he was certainly the first to believe that those impulses constituted genuine, objective data rather than instrumental artifacts.

To him, the neutrino telescopes were just another set of instruments which he knew intimately. They would not have been recognized a century or so earlier; they were far more sophisticated than the original tank of cleaning fluid in a mine. They still did not approach ordinary optical equipment in resolving power, but the word "telescope" was far more appropriate than it had once been. They even reported their data in the form of visual images on very conventional electron tubes, though their "optical" parts were warp fields.

Jeff Pardales, the physicist who made most use of the neutrino equipment, was never surprised to see ghost images on the tube, but he was never happy about them.

"Find it, please, Jeb," he said in a rather tired voice. "It's bad enough to have neutrinos at all from a supposedly dead white dwarf. It's worse when they come in separate bursts. It's worst of all when I can't tell whether they're actually coming from the dwarf or from some place as much as a million kilometers away from it. At least, though, I'd like to be sure that half of what I see isn't originating right in that circuit box."

"It shouldn't be." Garabed's voice was almost as tired. "I had it apart less than five days ago. What's the pattern that makes you worry?"

"Doubling of the image."

"That does sound embarrassing for me. What's the pattern? Horizontal? Vertical? Same brightness? Energy difference?"

"Energy about the same in original and ghost. Time difference varies from too close to distinguish—which may mean no ghost at all—up to just about one second. Position difference seems random—but at this range my resolving power in angle means more than one light-second."

Garabed frowned. "That doesn't sound like anything I've ever seen happen inside one of these things. Have you checked it out on the A star?"

"Yes. Nothing surprising. A steady image of what might be its active nucleus, blurred by resolution limit at this distance."

"Then I suggest you believe what you're getting here. I can't take apart everything on the ship every time someone is surprised by what he sees."

Embarrassment supplemented the fatigue on Pardales' face. "I know, Jeb. I wouldn't ask, except I've gone over it all myself, and can't find anything wrong with the telescope, and all of us have been beating our brains out without even a whisper of an idea of what could emit neutrinos in any such way. I'm not so much asking you whether there's anything wrong with the 'scope as I am asking what you can do to improve its resolution. In theory, inside tuning should give us another power of ten. I know we'll be that much closer in a couple of weeks, but if we have to wait that long some of us may not be in shape to work. I mean it."

Jeb's eyebrows started to imitate those of his former watchmate Sforza before he remembered and controlled them.

"That bad? I suppose that means one of you came up with the demon theory and no one else can think of anything to replace it—but you don't want to admit it."

"Just help us measure, please, Jeb." Garabed said nothing more; he nodded sympathetically and opened the case of the telescope. He understood perfectly. For Cro-Magnon man, it could be taken for granted that lightning was produced by a living being—one with special powers, but not entirely beyond man's comprehension. A few millennia later, the notion that disease was a divine punishment for sin was equally acceptable. Then the idea of an essentially human universe—one in which man was not only of central importance but of typical powers—began to fade as a more coherent concept of natural law was developed. Intelligent creators of the Martian canals, though popular as a concept, were not universally accepted; the flying saucer phenomenon a few decades later saw the "little green men" accepted by a minority, composed largely of the less disciplined imaginations. Very, very few seriously considered the pulsars as possible space beacons planted by star-faring races. And scarcely anyone interpreted the regular crystal-growth patterns, whose images were first transmitted to Earth by unmanned probes from the moons of Jupiter, as the remains of cities. Blaming things on intelligence had simply gone out of style.

This, of course, put the *Manzara*'s researchers at a profound disadvantage.

It also put Jeb Garabed to a great deal of unnecessary work. "I can't get you ten times the resolution," he said at last. "You'll have to settle for about seven, and get the rest by waiting. Look, I'm no psychologist, but why should you let this worry you now? Can't you just collect your measures, and not worry about explaining them until you've recorded everything you can expect to get? That's what Min would certainly advise, and—"

"And you would naturally be inclined to take her advice. I admit it's good; I just doubt that it's possible to follow. All right, Jeb. I'll be calling for you shortly, I'm sure."

"Not until that thing has been run for at least six hours," Garabed said firmly. "Unless you actually do go overboard and hit it with a torch, I refuse to believe that it can go wrong before then. Just get all your nice measures on the tapes, and don't—what do you scientists call it—theorize ahead of your data." He left hastily—there were two other calls for his services already.

He mentioned the conversation some hours later to the captain, not as a complaint or even an official report, but as an example of how things were going, in one of their rare private conversations. She proved more concerned than he had expected.

"I've heard a little about it," she agreed. "The star people seem terribly bothered at the idea of a white dwarf's putting out neutrinos, and even more so at the thought of their coming from the neutron star. The idea is that such bodies should be past that stage. I'd have thought that a real scientist would be delighted at the chance to discover something really new, but this crowd seems short on self-confidence; they can't convince themselves that the data aren't mistakes."

"That's what it looked like to me," agreed her husband. "I suggested to Jeff that he just collect measures for a while, hoping that the bulk of material would convince him there must be something to it, but I don't know whether it'll work."

Sarjuk pondered for a minute or two. "I can't think of anything better, myself," she admitted finally, "except that you'd better do everything you can to keep up their confidence in the equipment—even if it takes more than its fair share of your time. If necessary, I'll juggle watch assignments even further."

"Hmph. I hope it won't be. I like my work, but enough is as good as too much. That telescope *is* working; there are bursts of neutrinos coming from somewhere near that whirligig pair, whether Jeff and his friends want to believe it or not."

"I'm willing to take your word for it—so far." He looked at her sharply as she made the qualification. She smiled. "I just hope you don't have to do their work as well, and come up with a theory to satisfy them. But forget all that for a few hours—no one can work all the time."

Sarjuk did not actually have to reassign watches, but Garabed spent a great deal of time on the neutrino telescope during the next ten days. By that time, every one of its component modules had been replaced at least once, and the decreasing distance had improved image resolution to the point where it began to look as though at least some of the bursts were centered on, if not actually originating in, the neutron star.

By that time, also, the *Manzara* had made two minor—very minor—orbit corrections. The fusers had been used, and Feroxtant had seen for himself that his assistant had not been hallucinating. He did not stop his casts, however; there seemed no point in debating the matter until more data could be secured. Therefore, the *Longline* continued to emit its own neutrino bursts as it left the neutron star and when it made its reversal some three hundred thousand kilometers away.

To the surprise of Garabed and the relief of the captain, the physicists were beginning to accept the reality of their data, and were eagerly awaiting the completion of the capture maneuvers. The plan was to place the *Manzara* at the mass center of the white dwarf-neutron star pair, holding the umbrella toward the dwarf; in effect, this would place the ship's instruments at the origin of a system-centered coordinate set, and the observers relative motion should be zero. This would avoid a lot of variables...

The capture maneuver was artistic, though hard for nonspecialists to appreciate. Sforza cut as closely as he could first to one of the bodies and then the other, choosing his vectors so that the inevitable gain in kinetic energy as he approached each would be more than offset by the loss as he withdrew, and combining this with an initial approach direction which caused each near-parabolic deflection to carry the *Manzara* from one body towards the other. It would have been elegant, as Sforza admitted, to do the whole job with a single application of steering power to get them into the proper initial approach curve; unfortunately, it was impossible. The period of the system remained just below thirteen minutes—which cut things tight enough as it was—while that of the ship was constantly decreasing as it surrendered energy to the little stars.

The job was finally finished, with the umbrella warding off the radiation flood from the hot star some twenty thousand miles off the bow and the vessel's stem pointing toward the invisible mystery a little more than twice as far away. The data continued to flood in.

Feroxtant had also received a flood of data. It was not easy to interpret; one fact common to both his and the human universe is that the number of independent equations must equal or exceed the number of unknowns before any certainty is possible. The actual power drain on the *Manzara's* fusers had been varying in complex fashion; so had the ship's distance from the neutron star. Hence, the neutrino flux recorded by the *Longline's* sensing equipment had varied widely and erratically during the many minutes of Sforza's maneuvering. Feroxtant felt subjectively that the variation was not random, but could find no pattern in it. He had stopped casting very quickly, and called Wattimlan back aboard. The youngster was equally mystified, though happy that his commander had also seen the strange readings.

"No star ever acted like that." Feroxtant was firm. "I don't know what we've found—well, what you've found, to be honest—but it's new."

"But—stars aren't the only things that give off neutrinos," Wattimlan pointed out rather timidly. "Ship's accelerators—food factories—"

"I thought of that. Of course artificial processes emit neutrinos, too; but what imaginable process would produce them in a pattern which varies like this?"

Wattimlan had no answer.

Oddly enough, Garabed's work load eased off; the physicists were accepting the information and had turned back into scientists. Sarjuk felt that the earlier problem must have been mere inertia—their minds had been running free, except for the planning of possible experiments, for nearly a year and a half; they had simply slipped clutches briefly at the first contact with reality in so many months,

She might have been right. Garabed wasn't sure, but didn't argue; he enjoyed the respite, and listened with interest to the questions flying about. Why should a neutron star emit neutrinos at all? Why in separate bursts? Why, if the Sirius system had started as a single unit, had its least massive member reached the neutron star stage first? Why were the white dwarf and its companion so close together—so close that when both were main sequence stars their radii would have overlapped? Why, if its magnetic field meant anything, was the neutron star in locked rotation facing the dwarf rather than spinning several times a second like all the others known? Answers were not forthcoming. Physical data—size, mass, detailed motion, even temperature and conductivity—were flowing in nicely; but any question beginning with "why" remained wide open.

The white dwarf was being very cooperative, though it was not much to look at through a filter—no sunspots, no corona, no prominences or faculae; simply a featureless disc, Nevertheless, information about its internal structure was coming in very well, and none of it was very surprising. It was now clear that the neutrino bursts were not coming from this body; as far as nuclear activity was concerned, it was dead.

The neutrino telescope had been shut down during the capture maneuvers, and the pause when Feroxtant had stopped casting for a time had been missed.

It was equally clear that not all of the bursts were coming from the neutron star, either. Just half of them were—or at least, from a region within about eight hundred kilometers of it, that being the resolution limit of the telescope at this distance. The other half appeared to originate randomly at any point within about a light-second of the same center. They still came in pairs, one of each pair at the center and one away from it, with pauses of a few seconds every ten to twenty minutes—not completely random, but not orderly enough for anyone to have worked out a system yet.

"You have the betting look on your face again. I thought you were going to stop until the work let up." Garabed looked at the captain, trying to decide how serious she might be.

"It has been easier lately. This isn't to take care of boredom, though. It's just one of those sure things. Would you care to allow any odds that the astrophysics crowd won't be begging, within the next twenty-four hours, that we go into a parking orbit around the neutron star at tidal limit distance?"

Sarjuk gave a snort of disbelief. "They must know better. A few thousand more kilograms of hydrogen and we'll have to get fuel from one of the planets to get home."

"Well, we probably can. The big one seems to have water."

"With enough deuterium already? Or do we build a separator?"

"We could. We expected to be here for as much as three years anyway, and personally I wouldn't mind settling down into a less hectic life than this for a while."

"The idea was, and remains, to make a preliminary survey and get the results home. The three-year plan was contingent on either unforeseen complication—just a safety margin—or on the making of some really fundamental discovery important enough to demand immediate work, rather than wait for the next expedition."

"And how important would that have to be?" asked her husband.

"That will have to be settled when—and if—it happens. Until something of the sort comes up, we plan to return as soon as the planned operation—"

"Was the neutron star part of anyone's plan?"

"No, but you know as well as I that it can really be handled only by a group set up specifically for it. No one even dreamed that such a thing would be here, I can't see staying on and trying to do that job ourselves, even though we could live in the *Manzara* indefinitely. And, as I still think they know too well to ask, I will not sanction the fuel expense of getting into a parking orbit as far down in a gravity well like this as they'd need. And I won't do any betting on the matter, dear husband."

"I didn't really think you would. I'll cook up something even more certain."

He refused to be more specific, and the captain knew him well enough by now not to try very hard.

The *Manzara*'s station between the two ex-stars was of course unstable, so Sforza and his colleagues would permit no interruption in their constant watch of the ballistics computer and its display. There were other, equally versatile units on board, however, and Garabed had no trouble getting time on one of these; he had an idea to check. He would have been as reluctant as any physicist to describe it to anyone; he would have admitted at the time, as was charged later by amateur psychologists, that it stemmed purely from wishful thinking. He made a point of setting it up in private, and looked for a long time at the display when the computer had done its work. Then he cleared the setup, and spent some time trying to decide whether to break it first to his wife or to Pardales.

The decision brought a smile to his face.

"Jeff," he remarked to the physicist a few minutes later, "I don't see why you fellows have had so much trouble with those pairs of neutrino bursts. I was just running your records through to check out one of the computer cores, and it seems perfectly straightforward to me."

"Straightforward? How do you mean?"

"Well, the pattern is so simple. One of each pair is at the neutron star, as you've been admitting, and the other is always on the surface of a hemisphere just over a light-second in radius, centered on the neutron star and with its axis pointing—"

"Show me!" The physicist was satisfyingly jolted.

Garabed led him back to the station where he had tried his idea, and set up the material again. It showed as he had said; he had arranged the plot on a coordinate system which rotated with the Sirius B doublet, so the two main bodies showed no motion. The hundreds of luminous points which represented the records of the neutrino bursts were indeed arranged in a nearly perfect hemisphere for the one part, and concentrated around the neutron star for the other.

"Our plot was all over the place—nothing like that regular!" exclaimed Pardales. "What did you plug in there? You must have put in some extra data—"

"Not exactly," replied Garabed. "There's my program. Actually, I left something out. Look it over." There was silence for a minute or two.

"You took for granted, as we did, that there was a causal relation between the members of each pair. You allowed for travel time from point of origin of each flash to the ship; you allowed for travel time from one of each pair to the other—wait a minute! No, you didn't! You assumed they were really simultaneous!"

"Right," grinned Garabed. "No travel time. Think it over, friend; I have to talk to the captain." Pardales did not notice his departure. It is all very well to admit that coincidence can account for only so much; but when nothing else believable can account for it either...

"Captain!" called the instrument technician. Sarjuk was on the bridge, and there were others present, so he automatically avoided familiarity. "I think you'll be having another request from Physics very shortly. I think I can forestall a suggestion of moving the ship, if you'll let me take a tender out for a while."

Sarjuk frowned. "That will take fuel, and are you a good enough pilot to play around in a gravity well this deep?"

"I don't insist on driving it myself. Look, they are going to have another spell of doubting the neutrino telescope—I'll bet on that. I want to take out the tender so they can check the scope against its engine emissions, and kill that argument before it gets started. Isn't that worth a kilogram or two of hydrogen?"

Garabed's words were very straightforward, but his wife thought she could detect something under them. She looked at him sharply. "Is that the whole thing?" she asked.

He knew better than to lie to her. "Not entirely," he admitted, "but isn't it enough?" Their eyes locked for several seconds; the others on the bridge carefully concentrated on their own jobs for the moment. Then she nodded.

"All right. Plan to stay inside one kilogram. Sforza will drive you."

Minutes later the tender was hurtling away from the dying stars. Garabed would have climbed straight out along their orbital axis, with little regard for energy expenditure; Sforza, as a matter of habit and policy, cut out in the plane of their common orbits, slipped behind the neutron star at minimum safe distance, and let it sling them outward. Once he could see that they were safely away, Garabed made his key request.

"Will you let me have it for a few minutes? I want to change thrust patterns so Jeff and his friends can check their gear. There's no damage I can do, I take it."

"None that I can guess at," replied the ballistician. "If there's anything here to run into, I don't know about it either. Go ahead."

Garabed fingered the thrust potentiometer and began changing it in a careful pattern—alternately high and low, once, once again; twice, then four times; thrice, then nine times. Again and again he went through the cycle, while Sforza watched in amusement.

"It's lucky this is a warp drive. You'd have broken our straps with straight reaction. If I were a mystery fan, I'd say you were playing spy sending code."

"It does suggest that a little, doesn't it?" acknowledged Garabed.

It was not the code which first caught Feroxtant's attention; the drive units of the *Manzara* had bothered him enough, and. the addition of the tender's power plant gave him at least as much of a shock as Garabed had just given Pardales. The notion that anything could travel less rapidly than neutrinos was as hard for him to swallow as the demon hypothesis. Since neither his senses nor his imagination could provide data on the direction of the human machines, he could not be sure of their slow motion; but his attention, and Wattimlan's, were firmly focused on them while the two explorers continued their casting for the white dwarf—or rather, for its slowly developing neutronium core, still so small that their thousands of random shots had not struck it.

Garabed's code—the squares of the first three numbers—started the two on an argument which, by human standards, would have gone on for hours. Eventually, more to prove Wattimlan wrong than because he expected any results, Feroxtant performed a multiple reversal in open space which produced neutrino bursts closer to the neutron star; and he deliberately produced a set of four, followed by sixteen. He then brought the *Longline* back to her mooring in the neutron star's surface film, and sent a frantic report to his home star. By the time Garabed's five-twenty-five reply was spreading into space, the word had come that scientists were on the way. Not even the most conservative of beings could doubt that a series of numbers followed by their squares could originate in anything but a living mind—perhaps acting indirectly, but still a mind. It might have been some sort of recording—but it had responded when Feroxtant extended the number series. It responded with neutrinos, which had reached Feroxtant's ship very quickly, in spite of the fact that they traveled with the ultimate slowness, so the mind—or minds—must be close to the newly discovered star. The discovery of an unknown intelligent race was worth a major research project—even if no one believed that they could travel slower than neutrinos.

"Just a minute." Jeb Garabed was not a member of Policy, but he had the common right to speak up to the group. "We don't dare go back to the Solar system at this stage, and you know it. We are sure now that these faster-than-light things have a different time rate than we do; if we disappeared from here for twenty years, without any more attempt to talk with them, they might be extinct—or at least, their culture might be, and they could have forgotten us. I know it takes fuel to talk to them, and we're running low—though we could certainly build smaller fusion generators if all that's needed is neutrino output. The only sensible thing to do is get over to planet Four, which we're sure has water, set up a deuterium plant so we have no power problems, and just settle down to do research—which is what we're here for anyway. We can stay right here, and keep sensibly and happily busy, and live very good lives for nineteen years until the next expedition gets here."

"If they come," interjected his wife.

"You know they'll come." Garabed spoke directly to her, but did not forget the others. "They can't do anything else. The whole argument against interstellar flight has been the time it would take, as long as we thought the speed of light was a limit. Now we know it isn't, and however shortsighted human beings may be, they don't live happily with the certainty that someone can do something they can't. Remember your history! What made it impossible to keep the nuclear bomb a secret? Leaky spy shielding? Balloon juice! The only important piece of information was given away free by the original builders—*the fact that it could be done!* There'll be shiploads of people here from the Solar system as soon as they can make it. They'll start so fast after our waves get there that we'll probably have to rescue the first few—they'll have set out without proper preparation. Sirius A-IV may not be really habitable, but there'll be a human colony here in twenty years—or sooner, if my old idea is right. That radio message of ours may be all that's needed, after all. Anyone want to bet whether it's ten years or twenty before they get here?"

"You and your everlasting betting!" growled Sforza. "You know perfectly well that the reason you want to settle down in a colony and work only twelve hours a day has nothing to do with getting in touch with these tachyon people."

"That," said Garabed, "is irrelevant. The main thing is that we have to do it—not just that I want to." He looked at his captain as he spoke, and even she couldn't tell whether his grin meant triumph or merely contentment. She nodded slowly. "We stay. Mr. Sforza, plot a minimum-fuel course to A-IV. Chemistry, check practicability of a surface base as soon as we're close enough for you to work. Mr. Garabed, report to me at the end of the watch."

Garabed nodded absently. He was not really listening. He was looking into the display tank, seeing with his imagination more of the details of Sirius A-IV than the sensors had yet determined. The planet might not turn out to be as Earthlike as its color suggested, and he knew perfectly well that wishful thinking was painting a lot of his mental picture—but he was ready to bet that the next decade or two would be fun.

PLANETFALL

Satellite Science Fiction, February 1957

1

A Conservation Service vessel is quite fast and maneuverable as craft of that general type go. But there was little likelihood that this one would catch up with its present target. Its pilot knew that. He had known it since the first flicker of current in his detectors had warned him of the poacher's presence. But with the calm determination so characteristic of his race, he made the small course-correction which he hoped would bring him through the target area at action speed.

The correction had to be small. Had the disturbance been far from his present line of flight, he would never have detected it, for his instruments covered only a narrow cone of space ahead of him. Too many pilots in the old days, with full-sphere coverage, had been unable to resist the temptation of trying to loop back to investigate disturbances whose source-areas they had already passed.

At one-third the speed of light, such a reversal of course would have wasted both energy and time. No one could make a reversal in any reasonable period, and, certainly, no poacher or other law-breaker was going to wait for the maneuver to be completed.

Even as it was, this pilot's principal hope lay in the possibility that the other vessel would be too preoccupied with its task of looting to detect and react to his approach in time. Detection was only possible if, like his own ship, the poacher carried but a single operator. Unfortunately, a freighter was quite likely to have at least two, even on a perfectly legal flight, and the Conservation pilot had known of cases where poaching machines had had crews as large as four.

Even the presence of two would render his approach almost certainly useless, since the loading and separating machinery would require only one manipulator, and the full attention of any others could be freed for lookout duty. Nevertheless, he bored on in, analyzing and planning as he traveled.

The poacher was big—as big as any he had ever viewed. It must have had a net load capacity of something like a half billion tons—enough to clean the concentrates off a fair-sized planet, particularly if it also boasted adequate stripping and refining apparatus. There was no way of making certain about this last factor, for no such equipment was drawing power as yet. And that, in a way, was peculiar, for the poacher must have been in his present position for some time.

Had the driving energies of the poacher been in use, the Conservation ship would have detected them long before, and would have experienced less difficulty in making the necessary course-change. With a scant five light-years in which to make the turn, the acceleration needed for the task was rather annoying. Not that it caused the pilot any actual physical discomfort. It was purely an emotional matter. His economy-conditioned mind was appalled by the waste of energy involved.

Four light-years lay behind him when the poacher reacted outrageously. For the barest instant the attacker dared to hope that he might still get within range. Them it became evident that the giant freighter had seen him long before, and had planned its maneuver with perfect knowledge of his limitations.

It began to accelerate almost toward him, at an angle which would bring it safely past. It would sweep past just out of extreme range if he kept on his present course—and probably well beyond trustworthy shooting distance, if he tried to intercept it. For an instant, the agent was tempted. But before a single relay had clicked in his own small craft he remembered what the poacher must already have known—that the planet, which had perhaps already been robbed, came first.

It *must* be checked for damage, even though it was uninhabited as far as anyone knew. The mere fact that the poacher had stopped there meant that it must have something worth taking. It must, therefore, be tied as soon as possible into the production network whose completeness and perfection was the only barrier between the agent's race and galaxy-wide starvation.

He held his course, therefore, and broadcast a general warning as he went. He gave the thief's specifications, its course, as of the last possible observation, plus the fact that it seemed to be traveling empty. The absence of cargo was an encouraging sign. Perhaps no damage had been done to the world ahead. Unfortunately, it might also mean that the raider had a higher power-to-mass ratio than any freighter the agent had ever seen or heard of. He assumed that the ship was without cargo, and worded his warning accordingly.

His temper was not improved by an incident which occurred just before the giant vessel passed beyond detection range. A beam, quite evidently transmitted from the fleeing mass of metal, struck his antenna, and the phrase—"Now, don't you just hope they get us!"—came clearly along the instrument.

Again, relays almost closed on the Conservation flier, but the agent contented himself with repeating his warning broadcast and adding to it the data which had inevitably come along with the poacher's taunt—data concerning the personal voice of the speaker. Then he turned his attention to the problem of the planet ahead.

He would need more energy, of course. The interstellar speed of his craft had to be reduced to the general velocity of the stars in this part of the galaxy, for he could not make the survey that would be needed, merely by viewing the planet as he flashed by. He could, of course, get a pretty good idea of the metals that were present through such flash-technique, but he needed information as to their distribution. If he were lucky—if the poacher had actually failed to load up—there would almost certainly be concentrates worth recording and reporting to Conservation.

The sun involved was obvious enough, since it was the only one within several light years. The agent thought fleetingly of the loneliness, even terror, which would descend upon the average ground-gripper in close proximity to the nearly empty space at the galaxy's rim, and timed and directed his deceleration to bring him to rest some twenty-four diameters from the sun's photosphere.

The poacher had begun to travel long before he drew close enough to detect individual planets, and he was faced with the problem of discovering just which planet or planetoid had been visited. There were certainly enough to choose among and he was reasonably sure he had detected them all as he approached.

The possibility that he had been moving directly toward one for the whole time, and had, as a result, failed to observe any apparent motion for it, was too remote to cause him concern, particularly since it turned out that he had been well away from the general orbital plane of the system. He had the planets, then. But which ones were important?

Since he would have to check them all anyway, he didn't worry too much about selection. After using up the energy and time needed to stop in this forlorn speck of a planetary system, it would be senseless to leave anything unexamined. Why, he reasoned, should anyone else have to come back later to do what he had left undone? Still, he thought, it would be pleasant to determine quickly what the poacher had accomplished, if anything.

The innermost planet was definitely not the plundered victim. It had plenty of free iron, of course, and the agent noted with satisfaction that the metal was not concentrated at its core. If it ever became necessary to seek iron so far out in the galaxy, stripping it from so small a world would be relatively easy.

However, the important metals seemed to be dissolved and distributed with annoying uniformity through the tiny globe—a fact which was hardly surprising. The planet was too small, and its temperature was too high, to permit either water or ammonia to exist in liquid form. The ordinary geological processes which produced ore deposits simply could not function here.

The second world was more hopeful—in fact, it seemed ideal on first survey. There was water, though not in abundance. Nevertheless, in the billions of years since the planet had formed a certain amount of hydrothermal activity had gone on in its crust, and a number of very good copper, silver, and lead concentrations appeared to exist. The agent decided to land and map these, after he had completed his preliminary survey of the system. If this were the world the poachers had been sweeping, they had evidently failed to get much, Venus might be the plundered planet.

It proved not to be, however. Earth's water is not confined to its lithosphere—it covers three-quarters of the planetary surface. It washes mountains into the seas, freezes at the poles and, at high elevations, even at the equator. It finds its way down into the rocks and joins other water molecules which have been there since the crust solidified. It picks up ions, carries them a little way, and trades them for others.

In short, Earth contains enough water to produce geological phenomena. The agent saw this almost in his first glance. He wasted a brief look at the encircling dry satellite, then he turned all of his attention on the primary planet itself. He even began to ease his ship outward from the orbit it had taken up, twenty million miles from Sol.

This, he decided, must be the world of the poacher's selection. Even without analysis, anyone with the rudiments of a geological education would know that there must be metal concentrations here—and a civilization that uses half a trillion tons of copper a year can be expected to have at least a few trained geologists.

The agent pointed the nose of his little cruiser at the tiny disc, shining brightly eighty million miles away. He drove straight toward it, combing its surface as he went with the highest-resolution equipment he could bring to bear. All over the surface, and for a mile below, those radiations probed and returned with their information. The agent swore luridly as the indicators told their tragic story

There *had* been concentrations, all right. There were still a few. But someone had been scraping busily at the best of them, and had left little that was economically worth recovering. It was the old story. If good deposits and poor ones were worked at the same time, the profit was of course smaller. But at least the deposits lasted longer.

An eternity had passed since any legal operator of the agent's race had worked the other way, stripping the cream for a quick profit and letting the others go. Such a practice would have crippled the industry of the agent's home planet millions of years before, had it not been checked sternly by the formation of the Conservation Board.

Crippled industry, to a race at the stage of development his had attained, was the equivalent of a death sentence. Not one in a thousand of his people could hope to escape death by starvation, if the tremendously complex system of commerce were to break down.

The agent knew that—like most of his profession, he had seen border worlds where momentary imperfections in the system had taken their toll.

His fury at the sight of this planet mingled with—and was fed by—the memory of the horrors he had seen. Apparently, he had been wrong. The poachers had gotten away with their load—in fact, scores of them must have been at work.

No one ship, not even the monster he had seen so recently, could have done such a job without assistance on a planet of this size. The Conservation Department had suspected, before now, that it faced a certain degree of organization among the poachers. Here was infuriating evidence that the suspicion was all too well-founded.

Thought followed reaction through the agent's reception apparatus and through his mind, before his ship was within a million miles of the planet.

At that range no precise mapping was possible. In a sense, surface-mapping was no longer necessary, since the surviving deposits were hardly worth the gathering—but the tectonic charts would have to be obtained as usual.

A world like this was in constant change. A million, or ten, or a hundred million years from now the natural processes within its crust would have brought new concentrations into being. These forces must be charted, so that proper predictions could be obtained. Only through such research and prediction could Conservation beat the poachers to the next crop of metal, when it appeared.

The agent began to decelerate again, now matching his velocity with that of the planet itself. At the same time, he began a more detailed analysis of the surface, refining it constantly as the distance diminished. The water he already knew about. He had supposed the gaseous envelope to consist of methane and water vapor, with perhaps some ammonia, formed at the same time as the rest of the planet. But his instruments told a different story.

Earth had lost its primary atmosphere. The tragedy had occurred before the first member of the agent's race had ventured away from his own planetary system. The agent found the free oxygen, and swore again. He knew what that meant—*photosynthesis*. The planet was infected by those carbon compounds that behaved almost like life, except for their ferociously rapid rate of reaction.

They were not very dangerous, of course, but due care had to be maintained. A good many planets in the liquid-ammonia–liquid-water temperature range had them, and techniques had long since been worked out for conducting analysis, and even for mining in their presence, destructive as they often were to machinery.

The Conservation vessel, naturally, was constructed of alloys reasonably proof against any attack by free oxygen or the usual run of the carbon compounds. In fact, if this world had any unique developments of the latter the agent could always lift his ship out of the atmosphere. Such a retreat seemed to put a stop to the growth of photosynthetic life.

It never occurred to the agent that concealment might be in order. In the first place, he was on a perfectly legal mission. In the second place, he didn't think that there might be anyone on the planet to observe his arrival.

Oxygen being what it is, he had automatically classified the world as uninhabited and uninhabitable. As a result, the events of the half-second following his machine's penetration of Earth's ozone layer demanded a rather drastic revision of his outlook.

The radar beams, for an instant, made him suppose that another ship was on this world, and was trying to communicate with him. He had almost begun to answer before he realized that the radiation was not modulated, and could hardly be speech—or, more accurately, that its modulation was too simple and regular to represent words. Even though such radiation did not mean intelligence, however, it obviously did imply the presence of life.

Somehow, an organism must have evolved in an oxygen atmosphere with the ability to reduce metal oxides or sulfides, and keep them reduced to free metal. At the moment, it seemed to be a low order of life. But if it continued to develop as the agent's own species had done, this corner of the galaxy might become rather an interesting place in time. A man might have drawn a somewhat similar conclusion from hearing the chirp of a cricket under analogous circumstances.

At first, the agent supposed the radiation to have meaning similar to that of the cricket's chirp, too—it came and it went, regularly and monotonously, from a seemingly fixed source, and had an apparent willingness to go on until the sun cooled. But, a few milliseconds after the first pulses struck his receptors, others began to come in. They shared the simplicity of pattern shown by the first, but there were more of them.

As the ship moved, and its distance from some of the sources changed, it became evident that the waves were being directed in beams, rather than broadcast in all directions—and that the beams were following the ship. Intelligent or not, *something* was at least aware of his presence.

A score of hypotheses ran through the agent's mind during the next few milliseconds, for thought can move rapidly, when the neurons involved are of metal, and the impulses they carry are electronic currents, rather than potential differences between the surfaces of a colloid membrane. But none of these theories managed to satisfy him.

Even he could not continue to theorize at the moment, either—for the hull of his vessel was glowing bright red, and the surface of the planet was coming up rather rapidly to meet him. He had to land within the next few seconds, assuming that he did not want to do his theorizing hanging motionless in the atmosphere.

The outer surface of his hull was a trifle hard to manage at its present temperature. But none of the myriads of relays further in had been affected, and the sliver of metal obeyed his thoughts as it always had, slowing to a dead halt a few yards above the surface and then settling down for a landing while the agent analyzed the material directly underneath.

It was pure luck that there was no vegetation below him—luck, at least, for any local fire-fighters. The hot walls did respond to control, albeit a trifle sluggishly. Particles of sand and clay, coming in contact with the hull, began to dance, like bits of sawdust on a vibrating plate. And like sawdust, the dance carried them into a particular pattern.

The pattern took the form of a hollow under the hull, while the excess soil heaped up around it on all sides. The ship eased gently downward into the crater thus formed, which deepened as it continued to sink. The settling of the vessel, and the deepening of the hole, continued for perhaps twenty feet, before the hull touched solid rock.

When it did, more relays moved, and the rock itself flowed away in fine dust. This continued for only another foot, and then the ship was resting in a perfectly fitting cradle of stone, and the displaced soil was drifting back around it, covering its still red-hot circumference. The sand smoothed itself into a low mound which almost, but not quite, covered the vessel.

Had the agent cared about concealment, of course, he could have dug a little deeper—but all he wanted was good contact with bedrock. There was much mapping to do, and the matter of local life would have to wait until it was done.

2

The radar beams had stopped—or had, at least, ceased to reach the Conservation Agent—before he had gone underground. The point where he had landed was not in line-of-sight range of any of their stations. Needless to say, however, their operators had not forgotten him.

The agent was not considering possible radar operators. In fact, he would not have considered them even if radar had been, to him, something produced by a machine. He was far too busy listening.

If a human being puts his ear close against a wall, or a door-jamb in a fairly large building, he will pick up a remarkable variety of sounds. He will hear doors closing, windows rattling, and assorted creaks and thuds whose origin is frequently difficult or impossible to determine. The one thing he will not hear is silence.

The crust of a planet is much the same on a vastly greater scale. It is always full of vibrations, ranging from gigantic temblors—as square miles of solid rock slip against similar areas on the two sides of a fault plane—to ghostly echoes of sound and the faintest of thermal oscillations as the sun's heat shifts from one side of a mountain to the other, and the rocks expand and contract to adjust to the new temperature.

These waves travel, radiating from their point of origin, being refracted and reflected as they enter regions of differing density or elasticity, losing energy as they go by heating infinitesimally the rock through which they pass. They may die out entirely in random motion—heat—while still inside the body of the planet. Or a good, healthy wave-train may get all the way to the other side.

If it does so on Earth, it takes about twenty minutes. Then a fair proportion of it bounces from the low-density zone that is the bottom of the atmosphere, or the top of the lithosphere, whichever you prefer, and starts back again.

And every variation in density, or crystal structure, or elasticity, or chemical composition, has some effect on the way such waves travel. They may speed up or slow down. Transverse waves, or the transverse components of complex waves, may damp out—have you ever tried to skip rope with a stream of water?—and the compressional waves alone go through. Transverse waves, polarized in one direction, may be refracted through an interface, where the same sort of wave striking the same interface—at the same angle but polarized differently—may be reflected from it.

The important thing is that constantly varying conditions affect the waves. And that means that the wave carry information.

It is confused, of course. Temblors come from all directions, from all distances, due to many different causes, and through all sorts of rock. Interpreting them is not just a matter of sitting down to listen. One might as well tune in a dozen different radios to as many different musical programs, while sitting in the middle of a battlefield with a thunderstorm going on, and try to decide how many flutes were being used in one of the orchestras. The information is there, but selectivity and analysis are needed.

The agent was equipped for such selectivity, such analysis. His sensitive gear could detect any motion of the rock, down to thermal oscillation of the ions, at frequencies ranging from the highest a silicate group could maintain, to the lowest harmonic of a planet the size of Jupiter.

If his instruments proved inadequate, he could listen himself. But since just listening would involve the projection of a portion of his own body through the hull and bringing it into contact with the rock, the act would put a crippling strain on his stone-like flesh, and would consume several millennia of time. He did not plan to take this alternative. Machines were built to be used. Why not use them?

His own senses reacted at electronic speed—were, in fact, electronic in nature, as were his thought patterns. The process of receiving a group of impulses, and of solving the multiple-parameter equations necessary to deduce all the facts as to their origin and transmission, called for just such a fast-acting computer as his mind, though even he took some time about it.

This, primarily, was because he was careful. A temblor originating nearby would naturally have fewer unknowns worked into its waveform by the time it reached him. Therefore, it represented a simpler problem.. Also, when solved, that problem provided quantities which could be fitted directly into the equations since their wave-trains must have come through the same rocks as they approached him.

His picture of the lithosphere around him grew gradually, therefore, and by concentric shells. He saw the layers of different sort of rock and, far more important, the stresses playing on each layer—stresses that sometimes damped out to zero in the endless, tiny twitchings of the planet's crust and that sometimes built up until the strength of the rocks, and the vastly greater weight of overlying materials, could no longer resist them, and something gave.

He sensed the change, as trapped energy built up the temperature in a confined volume, until the rock could no longer be called solid, even though the pressure kept it from being anything that could be called liquid. He saw the magma pockets formed in this way migrate, up, down and across in the crust, like monstrous jellyfish in an incredibly viscous sea.

He saw certain points on the planet where they had reached so nearly to the surface that the weight above could no longer restrain the pressure of their dissolved gases. An explosive volcanic eruption is quite a sight, even from underneath.

His senses, through the vessel's instruments, probed down toward the core of the world, where magma pockets were more frequent. In such pockets, held in solutions which might some day carry them to the upper crust, they would be accessible—the copper and silver and molybdenum, and other metals his people needed. They would lie diffused through the material of the planet.

Those were the things that interested him. He needed to know the forces at work down there—not in general, as a climatologist knows why Arizona is dry, but in sufficient detail to be able to predict when and where these metals would reach the upper crust and form ore bodies. The fastest electronic computers man has yet built would be a long time working out such problems, given the data. The agent was certainly no faster, and was less infallible.

He knew this to be so, and, therefore, spent much of his time checking and rechecking each step of the work. The task took all his attention, and, for the time being, he was totally indifferent to impulses originating near the surface—much less to a number of feeble ones which originated *above* the surface.

There was something a good deal more interesting than human reactions to claim the attention of the Conservation operative. He had, of course, confirmed long since his original impression that the ore beds of the planet had been looted. His principal job now was to decide how long the normal diastrophic and other geological processes would require to replace them.

On a purely general basis, replacement should take tens of millions of years for a planet of Earth's size and constitution. Magma pockets would have to work their way up from the metal-rich depths to the outer crust. Then they would have to come into contact with materials which would dissolve or precipitate, as might be the case, the particular metals he sought.

The geological processes which depended so heavily on water or ammonia, in the liquid state, and concentrated the metallic compounds into ore deposits, could occur only near the surface. Of course, a magma pocket, commencing five hundred miles down, may not go upward. It may travel in any direction whatever, or not at all.

The density, the chemical composition, the melting point of the surrounding material, its ability to retain, in solution, the radioactives which may have been responsible for the pocket in the first place, were all vital factors. Equally vital was the question of whether its crystalline makeup was such as to absorb or release energy as increasing temperature reorganized it—the proximity of one or more of the vast iron-pockets, whose coreward settling contributed its share of energy. All of these things influenced the path as well as the very existence of the pocket.

It would be relatively easy to predict, on a purely statistical basis, the number of ore-bodies to be formed in a given ten-million-year period. But the agent needed much more than that. When a freighter is dispatched to pick up metal at one specific point and deliver it to another, the schedule is apt to suffer if the ship has to wait a million years for its load. Interrupted schedules are not merely nuisances. In a civilization spread throughout the core of the galaxy, none of whose member worlds are self-sufficient, they can be catastrophic.

So the agent measured carefully, and, as he did so, something a trifle queer began to appear. Impulses that did not quite fit into the orderly pattern he had deduced kept arriving—impulses of a nature he found, at first, hard to believe.

Then he remembered that the poachers had been here for quite a while before his own arrival, and an explanation lay before him. The impulses were of the sort that his own hull must have broadcast, while he was digging his present refuge. There could be only one thing which the poachers would logically have left behind them. They could have left evidence of their digging.

They had shown, he decided, a rather unusual amount of foresight for their kind, coupled with a ruthlessness which made the agent wonder whether they had even felt the radar beams that had greeted his own arrival. What the poachers had done was not a thing to do to an inhabited planet.

The out-of-place impulses were from mole robots, slowly burrowing their way into the world's heart. Each one, as the agent patiently computed its position, course, and speed, was headed for a point where the release of a relatively minute amount of energy would swing delicately balanced forces in a particular direction. The direction was obvious enough. The poachers expected to be back for another load, and were stimulating Earth's diastrophic forces to provide it.

This was a technique often used by legitimate metal-producers, but only on worlds that were uninhabited. Orogeny, even when stimulated in this fashion, may take half a million years to raise a section of landscape a few thousand feet. That still would not provide time to escape for a being who, without mechanical assistance, would take something like the same length of time to travel a few hundred.

From the agent's point of view, the presence of such depth-charges meant that Earth was going to become, in a fairly short time, a writhing, buckling, seething surface of broken rock, molten lava and folding, crumpling, tilting rafts of silicate material on a fearfully disturbed sea of stress-fluid.

Such heartless behavior might prove unavoidable—since he wouldn't be there at the time. But—what had produced those radar beams?

It revolted him that any planet with life should be treated in such a manner. Whether or not the life was currently intelligent was beside the point. Few generations were needed to transform a life species, from something as unresponsive as the planet that had spawned them, into a species capable of understanding the internal mechanism of a star in detail, for any distinctions of that nature to carry weight. If those beams had originated from living bodies, something would have to be done about the moles.

The agent simply did not have the equipment to do a thing. He could fight his little ship. He could investigate and analyze. He could communicate all the way across the galaxy, if something like the ionized layers of a planet's atmosphere did not interfere.

But he had no mole robots on his vessel, no weapons that would penetrate rock, or even atmosphere, for any great distance. He could not himself stand the temperatures at depths to which some of the poacher's moles had already penetrated. Consequently, he could not follow them in his own ship, even if it were able to dig as rapidly as the robots. It was indeed a problem!

Sending for help was possible, but almost certainly useless. His patrol area was so far out near the galactic rim that any message would take several millennia to reach a point where it would do any good—and the ships which answered it would be at least three times as long in covering the distance as the radiation that summoned them.

By then most, if not all, of the robots would have reached their designated target points. They would have shut off the fields which held their shape against the pressure of the surrounding rock. Once that protection was gone, no material substance in the universe could keep the half-ton of fissionable isotopes forming their cargoes at subcritical separation. All that energy would come out, and the little that wasn't heat to start with soon would be.

Of course, even such amounts of energy are small in comparison with the usual supplies of a planet's crust. But once released in carefully calculated spots and at even more carefully calculated times they would do exactly what the poachers wanted. The Conservation agent, checking the placement of the moles, could find no fault with the computations of the poachers' geophysicist. He was in his own way an operator of genius!

He could, of course, arrange for official freighters to be on hand when the action bore fruit, and would certainly do so, as a last resort, But he must first attack the question of whether or not life was being endangered. For the first time since the beginning of his analysis, the agent directed his attention to the surface layers of the world.

Then he almost stopped again, as a new theory struck him. This planet had free oxygen in its atmosphere. Would its life, if any, be near the surface? But his hesitation was only momentary. He recalled the radar beams which were his only reason for suspecting life. They could not possibly have passed through any significant amount of rock. While his senses swept the surrounding crust, in ever-widening circles, he pondered the question of just how a living creature could endure such an environment. *Think hard now, concentrate!*

There was one obvious possibility. It might be riding a machine designed to protect it, as he was himself—which would imply that life was not native to this world. If that were the case, locating the creature or creatures should be easy. However, in such circumstances it would have to be assumed that the population was very small, since furnishing machines for all of a large population was a manifest impossibility. It would be unwise too—even if such a thing *were* possible.

A more fantastic idea was that, while the life of this world might have a carbon composition like his own, its metallic parts were of more inert substances—perhaps of the platinum-group metals. The agent knew no reason why these should not serve as well as calcium in a nervous system. He might have thought of aluminum, had he been familiar with its behavior in an oxygen-water environment.

Then, there was the notion that a ship of his own race might be down and crippled—the most fantastic of all. No such ship would be this far out in the galaxy, and it was hard to imagine a mishap which would leave the operator alive and safe from the environment, while crippling his communication facilities to the point where nothing but crude whistles came through.

Furthermore, there had been too many points of origin for the beams that had touched him. It might prove a difficult nut to crack.

In fact, it was simply impossible to decide whether one of these hypotheses, or something which had not yet occurred to him, would prove closest to the truth. For the time being, there was nothing to do but search. Naturally, it did not take long for the rhythmic impulses originating only a few miles away to catch his attention.

They were seismic, of course, since he was doing all his listening through the rock—but it quickly became evident that they were originating at the very boundary between lithosphere and atmosphere. Almost as quickly, he realized that the sources were moving.

This latter had complicated the analysis rather seriously. It took the agent some time to conclude that sets of more or less solid objects, apparently always in pairs, were striking the lithosphere from outside. Sometimes there were relatively long periods of regular, repeated thuds, as one or more of the pairs did its hammering, and such periods were always accompanied by motion of the point at which the blows were occurring.

At other times, the hammering was irregular, both in frequency and energy, and usually, though not always, these sequences radiated from a relatively fixed broadcasting point. There seemed to be six basic units producing the impulses. Well, he was making progress, at any rate. Systematic thought could be a joy in itself!

Quite evidently, if this disturbance were caused by local life, that life must be civilized to the point where it could design and build machines. Furthermore, six machines, machines so close together, really did call for thought. It suggested something about the population density of the planet.

On the worlds the agent knew, scarcely one individual in a thousand manned a machine capable of moving him about. To equip the rest similarly would not only be the height of folly, it would be impossible, because enough material could never be obtained; still more because very few of them were temperamentally suited to physical activity. Even if this race had equipped, say, one in a hundred of its members, the finding of such a number congregated in one spot implied either a tremendous population density or—*could it be that they were looking for him?*

He had never stopped to think what a two-dimensional search would be like. But these machines, he was beginning to think, must be confined to surface travel—perhaps sub-surface as well—and their operators were assuming that he was on or near the surface of the lithosphere.

The agent cast his memory back over the paths these things had been following, and decided that they might indeed be explained on the assumption they were seeking something and had a very restricted range of sensory perception. He dwelt for an instant on the last assumption, finding it unpleasant.

The radar beams, then, must have been used to track him. He had felt no such impulses since digging in, although a portion of his hull remained exposed. But his attention had been so completely taken up with his work that he might not have noticed. He began to listen more carefully for electromagnetic radiation, and heard it immediately. On the instant, any doubts that might have remained concerning the intelligence of this race were disposed of.

There was a single source, which seemed to accompany only one of the machines, though the agent found it a little harder to locate precisely than the seismic sources. Apparently radio waves were being reflected from surfaces not in his mental picture of this part of the planet, thus confusing slightly his attempts at orientation. He was disturbed by the seeming fact that only one of these operators talked—and wondered why there had been no answer.

That problem was quickly solved, however. More careful listening disclosed a response coming from a fixed point some distance away. The agent did not attempt to make a seismic check on the environs of this source of radiation, since there was already enough to occupy his attention.

Still, why should only one of these machines, or its driver, be engaged in a long-range conversation? Surely the others, if they could be trusted to drive such devices, must occasionally have ideas of their own. It did not occur to him that the impulses might not represent speech— their pattern complexity was too great for anything else, though their tone was rather monotonous—quite literally. The frequency was constant and only the amplitude was modulated.

One possibility, of course, was that there was only one operator present, who was reporting to or discussing matters with his more distant fellow while he controlled all six of the nearby machines. In that case, however, the impulses he was using to control the subsidiary vehicles should be detectable, and nothing of the sort had reached the agent's senses.

Could it be that the orders were transmitted by metallic connections instead of radiation? They would have to be flexible, of course, since the relative positions of the machines were constantly changing! Yes, that could be it!

3

It became increasingly evident to the Conservationist that he could lie there, until he was trapped in an earthquake, making up five hundred theories per second, without getting one whit closer to knowledge of what was happening around him. He was going to have to examine the machines more closely. The only question was one of tactics. Should he go to them, or have them come to him?

He decided first to try the second gambit, since it offered more promise of drawing out information as to their nature and abilities. He would thus be able to determine precisely what stimuli affected their sensory equipment, and the extent of their capability in analyzing what they did detect.

Naturally, not a wave of their radiation had, thus far, conveyed any meaning to the Conservationist. More accurately, the few patterns that even remotely matched patterns of his own language did not deceive him for an instant by such chance similarities. Nor did he suppose the natives would have any better luck with his language.

His first attempt at attracting their attention consisted merely of broadcasting sustained notes on a variety of frequencies, other than the one they were using. As he had rather expected, these produced no noticeable reaction. Travel and conversation went on unaffected. When he repeated the attempts, using the same wavelengths as the natives, however, the results were just as unsatisfactory. It was extremely frustrating.

Travel stopped, and after he had repeated the signal a few times, all six of the vehicles seemed to come together at one spot. In the pauses between his own transmissions, the native speech sounded almost continuously. Yet he felt doubt that he had even been heard.

He had rather expected that there might be an attempt to respond to him in kind, but this did not occur, even though he tried sending out his wave in various long and short pulses which should have been easy to copy. At least, he used lengths corresponding to those of the radar pulses which he had felt at his arrival, and which had, presumably, been emitted by members of this race.

They failed to respond to the patterns, however, even when in desperation he increased the lengths of the bursts of radiation to three or four thousand microseconds. The very speech patterns of the natives changed carrier amplitude in shorter periods than that—they must, he felt, be able to distinguish such intervals!

The agent began to speculate upon the general intelligence-level of this alien new race. He had to remind himself forcibly that, since they could move around so rapidly, they must be able to design and build complex machines. It was startling, to say the least.

Then it occurred to him that *all* the vehicles he was watching might be remote controlled, that the electromagnetic waves he was receiving were the control impulses. Yes, yes, that must be it! He spent some time trying to correlate the radio signals with the motions of the machines. The attempt, of course, failed completely, since men are at least as likely to talk while standing still, as while walking around.

This proving a poor check on his hypothesis—it did not disprove it, since the machines might be able to do many things besides move around—he tried duplicating some of their complete signal groups, watching carefully to see whether any motion of the vehicles resulted. He realized that the controlling entity might not like what he was doing, but he was sure that satisfactory explanations could be made, once contact was established.

The result of the experiment was a complete stoppage of motion, as nearly as he could tell. It was not quite what he had expected. But there was some gratification in getting any result at all. For several whole seconds there was silence, both seismic and electromagnetic.

Then the native speech—it had to be speech—began again, in groups which still seemed long to the agent, but which were certainly much shorter than most of those used before. He duplicated each group as it came.

"Who's that? *Hello?*"

"Who's that? *Hello?*"

"What in hell is going on? This isn't funny, Mack!"

"What in hell is going on? This isn't funny, Mack!"

"Cut it out, you joker! If you've got a message for us, unload it and take off!"

"Who's that? Hello?" The agent decided the last signal group was too long to be worth imitation, so he went back to one of the earlier groups. This action resulted in brief silence, followed by a pattern, brief, but with a fresh modulation, which he mimicked accurately. For several whole minutes, the conversation, if it could be called that, went on. He felt real pride now, a self-congratulatory kind of exaltation in being able to carry off his cleverly assumed masquerade with perfect confidence, vigor and, certainly, no small measure of success.

The Conservation agent had decided long since what the native machines would almost certainly do, and was pleased to detect them getting into motion once more. But when they had gone far enough for him to determine their direction of travel, he discovered, with some disappointment, that they were not moving toward him.

He would have had little trouble determining their motives, had they been moving straight *away* from him. But the angle they took carried them more or less in his direction, albeit considerably to one side. He found this a complete mystery, at first. Finally he noticed that the group was traveling along a depressed portion of the lithosphere's surface, and seized upon, as a working hypothesis, the idea that their machines found it difficult, or impossible, to climb slopes of more than a few degrees.

In that case, of course, they might not be able to reach him, directly or otherwise, since he had buried himself some distance up the side of a valley. He considered again leaving his position and coming to meet them, but reached the same decision as before—that he could learn more by seeing what they did on their own.

They spoke rarely as they traveled—but the agent found that he could always make them broadcast, by ceasing to radiate his own signal. Had they not been pursuing such an odd course, he would have supposed, from that fact, that they were using his radiation to lead them to him. His radiation! However, they kept on their course until they were somewhat past its nearest point to his position before they paused. Then there was a brief interchange of signals with some distant native, apparently in an atmosphere machine, and travel was resumed, at right angles to the original direction.

Now, however, the vehicles were heading away from the buried ship, had, in fact, turned left. The Conservationist gave up theorizing for the moment and contented himself with observing. He repressed his mounting excitement and became as still as a figure of stone.

They did not travel very far in the new direction. In less than half an hour they stopped again, held another brief conversation, and then began to retrace their steps to, and finally across, their original route. Apparently, they were still interested in the agent's broadcasts. At any rate, they continued repeating the early "Hello" and "Who's that" signals to which he had originally responded, whenever be stopped radiating. They were not following the radiation, but certainly—almost certainly—they had some interest in it.

Then, quite abruptly, they stopped traveling and appeared to lose interest in the whole matter. The group broke up, and its members wandered erratically about for some time. Then they drew together once more and gradually quieted down completely, or at least to the point where the agent could not sure that the occasional impulses coming from that area were due to their motion.

He had just developed another theory, and this new trick bothered him seriously. He would have preferred to ignore it, but he could not. It had occurred to him that these creatures might be able to detect electromagnetic radiation of the sort he had been broadcasting, but not be able to identify the direction from which it came. He had heard of cases of physical injury among his own people which had produced such a result.

The idea that such a disability might be universal in this race called for a severe stretch of the agent's imagination, but he toyed with it all the same. As a result, he had just come to realize that the peculiar motions of the things he had been observing could indeed be accounted for by the assumption that they were searching for him under some such handicap—when they stopped moving. This was hard to reconcile with any sort of search procedure. What possible reason could stop them? He wished sometimes there could be fewer complexities in his existence. What possible reason?

Lack of fuel? Inconceivable, assuming even minimum intelligence on the part of the operator or operators.

Surface impossible for the machines to travel over? Unlikely, since several of them had come some distance toward him during their erratic wandering after the halt of the main body. And there had been others in the atmosphere.

Sun-powered mechanisms, halted by the fact that night had fallen? It was possible, though it seemed a trifle odd for such a device to be used on a rotating planet, where it must be sunless half the time. Also, it seemed doubtful that the machines were large enough to intercept the requisite amount of solar radiation. The agent had a fair idea of their size and mass, from the minimum observed separation, plus the energy with which they struck the ground.

Not interested in him at all, and stopped simply because they had reached their intended destination? This seemed all too painfully probable, if the course of their travels were considered by itself—yet nearly impossible, if their reaction to his broadcasting were taken into account.

It was at this point that the agent began to consider seriously the possibility that he might never be able to get the information of their danger across to the inhabitants of this planet. Their behavior, so far, seemed to lack any element he could recognize as common sense. He was open-minded enough to realize that this might work both ways, yet such a possibility did not augur well for the chances of successful communication between the two intelligences involved. There were cynics even among his own people who claimed that folly and ignorance always went arm in arm, and were biological constants throughout space.

Once more, he was facing the question of whether he go to meet these gadgets, or wait where he was—and, in the latter case, how long he should wait. Certainly, if he were to check the possibility that they were sun-powered, he should not stir until after night was over.

But none of the other hypotheses could very well be tested without actually examining, at close hand, the natives and their machines. He decided, then, to wait until sunrise, and for a reasonable period thereafter. Then, if these things did not resume their journey in his general direction, he would seek them out

As it turned out, he did not have to move. The appearance of the sun saw the vehicles already in motion, which was informative in a negative way. After a brief period of random traveling, they congregated once more, seemed to confer silently for a time, and then resumed travel along their former route. Also, they broadcast once more the signal the agent had come to interpret as a request for him to start transmitting.

The events of the preceding afternoon were repeated in some detail. The group continued past the agent's station on their straight-line course for a short distance, then stopped, and once more made a right-angle turn. This time, it was to the right, toward the hidden alien—and the agent realized that his theory about their sensory limitations must be at least partly correct.

They had to go through elaborate maneuvers to locate the source of a radio broadcast—maneuvers which suggested that even their ability to judge the intensity of radiation was rather crude. It took them about a tenth of the planet's rotation period, this time, to narrow the field down as far as their radio senses appeared to permit.

Before mid-morning they had made two more right-angle turns, and then spread out to cover, individually, the remaining area of uncertainty. The agent settled comfortably in his hole and awaited discovery. That should tell him much.

Just how close would these things have to come to detect him directly? Would he be able to pick up their nerve-currents first? What would they do when they found him? How long would it take them to realize that he was not a native of their world? And, most important, would they have some constructive ideas about means of communication? Who did he think he was fooling? At the moment the agent would have admitted to anyone that he himself had none. And if he was up against a blank wall in that respect, how could he reasonably expect them to come up with something really new and brilliant?

He kept his own senses keyed up, striving to detect the first clue, other than radio and seismic waves, of the nearness of the Earthly machines. Presumably, they were more or less electrical in nature, and he knew that electric and magnetic fields must, sooner or later, draw close enough to give him a picture of their structure. A little closer than that, and the electric fields of the operators' nervous systems should permit him to deduce their shapes and structures—assuming, of course, that at least one operator was with the present group of machines, which could hardly yet be considered certain.

Although it was the machine with the radio that actually stumbled on the buried vessel, the radio was not in use at the time. As a result, the agent decided, rather quickly, that no operator was in fact present. The radio was, of course, put to use the moment the ship was sighted—but its structure and nature were obvious to the alien, and it was quite evidently not an intelligent being.

It was, however, the only object in the vicinity with functioning electrical circuits. Moreover, there was no direct sign of life in any of the machines which gathered quickly around the ship. Finding it a little hard to believe even his own theories, the agent once more examined the radio—only to reach the same conclusion.

Its organization was not sufficiently complex to compare with a single living crystal, much less an entire nervous system. The conclusion seemed inescapable. Not only was the machine carrying it being controlled from a distance, but even the vehicle itself operated *without detectable electrical forces.*

The machine, of course, could not be invisible. His failure to see it meant merely that he was employing the wrong means—*anything* material can be seen, in some way or other. There remained the question of just what *were* the proper means in this particular case.

Free metals affected electric or magnetic fields, or both, in ways which permitted their recognition. Only a few fragments of such material were present—fragments quite evidently shaped by intelligence, but not themselves part of either an intelligent body, or even a complex mechanism.

Non-conducting crystal reflected and refracted many kinds of radiation. Perhaps these things, then, could be *seen*. The only trouble with this idea was that eyes were not a normal part of the agent's physical makeup. While his ship possessed several which were used in navigation—stars were most easily detected and recognized by light waves—they all happened to be underground at the moment. He had never anticipated a use for them on the surface of the planet, not being himself a chemist.

The machines were now all moving about on the ground in his immediate vicinity. One of them even moved onto the exposed section of his hull for a few moments, and it gave him his first chance to approximate their mass really accurately. Unfortunately he could not determine precisely how much of the energy radiating from their footsteps was due to weight.

The machine on his hull carried a tiny ionization tube, whose behavior at the moment was being affected by the mild radioactivity of the ship—activity only natural after a million years in interstellar space. The purpose of the tube was no more obvious than that of the electromagnetic radiator. Neither could move or think. The only possibility seemed to lie in a connection with the remote control of these machines. Perhaps, they were sensing devices of some sort.

There seemed no logical reason for not raising the ship far enough to get a look at these alien machines. He had discovered all he could expect to learn, from where he was. They *did* receive him. They *were* interested, and they, therefore, had at least glimmerings of intelligence. They could *not*—or, at least, their machines could not—determine the direction from which radio-waves were coming.

It was still not clear to him whether these machines were under the control of one individual, or several. There seemed no way of investigating this important question for some time to come. What the agent wanted to know, as soon as possible, was just what sort of mechanism could operate *without perceptible electrical fields*—and that seemed to demand that he *see* them. Yes, he must see them.

His hull had long since cooled, and could be controlled without difficulty. He started it vibrating again, and, simultaneously, applied enough drive to counteract the weight of the ship and its contents. For a fleeting instant, he wondered whether the distant operators could detect the flickering of the myriads of relays that responded to his thoughts, or even the electrical fields of the thoughts themselves.

If the latter were true, they could certainly not interpret them properly. In that case, the machines would have found him much earlier, and the agent would, by now, have been holding a conference with them about the best means of intercepting the mole robots. That possibility, he decided, could be ignored.

The patrol flier lifted easily, until over half its bulk was above the ground. Its pilot held it there, briefly, while the rhythm of the hull packed and firmed the powdered soil that had drifted beneath it. Then he cut his power once more, and began to look about him with his newly uncovered eyes.

4

The star-traveler already knew, of course, that he was in a valley, partway up one of the sides. The hills bounding it were not particularly high, especially by the standards of this planet. In fact, the Conservationist had a pretty accurate idea of the dimensions of the Himalayas, distant as they were—though he had been more interested in determining the rate at which they were rising. He gave the local elevations only a passing thought, then sought to examine what lay closer to his vision-outlets—outlets which the Parsons group had quite correctly labeled "eyes."

He failed. The details five miles away were clear, and clouds of what must be water or ammonia droplets hanging at still greater distances in the atmosphere were still clearer. But, as he brought his attention to objects nearer and nearer to his ship, they grew, shapeless, and increasingly harder to examine,

Cursing himself for forgetting, he recognized the reason. His eyes were perfectly good instruments—for the purpose toward which they had been designed. They were carefully shaped lenses of calcium fluoride, designed with almost a full hemisphere of field, and their curved focal surface was followed faithfully by the photosensitive material of his own flesh. The tiny metallic crystals in his stony tissues would, of course, be affected electrically by light, and, like many of his race, he had learned to interpret the light-images formed by lenses.

There was just one catch. There was no provision for changing either the shape or the position of the lenses. But actually, why should there be? They were designed to enable him to determine the directions of the stars, whose distances were for all practical purposes always infinite. He had never needed focusing arrangements until now.

The eyes were a foot across and almost as great in focal length. Objects a hundred yards away were blurs. At six feet they were scarcely interruptions to the background. He could just tell, by sight, that there were moving objects in his vicinity, and get a vague idea of their size. Beyond that, details were indistinguishable.

The nearest repair-shop where his machinery could be modified was about six thousand light-years toward the galactic center. He could, of course, pull his flesh back from one or more of the lenses until the eye involved focused at a distance of a few feet—if the situation would wait for the necessary years or centuries. However, even if the situation did wait, the natives and their machines probably wouldn't.

He could wait until they departed, and examine them when they were far away. Better than this, he could fly to a distance at which they were reasonably distinct in his sight. The question raised in that connection was, of course, how the natives would react to such a move on his part. However, if he did not move, he would probably learn nothing. Therefore, he resumed his rise from the soil, cleared its surface, and hurled his vessel half a mile upward.

To observe, and, in effect, to photograph the details of what lay below took only a few microseconds. Then he moved a few hundred yards to one side and repeated the procedure. Three seconds after takeoff, he was settling back into his original location with a fairly clear picture of the strange equipment surrounding it firmly painted in his mind.

He understood now why the seismic impulses had come in pairs. Each of the machines was supported by two struts, which were so hinged as to permit several degrees of freedom of motion. During his brief period of observation, they had traveled enough—away from the point where his ship had been resting—to permit him to analyze their startling method of travel. This seemed to consist in balancing on one strut, falling in the desired direction, and catching one's mass with the other before collapsing completely. The process was repeated cyclically.

It appeared, mathematically, that the value of the planet's gravitational acceleration would put an upper limit on the rate of travel possible by this means. The agent found himself a little dubious about the engineering advantages of it. If one had to travel on the surface, wheels seemed easier—although an irregular surface might present further difficulties. Few Conservationists, surely, had confronted problems so difficult to resolve.

At least, he had eliminated the last possible doubt that the things were not-metallic, non-electric machines, since he had actually seen them move in a manner which verified and complemented his seismic observation. This implied that the natives were not merely cultured, *but had developed a physical science equal to, perhaps greater than, that of the agent's own race.* The latter was certainly possible, since he had not the faintest idea of what

was the operative principle of the devices. It was a disturbing speculation, but he refused to enlarge upon it emotionally. Obviously they had
some electrical equipment. The signal detector and broadcasting device,
as well as the ionization cylinder, were quite evidently as artificial as his
own ship. Their science, regardless of its development, could not be entirely alien. It might be possible for him to learn something about it. If
so, it was important that he begin—for the equipment needed to stop
the moles would have to be obtained from these people in rather short
order.

The agent examined once more, as precisely as his sensory equipment
permitted, every detail of the things around him, which were now returning slowly, after their hasty withdrawal. He broadcast his *"Hello"* again.
and carefully noted the way it affected the receiver. When the answer came,
he checked with equal care the source of the modulating energy.

The result was interesting. The receiver apparently did not consider
the carrier waves important. It damped them out and used, through most
of its circuitry, a secondary signal consisting of the original modulations.
This was caused to vary the strength of a magnetic field which, as nearly
as the agent could tell, was used to impart mechanical motion to an object principally non-metallic.

He could get only a rough idea of its size and shape from the space
left for it in the mechanism. The evidence seemed to indicate that the
whole device simply rebroadcast the modulation of the original signal
mechanically into the atmosphere.

He knew, of course, that a gas *could* carry compression waves, though
it had never occurred to him that they might be of any particular use. He
had simply never stopped to wonder why his method of digging was more
effective on a planet with atmosphere. It did no good to blame oneself
for such oversights when the fat was in the fire. Anyway, he was sure of
one thing. The waves were being used to carry the signals controlling the
machines. Certainly no others were.

They also served for communication, since similar waves appeared
to be received by the same disc in the signal device, and were used to
modulate its broadcast electromagnetic impulses. This process seemed
pointless, except as a means of long-distance communication. Probably
pressure waves did not transmit energy so effectively through a gas as electromagnetic radiation carried it through space. So far, so good.

It all tied in, more or less, with the evident fact that these machines
were not electrical, even if it did not begin to explain how they actually
worked. Some sort of more precise analysis would, of course, be needed.
The metal he could detect about the things seemed quite purposeless,
and he did not see that it was likely to help.

It was present in small, disconnected bits and was devoid of electrical energy, if you brushed aside the minute currents generated by its motion in the planet's magnetic field.

The machines, then, were made virtually entirely of non-conductors, and should be about as easy for the agent to examine as a device consisting exclusively of gas jets and magnetic fields would be for a human being.

This meant that the analysis would have to be by highly indirect methods. A chemist, with his laboratory machine, might be able to do the job in microseconds. But a traveling device, like the scoutship, had no equipment designed with any such purpose in mind,

He suspected that this was one of the situations where the sessile members of his race—the great majority—would leap at the chance to show their superiority over one who was bound to a machine. It had always been that way. It was a common enough feeling among those whose lives were primarily intellectual. The doers, like the agent, countered it with a clear recognition of the necessity for their work. At the moment, however, the agent rather wished that a normal person had been present, to show his intellectual superiority.

Then he realized that his own possession of machinery did not disqualify him as an intelligent being. If a member of his race could solve this problem, it was as likely to be himself as anyone else. He would have to use all his knowledge, of course, not just the specialized information which was all the millennia of flight demanded.

Enough knowledge should be there. He had, of course, been young when he elected this life, but he had had much thinking time before his career was actually begun. Also, there had been a good deal of time to think as he drifted among the stars, and opportunities to gather data that planetbound thinkers had never possessed.

He would have to go back to the most elemental principles of thought—if he could. First, he had decided, on the basis of what seemed adequate evidence, that the planet was inhabited—that its inhabitants used machines and, therefore, had freedom of motion—and that these machines were based on a technology almost, but not quite wholly, alien to his own.

Nevertheless, the devices must operate under the same physical laws that applied elsewhere in the universe. This meant that they must take in some form of energy, must perform a desired action, and must eventually account for the energy as heat.

The energy was not electric or magnetic, since he could have detected the presence of that kind of energy directly. It was not gravitational, since the gravitational potential of these machines—when measured as a function of their distance from the planet's center—had actually increased since he had first detected them. It was barely possible, of course, that some *primary* source beyond his detection-range might work on such a basis. But for the moment that hardly bothered him. It could be filed away for future reference.

There was almost certainly no direct mechanical link with a distant energy source. He felt sure that he would have seen any such, during his brief trip aloft.

Chemical energy, however, remained a distinct possibility. Normally— which usually meant, he reflected wryly, circumstances in which intelligence had not taken a hand—chemical reactions were too slow to provide useful energy, even though they were responsible for life. However, on a planet infested with such weirdly active carbon compounds, it would not do to be dogmatic on the matter.

It was known that reactions, in such circumstances, did go with enormous speed, though little actual quantitative work had been done on the matter of energy involved. It was quite conceivable, in any case, that there might be some method of turning chemical directly into mechanical energy, without involving electricity as an intermediate stage.

Looked at from this viewpoint, several more possibilities as to the planet became evident. Its natives could survive, either by nature or intelligent adaptation, in an oxygen-rich atmosphere. Oxygen was one of the most virulently active elements in existence. Hence, it might not be too surprising to find such a people developing a chemical technology and bypassing the electricity a living creature should logically use—but wait. They had *not* bypassed electricity.

There were auxiliary machines, among the vehicles facing him, which did use it. Perhaps, these people had originally developed a normal technology, but, for some unaccountable reason, had never mastered spaceflight! That was more than likely, if one assumed they did not merely tolerate oxygen, but *needed* it.

In that case, they would inevitably exhaust, in a relatively short time, the metal resources of a single planet.

They would be faced with the choice of developing machines that did not make demands on the metal supply, or of sinking to barbarism during the millions of years it would take new metal deposits to concentrate to usability.

This race might have succeeded in accomplishing the former—in which case, the exhaustion of the local ore veins could not be blamed on the poachers after all. The marauder might have planted the torpedoes in momentary pique, believing that a regular freighter had been there first and hoping to throw the production schedule of this planet out of step with that which had been recorded for it.

It was a very attractive idea, but the agent decided be should not go quite so far in pure speculation. There should be other possible sources of energy besides chemical activity, promising as such energy appeared to be. He could, for example, detect a pressure against his hull which seemed to be due to currents in the atmosphere. These must necessarily carry energy, though it seemed, at first estimate, that it could hardly be quantitatively adequate to run these machines.

There was nuclear energy. Obviously, these aliens did not use it directly, yet the possibility remained that it was their primary source and was stored in some non-self-destructive form within them. Strength was lent to this possibility by the presence of the ionization tube, which might well be used to locate radioactive materials. If, of course, the normal senses of the creatures were inadequate for the task. Atomic energy not under rigid control was always a rather frightening thing to contemplate, and he did not dwell on certain other unlikely possibilities concerning it.

He had already thought of solar energy, but had seen nothing to offset any of his earlier objections to this theory. On the whole, the chemical idea seemed the most worth following up.

He searched his memory for the little he knew about the high-speed chemical reactions of free-oxygen environments, and found a few helpful items. For one, they *did* involve solar energy—they employed it usually in breaking down water. The oxygen was freed to the surroundings, and the hydrogen combined with oxides of carbon to produce carbohydrates.

These, in turn, could react upon each other, with simple compounds and with some of the free oxygen, to produce incredibly complex substances whose detailed structure had never been worked out by any chemist of his people. This situation should, of course, result in a continual increase of free oxygen in the planet's atmosphere at the expense of the water.

Observation indicated that, actually, an equilibrium was usually attained in this respect. Whether the oxygen re-combined spontaneously with the hydrogen in the compounds, or whether still other high-speed reactions, of the same general type as the photosynthetic ones, did the trick, was still a matter of debate. Even the agent could understand, however, that the combination of oxygen with almost any of the complex carbon-hydrogen compounds would return the energy originally supplied by the sun.

If the compounds had any reasonable density, it should be possible to store quite a fuel supply in a very small space that way, using atmospheric oxygen to combine with it whenever desired. Even without precise figures, he felt sure that this would constitute an adequate energy-source for the machines he had been watching.

Was there anything he had overlooked? No—he was nothing if not thorough when he undertook a task of objective scientific analysis. A doer had his own pride to safeguard, and if he was not an intellectual in a strict sense, he did possess a first-rate mind.

How could this theory be checked experimentally? If it proved correct, there should be, somewhere on or within these machines, a store of hydrogen-carbon compounds. They should be absorbing atmospheric oxygen at a fairly high rate. And they should be exhausting water and, possibly, oxides of carbon.

He had no means for recognizing the hydrogen-carbon compounds, even if he found them, so there seemed little point in trying to take one of the mechanisms apart. No point even if its operator proved willing to allow it. However, there seemed to be a possible way of attacking the problem through the other facts. If an oxidizing reaction of the sort he had envisioned went on in a confined space, what would happen to the pressure? He pondered the problem.

Producing solid oxides would reduce pressure by removing oxygen. The formation of carbon dioxide would leave it unchanged, for there would be the same number of molecules after the reaction as before. Making water or carbon monoxide would give a pressure increase, since each molecule of oxygen would go into two molecules of the product.

All this, of course, assumed that water and the oxides of carbon were gases at this temperature. The method offered him two out of three chances of learning something—better, really, since it was likely that two, or all three, of the reactions occurred together. Only if CO_2 alone were produced, would there be a negative result? The catch seemed to be how one was to seal one of these devices in a gas-tight container, with a limited amount of atmosphere.

The container, of course, was available. His own ship had a good deal of waste space, left deliberately to allow for later modifications, if and when they were developed. He could open his hull for maintenance at virtually any point, and the openings were naturally designed to seal gas-tight, since his occupation was more than likely to lead him into corrosive atmospheres such as this.

He would have to be sure that he let the planet's air only into chambers where it could not reach either his own tissues or the ship's circuitry. No, wait. The test should take only minutes or hours, not years. Both his flesh and the silver wires could stand oxygen that long, and he could get rid of it later by opening the hull to the vacuum of space. That made matters easier—much easier.

But how could he detect the change in pressure, if it did occur? He did have manometers, of course. But they were vented to the outside of his hull. No one had foreseen a need for measuring internal pressure. He would have to do some more hard thinking.

What effects would pressure produce, besides merely mechanical ones? There would not be enough change, in the electrical properties of the exposed wires, for even the agent to detect. The change would probably not be fast enough to alter the temperature noticeably. And even if it did alter it, he would not be able to tell whether the change were due to gas laws, or simply the operation of the machine.

In the temperature range of this world, it was not really certain that all the products were gaseous, anyway. The mere fact that he had detected them in that form, during his approach, meant nothing. The infra-red spectrographic equipment he had used would have picked up trace quantities. It was unfortunate that its receivers were also aimed outward.

The agent could not, for the life of him, recall the vapor-pressure curves of any of the expected products—though, come to think of it, *something* was liquid here. The clouds he could see proved that, as did their precipitation on his hull. He could not assume that it was one of the products he sought, however, and his best bet was still to maintain pressure change. If he could do it...

As usual, the solution was ridiculously simple, once the traveler had thought of it. Most of the access-doors in the hull opened outward and all were operated electrically. He had perfect control over the current supplied to their operating motors. He knew that if he refrained from latching one or more of the doors, and simply held it shut with the motor, he could sense directly the amount of effort needed to keep it sealed against the internal pressure.

As far as he was concerned, it was a quantitative solution—if the pressure increased. If it decreased—well, he would know it, from the extra effort needed to open the door. He was concentrating on immediate small details now—and very wisely.

With his machine, action could follow thought without delay. The moment he had his answer, a door swung open in the side of the great metal egg he was driving, and Earth's air poured in. Good as his seals were, the ship had not, of course, retained any significant amount of gas in the millennia it had been in space.

He did not bother to develop a plan for enticing one of the machines through the opening. He assumed, quite justly, that any intelligent mind must have a fair proportion of curiosity in its make-up. The fact that self-preservation might oppose this influence did not, as far as the agent knew or suspected, apply to the present situation. The risk of sacrificing even an expensive remote-controlled machine should be well worth taking in such circumstances. He simply waited for one of the devices to be driven into his ship.

Before this happened, however, there was a good deal of conversation among the machines present and, he presumed, the distant broadcaster—if, of course, it could be called conversation. The agent was still unable to reconcile this supposition with the absence of intelligent life in the present group.

At last, however, the expected event occurred. One of the machines swung about and moved toward the opening in the hull. Just outside, it halted, and the agent guessed at a brief burst of atmospheric pressure waves, though his manometers did not react fast enough to catch them. Then it entered.

It traveled on four struts instead of two. It became completely horizontal and advanced on the supporting struts. Evidently the upper ones, which the agent had seen, could be used for locomotion when desirable. Its entrance was slower than by its usual rate of motion, though the agent could not imagine why. The suggestion that slower motion made detail observation easier would never have occurred to a being whose perception and recording operations occupied fractions of a microsecond. Whatever the reason for the delay, it finally managed to get inside.

The agent wasted no time. Ready to observe anything and everything that resulted, he shut the access hatch.

Results, by his reaction-time standards, were slow—additional evidence that remote control was involved. The electromagnetic unit burst into activity the instant things finally began to happen. Some of the machines outside began to tap on the hull with dimly perceptible solid fragments, apparently pieces of silicate rock. The agent tried to find regularities in the blows that might be interpreted as communication code of some sort. He failed.

One of the devices, standing a little distance away, moved one of its attached fragments of metal until a hollow cylinder—which formed part of it—was in line with the hull. After a long moment the more distant end of the cylinder filled with gas, sufficiently ionized to be clearly perceptible to the alien.

The gas must have been under considerable pressure, for almost instantly it began to expand, driving before it a smaller fragment of metal which had plugged the tube. This fragment became progressively easier to perceive as its speed through the planet's magnetic field increased.

It emerged from the near end of the cylinder with sufficient momentum to continue in a nearly linear course, until it made contact with the hull. The agent watched with mounting excitement as it flattened, spread out and finally broke into many pieces. Incredible! He analyzed it, both electrically and mechanically, from the way it broke up. But he could make no sense of the operation.

After a time, the pounding ceased, and the two machines remaining outside drew together. No obvious activity came from them for some time. Inside the hull, more interesting, possibly more understandable, events were taking place. The moment the door had closed, the machine trapped within had attempted to withdraw. Its action was a trifle faster than that of the ones still outside. The agent could not decide whether this meant that the escape reaction was automatic or that a distant controller had turned his attention to the captive machine first.

It had pounded aggressively on the inside of the door in the same seemingly planless fashion as its fellows. Then it had slowed down, and began to move another of the strangely fashioned pieces of metal distributed about its frame. This abruptly became clearly perceptible, as an electric current began to flow through portions of its structure.

The source of the current was a seemingly endless supply of metallic ions—quite evidently chemical energy could be used for something. The current's function was less obvious, since it was led through a conductor whose greatest resistance was concentrated in a tight metal spiral.

This must in some way have been shielded from atmospheric oxygen, at fairly high temperature if the ion cloud around it meant anything; it nevertheless remained uncorroded. Heating the wire seemed all that the device accomplished—the agent refused to believe that the ion cloud was intense enough to help either in action or perception. The light and heat radiated were inconsiderable, but—*wait!* Perhaps that was it—perhaps *this* machine had eyes!

The agent examined the electrical device more closely, and discovered that part of its uncharged structure consisted of a roughly paraboloidal piece of metal, which must certainly have been able to focus light into a beam of sorts.

A few moments later, it became evident that it did just that. The agent's body was exposed in several places in this part of the ship, and, time after time, one part would be struck by radiance, while the rest were in more or less complete darkness. Furthermore, a few minutes' observation showed that when the machine moved at all it followed the direction in which the light beam happened to be pointing at the time.

Sometimes it did not move, though the beam kept roving around the chamber. The agent deduced from that one of two things. Either the device had several eyes, or the one it had was movable over virtually the entire sphere of possible directions. The thing was making an orderly survey of the interior of the space in which it was trapped. But it was carefully refraining from touching anything except the floor on which it stood.

That portions of this floor consisted of the agent's tissue made no difference to either party—as far as either knew. But the agent began to wonder how much of the exposed machinery of the ship would be comprehensible to the presumed distant observer.

Still more, he wondered how this presumed observer maintained contact with his machine. There was no energy whatever—in any form that the agent could detect—getting though his hull, either to or from the trapped machine. A minor exception to this might be the pressure waves generated by the stones striking his hull. But he had already failed to find in these blows any pattern at all, much less one which could be correlated with the actions of the machine inside.

Naturally, the thought that this might be an automatic device, similar to the mole robots, could hardly help occurring to the Conservationist. If this were the case, its present behavior was far more complicated than that of any such machine he had ever encountered. But hold on— he had already faced the implications inherent in that idea. So the technology of this world was more advanced, in some ways, than his own. There were still things the natives didn't know—things which would most certainly hurt them. Any concern he might have felt about himself was drowned in this larger solicitude.

He wondered whether he could so operate any of his own machinery to or through his prisoner, so as to convey a message of any sort. Certainly, if it used light as a vehicle of perception, it could detect motion on the part of the relays. For example—they were larger by quite a margin than the wavelength of the radiation the hot wire was emitting in greatest strength.

There were several hundred thousand of them in the dozen square yards exposed to the direct-line vision of the captive, which should be enough to form some sort of pattern. Some sort of pattern, that is, if their owner could figure out how to operate them without making the ship misbehave.

He was still pondering this problem, along with the question of just what *would* be a meaningful pattern to the operators of the machine, when his attention was once more drawn to the outside.

The machines there seemed to have taken up a definite course of action. They had once more approached the hull, and were doing something to it which he could not at first quite understand. It quickly enough became evident, however. The brightness of the images he was receiving through the eyes, to which he had naturally been paying very little attention, began rapidly to decrease. Within a minute or so, the lenses ceased to transmit at all.

His tactile "sense" consisted in part of the ability to analyze the response of his hull to the vibrating impulses he applied to it. If such impulses were followed faithfully he could be sure that there was no mass in contact with the surface. On the other hand, if they were damped to any extent, he could form a fairly accurate idea of the amount and even some of the physical properties of such a mass.

In the present case, he discovered almost instantly that his eye lenses had been covered with a most peculiar substance. It not only adhered tenaciously to them, but seemed to absorb without noticeable reaction the same vibrations which had sent the soil dancing out of his way like summer chaff in a breeze. This did not particularly bother him, since the eyes were nearly useless for watching the machines anyway. But he kept trying to shake the material off, while he considered the implications of the move.

One was that the machines depended, far more heavily than he had suspected, on the sense of sight, and must suppose that he did likewise. Another was that they were about to take measures which they did not want observed by him. He did not worry seriously about anything they could do to his ship, but he began to listen very carefully for their footsteps all the same.

Another possibility was that they simply did not want him to fly away with the captive machine. To a race dependent upon sight, no doubt the idea of flying without it was unthinkable. He wondered, fleetingly, whether he should move a few hundred yards, just to see what effect the act had on them. Then the actions they were already performing caught his attention, and he shelved the notion. He became alarmed at what appeared to be an abrupt change of plan.

Two of the things were leaving the neighborhood, in a direction more or less toward the other electromagnetic radiator. Making allowances for the difficulty these machines apparently suffered in traveling over uneven terrain, the agent felt reasonably sure that this was their goal. The other two remained near him and settled down to relative motionlessness, as nearly as he could tell. He comforted himself with the thought that whatever plan they were attempting might demand some time to mature.

Perhaps the departing machines were going after additional equipment, though it appeared their goal might be attained more rapidly by sending other machines from the control point. However, it was quite possible that no others were available—such was likely enough to be the case on any of his own worlds, where only one individual in five hundred was machine-equipped, and over half of these were incapable of locomotion. Pride swelled in him at the thought, but he dismissed it as unworthy.

His soliloquy was interrupted by something that had not happened to him since his ship had first lifted from the world on which it had been built. The incident itself was minor, but its implications were not. The hull vibration, which he was still applying near all of his above-ground eyes, *stopped* near one of them.

He had not stopped it. The command for the carefully planned motion pattern was still flowing along his nerves. It should have been inducing the appropriate response in a fairly large group of relays. Something had gone wrong, and it produced a sudden crisis in his thinking.

The ship, of course, was equipped with a fantastic number of test-circuits, and he began to use them for all they were worth. It took him about three milliseconds to learn a significant fact. All the inoperative relays were close to, or actually within, the compartment where the captive machine was located. Closer checking showed that the trouble was mechanical—the tiny switches were being held in whatever position they had been in when the trouble struck.

Worse, the paralysis was spreading. It was spreading with a terrifying rapidity. The basic cause was not hard to guess, even with the details far from obvious. The agent instantly unsealed the door barring his captive from the outside world, and felt thankful that the controls involved still functioned.

The thing lost no time in getting out, and the pilot lost even less in getting the door securely sealed after it. For the time being, he completely ignored what went on outside, while he strove to remedy the weird disability. He was far from consoled by the thought, when it struck him, that he had proved what he wanted to know.

Something solid had blocked the relays—had, more accurately, *formed around* their microscopic moving parts. Whatever it was must have come in gas form, for he would have felt the localized weight of a liquid, even inside. Most of the interior of his ship, as well as his own flesh was still far colder than the planet on which he was lying.

Quite evidently one of the exhaust products of the captive machine, released as a gas, had frozen wherever it touched a cold surface. It might have been either water or one of the oxides of carbon. The agent neither knew nor cared. He proceeded to run as much current as possible through all his test-circuits, with the object of creating enough resistance-heat to evaporate the material.

The process took long enough to make him doubt seriously that his conclusion could be correct. But eventually the frozen relays began to come back into service. He could have speeded up the process, by going up a few miles and exposing his interior to the lowered pressure, and he knew enough physics to be aware of the fact.

It spoke strongly for the shock he had received that he never thought of this until evaporation was nearly complete. It was lucky for his peace of mind that he never realized what the liquid water formed in the process might have done to his circuits. Fortunately, formed as it had been, it contained virtually no dissolved electrolytes and caused no shorts.

He realized, suddenly, that he had permitted his attention to stray from the doings of the nearby machines for what might be an unwise length of time, and at once resumed his listening. Apparently, they were still doing nothing. No seismic impulses were originating in the area where he had last perceived them. That eased his mind a trifle, and he returned to the problem of the material covering his eyes.

This stuff seemed to be changing slightly in its properties. Its elasticity was increasing, for one thing, and the change seemed to be taking place more rapidly on the side from which the air currents were coming. The agent could think of no explanation for this. He tried differing vibration patterns on the stuff, manipulating them with the skill of an artist—but a long time passed before he had anything approaching success.

At last, however, a minute flake of the material cracked free and fell away—*and he could really see! He could actually make out what was going on!*

7

The reason was obvious, of course. With an aperture of thirty centimeters and a focal length of about twenty-seven, the focus of the Conservationist's eye-lenses was highly critical; with the aperture about half a millimeter, as it had been left by the fragment of clay he had broken off, it became a minor matter.

He recognized the machines easily, near the edge of his new field of view, and began to work on the covering of a better-located eye. He did not succeed quite so well here, as the fragment he finally detached was larger, and the image correspondingly less clear, but it was still a good-enough job to enable him to follow the actions of the devices visually.

They were not traveling, as he has deduced already. Furthermore, a fourth machine, hitherto unnoticed, had joined them. All four had settled to the ground, so that their main frames took the weight normally carried by the traveling struts, which appeared merely to be propping the roughly cylindrical shapes in a more or less vertical attitude. The different ways in which this was accomplished, in different cases, did not surprise the agent. It would not have occurred to him to expect any two machines to be precisely alike, except perhaps in such standard subcomponents as relays. And it was, of course, fortunate that every new development happened in sequence, enabling him to analyze carefully as he went along.

The upper struts were moving rather aimlessly in general, but it did not take long for him to judge that their primary function was manipulation. The objects being handled at the moment were for the most part meaningless—apparently stones, bits of metal without obvious function, utterly unrecognizable objects which might be aggregates of the unfamiliar carbon compounds, though the agent knew no way to prove it. There were one or two exceptions. The device that had projected the slug of metal at his hull was easy to recognize, even though he had not perceived all of it at the time it was being used.

He tried to decide what parts of the machines functioned as their eyes, and was able to find them. It was not difficult, for no other portion was reasonably transparent. He discovered that all these vision organs were now turned toward him, but saw nothing surprising in the fact. The operators must have been familiar with the rest of the landscape, and did not expect anything of interest to show up on it.

Then the traveler noticed that all four of the machines were rising to their struts. As he watched, they began to move toward him.

At the same time, one of them extended a handling member toward a smaller fabrication, which almost immediately turned out to be another electromagnetic radiator. It was put to use at once, being swiftly raised to the upper part of the largest machine in the vicinity of the eyes, while a minor appendage of the handling limb which held it closed a switch.

This started the carrier frequency, after a delay which the agent was able to identify as due to the slow growth of the ion-clouds in portions of the apparatus—apparently they were produced by heating metal—and to the inherent lag of mechanical operations. The relays in the device were fantastically huge. They took whole milliseconds to operate, and since they rather obviously had components consisting of multicrystalline pieces of metal, they must have had a sharply limited service life.

Evidently the natives had not gone far enough with metal technology even to get the most out of one world's supplies. This was a side-issue, however. A far more interesting development involved the modulation of the carrier. The agent found it possible actually to see the way this was being carried out

An opening in the machine, not far below the eyes, rimmed with a remarkably flexible substance at whose nature he could only guess, began to open, shut and go through a series of changes of shape. He found it possible to correlate many of these contortions with the modulation of the electromagnetic signal. Apparently the opening was part of a device for generating pressure-wave patterns in the atmosphere.

The agent supposed that whatever plan the distant observers had been maturing must be moving into action, and he wondered what the machines were about to do. He was naturally a little surprised, since he had not expected any developments of this sort so soon.

Then he wondered still more, for the advance toward him which had been commenced halted, as suddenly as it had begun. Whatever had motivated them had either ceased—or the whole affair was part of an operation whose nature was still obscure. It would be the better part of valor to assume the latter, he decided.

He watched all four of the machines with minute care. They were now balanced on their support struts. They were neither advancing nor retreating, and the upper members were moving in their usual random fashion. All eyes were still fixed on his ship.

Then he noticed that the pressure-wave assemblies of all four were functioning, although three did not possess any broadcaster whose signal could be modulated. He watched them in fascination. Sometimes—usually, in fact—only one would be generating waves. At others, two, three or all four would be doing so. Even the one with the broadcaster did not always have its main switch closed at such times. Something a little peculiar was definitely occurring.

It had already occurred to the agent that the atmospheric waves carried the control impulses for these machines. Why should the machines themselves be *emitting* them, however? Receivers should be enough for such machines. Then he recalled another of his passing thoughts, which might serve as an explanation. Perhaps there was only *one* operator for all of them. And after all, why not? It might be better to think of the whole group as a single machine.

In that case, the pressure waves, traveling among its components, might be coordination signals. They just might be. At any rate, some testing could be done along this line. Whatever limitations he and his ship might have on this world, he could at least set up pressure waves in its atmosphere. Perhaps he could take over actual control of one or more of these assemblies. He had had the idea earlier, in connection with radio waves, and nothing much had come of it. But there seemed no reason not to try it again with sound. Nothing could surpass the experimental method when it was pursued with one strongly likely probability in mind.

A logical pattern to use would be the one that had been broadcast back to the distant observer a few moments before. It had been connected with a fairly simple, definite series of actions, and he had both heard and seen its production. He tried it, causing his hull to move in the complex pattern his memory had recorded a few seconds before. He tried it a second time.

"The thing's howling like a fire-siren!"

Just as when he had tried the same test with radio waves, there was no doubt that an effect had been produced, though it was not quite the effect the agent had hoped for. The handling appendages on all four of the things dropped whatever they were holding and snapped toward the upper part of their bodies. Once there, their flattened tips pressed firmly against the sides of the turrets on which their eyes were mounted.

For a moment, none of them produced any waves of its own. Then, the one with the broadcaster began to use it at great length. The agent wondered whether or not to attempt reproduction of the entire pattern it used this time, and decided against it. It was far more likely to be a report than involved in control. He decided to wait and see whether any other action ensued.

What did result might have been foreseen even by one as unfamiliar with mankind as the Conservationist. The machine with the broadcaster began producing more pressure waves, watching the ship as it did so. The agent realized, almost at once, that the controller was also experimenting. He regretted that he could not receive the waves directly, and wondered how he could make the other—or others—understand that their signals should be transmitted electromagnetically.

As a matter of fact, the agent could have detected the sound waves perfectly well, had it occurred to him to extend one of his seismic receptor-rods into the air. A sound wave carries little energy and only a minute percentage of that will pass into a solid from a gas. But an instrument capable of detecting the seismic disturbance set up by a walking man a dozen miles away is not going to be bothered by quantitative problems of that magnitude. However, this fact never dawned on the agent. Yet few would deny that he had done very well.

As it happened, no explanation was necessary for the hidden observer. He must have remembered, fairly quickly, that all the signals the agent had imitated had been radioed, and drawn the obvious conclusion. At any rate, the broadcaster was very shortly pressed into service again. A signal would be transmitted by radio, and the agent would promptly repeat it in sound waves.

Since the Conservationist had not the faintest idea of the significance of any of the signals, this was not too helpful—but the native had a way around that. A machine advanced to the hull of the ship and scraped the clay from one of its eyes. The particular eye was the most conveniently located one, to the agent's annoyance. But fortunately it was not the only one through which he could see the things.

Then, an ordered attempt was begun to provide him with data which would permit him to attach meanings to the various signal groups. Once he had grasped the significance of pointing, matters went merrily on for some time.

They pointed at rocks, mountains, the sun, each other—each had a different signal group, confining the agent's earlier assumption that they were not identical devices. But there also seemed to be a general term which took them all in.

He was not quite sure whether this term stood for machines in general, or could be taken as implying that the devices present were part of a single assembly, as he had suspected earlier. While the lessons went on, two of them wandered about the valley seeking new objects to show him. One of these objects proved the spark for a very productive line of thought.

Its shape, when it was brought back and shown to him, was as indescribable as that of many other things he had been shown by them. Its color was bright green, and the agent, perceiving a rather wider frequency band than was usable by human eyes, did not see it or think of it as a green object. He narrowed its classification down to a much finer degree.

He did not know the chemical nature of chlorophyll, but he had long since come to associate that particular reflection spectrum with photosynthesis. The thing did not seem to possess much rigidity. Its bulbous extensions sagged away from either side of the point where it was being supported. The handling extension that gripped it seemed to sink slightly into its substance.

He had never seen such a phenomenon elsewhere, and had no thought or symbol for the term *pulpy*. However, the concept itself rang a bell in his mind, for the machines facing him seemed fabricated from material of a rather similar texture. It was a peculiarity of their aspect that had been bothering him subconsciously ever since he had seen them moving. Now a nagging puzzlement—subconscious frustration was always unpleasant—was lifted from his mind.

The connection was not truly a logical one. Few new ideas have strictly logical connection with pre-existing knowledge. Imagination follows its own paths. Nevertheless, there *was* a connection, and, from the instant the thought occurred to him, the agent never doubted seriously that he was essentially correct. The natives of this planet did not merely use active carbon compounds as fuel for their machines. They constructed the machines themselves of the same sort of material!

Under the circumstances it was a reasonable thing to do—if one could succeed at it. The reactions of such chemicals were undoubtedly rapid enough to permit speedy action as anyone could desire—at least as fast as careful thought could control. The agent's race had long since learned the dangers inherent in machines capable of responding to casual, fleeting thoughts, and his ship's pickup-circuits were less sensitive, by far, than they might have been.

It was obvious why these devices were controlled from a distance, instead of being ridden by their operators, too. There must be some dangerous reactions, indeed, going on inside them. The agent decided it was just as well that his temporary prisoner had merely looked at the inside of his ship, without touching anything, and resolved to take no more such chances.

At any rate, there should be no more need for that sort of experiment. Language lessons were well under way. He had recorded a good collection of nouns, some verbs the machines had acted out, even an adjective or two. He was puzzled by the tremendous length of some of the signal groups, and suspected them of being descriptions, rather than individual basic words.

But even that theory had difficulties. The signal which, apparently, stood for the machines themselves, one which should logically have called for a rather long and detailed description, was actually one of the shortest—though even this took several hundred milliseconds to complete. The agent decided that there was no point in trying to deduce grammar rules. He could communicate with memorized symbols, and they would have to suffice.

Of course, the symbols that could be demonstrated on the spot were hardly adequate to explain the nature of Earth's danger. The Conservationist had long since decided just what he wished to say in that matter, and was waiting impatiently for enough words to let him say it.

It gradually became evident, however, that if he depended on chance alone to bring them into the lessons, he was going to wait a long time. This meant little to him personally. But the mole robots were not waiting for any instruction to be completed. They were burrowing on. The agent tried to think of some means for leading the lessons in the desired direction.

This took a good deal of imagination on his part, obvious as his final solution would seem to a human being. The idea of having to learn a language had been utterly strange to him, and he was still amazed at the ingenuity the natives showed in devising a means for teaching one. It was some time before it occurred to him that *he* might very well perform some actions, just as *they* were doing. If he did *not* follow his own acts with signal groups of his own, these natives might not understand that he wanted theirs. The time had come for a more direct and audacious approach to the entire problem, and at the thought of what he was about to do his spirits soared.

He did it. He lifted the ship a few feet into the air, settled back to show that he was not actually leaving, and then rose again. He waited, expectantly.

"Fly."

"Up."

"Rise."

"Go."

Each of the watching machines emitted a different signal virtually simultaneously. Three of them came through very faintly, since the speakers were some distance from the radio. But he was able to correlate each with the lip-motions of its maker. He was not too much troubled by the fact that different signals were used. He was more interested in the evidence that a different individual was controlling each machine. This was a little confusing, in view of his earlier theories. But he stuck grimly to the problem at hand.

7

The agent dropped back to the ground and went through his actions again. This time only the individual with the radio spoke. The word it used was *rise*. This was not the one it had used the other time. To make sure, the agent went through the act still again, and got the same word. Evidently, once their minds were made up, they intended to stick to their decisions. What *could* he think?

Then he tried burrowing into the ground, which seemed a useful action to be able to mention. The word given on the radio was *dig*, though two of the other machines apparently had different ideas once more.

It did not occur to him that these things might be detecting the by-products of his digging as well as his deliberate attempts to produce sound waves, or that his efforts to focus his third eye lens, a little while before, had actually been the cause of their sudden interest in his ship at that moment. He was much too pleased with himself at this point to entertain such extraneous ideas.

Having taken over the initiative in the matter of language lessons, he concentrated on the words he wanted, and, within a fairly short time, felt sure that he could get the basic facts of Earth's danger across to his listeners. After all, only four signal groups were involved in the concept. Satisfied that he had these correctly, he proceeded to use them together. In his progress now he felt the surge of a very personal kind of pride.

"Man dig—mountain rise."

For some unexplained reason the listening machines did not burst into frantic activity at the news. For a moment, he hoped that the controllers had turned to more suitable equipment to cope with the danger, leaving inactive that which they had been using. But he was quickly disabused of that bit of wishful thinking. The machine with the radio began to speak again.

"Man dig." It bent over and began to push the loose dirt aside with the flattened ends of its upper struts.

The agent realized, with some dismay, that its operator must suppose he was merely continuing the language lesson. He spoke again, more loudly, the two signal groups which the other seemed to be ignoring.

"Mountain rise."

All the machines looked at the hill across the valley, but nothing constructive seemed likely to come from that. If they waited for that one to rise noticeably, it would be too late to do anything about enlightening them as to the robots. He tried, frantically. to think of other words he had learned, or combinations which would serve his purpose. One seemed promising to him.

"Mountain break—Earth break—man break." The verb did not quite fit what was to happen, according to its earlier demonstration, but it did carry an implication of destruction, at least. His audience turned back to the ship, but gave no obvious sign of understanding.

He thought of another concept which might apply, but no word for it had yet appeared in the lessons. So, to illustrate it, he turned his ship's weapon on a patch of soil, a hundred yards from the bow. Twenty seconds' exposure to that needle of intolerable flame reduced the ground which it struck to smoking lava.

Even before he had finished the word *fire* came from one of the watchers. The observer made no comment on the fact that the tube which threw slugs of metal had been leveled at his hull during most of the performance. He simply made use of the new word.

"Man dig—Earth fire—mountain fire."

One of the machines produced its ionization tube and cautiously approached the patch of cooling slag. This had a slight amount of radioactivity from the beam, and its effect on the tube gave rise to much mutual signaling on the part of the machines. This culminated in a lengthy radio broadcast, not addressed to the agent. Then the language lessons were resumed, with the natives once more taking the initiative.

"Iron—copper—lead." Samples were shown individually.

"Metal." All the samples were shown together.

"Melt," This was demonstrated, when they finally made him understand that the weapon should be used again.

"Big—little." Pairs of stones, of cacti, coins and figures scratched in the dirt, illustrated this contrast.

Numbers—no difficulty.

"Ship." This proved confusing, since the agent had supposed the word *man* covered any sort of machine.

Finally, slightly fuller sentences became possible.

"Fire-metal under ground," the men tried.

The agent repeated the statement, leaving them in doubt. More time passed, while *yes* and *no* were explained. Then the same phrase brought a response of "Yes."

"Men dig."

"Yes—men dig—mountain melt—mountain rise."

"Where?" This word took still more time, and was solved, at last, only by a pantomime involving all the men. *Here* and *there* were covered in the same act. However, knowing what the question meant did not make it much easier for the agent to answer it.

He had no maps of the planet, and would have recognized no man-made charts, with the possible exception of a globe, which is not standard equipment on a small field expedition.

After still more time, the men managed to get a unit of distance across to him, however, and he could use the ion beam for pointing. In this way, he did his best to indicate the locations of the moles.

"There! Eighty-one miles. Two miles down." And, in another direction, "There! Fifteen hundred-twelve miles. Eighteen miles down." He kept this up through the entire list of the forty-five moles he had detected and located.

The furious note-taking that accompanied his exposition did not mean anything to him, of course, though he deduced correctly the purpose of the magnetic compass one of the listening machines was using. He realized that giving positions to an accuracy of one mile was woefully inadequate for the problem of actually locating the moles.

But he could do the final close-guiding later, when the native machines approached their targets. He could come to their aid if they did not have detection equipment of their own which would work at that range. Just what possibilities in that direction might be inherent in organic engineering the agent could not guess. At any rate, the natives did not seem to feel greater precision was needed, They made no request for it.

In fact, they did not seem to want *anything* more. He had expected to spend a long time explaining the apparatus needed to intercept and derange the moles. But that aspect of the matter did not appear to bother the natives at all. Why, why? It *should* have bothered them.

In spite of appearances, the agent was not stupid. The problem of communication with an intelligence not of his own race had never, as far as he knew, been faced by any of his people. He had tried to treat it as a scientific problem. It was hardly his fault that each phenomenon he encountered had infinitely more possible explanations than ordinary scientific observation, and he could hardly be expected to guess the reason why.

Even so, he realized it could not be considered a proven fact that the natives had read the proper meaning from his signaling. He actually doubted that they had, in the way and to the extent that some mid-nineteenth-century human physicists doubted the laws of gravity and conservation of energy. He determined to continue checking as long as possible, to make sure that they *were* right.

The human beings, partly as a result of greater experience, partly for certain purely human reasons, also felt that a check was desirable. With their far better local background, they were the first to take action. To them, *fire metal,* when mentioned in conjunction with a positive test for radioactivity, implied only one kind of fire.

Man dig was not quite so certain. They apparently could not decide whether the alien being was giving information or advice—whether someone was already digging at the indicated points, or that they should go there themselves to dig. The majority inclined to the latter view.

To settle the question, one of them took the trench-shovel, which was part of their equipment, and arranged a skit that eventually made clear the difference between the continuative—*digging*—and the imperative *dig!*

While this was going on, another thought occurred to the agent. Since these things had used different words for the machines he was watching and the one he was riding, perhaps *man* was not quite the right term for the mole-robots he was trying to tell about. He wondered how he could generalize. By the end of the second run-through of the skit he had what he hoped was a solution.

"Man digging—ship digging," he said.

"Digging fire metal?"

"Man digging fire metal—ship digging fire metal."

"Where?"

He ran through the list of locations again, though somewhat at a loss for the reason it was needed, and was allowed to finish, because, though he did not know it, no one could think of a way to tell him to stop. He felt satisfied when he had finished—there could hardly be any doubt in the minds of his listeners now.

They were talking to each other again—the reason was now obvious enough. The operators must be in different locations, must be communicating with each other through their machines. He had little doubt of what they were saying, in a general way.

Which was too bad—in a general way.

"It's vague—infernally vague."

"I know—but what else can he mean?"

"Perhaps he's just telling about some of our own mines, asking what we get out of them or trying to tell us he wants some of it."

"But what can 'flame metal' mean but fissionables? And what mine of ours did he point out?"

"I don't know about all of his locations, but the first one he mentioned—the closest one—certainly fits."

"What?"

"Eighty-one miles, bearing thirty degrees magnetic. That's as close as you could ask to Anaconda, unless this map is haywire. There are certainly men digging there!"

"Not two miles down!"

"They will be, unless we find a substitute for copper."

"I still think this thing is telling us about beings of its own kind, who are lifting our fissionables. They could do it easily enough, if they dig the way this one does. I'm for at least calling up there, and finding out whether anyone has thought of drilling test cores under the mine level—and how deep they went. There's no point walking around here, looking for anything else. We've found our fireball, right here."

The agent was interested but not anxious when the machines turned back to him, and direct communication was brought once more into operation. He was beginning to feel less tense, and confident that everything was going to come out all right if he stuck with it.

"Eighty-one miles that way. Men digging. Go now."

They illustrated the last words, turning away from his ship and starting in the proper direction. The agent could not exactly relax, fitting as he did into the spaces designed for him in his ship, but he felt the appropriate emotion.

They were getting started on one of the necessary steps, at least.. Presumably, the other and more distant ones would be tackled as soon as the news could be spread. These machines moved slowly, but their control impulses apparently did not.

It occurred to him that, since none of the devices had been left on hand to communicate with him, the natives might be expecting him to appear at the nearest digging site—the one they had mentioned. The more he thought of it, the more likely such an interpretation of their last message seemed. So, with the men barely started on their walk back to the waiting jeep, the Conservationist sent his ship whistling upward on a long slant toward the northeast.

8

The moment he rose above the valley, the Conservationist picked up the radar beams again—the beams that had startled him when he first approached the strange planet. As had happened on the earlier occasion, a few milliseconds served to bring many more of them to bear upon him.

He was quite evidently being watched on this journey. But he no longer expected these beams to carry intelligent speech. More or less casually, he noted their points of origin. He wondered, for brief moments, whether it might not be worthwhile to investigate them later, but felt fairly certain that it wouldn't. He turned his full attention on his goal.

The crusts of clay had fallen from his eyes as he flew, and he was once again limited to long-distance vision. He could make out the vast, terraced pits of the great copper mine as he approached, but could not distinguish the precise nature of the moving objects within. He did not consider sight a particularly useful or convenient sense anyway, so he settled to the ground, half a mile from the pit's edge, bored in as he had before, and began probing with seismic detectors and electrical senses.

He had, of course, already known of the presence of the hole. A fair amount of seismic activity had reached his original landing-spot from this place, enabling him to deduce its shape fairly accurately. Now, however, he realized—and for the first time—the amount of actual work going on. There were many machines of the sort he had already seen, which was hardly surprising. But there were many others as well, and the fact that most of them were metallic in construction startled him considerably.

There was a good deal of electrical activity, and at first he had hopes of finding an actual native. But these hopes quickly faded when he discovered there was nothing at all suggestive of thought-patterns. Some of the machines were magnetically driven. Others used regular electrical impulses for, apparently, starting the chemical reactions which furnished their main supply of energy.

The really surprising fact was the depth of the pit. If this work had begun since the receipt of his information, the wretched, guilty robots would be caught without difficulty. It took some time, by his perception standards, for a truer picture of the situation to be forced on his mind.

The pit had *not* been started recently. The progress of the diggers was fantastically slow. Clumsy metal scoops raised a few tons of material at a time and deposited it in mobile containers that bore it swiftly away. Fragments of the pit-wall were periodically knocked loose by expanding clouds of ionized gas, apparently formed chemically. The shocks initiated by these clouds were apparently the origin of most of the temblors he had felt from this source, while he was still eighty miles away.

His electrical analysis finally gave him the startling, incredible facts. This was a copper mine—extracting ore far poorer in quality than his own people could afford to process. This race was certainly confined, for some reason, to its home planet, and had been driven to picking leaner and ever leaner ores to maintain its civilization.

The development of organic machines had given them a reprieve from barbarism and final extinction, but surely could not save them forever. *Why in the galaxy* did they not use the organic robots for digging directly, as he had seen them do, during the language lessons? One would think that metal would be far too precious to such planet-bound people, for them to waste even iron on bulky, clumsy devices such as those at work here!

Even granting that the machines he had originally seen, and which seemed the most numerous, were not ideally designed for excavation work, surely, surely, better ones could be made. A race that could do what this race had done with carbon compounds could have no lack of ingenuity—or, more properly, of creative genius.

Very slowly, he realized why they had not—and why his mission was futile. He realized why these people would be doomed, even if the moles had never been planted. He noticed something relevant during the conversation, but had missed its full staggering implication. The organic compounds were *soft*. They bent and sagged and yielded to every sort of external mechanical influence—it was a wonder, thinking about it, that the machines he had seen held their shapes so well. No doubt, there was a frame-work of some sort, perhaps partly metallic even though he had not perceived it.

But such things could never force their way through rock. The only way they *could* dig was with the aid of metallic auxiliaries—simple ones, such as those used to illustrate the verb to him, or more capacious and complex ones like those in use here.

This race was doomed, had been doomed long before the poachers ever approached their planet. They needed metal, as any civilization did. They were bound to their world, but kept from moving about even upon it, for not one in a thousand of these people could conceivably travel by machine, as the agent's race did. The organic engines could not possibly be used as vehicles. They could not be so used because their very essential nature of chemical violence made them *untouchable*.

These people were trapped in a vicious circle, using their metal to dig more metal, sparing what little they could for electrical machinery and other equipment essential to a civilization, always having less and less to spare, always using more and more to get it. The idea that they could survive, until the planet's natural processes renewed the supply, was ridiculous.

It was, in short, precisely the same tragic circle that the agent's own race was precariously avoiding, millennium after millennium, by its complex schedule of freighters that distributed the metal from each planet in turn among thousands of others; then either waited for nature to renew the supply, or "tickled up" uninhabitable worlds as the poachers had done to this one.

Metal kept the machines operating. The machines kept food flowing to that vast majority of individuals who could not travel in search of it. A single break in the transport schedule could starve a dozen worlds. It was a fragile system, at best, and no member of the race liked to think about—much less actually face—examples of its failure.

The agent's mounting discomfort as he considered the matter of Earth was natural and inevitable. This race was what his own might have been, hundreds of millions of years before, had means of space-travel not been developed. They would probably be extinct before the poachers' torpedoes began to take effect, which was, no doubt, a mercy.

The agent could not help them. Even if the communication problem were cracked, they could not be brought into the transport network of civilization for untold millennia. No, they were truly lost—a race under sentence of extinction. The reorganization necessary was *frightening* in its complexity, even to him. Teaching them to build and use the equipment of his ship would be utterly useless, since it was entirely metallic, and they would be even worse off than with their organic devices.

They were already, probably by chemical means, stripping ores more efficiently than his own people, so he could hardly help them there. No, it was a virtual certainty that, when the planet's crust began to heave as giant bathyliths built up beneath it, when rivers of lava poured from vents scattered over the planet, no one would be there to face it.

This was a relief, in a way. The agent could picture, all too vividly, the plight of seeing a close friend engulfed only a few miles away, and having to spend hours or years of uncertainty wondering, when his own area would be taken—*and then knowing*.

That was the worst. There was plenty of warning, as far as awareness was concerned. Anywhere from minutes to years and millennia, if one was a really good computer. You knew, and if you had a mobile machine, you could move out of the way. Even these organic machines traveled fast enough for that. But *only* machines would let a being get out of the way—and there would be no machines here by then.

He wished with every atom of his being that he had never detected the poachers, had never seen this unfortunate planet or heard of its race. No good had come of it—or very little, anyway. There would, admittedly, be metal here before long, brought up with the magma flows, borne by subcrustal convection-currents in the stress-fluid that formed most of the world's bulk.

The poachers would be coming back for it, and he could at least deprive them of that. He would beam a report in toward the heart of the galaxy, making sure it did not radiate in the direction they had taken. Then there would be freighters to forestall them.

It was ironic, in a way. If any of this race should have survived the disturbance that would bring back the metal, that disturbance would be the salvation both of their species and their civilization. Most probably, however, the only witnesses would be a few half-starved, dull-minded barbarians, who would wonder, dimly, what was happening for a little while before temblors shattered their bodies forever.

There was nothing to keep him here, and the place was distasteful. More of the organic robots were approaching his position, but he did not want to talk any more. He wanted to forget this planet, to blot the memory of it forever from his mind.

With abrupt determination, he sent the dirt boiling away from his hull in a rising cloud of dust, pointed his vessel's blunt nose into the zenith and applied the drive. He held back just enough to keep his hull temperature within safe limits, while he was still in the atmosphere.

Then, with detectors fanning out ahead, he swung back to the line of his patrol orbit, and began accelerating away from the Solar system. Ignorant of events behind him, he never sensed the flight of swept-winged metal machines that hurtled close below while he was still in the air, split seconds after he had left the ground.

He did not notice the extra radar beam that fastened itself on his bull, while the machine projecting it flung itself through the sky, computing an interception course. This was too bad, for the relays in that machine would have made him feel quite at home, and its propulsion mechanism would have given him more food for thought.

He might have sensed its detonation, for his pursuer had a nuclear warhead. But its built-in brain realized, as quickly as the agent himself could have, that no interception was possible within its performance limits. It gave up, shutting off its fuel and curving back toward its launching station. Even the aluminum alloys in its hull would have interested the agent greatly—but he was trying to think of anything except Earth, its inhabitants and their *appalling* technology.

His patrol orbit would carry him back to this vicinity in half a million years or so. The freighters would have been there by that time.

He wondered if he could bring himself to look at the dead world.

SUN SPOT

Astounding, November 1960

Ron Sacco's hand reached gently toward his switch, and paused. He glanced over at the commander, saw the latter's eyes on him, and took a quick look at the clock. Welland turned his own face away—to hide a smile?—and Sacco almost angrily thumbed the switch.

Only one of the watchers could follow the consequences in real detail. To most, the closing of the circuit was marked a split second later by a meaningless pattern on an oscilloscope screen; to "Grumpy" Ries, who had built and installed the instrument, a great deal more occurred between the two events. His mind's eye could see the snapping of relays, the pulsing of electrical energy into the transducers in the ice outside and the hurrying sound waves radiating out through the frozen material; he could visualize their trip, and the equally hasty return as they echoed back from the vacuum that bounded the flying iceberg. He could follow them step by step back through the electronic gear, and interpret the oscilloscope picture almost as well as Sacco. He saw it, and turned away. The others kept their eyes on the physicist.

Sacco said nothing for a moment. He had moved several manual pointers to the limits of the weird shadow on the screen, and was using his slide rule on the resulting numbers. Several seconds passed before he nodded and put the instrument back in its case.

"Well?" sounded several voices at once.

"We're not boiling off uniformly. The maximum loss is at the south pole, as you'd expect; it's about sixty centimeters since the last reading. It decreases almost uniformly to zero at about fifteen degrees north; any loss north of that has been too small for this gear to measure. You'll have to go out and use one of Grumpy's stakes if you want a reading there."

No one answered this directly; the dozen scientists drifting in the air of the instrument room had already started arguments with each other. Most of them bristled with the phrase "I told you—" The commander was listening intently now; it was this sort of thing which had led him, days before, to schedule the radius measurements only once in twelve hours. He had been tempted to stop them altogether, but realized that it would be both impolite and impractical. Men riding a snowball into a blast furnace may not be any better off for knowing how fast the snowball is melting, but being men they *have to know.*

Sacco turned from his panel and called across the room.

"What are the odds now?"

"Just what they were before," snapped Ries. "How could they have changed? We've buried ourselves, changed the orbit of this overgrown ice cake until the astronomers were happy, and then spent our time shoveling snow until the exhaust tunnels were full so that we couldn't change course again if we wanted to. Our chances have been nailed down ever since the last second the motors operated, and you know it as well as I do."

"I stand...pardon me, float...corrected. May I ask what our *knowledge* of the odds is now?" Ries grimaced, and jerked his head toward the commander.

"Probably classified information. You'd better ask the chief executive of Earth's first manned comet how long he expects his command to last."

Welland managed to maintain his unperturbed expression, though this was as close to outright insolence as Ries had come yet. The instrument man was a malcontent by nature, at least as far as speech went; Welland, who was something of a psychologist, was fairly sure that the matter went no deeper. He was rather glad of Ries' presence, which served to bring into the open a lot of worrying which might otherwise have simmered under cover, but that didn't mean that he liked the fellow; few people did. "Grumpy" Ries had earned his nickname well. Welland, on the present occasion, didn't wait for Sacco to repeat the question; he answered it as though Ries had asked him directly—and politely.

"We'll make it," he said calmly. "We knew that long ago, and none of the measures have changed the fact. This comet is over two miles in diameter, and even after our using a good deal of it for reaction mass it still contains over thirty billion tons of ice. I may be no physicist, but I can integrate, and I know how much radiant heat this iceberg is going to intercept in the next week. It's not enough, by a good big factor, to boil off any thirty billion tons of the stuff around us. You all know that—you've been wasting time making book on how much we'd still have around us after perihelion, and not one of you has figured that we lose more than three or four hundred meters from the outside. If that's not a safe margin, I don't know what is."

"You don't know, and neither do I," retorted Ries. "We're supposed to pass something like a hundred thousand miles from the photosphere.

You know as well as I do that the only comet ever to do that came away from the sun as two comets. Nobody ever claimed that it *boiled* away." "You knew that when you signed up. No one blackmailed you. No one would—at least, no one who's here now." The commander regretted that remark the instant he had made it, but saw no way to retract it. He was afraid for a moment that Ries might make a retort which he couldn't possibly ignore, and was relieved when the instrument man reached for a handhold and propelled himself out of the room. A moment later he forgot the whole incident as a physicist at one of the panels suddenly called out.

"On your toes, all of you! X-ray count is going up—maybe a flare. Anyone who cares, get his gear grinding!" For a moment there was a scene of confusion. Some of the men were drifting free, out of reach of handholds; it took these some seconds to get swimming. Others, more skilled in weightless maneuvering, had kicked off from the nearest wall in the direction of whatever piece of recording machinery they most cherished, but not all of these had made due allowance for the traffic. By the time everyone was strapped in his proper place, Ries was back in the room, his face as expressionless as though nothing had been said a few moments before. His eyes kept swiveling from one station to another; if anyone had been looking at him, they would have supposed he was just waiting for something to break down. He was.

To his surprise, nothing did. The flare ran its course, with instruments humming and clicking serenely and no word of complaint from their attendants. Ries seemed almost disappointed; at least Pawlak, the power plant engineer who was about the only man on board who really liked the instrument specialist, suspected that he was.

"C'mon, Grump," was this individual's remark when everything seemed to have settled down once more. "Let's go outside and bring in the magazine from the monitor camera. Maybe something will have gone wrong with *it;* you said you didn't trust that remote-control system."

Ries almost brightened.

"All right. These astronomers will probably be howling for pictures in five minutes anyway, so they can tell each other they predicted everything correctly. Suit up." They left the room together with no one but the commander noting their departure.

There was little space outside the ship's air lock. The rocket had been brought as close to the center of the comet as measurement would permit, through a tunnel just barely big enough for the purpose. Five more smaller tunnels had been drilled, along three mutually perpendicular axes, to let out the exhaust of the fusion-powered reaction motors which were to use the comet's own mass to change its course. One other passageway, deliberately and carefully zigzagged, had been cut for personnel. Once the sunward course had been established all the tunnels except the last had been filled with "snow"—crushed comet material from near the ship. The cavern left by the removal of this and the exhaust mass was the only open space near the vessel, and even that was not too near. No one had dared weaken the structure of the big iceberg *too* close to the rocket; after all, one comet *had* been seen to divide as it passed the sun.

The monitor camera was some distance from the mouth of the tunnel—necessarily; the passage had been located very carefully. It opened in the "northern" hemisphere, as determined by direction of rotation, so that the camera could be placed at its mouth during perihelion passage and get continuous coverage. This meant, however, that in the comet's present orbital position the sun did not rise at all at the tunnel mouth. Since pictures had to be taken anyway, the camera was at the moment in the southern hemisphere, about a mile from the tunnel mouth.

Some care was needed in reaching it. A space-suited man with a mass of two hundred fifty pounds weighed something like a quarter of an ounce at the comet's surface, and could step away at several times the local escape velocity if he wished—or, for that matter, if he merely forgot himself. A dropped tool, given only the slightest accidental shove sideways, could easily go into orbit about the comet—or leave it permanently. That problem had been solved, though, after a fashion. Ries and Pawlak attached their suits together with a snap-ended coiled length of cable; then they picked up the end of something resembling a length of fine-linked chain which extended off to the southwest and disappeared quickly over the near horizon—or was it around the corner? Was the comet's surface below them, or beside or above? There was not enough weight to give a man the comforting sensation of a definite "up" and "down." The chain had a loop at the end, and both men put one arm through this. Then Ries waved his free arm three times as a signal, and they jumped straight up together on the third wave.

It was not such a ridiculous maneuver if one remembered the chain. This remained tight as the men rose, and pulled them gradually into an arc toward the southwest.

Partway up, they emerged from the comet's shadow, the metal suits glowing like miniature suns themselves. The great, gaseous envelope of a comet looks impressive from outside, seen against a background of black space; but it means exactly nothing as protection from sunlight even at Earth's distance from the sun. At twenty million miles it is much less, if such a thing is possible. The suits were excellent reflectors, but as a necessary consequence they were very poor radiators. Their temperature climbed more slowly than that of the proverbial black body, but it would climb much higher if given time. There would be perhaps thirty minutes before the suits would be too hot for life; and that, of course, was the reason for the leap.

A one-mile walk on the surface of the comet would take far more than half an hour if one intended to stay below circular velocity; swinging to their goal as the bobs on an inverted pendulum, speed limited only by the strength of their legs, should take between ten and twelve minutes. There were rockets on their suits which could have cut even that time down by quite a factor, but neither man thought of using them. They were for *emergency;* if the line holding them to the comet were to part, for example, the motors would come in handy. Not until.

They reached the peak of their arc, the chain pointing straight "down" toward the comet. Their goal had been visible for several minutes, and they had been trying to judge how close to it they would land. A direct hit was nearly impossible; even if they had been good enough to jump exactly straight up, the problem was complicated by the comet's rotation. As it turned out, the error was about two hundred yards, fairly small as such things went.

The landing maneuver was complicated-looking but logical. Half a minute before touchdown, Ries braced his feet against Pawlak and pushed. The engineer kept his grip on the chain and stayed in "orbit" while his companion left him in an apparently straight line. About fifteen seconds sufficed to separate them by the full length of the connecting snap line; the elasticity of this promptly started them back together, though at a much lower speed than they had moved apart. Just before they touched the surface, Ries noted which side of the camera the snap line was about to land on, and deliberately whipped it so that it fell on the other side; then, when both men took up slack, it snubbed against the camera mounting. Even though both men bounced on landing—it was nearly impossible to take up exactly the right amount of energy by muscle control alone—they were secure. Ries sent a couple more loops rippling down the line and around the camera mount—a trick which had taken some practice to perfect, where there was no gravity to help—and the two men pulled themselves over to their goal. The tendency to whip around it like a mishandled yo-yo as they drew closer was a nuisance but not a catastrophe; both were perfectly familiar with the conservation of angular momentum.

Ries quickly opened the camera, removed the exposed part of the film in its take-up cartridge and replaced and rethreaded another, checked the mounting for several seconds, and the job was done. The trip back was like that out, except for the complication that their landing spot was not in sunlight and control was harder. Five minutes after getting their rope around the pole at the tunnel mouth, they were in the ship. There was no speed limit *inside* the comet.

Once they were inside the air lock, Ries' prophecy was promptly fulfilled. Someone called for pictures before his suit had been off for two minutes. Pawlak watched his friend's blood pressure start up, and after a moment's calculation decided that intervention was in order—Grumpy couldn't be allowed *too* many fights.

"Go develop the stuff," he said. "I'll calm this idiot down."

For a moment it looked as though Ries would rather do his own arguing; then he relaxed, and vanished toward the instrument shop. Pawlak homed on the voice of the complaining astrophysicist, and in the three minutes it took Ries to process the film managed to make the fellow feel properly apologetic. This state of affairs lasted for about ten seconds after the film was delivered.

A group of six or seven scientists were waiting eagerly and had it in a projector almost instantly. For a few seconds after the run started there was silence; then a babble of expostulating voices arose. The general theme seemed to be, "Where's that instrument maker?"

Ries had not gone far, and when he appeared did not seem surprised. He didn't wait to be asked any questions, but took advantage of the instant silence which greeted his entrance.

"Didn't get your flare, did you? I didn't think so. That camera has a half-degree field, and the sun is over two degrees wide seen from here—"

"We know that!" Sacco and two or three others spoke almost together. "But the camera was supposed to scan the whole sun automatically whenever it was turned on from here, and keep doing it until we turned it off!"

"I know. And it didn't scan. I thought it hadn't when I was getting the film—"

"How could you tell? Why didn't you fix it? Or did you? What was wrong, anyway? Why didn't you set it up right in the first place?"

"I could tell that there hadn't been enough film exposed for the time it was supposed to be on. As for fixing it out there, or even finding out what was wrong—don't sound any more idiotic than you can help. It'll have to be brought into the shop. I can't promise how long it'll take to fix it until I know what's wrong."

The expostulation rose almost to a roar at this last remark. The commander, who alone of the group had been silent until now, made a gesture which stilled the others.

"I know it's hard to promise, but please remember one thing," he said. "We're twenty million miles from the sun; we'll be at perihelion in sixty-seven hours. If we pass it without that camera, we'll be missing our principal means of correlating any new observations with the old ones. I don't say that without the camera we might as well not be here, but—"

"I know it," growled Ries. "All right. I knew we should have laid down a walk cable between here and the blasted thing when we first set it up, but with people talking about time and shortage of anchoring pins and all that tripe—"

"I think that last was one of your own points," interjected the commander. "However, we have better things to do than fix blame. Tell us what help you need in getting the camera back to the ship."

An hour later, the device came in through the air lock. Its mass had demanded a slight modification in travel technique; if the chain had broken during a "swing" the rockets would not have been able to return men and camera both to the comet, in all likelihood. Instead of swinging, therefore, the workers had pulled straight along the chain, building up speed until they reached its anchorage and then slowing down on the other side by applying friction to the chain as it unwound behind them. An extra man with a line at the tunnel mouth had simplified the stopping problem on the return trip with the camera.

Four hours later still, Ries had taken the camera completely apart and put it together again, and was in a position to say that there had been nothing wrong with it. He was not happy about this discovery, and the scientists who heard his report were less so. They were rather abusive about it; and that, of course, detonated the instrument man's temper.

"All right, *you* tell *me* what's wrong!" he snapped at last. "I can say flatly that nothing is broken or out of adjustment, and it works perfectly in here. Any genius who's about to tell me that *in here* isn't *out there* can save his breath. I know it, and I know that the next thing to do is take it back out and see if it still works. That's what I'm doing, if I can spare the time from listening to your helpful comments." He departed abruptly, donned his suit, and went outside with the instrument but without Pawlak. He had no intention of returning to the original camera site, and needed no help. The tunnel mouth was "outside" enough, he felt.

It took several more hours to prove that he was right. At first, the trouble refused to show itself. The camera tracked beautifully over any sized square of sky that Ries chose to set into its control. Then after half an hour or more, the size of the square began to grow smaller no matter what he did with the controls. Eventually it reached zero. This led him into its interior, as well as he could penetrate it in a spacesuit, but no information was forthcoming. Then, just to be tantalizing, the thing started to work again. On its own, as far as Ries could tell. He was some time longer in figuring out why.

Eventually he came storming back into the ship, fulminating against anyone who had had anything to do either with designing or selecting the device. He was a little happier, since the trouble was demonstrably not his own fault, but not much. He made this very clear to the waiting group as soon as his helmet was off.

"I don't know what genius indulged his yen for subminiaturization," he began, "but he carried it too far. I suppose using a balanced resistance circuit in a control is sensible enough; it'll work at regular temperatures, and it'll work at comet temperatures. The trouble is it won't work unless the different segments are near the *same* temperature; otherwise the resistors can't possibly balance. When I first took the thing outside, it worked fine; it was at ship's temperature. Then it began to leak heat into the comet, and went crazy. Later on, with the whole thing cooled down to comet temperature, it worked again. Nice design!"

"But it had been outside for days before—" began someone, and stopped as he realized what had happened. Ries pounced on him just the same.

"Sure—outside *in the sunlight*. Picking up radiant heat on one side, doing its best to get to equilibrium at a couple of hundred degrees. Conducting heat out into the ice four or five hundred degrees colder on the other side. Nice, uniform—aach!"

"Can't a substitute control be devised?" cut in the commander mildly. "That's your field, after all. Surely you can put something together—"

"Oh, sure. In a minute. We're just loaded with spare parts and gear; rockets always are. While I'm at it I'll try to make the thing wrist-watch size so it will fit in the available space—all we need is a research lab's machine shop. I'll do what I can, but you won't like it. Neither will I." He stormed out to his own shop.

"I'll buy his last remark, anyway," muttered someone. Agreement was general but not too loud.

At fifteen million miles from the sun, with another meter or so boiled off the comet's sunlit surface, Ries emerged with his makeshift. He was plainly in need of sleep, and in even worse temper than usual. He had only one question to ask before getting into his suit.

"Shouldn't the sun be starting to show near the tunnel mouth by now?"

One of the astronomers did a little mental arithmetic.

"Yes," he answered. "You won't need to travel anywhere to test the thing. Do you need any help?"

"What for?" growled Ries in his usual pleasant fashion, and disappeared again. The astronomer shrugged. By the time conversation had gotten back to normal the instrument specialist and his camera were in the air lock.

Taking the heavy device out through the tunnel offered only one danger, and that only in the last section—the usual one of going too fast and leaving the comet permanently. To forestall the risk of forcing people to pay final respects to him and regret the camera, he made full use of the loops of safety cable which had been anchored in the tunnel wall. He propped the instrument at the tunnel mouth facing roughly north, and waited for sunrise. This came soon enough. It was the display characteristic of an airless world, since the coma was not dense enough to scatter any light to speak of. The zodiacal light brightened near the horizon; then it merged into pearly corona; then a brilliant crimson eruptive arch prominence appeared, which seemed worth a picture or two to the nonprofessional; and finally came the glaring photosphere on which the test had to be made. It was here that another minor problem developed.

The photosphere, area for angular area, was of course no brighter than when seen from just above Earth's atmosphere; but it was no fainter either, and Ries could not look at it to aim his camera. The only finder on the latter was a direct-view collimating sight, since it was designed for automatic control. After a moment's thought, Ries decided that he could handle this situation too, but, since his solution would probably take longer than the sun would be above the horizon, he simply ran the camera through a few scanning cycles, aiming it by the shape of its own shadow. Then he anchored the machine in the tunnel mouth and made his way back to the ship.

Here he found what he wanted with little difficulty—a three-inch-square interference filter. It was not of the tunable sort, though of course its transmission depended on the angle of incidence of the light striking it, but it was designed for sixty-five hundred Angstroms and would do perfectly well for what he had in mind.

Before he could use it, though, another problem had to be solved. Almost certainly the lining up of the camera and its new control—that is, making sure that the center of its sweep field agreed with the line laid down by the collimator sight—would take quite a while. At fifteen million miles from the sun, one simply doesn't work for long with only a spacesuit as protection. The expedition had, of course, been carefully planned so that no one would have to do any such thing; but the plans had just graduated from history to mythology. Grumpy Ries was either going to work undisturbed in full sunlight, probably for one or two whole hours, or spend twenty minutes cooling off in the tunnel for every ten he spent warming up outside it; and that last would add hours and hours to the job time—with the heating period growing shorter with each hour that passed. A parabolic orbit has one very marked feature; its downhill half is very *steeply* downhill, and speed builds up far too quickly for comfort. It seemed that some means of working outside, if one could be found, would pay for itself. Ries thought he could find one.

He was an artisan rather than a scientist, but he was a good artisan. A painter knows pigments and surfaces, a sculptor knows metal and stone; Ries knew basic physics. He used his knowledge.

Limited as the spare supplies were, they included a number of large rolls of aluminum foil and many spools of wire. He put these to use, and in an hour was ready with a six-foot-square shield of foil, made in two layers a couple of inches apart, the space between them stuffed with pulverized ice from the cavern. In its center was mounted the filter, and beside this a hole big enough to take the camera barrel. The distance between the two openings had been measured carefully; the filter would be in front of the camera sight.

Characteristically, he showed the device to no one. He made most of it outside the ship, as a matter of fact; and when it was done he towed it rather awkwardly up the tunnel to the place where the camera was stored. Incredibly, twenty minutes later the new control was aligned, the camera mounted firmly on its planned second base at the tunnel mouth, and a control line was being run down the tunnel to the ship. With his usual curtness he reported completion of the job; when the control system had been tested from inside, and the method Ries had used to accomplish the task wormed out of him, the reaction of the scientists almost had him smiling.

Almost; but a hardened grouch doesn't change all at once—if ever.

Ten million miles from Sol's center. Twenty-one hours to go—people were not yet counting minutes. The sun was climbing a little higher above the northern horizon as seen from the tunnel mouth, and remaining correspondingly longer in view each time it rose. Some really good pictures were being obtained; nothing yet which couldn't have been taken from one of the orbital stations near Earth.

Five million miles. Ten hours and fifty minutes. Ries stayed inside, now, and tried to sleep. No one else had time to. Going outside, even to the mouth of the tunnel, was presumed impossible, though the instrument maker had made several more shields. Technically, they were within the corona of the sun, though only of its most tenuous outlying zones—there is, of course, a school of thought that considers the corona as extending well past the Earth's orbit. None of the physicists were wasting time trying to decide what was essentially a matter of definition; they were simply reading and recording every instrument whose field of sensitivity seemed to have the slightest bearing on their current environment, and a good many which seemed unlikely to be useful, but who could tell?

Ries was awake again when they reached the ninety-degree point—one quarter of the way around the sun from perihelion. The angular distance the earth travels in three months. Slightly over one million miles from the sun's center. Six hundred thousand miles from the photosphere.

Well within *anyone's* definition of the corona; within reach of a really healthy eruptive prominence, had any been in the way. One hour and eighteen minutes from their closest approach—or deepest penetration, if one preferred to put it that way. Few did.

They were hurtling, at some three hundred ten miles per second, into a region where the spectroscope claimed temperatures above two million degrees to exist, where ions of iron and nickel and calcium wandered about with a dozen and more of their electrons stripped away, and where the electrons themselves formed almost a gas in their own right, albeit a highly tenuous one.

It was that lack of density on which the men were counting. A single ion at a "temperature" of two million degrees means nothing; there isn't a human being alive who hasn't been struck by vast numbers of far more energetic particles. No one expected to pick up any serious amount of heat from the corona itself.

The photosphere was another matter. It was an opaque, if still gaseous, "surface" which they would approach within one hundred fifty thousand miles—less than its own diameter by a healthy factor. It had a radiation equilibrium temperature of some six thousand degrees, and would fill a large solid angle of sky; this meant that the black-body equilibrium temperature at their location would not be much below the same value. The comet, of course, was not a black body—and did not retain even the heat which it failed to reflect. The moment a portion of its surface was warmed seriously, that portion evaporated, taking the newly acquired heat energy with it. A new layer, still only a few degrees above absolute zero, was exposed in its turn to the flood of radiation.

That flood was inconceivably intense, of course; careless, non-quantitative thought could picture the comet's vanishing under that bombardment like a snowball in a blast furnace—but the flood wasn't infinite. A definite, measurable amount of energy struck the giant snowball; a definite amount was reflected; a definite, measurable amount was absorbed and warmed up and boiled away the ices of water and ammonia and methane that made it up.

And there was a lot to boil away. Thrust-acceleration ratios had long ago given the scientists the mass of their shelter, and even at a hundred and fifty thousand miles a two-and-a-half-mile-thick bar of sunlight will take some time to evaporate thirty-five billion tons of ice. The comet would spend only a little over twenty-one hours within five million miles of the sun, and unless several physicists had misplaced the same decimal point, it should last with plenty to spare. The twelve-hour rule on Sacco's echo sounder had been canceled now, and its readings were common knowledge; but none of them caused anxiety.

In they drove. No one could see out, of course; there was nothing like the awed watching of an approaching prominence or gazing into the deceptively pitlike area of a sunspot of which many of them had unthinkingly dreamed. If they could have seen a sunspot at all, it would have been as blinding as the rest of the photosphere—human eyes couldn't discriminate between the two orders of overload. For all any of them knew, they might be going through a prominence at any given second; they wouldn't be able to tell until the instrument records were developed and reduced. The only people who could "see" in any sense at all were the ones whose instruments gave visible as well as recorded readings. Photometers and radiometers did convey a picture to those who understood them; magnetometers and ionization gauges and particle counters meant almost as much; but spectrographs and interferometers and cameras hummed and clicked and whirred without giving any clues to the nature of the meals they were digesting. The accelerometers claimed their share of watchful eyes—if there were any noticeable drag to the medium outside, all bets on the comet's future and their own were off—but nothing had shown so far.

They were nineteen minutes from perihelion when a growing sense of complacency was rudely shattered. There was no warning—one could hardly be expected at three hundred twenty-five miles a second.

One instant they were floating at their instruments, doing their allotted work, at peace with the universe; the next there was a violent jolt, sparks flew from exposed metal terminals, and every remote indicator in the vessel went dead.

For a moment there was silence; the phenomenon ended as abruptly as it had started. Then there was a mixed chorus of yells, mostly of surprise and dismay, a few of pain. Some of the men had been burned by spark discharges. One had also been knocked out by an electric shock, and it was fortunate that the emergency lights had not been affected; they sprang automatically to life as the main ones failed, and order was quickly restored. One of the engineers applied mouth-to-mouth respiration to the shock victim—aesthetic or not, it is the only sort practical in the weightless condition—and each of the scientists began trouble shooting.

None of the remote gear registered in any way, but much of the apparatus inside the ship was still functioning, and a tentative explanation was quickly reached.

"Magnetic field," was Mallion's terse comment, "size impossible to tell, just as impossible to tell what formed or maintained it. We went through it at three hundred twenty miles a second, plus. If this ship had been metal, it would probably have exploded; as it was, this general sort of thing was a considered possibility and there are no long conducting paths anywhere in the ship—except the instrument controls. The field intensity was between ten and a hundred Gauss. We've taken all the outside readings we're going to, I'm afraid."

"But we can't stop now!" howled Donegan. "We need pictures—hundreds more of them. How do we correlate all the stuff we have, and the things that will still show on the inside instruments we can still use, unless there are pictures—it's fine to say that this or that or the other thing comes from a prominence, or a flare, or what have you, but we won't *know* it does, or anything about the size of the flare...

"I understand, sympathize, and agree; but what do you propose to do about it? I'd bet a small but significant sum that the cable coming in through the access tunnel *did* explode. Something certainly stopped the current surge before all the instruments here burned up."

"Come on, Dr. Donegan. Get your suit." It was Ries, of course. The physicist looked at him, must have read his mind, and leaped toward his locker.

"What are you madmen up to?" shouted Mallion. "You can't go out to that camera—you'd be a couple of moths in a candle flame, to put it mildly!"

"Use your brain, not your thalamus, Doc," Ries called over his shoulder. Welland said nothing. Two minutes later the pair of madmen were in the air lock, and sixty seconds after that were floating as rapidly as they dared out the tunnel.

The lights were out, but seeing was easy. There was plenty of illumination from the mouth of the tunnel, crooked as the passage was; and the two had to use the filters on their face plates long before they reached the opening. By that time, the very snow around them seemed to be glowing—and may very well have been doing just that, since light must have filtered for some distance in through the packed crystalloids as well as bounced its way around the tunnel bends.

Ries had left his foil shelters at the first bend. There was some loose snow still on hand from his earlier experiments, and they stuffed as much of this as they could between the thin metal layers, and took several of the sandwiched slabs with them as they gingerly approached the opening. They held one of the larger of these—about four feet square—ahead of them as they went; but it proved insufficient when they got within a few yards of the mouth. The trouble was not that the shield failed, but that it wasn't big enough; no matter how close to the opening they came, the entire sky remained a sea of flame. They retreated a little way and Ries rapidly altered the foil armor, bending the sheets and wiring them together until he had a beehive-shaped affair large enough to shield a man. He used the last of their snow in this assembly.

Covered almost completely, he went alone to the tunnel mouth, and this time had no trouble. He was able to use a loop of control wire as a safety, and by hooking his toes under this reached the instrument. It had settled quite a bit—its case and mounting bad transmitted heat as planned to the broad silver feet, and these had maintained good surface contact. Naturally a good deal of comet material had boiled away from under them, and the whole installation was in a pit over two feet deep and eight in width. The general lowering of the comet's surface was less obvious.

The vanes of the legs were fairly well sunk into the surface, but with gravity as it was, the only difficulty in freeing them was the perennial one—the risk of giving too much upward momentum. Ries avoided this, got camera and mounting loose, and as quickly as possible brought them back into the tunnel. There was no need to disconnect the control wire from the main cable; as Mallion had predicted, both had disappeared. Their explosion had scarred a deep groove along the tunnel wall at several points where they had been close to the side. Ries regretted their loss; without them he had some difficulty getting himself and his burden started downward, and he wanted the camera into the tunnel's relative shelter as quickly as possible. With its heat-shedding "feet" out of contact with the ground, it would not take long to heat up dangerously. Also, with the comet now whipping closer and closer to perihelion, there was already an annoyingly large gap in the photographic record.

Back in the tunnel, Ries improvised another set of shields for the camera and its operator, and checked the one he had used to see how much snow remained in it. There was some, but discouragingly little. He placed his helmet against that of Donegan and spoke—the radios were useless in the sun's static.

"You can't go out until we get more snow for this thing, and you'll have to come back every few minutes for a refill. I'd do the photography, but you know better than I what has to be taken. I hope you can make out what you need to see through the sixty-five-hundred filter in the shield I made for the finder. I'll be back."

He started back down the tunnel, but at the second turn met another suited figure coming out—with a large bag of snow. He recognized Pawlak by the number on the suit, since the face of the occupant was invisible behind the filter. Ries took the bag and gestured his thanks; Pawlak indicated that he would go back and bring more, and started on this errand. Ries reappeared at the camera soon enough to surprise his companion, but the physicist wasted no time in questions. The two men restuffed the shields with snow, and Donegan went back to the tunnel mouth to do his job.

Through the filter, the angry surface of the sun blazed a fiery orange. Features were clear enough, though not always easy to interpret. Individual "rice grains" were clearly visible; a small spot, badly foreshortened, showed far to one side. By moving his head as far as the shield allowed, the observer could see well away from the camera's line of sight; doing this, of course, blued the sun as the ray path difference between the reflecting layers in the filter was shortened. He could not tell exactly what wave length he was using at any given angle, but he quickly learned to make use of the rather crude "tuning" that angle change afforded. He began shooting, first the spot and its neighborhood, altering the camera filter wave length regularly as he did so. Then he found something that might have been a calcium flocculus and took a series around it; then feature after feature caught his eye, and he shot and shot, trying to get each field through the full wavelength range of the camera at about fifty-Angstrom intervals plus definite lengths which he knew should be there—the various series lines of hydrogen and of neutral and ionized helium particularly, though he did not neglect such metals as calcium and sodium.

He was distracted by a pull on his armored foot; Ries had come up, inadequately protected by the single remaining sheet of "parasol," to warn him to recharge his own shield. Reluctantly he did so, grudging the time. Rica packed snow against the feet of the camera mounting while Donegan stuffed it between the foil layers of his shield as rapidly as his spacesuited hands could work. The moment this was done he headed back to the tunnel mouth, now not so far away as it had been, and resumed operations.

They must have been almost exactly at perihelion then. Donegan neither knew nor cared. He knew that the camera held film enough to let him take one picture a second for about ninety minutes, and he intended to use all of it if he could. He simply scanned the sun as completely as his eyesight, the protecting filter, and his own knowledge permitted, and recorded as completely as possible everything even slightly out of the ordinary that he saw. He knew that many instruments were still at work in the ship, even though many were not, and he knew that some of the devices on the comet's surface would function—or should function—automatically even though remote control was gone; and he intended that there should be a complete record in pictures of everything which might be responsible for whatever those machines recorded. He did a good job.

Not too many—in fact, as time went on, too few—yards below him Ries also worked. If being an instrument maintenance specialist involved moving snow, and in this part of the universe it seemed to involve little else, then he would move snow. He had plenty of it; Pawlak kept bringing more and more bags of the stuff. Also, on his second trip, the engineer produced a lengthy coil of wire; and at the first opportunity Ries fastened one end of this to Donegan's ankle. It served two purposes—it was no longer necessary to go out to let the fellow know by physical contact that his time was getting short, and it let the observer get back to work more quickly. Since he was belayed to Ries, who could brace himself against the tunnel walls beyond the bend, there was no worry of going back to the surface too rapidly and being unable to stop.

Ries kept busy. No one ever knew whether he did it silently or not, since the radios were unavailable. It was generally taken for granted that he grumbled as usual, and he may very well have done just that, or even surpassed himself. Hanging weightless in a white-glowing tunnel, trying to read a watch through the heaviest solar filter made for space helmets, holding one end of a line whose other end was keeping a man and a fantastically valuable camera from drifting away and becoming part of the solar corona, all the while trying to organize a number of large plastic sacks of pulverized frozen water, ammonia, and methane which persistently gathered around him would have driven a more self-controlled man than Ries to bad language.

Of course, Donegan didn't map the whole surface. This would take quite a while, using a camera with a half-degree field on a surface over ninety-five degrees across, even when the surface in question is partly hidden by the local horizon. It was made even more impossible by their rate of motion; parabolic velocity at a distance of five hundred eighty thousand miles from Sol's center is just about three hundred thirty miles per second, and that produced noticeable relative motion even against a background a hundred and fifty thousand miles away. Features were disappearing below the solar horizon, sometimes, before Donegan could get around to them. Even Ries could think of no solution to this difficulty, when the physicist complained of it on one of his trips for more snow.

At this point, the sun's apparent motion in latitude was more rapid than that in longitude—the comet was changing its direction from the sun more rapidly than it was rotating. The resultant motion across the sky was a little hard to predict, but the physicist knew that the center of the solar disk would set permanently at the latitude of the tunnel mouth an hour and three-quarters after perihelion. The angular size of the disk being what it was, there would be *some* observing after that, but how much depended on what might be called the local time of day, and he had not attempted to figure that out. He simply observed and photographed, except when Ries dragged him forcibly back to get his shield recharged.

Gradually the gigantic disk shrank. It never was far above the local horizon, so there was always something with which to compare it, and the shrinking could be noticed. Also, Ries could tell as time went on that there was a little more snow left in Donegan's shield each time it came back for refilling. Evidently they were past the worst.

But the sun had taken its toll. The mouth of the tunnel was much closer to the ship than it had been; several times Ries had been forced back to another section of tunnel with his snow bags, and each resumption of observation by Donegan had involved a shorter trip than before to the surface. Ries, Donegan, and Pawlak were the only members of the expedition to know just how far the evaporation was progressing, since the echo-sounder had been wrecked by the magnetic field; they were never sure afterward whether this was good or not. Those inside were sustained, presumably, by their faith in mathematics. For the physicists this was adequate, but it might not have been for Ries if he had been with them. In any case, he didn't worry much about the fate of the comet after perihelion had been passed; he had too many other troubles, even though his activity had quickly become routine. This left him free to complain—strictly to himself.

Donegan was furious when he finally realized that the sun was going to set at his observing station while it was still close enough to photograph. Like Ries, however, he had no way of expressing his annoyance so that anyone could hear him; and as it turned out, it would have been wasted breath. Observation was cut even shorter by something else.

They had been driven down to what had been originally the third bend in the tunnel, and at this point the passage ran horizontally for a time. Pawlak had just come to the other end of this straight stretch with what he hoped would be his last load of snow when something settled gently through its roof between him and Ries. He leaped toward it, dropping his burden, and discovered that it was one of the instruments which had been on the surface. Its silver cover was slightly corroded, and the feet of its mounting badly so. Apparently its reflecting powers had been lowered by the surface change, and it was absorbing more energy than an equivalent area of comet; so its temperature had gone up accordingly, and it had melted its way below the rest of the surface.

Low as the sun was, it was shining into the hole left by the instrument; evidently the pit it had made was very broad and shallow. Pawlak made his way around the piece of gear and up to Ries, whose attention was directed elsewhere, and reported what had happened. The instrument man looked back down the tunnel and began to haul in on the line attached to Donegan. The physicist was furious when he arrived, and the fact became evident when the three helmets were brought together.

"What in blazes is going on here?" he fulminated. "You can't make me believe my shield had boiled dry again—I haven't been out five minutes, and the loads are lasting longer now. We're losing the sun, you idiot; I can't come back because someone had a brainstorm or can't read a watch—"

Pawlak interrupted by repeating his report. It did not affect Donegan.

"So what?" he blazed. "We expected that. All the gear around the tunnel mouth has sunk—we're in a big pit now anyway. That's making things still worse—we'll lose sight of the sun that much sooner. Now let me get back and work!"

"Go back and work if you want, provided you can do anything with the naked eye," retorted Ries, "but the camera's going back to the ship pronto. That's one thing we forgot—or maybe it was just assumed that gaseous ammonia in this concentration and at this temperature wouldn't do anything to silver. Maybe it isn't the ammonia, for all I know; maybe it's something we've been picking up from the corona; but look at that camera of yours! The polish is gone; it's picking up heat much faster than it was expected to, and not getting rid of it any quicker. If that magazine of exposed film you have in there gets too hot, you'll have wasted a lot of work. Now come on, or else let me take the camera back." Ries started along the tunnel without further words, and the physicist followed reluctantly.

Inside, Donegan disappeared with his precious film magazine, without taking time to thank Ries.

"Self-centered character," he muttered. "Not a word to anyone—just off to develop his film before somebody opens the cartridge, I suppose."

"You can't blame him," Ries said mildly. "He did a lot of work for it."

"*He* did a lot of work? How about us? How about you; it was all your idea in the first place—"

"Careful, Joe, or they'll be taking my nickname away from me and giving it to you. Come on; I want to see Doc Sonne. My feet hurt." He made his way to the main deck, and Pawlak drifted after him, grumbling. By the time the engineer arrived, the rest of the group was overwhelming Ries with compliments, and the fellow was grinning broadly. It began to look as though the name "Grumpy" *would* have to find a new owner.

But habit is hard to break. The doctor approached, and without removing his patient's shoes dredged a tube of ointment out of his equipment bag.

"Burn ointment," the doctor replied. "It'll probably be enough; you shouldn't have taken too bad a dose. I'll have you patched up in a minute. Let's get those shoes off."

"Now wouldn't you know it," said Ries aloud. "Not even the doctor around here can do the right thing at the right time. Physicists who want A's gear fixed on B's time—won't let a man go out to do a job in the only way it can be done—won't give a person time to rest—and now," it was the old Grumpy back again, "a man spends two hours or so swimming around among sacks of frozen methane, which melts at about a hundred and eighty-five degrees Centigrade below zero—that's about two hundred and ninety below, Fahrenheit, doctor—and the doctor wants to use *burn ointment*. Break out the frostbite remedy, will you, please? My feet hurt."

THE MECHANIC

Analog, September 1976

Drifting idly, the *Shark* tended to look more like a manta ray than her name suggested; but at high cruise, as she was now, she bore more resemblance to a flying fish. She was entirely out of the water except for the four struts that carried her hydroplanes; the air propellers which drove her were high enough above the surface to raise very little spray. An orbiting monitor satellite could have seen the vessel herself from a hundred miles up, since her upper hull was painted in a vividly fluorescent pattern of red and yellow; but there was not enough wake to suggest to such a watcher that the wedge-shaped machine was traveling at nearly sixty-five knots.

Chester V. Winkle—everyone knew what the middle initial stood for, but no one mentioned it in his presence—sat behind the left bow port of his command with his fingers resting lightly on the pressure controls. He was looking ahead, but knew better than to trust his eyes alone. Most of his attention was devoted to the voice of the smaller man seated four feet to his right, behind the other "eye" of the manta. Yoshii Ishihara was not looking outside at all; his eyes were directed steadily at the sonar display screen which was all that stood between the *Shark* and disaster at her present speed among the ice floes and zeowhales of the Labrador Sea.

"Twenty-two targets in the sweep; about fourteen thousand meters to the middle of the group," he said softly.

"Heading?" Winkle knew the question was superfluous; had a change been in order, the sonarman would have given it.

"As we go, for thirty-two hundred meters. Then twenty-two mils starboard. There's ice in the way."

"Good. Any data on target condition yet?"

"No. It will be easier to read them when we stop, and will cost little time to wait. Four of the twenty-two are drifting, but the sea is rich here and they might be digesting. Stand by for change of heading."

"Ready on your call." There was silence for about a minute.

"Starboard ten."

"Starboard ten." The hydroplanes submerged near the ends of the *Shark*'s bow struts banked in response to the pressure of Winkle's fingers, though the hull remained nearly level. The compass needle on the panel between the view ports moved smoothly through ten divisions. As it reached the tenth Ishihara, without looking up from his screen, called, "Steady."

"Steady she is," replied the commander.

"Stand by for twelve more to starboard—now." The *Shark* swung again and steadied on the new heading.

"That leaves us a clear path in," said the sonarman. "Time to engine cut is four minutes."

In spite of his assurance that the way was clear, Ishihara kept his eyes on his instruments—his standards of professional competence would permit nothing less while the *Shark* had way on her. Winkle, in spite of the sleepy appearance which combined with his name to produce a constant spate of bad jokes, was equally alert for visible obstructions ahead. Several ice floes could be seen, but none were directly in the vessel's path, and Winkle's fingers remained idle until his second officer gave the expected signal.

Then the whine of turbines began to drop in pitch, and the *Shark*'s broad form eased toward the swell below as the hydrofoils lost their lift. The hull extensions well out on her "wings" which gave the vessel catamaran-type stability when drifting kissed the surface gently, their added drag slowing the machine more abruptly; and twenty feet aft of the conning ports the four remaining members of the crew tensed for action.

"Slow enough for readings?" asked Winkle.

"Yes, sir. The homing signal is going out now. I'll have counts in the next thirty seconds." Ishihara paused. "One of the four drifters is underway and turning toward us. No visible response from the others."

"Which is the nearest of the dead ones?"

"Fifteen hundred meters, eight hundred forty mils port." Winkle's fingers moved again. The turbines that drove the big, counter-rotating air propellers remained idle, but water jets playing from ducts on the hydrofoil struts swung the ship in the indicated direction and set her traveling slowly toward the drifter. Winkle called an order over his shoulder.

"Winches and divers ready. The trap is unsafetied. Contact in five minutes?"

"Winch ready," Dandridge's deep voice reported as he swept his chessboard to one side and closed a master switch. Mancini, who had been facing him across the board, slipped farther aft to the laboratory which occupied over half of the *Shark*'s habitable part. He said nothing, since no order had been directed at him, and made no move to uncage any of his apparatus while the vessel was still in motion.

"Divers standing by." Farrell spoke for himself and his assistant after a brief check of masks and valves—both were already dressed for Arctic water. They took their places at either side of the red-checkered deck area, just forward of the lab section, which marked the main hatch. Dandridge, glancing up to make sure that no one was standing on it, opened the trap from his control console. Its halves slid smoothly apart, revealing the chill green liquid slipping between the hulls. At the *Shark*'s present speed she was floating at displacement depth, so that the water averaged about four meters down from the hatch; but this distance was varied by a swell of a meter or so. Farrell stood looking down at it, wailing patiently for the vessel to stop; his younger assistant dropped prone by the edge of the opening and craned his neck through it in an effort to see forward.

Ishihara's voice was barely audible over the wind now that the hatch was open, but occasional words drifted back to the divers. "Six hundred... as you go...four...three..."

"I see it," Winkle cut in. "I'll take her." He called over his shoulder again, "Farrell...Stubbs...we're coming up on one. You'll spot it in a minute. I'll tell you when I lose it under the bow."

"Yes, sir," acknowledged Farrell. "See it yet, Rick?"

"Not yet," was the response. "Nothing but jellyfish."

"Fifty meters," called the captain. "Now thirty." He cut the water jets to a point where steerage way would have been lost if such a term had meant anything to the *Shark,* and continued to inch forward. "Twenty."

"I see it," called Stubbs.

"All right," answered the captain. "Ten meters. Five. It's right under me; I've lost it. Con me, diver."

"About five meters, sir. It's dead center...four...three...two...all right, it's right under the hatch. Magnets ready, Gil?"

The magnetic grapple was at the forward end of its rail, directly over the hatch, so Dandridge was ready; but Winkle was not.

"Hold up...don't latch on yet. Stubbs, watch the fish; are we drifting?"

"A little, sir. It's going forward and a little to port...now you're stopping it...there."

"Quite a bit of wind," remarked the captain as his fingers lifted from the hydrojet controls. "All right. Pick it up,"

"Think the magnets will be all right, Marco?" asked Dandridge. "That whale looks funny to me." The mechanic joined the winchman and divers at the hatch and looked down at their floating problem.

At first glance the "whale" was ordinary enough. It was about two meters long, and perfectly cigar-shaped except where the intake ring broke the curve some forty centimeters back of the nose. The exhaust ports, about equally far from the tail end, were less visible since they were merely openings in the dark gray skin. Integument and openings alike were hard to see in detail, however; the entire organism was overgrown with a brownish, slimy-looking mass of filaments reminiscent both of mold and of sealskin.

"It's picked up something, all right," Mancini conceded. "I don't see why your magnets shouldn't work, though...unless you'd rather they didn't get dirty."

"All right. Get down the ladder and steer 'em, Rick." Dandridge caused a light alloy ladder to extend from the bow edge of the hatch as he spoke; then he fingered another switch which sent the grapples themselves slowly downward. Stubbs easily beat them to the foot of the ladder, hooked one leg through a rung, reached out with both arms and tried to steady the descending mass of metal. The *Shark* was pitching somewhat in the swell, and the eighty pounds of electromagnet and associated wiring was slightly rebellious. The youngest of the crew and the only nonspecialist among its members—he was still working off the two-year labor draft requirement which preceded higher education—Rick Stubbs got at least his share of the dirty work. He was not so young as to complain about it.

"Slower...slower...twenty c's to go...ten...hold it now...just a touch lower all right, juice!" Dandridge followed the instructions, fed current to the magnets, and started to lift,

"Wait!" the boy on the ladder called almost instantly. "It's not holding!"

The mechanic reacted almost as fast.

"Bring it up anyway!" he called. "The infection is sticking to the magnets. Let me get a sample!" Stubbs shrank back against the ladder as the slimy mass rose past him In response to Mancini's command. Dandridge grimaced with distaste as it came above deck level and into his view.

"You can have it!" he remarked, not very originally.

Mancini gave no answer, and showed no sign of any emotion but interest. He had slipped back into his lab as the material was ascending, and now returned with a two-liter flask and the biggest funnel he possessed.

"Run it aft a little," he said briefly. "That's enough...I'll miss some, and it might as well fall into the water as onto the deck." The grapple, which had crawled a few inches toward him on its overhead rail, stopped just short of the after edge of the hatch. Mancini, standing unconcernedly at the edge of the opening with the wind ruffling his clothes, held funnel and flask under the magnets.

"All right, Gil, drop it," he ordered. Dandridge obeyed.

Most of the mess fell obediently away from the grapple. Some landed in the funnel and proceeded to ooze down into the flask; some hit Mancini's extended arm without appearing to bother him; a little dropped onto the deck, to the winchman's visible disgust. Most fell past Stubbs back into the sea.

The mechanic took up some of the material from his arm and rubbed it between thumb and forefinger. "Gritty," he remarked. "And the magnets held this stuff, but not the whale's skeleton. That means that most of the skeleton must be gone, and I bet this grit is magnetite. I'll risk a dollar that this infection comes from that old 775-Fe-DE6 culture that got loose a few years ago from Passamaquoddy. I'll give it the works to make sure, though. You divers will have to use slings to get the fish aboard, I'm afraid."

"Rick, I'll send the magnets down first and you can rinse 'em off a bit in the water. Then I'll run out the sling and you can get it around the whale."

"All right, sir. Standing by." As the grapple went down again Dandridge called to the mechanic, who had turned back toward the lab.

"I suppose the whale is ruined, if you're right about the infection. Can we collect damages?" Mancini shook his head negatively.

"No one could collect from DE: they went broke years ago—from paying damages. Besides, the courts decided years ago that injury or destruction of a piece of pseudolife was recoverable property damage only if an original model was involved. This fish is a descendant of a model ten years old; it was born at sea. We didn't make it and can't recover for it." He turned to his bench, but flung a last thought over his shoulder. "My guess that this pest is a DE escapee could be wrong, too. They worked out a virus for that strain a few months after it escaped, and I haven't heard of an iron infection in four years. This may be a mutation of it— that's still my best guess—but it could also be something entirely new." He settled himself onto a stool and began dividing the material from the flask into the dozens of tiny containers which fed the analyzers.

In the water below, Stubbs had plunged from the ladder and was removing slime from the grapple magnets. The stuff was not too sticky, and the grit which might be magnetite slightly offset the feeling of revulsion which the boy normally had for slimy materials, so he was able to finish the job quickly enough to keep Dandridge happy. At Rick's call, the grapple was retracted; a few moments later the hoist cable came down again with an ordinary sling at its extremity. Stubbs was still in the water, and Farrell had come part way down the ladder. The chief diver guided the cable down to his young assistant, who began working the straps around the torpedo-like form which still bobbed between the *Shark*'s hulls,

It was quite a job. The zeowhale was still slippery, since the magnets had not come even close to removing all the foreign growth. When the boy tried to reach around it to fasten the straps it slithered away from him. He called for more slack and tried to pin it against one of the hulls as he worked, but still it escaped him. He was too stubborn to ask for help, and by this time Farrell was laughing too hard to have provided much anyway.

"Ride him, Buster!" the chief diver called as Stubbs finally managed to scissor the slippery cylinder with his legs. "That's it...you've got him dogged now!"

The boy hadn't quite finished, actually, but one strap did seem secure around the forward part of the hull. "Take up slack!" he called up to the hatch, without answering Farrell's remark.

Dandridge had been looking through the trap and could see what was needed; he reached to his control console and the hoist cable tightened.

"That's enough!" called Stubbs as the nose of the zeowhale began to lift from the water. "Hold it until I get another strap on, or this one will slip free!"

Winches obediently ceased purring. With its motion restrained somewhat, the little machine offered less opposition to the attachment of a second band near its stern. The young swimmer called, somewhat breathlessly, "Take it up!" and paddled himself slowly back to the ladder. Farrell gave him a hand up, and they reached the deck almost as quickly as the specimen.

Dandridge closed the hatch without waiting for orders, though he left the ladder down—there would be other pickups in the next few minutes, but the wind was cold and loud. Stubbs paid no attention; he barely heard the soft "Eight hundred meters, seventy-five mils to starboard," as he made his way around the closing hatch to Mancini's work station. The mechanic's job was much more fascinating than the pilot's.

He knew better than to interrupt a busy professional with questions, but the mechanic didn't need any. Like several other men, not only on the *Shark* but among the crew of her mother ship, Mancini had come to like the youngster and respect his general competence; and like most professionals, his attitude toward an intelligent labor draftee was a desire to recruit him before someone else did. The man, therefore, began to talk as soon as he noticed the boy's presence.

"You know much about either chemical or field analysis, Rick?"

"A little. I can recognize most of your gear—ultracentrifuge, chromatographic and electrophoretic stuff, NMR equipment, and so on. Is that," he pointed to a cylindrical machine on another bench, "a diffraction camera?"

"Good guess. It's a hybrid that a friend of mine dreamed up which can be used either for electron microphotography or diffraction work. All that comes a bit later, though. One thing about analysis hasn't changed since the beginning; you try to get your initial sample into as many different homogeneous parts as possible before you get down to the molecular scale."

"So each of these little tubes you're filling goes through centrifuge, or solvation, or electrophoresis—"

"More usually, through all of them, in different orders."

"I should think that just looking at the original, undamaged specimen would tell you *something*. Don't you ever do that?"

"Sure. The good old light microscope will never disappear; as you imply, it's helpful to see a machine in its assembled state, too. I'll have some slides in a few more seconds; the mike is in that cabinet. Slide it out, will you?"

Stubbs obeyed, literally since the instrument was mounted on a track. The designers of the *Shark*'s laboratory had made it as immune to rough weather as they could. Mancini took the first of his slides, clipped it under the objective, and took one look.

"Thought so," he grunted. "Here, see for yourself."

Stubbs applied an eye to the instrument, played briefly with the fine focus—he had the normal basic training in fundamental apparatus—and looked for several seconds.

"Just a mess of living cells that don't mean much to me, and a lot of little octahedra. Are they what you mean?"

"Yep. Magnetite crystals, or I'm a draft-dodger." (His remark had no military significance; the term now referred to individuals who declined the unskilled-labor draft, voluntarily giving up their rights to higher education and, in effect, committing themselves to living on basic relief.) "We'll make sure, though." The mechanic slid another piece of equipment into position on the microscope stage, and peered once more into the field of view. Stubbs recognized a micromanipulator, and was not surprised when Mancini, after two minutes or so of silent work, straightened up and removed a small strip of metal from it. Presumably one of the tiny crystals was now mounted on the strip.

The mechanic turned to the diffraction camera, mounted the bit of metal in a clamp attached to it, and touched a button which started specimen and strip on a journey into the camera's interior. Moments later a pump started to whine.

"Five minutes to vacuum, five more for scanning," he remarked. "We might as well have a look at the fish itself while we wait; even naked-eye examination has its uses." He got up from his seat, stretched, and turned to the bench on which the ruined zeowhale lay. "How much do you know about these things, Rick? Can you recognize this type?"

"I think so. I'd say it was a copper-feeder of about '35 model. This one would be about two years old."

"Good. I'd say you were about right. You've been doing some reading, I take it."

"Some. And the *Guppy*'s shop is a pretty good museum."

"True enough. Do you know where the access regions are on this model?"

"I've seen some of them opened up, but I wouldn't feel sure enough to do it myself."

"It probably wouldn't matter if you did it wrong in this case; this one is safely dead. Still, I'll show you; better see it right than do it wrong." He had removed the straps of the sling once the "fish" had been lowered onto a rack on the bench, so nothing interfered with the demonstration. "Here," he pointed, "the reference is the centerline of scales along the back, just a little lighter in color than the rest. Start at the intake ring and count eight scales back; then down six on either side, like that. That puts you on this scale…so…which you can get under with a scalpel at the start of the main opening." He picked up an instrument about the size of a surgical scalpel, but with a blunt, rounded blade. This he inserted under the indicated scale. "See, it comes apart here with very light pressure, and you can run the cut back to just in front of the exhaust vents—like that. If this were a living specimen, the cut would heal under sealant spray in about an hour after the fish was back in the water. This one…hm-m-m. No wonder it passed out. I wonder what this stuff is?"

The body cavity of the zeowhale was filled with a dead-black jelly, quite different in appearance from the growth which had covered the skin. The mechanic applied retractors to the incision, and began silently poking into the material with a variety of "surgical" tools. He seemed indifferent to the feelings which were tending to bring Stubbs' stomach almost as much into daylight as that of the whale.

Pieces of rubbery internal machinery began to litter the bench top. Another set of tiny test tubes took samples of the black jelly, and followed their predecessors into the automatic analyzers. These began to hum and sputter as they went to work on the new material—they had long since finished with the first load, and a pile of diagrams and numerical tables awaited Mancini's attention in their various delivery baskets. He had not even taken time to see whether his guess about magnetite had been good.

Some of the organs on the desk were recognizable to the boy—for any large animal, of course, a heart is fairly obviously a heart when it has been dissected sufficiently to show its valve structure. A four-kilogram copper nugget had come from the factory section; the organism had at least started to fulfill its intended purpose before disease had ended its pseudolife. It had also been developing normally in other respects, as a twenty-five-centimeter embryo indicated. The zeowhales and their kindred devices reproduced asexually; the genetic variation magnification, which is the biological advantage of sex, was just what the users of the pseudo-organisms did not want, at least until some factor could be developed which would tend to select for the characteristics they wanted most.

Mancini spent more than an hour at his rather revolting task before he finally laid down his instruments. Stubbs had not been able to watch him the whole time, since the *Shark* had picked up the other two unresponsive whales while the job was going on. Both had been infected in the same way as the first. The boy was back in the lab, though, when the gross dissection of the original one was finished. So was Winkle, since nothing more could be planned until Mancini produced some sort of report.

"The skeleton was gone completely," was the mechanic's terse beginning. "Even the unborn one hadn't a trace of metallic iron in it. That was why the magnets didn't hold, of course. I haven't had time to look at any of the analysis reports, but I'm pretty certain that the jelly in the body cavity and the moldy stuff outside are part of the same life form, and that organism dissolved the metallic skeleton and precipitated the iron as magnetite in its own tissues. Presumably it's a mutant from one of the regular iron-feeding strains. Judging by its general cellular conformation, its genetic tape is a purine-pyrimidine nucleotide quite similar to that of natural life—"

"Just another of the original artificial forms coming home to roost?" interjected Winkle.

"I suppose so. I've isolated some of the nuclear material, but it will have to go back to the big field analyzer on the *Guppy* to make sure."

"There seem to be no more damaged fish in the neighborhood. Is there any other material you need before we go back?"

"No. Might as well wind her up, as far as I'm concerned—unless it would be a good idea to call the ship first while we're out here to find out whether any other schools this way need checking."

"You can't carry any more specimens in your lab even if they do," Winkle pointed out, glancing around the littered bench tops.

"True enough. Maybe there's something which wouldn't need a major checkup, though. But you're the captain; play it as you think best. I'll be busy with this lot until we get back to the *Guppy* whether we go straight there or not."

"I'll call." The captain turned away to his own station.

"I wonder why they made the first pseudolife machines with gene tapes so much like the real thing," Stubbs remarked when Winkle was back in his seat. "You'd think they'd foresee what mutations could do, and that organisms too similar to genuine life might even give rise to forms which could cause disease in us as well as in other artificial forms."

"They thought of it, all right," replied Mancini. "That possibility was a favorite theme of the opponents of the whole process—at least, of the ones who weren't driven by frankly religious motives. Unfortunately, there was no other way the business could have developed. The original research of course had to be carried out on what you call 'real' life. That led to the specific knowledge that the cytosine-thiamine-adenine-guanine foursome of ordinary DNA could form a pattern which was both self-replicating and able to control polypeptide and polysaccharide synthesis—"

"But I thought it was more complex than that; there are phosphates and sugars in the chain, and the DNA imprints RNA, and—"

"You're quite right, but I wasn't giving a chemistry lecture; I was trying to make an historical point. I'm saying that at first, no one realized that anything except those four specific bases could do the genetic job. Then they found that quite a lot of natural life forms had variations of those bases in their nucleotides, and gradually the reasons *why* those structures, or rather their potential fields, had the polymer molding ability they do became clear. Then, and only then, was it obvious that 'natural' genes aren't the only possible ones; they're simply the ones which got a head start on this planet. There are as many ways of building a gene as there are of writing a poem—or of making an airplane if you prefer to stay on the physical plane. As you seem to know, using the channels of a synthetic zeolite as the backbone for a genetic tape happens to be a very convenient technique when we want to grow a machine like the one we've just taken apart here. It's bulkier than the phosphate-sugar-base tape, but a good deal more stable.

"It's still handy, though, to know how to work with the real thing—after all, you know as well as I do that the reason you have a life expectancy of about a hundred and fifty years is that your particular gene pattern is on file in half a cubic meter of zeolite mesh in Denver under a nice file number..."

"O26-18-5633," muttered the boy under his breath.

"...which will let any halfway competent molecular mechanic like me grow replacement parts and tissues if and when you happen to need them."

"I know all that, but it still seems dangerous to poke around making little changes in ordinary life forms," replied Rick. "There must be fifty thousand people like you in the world, who could tailor a dangerous virus, or germ, or crop fungus in a couple of weeks of lab and computer work, and whose regular activities produce things like that iron-feeder which can mutate into dangerous by-products."

"It's also dangerous to have seven billion people on the planet, practically every one of whom knows how to light a fire," replied Mancini. "Dangerous or not, it was no more possible to go from Watson and Crick and the DNA structure to this zeowhale without the intermediate development than it would have been to get from the Wright brothers and their powered kite to the two-hour transatlantic ramjet without building Ford tri-motors and DC-3's in between. We have the knowledge, it's an historical fact that no one can effectively destroy it, so we might as well use it. The fact that so many competent practitioners of the art exist is our best safeguard if it does get a little out of hand at times."

The boy looked thoughtful.

"Maybe you have something there," he said slowly. "But with all that knowledge, why only a hundred and fifty years? Why can't you keep people going indefinitely?"

"Do you think we should?" Mancini countered with a straight face. Rick grinned.

"Stop ducking. If you could, you would—for some people anyway. Why can't you?" Mancini shrugged.

"Several hundred million people undoubtedly know the rules of chess." He nodded toward the board on Dandridge's control table. "Why aren't they all good players? You know, don't you, why doctors were reluctant to use hormones as therapeutic agents even when they became available in quantity?"

"I think so. If you gave someone cortisone it might do what you wanted, but it might also set other glands going or slow them down, which would alter the levels of other hormones, which in turn...well, it was a sort of chain reaction which could end anywhere."

"Precisely. And gene-juggling is the same only more so. If you were to sit at the edge of the hatch there and let Gil close it on you, I could rig the factors in your gene pattern so as to let you grow new legs; but there would be a distinct risk of affecting other things in your system at the same time. In effect, I would be taking certain *restraints* which caused your legs to stop growing when they were completed *off* your cell-dividing control mechanisms—the sort of thing that used to happen as a natural, random effect in cancer. I'd probably get away with it—or rather, you would—since you're only about nineteen and still pretty deep in what we call the stability well. As you get older, though, with more and more factors interfering with that stability, the job gets harder—it's a literal juggling act, with more and more balls being tossed to the juggler every year you live.

"You were born with a deep enough stability reserve to keep yourself operating for a few decades without any applied biochemical knowledge; you might live twenty years or ninety. Using the knowledge we have, we can play the game longer; but sooner or later we drop the ball. It's not that we don't know the rules; to go back to the chess analogy, it's just that there are too many pieces on the board to keep track of all at once."

Stubbs shook his head. "I've never thought of it quite that way. To me, it's always been just a repair job, and I couldn't see why it should be so difficult."

Mancini grinned. "Maybe your cultural grounding didn't include a poem called the 'The Wonderful One-Hoss Shay.' Well, we'll be a couple of hours getting back to the *Guppy*. There are a couple of sets of analysis runs sitting with us here. Maybe, if I start trying to turn those into language you can follow, you'll have some idea of why the game is so hard before we get there, Maybe, too"—his face sobered somewhat—"you'll start to see why, even though we always lose in the end, the game is so much fun. It isn't just that our own lives are at stake, you know; men have been playing that kind of game for two million years or so. Come on."

He turned to the bench top on which the various analyzers had been depositing their results; and since Stubbs had a good grounding in mathematical and chemical fundamentals, their language ceased to resemble Basic English. Neither paid any attention as the main driving turbines of the *Shark* came up to quarter speed and the vessel began to pick her way out of the patch of ice floes where the zeowhales had been collecting metal.

By the time Winkle had reached open water and Ishihara had given him the clearance for high cruise, the other four had lost all contact with the outside world. Dandridge's chess board was in use again, with Farrell now his opponent. The molecular mechanic and his possible apprentice were deeply buried in a task roughly equivalent to explaining to a forty-piece orchestra how to produce *Aida* from overture to finale—without the use of written music. Stubbs' basic math was, for this problem, equivalent to having learned just barely his "do, re, mi."

There was nothing to distract the players of either game. The wind had freshened somewhat, but the swells had increased little if at all. With the *Shark* riding on her hydrofoils there was only the faintest of tremors as her struts cut the waves. The sun was still high and the sky almost cloudless. Between visual pilotage and sonar, life seemed as uncomplicated as it ever gets for the operator of a high-speed vehicle.

The *Guppy* was nearly two hundred kilometers to the south, far beyond sonar range. Four of her other boats were out on business, and Winkle occasionally passed a word or two with their commanders; but no one had anything of real importance to say. The desultory conversations were a matter of habit, to make sure that everyone was still on the air. No pilot, whether of aircraft, space vessel, surface ship, or submarine, attaches any weight to the proverb that no news is good news.

Just who was to blame for the interruption of this idyll remains moot. Certainly Mancini had given the captain his preliminary ideas about the pest which had killed their first whale. Just as certainly he had failed to report the confirmation of that opinion after going through the lab results with Stubbs. Winkle himself made no request for such confirmation—there was no particular reason why he should, and if he had it is hard to believe that he would either have realized all the implications or been able to do anything about them. The fact remains that everyone from Winkle at the top of the ladder of command to Stubbs at the bottom was taken completely by surprise when the *Shark's* starboard after hydrofoil strut snapped cleanly off just below the mean planing water line.

At sixty-five knots, no human reflexes could have coped with the result. The electronic ones of the *Shark* tried, but the vessel's mechanical I.Q. was not up to the task of allowing for the lost strut. As the gyros sensed the drop in the right rear quadrant of their field of perception, the autopilot issued commands to increase the angle of attack of the control foils on that strut. Naturally there was no response. The dip increased. By the time it got beyond the point where the machine thought it could be handled by a single set of foils, so that orders went out to decrease lift on the port-bow leg, it was much too late. The after portion of the starboard flotation hull smacked a wave top at sixty-five knots and, of course, bounced. The bounce was just in time to reinforce the letdown command to the port-bow control foils. The bow curve of the port hull struck in its turn, with almost undiminished speed and with two principal results.

About a third of the *Shark's* forward speed vanished in less than the same fraction of a second as she gave up kinetic energy to the water in front, raising a cloud of spray more than a hundred meters and subjecting hull and contents to about four gravities of acceleration in a most unusual direction. The rebound was high enough to cause the starboard "wing" to dip into the waves, and the *Shark* did a complete double cartwheel. For a moment she seemed to poise motionless with port wing and hull entirely submerged and the opposite wing tip pointing at the sky; then, grudgingly, she settled back to a nearly horizontal position on her flotation hulls and lay rocking on the swell.

Externally she showed little sign of damage. The missing strut was, of course, under water anyway, and her main structure had taken only a few dents. The propellers had been twisted off by gyroscopic action during the cartwheel. Aside from this, the sleek form looked ready for service.

Inside, things were different, Most of the apparatus, and even some of the men, had been more or less firmly fixed in place; but the few exceptions had raised a good deal of mayhem.

Winkle and Ishihara were unconscious, though still buckled in their seats. Both had been snapped forward against their respective panels, and were draped with sundry unappetizing fragments of the dissected zeowhale. Ishihara's head had shattered the screen of his sonar instrument, and no one could have told at first glance how many cuts were supplying the blood on his face.

The chess players had both left impressions on the control panel of the winch and handling system, and now lay crumpled beside it. Neither was bleeding visibly, but Farrell's arms were both twisted at angles impossible to intact bones. Dandridge was moaning and just starting to try to get to his feet; he and Mancini were the only ones conscious.

The mechanic had been seated at one of his benches facing the starboard side of the ship when the impact came. He had not been strapped in his seat, and the four-G jerk had started to hurl him toward the bow. His right leg had stopped him almost as suddenly by getting entangled in the underpinning of the seat The limb was not quite detached from its owner; oddly enough, its skin was intact. This was about the only bit of tissue below the knee for which this statement could he made,

Stubbs had been standing at the mechanic's side. They were to argue later whether it had been good or bad luck that the side in question had been the left. It depended largely on personal viewpoint. There had been nothing for Rick to seize as he was snatched toward the bow or, if there was, he had not been quick enough or strong enough to get it. He never knew just what hit him in flight; the motions of the *Shark* were so wild that it might have been deck, overhead, or the back of one of the pilot seats. It was evident enough that his path had intersected that of the big flask in which Mancini had first collected the iron-feeding tissue, but whether the flask was still whole at the time remains unclear. It is hard to see how he could have managed to absorb so many of its fragments had it already shattered, but it is equally hard to understand how he could have scattered them so widely over his anatomy if it had been whole.

It was Stubbs, or rather the sight of him, that got Mancini moving. Getting his own shattered leg disentangled from the chair was a distracting task, but not distracting enough to let him take his eyes from the boy a few meters away. Arterial bleeding is a sight that tends to focus attention.

He felt sick, over and above the pain of his leg; whether it was the sight of Rick or incipient shock he couldn't tell. He did his best to ignore the leg as he inched across the deck, though the limb itself seemed to have other ideas. Unfortunately these weren't very consistent; sometimes it wanted—demanded——his whole mind, at others it seemed to have gone off somewhere on its own and hidden. He did not look back to see whether it was still with him; what was in front was more important.

The boy still had blood when Mancini reached him, as well as a functioning heart to pump it. He was not losing the fluid as fast as had appeared from a distance, but something would obviously have to be done about what was left of his right hand—the thumb and about half of the palm. The mechanic had been raised during one of the periods when first-aiders were taught to abjure the tourniquet, but had reached an age where judgment stands a chance against rules. He had a belt and used it.

A close look at the boy's other injuries showed that nothing could be done about them on the spot; they were bleeding slowly, but any sort of first aid would be complicated by the slivers of glass protruding from most of them. Face, chest, and even legs were slashed freely, but the rate of bleeding was not—Mancini hoped—really serious. The smaller ones were clotting already.

Dandridge was on his feet by now, badly bruised but apparently in the best shape of the six.

"What can I do, Marco?" he asked. "Everyone else is out cold. Should I use—"

"Don't use anything on them until we're sure there are no broken necks or backs; they may be better off unconscious. I know I would be."

"Isn't there dope in the first-aid kit? I could give you a shot of pain-killer."

"Not yet, anyway. Anything that would stop this leg from hurting would knock me out, and I've got to stay awake if at all possible until help comes. The lab equipment isn't really meant for repair work, but if anything needs to be improvised from it. I'll have to be the one to do it.

I could move around better, though, if this leg were splinted. Use the raft foam from the handling locker."

Five minutes later Mancini's leg, from mid-thigh down, was encased in a bulky, light, but reasonably rigid block of foamed resin whose original purpose was to provide on-the-spot flotation for objects which were inconvenient or impossible to bring aboard. It still hurt, but he could move around without much fear of doing the limb further damage.

"Good. Now you'd better see what communication gear, if any, stood up under this bump. I'll do what I can for the others. Don't move Ishi or the captain; work around them until I've done what I can."

Dandridge went forward to the conning section and began to manipulate switches. He was not a trained radioman—the *Shark* didn't carry one—but like any competent crew member he could operate all the vessel's equipment under routine conditions. He found quickly that no receivers were working, but that the regular transmitter drew current when its switches were closed. An emergency low-frequency beacon, entirely separate from the other communication equipment, also seemed intact; so he set this operating and began to broadcast the plight of the *Shark* on the regular transmitter. He had no way of telling whether either signal was getting out, but was not particularly worried for himself. The *Shark* was theoretically unsinkable—enough of her volume was filled with resin foam to buoy her entire weight even in fresh water. The main question was whether help would arrive before some of the injured men were beyond it.

After ten minutes of steady broadcasting—he hoped—Dandridge turned back to the mechanic, to find him lying motionless on the deck. For a moment the winchman thought he might have lost consciousness; then Mancini spoke.

"I've done all I can for the time being. I've splinted Joe's arms and pretty well stopped Rick's bleeding. Ishi has a skull fracture and the captain at least a concussion; don't move either one. If you've managed to get in touch with the *Guppy,* tell them about the injuries. We'll need gene records from Denver for Rick, probably for Ishi, and possibly for the captain. They should start making blood for Rick right away, the second enough gene data is through; he's lost quite a bit."

"I don't know whether I'm getting out or not, but I'll say it all anyway," replied Dandridge, turning back to the board. "Won't you need some pretty extensive repair work yourself, though?"

"Not unless these bone fragments do more nerve damage than I think they have," replied Mancini. "Just tell them that I have a multiple leg fracture. If I know Bert Jellinge, he'll have gene blocks on all six of us growing into the machines before we get back to the *Guppy* anyway."

Dandridge eyed him more closely. "Hadn't I better give you a shot now?" he asked. "You said you'd done all you could, and it might be better to pass out from a sleepy shot than from pain. How about it?"

"Get that message out first. I can hold on, and what I've done is the flimsiest of patchwork. With the deck tossing as it is any of those splints may be inadequate. We can't strap any of the fellows down, and if the wave motion rolls one of them over I'll have the patching to do all over again. When you get that call off, look at Rick once more; I think his bleeding has stopped, but until he's on a repair table I won't be happy about him."

"So you'd rather stay awake."

"Not exactly, but if you were in the kid's place, wouldn't you prefer me to?" Dandridge had no answer to that one; he talked into the transmitter instead.

His words, as it happened, were getting out. The *Conger*, the nearest of the *Shark's* sister fish-tenders, had already started toward them; she had about forty kilometers to come. On the *Guppy* the senior mechanic had fulfilled Mancini's prediction; he had already made contract with Denver, and Rick Stubbs' gene code was about to start through the multiple-redundant communication channels used for the purpose—channels which, fortunately, had just been freed of the saturation caused by a serious explosion in Pittsburgh, which had left over five hundred people in need of major repair. The full transmission would take over an hour at the highest safe scanning rate; but the first ten minutes would give enough information, when combined with the basic human data already in the *Guppy's* computers, to permit the synthesis of replacement blood.

The big mother-ship was heading toward the site of the accident so as to shorten the *Conger's* journey with the victims, The operations center at Cape Farewell had offered a "mastodon"—one of the gigantic helicopters capable of lifting the entire weight of a ship like the *Shark*. After a little slide-rule work, the *Guppy's* commander had declined; no time would have been saved, and the elimination of one ship-to-ship transfer for the injured men was probably less important than economy of minutes.

Mancini would have agreed with this, had he been able to join in the discussion. By the time Dandridge had finished his second transmission, however, the mechanic had fainted from the pain of his leg.

Objectively, the winchman supposed that it was probably good for his friend to be unconscious. He was not too happy, though, at being the only one aboard who could take responsibility for anything. The half hour it took for the *Conger* to arrive was not a restful one for him, though it could not have been less eventful. Even sixty years later, when the story as his grandchildren heard it included complications like a North Atlantic winter gale, he was never able to paint an adequate word picture of his feelings during those thirty minutes—much less an exaggerated one.

The manta-like structure of the tenders made transshipping most practical from bow-to-bow contact, but it was practical at all only on a smooth sea. In the present case, the *Conger's* commander could not bring her bow closer than ten meters to that of the crippled ship, and both were pitching too heavily even for lines to be used.

One of the *Conger's* divers plunged into the water and swam to the helpless vessel. Dandridge saw him coming through the bow ports, went back to his console, and rather to his surprise found that the hatch and ladder responded to their control switches. Moments later the other man was on the deck beside him.

The diver took in the situation after ten seconds of explanation by Dandridge and two of direct examination, and spoke into the transmitter which was part of his equipment. A few seconds later a raft dropped from the *Conger's* hatch and two more men clambered down into it. One of these proved on arrival to be Mancini's opposite number, who wasted no time.

"Use the foam," he directed. "Case them all up except for faces; that way we can get them to the bench without any more limb motion. You say Marco thought there might be skull or spine fractures?"

"He said Ishi had a fractured skull and Winkle might have. All he said about spines was that we'd have to be careful in case it had happened."

"Right. You relax; I'll take care of it." The newcomer took up the foam generator and went to work.

Twenty minutes later the *Conger* was on her hydroplanes once more, heading for rendezvous with the *Guppy*.

In spite of tradition, Rick Stubbs knew where he was when he opened his eyes. The catch was that he hadn't the faintest idea how he had gotten there. He could see that he was surrounded by blood-transfusion equipment, electronic circulatory and nervous system monitoring gear, and the needle-capillary-and-computer maze of a regeneration unit, though none of the stuff seemed to be in operation. He was willing to grant from all this that he had been hurt somehow; the fact that he was unable to move his head or his right arm supported this notion. He couldn't begin to guess, however, what sort of injury it might be or how it had happened.

He remembered talking and working with Mancini at the latter's lab bench. He could not recall for certain just what the last thing said or done might be, though; somehow the picture merged with the foggy struggle back to consciousness which had culminated in recognition of his surroundings.

He could see no one near him, but this might be because his head wouldn't turn. Could he talk? Only one way to find out.

"Is anyone here? What's happened to me?" It didn't sound very much like his own voice, and the effort of speech hurt his chest and abdomen; but apparently words got out.

"We're all here, Rick. I thought you'd be switching back on about now." Mancini's face appeared in Stubbs' narrow field of vision.

"We're *all* here? Did everyone get hurt somehow? What happened?"

"Slight correction—most of us are here, one's been and gone. I'll tell you as much as I can; don't bother to ask questions, I know it must hurt you to talk. Gil was here for a while, but he just had a few bruises and is back on the job. The rest of us were banged up more thoroughly. My right leg was a jigsaw puzzle; Bert had an interesting time with it. I thought he ought to take it off and start over, but he stuck with it, so I got off with five hours of manual repair and two in regeneration instead of a couple of months hooked up to a computer. I'm still splinted, but that will be for only a few more days.

"No one knows yet just what happened. Apparently the *Shark* hit something going at full clip, but no one knows yet what it was. They're towing her in; I trust there'll be enough evidence to tell us the whole story."

"How about the other fellows?"

"Ishi is plugged in. He may need a week with computer regeneration control, or ten times that. We won't be able to assess brain damage until we find how close to consciousness he can come. He had a bad skull fracture. The captain was knocked out, and some broken ribs I missed on the first-aid check did internal damage. Bert is still trying to get him off without regeneration, but I don't think he'll manage it."

"You didn't think he could manage it with you, either."

"True. Maybe it's just that I don't think I could do it myself, and hate to admit that Jellinge is better at my own job than I am."

"How about Joe?"

"Both arms broken and a lot of bruises. He'll he all right. That leaves you, young fellow. You're not exactly a critical case, but you are certainly going to call for professional competence. How fond are you of your fingerprints?"

"What? I don't track."

"Most of your right hand was sliced off, apparently by flying glass from my big culture flask. Ben Tulley from the *Conger*, which picked us up, found the missing section and brought it back; it's in culture now."

"What has that to do with fingerprints? Why didn't you or Mr. Jell-inge graft it back?"

"Because there's a good deal of doubt about its condition. It was well over an hour after the accident before it got into culture. You know the sort of brain damage a few minutes without oxygen can do. I know the bone, tendon, and connective tissue in a limb is much less sensitive to that sort of damage, but an hour is a long time, chemically speaking. Grafting calls for healing powers which are nearly as dependent on genetic integrity as is nerve activity; we're just not sure whether grafting is the right thing to do in your case. It's a toss-up whether we should fasten the hand back on and work to make it take, or discard it and grow you a new one. That's why I asked how much you loved your fingerprints."

"Wouldn't a new hand have the same prints?"

"The same print classification, which is determined genetically, but not the same details, which are random."

"Which would take longer?"

"If the hand is in shape to take properly, grafting would be quicker—say a week. If it isn't, we might be six or eight times as long repairing secondary damage. That's longer than complete regeneration would take."

"When are you going to make up your minds?"

"Soon. I wondered whether you'd have a preference."

"How could I know which is better when you don't? Why ask me at all?"

"I had a reason—several, in fact. I'll tell you what they were after you've had two years of professional training in molecular mechanics, if you decide to come into the field. You still haven't told me which you prefer."

The boy looked up silently for a full minute. Actually, he spent very little of that time trying to make his mind up; he was wondering what Mancini's reasons might be. He gave up, flipped a mental coin, and said, "I think I'd prefer the original hand, if there's a real chance of getting it back and it won't keep me plugged in to these machines any longer than growing a new one would."

"All right, we'll try it that way. Of course, you'll be plugged in for quite a while anyway, so if we do have trouble with the hand it won't make so much difference with your time."

"What do you mean? What's wrong besides the hand?"

"You hadn't noticed that your head is clamped?"

"Well, yes; I knew I couldn't move it, but I can't feel anything wrong. What's happened there?"

"Your face stopped most of the rest of the flask, apparently."

"Then how can I be seeing at all, and how is it that I talk so easily?"

"If I knew that much about probability, I'd stop working for a living and take up professional gambling. When I first saw you after your face had been cleaned off and before the glass had been taken out, I wondered for a moment whether there hadn't been something planned about the arrangement of the slivers. It was unbelievable, but that's the way it happened. They say anything can happen once, but I'd advise you not to catch any more articles of glassware with your face,"

"Just what was it like, Marco? Give me the details."

"Frankly, I'd rather not. There are record photos, of course, but if I have anything to say about it you won't see them until the rebuilding is done. Then you can look in a mirror to reassure yourself when the photos get your stomach. No"—as Stubbs tried to interrupt—"I respect what you probably think of as your clinical detachment, but I doubt very strongly that you could maintain it in the face of the real thing. I'm pretty sure that I couldn't, if it were my face." Mancini's thoughts flashed back to the long moments when he had been dragging his ruined leg across the *Shark*'s deck toward the bleeding boy, and felt a momentary glow—maybe that disclaimer had been a little too modest. He stuck to his position, however.

Rick didn't argue too hard, for another thought had suddenly struck his mind. "You're using regeneration on my face, without asking me whether I want it the way you did with my hand. Right?"

"That's right," Mancini said.

"That means I'm so badly damaged that ordinary healing won't take care of it,"

Mancini pursed his lips and thought carefully before answering. "You'd heal, all right," he admitted at last. "You might just possibly, considering your age, heal without too much scarring. I'd hesitate to bet on that, though, and the scars you could come up with would leave you quite a mess."

Stubbs lay silent for a time, staring at the featureless ceiling. The mechanic was sure his expression would have been thoughtful had enough of the young face been visible to make one. He could not, however, guess at what was bothering the boy. As far as Mancini could guess from their work together there was no question of personal cowardice—for that matter, the mechanic could not see what there might be to fear. His profession made him quite casual about growing tissue, natural or artificial, on human bodies or anywhere else. Stubbs was in no danger of permanent disfigurement, crippling damage, or even severe pain; but something was obviously bothering the kid,

"Marco," the question came finally, "just where does detailed genetic control end, in tissue growth, and statistical effects take over?"

"There's no way to answer that both exactly and generally. Genetic factors are basically probability ones, but they're characterized by regions of high probability which we call stability wells. I told you about finger-prints, but each different situation would call for a different specific an-swer."

"It was what you said about prints that made me think of it. You're going to rebuild my face, you say. You won't tell me just how much re-building has to be done, but you admitted I *could* heal normally. If you rebuild, how closely will you match my original face? Does that statisti-cal factor of yours take over somewhere along the line?"

"Statistical factors are everywhere, and work throughout the whole process," replied Mancini without in the least meaning to he evasive. "I told you that. By rights, your new face should match the old as closely as the faces of identical twins match each other, and for the same reason. I grant that someone who knows the twins really well can usually tell them apart, but no one will have your old face around for close comparison. No one will have any doubt that it's you, I promise."

"Unless something goes wrong."

"If it goes wrong enough to bother you, we can always do it over."

"But it might go really wrong."

Mancini, who would have admitted that the sun might not rise the next day if enough possible events all happened at once, did not deny this, though he was beginning to feel irritated. "Does this mean that you don't want us to do the job? Just take your chances on the scars?" he asked.

"Why do scars form, anyway?" was the counter. "Why can't regular, normal genetic material reproduce the tissue it produced in the first place? It certainly does sometimes; why not always?"

"That's pretty hard to explain in words. It has to do with the factors which stopped your nose growing before it became an elephant's trunk— or more accurately, with the factors which stopped your overall growth where they did. I can describe them quite completely, and I believe quite accurately, but not in Basic English."

"Can you measure those factors in a particular ease?"

"Hm-m-m, yes; fairly accurately, anyway." Stubbs pounced on this with an eagerness which should have told the mechanic something.

"Then can't you tell whether these injuries, in my particular case, will heal completely or leave sears?"

"I...well, I suppose so. Let's see; it would take...hm-m-m; I'll have to give it some thought. It's not regular technique. We usually just rebuild. What's your objection, anyway? All rebuilding really means is that we set things going and then watch the process, practically cell by cell, and cor-rect what's happening if it isn't right—following the plans you used in the first place."

"I still don't see why my body can't follow them without your help."

"Well, no analogy is perfect; but roughly speaking, it's because the cells which will have to divide to produce the replacement tissue had the blueprints which they used for the original construction stamped 'production complete; file in reference storage' some years ago, and the stamp marks covered some of the lines on the plans." Mancini's temper was getting a little short, as his tone showed. Theoretically his leg should not have been hurting him, but he had been standing on it longer than any repairman would have advised at its present stage of healing. And why did the kid keep beating around the bush?

Stubbs either didn't notice the tone or didn't care.

"But the plans—the information—that's still there; even I know that much molecular biology. I haven't learned how to use your analysis gear yet, much less to reduce the readings; but I can't see why you'd figure it much harder to read the plans under the 'file' stamp than to work out the ability of that magnetite slime to digest iron from the base configuration of a single cell's genes."

"Your question was why your body couldn't do it; don't change the rules in the middle of the game. I didn't say that *I* couldn't; I could. What I said was that it isn't usual, and I can't see what will be gained by it; you'd at least double the work. I'm not exactly lazy, but the work at best is difficult, precise, and time consuming. If someone were to paint your portrait and had asked you whether you wanted it on canvas or paper, would you dither along asking about the brand of paint and the sizes of brushes he was going to use.

"I don't think that's a very good analogy. I just want to know what to expect—"

"You can't *know* what to expect. No one can. Ever. You have to play the odds. At the moment, the odds are so high in your favor that you'd almost be justified in saying that you know what's going to happen. All I'm asking is that you tell me straight whether or not you want Bert and me to ride control as your face heals, or let it go its own way."

"But if you can grow a vine that produces ham sandwiches instead of pumpkins, why—" Mancini made a gesture of impatience. He liked the youngster and still hoped to recruit him, but there are limits.

"Will you stop sounding like an anti-vivisectionist who's been asked for a statement on heart surgery and give me a straight answer to a straight question? The chances are all I can give you. They are much less than fifty-fifty that your face will come out of this without scars on its own. They are much better than a hundred to one that even your mother will never know there's been a controlled regeneration job done on you unless you tell her. You're through general education, legally qualified to make decisions involving your own life and health, and morally obligated to make them instead of lying there dithering. Let's have an answer."

For fully two minutes, he did not get it. Rick lay still, his expression hidden in dressings, eyes refusing to meet those of the man who stood by the repair table. Finally, however, he gave in.

"All right, do your best. How long did you say it would take?"

"I don't remember saying, but probably about two weeks for your face. You'll be able to enjoy using a mirror long before we get that hand unplugged, unless we're remarkably lucky with the graft."

"When will you start?"

"As soon as I've had some sleep. Your blood is back to normal, your general pattern is in the machine; there's nothing else to hold us up. What sort of books do you like?"

"Huh?"

"That head's going to be in a clamp for quite a while. You may or may not like reading, but the only direction you can look comfortably is straight up. Your left hand can work a remote control, and the tape reader can project on the ceiling. I can't think of anything else to occupy you. Do you want some refreshing light fiction, or shall I start you on Volume One of *Garwood's Elementary Matrix Algebra for Biochemists?*"

A regeneration controller is a bulky machine, even though most of it has the delicacy and structural intricacy possible only to pseudolife—and, of course, to "real" life. Its sensors are smaller in diameter than human red blood cells, and there are literally millions of them. Injectors and samplers are only enough larger to take entire cells into their tubes, and these also exist in numbers which would make the device a hopeless one to construct mechanically. Its computer-controller occupies more than two cubic meters of molecular-scale "machinery" based on a synthetic zeolite framework. Mating the individual gene record needed for a particular job to the basic computer itself takes nearly a day—it would take a lifetime if the job had to be done manually, instead of persuading the two to "grow" together.

Closing the gap between the optical microscope and the test tube, which was blanketed under the word "protoplasm" for so many decades, also blurred the boundary between such initially different fields as medicine and factory design. Marco Mancini and Bert Jellinge regarded themselves as mechanics; what they would have been called a few decades earlier is hard to say. Even at the time the two had been born, no ten Ph.D.'s could have supplied the information which now formed the grounding of their professional practice.

When their preliminary work—the "prepping"—on Rick Stubbs was done, some five million sensing tendrils formed a beard on the boy's face, most of them entering the skin near the edges of the injured portions. Every five hundred or so of these formed a unit with a pair of larger tubes. The sensors kept the computer informed of the genetic patterns actually active from moment to moment in the healing tissue—or at least, a statistically significant number of them. Whenever that activity failed to match within narrow limits what the computer thought should be happening, one of the larger tubes ingested a single cell from the area in question and transferred it to a large incubator—"large" in the sense that it could be seen without a microscope—just outside Rick's skin. There the cell was cultured through five divisions, and some of the product cells analyzed more completely than they could be inside a human body. If all were well after all, which was quite possible because of the limitations of the small sensors, nothing more happened.

If things were really not going according to plan, however, others of the new cells were modified. Active parts of their genetic material which should have been inert were incited, quiet parts which should have been active were activated. The repaired cells were cultivated for several more divisions; if they bred true, one or more of them was returned to the original site—or at least, to within a few microns of it. Cell division and tissue building went on according to the modified plan until some new discrepancy was detected.

Most of this was, of course, automatic; too many millions of operations were going on simultaneously for detailed manual control. Nevertheless, Mancini and Jellinge were busy. Neither life nor pseudolife is infallible; mutations occur even in triply-redundant records. Computation errors occur even—or especially—in digital machines which must by their nature work by successive-approximation methods. It is much better to have a human operator, who knows his business, actually see that connective tissue instead of epidermis is being grown in one spot, or nerve instead of muscle cells in another.

Hence, a random selection of cells, not only from areas which had aroused the computer's interest but from those where all was presumably going well, also traveled out through the tubes. These went farther than just to the incubators; they came out to a point where gross microscopic study of them by a human observer was possible. This went on twenty-four hours a day, the two mechanics chiefly concerned and four others of their profession taking two-hour shifts at the microscope. The number of man-hours involved in treating major bodily injury had gone up several orders of magnitude since the time when a sick man could get away with a bill for ten dollars from his doctor, plus possibly another for fifty from his undertaker.

The tendrils and tubes farthest from the damaged tissue were constantly withdrawing, groping their way to the action front, and implanting themselves anew, guided by the same chemical clues which brought leukocytes to the same area. Early versions of the technique had involved complex methods of warding off or removing the crowd of white cells from the neighborhood; the present idea was to let them alone. They were good scavengers, and the controller could easily allow for the occasional one which was taken in by the samplers.

So, as days crawled by, skin and fat and muscle and blood vessels, nerves and bones and tendons, gradually extended into their proper places in Stubbs' face and hand, The face, as Mancini had predicted, was done first; the severed hand had deteriorated so that most of its cells needed replacement, though it served as a useful guide.

With his head out of the clamp, the boy fulfilled another of the mechanic's implied predictions. He asked for a mirror. The man had it waiting, and produced it with a grin; but the grin faded as he watched the boy turn his face this way and that, checking his appearance from every possible angle. He would have expected a girl to act that way; but why should this youngster?

"Are you still the same fellow?" Mancini asked finally. "At least, you've kept your fingerprints." Rick put the mirror down.

"Maybe I should have taken a new hand," he said. "With new prints I might have gotten away with a bank robbery, and cut short the time leading to my well-earned retired leisure."

"Don't you believe it," returned Mancini grimly. "Your new prints would be on file along with your gene record and retinal pattern back in Denver before I could legally have unplugged you from the machine. I had to submit a written summary of this operation before I could start, even as it was. Forget about losing your legal identity and taking up crime."

Stubbs shrugged. "I'm not really disappointed. How much longer before I can write a letter with this hand, though?"

"About ten days; but why bother with a letter? You can talk to anyone you want; haven't your parents been on the 'visor every day?"

"Yes. Say, did you ever find out what made the *Shark* pile up?"

Mancini grimaced. "We did indeed. She got infected by the same growth that killed the zeowhale we first picked up. Did you by any chance run that fish into any part of the hull while you were attaching the sling?"

Rick stared aghast. "My gosh, Yes, I did. I held it against one of the side hulls because it was so slippery...I'm sorry...I didn't know—"

"Relax. Of course you didn't. Neither did I, then; and I never thought of the possibility later. One of the struts was weakened enough to fail at high cruise, though, and Newton's Laws did the rest."

"But does that mean that the other ships are in danger? How about the *Guppy* here? Can anything be done?"

"Oh, sure. It was done long ago. A virus for that growth was designed within a few weeks of its original escape; its gene structure is on file. The mutation is enough like the original to be susceptible to the virus. We've made up a supply of it, and will be sowing it around the area for the next few weeks wherever one of the tenders goes. But why change the subject, young fellow? Your folks *have* been phoning, because I couldn't help hearing their talk when I was on watch. Why all this burning need to write letters? I begin to smell the proverbial rat."

He noticed with professional approval that the blush on Rick's face was quite uniform; evidently a good job had been done on the capillaries and their auxiliary nerves and muscles. "Give, son!"

"It's .,.it's not important," muttered the boy.

"Not important...oh, I see. Not important enough to turn you into a dithering nincompoop at the possibility of having your handsome features changed slightly, or make you drop back to second-grade level when it came to the responsibility for making a simple decision. I see. Well, it doesn't matter; she'll probably do all the deciding for you."

The blush burned deeper. "All right, Marco, don't sound like an ascetic; I know you aren't. Just do your job and get this hand fixed so I can write—at least there's still one form of communication you won't be unable to avoid overhearing while you're on watch."

"What a sentence! Are you sure you really finished school? But it's all right, Rick—the hand will be back in service soon, and it shouldn't take you many weeks to learn to write with it again—"

"What?"

"It is a new set of nerves, remember. They're connected with the old ones higher up in your hand and arm, but even with the old hand as a guide they probably won't go to exactly the same places to make contact with touch transducers and the like. Things will feel different, and you'll have to learn to use a pen all over again." The boy stared at him in dismay. "But don't worry. I'll do my best, which is very good, and it will only be a few more weeks. One thing, though—don't call your letter-writing problem my business; I'm just a mechanic. If you're really in love, you'd better get in touch with a doctor."

ATTITUDE

Astounding, September 1943

Dr. Little woke up abruptly, with a distinct sensation of having just stepped over a precipice. His eyes flew open and were greeted by the sight of a copper-colored metal ceiling a few feet above; it took him several seconds to realize that it was keeping its distance, and that he was not falling either toward or away from it. When he did, a grimace of disgust flickered across his face; he had lived and slept through enough days and nights in interstellar space to be accustomed to weightlessness. He had no business waking up like a cadet on his first flight, grasping for the nearest support—he had no business waking up at all, in these surroundings! He shook his head; his mind seemed to be working on slow time, and his pulse, as he suddenly realized as the pounding in his temples forced itself on his awareness, must be well over a hundred.

This was not his room. The metal of the walls was different, the light was different—an orange glow streaming from slender tubes running along the junction of wall and ceiling. He turned his head to take in the rest of the place, and an agonizing barrage of pins and needles shot the length of his body. An attempt to move his arms and legs met with the same result; but he managed to bend his neck enough to discover that he was enveloped to the shoulders in a sacklike affair bearing all the earmarks of a regulation sleeping bag. The number stenciled on the canvas was not his own, however.

In a few minutes he found himself able to turn his head freely and proceeded to take advantage of the fact by examining his surroundings. He found himself in a small chamber, walled completely with the coppery alloy. It was six-sided, like the cells in a beehive; the only opening was a circular hatchway in what Little considered the ceiling—though, in a second-order flight, it might as well have been a floor or wall. There was no furniture of any description. The walls were smooth, lacking even the rings normally present to accommodate the anchoring snaps of a sleeping bag.

There was light shining through the grille which covered the hatchway, but from where he was Little could make out no details through the bars. He began to wriggle his toes and fingers, ignoring as best he could the resulting sensations; and in a few minutes he found himself able to move with little effort. He lay still a few minutes longer, and then unsnapped the top fasteners of the bag. The grille interested him, and he was becoming more and more puzzled as to his whereabouts. He had no recollection of any unusual events; he had been checking over the medical stores, he was sure, but he couldn't recall retiring to his room afterward. What had put him to sleep? And where had he awakened?

He grasped the top of the bag and peeled it off, being careful to keep hold of it. He started to roll it up and paused in astonishment. A cloud of dust, fine as smoke, was oozing from the fibers of the cloth with each motion, and hanging about the bag like an atmosphere. He sniffed at it cautiously and started coughing; the stuff was dry, and tickled his throat unpleasantly. There could be only one explanation; the bag had been drifting in open space for a length of time sufficient to evaporate every trace of moisture from its fibers. He unrolled it again and looked at the stenciled number—GOA-III-NA12-422. The first three groups confirmed his original belief that the bag had belonged to the *Gomeisa;* the last was a personal number indicating the identity of the former owner, but Little could not remember whose number it was. The fact that it had been exposed to the void was not reassuring.

Dismissing that phase of the problem for the moment, the doctor rolled the bag into a tight bundle. He was drifting weightless midway between ceiling and floor, almost in the center of the room; the hatchway was in one of the six corners of the ceiling. Little hurled the bundle in the opposite direction. It struck the far corner and rebounded without much energy; air friction brought it to a halt a few feet from the wall. The doctor drifted more slowly in the direction of the grating. His throw had been accurate enough to send him within reach of it; he caught hold of one of the bars and drew himself as close as possible.

Any lingering doubt that might have remained in his still befuddled brain as to whether or not he were still on board the *Gomeisa* was driven away as he caught his first glimpse through the grille. It opened—or would have opened had it been unlocked—onto a corridor which extended in two directions as far as the doctor's limited view could reach. The hallway was about thirty feet square, but there its orthodox characteristics terminated. It had been built with a sublime disregard for any possible preferred "up" or "down" direction. Hatches opened into all four sides; those opposite Little's station were circular, like his own, while those in the "side" walls were rectangular. From a point beside each opening, a solidly braced metal ladder extended to the center of the corridor, where it joined a heavy central pillar plentifully supplied with grips for climbing. Everything was made of the copperlike material, and the only light came from the orange-glow tubes set in the corners of the corridor.

Dr. Little maintained his position for several minutes, looking and listening; but no sound reached his ears, and he could perceive nothing through the gratings which covered the other hatchways. He also gave a few moments' attention to the lock on his own grating, which evidently was operated from either side; but it was designed to be opened by a complicated key, and the doctor had no instruments for examining its interior. With a sigh he hooked one arm about a bar of the grating and relaxed, trying to reason out the chain of events which had led up to these peculiar circumstances.

The *Gomeisa* had been a heavy cruiser, quite capable of putting up a stiff defense to any conceivable attack. Certainly no assault could have been so sudden and complete that the enemy would be in a position to use hand weapons on the crew before an alarm was raised—the idea was absurd; and fixed mount projectors of any type would have left more of a mark on the doctor than he could find at this moment. Furthermore, the ship had been, at the last time of which Little had clear recollection, crossing the relatively empty gulf between the Galaxy proper and the Greater Magellanic Cloud—a most unpropitious place for a surprise attack. The star density in that region is of the order of one per eight thousand cubic parsecs, leaving a practically clear field for detector operations. No, an attack did not seem possible; and yet Little had been deprived of consciousness without warning, had been removed from the *Gomeisa* in that state; and had awakened within a sleeping bag which showed too plainly the fact that part, at least, of the cruiser had been open to space for some time.

Was he in a base on some planet of one of those few stars of the "desert," or in some ship of unheard-of design? His weightlessness disposed of the first idea before it was formulated; and the doctor glanced at his belt. Through the glass window in its case, he could see the filament of his personal equalizer glowing faintly; he was in a ship, in second-order flight, and the little device had automatically taken on the task of balancing the drive forces which would, without it, act unequally on each element in his body. As a further check, he felt in his pocket and drew out two coins, one of copper and one of silver. He held them nearly together some distance from his body, released them carefully so as not to give them velocities of their own, and withdrew his hand. Deprived of the equalizer field, they began to drift slowly in a direction parallel to the corridor, the copper bit moving at a barely perceptible crawl, the silver rapidly gaining. The corridor, then, was parallel to the ship's line of flight;

and the coins had fallen forward, since the silver was more susceptible to the driving field action.

Little pushed off from the ceiling and retrieved the coins, restoring them to his otherwise empty pocket. He had not been carrying instruments or weapons, and had no means of telling whether or not he had been searched while unconscious. Nothing was missing, but he had possessed nothing worth taking. The fact that he was locked in might be taken to indicate that he was a prisoner, and prisoners are customarily relieved of any possessions which might prove helpful in an escape. Only beings who had had contact with humanity would logically be expected to identify which of the numerous gadgets carried by the average man are weapons; but the design of this craft bore no resemblance to that of any race with which Little was acquainted. He still possessed his wrist watch and mechanical pencil, so the doctor found himself unable to decide even the nature of his captors, far less their intentions.

Possibly he would find out something when—and if—he was fed. He realized suddenly that he was both hungry and thirsty. He had been unconscious long enough for his watch to run down.

Little's pulse had dropped to somewhere near normal, he noticed, as he drifted beside the hatch. He wondered again what had knocked him out without leaving any mark or causing some sensation; then gave up this line of speculation in favor of the more immediate one advocated by his empty stomach. He fell asleep again before he reached any solution. He dreamed that someone had moved Rigel to the other side of the Galaxy, and the navigator couldn't find his way home. Very silly, he thought, and went on dreaming it.

A gonglike note, as penetrating as though his own skull had been used as the bell, woke him the second time. He was alert at once, and instantly perceived the green, translucent sphere suspended a few feet away. For a moment he thought it might be one of his captors; then his nose told him differently. It was ordinary lime juice, as carried by practically every Earth cruiser. A moment's search served to locate, beside the hatchway, the fine nozzle through which the liquid had been impelled. The doctor had no drinking tube, but he had long since mastered the trick of using his tongue in such circumstances without allowing any other part of his face to touch the liquid. It was a standard joke to confront recruits, on their first free flight, with the same problem. If nose or cheek touched the sphere, surface tension did the rest.

Little returned to the door and took up what he intended to be a permanent station there. He was waiting partly for some sign of human beings, partly for evidence of his captors, and, more and more as time wore on, for some trace of solid food, He waited in vain for all three. At intervals, a pint or so of lime juice came through the jet and formed a globe in the air beside it; nothing else. Little had always liked the stuff, but his opinion was slowly changing as more and more of it was forced on him. It was all there was to drink, and the air seemed to be rather dry; at any rate, he got frightfully thirsty at what seemed unusually short intervals.

He wound his watch and discovered that the "feedings" came at intervals of a little over four hours. He had plenty of chance to make observations, and nothing else to observe; it was not long before he was able to predict within a few seconds the arrival of another drink, Later, he wished he hadn't figured it out; the last five or ten minutes of each wait were characterized by an almost agonizing thirst, none the less painful for being purely mental. Sometimes he slept, but he was always awake at the zero minute.

With nothing to occupy his mind but fruitless speculation, it is not surprising that he lost all track of the number of feedings. He knew only that he had slept a large number of times, had become deathly sick of lime juice, and was beginning to suffer severely from the lack of other food, when a faint suggestion of weight manifested itself. He looked at his equalizer the instant he noticed the situation and found it dark. The ship had cut its second-order converters, and was applying a very slight first-order acceleration in its original line of flight—the barely perceptible weight was directed toward what Little had found to be the stern. Its direction changed by a few degrees on several occasions, but was restored each time in a few seconds. The intensity remained constant, as nearly as Little could tell, for several hours.

Then it increased, smoothly but swiftly, to a value only slightly below that of Earthly gravity. The alterations in direction became more frequent, but never sudden or violent enough to throw Little off his feet— he was now standing on the rear wall, which had become the floor. Evidently the ship's pilot, organic or mechanical, well deserved the name. For nearly half an hour by the watch, conditions remained thus; then the drive was eased through an arc of ninety degrees, the wall containing the hatchway once more became the ceiling, and within a few minutes the faintest of tremors was perceptible through the immense hull and the direction of gravity became constant. If this indicated a landing, Little mentally took off his hat to the entity at the controls,

The doctor found himself badly placed for observation. The hatch was about four feet above the highest point he could reach, and even jumping was not quite sufficient to give him a hold on the bars. He estimated that he had nearly all of his normal hundred and ninety pounds Earth weight, and lack of proper food for the last several days had markedly impaired his physical powers. It was worse than tantalizing; for suddenly, for the first time since he had regained consciousness in this strange spot, he heard sounds from outside. They were distorted by echoes, sounding and reverberating along the corridor outside, and evidently originated at a considerable distance, but they were definitely and unmistakably the voices of human beings.

For minutes the doctor waited. The voices came no nearer, but on the other hand they did not go any farther away. He called out, but apparently the group was too large and making too much noise of its own to hear him. The chatter went on. No words were distinguishable, but there was a prevailing overtone of excitement that not even the metallic echoes of the great hull could cover. Little listened, and kept his eyes fixed on the hatchway.

He heard nothing approach, but suddenly there was a faint click as the lock opened. The grille swung sharply inward until it was perpendicular to the wall in which it was set; then the side bars of its frame telescoped outward until they clicked against the floor. The crossbars separated simultaneously, still maintaining equal distances from each other, and a moment after the hatch had opened a metal ladder extended from it to the floor of the room. It took close examination to see the telescopic joints just below each rung. The metal tubing must be paper-thin, Little thought, to permit such construction.

The doctor set foot on the ladder without hesitation. Presumably, his captors were above, and wanted him to leave the room in which he was imprisoned. In this wish he concurred heartily; he was too hungry to object effectively, anyway. He made his way up the ladder to the corridor, forcing his shoulders through the narrow opening. The human voices were still audible, but they faded into the background of his attention as he examined the beings grouped around the hatch.

There were five of them. They bore some resemblance to the nonhumans of Tan Ceti's first planet, having evidently evolved from a radially symmetric, starfishlike form to a somewhat more specialized type with differentiated locomotive and prehensile appendages. They were five-limbed and headless, with a spread of about eight feet. The bodies were nearly spherical; and if the arms had been only a little thicker at the base it would have been impossible to tell where body left off and arm began. The tube feet of the Terrestrial starfish were represented by a cluster of pencil-thick tendrils near the tip of each arm and leg—the distinction between these evidently lying in the fact that three of the appendages were slightly thicker and much blunter at the tips than the two which served as arms. The tendrils on the "legs" were shorter and stubbier, as well. The bodies, and the appendages nearly to their tips, were covered with a mat of spines, each several inches in length, lying for the most part nearly flat against the skin. These either grew naturally, or had been combed away from the central mouth and the five double-pupiled eyes situated between the limb junctions.

The beings wore metal mesh belts twined into the spines on their legs, and these supported cases for what were probably tools and weapons. Their "hands" were empty; evidently they did not fear an attempted escape or attack on the doctor's part. They made no sound except for the dry rustle of their spiny armor as they moved. In silence they closed in around Little, while one waved his flexible arms toward one end of the passageway. A gentle shove from behind, as the doctor faced in the indicated direction, transmitted the necessary command, and the group marched toward the bow. Two of the silent things stalked in front, two brought up the rear; and at the first opportunity, the other swarmed up one of the radial ladders and continued his journey directly over Little's head, swinging along by the handholds on the central beam.

As they advanced, the voices from ahead grew slowly louder. Occasional words were now distinguishable. The speakers, however, were much farther away than the sound of their voices suggested, since the metal-walled corridor carried the sounds well if not faithfully. Nearly three hundred yards from Little's cell, a vertical shaft of the same dimensions as the corridor interrupted the latter. The voices were coming from below. Without hesitation, the escort swung over the lip of the shaft and started down the ladder which took up its full width; Little followed. On the way, he got some idea of the size of the ship he was in. Looking up, he saw the mouths of two other corridors entering the shaft above the one he had traversed; at the level of the second, another hallway joined it from the side. Evidently he was not near the center line of the craft; there were at least two, and possibly three, tiers of longitudinal corridors. He had already seen along one of those corridors; the ship must be over fifteen hundred feet in length. Four vessels the size of the *Gomeisa* could have used the immense hull for a hangar, and left plenty of elbow room for the servicing crews.

Below him, the shaft debouched into a chamber whose walls were not visible from Little's position. His eyes, however, which had become exceedingly tired of the endless orange radiance which formed the ship's only illumination, were gladdened at the sight of what was unquestionably daylight leaking up from the room. As he descended, two of the walls became visible—the shaft opened near one corner—and in one of them he finally saw an air lock, with both valves open. He went hastily down the remaining few feet and stopped as he touched the floor. His gaze took in on the instant the twenty-yard-square chamber, which seemed to occupy a slight outcrop of the hull, and stopped at the corner farthest from the air lock. Penned in that corner by a line of the starfish were thirty-eight beings; and Little needed no second glance to identify the crew of the *Gomeisa*. They recognized him simultaneously; the chatter stopped, to be replaced by a moment's silence and then a shout of "Doc!" from nearly two score throats. Little stared, then strode forward and through the line of guards, which opened for him, A moment later he was undergoing a process of handshaking and backslapping that made him wonder. He didn't think he had been that popular.

Young Captain Albee was the first to speak coherently.

"It's good to see you again, sir. Everyone but you was accounted for, and we'd begun to think they must have filed you away in formaldehyde for future reference. Where were you?"

"You mean I was the only one favored with solitary confinement?" asked Little. "I woke up in a cell upstairs, about two thirds of the way back, with less company than Jonah. I could see several other sets of bars from my stateroom door, but there was nothing behind any of them. I haven't seen or heard any living creature but myself since then. I can't even remember leaving, or being removed from, the *Gomeisa*. Does anyone know what happened?"

"How is it that you don't?" asked Albee. "We were attacked; we had a fight, of a sort. Did you sleep through it? That doesn't seem possible."

"I did, apparently. Give me the story."

"There's not much to give. I was about to go off watch when the detectors picked up a lump that seemed highly magnetic, and something over eighty million tons mass. We hove to, and came alongside it while Tine took a couple of pictures of the Galaxy and the Cloud so that we could find it again. I sent out four men to take samples, and the instant the outer door was opened these things"—he jerked his head toward the silent guards—"froze it that way with a jet of water on the hinge and jamb. They were too close to use the heavy projectors, and we still had no idea there was a ship inside the meteoric stuff. They were in space-suits, and got into the lock before we could do anything. By the time we had our armor on they had burned down the inner lock door and were all through the ship. The hand-to-hand fighting was shameful; I thought I knew all the football tricks going, and I'd taught most of them to the boys, but they had every last one of us pinned down before things could get under way. I never saw anything like it.

"I still can't understand what knocked you out. They used no weapons—that annoyed me—and if you didn't put a suit on yourself I don't see how you lived when they opened up your room. The air was gone before they started going over the ship."

"I think I get it," said Little slowly. "Geletane. Four cylinders of it. Did you broadcast a general landing warning when you cut the second-order to examine that phony Bonanza? You didn't, of course, since we weren't in a gravity field of any strength. And the 'meteor' was magnetic, which made no difference to our beryllium hull, but made plenty to the steel geletane cylinders, one of which I had unclamped for a pressure test and had left in the tester. I went on about my business, and the field yanked the cylinder out of the tester and against the wall. It didn't make enough noise to attract my attention, because I was in the next room. With the door open. And the valve cracked just a trifle—just enough. I didn't need a suit when these starfish opened my room; I must have been as stiff as a frame member. I had all the symptoms of recovery from suspended ani-mation when I woke up, too, but I never thought of interpreting them that way. The next ship I'm in, see if I don't get them to rig up an auto-matic alarm to tell what the second-order fields are doing—"

"You might also put your geletane cylinders back in the clamps when, and if, this happy state of affairs eventuates," remarked Goldthwaite, the gloomy technical sergeant. "May I ask what happens now, captain?"

"I'm afraid it isn't up to me, Goldy," returned Albee. "But I don't suppose they plan to keep us in this corner indefinitely."

Probably they didn't, but Albee was beginning to doubt his own state-ment before anything else happened. The sun had risen so that it was no longer shining directly into the port, and the great chamber had grown darker as the shadow of the vast interstellar flier crept down and away from its outer wall, when a new party came through the air lock from outside. Two of the pentapods came first, and came to a halt on either side of the inner door; after them crept painfully the long, many-legged, gorgeously furred body of a Vegan. Its antennae were laid along its back, blending with the black and yellow stripes; the tiny, heavily lidded eyes opened wide in the effort to see in what, to the native of the blue star, was nearly total darkness. The line of guards penning in the Earthmen opened and formed a double-walled lane between humans and Vegan.

Albee stepped forward, and at the same moment the interior lights of the chamber flashed on. The Vegan relaxed for a moment as its eyes readjusted themselves; then its antennae snapped erect and began to sway slowly in the simple patterns of the sign language of its race.

"I assume that some of you, at least, understand me," it said. "Our captors, having learned a little of my language in the months I have spent here, hope to save themselves trouble by using me as an interpreter. Do you wish to acknowledge acquaintance with my speech, or do you think it better to act as though our races had never encountered each other? I was not captured near my home planet, so you might get away with such an act."

Most of the Earthmen had some knowledge of Vegan speech—the two systems are near neighbors, and enjoy lively commercial relations—and all looked to Albee for a decision. He wasted little time in thought; it was evident that they would be better off in communication with their captors than otherwise.

"We might as well talk," he answered, forming the signs as well as he could with his arms. "We should like to find out all you can tell us about these creatures, and it is unlikely that we would be given the chance to communicate secretly with you. Do you know where we are, and can you tell us anything about this planet and its people?"

"I know very little," was the answer. "I believe this world is somewhere in the Cloud, because the only time one of us was ever outside the fort at night he could see the Galaxy. Neither I nor my companions can tell you anything about the planet's own characteristics, for we have been kept inside the base which these creatures have established here ever since our capture. We move too slowly in this gravity to escape from them, and, anyway, the sun has not sufficient ultraviolet light to keep us alive. Our captors, we are sure, are not natives of the planet; they seldom venture outside the walls themselves, and always return before nightfall. Furthermore, they live on provisions brought by their interstellar ships, rather than native food.

"They have not told us the reason for our capture. They allow us to prepare everything we need for existence and comfort, but every time we try to divert supplies to the production of weapons, they seem to know it. They let us nearly finish, and then take it away from us. They never get angry at our attempts, either. We don't understand them."

"If they are so careful of your well being, why do they try to drive us crazy on a steady diet of lime juice?" interrupted Little.

"I could not say; but I will ask, if you wish," returned the Vegan. He swung his fusiform body laboriously around until he was facing one of the creatures who had accompanied him to the ship, and began semaphoring the question. The men watched silently; those who had not understood the preceding conversation were given the gist of it in brief whispers by their fellows. Little had not had a chance to ask if the others had been fed as he had been; their silent but intense interest in the answer to his question indicated that they had. The chronic slowness of Vegan communication rendered them all the more impatient to know the reason, as the black and yellow creature solemnly waved at the motionless pentapod.

There was a brief pause before the latter began to answer. When it did, the Earthman understood why an interpreter was necessary, even though both sides knew the same language. The arms of the creature were flexible enough in front-to-rear motion, as are human fingers; but their relatively great width hampered them in side-to-side waves, and put them at a severe disadvantage in using the Vegan language. The Vegan himself must have had difficulty in comprehending; the Earthman could not make out a single gesture.

Finally the interpreter turned back to the human listeners and reported the result of his questioning:

"The green liquid is all that our captors found in the canteens of your space armor. Since there was a large supply of it on your ship, they assumed it was the principal constituent of your diet. They have, however, salvaged practically all of the contents of your vessel, and you will be allowed shortly to obtain your foodstuffs, cooking equipment, and personal belongings, with the natural exception of weapons. I might add, from my own experience, that their unfamiliarity with your weapons will not help you much if you attempt to smuggle any from the stores. We never could get away with it."

"What surprises me," remarked Albee in English, "is that we are allowed at the supplies at all. These creatures must be extremely confident in their own abilities to take a chance."

"From what you told me of the hand-to-hand fighting, such confidence may be justified," remarked Little with a grin. "Didn't you say that they more or less wiped up the floor with the boys?"

"True," admitted the captain, "but there's no need to rub it in. Why are they so stuck up about it?"

"Stuck up? I was getting a strong impression that, as a race, they must be unusually modest." Albee stared at the doctor, but could not get him to amplify the remark. The Vegan interrupted further conversation, attracting their attention with a flourish of its long antennae.

"I am told that your supplies have been unloaded through another port, and are lying on the ground outside the fort. You are to accompany me and the guards to the pile, and take all the food you wish—you may make several trips, if necessary, to get it all to your quarters in the fort."

"Where is this fort, in relation to the ship?" asked Albee. "What sort of land is around it?"

"The ship is lying parallel to the near wall of the fort, about two hundred yards from it. This air lock is near the nose of the ship, and almost opposite the main valves of the fort. In front of the ship the ground is level for about a quarter of a mile, then dips down into what seems to be a heavily forested river valley. I don't know what lies beyond, in that direction; this sunlight is too dim for me to make out the details of objects more than a mile or two distant. I do get the impression of hills or mountains—you will be able to see for yourselves, outside. Your eyes are adapted to this light.

"In the other direction, toward the stern, the level plain extends as far as I can see, without any cover. Anyway, you'd be between the ship and the fort for the first five hundred yards, if you went that way, and could easily be cornered. I warn you again that these creatures will outguess you, but—good luck. I've told you all I know."

"I guess we might as well go along and get our stuff, then," remarked Albee to his crew. "Don't do anything rash without orders, We'll wait until we see how the supplies are arranged. Maybe we'll have to move some apparatus to get at the food."

The black bodies of the guards had ringed them, almost statuesque in their motionlessness, during the conversation. As the Vegan concluded his speech, he had turned toward the lock; Albee had spoken as the men began to follow. The air of the planet was evidently similar to that of Earth, Vega Five, and the home planet of the pentapods, since both valves of the air lock were open. It had the fresh-air smell which the filtered atmosphere of a spaceship always seems to lack, and the men almost unconsciously squared their shoulders and expanded their chests as they passed down the ramp in the wake of the heavily moving Vegan. The scene before them caught all eyes; the interpreter's description had been correct, but inadequate.

The hull of the interstellar cruiser curved high above their heads. The lock chamber occupied a relatively tiny gondola that projected far enough, from its location well to one side of the keel, to touch the ground. The outside of the vessel gleamed with a brilliant silvery luster, in contrast to the coppery glow of the interior. The fort, directly in front of them, was an imposing structure of stone composition half a mile in length and two hundred feet high on the side facing them. The walls were smoothly polished, and completely lacking in windows.

To the left, beyond the nose of the craft, the level meadow continued for several hundred yards, and then dipped abruptly downward. As the Vegan had intimated, the background was filled by a range of rugged-looking mountains, the nearest several miles away. The sun was now nearly overhead, thereby robbing the landscape of the shadows that would have given the Earthman a better idea of its relief. Albee wasted little time looking for what he wouldn't be able to see; he strode on toward the great gate of the fort. In front of the portals were several large heaps of articles, and even at this distance some of them could be recognized as pieces of equipment from the unfortunate *Gomeisa*. The guards closed around the group of human beings and proceeded at the pace set by the captain, leaving the Vegan prisoner to follow at his own speed.

It was evident that a thorough job of looting had been done on the Terrestrial warship. Food and medical supplies, bunks, kitchen equipment, blankets and miscellaneous items of field apparatus were included in the half dozen heaps laid out beneath the glistening black walls. Mixed in with the rest were hand tools and weapons, and Albee, in spite of the Vegan's warning, began promptly to make plans. At his orders, each of the men dragged a shoulder pack out of one of the piles and began filling it with containers of food and drink. The pile of lime-juice bottles was pointedly ignored until Albee, glancing at it, noticed that one case of bottles was not green in color. He went over for a closer look, then extracted one of the plastic containers, opened it and sniffed. His voice, as he turned to the watching men, was just a little louder than usual:

"Would anyone know where they found this stuff?" His eyes wandered over the faces of the crew. It was Sergeant Goldthwaite who finally answered, hesitantly.

"They *might* have looked between the bulkheads at the cap end of the storage room, cap'n. It was pretty cool there, and seemed like a good place—"

"Not too easy to visit often, in flight," remarked the captain quizzically.

"I never visited it, sir—you can see it hasn't been touched. But you said we would probably touch at Ardome, and I was thinking it might be possible to get rid of it there."

"It probably would. But they have good customs inspectors, and war vessels aren't immune to search. I shudder to think of what would have happened to our reputation if we had made Ardome. Consider yourself responsible for this stuff."

The sergeant gulped. The case of liquor weighed eighty pounds, and could not possibly be crammed into a shoulder pack. He realized gloomily that the captain had inflicted about the only possible punishment, under the circumstances. He put five of the bottles into his pack and began a series of experiments to find out which way his arms went most easily around the case. A small group of pentapods regarded the struggle with interest, their spines waving slowly like a field of wheat in a breeze.

Albee watched, too, for a moment; then he went on, without altering the tone of his words:

"Most of you should have a decent supply of food by now. This planet probably has good water, since the vegetation and clouds appear normal.

We should be able to live here without the aid of our generous captors, but we may have some difficulty an avoiding their well-meant ministrations. The Vegan said his people had never been able to fool these pincushions into letting them make or steal a weapon. Remembering that, use every caution in carrying out the orders I am about to give.

"When I have stopped talking, each of you count thirty, slowly, meanwhile working your way toward the handiest tool or weapon in the neighborhood. When you reach thirty, dive for the object of your choice and do your best to get to that forest. You have all, except the doctor, had some experience of the rough-and-tumble tactics of these creatures; the problem, I should say, is to get past them without a fight and into the open. I think we can outrun, on the level, any invertebrate alive. If someone is caught, don't stay to help him; right now, I want to get at least a small crew away from here, where we can work out at our leisure rescue plans for the unlucky ones. Don't all try to get guns; we'll find cutting tools just as useful in the woods. You may start counting."

Without haste, Albee counted over the contents of his pack, swung it to his shoulders. The guards. spines twitching slowly, watched. Reiser, the senior navigator, was helping one of Goldthwaite's engineers drag the ship's electric stove from a pile which chanced also to contain several ion pistols. Little picked up and tested briefly a hand flash, conscious of the fact that guards were watching him closely. The action had some purpose; the flash was almost exactly similar to the pistols. He tightened the straps of his own pack—and someone reached the count of thirty. Albee had chosen that number to give the men time enough to prepare, but not enough to get very far out of pace in the counting.

Almost as one, the human beings turned and sprinted for the bow of the warship. Almost simultaneously, the guards went into action, each singling out a man and going to work. Little, who had not experienced the tactics of the creatures, managed to avoid them for perhaps five yards; then one of them twined its tendrils about his wrist and literally climbed up onto his back. A moment later, the doctor was face down on the grass, arms and legs held motionless in the grip of the clumsy-looking, stubby limbs. The spines of his captor were not stiff enough to penetrate clothing or skin, but their pressure on the back of his neck was unpleasant. He managed to turn his head sufficiently to see what was going on.

Four men, who had been at the pile nearest the forest, had moved fast enough to avoid contact with their guards. They were now running rapidly toward the declivity; none of the creatures was in pursuit. Albee and a dozen others were practically clear, but one of these was pulled down as Little watched. One man found himself in a relatively clear space and made a dash. Guards closed in from either side, but realized apparently that they were not fast enough to corner the fellow. They turned back to other prey, and the runner was allowed to escape.

Goldthwaite had been in a bad position, with almost the whole group to fight through on his way to the woods. Apparently he never thought of disobeying orders, and going the other way, he dropped the case he had been trying to lift, seized a bottle from it with each hand and headed into the melee. Curiously enough, he was the only one using weapons; the guards, festooned with implements snapped to their leg belts, fought with their bare "hands," and the men all ignored their guns and knives in the effort to run. Most of the pentapods at the sergeant's end of the group were engaged, and he got nearly halfway through the group before he was forced to use his clubs.

Then a guard saw him and closed in. Goldthwaite was handicapped by the creature's lack of a head, but he swung anyway. The blow landed between the two upper limbs, just above one eye. It didn't seem to bother the pentapod, whose flexible legs absorbed most of the shock, and the tough plastic of the bottle remained unbroken; but the stopper, urged by interior pressure and probably not closed tightly enough—it may have been the bottle investigated by the captain—blew out, soaking the sergeant's sleeve and jacket with liquor. This particular fluid had some of the characteristics of Earthly champagne, and had been considerably shaken up.

Another of its qualities was odor. This, like the taste of Roquefort, required a period of conditioning before one could become fond of it; and this may have been the reason that the guard fell back for a moment as the liquid foamed out. It is more likely, however, that he was merely startled to find an object his people had decided was harmless suddenly exhibit the characteristics of a projectile weapon. Whatever the reason, he hesitated a split second before pressing the attack; and in that moment the sergeant was past.

Ahead of him, three or four more guards—all who remained unoccupied—converged to meet him. Without waiting for them to charge, Goldthwaite swung the other bottle a few times and hurled it into their midst. He was a man quick to profit by experience. Unfortunately, so were the guards. They saw the liquid which had soaked into the sergeant's clothes, and needed no further assurance that it was harmless. They paid no attention to the flying bottle until it landed.

This flask was stoppered more tightly and did not blow out. The pentapods, who had either seen the behavior of the first bottle or had been told of it, decided that the latest arrival was a different sort of weapon and prudently changed course, avoiding the spot where it lay, and the sergeant, with no such scruples, passed over it like a racehorse. It was several seconds before the guards overcame their nervousness over this new form of delayed-action bomb, and before they could circle around it. Goldthwaite was well out of reach across the plateau. By that time the action was over.

Albee had gotten away with about a dozen men. One of these had escaped through the co-operation of the Vegan, who, unable to run himself, had tripped up with an antenna the only guard in position to catch the man. Some twenty-five human beings lay about on the field, each held down by a single pentapod. Two swarms of the creatures were coming rapidly toward them, one from the ship and one from the fort. These formed a ring about the area, and Little found himself once more free to get to his feet. He did so, the others gathering round him.

All guns had disappeared, it seemed. One of the men had tried to use his when he had been intercepted, but his opponent had relieved him of the weapon before any damage had been done. Evidently the information had been broadcast, for all the other ion pistols had been confiscated, though the very similar flash tubes had not been touched. Injuries were confined to bruises.

Little was beginning to get ideas about his captors—he had, indeed, begun to get them some time since, as his cryptic remark to Albee had indicated. Every action they performed gave evidence of most peculiar motivation and thought processes, evidence which was slowly sifting its way through Little's mind. He continued to let it sift as the men, still ringed by pentapods, began to march toward the fort.

The great outer gate opened into a chamber large enough to hold the entire group with room to spare. It was about fifteen feet high, metal walled, and possessed but two doors—the outer valve and another, smaller, in the opposite wall, giving access to the interior of the structure. As though the room were an air lock, the inner portal was not opened until the outer had shut. Then the group passed into a brilliantly lit corridor, stretching on ahead of them far into the bowels of the fort. Hallways branched from this at intervals of a few yards, some brightly lighted like the main passage, others in nearly total darkness. They had gone only a short distance when the men were stopped by their escort in front of a small doorway in the left-hand wall.

One of the guards activated a small control in the wall beside the door, causing the latter to slide open. The small chamber disclosed was evidently an elevator car, into which five of the pentapods beckoned an equal number of the men. The door slid to behind them, and several minutes of uneasy silence ensued. Little asked the Vegan if it knew where they were being taken.

"Our quarters are in a superstructure on the roof," gestured the creature. "They may put you there, or on the roof itself. You can live in the open under this sunlight; we need supplementary lighting, both visual and ultraviolet. They have told me nothing. I do not even know whether we will be allowed to communicate any further—though I hope so. My companions and I have long wanted to have someone besides ourselves to talk to."

"I suspect we shall be allowed as much contact as we wish—they may even quarter us in adjoining rooms," remarked Little hesitantly. The Vegan eyed him closely for a moment.

"Ah, you have found a way into their minds, Earthman?" it asked. "I congratulate you. We have never been able to understand their motivation or actions in the slightest degree. It may, of course, be that they think more after your fashion than ours—but that seems unlikely, when your minds and ours are sufficiently alike to agree even on matters of philosophy."

"I am not at all sure I have penetrated their minds," answered Little. "I am still observing, but what I see has so far strengthened the impression I obtained almost at the first. If anything constructive results from my ideas, I will tell, but otherwise I should prefer to wait until I am much more certain of my conclusions."

The return of the elevator interrupted the laborious exchange of ideas. It had been gone many minutes, but the Vegan sign language is much slower than verbal speech, and the two allies had had time for only a few sentences. They watched silently as five more men and their guards entered the car and disappeared. There was little talk in the ensuing wait; most of the beings present were too fully occupied in thinking. One or two of the men exchanged low-voiced comments, but the majority kept their ideas to themselves. The Vegan, of course, was voiceless, and the guards stood about patiently, silent as ever, rock-still except for the slow, almost unceasing, wave of the black, blunt spines. They did not seem even to breathe.

The silence continued while the elevator returned and departed twice more. Its only interruption consisted of occasional faint metallic sounds of indeterminable origin, echoing and reechoing along the corridors of the vast pile. To Little, they were interesting for the evidence they provided of activity through the place, and therefore of the presence of a very considerable garrison. Nothing was seen to substantiate this surmise, however, although it was possible to view objects at a considerable distance along the well-lighted passage.

The elevator returned for the last time. Little, the few remaining men, and the Vegan entered, accompanied this time by only two of the pentapods, and the upward journey began. The car was lifted by an extremely quiet—or extremely distant—motor; the continuous silence of the place, indeed, was beginning to jar on human nerves. The elevator rose smoothly; there was no sense of motion during the five or six minutes of the journey. Little wondered whether the creatures had some ulterior motive, or were simply economizing on power—if the fort were only two hundred feet high, an elevator journey from ground to roof should take seconds, not minutes. He never discovered the answer.

The car door slid open to reveal another corridor, narrower than the one below. To the right it came to an end twenty yards away where a large circular window allowed the sunlight to enter. Little decided that they must be above the level of the outer wall, since no openings had been visible in it. The wall at this level must be set back some distance, so as to be invisible from a point on the ground near the building.

The party was herded in the opposite direction toward several doors which opened from the hallway. Through a number of these, light even brighter than the daylight was streaming; from others there emerged only the sound of human voices. The party paused at one of the brightly lighted doorways, and the Vegan turned to Little.

"These are our quarters," telegraphed the creature. "They have permitted us to set up everything we needed for comfort. I would invite you to enter, but you should first find some means of protecting your skin against the ultraviolet radiators we have arranged. Dark goggles, such as Earthmen usually wear on Vega Five, would also be advisable. I shall tell my friends about you; we will converse again whenever possible. If my ears do not deceive me, your people are quartered along this same corridor, so we can meet freely—as you guessed we might. Farewell." The bulky form turned away and hitched itself through the blue-lit entrance.

The creature's auditory organs had not lied; the human crew was found occupying a dozen of the less strongly illuminated rooms along the corridor. Magill, who as quartermaster was senior officer present, had taken charge and had already begun to organize the group when Little and his companions arrived. One chamber had already been set aside as a storeroom and kitchen, and the food was already being placed therein. When the quartermaster caught sight of Little, he wasted no time in greetings.

"Doctor, I seem to recall that the Vegan said we could make several trips for supplies, if necessary. I wish you'd take a dozen men, try to make these creatures understand what you want, and bring up the rest of the food. Also, Denham wants that stove—he promises a regular meal half an hour after you get it here. Can do?" Little nodded; and the officer told off a dozen men to go with him. The group retraced their steps to the elevator.

Several of the pentapods were loitering at this end of the corridor. They made no objection as the doctor investigated the control beside the elevator door, and finally manipulated it; but two of them entered the car with Little and half of his crew, and accompanied them to the ground level. Little obtained one more bit of information as they started down: the elevator controls were like those of an Earthly automatic car, simply a row of buttons. He indicated the lowest, and made a motion as though to push it, meanwhile looking at one of the guards. This creature came over beside him, and with one of its tendrils touched a stud less than a third of the way down the panel. Little smiled. Evidently the fort was more underground than above, and must be a far larger structure than he had thought. It was nice to know.

They waited at the lower level, while one of the men took the car back for the others; then, accompanied by several more of the guards, they went outside. None of the men could discover how the doors of the entrance chamber were manipulated; none of the creatures accompanying them appeared to touch a control of any sort. The piles of supplies and equipment were still in front of the gate; nothing had been touched. Squads of the pentapods were hurrying this way and that around the great ship; some were visible, clinging to nets suspended far overhead against the hull, evidently repairing, cleaning, or inspecting.

A long line of the creatures was passing continually back and forth between one of the ports of the vessel and a small gate, which the men had not previously noticed, in the wall of the fort. They were bearing large crates, which might have contained anything, and various articles of machinery. Little watched them for a moment, then turned his attention to their own supplies.

The men loaded up and returned to the elevator, into which the food was piled. One man started up with the load and the others went back to the piles. This time Little turned his attention to the stove, which the cook had demanded. It had already been worked out of its pile and was awaiting transportation. The doctor first inspected it carefully, however.

It was an extremely versatile piece of equipment. It contained a tiny iron converter of its own, but was also designed to draw power from any normal standard, if desired. Being navy equipment, it also had to be able to work without electric power, if circumstances required precautions against detection; and a tube connection at the back permitted the attachment of a hydrogen or butane tank—there was even a clamp for the tank.

Little saw a rack of three gas tanks standing by a nearby pile, and was smitten with an idea. He detached one of them and fastened it into the stove clamp, which, fortunately, it fitted. Four men picked up the stove and carried it inside. The other tanks were removed from the rack and carried after it. They contained, it is needless to say, neither hydrogen nor butane. Little hoped that none of the watching guards had been present at the actual looting of the *Gomeisa,* and knew where those tanks came from. He had tried to act normally while he had fitted the cylinder and given orders to bring the others.

The elevator had not yet returned when they reached its door. The men set their burden down. To Little's surprise, none of the guards had accompanied them—they had deduced, from the weight and clumsiness of the device the men were carrying, that watching them would be superfluous until the machine was set up. Or, at least, so reasoned the doctor. He took advantage of the opportunity to tell the men to be very careful of the cylinders they were carrying. They asked no questions, though each man had a fairly good idea of the reason for the order. They already knew that the atomic converter of the stove was in working order, and that heating gas was, therefore, superfluous.

When the elevator finally arrived, Little ordered the man who had brought it to help the others bring the rest of the food from outside. There was still a good deal of it, and it might as well be brought in, though a large supply had already accumulated in the storeroom. He finished his orders with:

"You're free to try any smuggling you want, but be careful. They already know what an ion gun looks like, and we have been told that they're very good at guessing. We don't know, of course, what articles besides weapons they don't want us to have; so be careful in taking anything you think they might object to. I'm going to take this load up." He slid the door to and pressed the top button.

The same group of guards were waiting at the top. They watched with interest as several men helped the doctor carry the stove to the room which was to serve as the kitchen. There was not too much space left, for food supplies filled all the corners. Little smiled as he saw them—it seemed as though Magill were anticipating a long stay. He was probably justified.

Denham, the cook, grinned as he saw the stove. He had cleared a narrow space for it and fussily superintended the placing. He looked at the gas tank attached to it, but before he could express any surprise, Little spoke. He kept his voice and expression normal, for several pentapods had followed the stove into the room.

"Act as if the tank were just part of the stove, Den," he said, "but use the iron burner. I assure you that the gas won't heat anything."

Denham kept his face expressionless and said, "O.K., Doc. Good work." As though nothing unusual were occurring, he began digging supplies from the surrounding heaps, preparing the promised dinner. The doctor sought out Magill, who had just completed the task of assigning men to the rooms.

"Have you found out how this place is ventilated?" asked Little, as soon as he could get the quartermaster's attention.

"Hello, Doc. Food in? Yes, we located the ventilators. Ceiling and floor grilles. Too small to admit a pair of human shoulders, even if we got the bars out."

"I didn't mean that, exactly. Do you know if the same system handles the rest of the building? And whether those grilles keep blowing if we open the window in a room?"

"We can find out the answer to the second, anyway. Come along."

The two entered one of the rooms, which had been set aside as a sleeping room for three men. All the chambers on this side of the corridor had transparent ports opening onto the roof; after some juggling, Magill got one open. Little, standing beneath the ceiling inlet, was gratified to feel the breeze die away. He nodded slowly.

"I think we should form the habit of keeping the windows open," he remarked. "Of course, not being too pointed about it. It may get a trifle cool at night, but we can stand that. By the way, I forgot to have the men bring up those sleeping bags; I'll tell them the next time the elevator comes up. Do you think our faithful shadows"—Little nodded toward the two pentapods standing in the doorway—"would object if we went out on the roof? They let us open the window, and we could go out that way, in a pinch. There must be some more regular exit."

"No harm in trying," replied Magill. He led the way into the corridor, the two watchers moving aside for them, and after a moment's hesitation turned left, away from the elevator. The guards fell in behind. The room they had been in was the last of those occupied by the Earthmen, and several lightless doorways were passed before the end of the passage was reached. They found it similar in arrangement to the other end, containing a large, transparent panel through which was visible a broad expanse of roof.

Magill, who had opened the window in the room, began to examine the edges of the panel. It proved openable, the control being so high above the floor as to be almost out of reach. The pentapods could, without much effort, reach objects eight feet in the air. The quartermaster, with a little fumbling, finally released the catch and pushed the panel open.

The guards made no objection as the men went out on the roof, merely following a few yards behind. This end of the hall opened to the southeast—calling the sunrise point east—away from the ship. From a position a few yards outside the panel, it was evident that the prison quarters occupied a relatively small, rectangular pimple near the north corner of the half-mile-square roof. The men turned left again and passed along the side of the protuberance. Some of the crew saw them through the windows, which Magill beckoned them to open. Denham had already opened his, and cooking odors were beginning to pour forth.

Crossing the few yards to the five-foot parapet at the edge of the roof, the men found a series of steps which raised them sufficiently to lean over the two-foot-thick wall. They were facing the forest to which Albee and the others who had escaped had made their dash. From this height they could see down the declivity at its edge, and perceive that a heavy growth of underbrush was present, which would probably seriously impede travel. No sign of the refugees caught the eye.

The bow of the ship protruded from behind the near corner of the structure. Little and Magill moved to this wall and looked down. The line of pentapods was still carrying supplies to the vast ship, whose hull towered well above the level of the two watchers. It hid everything that lay to the northwest. After a few minutes' gaze the officers turned back to the quarters. They were now at the "elevator" end of the superstructure, and found themselves facing the panel which had not yet been opened. Two of the men were visible, watching them from within; and Magill, walking over to the entrance, pointed out the catch which permitted it to open. No outside control was visible.

"The men have come with the rest of the food, sir," said one as soon as the panel opened, "and Denham says that dinner is nearly ready."

"We'll be in shortly," said the quartermaster. "You may tell the men they are free to come out and explore, if they wish."

"I would still like to know if the ventilator intake is on this roof," remarked Little as they walked on. "It must be somewhere, and the wall we saw was perfectly smooth. There doesn't seem to be anything out in the middle of this place, so if it's anywhere, it must be hiding in the shadow of the parapet. Can you see any irregularities near the edges?"

"No," said Magill after straining his eyes in every direction, "I can't. But we're half a mile from two of the walls, and might easily miss such a thing at a much shorter distance. If it's here, one of the men will find it sooner or later. Why do you worry about it, if you want us to use out-door air directly?"

"I thought it might be a useful item of knowledge," replied Little. "I succeeded in smuggling up my three remaining cylinders of geletane, dis-guised as part of the stove. I don't suppose there's enough to put the whole garrison out—but still, it would be nice to know their ventilating sys-tem."

"Good job, doctor. After we eat we'll find out what else, if anything, the boys succeeded in bringing up, and more or less take inventory. Then perhaps we can arrange some plan for getting out of here. I wish we knew what has become of the *Gomeisa;* I don't suppose we could manage the controls on that ship outside." Magill made this remark with such perfect seriousness that Little was forced to grin.

"You may be a little optimistic, Keys. Remember the Vegans, who are far from stupid creatures, have been here for some time and have failed to get to first base to date."

"They are handicapped physically, Doc. They can't live for long outside without supplementary ultraviolet sources, and they have to plan with that in mind. Furthermore, this gravity is nearly twice that of Vega Five, and they can't move at any rate better than a crawl."

Little was forced to admit the justice of this argument, but remained, in Magill's opinion, pessimistic. He had developed a healthy respect for their captors, along with a slight comprehension of their motives. The trouble was, the Vegan's description of the way the pentapods seemed to guess the purpose of a device before it was completed did not tie in very well with his theory concerning those motives. More thought was indicated. He indulged in it while Magill steered him back to the prison and dinner.

The meal was good. There was no reason why it shouldn't be, of course, since the cook had all the usual supplies and equipment; but Little was slightly surprised to find himself enjoying dinner while in durance vile as much as if he were on his own ship. It didn't seem natural. They ate in the hallway, squatted in a circle in front of the kitchen door. The Vegans, whose quarters were directly opposite, watched from their doorways. They also commented from time to time, but were very seldom answered, since both hands are required to speak Vegan. They would probably have felt slighted if one of them—not the one who had acted as interpreter—had not understood some English. He got about two words in every five, and succeeded in keeping his race in the conversation.

The meal concluded, the meeting of the ways and means committee, which consisted of all human beings and Vegans in the neighborhood, was immediately called to order. The presence of nonmembers, though resented, was perforce permitted, and discussion began under the watchful eyes of eight or ten pentapods. Little, rather than Magill, presided.

"The first thing we need to know," he said, "is everything possible about our five-sided friends. The Vegans have been with them longer, and probably know more than we; but owing to the relative slowness of their speech, we will save their contribution until last. You who understand English may translate the substance of our discussion to your fellows if you wish, but we will hold a second meeting afterward and go over everything in your own language. First, then, will anyone who suc-

ceeded in smuggling any weapons or probable-contraband tools up here
please report? Keep your hands in your pockets and your eyes on me while
you do so; there is a high order of probability that our friends are very
good at interpreting gestures—even human gestures."

A man directly across the circle from Little raised a hand. The doctor
nodded to him.

"When we were loading food, before we made that break, I dropped
my testing kit into my pack first of all. I didn't try to cover it up and I
concentrated on boxed articles of food afterward to make it look natural."
The speaker was one of Goldthwaite's assistants, a tall fellow with the in-
signia of a technician's mate. Little knew him fairly well. He had been born
on Earth but showed plainly a background of several generations on the
colony-planet Regulus Six—big bones, dark skin, quick reactions.

"Good work, Dennis. What is in the kit?"

"Pliers, volt-ammeter, about sixty feet of assorted sizes of silver wire,
two-thousand-line grating, midget atomic wire-welder, six plano-convex
lenses of various focal lengths, support rod and two mirrors to go with
them, and a small stroboscope."

"Item, one portable laboratory," remarked Little. "Congratulations.
Leo, I suppose you have outdone your brother?"

Leo Dennis, the twin brother of the first speaker, shook his head.
"Just an old-fashioned manual razor. I'll start accepting offers tomorrow."
Little smiled and fingered his chin.

"You're too late, unless someone brought scissors to start with. Safety
razors weren't built to cope with a ten-day growth, more or less. Never
mind, we may find a use for it—it's a cutting tool, anyway. Next?"

There was a pause, with everybody looking expectantly at his neighbor. Evidently the total had been reached. Little spoke again.

"Did anybody try to smuggle something and fail?"

"I tried to salvage Goldy's liquor, and had it taken from me," answered another man. "I guess they're firmly convinced it's lethal. I wish
them luck in analyzing the stuff—we never could."

"How far did you get before they took it from you?"

"They let me pick up the bottles that were lying around, and put
them in the case; half a dozen of them watched me while I did that. But
when I started to carry the case toward the gate—of course, that was some
job, as Goldy found out—they all walked up and just took it away. They
didn't get violent or anything like that."

"Then it wasn't really a case of detected smuggling; you made no effort to mask your real intentions. Is that right?"

"Yes, sir. I don't quite see how anyone could hide either that case or
the bottles; I was just sort of hoping against hope."

Little nodded and called for more contributions. A gunner responded. "I found a couple of cases of grenades and stuck several into my pockets. The next thing I knew, one of the starfish was holding my arms, and another taking them out again. He handled them as though he knew what they were."

"1 suppose you checked the safeties before you pocketed the bombs?"

"Of course, sir,"

Little nodded wearily. "Of course. And that was enough for our admittedly astute friends. I admit it's usually a very good idea to obey regulations, but there are exceptions to every rule. I think the present circumstances constitute an exception to most of them. Any others?"

Apparently no one else had seen anything he coveted sufficiently to attempt to sneak out of the piles. The doctor didn't care particularly; he believed he had enough data from that source, and an idea was rapidly growing. Unfortunately, the primary principle of that idea required him to learn even more, though not about his captors. Possibly the Vegans could supply the information, but Little was not prepared to bet on it.

Magill closed the discussion by mentioning the anesthetic which Little had made available, and requesting an early communication of all ideas. The men withdrew into smaller groups, talking in low tones among themselves, and gradually drifted through the doors to their rooms, or out onto the roof. Magill followed to take a small group down again for the sleeping bags.

Little remained with the Vegans. He had a good deal to ask them, and material which could be covered in an hour of verbal conversation would probably take three or four hours of arm-waving. He sat just outside the fan of intense light from one of the doorways, and the creatures formed a semicircle just inside—the door was wide enough for the four of them, since it had been constructed to admit the pentapods. The doctor opened the conversation.

"How long have you been here?" was his first question. It was answered by the individual who had acted as interpreter.

"Since our arrival there have passed about two hundred of the days of this planet. We are not sure just how long they are, but we believe they are about thirty of your hours. We have no idea of the length of time that elapsed between our capture and our arrival at this place, however. We were driving a small private ship on a sightseeing trip to a world which had recently been reported near the galactic center by one of our official exploring vessels, and were near its reported position when we were taken. They simply engulfed us—moved up and dragged our ship into a cargo lock with magnets. We were on their ship a long time before they put us off here and left again, and we were not allowed to obtain any of our belongings except food and ultraviolet lamps until we arrived; so we don't know how long the trip lasted. One of us"—the Vegan indicated the individual—"got up courage enough to venture onto the roof one night and saw what he thinks was the Galaxy; so we believe this world lies in the Cloud. You will be able to tell better for yourselves—you can stand the dark longer than we, and your eyes are better at locating faint details."

"You may be right. We were heading toward the Cloud when we were taken," answered Little. "How freely have you been permitted to move about this fort?"

"We may go almost anywhere above ground level," was the answer. "Some of these watchers"—a supple antenna gestured toward the ever-present guards—"are always with us, and they prevent us from taking the elevators any lower. Then there are a few rooms on the upper levels which are always sealed, and two or three which are open but whose thresholds we are not permitted to cross."

"How do they prevent your entering?"

"They simply get in front of us, and push us back if we persist. They have never used violence on us. They never need to; we are in no position to dispute their wishes. There is no comparison between them and us physically, and we are very much out of our natural environment."

"Have you been able to deduce the nature or purpose of the rooms from which you are barred?"

"We assume that they are control rooms, communication offices, or chart rooms. One of them contains several devices which look like ordinary television screens. Whether they are for long-range use or are merely part of a local system, of course we cannot tell." Little pondered for several moments before speaking again.

"You mentioned constructing several devices to aid in escape, only to have them taken away from you just before they were completed. Could you give me more details on just what happened? What were you doing, and at what stage were you interrupted? How did you expect to get away from the planet?"

"We did not expect to get away. We just wanted to make them go, so we could take over the fort. When we disconnected their tube lights to put in our own, he"—indicating the creature beside him—"managed to retain a sample of the tube. On its walls were absorbed layers of several gases, but neon was the chief component. We had smuggled in the neutrino converters and stabilizers from our ship"—and Keys said these fellows were helpless, thought Little—"and it occurred to us that we might set up a neon-oxygen reaction which would flood the place with ultraviolet. We had already noticed that they could not stand it any better than you. The half life of the process would have been of the order of twelve hours, which should have driven them out for a period of time ample for our purpose. A neutrino jet of very moderate power, correctly tuned, could easily have catalyzed such a reaction in every light tube in the place. We had built the projector, disguising it as another ultraviolet lamp, and were connecting the converter when about fifty of the guards dived in, took the whole thing away, and ran out before the lamps we already had going could hurt them."

Little heroically forbore to ask the creatures why they had not smuggled in their ship while they were about it and flown away. The Vegans wouldn't have appreciated the humor.

"I believe I understand the purpose of the actions of these creatures," he said. "But some of their characteristics still puzzle me. Their teamwork is perfect, better than that of well-trained human fighters, but if my idea is correct their technical knowledge is inferior to ours. I have already mentioned to my captain their apparent lack of conceit—that is also based on my guess as to their motives in capturing us. One thing, however, I do not understand at all. How do they communicate? I have always been reluctant to fall back on the 'explanation' of telepathy; there are reasons which make me doubt that it can ever be a satisfactory substitute for a language."

The Vegans looked at him for a moment, astonishment reflected in the tenseness of their antennae.

"You do not see how they talk?" signaled one at length. "That is the first and only thing we have been able to appreciate in their entire make-up."

Little leaned forward. "Explain, please," he waved tensely. "That may be the most important thing any of us has yet ascertained."

The Vegans explained at length. Great length. The recital was stretched out by Little's frequent questions, and once or twice delayed by his imperfect comprehension of the Vegan language. The sun was low in the west when the conversation ended, but the doctor had at last what he believed to be a complete mental picture of the habits, thoughts, and nature of the pentapods, and he had more than the glimmerings of a plan which might set the human and Vegan prisoners free once more. He hoped.

He left his nonhuman allies, and sought out Magill. He found him at the western corner of the roof, examining the landscape visible beyond the tail of the spaceship. A couple of pentapods were on hand, as usual. Leo Dennis was making himself useful, sketching the western skyline on a pad he carried, with the apparent intention of marking the sunset point. Magill had evidently decided that an assistant navigator should be able to get his own location on a planet's surface as well as in space. Dennis was slightly handicapped by a total lack of instruments, but was doing his best. Little approached the quartermaster.

"Has anything new turned up, Keys?"

The officer shook his head without turning. "The men are all over the roof, to see if there are any ventilator intakes or anything else. One of them pointed out that the lack of superstructure suggested that the roof might be used as a landing place for atmosphere craft, and found some blast marks to back up the idea. No one else has made any worth-while reports. If there are any aircraft, though, I'd like to know where they stow them."

"It might help, though I hope we won't be driven to using them. I suppose the boys have their eyes open for large, probably level-set trapdoors in the roof. But what I wanted to find out was: with whom am I sharing a room?"

"Don't recall, offhand," replied Magill. "It doesn't matter greatly. If there is anyone in particular you want—or don't want—to be with, you're at liberty to trade with someone. I told the boys that."

"Thanks. I want to spend some time with the Dennis boys, without making it too obvious. I suppose they're already together. By the way, seeing I'm still a medical officer, has anyone reported sick? The air is just a shade on the thin side, and we've been breathing it long enough for effects to show, if there are going to be any."

Magill shook his head negatively, and Little strolled over to Leo, who had completed his sketch and was trying to mark the position of the sun at five-minute intervals. He was wearing one of the few watches possessed by the party. He was perfectly willing to have his erstwhile roommate replaced by the doctor, especially when Little promised work to be done. He agreed to speak to his brother and to Cauley, who had originally been assigned to their room.

"Tell Arthur to bring his pack, with the kit he sneaked along," added the doctor. "We will probably have use for it." Leo nodded, grinning, and resumed his attempts to fix the position of an object, much too bright to view directly, which had an angular breadth on the order of half a degree. He didn't appear discouraged yet.

Little wandered off across the roof, occasionally meeting and speaking to one of the men. Morale seemed to be good, he noted with relief. He had always considered that to be part of the business of a medical officer, since it was, after all, directly reflected in the health of the men.

A motion in the direction of the setting sun caught his eye. He turned to face it and saw a narrow, dazzling crescent low in the western sky, a crescent that rose and grew broader as he watched. The planet had a satellite, like Mars, so close that its period of revolution was less than one of its own days. Little wondered if a body so close to the planet might not prove useful. He filed the thought away for future reference.

The sun set as he watched, and he realized he had been right about the thinness of the air. Darkness shut down almost at once. The moon sprang into brilliance—brilliance that was deceptive, for details on the landscape were almost impossible to make out. Stars, scattered at random over the sky, began to appear; and as the last traces of daylight faded away, there became visible, at first hazily and then clear and definite, the ghostly shape of the Galaxy. Its sprawling spiral arms stretched across a quarter of the sky, the bulk of the system inclined some thirty degrees from the edge-on position—just enough to show off the tracing of the great lanes of dust that divided the arms.

The men began to drift toward the orange glow that shone through the entrance panels and windows of the "penthouse." They were greeted by the whistle of Denham, who had just completed preparation of another meal. It was eaten as the first had been, in the corridor with a silent audience of guards. The men had grown used to the creatures, and were no longer bothered by their presence. The conversation was desultory, except when Arthur Dennis offered to take the place of Denham's helper for the evening. It was the most plausible excuse for entering the kitchen-storeroom, where the packs had been stowed. No one commented, though everybody guessed the reason.

Windows and doors of all rooms were left open, the first because of Little's advice, the second because the pentapods had removed all means of closing the entrances—privacy was impossible, which did not in the least surprise Little. At the conclusion of the meal, he accompanied Leo Dennis to the latter's room, which was near the end of the corridor farthest from the elevator, and waited for the arrival of Arthur. A little investigation solved the secret of turning out the room's tube lights, which darkened the place somewhat, but the light from the corridor was sufficient to move around by.

Arthur entered after about fifteen minutes, carrying three packs under his arms. Two of these he tossed to his brother and the doctor, remarking, "Pillows in one suite, anyway!" The other he retained. The three men rolled up the packs and placed them under the canvas at the heads of their sleeping bags, conscious meanwhile of the never-ending scrutiny from the door; then they leaned back against the wall and relaxed.

The twins had tobacco, and all three smoked as they talked. A remark of Leo's, which opened the conversation, eased Little's mind of one problem which had been bothering him.

"Before we do or say anything else, Doc," said the navigator, "please think carefully before you tell us anything. I suppose you found out a good deal from the Vegans, and I wouldn't be surprised to know you have a campaign all mapped out; but I don't want to know more than necessary. I have developed, from what the Vegans said and from what I've seen myself, a very healthy respect for the intuition, or guessing powers, or whatever it is, of our silent watchers. It makes me uncomfortable. And the less I know the more natural I can let myself act. All right?"

"All right; that was my own idea, too," answered the doctor. "I will tell you no more than necessary. In the first place I should, like Magill, like to know our location on this planet and the planet's location in space. That, unquestionably, is your job, Leo. Then I want to get the information to the handiest Union base or ship. That's all. I don't believe we could break out of here, though probably Keys will try. I pin my hope on our broadcasting a message from inside and letting people already outside do the rest."

The brothers nodded. "That's clear enough," said Leo, "and I can probably locate us fairly well if...Art, did you say you had a grating in that kit of yours?"

"Yes," was the answer. "Do you need it?"

"Uncertain, but probably. I'll have to identify the local navigation beacon somehow, and its spectrum will be the most outstanding hallmark. Why don't Doc and I go outside now and do some star-gazing, while you curl up in your sleeping bag and see if the shadows don't follow us? If they do, you can rummage in the kit without being seen, and come out in a few minutes with the grating and a couple of the lenses you mentioned. If they don't, we'll do what we can with the naked eye and come back. Sound?"

"Solid. Be seeing you."

Arthur extinguished the stub of his cigarette, loosened his belt and shirt, and began removing his boots, while Leo and Little rose and went out into the hallway. Pentapods, scattered along the corridor, eyed them as they emerged, but made no move to intercept them. The door opening outside had been left ajar by the Earthmen in their policy of avoiding the use of the building's ventilation system, and the guards were evidently following a policy of noninterference with regard to everything but weapons. The panel was still partly open.

Little pushed it wide, and the two human beings went out onto the roof. To their surprise they were not followed; but both realized that there might already be guards on the roof. They moved out of the path of the light from the door and approached the nearest wall.

The mountains to the northeast were silhouetted against the almost equally dark sky; the forest at their feet was indistinguishable. No glow or spark of light suggested the presence, anywhere in the scene, of the men who had escaped nine hours before, though Little and Dennis strained their eyes looking. Not even a reflection from the river the doctor believed must be present broke the dark expanse.

The sky offered more material for comment. The Galaxy was lower in the west and the moon higher. Dennis, looking at the latter, did some rapid mental arithmetic. It had risen about an hour and a half ago, and would probably reach the zenith in a little more than another hour. Its sidereal period, then, must be about eight hours, and its distance, if this world had the same size and mass as Earth, a little over eight thousand miles from the surface. It was now nearly at "first quarter," but its dark side was faintly visible, presumably illuminated by the reflected light of the planet. Somewhat less than four hours after sunset, the satellite should enter the planet's shadow and be eclipsed for about forty minutes, unless its orbit were more highly inclined to that of the planet than appeared to be the case.

Little was looking at the stars, spread over the sky in unfamiliar constellations. "Which of these is the local navigation beacon, and how do you identify it?" he asked. "And why do you pick out one star to call a beacon?"

"It would be possible to obtain our position from any three stars whose location is on the charts," answered Dennis, "but it is much easier, as a rule, to use certain individuals, because tables have been computed for use with them, and they are easier to identify. I don't have the tables with me, of course, but the beacon for this neighborhood and the Galaxy, together, would give me a fairly good idea. We use the brightest available stars for beacons, naturally—Rigel and Deneb in the Solar sector, for example. For navigation in the Larger Cloud we use a slightly different system, which employs two super-giant stars back in the Galaxy and the one local beacon which covers the whole Cloud—S Doradus. It shouldn't be hard to find, even without instruments, since it's a first-magnitude star at a thousand parsecs; but we always like to check the spectrum, if possible. Most beacon stars, of course, are O, B, or A supergiants, but there are usually detectable individual differences which can be picked out by a good instrument. We haven't a good instrument, but fortunately S Doradus has a very distinctive spectrum."

Little nodded. "I can see that much. Don't tell me how you reduce the observations to get your position; it would certainly go beyond my mathematical limit, and I don't like to be shown up."

"It's not difficult—elementary spherical trig. If you know what a direction cosine is, you're all right. Matter of fact, that's how positions are indicated—three direction cosines from a given beacon, plus distance. I don't know how we'll get the distance—I can estimate brightness to a tenth of a magnitude, but that may answer to a small percentage of an awful distance. We usually can triangulate, but not in the Cloud."

"I'll take your word for it," replied the doctor. "Can you see anything that might be your beacon?"

"There's a fairly bright specimen sitting just above the north horizon, that seems to have a tinge of yellow; and there's another right overhead. If Art ever gets here with the lenses and grating I'll test them. I suppose he can't make it, since the dumb chums didn't follow us out here and give him a chance to burrow into the kit."

"He may find a way to do it anyway," remarked the doctor.

"It would be just like him to try, and lose the kit," was the pessimistic answer.

Even Little was growing discouraged by the time Arthur finally arrived. They had been out nearly an hour, Little amusing himself by strolling along the walls to see whether anything were visible below, and Leo observing the satellite as it approached the zenith. He had already come to the conclusion, from the fact that the sun had set practically "straight down," that they were near the equator of the planet. It now seemed that the moon was in the equatorial plane, since it was rising to a point directly overhead. It was well past first quarter now, but the unlighted crescent was still visible. Leo had just noticed this fact when Arthur's voice interrupted his pondering.

"I assumed you wanted the lenses for a telescope of sorts, and chose accordingly," said the technician. "It took me a long time to work the kit out of the pack and into the sleeping bag because the guards were looking in every two or three minutes. I don't know what will happen when they find me gone."

"I do, you chump," answered Leo. "Two or three of them will drift out here after us, and some more will seize the chance to investigate the pack whose position you changed so often."

"Think so?" asked Arthur. "Here are the lenses and grating. I brought the rod and lens clamps, too, but I'm afraid you'll have to get along without a tube." His brother accepted the assortment and fell to work. The doctor looked on silently. Arthur had brought a light also, and held it on the step which served as a workbench.

Leo, after a moment's thought, discarded one lens and used the other—the one of longer focal length. He clamped this at one end of the rod, with the plane side toward the center. The grating was smaller than the lens, and he clamped it against the plane face of the latter with the excess glass blocked off with paper. Another sheet of paper—a leaf torn from his sketch pad—was clamped to the rod at the focal distance of the lens, completing the crude spectroscope.

He set the instrument on the wall, propping it so that it was pointed toward the northern horizon and one of the stars he had mentioned. He leaned over it, to cut off the moonlight. The other two also leaned forward to see the results.

A little streak of color, narrow as a pencil line, was just visible on the paper screen. Leo brought his eyes as close as he could, striving to perceive the tiny dark gaps that should have existed; but the resolution of the instrument was not sufficient. After a moment's pause, he returned to the original idea, removing the paper and clamping the other lens in normal eyepiece position. This proved successful. He could make out enough to identify both the stars he had counted on as unquestionably sun-type G stars, probably no more than a few parsecs distant, and definitely not the giant he sought.

The navigator began to wear a worried expression. There were several thousand stars visible to the naked eye, and only a few of them were obviously not the object of his search. After a few minutes, however, he began a methodical examination of all the brighter yellow and white stars, one after another. Arthur and the doctor saw that interruption would not be helpful, so they withdrew a few yards and conversed in low tones.

"What will you do if Leo does get our position?" asked the technician. "I suppose you have some idea."

"The idea I have depends almost entirely on you," answered Little. "I have been told that a second-order transmitter is less complicated than an ordinary radio. Could you build one?"

Dennis frowned and hesitated. "If I had all the materials and no interruptions, yes. Here and now, I don't know if the necessary equipment is available, and I'm reasonably sure we wouldn't be allowed to do it, anyway."

"You said there were two atomic tools in your kit, a heater and a stroboscope," said Little. "Would their parts be enough?" Once again Dennis paused to think.

"The welder wouldn't—it's just a converter and a tungsten element. The stroboscope converts with a direct electron current and a variable oscillator and—I believe it could be done. But it wouldn't handle much power, and the range would be nothing to speak of."

"That doesn't matter, as I see it. All I want to know is that you can build a vision transmitter with the material on hand—"

"Wait a minute!" interrupted Arthur. "I didn't say a vision unit. What do you need that for? All I was counting on was voice transmission. That won't be very difficult."

Little shook his head. "Vision or nothing. I don't want to tell you why, for the reason Leo gave. But please, if you don't want me to have to redesign the whole plan, find a way to construct a vision transmitter. And I hate to be too exacting, but I'd like it done before that ship leaves again. I don't know how long they usually stay here, but I notice they're stocking up."

"Sure," groaned Dennis. "Right away. Doc, if it were anyone else I'd know he was crazy, but with you it's only a strong suspicion. I'll try—but Lord knows where I can come by an icon tube."

Little grinned invisibly in the darkness. "The Vegans said they smuggled up a complete neutrino assembly. It was taken away from them later, but it gives you an idea of what can be done."

"They didn't give you an idea of their technique, I suppose? I'm not too proud to learn."

"I didn't ask them. There were guards around. Good luck!"

Little went back to Leo, who was resting his arms. Not a single O-class spectrum had yet been picked up by the instrument.

"If I were sure it were there, I wouldn't mind so much," he said, wiping his forehead. "But it's just as likely to be in the daylight half of the sky. I'd rather not have to wait here half of whatever time it takes this world to amble around its sun, just to get a rough idea of where I am."

Little nodded sympathetically—after all, he was the one who wanted their location. "Does the moonlight interfere any?" he asked.

"It did, until I made a rough tube out of paper. It's a little hard to hold together. But speaking of the moon, Doc, have you noticed anything strange about it?"

"I wouldn't," answered Little. "Is something wrong? It looks natural to me."

"It doesn't to me. It did right after sunset, when it was a narrow crescent. We could see the rest of it then, but reflection from this planet could have accounted for that. But it doesn't now! The darn thing's nearly full, and you can still see the strip that the sun doesn't reach. This world can't possibly reflect enough light for that. What's lighting it up?"

"I'm afraid it's no use to ask me," said the doctor. "I can guarantee it's not radioactivity, because that much radioactive matter so close would have prevented the existence of life on this world. It would have been burned sterile; we'd probably be dead now ourselves. I don't know any astronomy, but I can tell you all you want to know about gamma-ray burns."

"That occurred to me, too," agreed Leo. "It seems that there must be something, at present invisible to us, shining on that satellite. I think in a few minutes we'll be able to get an idea of where it's shining from, too."

"How?" asked Little and Arthur with one voice.

"The moon should pass into this planet's shadow very shortly," answered Leo. "A lunar eclipse. The satellite must have one every revolution—

almost four times a day, I should say. The sun's light will be cut off, except for the fraction scattered by the atmosphere of this world, and we should be able to tell from the shape of the part illuminated by this mystery source, the direction of the source. We'll wait." The other two nodded. Even Little. who was no astronomer, understood the mechanism of an eclipse. The three settled themselves on the broad steps inside the wall.

They had not long to wait. It was about three and a quarter hours after sunset, and the first outlying tentacles of the looming Galaxy were just dipping below the western horizon, when Leo marked the first darkening of the eastern limb of the nearly full moon. It was not like the protracted lunar eclipse of Earth; the satellite was moving far more swiftly, and took less than a minute to travel its own diameter. There was a feeble, preliminary reddening as it plunged into the region illuminated only by air-scattered light; then this was gone, as the little body passed on into the umbra of the planet's shadow.

It should have disappeared. No possible reflection from the planet it circled could have given it a touch of illumination, for it looked down only on the night side of the world. Yet part of it was still to be seen—a ghostly, dim-lit crescent, a little less than half full, its convex side facing *east*. There was no possible question of the nature of the light source. Leo estimated the distance of the moon above the eastern horizon, and the angular breadth of illuminated surface; there was only a small difference.

"It will rise before long," he said. "I'm staying to see. You fellows can go back to sleep if you wish; we've been out over two hours and we'll need some sleep."

"We'll stay," said Little. "This gets interesting. Do you think there's another, very bright moon? Large enough, perhaps, to be habitable?"

Leo shook his head. "I don't believe any possible moon could do that," he said. Arthur nodded in silent agreement, and for many minutes the three sat without speaking as the dimly lit crescent dipped lower toward the eastern horizon. Leo had judged roughly that the eclipse should last about forty minutes.

It had not ended when Arthur pointed silently to the east. A spur of the mountain range whose principal peaks lay to the northeast had become a little clearer, silhouetted against a suddenly brighter patch of sky. The brilliance grew and spread, paling the stars in that quarter of the heavens as though dawn were breaking; and quite suddenly the source rode clear of the concealing hill and presented itself to view. The undulations of the landscape were abruptly visible, standing out against the long shadows cast by the light of the newcomer, which hung, far brighter than the moon at its best, just above the peaks.

The men looked on in awe. They had seen the mad splendor of the spiraling gas streams hurled forth from binaries like Beta Lyrae; they had driven through the hearts of globular clusters, with giant suns by the myriad on every hand; but somehow the lonely, majestic grandeur of this object was more impressive. A star—too distant to show a perceptible disk—too bright to be gazed at directly, putting to shame the surrounding celestial objects. Even the moon, sliding out of the shadow in an apologetic fashion, no longer seemed bright.

Arthur Dennis was the first to speak. "It gets you, doesn't it? I suppose it's a companion to the sun, or else—"

"Or *else,*" said Leo flatly, snatching the spectroscope. The great star was white, with just a suspicion of topaz in its glow, and Leo was prone to jump to conclusions. One glance through the instrument, sweeping it slightly from left to right, was enough. He grinned, removed the eye lens, and replaced the paper screen of the original arrangement, and three heads bent once more to look at the streak of color.

It wasn't a streak this time. A single bright point centered itself directly behind the objective lens, and to either side of this there extended a broken series of dashes—the intense emission bands, bordered on the violet side by relatively sharp dark lines, which characterize what the early astronomers called a "P Cygni" star. The continuous background spectrum was too faint to show; the grating was so coarse that several orders of the spectrum fell on the paper at once.

"And that's your beacon!" remarked Little after a few moments of silence. "Well, it certainly earns the name."

"You can get our location now?" asked Arthur. I should think you wouldn't need to say much but 'Near S Doradus,' from the looks of that thing."

"Wrong, blast it," answered Leo. "When I said I could judge brightness to a tenth of a magnitude, I was thinking of decent stars with visual mags between zero and plus six. For this thing, I don't know whether it's minus five or minus fifteen—whether the blasted thing is three quarters of a parsec or eighty parsecs away. I'll get the direction, though, and maybe I'll find a way to measure the brightness. I'll look after that, you people worry about what to do with it if I get it. Good night."

The dismissal was rather pointed, and Leo turned his full attention to the pad on which he was computing, so Little and Arthur silently retired. So did all but one of the guards who had been watching, invisible in the shadow of the superstructure.

Dr. Little opened his eyes with a start and realized it was full daylight. It had been the first sleep under normal gravity in several weeks, and his body had made the most of it. The other two sleeping bags were empty, but the Dennis brothers were both present. They were by the window, removing a piece of canvas that had apparently been draped across it. Little sat up.

"What are you fellows up to now?" he asked. "Leo, don't you ever sleep?"

"Sure, when necessary. You have been sleeping for twelve hours, Doc. Did we wake you up?"

"Twelve hours! No, it was probably my conscience. What's the idea of window curtains? We haven't even a door, so it can't be privacy."

"We were screening out the sunlight Leo didn't want," answered Arthur. "He was trying to get the sun's spectrum, and just wanted a narrow beam through the grating."

"Did you get it?"

"Sure." It was Leo speaking again. "And we found a use for the razor. The edges of the blades are good for making a slit for the beam. This fellow, of course, didn't have anything in that wonderful testing kit that would do. By the way, Art, have you still got the kit, or did our friends take it last night?"

"Someone poked around in it," Arthur answered, "but they left it here. Maybe they thought there was nothing in it that we could put to use."

"I think they would have left it, anyway," remarked the doctor, grinning at the expressions of unbelief on the two faces.

Leo walked over to his brother's sleeping bag and took the kit box from the pack. "You know best, Doc. In that case, I'm going to have a look, and find out if there's anything useful that Art forgot to mention— Art, you dope!"

"What's wrong now?" asked the technician, without moving.

"The welder and the stroboscope you spoke of—they're gone! And you said the guards must have decided the stuff was harmless. What do we do now?"

"The welder and stroboscope are in my pockets, and have been since last night. You thought of the stuff's being taken, didn't you? And did you *ever* think of anything without my beating you to it? You worry about your own department; I can take care of mine, I hope." The last phrase was stimulated by an amused glance from the doctor.

They strolled out into the mixed crowd of humans and pentapods in the corridor, and Arthur went over to the kitchen. He appeared to have taken on permanently the job of cook's helper. Little located the quartermaster, and began discussing the day's possibilities. They seemed to be few. Most of the crew were specialists of one sort or another, experts in the fields of knowledge and activity necessary to fly and fight an interstellar cruiser; but one and all were hampered by lack of materials and tools. The only way to get these appeared to be theft, at which the crew of the *Gomeisa* were not specialists. The only advice Little could give was that the men should do their best to smuggle in materials, to the exclusion of other occupations, and anyone who had a workable idea should let the others know what he needed to work it. Not very helpful, since everybody already had that idea. It looked as though time would pass rather boringly.

It did. The men wandered more or less freely about the roof and the corridors of the building below, and occasionally went out to the supply piles for material they wanted. To Magill's surprise, but not to Little's, they were allowed to take even pieces of scientific apparatus without interference.

"1 don't get it," said the quartermaster when a man reported bringing in a portable atomic melting furnace. "Anyone could see that that was a dangerous tool in the hands of a prisoner. Why do they let us get away with it?"

"To me," answered Little, "that is the least puzzling factor. The treatment we are getting shows that there can be only one reason for our capture—to learn from us. Naturally, we must be allowed access to tools and scientific equipment. Then they watch our efforts to escape, and help themselves to the results of our labor. What is so puzzling about that?"

Magill was silent for several minutes. "Put that way," he said at last, "it's obvious. I don't know why I didn't think of it before. That, I suppose, is why you said they weren't a conceited race—they go to such lengths to take the knowledge of others. But what happens if they're a little slow in taking a weapon away from us?"

"Apparently they are prepared to take that risk. They have succeeded so far with the Vegans, and they have all our standard weapons, you'll note. That ability of theirs to guess the purpose of our actions is our chief bugbear. It's unusual; most of the time it's almost impossible for two races meeting for the first time to understand even each other's standard gestures, let alone natural, unstereotyped face and body motions. But do your best with that in mind."

Little did not say that, with the aid of the information given by the Vegans, he had been able to deduce the reason for the almost telepathic guessing ability of the pentapods; and he did not mention the plan that he and the Dennis brothers were trying to put into operation. If Magill went ahead with ideas of his own, it would probably occupy much of the attention of their guards. Not that Little wanted it *all* occupied.

The reports of the men who had wandered through the building agreed with the statements of the Vegans—most places were permitted, below ground was not, some rooms were locked, and some were open but the men had been kept out. One room, on the top floor almost directly below the prison quarters, appeared to be a communications office—which was a natural situation, if the roof had originally been used as a landing platform. The purpose of most of the others was not cleat. Little did some wandering himself, and personally checked most of the information.

That evening the Vegans ate with the men; their own supplies had given out long before, of course, and they had been living on food supplied by the pentapods. It was evidently harmless, but far from enjoyable, according to the Vegans. Arthur Dennis served the food to them at their doorway, and brought the mess kits back to the kitchen after the meal. The guards usually withdrew some distance while the men were eating; the odors evidently did not appeal to them. Consequently, there was none of the creatures in the kitchen when Arthur brought back the kit. His self-assigned position as cook's helper was becoming constantly more useful, he reflected.

Days in prison tend to be rather boring. Nights are better because one can sleep and forget the boredom for a while; but from this night on Arthur Dennis knew he would sleep very little, though he planned to trade his sleeping bag for one several sizes larger and retire completely into it. He decided to develop the habit of keeping his face partly covered by the canvas flap, and have his companions emulate him to make the action seem more natural. He was jubilant when the others came to the room.

"I have an icon tube, Doc," he said from the depths of the sleeping bag. "That's what worried me most. I can build the second-order converter from the stuff I already had, and I can probably dig up enough from the other boys to make the tube connections. It's lucky they let us keep the hand lights. I don't know how I'd put this stuff together in the dark."

"How did you get the tube?" asked Little. "I didn't see you go downstairs all day, and I don't think many of the men knew about the guards' having let a good deal of apparatus by without trouble, so they wouldn't have done it for you."

Arthur grinned in the darkness. "Since I didn't have the Vegan technique we mentioned. I bet one of the Vegans fifty Union credits it couldn't be done—thus implying my doubt of his story of smuggling up a neutrino unit. He slipped it into his mess kit this evening after the meal, and I got it in the kitchen. He was a little touchy about my rudeness, but I apologized this evening and he's cooled off. I pay the bet if and when we reach a Union planet and can get some money," The technician ceased speaking, and the flap fell again across the opening of the bag.

Silence fell throughout the room, broken by the even breathing of two people and the occasional almost inaudible footfalls of the guard outside. Once or twice a shadow fell across the doorway as one of the creatures looked in, but it defeated its own purpose by blocking the light, and saw nothing. Dennis was careful, anyway, and allowed no motion to show through the padded canvas of die sleeping bag.

He was not interrupted that night, and worked for two or three hours before placing the partly completed unit in his kit and going to sleep.

The next morning it occurred to Little that the Vegans might have some idea of the probable length of stay of the ship. After the morning meal he squatted in front of the doorway of their quarters and questioned the creatures.

"They usually remain about ten days," was the answer. "But it is impossible to tell for sure. This is the first time prisoners have been brought since we came. We didn't notice how long they stayed on our arrival—we were too worried about other things."

"How long do they remain away, usually?"

"There is no 'usually' about it, the duration is absolutely unpredictable as far as we can see. Sometimes the ship is gone for only a day, sometimes for several weeks. It is evidently not a patrol cruiser with a regular beat."

Little thanked the creature and left, to ponder the effect of the new facts on his plans. He returned almost at once, to ask another question:

"Does the garrison of the fort appear to expect the ship at any time before its actual arrival?"

"Not obviously, if at all," was the answer.

Little nodded, satisfied. He sought out the Dennis brothers. Leo was in their sleeping room, trying to manufacture a photometer from the lenses of a pair of dark goggles an atomic engineer had found in his pocket. The doctor located Arthur and brought him back to the room, and asked if either one knew anything about geletane.

"Not much," answered Leo. "I gathered that it was more than an ordinary anesthetic when I heard you had lived through an exposure to space while under its influence."

"Right," nodded Little. "It produces, to put it crudely, suspended animation. It is adsorbed, apparently, on all the cell surfaces in the body, foreign bacteria included, and seals them from chemical influence. One would expect that to produce death, since the destruction of the gas film could not start the vital processes again; but the patient always revives. I could put my finger on ten different theses in the New York Medical Library, each suggesting a different mechanism and none completely satisfactory. The film, when it breaks, seems to do so everywhere at once, and there is an abnormal amount of carbon dioxide in the blood immediately thereafter; but the whole process is not thoroughly understood.

"It seems, however, that the cell walls themselves tend to cause the breakdown of the film; and if a person exposed to the gas is exercising violently, that action is increased to a point where he is *not affected at all.* If he holds his breath, and otherwise suspends body activity, it gets him almost instantly. The gas, as you can see, has an all-or-none nature. I wanted you to understand this, because it is possible we may have to use the gas in the near future. Think it over." The brothers kept their faces nearly expressionless, but it was perceptible that they thought the matter over with some pleasure. Arthur, slightly the more imaginative of the two, immediately assumed that the gassing was to take place when the communicator was finished, so that they would have a chance to use it.

With this pleasant prospect in mind, Arthur worked even longer that night. The converter was completed, and he began to construct a support for the tube and its connections before he was forced to sleep. Again, his work apparently went undetected by the ever-prowling guards. His hopes showed so clearly on his face the next morning that his brother kicked him firmly and ungently in the shins as a reminder of the unbelievable expression-comprehension of the pentapods.

He reported to Little that the device would probably be completed that night. The doctor nodded and said:

"Good work, Art. We probably had another week before the ship left, but this is better than I expected. As soon as Leo gets his photometer done and finds our distance from S Doradus, things should start to pop; and that should be fairly soon." In this statement Little was half right; things started happening quite soon, but they did not wait for the navigator's mate to complete his tasks.

The doctor found Leo seated on one of the steps which lined the outer wall. He was examining closely an object, consisting chiefly of several small fragments of darkened glass, which proved to be his photometer; and like his brother, he was obviously in good humor.

"All done, Doc," he said on sighting Little. "I can measure tonight—calibrate this thing on stars I can estimate, and then do the beacon. It's lucky I already know its absolute magnitude. What do you think are the chances of that gadget of Art's reaching a Union receiver?"

Little smiled without speaking, and shrugged his shoulders. His opinion was that the question was unimportant, but it would not do to say so. He might be misunderstood. He fully believed that they would be caught the moment they attempted to start broadcasting. Without committing himself, he admonished Leo not to lose the photometer, and went in search of Magill.

To that officer he spoke earnestly for several minutes, making several requests which were granted only after persuasion. One of them had to do with the disposal of kitchen waste, and for once the doctor's interest was not in sanitation.

The rest of the day passed in as boring a fashion as had the two preceding.

Evening found the three conspirators in their room, planning the night's activities. Arthur, of course, would remain to "sleep." They found difficulty in deciding whether Little should remain with him, or accompany Leo on his astronomical expedition. If he went without an obvious purpose, the guards might wonder why he was the only curious sightseer and why Arthur didn't go, too; if he remained, they might wonder why he behaved differently from the previous occasion, and investigate the sleepers. Even the insight Little had gained into their thought processes could throw no light on this question.

Finally, he accompanied Leo, carrying the latter's pencil and pad to provide himself with an excuse. As on the previous occasion, none of the guards followed them through the door. They took up their former station by the wall and seated themselves on the steps until S Doradus should rise. The moon was only a little past first quarter, and the beacon would not rise tonight until some two hours after the eclipse, so they had a wait of nearly four hours. They had chosen to come out early, to avoid falling asleep and missing their chance.

For the first time since their arrival on the planet, there were clouds in the sky. These provided matter for conversation and anxiety for nearly three hours, as they completely covered the heavens on two occasions; but by the time the waning moon was sinking low in the east they had disappeared. The remaining time before observation could be started was passed in silence.

As the glow on the eastern horizon warned of the mighty star's advent, Leo went to work. Each of the fragments of glass he had obtained from the engineer's goggles was tested in turn, a star viewed through the darkened glass being compared with another seen directly. Little noted the results on the pad, though there was little need. The lenses had originally been very evenly darkened, and as nearly as Leo could estimate, a single thickness of the glass cut about three and five-tenths magnitudes from the brightness of an object.

When the beacon rose, his only task was to find the number of layers necessary to reduce its apparent brightness to that of a star lying in the range where his own judgment was good. The method obviously gave room for error, which increased with each additional thickness used, but it was better than guessing; and anyway, as Leo remarked, since S Doradus is an irregular variable, the best instruments in Civilization would still have left them with a probable error of over half a magnitude.

He measured and computed. "Art was almost right, at that," he remarked finally. " 'Near S Doradus' would almost be enough. I get an apparent magnitude of minus fourteen, which means a distance of just under one parsec." He took a fresh sheet of paper from the pad and wrote rapidly. "Here," he said, handing it to Little, "is the complete specification of our position, to two decimal places—I can't guess closer. It also includes the type of this planet and sun in standard terms, and a rough idea of our latitude on the planet. If you broadcast that and anyone hears you, they'll find us."

"And he can go right ahead and broadcast it, as soon as the rubbernecks are out of the way," broke in a new voice. "The gadget's done. I haven't tested it, naturally, but it can't help working. Say the word, Doc."

Little shook his head. "Not tonight. We must arrange some way to keep the broadcast from being too obvious. Come on to bed and we'll talk as we go. It would be too bad to slip up now."

They arose and walked slowly toward the lighted doorway.

"It seems to me that we only need to gas the guards in the immediate neighborhood, and lock ourselves into the quarters with them outside. There are no outside catches on the main doors, and I could seal the elevator panel with the welder—I didn't use it for the broadcaster, and it should stand the overload long enough."

They passed into the corridor. "That might work," mused the doctor. "There is only the one elevator, and no other entrances to the roof, from below, anyway. But we'd want as many hours as we could get, and I should think they could burn out the elevator door in a few minutes."

They entered the room in which they slept. "That could be prevented by simply leaving that door open when the elevator was up and going into action at that time," contributed Leo as they pulled off their boots. "Then they couldn't get at either the elevator or its door."

"How about the other men?" asked Little. "It will be difficult to tell them all about the geletane, and how to avoid its effects. What will—"

"Stop worrying about it," interrupted Arthur. He had lain down with the pack for a pillow, moved it to a more comfortable spot, noticed the ease with which it moved and, with a horrible suspicion in his mind, looked into the kit box inside. "The communicator is gone."

Possibly the guards in the corridor and on the roof were laughing, if their unhuman cerebral processes had ever evolved an emotion akin to humor. Certainly, they were pleased with themselves.

"You loon," growled Leo. "Why did you have to celebrate finishing the thing by tearing outside to tell us? It would have been simpler just to step outside our door and hand it to a guard."

The night had not passed too peacefully, in spite of Little's advice to save recriminations until morning. Relations between the twins were slightly strained. The sunlight coming through the window revealed only too clearly on Leo's face that expression of smug, "I wouldn't do such a thing" superiority that tends to drive repentant sinners to homicide.

"The meeting will please come to order," interrupted the doctor. "Leo, lay off Arthur. If it will make you any happier, Art, I'll tell you that if neither of you boys had spilled the beans in a day or two, I should have done so myself—carefully, of course. It was better for it to happen naturally. Now sit around, and wear a disgusted expression for the benefit of the guards if you like, and listen. This will take some time.

"In the first place, I suppose you've realized by now that we were captured simply for observation purposes; the pentapods hoped to learn about our weapons and science from our efforts to escape. They have, we must admit, been rather successful. Our activities have probably been evident to them from the first, but they waited until the communicator was completed before taking it, naturally. That habit of theirs struck me when the Vegans first described the way in which their plans were never interfered with until nearly mature.

"There was also the question of the surprising ease with which they were able to divine our feelings and intentions. It took me longer to discover the reason for that; but information supplied by the Vegans again provided the key.

"Their language is not verbal. None of us has yet heard them utter a vocal sound. We couldn't understand how they communicated, but to the Vegans it was so evident as to be unworthy of comment—their captors' language was of the same type as their own, visual rather than audible, a sign language in which the thousands of mobile spines with which their bodies are covered replaced the two antennae of a Vegan. It was so complex that the Vegans couldn't begin to learn it, but the method was obvious to them.

"That, to me, gave a nearly complete picture not only of their language, but of their thought; not only of the way they exchanged ideas, but of the very nature of those ideas.

"You have heard, no doubt, that thoughts may be considered as unuttered words. Of course, we do think in visual images, too, but *logical reasoning*, in human minds at least, takes the form of an unuttered conversation with oneself. Think through the proof of a theorem in grade-school geometry, if you don't believe it. With creatures like the Vegans, an analogous process takes place; they think in terms of the visible symbols of their language. The language, as you know, is slow—takes much longer to get ideas across. Also, it takes longer for a Vegan to comprehend something, though they certainly can't be called stupid.

"The same thing should happen, and does happen, with our captors. They think and talk immeasurably *faster* than we do; and their thoughts are not in arbitrary word or picture symbols, but in attitudes. Watching them, I have come to the conclusion that they don't have a language as we understand it at all; the motions and patterns of the spines, which convey thought from one to another, are as unconscious and natural as expressions on our faces. The difference being that their 'faces' cover most of their bodies, and have a far greater capacity for expression. The result is that they have as easy a time learning to interpret expressions and bodily attitudes of other creatures, as we would have learning a simple verbal tongue. What the psychologists call attitude—or expression, to us—is the key to their whole mental activity. Until we understood that, we had no chance of using their own methods to defeat them, or even of understanding the methods.

"When Albee and the others made that break, you noticed that the pentapods wasted no time in pursuing a man who was even slightly out of reach; they were able to reason with extreme rapidity even in a situation like that, and realized that they couldn't catch him. A man would have tried, at least.

"Like everything else, this high-speed communication has its disadvantages. These creatures could never have invented the telephone, any more than the Vegans could; and they'd have had the same difficulty with gadgets such as the telegraph. I don't know anything about their written language, but it must be ideographic and contain, unless I underestimate their capacity for bringing order out of chaos, a perfectly appalling number of symbols. Who could make up a dot-and-dash code for that? The Orientals of Earth had the same trouble. That would interfere with the 'evolution' of communication devices.

"Their long-distance communication, therefore, must be purely visual transmission. We have seen the television screens in their office downstairs—ten feet square, enough to picture any of the creatures full length. I'm sure that they can't broadcast their vision for two reasons: the Vegans say the ship always returns unexpectedly, and preparations are never made a few hours in advance of its arrival—as they would be if they could broadcast news of their approach. Also, there is no sign anywhere on this building of a beam-type second-order projector, or even the loop of a general field broadcaster such as Art was making. The images are transmitted by wire, and only inside this building. That was the reason, Art, that I insisted on your making a visual transmitter. They would have no desire to copy a telephone unit. They have it now; they'll have a full-size visual before that ship leaves; and their communications room is right below here, and should contain emergency accumulators in case the regular power goes.

"When the ship leaves, we wait a day. Then we collect the kitchen refuse, which Denham is accumulating, and pile it into the elevator to take outside—Leo, get that happy expression off your face—making the load big enough so that none of the guards can ride with us, though they don't usually these days anyway. Just before we go, the stove will break down, and Denham will come kicking about it. Arthur will go back, tinker with the stove, remove the geletane tank now clamped to it and replace it with another, and toss the 'used' tank in with the rest of the waste. The elevator will descend one floor, and we will emerge with the tank open. We will *run* toward the office, which is just down the hall, in order to avert the effects of the geletane by activity; we will hold handkerchiefs over our faces to let the guards know we have gas, and hold their breaths. Two of us will enter the communication office, while the third will remain outside to destroy the door control. He can spend the rest of his time welding the door shut, until that welder gives out.

"The guards and operators inside should be under the influence of the gas by then, and will be thrown out before the welding starts. The two of us who are inside will keep exercising until the ventilators clear the air in the room; then we can use the vision transmitter to our heart's content, until the starfish can bring up heavy tools and burn through the door. There are a dozen Union bases within five hundred parsecs, even I know; and five minutes should be ample to contact one of them and give our situation.

"Art, did you really think I hoped to get anywhere with that pint-sized thing you built? The pentapods have us here so that we can build equipment for them; I decided that turn about was fair play. I only hope those infernally quick minds of theirs don't grasp the fact that two can play at one game. In case they should, I think we had better start working with Magill on whatever plan he has evolved; that will keep us occupied, reduce the chance of our betraying our secret, and may prove a valuable second string to the bow if our plan falls through. Let's have breakfast."

Little had spoken lightly of "working in" with Magill on whatever plan of escape that worthy might have evolved; at breakfast he discovered that no less than four lines of attack were being developed simultaneously. The quartermaster was hoping that one of them would go undiscovered long enough to reach a climax. He had not divided the men into separate groups for each job; the idea was to confuse the guards by having everybody work on all the plans at once. Confusion had certainly resulted, though none of the pentapods showed the symptoms. Little, first making sure that his own private plan would not be affected by any of the others, plunged joyfully into the conflicting tasks of (1) finding and using one or more of the aircraft which Magill was positive were stored beneath the roof; (2) getting an armed party of human beings into the interstellar flier of the pentapods; (3) carrying out the original Vegan plan of flooding the building with ultraviolet light without at the same time forcing out the men; and (4) locating an arsenal of the pentapods and simply clearing a section of the building by brute force. Magill intended to use whichever of these plans first attained practicability.

Four days were spent in this fashion. Work at least prevented them from being as boring as the preceding three, though little or no progress was made. On the morning of the fifth day, however, just after the morning meal, an event occurred which opened a fifth line of procedure, and almost caused Magill to abandon the others.

One of the men had gone out onto the roof; and the others were attracted by his cry. Little, following the others to the edge of the roof, looked over; and was rewarded with a clear view of nothing at all. The line of pentapods which had been loading supplies into the vast cruiser was not to be seen, and the vessel's ports were closed. The men watched silently and expectantly, reasonably sure of what was to happen.

Perhaps ten minutes passed without a word being spoken; then, without sound or ceremony, the tremendous cylinder of metal drifted lightly upward. The men followed it for a short distance with their eyes; they might have watched longer, if their attention had not been distracted by an object revealed by the cruiser's departure.

Just beyond the depression in the soil left by the great ship there appeared a second, much smaller, silvery metal torpedo; and a howl of surprise burst from almost every human throat on the rooftop. It was the *Gomeisa,* her ports open, apparently unharmed, and—apparently deserted.

For several seconds after that involuntary expression of astonishment there was dead silence; then Magill spoke.

"This puts a new light on the situation. Don't do anything rash until we decide just how this affects our position; our plans will certainly need modification. I'll be in the market for ideas all morning; we'll have a general discussion meeting after dinner," He turned away from the edge and walked back toward the doorway.

Denham had long since been coached in his part,; he played it without a hitch. The load of refuse and the tank of geletane were tossed into the elevator; the three men followed. No guards entered; since the departure of their ship they had concentrated on guarding the lower doors rather than preventing the prisoners from wandering about the fort. Little slid the door of the cage closed and touched the button next to the top, and Arthur took the welder from his pocket.

Slow as it was, the car took but a few seconds to reach the next level. It stopped; Little looked at his companions and slid open the door, at the same instant opening the valve of his gas tank. The three dashed into the corridor and toward the office, handkerchiefs pressed over their mouths and noses.

Two pentapods stood at the open door of the communication room. They swept instantly toward the approaching men, but must have conversed with others inside the room even in that time, for three more emerged after them.

Fast as the men were running, the gas diffused ahead of them; and the rearmost guards, who were moving more slowly than the others, were paradoxically the first to go down under the invisible attack. The others heard them fall, deduced the cause, presumably held their breath—and dropped as though shot. The men hurtled into the room, Little still leading, and found it empty. Evidently the communication officers had joined the guards and, confident of their ability to overcome three human beings, had not even sounded an alarm,

Leo Dennis leaped toward a mass of equipment that was all too plainly of recent installation; Little reversed his motion, snatched the welder from Arthur's hand, and darted back through the door.

"I'll look after this end," he said, "and saturate the air in the corridor while I'm at it. I'm more used to gas and can probably avoid its effects longer than you, Art." He slid the metal portal shut with a clang, tossed the still-open gas cylinder across the hall, and set to work with the welder. He jumped up and down, kicking, dancing, and waving his free arm as he worked; but the hand holding the torch remained steady.

Reluctantly, the metal of door and frame fused and flowed under the heat. The tiny lever that had actuated the opening mechanism dripped away. Slowly a glowing line of red marked the edge of the door and extended around it, a line that did not cease its slow growth as a dozen guards raced around a corner and collapsed as one the moment they paused to take in the situation. One, at least, must have been far enough behind to signal to others; seconds later, another group, clad in transparent, baggy air suits, sped into sight. At almost the same instant the little torch expired.

Little straightened, dropping the instrument, and saw the approaching guards. He turned to run toward the elevator, and saw another group rapidly approaching from that direction. Knowing the futility of the attempt, he tried to dodge past them; one swerved, reached, and an instant later he was pinned motionless as he had been once before in the first break for freedom. But he was still in the region of geletane-impregnated air.

Dr. Little opened his eyes with that peculiar feeling of having done the same thing before. This time memory returned almost instantly; he struggled to his feet, helped by the men clustered around him. He was on the roof of the fort, where a stiff breeze had cleared the last of the gas from his lungs and cell walls. No guards were in evidence.

"How did it go?" he asked, seeing the grinning features of the Dennis brothers beside him. "Did you get through?"

"We did. It took them nearly an hour to get heavy tools and cut in— after all we had control of their local 'telephone' central. They must have called their own ship back at once; it came in ten minutes ago, and they're rushing stuff aboard. I think they're going to abandon this place before help arrives for us. The Ardomese I talked to promised a squadron in fifteen hours.

"I wish that starfish ship had been farther away—we might have been able to take some prisoners of our own. But I'm afraid they'll have time to clear out."

"You're not annoyed, are you?" asked Little. "After all, they didn't hurt you fellows when they found you in the communication room. I think they're rather good sports, myself. After all, they've been risking all along the chance that we might do just what we did; they haven't hurt anyone; and the *Gomeisa* is not seriously damaged."

"Nevertheless, they committed an act of war against the Union," cut in Magill, "and they have stolen a lot of valuable information. The *Gomeisa* carried stuff that could make them dangerous enemies."

"They have had plenty of time to duplicate that armament, and unquestionably have done so," returned Little, "but they seem to have no intention of staying and using it on our ships. I think their curiosity was purely academic; perhaps this was all a game to them. In any case, I can't make myself feel anger toward them. I'm curious, myself, and personally I rather like the creatures. You can make yourself do the same, Keys; the whole thing is only a question of attitude." The doctor traded knowing winks with the Dennis brothers.

HALO

Galaxy, October 1952

"You disappoint me," the class superintendent said with some feeling. "I have a personal as well as a professional dislike of wastefully run farms, and you seem to have furnished a prime example." He paused briefly, watching in silence as the spheroidal forcing beds drifted smoothly about their central radiator. "Of course, I would be much more sympathetic with *you* if your own ill-advised actions were not so largely responsible for this situation." He checked his young listener's half-uttered protest. "Oh, I realize that youngsters have to learn, and experiment is the only source of knowledge; but why not use the results of other people's experiments? This sort of thing has happened before, I think you'll find."

"I didn't know." The answer was sullen despite the grudging respect. "How was I supposed to?"

"Did you get an education or not?" There was some heat in the query. "I can't imagine what the primary teachers do these days. Even though you are so young, I understood that you had some qualifications and even a bit of promise in agriculture. That's why I thought you could be trusted without supervision for a few years. Am I to assume that you became dissatisfied with the yield of this farm?"

"Of course. Why else study agriculture?"

"Until you can answer that for yourself, I won't try to. Tell me in detail what you did. Did you try to step up the output of the central radiator?"

"What do you think I am?" The younger being's indignation flared abruptly.

The other remained calm and exhibited faint traces of amusement, permitting the feeling to show in his answer rather more plainly than was strictly tactful.

"Don't boil your crust off. You might not be able to spare it next time you go in to harvest. People still do try the stunt I mentioned, you know.

Every now and then it works for someone after a fashion, so the rest feel it's still worth trying. If it wasn't that, just what did you do? You're missing a culture unit, if I remember this solar system correctly."

The student took a moment to find just the right words. "One of the lots seemed to be practically ideal. When it first solidified, it was just far enough from the radiator and just large enough to retain a thin surface film of light elements; and it responded beautifully to culturing with water-base growths. On the colder ones, by the way, I had good luck with ammonia cultures."

"Quite possible, in that sort of bed. I noticed a couple of them were bare, though. Was that another result of this experiment of yours?"

"Indirectly, yes." The young farmer looked a trifle apprehensive. "There was another plot, a good deal farther out and colder than my ideal one. But it was too hot for ammonia growths and too small to furnish the pressure they seem to need—at least the ones I'm familiar with." The addition was made hastily.

"I judged that it should have a good supply of food elements, cooling where it did; and since it wasn't doing well where it was, I thought it would be a good idea to move it farther in."

The listener's manner lost some of its amused aspect.

"Just how did you decide to go about that? The energy involved would have demanded several times the mass of your own body, even with total conversion—which I can't believe you've mastered."

"I don't suppose I have. It seemed to me that the unit itself could furnish the mass without serious loss, though."

"I see." The comment was grim. "Go on."

"Well, I went in and set up a conversion reaction. I touched it off as well as I could on the forward side of the unit, though that was a little hard to arrange—the thing was spinning like mad, as most of them do. Maybe that was the reason I let a little too much mass get involved, or maybe the globe wasn't as massive as I had thought."

"You mean you were uncertain of its mass? Is something wrong with your perceptive faculties as well as your judgment? Just how old are you, anyway?"

"Fifteen." The sullenness, which had began to depart from the youngster's tone as he warmed to his narrative, returned in full strength. The questioner noted it and realized that he was not being as tactful as he might be; but under the circumstances he felt entitled to a little emotion.

"Fifteen years on what scale?"

"Local—this furnace, around the mass-center of the system."

"Hmph. Continue."

"Most of the sphere was volatilized, and most of what wasn't was blown completely out of the system's gravitational influence. The rest—well, it's still circling the furnace in quite a wide variety of orbits but it's not much good to anyone."

There was a pause while the nearly useless outermost unit swung beneath the two speakers, then on to the far side of the glowing sphere of gas that held it with unbreakable fingers of gravity. The supervisor was not actually boiling—that would be difficult even for a body composed largely of methane, oxygen, and similar solids when it is at a temperature of about half a degree absolute—but his temper was simmering. After a moment he spoke again.

"Let me get this straight. You sent a slave with a message that your farm had gotten out of hand and that you would like advice. Am I to understand that you spent so much time ruining one of your units that some of the others developed culture variations whose taste didn't appeal to you? I'm afraid my sympathy grows rapidly less."

"It's not that I don't like the stuff; it's that I can't eat it." The youngster must have been angry, too; there was no other imaginable reason why he should have made a statement at once so true in fact and so misleading in implication. The superintendent, swallowing the implication whole, permitted the remains of his temper to evaporate completely.

"You can't eat it? That is really too bad. Pardon me while I go to sample some of this repulsive chemical—or perhaps you would like to come along and show me what you *have* been eating. There is hardly enough drift in this area to support you, particularly with a decent-sized crew of slaves. What have you been feeding them? Perhaps you ought to let someone else take over this farm and get yourself a research job out in one of the drift clouds, soaking up your nourishment from a haze of free atoms ten parsecs across for a few years. You youngsters!"

"I've been eating from the ammonia units. So have the slaves."

"Very well, then I shall look over your water culture, which by elimination must be the one that's been giving trouble. On second thought, you needn't come along. It's the third plot from the furnace. I can find my way." He moved off abruptly, not even waiting for an answer.

And the student, with no slightest shadow of an excuse, simply because of his own childish loss of temper, let him go without a word of warning.

It might, of course, have made no difference if he had spoken. The superintendent was annoyed, too, and might understandably have chosen to ignore his junior. His attention, as he permitted himself to fall toward the central radiator, was divided between his own irritation and the condition of the various plots. Only gradually did the latter feeling predominate.

He had to admit the outermost was too cold for much chemical action except actual life processes which were too slow to be useful. The fact that the youngster he had left above had induced anything at all to grow there was at least one point to his credit. It swung past only once while he was falling by its orbit. Though his gravity-given speed was slow, its speed was slower—and it had farther to go.

The next two he had noted earlier were bare of useful growths. He remembered now that the student had admitted this fact to be an indirect result of his experiment. The superintendent could not see the connection. The plots themselves, on closer inspection, seemed physically undamaged, and the student himself could not possibly have eaten them both clean, no matter what his hunger. Of course, a crowd of slaves might—but he was not going to accuse anybody *yet* of letting slaves get that far out from under control. They were not even allowed to approach a culture plot in person, being fed from its produce by their master.

The plots themselves were large bodies, though not the largest in the system, with their solid bulks veiled under mile after mile of hydrogen compounds. The superintendent's senses probed in vain for the enormously complex compounds that were the preferred food of his kind. Several much smaller bodies were gravitating about each of these plots, but none was large enough to hold the light elements in the liquid or gaseous form necessary for food culture.

The next unit had the merit of interesting appearance, if nothing else. In addition to the more or less standard quota of bodies circling it, it possessed a regular halo of minute particles traveling in a solidly interwoven maze of orbits just outside the atmosphere. On the surface, and even in the atmosphere itself, its cultures were flourishing. The superintendent paused to take a sample, and had to admit that once again the youngster had not done too badly.

His temper cooling, he rode the farm plot most of the way around its orbit, taking an occasional taste and growing calmer by the moment. By the time he left the limits of its atmosphere, he was almost his normal self.

This, however, did not last long enough even for him to get rid of the globe's orbital speed, to say nothing of resuming his drop toward the sun. He had slanted some distance inward and fallen well behind the ringed sphere when his attention was drawn to another, much smaller object well to one side of his line of flight.

Physically, there was little remarkable about it. It was less massive even than his own body, though a short period of observation disclosed that it was in an orbit about the central furnace, just as the farm plots were. Sometimes its outline was clear, at others it blurred oddly. Its brightness flickered in an apparently meaningless pattern. Merely on its physical description, there was nothing remarkable about it, but it seized and held the superintendent's puzzled attention. Off his planned course though it was, he swung toward it, wondering. The student had mentioned no friends or co-workers—

Gradually, details grew clearer and the superintendent's feelings grew grimmer. He did not like to believe what he saw, but the evidence was crowding in.

"Help! Please help! Master!"

The bubble of horror burst, and one of anger grew in its place. Not one of his own kind, injured or dying and an object of terror and revulsion thereby; this thing was a slave. A slave, moreover, well within the limits of the farm, where it had no business to be without supervision; a slave who dared call on him for help!

"What are you doing here?" The superintendent sent the question crackling along a tight beam toward the apparently helpless creature. "Did you enter this region without orders?"

"No, Master. I was...ordered."

"By whom? What happened to you? Speak more clearly!"

"By—I cannot, Master. Help me!" The irregular flickering of the slave's auroral halo brightened fitfully with the effort of radiating speech.

Unsympathetic as the superintendent normally was to such beings, he realized that help must be given if he were to learn anything. Conquering a distinct feeling of repugnance, he moved up beside the slave to investigate its injuries. He expected, naturally, to find the visible results of a thorough ion-lashing, that being the principal occupational hazard faced by the slaves; but what he actually saw almost made him forget his anger.

The unfortunate creature's outer crust was *pitted*—dotted and cratered with a pattern of circular holes which resembled nothing the superintendent had ever encountered. He knew the long, shallow scars of an ion-lashing and the broad, smoothed areas which showed on the crust of one of his people when close exposure to a sun had boiled away portions of his mass. These marks, however, looked almost as though the slave had been exposed to a pelting by granules of solid *matter!*

A ridiculous thought, of course. The stupidest slave could detect and avoid the occasional bits of rock and metal which were encountered in the interstellar void. After all, they had the same sensory equipment and physical powers as the masters. An unprejudiced judge might even have said they were of the same species as the masters.

Whatever had caused the creature's injury, there was little that could be done for it. Grudgingly, inspired far more by curiosity than by sympathy, the superintendent did that little, supplying hydrocarbons and other organic matter lately skimmed from the ringed planet.

Food, however, was not enough. Bits of extraneous metal were imbedded in its body, altering the precise pattern of charged metal nodes that spelled life to these beings. Some of its own field nodes had apparently been chipped or blown away, and others were discharged. The creature's body was only a fraction of its normal size—the regular reserve of "food" compounds that ordinarily made up so much of even a slave's bulk had long since been consumed or had evaporated.

There was no doubt that it was dying. But there was some chance that it might gain strength enough to impart information if it were fed. It was—sparingly, of course.

"No sense wasting food on a slave that's about to die," the superintendent explained without brutality.

"Certainly not, Master," the slave agreed without resentment.

"What happened to you?" the superintendent repeated. The slave was in no condition to be coherent; but a lifetime of conditioning brought some order to its agony-dazed mind, and it answered.

"I was ordered to the inner plots—to harvest." The word-symbols came haltingly, but with sufficient clarity to be unmistakable, shocking as their implication was.

So the student had trusted slaves near a food supply! Perhaps that accounted for the two stripped planets.

"You went to harvest when a young fool like this orders it?"

"He was a master, and he gave the order. Many of us went; many of us have been going for years—and seldom returning. We did not wish it, Master, but he ordered it. What could we do?"

"You could have asked the first superintendent who came here whether it was better to disobey a Prime Order or a young master."

"You are the first to come, Master, as far as I know. And the young master said we were not to speak of this order to anyone. It is only because you command me to speak that I do so now—that and the fact that there is little more that he could do to me, anyway."

The overseer ignored the pointed closing sentence. "You say many of you have been ordered to do this, but few have returned from the errand? What happened to them? What happened to you?"

"They die. I did not know how; now I suppose it must be—this way."

There was a pause, and the supervisor was moved to sarcasm. "I suppose they are struck by meteoric particles, as you seem to have been. Do slaves absorb personal characteristics such as stupidity from their masters? Could you not dodge the meteors?"

"No, not all of them. The region near the central furnace has more of such matter than any other place I have ever seen. Some pieces are iron, some are of other matter; but they cannot be avoided. They strike too hard. They cannot be absorbed in normal fashion, but simply boil off one's body material into space. The shock is so tremendous that I, at least, could do nothing toward recovering the material until it had dissipated beyond hope of salvage. That is the reason so much of my mass is gone; it was not merely starvation.

"Some of the other slaves did better than I—as I said, some of them have survived—but others did much worse. They would dive in toward the furnace, and their bodies would come falling back out in just about the shape I am."

"And still he sends his slaves in to harvest?"

"Yes. We did not do too badly, actually, on the largest plots; but then he got interested in the others farther in. After all, they're hotter. He ventured in himself almost to the orbit of the plot that was destroyed—did you know that?—but came out very quickly and sent us on all such journeys thereafter.

"We—or, rather, those who preceded me—cleaned off the next inner plot, the fourth from the central furnace, fairly well, though the loss of slaves was high. Then he wanted to start on the third. I was one of the first to work on this project.

"I did not expect to live, of course, after what I had heard from the others; but the order came, and I let myself fall toward the sun. My orbit passed close to the greatest of the plots, which the master has been harvesting himself, and I hoped to strengthen myself with a little food from it as I passed."

That confession showed how certain the slave felt of his own imminent death, as well as the state of demoralization into which the student's activities had permitted his servitors to fall.

"But I did not dare take any food when the time came," the slave went on feebly. "As I passed through the region where the destroyed plot had been, drifting particles began to grow more numerous. At first there would be an occasional bit of stone or iron, which I could dodge easily. Then they came in twos and threes, and sometimes I would have to change an escape curve in mid-maneuver. Then they came in dozens and clusters, and at last I could avoid them no longer. I was struck several times in rapid succession.

"For a moment I almost turned back—I had never dreamed that anything could feel like that—and then I remembered the order and went on. And I was struck again, and again, and each time the order faded in my mind. I reached the orbit of the fourth planet, crossed it—and turned out again. It didn't seem to help; I was still being pelted. For a time I must have almost lost orientation; but at last I won out to a place near the orbit of the giant planet. That was where I remembered the order again.

"I had never disobeyed a master before, and I didn't know what to do, or say, or think. I'd start back toward the sun, and remember what had happened, and come back out. Then I'd remember the master, and head in again. I didn't dare go out in the cold where he would be waiting. I didn't dare dive back into that storm of rock and metal from the old fifth planet. But I had to do something. I couldn't float by the orbit of the giant planet forever. He would find me there sooner or later, and that would be worse than if I had come out to him. I had to think."

That word struck the superintendent like a shock. The very idea of a slave's thinking—making a decision for himself concerning an action he was to perform—was repugnant to a member of the dominant race. They preferred to think of their slaves as mindless creatures relying on their masters for the necessities of existence—a comforting fiction that had been maintained for so many rotations of the Galaxy that its originators had come to believe it themselves. He had suspected that this particular slave must be an unusual specimen in many ways; now he was sure of it.

It was this that kept him silent while the creature paused, visibly collected its waning energies, and resumed the tale.

"I found what I thought was the answer at last. Since the tremendous number of particles must have come from the farm that had been blown up, it seemed likely that their orbits would be more or less controlled by that and would have at least a slight family resemblance. If I were to take up a powered, nearly elliptical path through that region, matching velocities with most of them instead of falling in a practically parabolic orbit across their path, I should be able to avoid the worst of the blows."

Weakly, the shattered creature shuddered and paused, mustering strength to continue.

"I had about made up my mind to try this when I detected another slave inbound," it went on, "and it occurred to me that two would be better than one. If one died, at least the other could learn from what had happened. I caught him easily since he was in free fall and explained the idea. He seemed willing to follow any suggestion, not thinking for himself at all, so he went with me.

"For a while it worked. We got inside the orbit of the fourth planet without being hit more than a few times each—that was harder on me than on him, because I'd already been hurt quite a lot on the first trip. In to that level, a great deal of the wreckage is formed of quite large particles, anyway; it's easy to see and avoid. Farther in, though, where most of the heavy stuff either never went or was cleared out by collision with the inner planets in a few million of their revolutions, there was much more extremely fine stuff. It actually seems to increase in concentration near the sun. Maybe radiation pressure has something to do with it.

"Anyway, we began to take a bad beating again. It was a little better than before. My idea must have had something to it, but it still wasn't good. The other slave wasn't used to it, either, and lost control of himself just as I had. We were almost to the third farm plot then, but he must have gone completely blind from pain. He apparently never sensed the food so near by—that plot is incredibly rich.

"He went blundering squarely into another, useless plot that accompanies the third one in its orbit; an object too small to hold culture material in that temperature range, though still several hundred times the diameter of my body or his. He rammed it hard, and the energy involved in matching velocities was more than enough to volatilize his mass completely. The object was pretty well scarred with impact craters, but he made one of the neatest.

"I was close enough then to the third planet to start harvesting—at least, I would have been under normal circumstances. I tried, but couldn't concentrate on one course of action long enough. The bombardment was endless. There are simply no words to describe what it was like. I was not twenty of its own diameters from the most amazingly rich farm plot I have ever seen, and was not able to touch a *bit* of it!

"It had been so long since it was harvested that substances completely strange to me had developed in its surface layers. There were carbohydrates, of course, and light-element oxides and carbonates which anyone would expect; but there were proteins more fantastically complex than anyone could well imagine. Their emanations nearly drove me wild. They must have been building up and breaking down at incredible speed at that temperature—I had quite an atmosphere out, as a result of boiling off surface matter to use up incoming radiant energy—and they had evolved to an unheard-of degree. And I couldn't get a taste!

"I could sense them, though, and in spite of the pain of the meteor bombardment, I stayed near the planet, vacillating as I had done before, for a couple of hundred of its trips around the Sun. That may seem like a short time, but it was long enough to ruin my body past saving. It was only when my senses began to fail that I was able to turn away from it and fight my way out this far. I just managed to get into a stable orbit that would keep me clear of that hellish halo of planet fragments, and every now and then I succeeded in mustering enough energy to call for help, but I knew it was useless. Even had you come much sooner, it would still have been too late for me.

"I live to warn you, however. *Do not go within the orbit of the old fifth planet!* Do not even look within it, for if you sense what lies on that un-harvested third world, you will be drawn to your doom as surely as I was ordered to mine!"

The slave fell silent, and the superintendent pondered its tale as they drifted on about the Sun. He could not, offhand, think of any adequate punishment for the student whose recklessness had brought about this state of affairs. The mere cruelty of ordering endless crowds of slaves to nearly certain death did not affect him particularly; but the waste of it did, very much. To him the thought of hundreds of lifeless bodies drift-ing endlessly about the Sun, boiling off a little more of their masses with each perihelion passage until nothing was left but a loose collection of high-melting-point pebbles, was a painful picture of economic loss. The fact that the best farm plot in the system had apparently become un-attainable was also to be considered, and the driving of at least one slave to the extreme of thinking for himself was not to be ignored.

Of course, everything should be checked before confronting the stu-dent with such charges. Only the last, after all, could be considered as yet a matter of objective knowledge.

The overseer moved abruptly away from the slave—sunward. The dying creature, seeing him depart, called once more for aid, and was si-lenced instantly and permanently by a slashing beam of ions. For an in-stant the overseer regretted the impulsive act—not from gratitude for the warning, to which he attached little weight and which was part of a slave's duty, but simply because it *was* impulsive rather than reasoned. But then he reflected that the creature could probably not have told much more anyway, even if it had survived until his return.

He was in no hurry. He let the gravity of the central furnace draw him in to the orbit of the giant planet, his senses covering the half-bil-lion-mile sphere of space ahead where death was reputed to lurk.

At this range, all seemed innocuous. He watched the inner planets circling rapidly in their paths—even the giant one made most of a revo-lution during his fall—and noted that the slave had spoken the truth about a companion body to the third planet. But space seemed otherwise empty.

He did not completely abandon caution, however. What had proven fatal to slaves might be inconvenient or even dangerous to a master.

He stopped at the fifth planet's orbit and began a more minute ex-amination of that suspicious volume of space.

The small bodies were there, all right. Thousands of them, even though he was not trying to detect anything less than a twentieth of his own diameter. They did show a rather vague preference for the orbit of the old fifth planet, as the slave had said. The greater number circled between the present fourth and fifth orbits, at any rate. There seemed no reason why he could not match velocities well enough to keep out of trouble. Why, chance alone could be trusted to protect him from collision with a few thousand asteroids, when they were scattered through something like ten-to-the-twenty -fourth-power cubic miles of space!

Still, there was little wisdom in going into possible danger without a very sound reason. It would be well to judge from his present position if such reason existed. His finer senses could easily operate at the half billion miles that separated him from the farthest point of the third planet's orbit. So, holding his position, he focused his attention on the elusive farm plot in question.

Being so close to the central furnace, it revolved rapidly. He faced somewhat the same problem in examining it that a man would have trying to recognize a friend on a merry-go-round—assuming that the friend were spinning in his seat like a top at the same time.

It took the superintendent only a few revolutions of the body to adjust to this situation, however, and as details registered more and more clearly on his consciousness, he began to admit grudgingly that the slave had not exaggerated.

The plot was fabulous!

Substances for which he had no name abounded, impressing themselves on the analytical sense that was his equivalent of both taste and smell. Strange as they were, he could tell easily that they were foods— packed with available energy and carrying fascinating taste potentialities, organized to a completely unheard-of degree. They were growths of a type and complexity which simply never had a chance to evolve on the regularly harvested worlds of the Galaxy.

The overseer wondered whether it might not be worth while to let other plots run wild for a few years. His principal vice, by the standards of his people, was gluttony; but the most ascetic of his species would have been tempted uncontrollably by that planet.

He almost regretted the few tons of food he had taken on from the ringed planet—though he had, he told himself quickly, sacrificed much of that in helping the slave and would lose still more if he decided actually to penetrate into the high-temperature zones near the Sun.

Huge as his mass was, his normal temperature was so low that life processes went on at an incredibly slow pace. To him, a chemical reaction requiring only a few millennia to go to completion was like a dynamite explosion. A few pounds of organic compounds would feed his miles-thick bulk for many human lifetimes of high activity.

In short, the slave had been quite right.

Almost involuntarily, rationalizing his appetite as he went, the superintendent permitted himself to drift into the asteroid zone. With only the smallest part of his attention, he assumed a parabolic, free-fall orbit in the general plane of the system, with its perihelion point approximately tangent to the orbit of the third planet. At this distance from the Sun, the difference between parabolic and circular velocities was not too great to permit him to detect even the tiniest particles in time to avoid them. That fact, of course, changed as he fell sunward.

Perhaps he had been counting on a will power naturally superior to that of the slave who had warned him. If so, he had forgotten the effects of an equally superior imagination. The pull of the third planet was correspondingly stronger and, watching the spinning globe, he was jarred out of an almost hypnotic trance by the first collision. It awakened him to the fact that his natural superiority to the slave race might not be sufficient to keep him out of serious trouble.

The space around him—he was now well inside the orbit of the fourth planet—was literally crowded with grain-of-dust meteors, each, as he had seen on the slave's crust, able to blast out a crater many times its own volume in a living body. Individually, they were insignificant; collectively, they were deadly.

His attention abruptly wrenched back to immediate problems of existence, the superintendent started to check his fall and veer once more toward the safe, frozen emptiness of interstellar space. But the spell of the gourmet's paradise he had been watching was not that easily thrown off. For long moments, while the planet circled its primary once and again, he hung poised, with gluttony and physical anguish alternately gaining the upper hand in a struggle for possession of his will. Probably he would have lost, alone; but his student did have a conscience.

"Sir!" The voice came faintly but clearly to his mind. "Don't stay! You mustn't! I should never have let you come—but I was angry! I know I was a fool; I should have told you everything!"

"I learned. It was my own fault." The superintendent found it curiously difficult to speak. "I came of my own free will and I still think that plot is worth investigation."

"No! It's not your own free will—no will could remain free after seeing what that planet has to offer. I knew it and expected you to die—but I couldn't go through with it. Come, and quickly. I will help."

The student was in an orbit almost identical with that of the superintendent, though still a good deal farther out. Perhaps it was the act of looking at him, which took his attention momentarily from the alluring object below, that made the older being waver. Whatever it was, the student perceived the break and profited by it.

"Don't even look at it again, sir. Look at me, and follow—or if you'd rather not look at me, look at *that!*"

He indicated the direction plainly, and the dazed listener looked almost involuntarily.

The thing he saw was recognizable enough. It consisted of a small nucleus which his senses automatically analyzed. It consisted of methane and other hydrocarbons, some free oxygen, a few other light-element compounds, and had nuggets of heavier elements scattered through it like raisins in a plum pudding. Around it for thousands of miles there extended a tenuous halo of the more volatile of its constituent compounds. The thing was moving away from the Sun in an elliptical orbit, showing no sign of intelligent control. A portion of its gaseous envelope was driven on ahead by the pressure of sunlight from below.

It was a dead slave, but it could as easily have been a dead master.

A dead slave was nothing; *but the thing that had killed it could do the same to him.*

It was the first time in his incredibly long life that the *personal* possibility of death had struck home to him; and probably nothing less than that fear could have saved his life.

With the student close beside, he followed the weirdly glowing corpse out to the farthest point of its orbit; and as it started to fall back into the halo of death girdling that harmless-looking star, he pressed on out into the friendly darkness.

Perhaps some day that third planet would be harvested; but it would not be by one of his kind—not, at least, until that guarding haze had been swept up by the planets that drifted through its protecting veil.

It was not a very good group, Wright reflected. That always seemed to be the case. When he had luck with observing weather, he had no one around to appreciate the things that could be seen. He cast a regretful glance toward the dome of the sixty-inch telescope, where a fellow candidate was taking another plate of his series, and wondered whether there were not some better way than part-time instructing to pay the expenses of a doctorate program.

Still, the night *was* good. Most of the time in the latitude—

"Mr. Wright! Is that a cloud or the Aurora?"

"If you will stop to consider the present position of the Sun below the horizon," he answered indirectly, "you will discover that the patch of light you are indicating is directly opposite that point. It lies along the path of the Earth's shadow, though, of course, well beyond it. It is called the *Gegenschein* and, like the Zodiacal Light, is not too commonly visible at this latitude. We did see the Light some time ago, if you remember, on an evening when we started observing earlier. Actually, the *Gegenschein* is a continuation of the luminous band we call the Zodiacal Light. The latter can sometimes be traced all the way around the sky to the point we are now watching."

"What causes them?"

"The most reasonable assumption is that they are light reflected from small, solid particles—meteors. Apparently a cloud of such matter extends outward for some distance past the Earth's orbit, though just how far, it is hard to say. It grows fainter with distance from the Sum, as would be expected, except for the patch we call the *Gegenschein*."

"Why the exception?"

"I think one of you can answer that."

"Would it be for the same reason that the full Moon is so much more than twice as bright as either quarter? Simply because the particles are rough, and appear dark in most positions because of the shadows of irregularities on their own surfaces—shadows which disappear when the light is behind the observer?"

"I think you will agree that that would account for it," Wright said. "Evidently the meteors are there, are large compared to wavelengths of visible light, and form a definite part of the Solar System. I believe it was once estimated that if the space inside the Earth's orbit contained particles one millimeter in diameter and five miles apart, they would reflect enough light to account for what we are observing. They might, of course, be smaller and more numerous. Only that amount of reflecting surface is necessary."

"You had me worried," another voice broke in. "I'd been hearing for years that there would be little reason to fear collisions with meteors when we finally get a rocket out of the atmosphere. For a moment, I though a cloud such as you were working up to would riddle anything that got into space. One pinhead every five miles isn't so bad, though."

"There is a fairly good chance of collision, I would say," returned Wright, "but just what damage particles of that size would do, I am not sure. It seems rather likely that they would be volatilized by impact. How the hull of a rocket would react, we will have to find out by experience. I wouldn't mind taking the risk myself. I think we can sum up the greatest possibilities by saying that the meteoric content of the Solar System has and will have nothing but nuisance value to the human race, whether or not we ever leave our own planet."

A streak of white fire arced silently across the sky, putting a fitting period to the subject.

Wright wondered whether it would appear on his friend's photographic plate.

Impediment

Astounding, August 1942

Boss ducked back from the outer lock as a whir of wings became audible outside. The warning came barely in time; a five-foot silvery body shot through the opening, checking its speed instantly, and settled to the floor of the lock chamber. It was one of the crew, evidently badly winded. His four legs seemed to sag under the weight of the compact body, and his wings drooped almost to the floor. Fight, or any other severe exertion, was a serious undertaking in the gravity of this world; even *accelerine,* which speeded up normal metabolism to compensate for the increased demand, was not perfect.

Boss was not accustomed to getting out of anyone's way, least of all in the case of his own underlings. His temper, normally short enough, came dangerously near the boiling point; the wave of thought that poured from his mind to that of the weary flier was vitriolic.

"All right, make it good. Why do I have to dodge out of the path of every idiotic spacehand who comes tearing back here as though the planet was full of devils? Why? What's the rush, anyway? This is the first time I ever saw you in a hurry, except when I told you to hop!"

"But you told me this time, Boss," was the plaintive answer. "You said that the moment that creature you were after turned into the path leading here, I was to get word to you. It's on the way now."

"That's different. Get out of sight. Tell Second to make sure everybody's in his quarters, and that all the doors along the central hall are locked. Turn out all lights, except for one at each end of the hall. No one is to be visible from that hallway, and no other part of the ship is to be accessible from it. Is that understood?"

"Yes, Boss."

"Clear out, then. That's the way you wanted things, isn't it, Talker?"

The being addressed, who had heard the preceding dialogue with more amusement than respect, was watching from the inner door of the airlock.

Like the blustering commander and the obsequious crew member, he supported his body almost horizontally on four slender legs. Another pair of appendages terminated in prehensile organs as efficient as human hands, and a double pair of silvery-gray, membranous wings were folded along the sides of his streamlined, insectile body.

He could best be described to an Earthman as a giant hawk moth, the resemblance being heightened by the broad, feathery antennae projecting some eighteen inches from a point above his eyes. Those appendages alone differentiated him from the others of his kind; those of the captain and crew were a bare eight inches in length, narrower, and less mobile.

His eyes were the most human characteristics—more accurately, the only ones—that he possessed. Two disks of topaz, more than three inches across, they lent a strangely sagacious expression to the grotesque countenance.

"You have understood well, Commander," radiated Talker, "even though you seem unable to realize the necessity for this action. The creature must see enough of the ship to arouse his curiosity; at the same time he must gain no inkling of our presence."

"Why not?" asked Boss. "It seems to me that we could learn to communicate much more quickly if we capture him. You say he must be allowed to come and go as he pleases for many days, and must remain under the impression that this ship is deserted. I know you've been trained to communication all your life, but—"

"But nothing! That one fact should make it evident that I know more than you can hope to understand about the problem we're facing. Come up to the control room—that native will arrive shortly, and that's the only place from which we can watch him without being seen ourselves."

Talker led the way forward along the dimly lit main corridor, into which the inner door of the airlock opened directly. At its end, a low doorway opened, and a spiral ramp led to the control deck, half a level higher. Here the two paused. Metal grillwork, its interstices filled with glass, formed the rear wall of the room and afforded a view the whole length of the corridor. Talker extinguished the control-room lights, and settled himself at this vantage point.

His name was no indication of his temperament. The narrator, in fact, must accept full blame for the former. Had it been merely a question of translating from one vocal language to another, it would have been possible to set down a jumble of vowels and consonants, the more unpronounceable the better, and claim that the English alphabet provided no means of coming closer to the true pronunciation. Unfortunately, these beings were able to sense directly the minute electrical disturbances that accompany nerve currents; they conversed by broadcasting reproductions of the appropriate sensory impressions. The "language," if it could be so called, might be thought of as possessing the elements of a vocal tongue—nouns, verbs, and modifiers; interjections were replaced by the appropriate emotions, but most of the conversation was reproduced visual imagery.

Obviously, personal names were nonexistent; but the knowledge of identity was in no way impaired. An individual was thought of with respect to his position, temporary or permanent, in the group, or by his personal characteristics. The names used are attempts to show this fact.

No name would suit the arrogant, peppery commander of the vessel, other than the one we have used; but the cognomen "Talker" merits further explanation.

The rulers of his home planet had many of Boss's characteristics. They were the outcome of ages of government similar to the feudal systems of Earth's Middle Ages. Ranks corresponding to kings, lords, and dukes existed; warfare was almost continuous. Talker belonged to a class having almost exactly the same duties as medieval heralds; he had been trained from infancy in the traditions, obligations, and special abilities of that class. He was one of a clique which, within itself, formed an international fraternity almost as powerful as any of the governments. Their indispensability protected them; they formed, in addition, probably the most intelligent group in the world. The rulers, and through them, the other inhabitants, looked up to them, and perhaps even feared them a little. The enormously developed faculty of communication implied an unparalleled ability to catch and decipher the mental radiations of others; the development of that power was the "herald's" chief exercise. These last facts should suffice to explain the power of the group, as well as the origin of Talker's name.

Once comfortably settled, Talker again addressed the captain.

"I can't blame you too much for failure to understand the need for this procedure. You lack the training, as you have said; and in addition, there is a condition present whose very possibility never before occurred to me. Tell me, Boss, could you imagine someone—one of your engineers, let us say—acting quite normally, and yet radiating impulses that meant absolutely nothing to you?"

"None of them knows enough to think anything I couldn't understand," was the incredulous answer. "If one of them did, I'd lock him up for examination."

"Exactly. You can't imagine a perfectly sane mind giving off anything but clear thoughts. But what are the thoughts, the waves, that you hear?"

"I hear what he's thinking."

"You don't. Your antennae pick up waves which are generated by the chemical processes going on in his brain. Through long practice, you have learned to interpret those waves in terms of the original thoughts; but what thought actually is, neither you nor I nor anyone else knows. We have 'thought' in the same fashion all our lives; one brain radiates just like another. But this creature, with whom we have to communicate, is a member of another race; the same thoughts in his mind produce different radiations—the very structure of his brain is, quite likely, different from ours. That is why I was so long finding him; I could not disentangle his radiations from the nerve waves of the other relatively unintelligent life forms around here, until I actually saw him performing actions that proved unquestionably that he does possess a reasoning brain. Even then, it was some time before I realized just what was wrong—it was so new and different."

"Then what can you do? What good will those observations do us!" asked Boss, almost tremulously. "I don't get it entirely, but you seem to. If you can't talk to him, how can we get the stuff we need? And if we don't get it, please tell me how we dare show our faces again within five light-years of home!"

"I am far from sure of just how much can be done," replied the other. "It will be necessary to determine, if possible, the relation between what this creature thinks and what he radiates; I don't think it will be easy. These observations are for the purpose of getting a start in that direction.

"As to the other questions, they are entirely your business. You command this ship; and this is the first time I ever saw you want to talk to someone before you helped yourself to his belongings. If you find yourself unable to do so, we can go back, anyway—if labor is scarce, we might get off with a life sentence in the King's mines on the big moon."

"If they still belong to the King by then. I think I'd rather die here, or in space."

"At least, there would be no trouble in getting hold of arsenic," said Talker dryly. "Those mines produce more of that stuff than anything else. If there is any at all on this planet, we have no time to waste on a probably fruitless search; we must get it from the natives, if they know what it is and have any."

"And to find out if they have any, we must talk to them," answered Boss. "I wish us luck, Talker, Go to it."

The astroplane rested in a small arroyo not much wider than its own hull. The banks of this gully rose nearly to the control-room ports, and from where he lay, Talker could see the gap which marked the point where the trail across the main valley emerged from among the trees. Down that trail the native must come; he had been seen coming through the gap in the hills that bounded the valley on the south side, and no other trail led to the pass in the northern boundary, which was marked by even higher and far steeper cliffs. There seemed little in the valley itself to attract an intelligent being, except animals of various species; and the Talker knew that the camp on the other side of the southern hills was well supplied with food, so that the native would probably not be hunting. Would he be superstitiously afraid of the ship, or intelligently curious enough to examine it more closely?

The question was not long in being answered. Talker sensed the nearness of the creature some time before it became visible; the herald judged, correctly, that it had seen the vessel first and was approaching cautiously, under cover. For several minutes, nothing happened; then the man walked boldly to the edge of the bank and stood there, carefully examining the long metal hull.

Both aliens had seen him before, but only at a considerable distance. Talker's chief surprise at the human form was that a being should support a mass about four times his own, against the relatively enormous gravity of Earth, on but two legs—though the legs, it is true, resembled tree trunks when compared to the stalklike limbs of the visitors.

The man held a rifle in one hand. The watchers recognized it as a weapon of some sort, but were unable to make out its details even in the midmorning sunlight that shone upon the native. They waited, even Boss maintaining an unaccustomed silence, while the newcomer took in the details of the forty-meter, cigar-shaped spaceship. He noticed that there were ports—round windows along the sides; these were covered, except for some near the bow, with metal shutters. The exposed windows contained round panes of glass or quartz; the room or rooms within were dark, however, and he could see nothing through them.

A little more than a quarter of the vessel's length back from the nose was a larger port, evidently an entrance. It was elliptical, and about five feet high and twice as wide. It was half open, giving a curiously deserted appearance to the ship.

Talker and Boss could see the indecision in the man's attitude, although his thought waves, which the former could perceive clearly, were completely indecipherable. The doubt manifested itself in restless motion; the man paced toward the stern of the ship, passing out of the watchers' sight, and reappeared a few minutes later on the opposite bank of the gully. He crossed once more, under the curve of the ship's nose, but this time did not climb the bank. Instead, he disappeared sternward again, evidently having made up his mind.

Talker was sure he knew the decision that had been reached; for a moment he was jubilant, but an instant later he came as close to cursing himself as anyone can without benefit of language. The being quite evidently could not fly; the port was ten feet above its head and fifteen feet from the bank. Even if the man wished to, how could he enter? Climbing, for obvious reasons, did not occur to Talker; he had never in his life had to climb, except in buildings too cramped for flying. He caught a glimpse of the man disappearing among the trees, and toyed with the idea of moving to some other part of the planet and trying again.

He did not crystallize this thought sufficiently to mention it to Boss; before he could do so, his attention was caught by something in motion. The man slowly reappeared, dragging a hardwood sapling pole nearly twenty feet in length. He tossed this down the bank, and scrambled after it; then he picked up one end and dragged the pole out of sight along the hull.

Talker realized the plan and gained new respect for the strength, to him almost inconceivable, that lay in those blocky arms and legs. He heard and correctly interpreted the scraping sound as the pole was laid against the lower sill of the airlock; and moments later, an indicator on the control panel showed that the outer door had been swung a little wider, to admit a pair of human shoulders.

Both aliens glued their eyes to the grillwork, looking down the dimly lighted length of corridor to the place where the inner lock door swung wide open, partly blocking further vision. The hinge was to the rear, fortunately; the man would not be hidden from them by the door, if and when he stepped into the hallway,

Boss grew impatient as moments slipped uneventfully by; once he shifted his position, only to freeze motionless again at a warning flicker of radiation from Talker. He thought the latter had seen something, but another minute rolled by before the shadow dimming the light that came through the lock moved enough to show that the man had really entered.

An instant later he had stepped into view. He moved soundlessly, and carried his weapon in a manner that showed it was certainly something more than a club. He was evidently ill at ease; his cramped position accounted largely for that fact—the ceiling of the corridor was barely five feet above the floor. The owners of the ship, with their nearly horizontal carriage, needed little head room.

The man's first action was to peer behind the inner door, rifle held ready. He saw at once that, except for himself, the corridor was empty; but numerous low doors were visible along its full length, with larger portals at each end, and one directly opposite him. The one by which he had entered was the only one open; that immediately facing led, he judged, to a similar airlock on the port side of the ship.

For a minute or two he listened. Then he partly closed the inner door of the lock, so as to allow an unimpeded view the full length of the hall, and walked cautiously forward. Once he raised his hand as though to pound on one of the doors, but evidently thought better of it. Two or three times he looked quickly behind him, turning his head to do so, much to Boss's astonishment. Talker had already deduced from the location of the eyes that the head must be mobile.

The light, set in the ceiling near the front end of the hall, was made the subject of a careful examination. The man looked back along the corridor, noting the row of similar, unlighted bulbs at equal intervals along the ceiling, and the single other lighted one at the far end. Talker was unable to tell from his attitude whether they were something utterly new or completely familiar to him.

Caution had by now succumbed entirely to curiosity. Several doors, including that which led to the control room, were tried. In accordance with Boss's orders, all were locked. For a few moments the man's face stared through the grillwork not two feet from his observers; but the control room was in complete darkness, Talker having closed the shutters the instant he was sure the man had entered the lock. The reflection of the ceiling lamp from the glass filling helped to conceal them from the tiny human eyes, and the man turned away without realizing the nearness of the two.

He wandered down to the far end of the hallway, trying a door here and there. None yielded to his efforts, and eventually he swung open the airlock door and passed out. Talker hastily opened the control-room shutters, in case the being had noticed their previous condition, and saw him disappear in the direction from which he had come. Evidently whatever plans he had formed for the day had been given up.

"Did you get anything?" asked Boss eagerly, as the tension relaxed. He watched impatiently as Talker walked to the control desk, opened a drawer, and helped himself to a tablet of accelerine before answering.

"As much as I expected," he replied finally. "I was able to isolate the radiations of his optical section, when he first looked at the single light at this end—that was why I arranged it that way. Concentrating on those emanations, I think I know the patterns corresponding to some of the more simple combinations of straight lines and circles—the impressions he got while examining the corridor and doors. It is still difficult, because he is highly intelligent and continuously radiates an extremely complex and continually changing pattern which must represent not only the integration of his various sensory impressions, but the thought symbols of abstract ideas; I don't see how I can master those. I think all we can hope to do is to learn his visual pattern, and try to broadcast to him pictures that will explain what we want. That will take long enough, I fear."

"It better not take too long," remarked Boss. "We can breathe the air and eat the food of this planet, tough as the latter is. But we will live under this gravity just as long as the accelerine holds out, which won't be too many weeks."

"You can synthesize accelerine out of those plants with the straight needlelike leaves," answered Talker. "Doc told me this morning; that was some of his product that I just ate. Accelerine won't be enough, however. It speeds up our metabolism, makes us eat like power furnaces, and gives us enough muscular strength to stand up and walk, or even fly; but if we keep taking it too long, it's an even bet whether we die young of old age, or get so accustomed to it that it becomes useless. Also, it's dangerous in another way—you were telling me that two of the fighters have broken legs, from landing too hard or trying to stand up too quickly. Our muscles can stand the gravity, helped by the dope, but our skeletons can't."

"Can't you ever deliver a little good news, without mixing it so thoroughly with bad that I feel worse than ever?" asked Boss. He stalked aft to the engine room, and relieved his feelings by promising a couple of unfortunate workers the dirty job of replacing the main attractor bar in the power converter, the next time the flood of incoming radiation from space riddled it into uselessness.

Talker squatted where he was, and thought. Learning a language was a new form of exercise to one who had never before dreamed of its necessity. He guessed, from the attitude of the native as he departed, that it would be necessary to reveal the presence of the aliens aboard if the man's interest in the ship was to be maintained. Thinking the matter over, it suddenly occurred to Talker that the man himself must have some means of communicating with his kind; and there had been no antennae visible. If the method were different from that employed by Talker's people, it might be more suited to present requirements. Yes, revealing their presence was definitely indicated, the more so since, finding himself unable to solve the ship's mystery alone, the man might go off to obtain others of his kind. It was no part of Boss's plan to reveal his presence to the main population of the planet in his present, nearly defenseless condition.

It would be easy enough to induce the man to return. One of the crew, flying toward the ship, could "accidentally" pass over his camp. Whether on finding the vessel inhabited, he would be bold enough to venture near any of the aliens, was a matter that could be tested only by experiment; Talker believed he would, since he had shown sufficient courage to enter the ship in ignorance of what lay within.

The herald crept to the controls, and pressed the signal switch indicating that the commander's presence was desired in the control room.

Perhaps a minute later, Boss struggled up the spiral, air hissing from his breathing vents as his lungs tried to cope with the results of his haste. If he had had to rely on vocal speech, he probably couldn't have spoken at all.

"Careful," warned Talker; "remember those broken legs among the crew."

"What is it now?" asked the captain. "Come to think of it, why do I always have to come to you? I'm in command here."

Talker did not bother to dispute the statement. The feeling of superiority ingrained in every member of his class was, through motives of prudence, kept very much under cover. He informed the captain of the results of his cogitation, and let him give the necessary orders—orders which had to be relayed through Talker, in any case.

There were no communicating devices on the ship; the herald had to radiate all of Boss's commands to the proper individuals. There was no machine known to these beings which was capable of receiving, analyzing, and transmitting through wires or by wave the delicate impulses radiated by their minds. They had the signal system already referred to, which was limited to a few standard commands; but in general, messages to be transmitted more than a few yards, or through the interference of metal walls, had to pass through the antennae of a herald. It is conceivable that the heralds themselves had subtly discouraged, for their own ends, research in mechanical communication.

One of the fighters was ordered to the airlock. Talker and Boss met him there, and the former carefully explained the purpose of the flight. The soldier signified his understanding, made sure that his tiny case of accelerine tablets was securely fastened to his leg, and launched himself from the sill. He rose almost vertically, and disappeared over the trees. Talker, after a moment's thought, rose also, and settled on the bank opposite the airlock door. Boss started to follow, but the other "advised" him not to.

"Stay in the doorway," said Talker, "but be sure you are in plain sight. I want him to concentrate his attention on me, but I don't want to give him the impression that you are trying to hide. He might misinterpret the action. When he gets here, keep quiet. I'll have other things to do than listen to you."

The wait, which Talker had expected to be a few minutes, grew into half an hour, without any sign from the decoy. Boss, true to his nature, fumed and fidgeted, providing his companion with a good deal of—well-concealed—amusement. His temper did not improve when the fighter, appearing with a rush of wings, settled in front of Talker, instead of the commander, to make his report.

"He was still in the woods when I went out, sir," said the flier. "I found a spot where I could watch an open place on the trail. I was sure he hadn't come by yet, so I landed on a ridge—the place was near the cliffs—and waited. When he appeared at the edge of the clearing, I flew low, out of sight from the ground, to the other side of the hills; then I came back, quite high, toward here. I'm sure he saw me; I passed directly over him, and he stopped in the middle of the clearing with his whole head tipped up—I suppose he had to, in order to look up with those sunken-in little eyes."

"You have done well. Did you see the creature turn, as though to come back this way?"

"He turned to watch me as I passed overhead; he was still standing motionless the last I saw of him. I don't know what he was going to do. So far as I can tell, he doesn't think at all."

"All right. You may return to your quarters, and eat if you wish. Tell the rest of the crew they are free to move about in the ship, but the ports must be left closed—no one but Boss and me must be visible from the outside."

The soldier vanished into the vessel, showing his near exhaustion in the clumsiness of his movements. Boss looked after him.

"We can't get away from this place too soon to suit me," he commented finally. "A few more weeks and I won't have a single soldier or engineer fit for action. Why did you pick this ghastly planet as a place to restock, anyway? There are eight others in this system."

"Yes," replied Talker sarcastically, "eight others. One so far from the Sun we'd never have noticed it if our course hadn't taken us within half a million miles; four almost as cold, the smallest of them four times the size of this world; two with decent gravity, but without air enough to activate a lump of phosphorus—one of them near the Sun and continually facing it with one hemisphere; and one like this one, with air that would have mummified you at the first attempt to breathe. If you want to go to one of the others, all right—maybe it would be a better way to die, at that."

"All right, forget it—I was just wondering," answered Boss. "I'm so full of this blasted dope we have to take that I can't think straight, anyway. But when is that native coming back?"

"I'm not sure he is, just yet. The soldier flew so as to make it appear that he was coming from the other side of the hills; possibly the creature went to make sure his camp had not been molested. In that case, he may not return today; it's quite a trip for a ground animal, you know."

"Then what are we waiting here for? If he is very long coming, you won't be able to stay awake to meet him. You should have told the soldier to stay out until he was sure what the creature was going to do."

"That would probably have cost us the soldier. You saw the condition he was in when he came back. If you feel energetic, you can send out watchers in relays; but on a day like this, I don't see how they can keep out of sight—there's not a cloud in the sky. I was planning to allow a reasonable time for the native to come back from the point where he saw our soldier. If he doesn't show up, I'll get a night's sleep and expect him tomorrow morning."

"How do you know how long he'll take? You don't know the turns and twists in the trail, and you don't know how fast he walks when he's going somewhere."

"I know how long it took him to come from the pass this morning," answered Talker. "He was near there when the soldier saw him."

"Well, it's your idea, but I don't mind waiting. This sunlight is comfortable." Boss swung the airlock door wide open, letting the sun shine some distance into the lock chamber, and settled himself on the smooth metal floor. Any long period of inactivity had one inevitable result; for it was necessary to sleep some sixteen hours out of twenty-four to offset the enormous consumption of energy exacted by Earth's gravity. Boss may have intended to watch, but he was asleep in two minutes.

Talker remained awake longer. He had indulged in less physical activity than anyone else on the ship, and his mind was normally by far the most active. He squatted on the soft carpet of grass, legs spread spiderwise on either side of his body, while the great topaz eyes took in the details of the surroundings.

Numerous living creatures were visible or audible. Birds were everywhere, as were the insects upon which many of them fed; for in August even Alaska knows that summer has been present for quite a while. The insects, naturally, interested Talker. Some of them bore rather close resemblance to himself, except in the matter of size. A few butterflies fluttered near him in erratic circles; he radiated a thought to them, but got no answer. He had expected none; but he continued to think to them, as a man thinks aloud to a dog, until their intoxicated flight carried them away from the neighborhood.

The flowers, too, caught his eye. They were "not much," as a human florist might have told him, but all were strange to Talker—his home planet had flowers, but they grew in the wilder regions, where it was decidedly unsafe to venture at any time. The only plants allowed in the vicinity of the castlelike fortresses, in which all civilized beings dwelt, were those which were of use in sustaining life. The few vegetables of this variety which bore attractive blooms were too common to be appreciated.

Talker himself was half asleep when he became aware of the man's approach. Had the alien known more of Earthly conditions, he would have realized, from the fact that the man was audible at all at fifty yards, that he was a city dweller.

Talker folded his wings tight against his streamlined body and watched the opening of the trail. The native was even more cautious in his approach than he had been the first time; but in spite of this, the two saw each other almost simultaneously. The man had stepped from the forest with his eyes fixed on Boss, asleep in the airlock, and did not see Talker until the shelter of the trees was behind him.

He stopped instantly, rifle halfway to his shoulder; but Talker carefully refrained from moving anything but his eyes until the weapon was lowered again. To his surprise, the gun was not merely lowered, but slung across the man's back; the man himself took a step or two forward and stopped about fifteen feet away from the alien.

Talker was wondering just how far he could go without alarming the other into flight. Allen Kirk was wondering exactly the same thing. The human being was on the less comfortable side of the exchange, for he was seeing for the first time a creature who had obviously not originated upon his own planet. He felt uncomfortable under the unwinking stare of two pairs of eyes—the optical organs of Talker's kind are lidless, and Kirk had no means of knowing that Boss was asleep—and the uncanny stillness of the two strange beings got on his nerves. In spite of this, Talker was the first to break down the tension.

His antennae had been folded back, unnoticeable against the silver-gray fur of his body. Now they swung forward, expanding into two iridescent plumes as their owner sought to interpret the mental radiations from the human brain.

Kirk was at first startled, then interested. He knew that the antennae of terrestrial moths were strongly suspected of acting as organs of communication, in some cases at least. It was possible, then, that this moth-like entity was interested solely in conversing with him—a possibility made more probable by the fact that neither creature had as yet made a hostile move, as far as the Earthling could tell.

Talker was fortunate in encountering Kirk, instead of a member of one of the several small tribes dwelling in the surrounding territory. Kirk was educated—he had just completed his third year of university study and was working during the summer recess at plotting the activities of a minor insect pest which was threatening to spread south and east into Canada. He had majored in sociology, and had taken courses in biology, astronomy and psychology—though the last subject had bored him excessively.

He had realized from the first, of course, that the object in the gully was a flying machine of some sort; nothing else could have reached this spot without leaving traces in the surrounding forest. He had noticed the air-tight construction of the doorway, but subconsciously refused to consider its full implication until he was actually confronted by one of the vessel's owners, and realized that neither ship nor navigators could possibly have originated on Earth.

With the realization that the being before him wanted to communicate, Kirk bent his thoughts in that direction. He regretted the nearly wasted psychology course; it was practically certain that none of the languages he knew would be of use. Nevertheless, he uttered a few words, to see if they produced any effect; for all he knew, the alien might not be able to hear.

Talker did hear, and showed the fact by a slight start; but the auditory impression he received was unimportant. As he had mentioned to Boss, he had managed to disentangle the cerebral radiations corresponding to a few simple line patterns, as received by the human eyes and symbolized in the brain; and he received, coincidentally with the vocal sounds, a thought-wave which he could translate easily into a series of just such patterns. Kirk, like many people, involuntarily visualized the written form of the words he uttered—not perfectly, but in sufficient detail for the keen mind of the listener to decipher.

Kirk saw the start, though he misinterpreted it. The motion that caught his attention was the sudden stiffening of the antennae as he spoke, the two plumelike organs expanding sideways and pointing diagonally forward, as though to bring his head between their tips. For almost a minute the two creatures remained absolutely motionless, Talker hoping for and expecting further speech, and Allen Kirk watching for some understandable signal. Then the antennae relaxed, and Talker considered the possible meaning of the images he had received.

His own race had a written language—or rather, a means for permanently recording events and ideas; since they had no vocal speech, their "writing" must have been utterly different in basis from that of any Earthly people, for the vast majority of terrestrial written languages are basically phonetic. At any rate, it is certain that Talker had severe difficulty in connecting with any, to him, normal means of communication the symbols he learned from Kirk; for a time, at least, he did not realize that they were arbitrary line arrangements.

Kirk watched the nearly motionless insect for several minutes, without any idea of the true nature of the difficulty. Then, since speech had produced some effect the first time, he tried it again. The result caused him to doubt his own sanity.

Talker knew that he needed further data; in an attempt to obtain it, he simply reached forward to a bare spot of earth and scratched with his odd "hand" the line pattern he had last seen in the human mind. Like Kirk's speaking, it was purely an experiment.

To the man, it was a miracle. He spoke; and the grotesque thing before him wrote—crudely and clumsily, to be sure, for Talker's interpretation was still imperfect, and he was, to put it mildly, unpracticed in the art of penmanship—the last few words that the man had uttered. Kirk was momentarily dumbfounded, unable for an instant to think coherently; then he jumped to a natural, but erroneous, conclusion. The stranger, he decided, must lack vocal cords, but had learned written English from someone else. That implied previous friendly relationships with a human being, and for the first time Kirk felt fully at ease in the presence of the strange creatures.

He drew his knife, and with the tip scratched, "Who are you?" on the ground beside Talker's line. The meaning of the question lay in his mind; but it was couched in terms far too abstract for Talker to connect directly with the marks. A problem roughly similar would be faced by a three-year-old child, not yet literate, presented with a brick covered with cuneiform writing and told that it meant something. Talker saw the same letters in the man's brain, but they were as utterly meaningless there as on the ground. The conference seemed to have reached an impasse.

In spite of his relatively deep-set eyes, which should, in Talker's opinion, have limited his range of vision to what lay before him, Kirk was the first to see Boss move. He turned his head to see more clearly, and Talker followed his gaze with one eye. Boss had awakened, and was standing as high as his legs would lift him in an effort to see the marks on the ground— the top of the bank was about on the same level as the airlock floor. He saw the attention of the other two directed his way, and spoke to Talker.

"What is that? Have you got in touch with him? I can't see what you have on the ground there."

Talker turned his antennae toward the air lock, not that it was necessary, but to assure the human being that Boss was being included in the conversation. "Come on over," he said resignedly, "though it won't do you much good to see. Don't fly too close to the native, and don't get nearer to him than I do at any time."

Kirk watched Boss spread his wings and launch himself toward Talker. The pinions moved too fast to be visible; it occurred to Kirk that these creatures were heavier than any Earthly bird, except for flightless forms like the ostrich, yet their wings spanned less than eight feet.

Boss took a single glance at the letters on the ground, and turned his attention to the Earthman. This was the first time he had seen him in full daylight, and he made the most of the opportunity, mercifully remaining silent the while. Talker promptly forgot him, as nearly as such an individual can be forgotten, and brought himself back to the matter in hand.

The "natural" method of learning a language consists of pointing out objects and having their names repeated until one can remember them. This is the first method that suggests itself to a human being, if no printed grammar is available. Talker hit upon it only after long and profound cogitation, when he suddenly realized that he had learned to interpret the human visual impressions in just that fashion—placing the subject in contact with simple objects, and examining the resulting mental radiations. He tried it.

Normally, the teacher of a language, whatever method he uses, knows what is being done. Kirk did not, for some time. Talker pointed at the ship with one of his hands, watching the man's mind intently for a series of marks such as had accompanied the sounds from his mouth. Kirk looked in the indicated direction, and then back at Talker. The latter pointed again; and a distinct picture, such as he had been seeking, appeared for an instant in the man's mind, to be replaced almost at once by an indecipherable complex of abstract thoughts.

Talker scratched the first impression on the ground—a perfectly recognizable word, "ship"—and looked up again. The man had disappeared. For an instant Talker was confused; then he heard various sounds from the gully, and crawled to the edge to look over. Kirk was below, raising his pole, which had been lying where he had left it, to the sill of the airlock. Still believing that Talker was able to write English, he had completely misinterpreted the gestures and writing, and supposed he was being requested to enter the craft.

Talker had a feeling of helplessness, in the face of his troubles; then he pulled himself together, forcing himself to remember that his life, and the other lives on the ship, depended on his efforts. At least, he now knew the marks had a definite meaning, and he had learned the symbol for "ship." It was, he tried to convince himself, a fair beginning.

The man was crouching in the lock entrance—it was not high enough for him to stand—watching expectantly. Talker beckoned him back. If the man misunderstood his first attempt, now was the time to straighten it out. Kirk looked annoyed, though the aliens could not interpret the expression, slid down the pole, and scrambled back up the bank.

Talker tried again, pointing this time to the early-afternoon sun, and writing the word when it formed in Kirk's mind. The Earthman looked down at the result.

"If that job were necessary, it would be hopeless, friend," he said, "but it isn't necessary. I can speak English, and read it, and write it, thank you. If you can't talk, why don't you just write out what you want me to know?"

Not a word of this was understandable to Talker; in a rather hopeless fashion, he wrote the word or two which had been pictured clearly enough for him to catch, and succeeded in exasperating Kirk still further.

The man certainly cannot be accused of stupidity; it was not his fault that he failed to experience a flash of insight that would give the clue to the alien's meaning. The great majority of people would have done no better, except, perhaps, for some lucky chance. Human experience of thought transference is limited to the claims of "psychics" and to fantastic literature, except for a few scientific experiments of doubtful value; Kirk was not addicted to the reading of any of these products of mental aberration, and made no claim to be any sort of scientist. He had begun by jumping to a conclusion, and for some time it simply did not occur to him that the conclusion might be erroneous—the evidence had been quite convincing, to him, that Talker was acquainted with the English language. It followed that the mothlike one's intentions, motivating all this gesticulation and writing, were to teach Kirk the same tongue: an idea so exactly opposite the true state of affairs as to be almost comical.

Twice more Talker repeated his forlorn attempt to get his idea across to the other; twice Kirk repeated his expostulation, once going so far as to write it out on the ground, when it occurred to him that Talker might be deaf. The third time, the Earthling's temper broke free of its moorings—almost. He was not accustomed to using profanity; his family, whose elder members had carefully controlled his upbringing, was almost puritanical in that respect, and habit got control of his reactions in time to prevent his speaking aloud the words in his mind. His reaction may be imagined when, without Kirk's having uttered a sound, except for a strangled snort, Talker extended a forelimb and scratched a perfectly legible "damn" on the bare patch of ground.

The word "insight" provides a psychologist with material for hours of talk. Its precise meaning cannot be given without tacit assumption of understanding of its nature; neither Kirk nor the narrator possesses that understanding. It is assumed that the readers have had experience of insight, and can understand the habit of cartoonists of symbolizing its presence by an incandescent bulb—whether this habit antedates or succeeds the coining of the phrase "to see light" is a purely academic question. All that matters to us is the fact that Kirk abruptly saw the light—dimly at first, and then, though it strained his credulity to the breaking point, with something like comprehension. Why that particular incident should have served to unlock the door we cannot say: certainly Talker's knowledge of a bit of English profanity could have had many other explanations. Insight, as we have intimated, is a rather obscure process.

For almost a full minute, Earthling and alien stared at each other, the former struggling with his own prejudices and the latter wondering what had happened—even he, unused to interpreting human attitudes, could perceive that Kirk was disturbed. Then the Earthman, with the seeds of truth rapidly maturing in his mind, deliberately visualized a simple design—a circle inscribed in a square. Talker promptly and accurately reproduced it on his improvised backboard. Kirk tried various letters of the English and Greek alphabets, and finally satisfied himself that Talker was actually obtaining the impressions directly from the thoughts. Talker, for his part, discovered that the visual impressions were almost as clear to him now as those of Boss, who had lost his patience and temper long before the Earthman, and had withdrawn by request. He was now sulking, once more squatting in the airlock.

The auditory impressions and abstract thoughts were still a hopeless confusion, so far as Talker was concerned; he never did make a serious attempt to unravel them. Both he and Kirk were satisfied to have found a common ground for expression, and completely ignored lesser matters. Kirk seated himself on the ground beside Talker, and an intensive course in English was rapidly embarked upon.

Not until the Sun was low did Kirk abandon the task, and then it was only because of hunger. Talker had already learned enough to understand the man's declaration that he would return in the morning; and Kirk went back to his camp in the gathering dusk, to prepare a meal and obtain a few hours' sleep—very few, as may well be imagined. He spent a good deal of the night awake in his blankets, staring up at the clear sky and wondering, at times aloud, from which of the thousands of points of light his new acquaintance had come. He was sufficiently adventurous by nature not to ask himself why they had come.

Talker watched the man disappear into the woods, and turned wearily toward the ship. He was overtired; the effects of the earlier dose of accelerine were beginning to abate, and he had a well-founded objection to taking more of the stuff than was necessary to keep him alive. With an effort, he flew the few yards between the bank and the airlock, settling heavily beside Boss. The sound of his wings woke the commander, who eagerly demanded a report on progress in communication. Talker obliged, somewhat shortly; his fatigue had brought him unusually close to anger.

"I have made a beginning, in spite of your aid. How long it will take to set up working communication, I don't know; but I will try to direct the conversations so that the ideas we need to impart are used. He will be back when the Sun rises again; in the meantime, I need sleep. Don't disturb me until the native returns."

Boss was too elated at Talker's news to take offense at his manner. He allowed the herald to depart to his own quarters, and went off himself to spread the news, after closing the outer airlock door. The second in command received the information with glee, and in short order the crew was in better spirits than it had enjoyed since landing on this unhealthy and uncomfortable planet. Even the inhabitants of the sick bay, now three in number since the decoy who had gone after Kirk had returned with a complete set of pulled wing ligaments, began to feel that they were suffering in a good cause, and ceased thinking uncomplimentary thoughts about their officers. The doctor, too, usually by far the most pessimistic member of the ship's personnel, ceased making pointed remarks about "wasted effort" as he worked over his patients. Not one of them appreciated the very real difficulties that still lay ahead, before Talker would have any chance of making the human being understand their needs. None thought that anything more than the transmission of that knowledge would be necessary; and all, except Talker, regarded that matter as practically solved,

The herald had a better appreciation of what lay before him, and was far from sure of his course of action. He had promised Boss to arrange matters so that their needs would be among the first things to be transmitted to the Earthling; but he could not see how he was to fulfill the promise. Had it been merely a matter of keeping his word to the commander, Talker would not have been bothered in the least; he considered anything said to Boss was justified if it succeeded in silencing him. Unfortunately, Talker's own future existence depended on his ability to carry out the terms of that promise. Even with his lack of experience in learning, or teaching, languages, it occurred to him that making advanced chemistry the subject of the lessons was bound to be rather awkward. One cannot point out atoms and molecules individually; it would be pure chance if the man recognized either diagrams or samples, since the latter would be of value only to a chemist with a laboratory, and the former might not—probably would not—conform to human theories of atomic formation. It did not occur to Talker that the ship's pharmacist might be of help; he had been out of contact with his own class for so long that an unfortunate, but almost inevitable, sense of his own superiority had grown up within him. The rest of the crew, to him, were mere laborers; he had never talked with any of them as friend to friend; he had solved all his own problems since joining the crew, and would undoubtedly continue to do so unless and until something drastic forced him out of his rut. Be it said for him that he was not conceited in the ordinary sense of the word;

the feeling of superiority was the result of class training; and the ignoring of others' abilities was completely unconscious.

At the moment, Talker was not worrying about his course of action. He was sound asleep, crouched on the padding of the floor of his quarters. Boss, having made sure that his own contributions toward the present state of near-success were not being minimized in the rapidly spreading news, also retired. The second officer made sure that both airlocks were fast, and made his way to the long wardroom in the lower part of the ship. Most of the soldiers and several engineers were gathered there, discussing the day's events and the chances of reaching their original planetary system—they no longer had "homes" since Boss had broken allegiance with his overlord. The officer's presence did not interrupt the conversation; the Second was a member of the soldier class, and entered the discussion on an equal plane with the others.

It is exceedingly doubtful if any of the crew had ever objected to Boss's dereliction; the act had made little or no change in the course of their existence, and they cared little for whom they worked and fought. If anything, they preferred the new state of affairs, for the constant internecine warfare between the rulers of their home world resembled organized piracy more than anything else, and there was now no need to turn over most of the loot to their own overlord. Boss, of course, had acted almost on impulse, giving little or no thought to such matters as the problem of replenishing exhausted food and ammunition—he expected to supply those wants from his victims. Unfortunately, an unexpected encounter with a full-armed ship belonging to his erstwhile ruler had left him in no condition to fight anybody; after three or four attempts to bluff supplies from isolated stations in his own system, he had made matters a little too hot for himself and fled in the handiest direction, which happened to be straight away from four pursuing warships. Near the speed of light, his vessel became undetectable; and once out of his own system, he had not dared to stop until Sol was bright on his navigation plates. His reasons for landing on Earth have already been made clear. He had food in plenty, and his ship drew its power from stellar radiations; but not a locker on his ship contained a round of ammunition.

If the discomfort of their environment had turned any of Boss's crew against him, Talker's recent efforts had brought them back. The second officer found himself in complete agreement with the crew—it was good to have a commander like Boss, to keep things under control! There passed a peaceful and happy evening on Boss's vessel.

Boss had found it almost impossible to set regular watches. No matter how often he relieved his men, the inactivity of the job promptly put the relief to sleep. The bodies of the crew, exhausted by the constant battle against Earth's savage gravity, would give up and drop the individuals into a coma before they realized that the stimulant accelerine had worn off. The sleep was short, but apparently unavoidable; Talker, alone, had been able to force himself to more or less regular waking and sleeping hours, simply because he did practically no manual labor. For this reason, as soon as he was convinced that there was nothing in the neighborhood that constituted a menace to the ship itself, Boss ceased setting watches and merely closed the ports at night. There were enough differences in physique among the crew members to make it practically certain that someone would always be awake, day or night. The whole thing was horribly unmilitary by any standards, but it was typical of Boss's line-of-least-resistance nature.

It chanced that Boss himself was asleep when Kirk showed up the next morning, and the ports were still sealed. The man threw a stone at the airlock door, and examined the ship more closely while he waited for something to happen. The sun had just cleared the trees and was shining directly on the bow of the vessel. This time, Kirk found that he could see a little through the control-room ports—a few glimpses of boards, covered with dials and levers, the latter oddly shaped to conform to the peculiar "hands" of the operators. He was not close enough to the ship to obtain a very wide vision angle through the ports, and he had to move around to see the various parts of the chamber. While he was thus improving his knowledge, his eye caught a flash of reflected sunlight from the beveled edge of the airlock door, and he turned to see who or what was emerging.

The sound of the stone Kirk had thrown had echoed through the main corridor and reached the "ears" of a party of engineers in the wardroom below. These individuals had interrupted a form of amusement startlingly similar to contract bridge, in which they were engaged, and one had gone to inform Boss. The latter cursed him, told him to rouse Talker, and went back to sleep.

It was Talker, therefore, followed by some of the more curious engineers, who emerged from the lock. Kirk was able to recognize the herald by his antennae, but could discern no difference between the other members of the group. The meeting adjourned, at Talker's direction, to a spot in the gully, in front of the ship, which bore a large and exceptionally smooth area of sun-dried clay, and lessons began. Talker had brought the appropriate materials with him, and had planned to take notes in his own form of "writing"; but he delegated this task to a member of the audience, and gave his full attention to the delicate matter of guiding the choice of words in the proper direction.

This task was no sinecure, since Talker was still extremely uncertain as to the precise nature of words. The meaning covered by a single word in English sometimes requires several in another language; the reverse is also true. Talker had learned the symbol that indicated the ship; he discovered later, to his confusion, that there exist such things as synonyms, other words that meant the same thing. He never did discover the variety of objects that could have been meant by "ship." Kirk saw these sources of difficulty almost from the beginning, and went to considerable trouble to avoid them.

Each written word, to Talker, was a complete unit; it is doubtful if he ever discovered that they were made of twenty-six simple marks, in various combinations. Obviously this fact complicated his task enormously, but there was nothing to be done about it. To explain the individual letters would have been tantamount to teaching the verbal language; and months, or even years, would have been necessary to teach Talker's auditory organs to recognize the innumerable fine distinctions of pitch and overtone to be found in a single sentence.

The details of the weeks that were taken up in the learning would be of interest to psychologists and semanticists, but would extend the present narrative to an unjustifiable length. There were several short interruptions when Kirk had to forage for food, and once he was forced to absent himself for nearly a week, in order to turn in his parasite report at the nearest center of civilization. He told no one of his find in the forest, and returned there as quickly as he could. He found the aliens impatiently waiting for him, and the herald at once returned to the task. Kirk had long since perceived that some tremendous anxiety was behind Talker's insistence, but no amount of effort served to make clear any details.

September and Kirk's patience were drawing to an end by the time that exchange of ideas had progressed to a point where it could be called conversation. Talker wrote with considerable facility, using a pencil and pages from Kirk's notebooks; the man spoke aloud, since he had discovered that this apparently resulted in a sharper mental image of the words. To him, the herald's need was less urgent than the satisfaction of his own curiosity; he asked, so far as Talker's rapidly increasing vocabulary would permit, questions designed to fill that want. He learned something of the physical and sociological nature of the alien's home world—not too much, for Talker had other ideas than the telling of his life story, and Boss became suspicious and almost aggressive when informed of the nature of the Earthman's curiosity. He could conceive of only one use to which such information could possibly be turned.

Kirk finally accepted the inevitable, and permitted Talker to run the conversation in his own fashion, hoping to get a few words of his own into the discussion when the herald's "urgent business" was completed. Talker had kept the man ignorant of Boss's attitude, justly fearing detrimental effects on Kirk's willingness to cooperate.

The attempts at explanation, however, seemed as futile as the first words had been. Talker's premonition of the futility of drawings and diagrams was amply justified; not only were the conventions used in drawing by the engineers of his people utterly different from those of Earth, but it is far from certain that the atoms and molecules the aliens tried to draw were the same objects that a terrestrial chemist would have envisioned. It must be remembered that the "atoms" of physics and of chemistry, used by members of the same race, differ to an embarrassing extent; those conceived in the minds of Talker's people would have been simply unrecognizable, even had Kirk possessed any knowledge of chemistry.

The supply of the requisite arsenic was completely exhausted, so that no samples were available; in any case, Kirk's lack of chemical knowledge would undoubtedly have rendered them valueless.

"There is no use in trying to make your needs known in this manner," the human being finally stated. "The only way in which I am at all likely to hit upon the proper word is for you to describe the more common characteristics of the substance, and the uses to which you put it. Your pictures convey no meaning."

"But what characteristics are you likely to recognize?" asked Talker, on the paper. "My engineers have been striving to do that very thing, since we started."

"They have sought to describe its chemical nature," responded Kirk. "That means nothing to me in any case, for I am not a chemist. What I must know are things like the appearance of the stuff, the appearance of the things that can be made from it, and the reasons you need it so badly. You have not told me enough about yourselves; if I met a party of my own kind stranded on an uninhabited land, I would naturally know many of the things of which they might stand in need, but there is no such guide for me in this case. Tell me why you are here, on a world for which you are so obviously unfitted; tell me why you left your own world, and why you cannot leave this one. Such things will guide me, as could nothing else you might do."

"You are probably right, man, My captain forbade me to divulge such knowledge to you, but I see no other way to make clear our need."

"Why should the commander forbid my learning of you?" asked Kirk. "I see no harm which could result; and I have certainly been frank enough with you and your people. Mothman, I have considered you as being friendly, without seeking evidence of the fact; but I think it would be well for you to tell me much about yourselves, and tell it quickly, before any more efforts are made to supply your wants."

Kirk's voice had suddenly grown hard and toneless, though the aliens could neither appreciate nor interpret the fact. It had come as an abrupt shock to the man, the idea that the helpless-seeming creatures before him could have any motive that might augur ill to humanity, and with it came a realization of the delicacy and unimportance of his own position. Were these beings using him as a tool, to obtain knowledge of humanity's weaknesses, and to supply themselves with means to assault the race? Unbelievable as it may seem, the thought of such a possibility had not entered his head until that moment; and with its entrance, a new man looked forth at the aliens from Kirk's eyes—a man in whom the last trace of credulity had suddenly vanished, who had lost the simple curiosity that motivated the student of a few minutes before, a man possessed and driven by a suspicion of something which he himself could not fully imagine. The doubts that had failed to appear until now were making up for lost time, and were reinforced by the uncomfortable emotion that accompanies the realization that, through no act or idea of one's own, one has barely been diverted from the commission of a fatal blunder.

Talker realized his own error before the Earthman had finished speaking, and wasted no time in endeavoring to repair it. His ignorance of human psychology was an almost insuperable obstacle in this attempt.

"We need the substance which I am trying to describe, far more urgently than we can say," he wrote. "It was the commander's idea, and my own, that it would be a fatal waste of time to allow the conversation to move to other topics, which I can well understand must interest you greatly. Had we learned where it might be found, there would have been no objection to answering any questions you might ask, while we were obtaining it; but we cannot remain here very long, in any case. You must have noticed—indeed your words have shown that you have noticed—how uncomfortable we are on this planet. Nearly half of us, now, are disabled from fractured limbs and strained tendons, fighting your terrible gravity; we live at all only through the use of a drug, and too much of that will eventually prove as dangerous as the condition it is meant to counteract."

"Is your vessel disabled, then?" asked Kirk.

"No, there is no mechanical trouble, and its power is drawn from the matter around it in space. We could travel indefinitely. However, before we dare return to a region where our enemies may locate us, we need a large store of—the material we seek."

"Have you no friends in that neighborhood, to whom you could have fled, instead of making such a long voyage to this solar system?"

"The voyage was not long—perhaps four hundred of your days. Our ship is powerful, and we used full acceleration until your sun showed its nearness by increasing rapidly in brilliance. We would have risked—did risk, since we had no idea of the distance—a much longer flight, to get away from that system. We had a ruler, but the captain decided we would do better on our own, and now there is no armed vessel within the orbit of the outermost planet that would not fire on us at sight."

"It would seem that you lack ammunition, then, and possibly weapons." Kirk proceeded to make clear the difference in meaning between the words, using his rifle as an example.

"Weapons we have; it is the ammunition we lack," affirmed Talker. "I see how your rifle works; ours are similar, throwing a projectile by means of explosives. We have already manufactured the explosives from organic materials we found here; but the element we use in our projectiles is lacking."

"It would, I suppose, be a metal, such as that from which my bullets, or possibly the gun, are made," decided Kirk. "I know where these substances may be found, but you have not yet convinced me that my people can trust you with them. Why, if you are an outlaw in your own system as you claim, do you wish to return at all? You could not, so far as I can see, hope for security there, even with weapons at your disposal."

"I do not understand your question," was the reply. "Where else would we go? And what do you mean by 'security'? Our lot would be better than before, for we would not have to render up the greater portion of what we obtain to our ruler—we can keep it ourselves. There are many uninhabited portions of our world where we can make a base and live in ease."

"Something tells me that your way of life is different from ours," remarked Kirk dryly. "What is the metal you seek?" He wanted to know this for the sake of the knowledge; he had as yet no intention of helping the mothmen to obtain the substance. He wished that Talker's pencil could convey some idea of what the herald was really thinking. Writing, by one who barely knows a language, is not an extraordinarily efficient method of conveying emotions. "If you will show me one of your weapons, it may help," the man added as an afterthought.

Talker, naturally, had suspicions of his own arising from this suggestion. Unlike Boss, however, he was not blinded by them; and remembering that he had already divulged probably the most important characteristic of the weapons—the fact that they were projectile-throwers—he answered after a moment, "Come, then, and see."

It was characteristic of the herald that he tendered the invitation without consulting Boss, or even mentioning to Kirk the objections that the commander would probably raise. He had a contempt, born of long experience, for the captain's resolution, and it never occurred to Talker to doubt his own ability to override any objections. His confidence was justified. If Boss had possessed a heart, instead of a system of valves and muscle rings along the full length of his arterial and venous systems, he would probably have had heart failure when Talker coolly announced his intention of displaying the ship's armament to the Earthling; he was still sputtering half-formed thought waves as he followed the pair toward the airlock. Talker had merely explained the reason for his action, and acted; Boss would never have admitted, even to himself, that he considered Talker's opinion superior to his own, but he invariably accepted it as though it were. He was firmly convinced that his own genius was responsible for their successes to date, and Talker saw no reason to disillusion him.

Kirk learned little from the ship's guns, though the sighting apparatus would have given an artilleryman hours of ecstasy. The weapons themselves were simply ordinary-looking small-caliber, smooth-bore cannon, but with extremely ingenious mountings which permitted them to be loaded, aimed, and fired without losing air from the ship. The turret rooms were divided by bulkheads into two parts, one containing the gun and auxiliary mechanisms, and the other, to Kirk's surprise, piled high with metal cylinders that could be nothing but projectiles. He picked up one of these, and found it to be open at one end, with an empty hollow taking up most of its interior. Talker, who had made explanations from time to time, began to write again.

"We need material to manufacture the filling of that projectile," were his words. "Empty, it is useless for any purpose whatsoever."

"And when it is full—" asked Kirk.

"The shell penetrates the walls of a ship, leaving only a small hole which is promptly sealed by the material between the inner and outer hulls. The projectile is ruptured by a small explosive charge, and its contents evaporate, releasing an odorless gas which takes care of the crew. The ship can then be towed to a planet and looted without opposition and without danger—if you can reach a habitable world unseen."

"Why can you not use an explosive charge which will open a large hole in the hull, and do your looting in space?" asked the man.

"Air extends only a short distance outward from each world," explained Talker, his respect for the Earthman's knowledge dropping about fifty points, "so it is impossible to leave a ship or change ships while in space. An explosive shell, also, would probably destroy much of the interior, since the hull of a ship is far stronger than the inner partitions, and we want what is inside as nearly intact as possible."

Kirk waited rather impatiently for the herald to finish scrawling this message, and snapped, "Of course, I know about the airlessness of space; who doesn't? But have you no protective garment that will permit you to carry air and move about more or less freely, outside a ship?"

"Many attempts have been made to devise such a suit," was the answer, "but as yet there is nothing which can be trusted to permit all our limbs to move freely, carry air to our breathing orifices, and possess airtight joints and fastenings. I can see that there might be very little difficulty in designing such a garment for your simply constructed body, but Nature built us with too many appendages."

Kirk said nothing as he half-crawled down the low corridor to the airlock, but he did a lot of thinking. He was reasonably sure that most of his cerebral operations were indecipherable to the alien, though it was chiefly mental laziness which kept him from making any particular effort to couch his thoughts in nonvisual terms—such an effort would have been a distinct bar to constructive thinking, in any case. The herald's story, while strange from Kirk's Earthly point of view, was certainly not impossible; the conditions of life he had described had, in large measure, existed on Earth at various times, as the Earthling well knew. Kirk had gained considerable appreciation of Talker's rather cynical character, and had been somewhat amused at the unconscious egotism displayed by the herald.

The sun was low in the west when the group emerged from the airlock, and a stiff northeast wind made its presence felt at the top of the bank, out of the shelter of the hull. Kirk looked at the sky and forest for a few minutes, and then turned to Talker.

"I will return to my camp now, and eat. You have given all the help you can, I guess. I will try to solve the problem tonight. I can make no promise of success, and, even if I do discover what your chemical is, there is the possibility that I will still fear to trust you with it. Your people are peculiar, to me; I don't pretend to understand half of your customs or ideas of propriety, and my first consideration must be the safety of my own kind.

"Whatever happens, I cannot remain much longer in the territory. You may not be acquainted with the seasonal changes of this planet, but you must have noticed the drop in temperature that has been evident at night the last week or two. We are located almost upon the Arctic Circle"— Kirk pictured mentally just what he meant—"and I could not live very far into the winter with my outfit. I should have returned to my own country several weeks ago."

"I cannot control your actions, even if I wished to do so," answered Talker, "I can but hope for the best—an unusual situation, all around, for me."

Kirk grinned at the herald's wry humor, turned, and strode away in the direction of his camp—he had not moved it closer to the ship, because of the better water supply at its original location. As he walked, the grin melted quickly from his features, to be replaced by the blank expression which, for him, indicated thought. He had no idea of what he should do; as he had told the herald, the man's first consideration was his own kind, but he wanted to believe and trust in the alien, whom he had come to like.

It was evident that Talker had not exaggerated the seriousness of his own position. Kirk had seen members of the crew moving painfully about their duties on board the ship, and had seen one of them collapse as the horny exoskeleton of his absurdly thin legs gave way under a body weighing more than three times what it should have. On the other hand, a crew of Earthmen under such conditions would have left long since, weapons or no weapons. Kirk found himself unable to decide whether the stubbornness of these creatures was an admirable trait, or an indication of less worthy natures. It occurred to him, fleetingly, that their idea of a "worthy" trait probably differed widely from his own.

Possibly, if the man decided to refuse aid to the strangers, he could quiet his conscience by comparing them to children refusing to come in out of the rain until mother promised them some candy—but a scientist, working overtime in his laboratory, could be described by the same simile, and Kirk knew it. No, the need was surely real enough to them.

And why should they want to attack mankind? Earth was useless to them, as a dwelling place; if, as they claimed, their own king were against them, only fools would make such an attempt, however armed. And Kirk was not impressed with the gas guns of the aliens—they were, even he could realize, worth absolutely nothing except in the confined space of an ether ship. On the other hand, Talker might have stretched the truth beyond its yielding point; and the "king," whom he might still be serving, would not need excuses such as the possible utility of a world in order to attack it, unless he differed greatly from Earthly rulers. The chance to extend his dominions would be motive enough.

Well, let that go for a minute. Kirk had arrived at his camp, and prepared a light meal. He ate slowly, still thinking, and washed the few utensils in the same fashion, The Sun had long been gone, and he sought his blankets with the intention of sleeping on the problem.

Sleep refused to come. He would absolutely refuse to consider one angle, and another promptly rose to torment him. What was the gas the aliens used? Kirk was not sure whether or not he regretted his ignorance of chemistry. The train of thought led by imperceptible, but perfectly natural, steps to the idea of insect poisons, his own original job in the territory, and the stock of copper sulfate and arsenate of lead which was stored at the river mouth port, for use the following spring. The idea left his mind as quickly as it had entered; for such materials did not, so far as Kirk knew, form any kind of gas. The job recalled his other occupation, which was still that of acquiring an education. The imminent opening of college presented itself as an additional reason for immediate departure; it was doubtful even now whether he could return to the States in time for registration—unless, he thought with a flicker of amusement, the aliens performed the necessary transportation. And so the trail of thought led itself in a circle, and he was once again considering the matter of the requirements of those on the spaceship.

And then another thought struck him. Let it be granted that the herald had adhered strictly to the truth at all times. He might, then, be a likable individual; he might be a shepherd trying to save the lives of his flock; he might be an officer worthy of respect for his ability and devotion to duty—no matter what he might be in his character, the simple and undeniable fact remained that, by his own admission of past activities and by his declaration of the uses to which he intended to put the weapons he hoped to acquire, he was neither more nor less than a pirate. He had stated plainly that Boss had revolted against the authority of his original ruler; he had tacitly admitted that he himself had concurred in the expression of independence: and he had used the term "outlaw" in describing the ship and its crew.

If Earth were to have any dealings with the herald's people, they would normally be with the law-abiding section of society. Kirk had no moral right to give assistance to that crew, no matter what his personal feelings might be. For a while, the Earthman pondered the matter, seeking flaws in the argument, seeking them solely because of the friendship he had commenced to feel for Talker, for any sort of decision would be a boon to his tortured mind.

But the fact stood; and eventually Kirk ceased attempting to argue it away, and accepted the simple idea that aiding the strangers would be, legally and morally, an offense against justice. Owing to the natural contrariness of human nature, he now found himself wishing he could help the alien with whom he had conversed so long, but the attainment of a decision had eased the tension in his mind, and at long last the man succeeded in falling asleep. He might have slept even more peacefully had he known a single fact—one of which not even Talker and Boss had dreamed.

Their interstellar voyage had consumed, not four hundred days, but more nearly forty years. The greater part of the flight had been made at a speed near that of light; hours of ship's time had been days outside. A similar period was certain to elapse on the return; and the ruler who had been defied would certainly have been succeeded by another. Talker and Boss could easily have passed themselves off as returning members of a legitimate interstellar expedition; even had they failed to do so, it is unlikely that they would have been punished for defying a ruler whose place their judge, as likely as not, would have inherited either by private assassination or conquest in war.

Unfortunately, Talker's race had no inkling of relativity, as their science was of the type which develops better guns and faster ships, without bothering too much with theory: and Kirk's only acquaintance with the concept had been made through the pages of a classic novel on time travel—the only such work he had ever read, and one which had emphasized the fourth dimension rather than velocity-mass ratios.

When Kirk awoke, therefore, it was with a distinctly uncomfortable feeling connected with the day's probable events. He rose, shivering in the biting cold of early morning, washed and ate, and broke camp. Whatever happened, he intended to head south that day, and he carefully made tent, blankets, and the other gear into a single large pack. This he cached near the campsite; then he picked up his rifle and took the trail over the hill into the next valley. He was fairly sure that the aliens could not harm him, except by landing their vessel on top of him, since they were without weapons and far inferior to him in physical strength.

But why, he suddenly thought, should there be any trouble? He need not refuse to help; it was simple truth that he had not been able to solve the problem—he still had no idea of the identity of the substance they desired. He could keep to himself his opinion of their occupation. Kirk was sure that the words describing that opinion had not been used in any of his conversation with Talker, and the herald must by this time be accustomed to receiving untranslatable waves from the Earthman's mind.

Thus determined, Kirk now emerged from the forest to the bank of the arroyo where the interstellar flier lay. As usual at this time of day, none of the crew was visible; also as usual, Kirk attracted attention to the fact of his presence by sending a stone clattering against the outer hull.

Talker, in spite of the ever-mounting fatigue that was threatening the lives of his party as much as any other single trouble, had also spent a portion of the night in thought. He had seen, more and more clearly in the last few days, that the chances of Kirk's learning the name of the poison were microscopic. A practical chemist, given a sample of the substance, could have identified it without difficulty; but without even a milligram sample on board, it seemed doubtful whether anyone could tell what was needed. The natives of this planet had, and used, poison gases; Kirk had told him that much, In their case, however, it was necessary in general to use them outdoors, and special characteristics of density and effectiveness were thus required. Talker knew that his gas was about twice as dense as the air of this world, under the same conditions of temperature and pressure; but he had no idea of the extent of its toxic qualities on terrestrial life.

The only chance, it seemed, if Kirk failed in his task, was to have him direct the voyagers to a place where someone skilled in chemistry, or warfare, or both, might be found, The herald had learned to communicate; the rest should not be difficult.

So it came about that Talker answered the bell-like clang on the hull with his mind set to expect the worst, and prepared to do something about it. He noticed at once that the human being was carrying his rifle, which he had not done since the first day, and the alien partially interpreted the reason for the act. He flew to the bank, and squatted in front of Kirk, antennae alertly spread. The Earthling, his mind made up, wasted no time.

"I have not solved the problem," he stated flatly.

"I am not surprised," wrote Talker, "nor am I angered. There was no need to bring the weapon—you cannot be blamed for failure at a task where one better trained than you could probably have done no more. It would be childishly stupid to hold animosity against you, in spite of our disappointment.

"But you can still help us. There must be, somewhere on this planet, individuals who are trained in such matters. You have mentioned your own need of getting out of this region before the onset of winter. We could easily transport you to your own place, and you in return can direct us to such a person as I have described. Are you willing?"

The herald's attitude at his failure had taken Kirk completely by surprise, and had added much to his opinion of the creature. The new suggestion found him unprepared, for his intended refusal seemed now even more unpleasant than before. Some inner guardian made him say simply, "I have left my equipment at the camp," and then he turned and strode, as rapidly as he dared, into the forest and away from the danger of betraying the thoughts whirling about in his mind.

A mile from the ship, Kirk stopped and tried to settle the recent happenings into his picture of the alien's personality. He had felt friendship of a sort for Talker, even after deciding he was a pirate and unworthy of such feeling; the attitude the herald had shown, in the face of what must have been a bitter disappointment, had strengthened Kirk's respect. Refusing to help was going more and more against the grain.

He tried to argue down his feelings. It was evident, from Talker's conversation, that the human-admired characteristics of altruism and sympathy were foreign to his makeup. He was perfectly selfish, and Kirk had no doubt that he would have seized any chance of saving his own neck, whether or not that chance also included the necks of his fellows. He looked on those others with tolerance, since they made life easier for him, but there was certainly no trace of fellowship in his feelings toward them. Kirk had repeatedly sensed the amusement in Talker's mind as he spoke of Boss and others of the crew, and was reminded of the interested contempt with which he himself had sometimes watched a child building sand castles at the seashore.

No, Talker was not an ideal character from a human point of view; but Kirk still felt attracted to him. Could he go back and tell the alien that it was useless to ask him for further aid? The man shrank from the thought; and yet what else could he do? Nothing. Slowly the human being finished the walk to his former campsite, shouldered the heavy pack, and turned back toward the ship. He walked sturdily, but the morning sunlight filtered through the leaves onto a face that looked far older than Kirk's twenty years would demand.

Talker was still waiting on the bank, both his great yellow eyes fixed upon the opening of the trail. He saw Kirk coming with his burden, and at once turned and flew to the airlock, disappearing within. Kirk saw him go, and called; the herald's head and antennae reappeared at the portal. The man dropped his pack to the ground, and stood motionless and silent, looking at the mothman and trying to find words in which to express the thing he had to make clear. He couldn't do it.

The thoughts were enough. Talker spread his wings and, concealing the frightful effort the act cost him, returned to the place where Kirk was standing. He still carried the writing materials, and, as the Earthling commenced to realize the extent to which he had been analyzed, he began writing.

"What is it that we have done to offend your customs?" asked the herald. "What possible interest can you have in those of my kind whom you have never seen, of whom you would never have heard except for me?"

Kirk tried to explain his attitude on the subject of piracy, but failed signally. To the alien, raiding and looting were the natural means of making a living; his ideas of right and wrong simply did not match those of human civilization, any more than could be expected. It was Talker who finally decided that further effort in that direction was useless.

"When I first discovered you," he said, "it took some time for me to realize that the waves you radiated represented a pattern of intelligence. Your behavior eventually showed the truth, and with much effort I learned to interpret, to a certain extent, those thought waves. I fear that we are up against the same problem here. Just as it took me some time to comprehend that my thoughts were not the only possible kind, I am just beginning to understand that my behavior pattern is not the only possible one. With time, perhaps I may understand yours; I must, if to do so lies within the powers of intelligence. Therefore, I invite you to come with us, anyway, to the southern regions from which you say you have come. On the way, you will tell me more about your people, as I have told you of mine. Perhaps, with that background, I shall begin to appreciate your point of view and find a means of persuading you to help us. In any case, the knowledge will be of great interest for its own sake.

"Until I do have some understanding of your reasons for refusal, I shall not repeat our request; nor shall I inform the commander of what has occurred. The less he knows, the better for both of us, as well as himself. He could never appreciate what I am now trying to do, and he has no understanding of how a mind can seek pure knowledge without some immediate use for it—curiosity and imagination are unknown to him.

"Come, then; we will travel southward slowly, and converse as we fly. Some time at least will be saved; and we do not dare spend more than a few more days on this planet. We would not have enough of the crew left to man the engines—there are few enough of us now who remain able."

Kirk accepted, though never thereafter could he account for his reasons for doing so. Unconsciously, he wanted to give the creature a chance to justify itself; more and more the idea was winning ground that a being so generally reasonable and so utterly imperturbable in the face of telling disappointment could not be a criminal on any code. Such a belief, of course, is unreasonable and unjustifiable even when considered with respect to a single culture. Applied by a member of one civilization to a creature of another, such an emotional attitude is sheer lunacy. Logic alone stands a chance, and even that is likely to be badly crippled for lack of data.

Earthman and alien entered the airlock, and closed both doors—for nearly the last time on Earth, the herald hoped. Talker relaxed for a moment in the corridor, fervently vowing never again to spread his wings on a world where he couldn't fly without stimulants; then he crawled forward and up the ramp to the control room, Kirk following.

They found themselves alone in the control chamber, for it was still early morning. Talker sounded the signal intended to let Boss know he was wanted, and the oddly assorted pair waited in silence. Several repetitions of the call were necessary before Boss finally appeared from below. His attitude was even more domineering than usual, partly because he had just been awakened by the signal, and partly because he never missed an opportunity to try to impress the native with his importance; he never fully appreciated the fact that the human being could neither "hear" his speech nor interpret his bodily attitude.

Talker told him to get the ship into the air, and cruise slowly toward the equator of the planet until ocean was reached. Boss promptly began asking questions about the state of progress in locating the object of their search; and the herald replied that at the moment no progress was being made because the individual who should be working was talking instead. That silenced the captain, and he moved to the control board to call the engineers to their stations. Talker took his place at the commander's side, ready to transmit more detailed instructions if and when necessary. The signal board was a sufficiently versatile affair to transmit the relatively simple commands involved in raising the ship, however; as a matter of fact, the actual takeoff, as would be expected, was handled from the control room, and orders were given merely to start the proper generators below.

Kirk laid his pack on the floor beside the captain and sat on it, thus bringing his head down to within about two feet of the other's. The glass ports, larger than any others in the ship, permitted him to see in all directions forward, while a periscope, which he quickly noticed, gave a partial view backward, leaving the lower rear the vessel's only blind spot. The periscope eyepiece was made to accommodate the huge optics of the ship's owners, and transmitted a decidedly distorted image to Kirk's eyes, as he found by experiment. The field of view could not be shifted, and its lower half was occupied by the hull. The man turned his attention to the great port which gave a clear view of what lay below and in front.

He settled himself more solidly as the ground slid smoothly away from him. There was no takeoff run; the vessel rose straight for two thousand feet, turned the streamlined bow southward, and followed its nose. Boss relaxed at his post as soon as they were on course, and merely kept his eyes on a row of dials supposed to indicate the behavior of the generators. An engineer was watching a duplicate set below, and it made little difference whether or not Boss stuck to his job—though he would not have admitted that fact to Kirk had he been able to speak to him.

The human being and the herald watched and commented upon the terrain below, as it drifted sternward. Talker drew attention to the deserted appearance of the forest, and compared it to the similar vast, uninhabited regions of his own planet. This, as intended, drew from Kirk a description of the more densely populated countries, of the different peoples who inhabited them, and the various relationships existing between them. On this last point he was a fair lecturer, for he had spent a good deal of time on sociology. The herald kept him talking, asking questions whenever the man seemed to be running down, and in general doing everything which was likely to result in the production of any information that might be of use.

Their pace was only moderately rapid. The sound of the ship's passage through the air could not have been heard on the ground, and was inaudible through the double hulls; whatever power drove and supported them was efficient enough to be soundless, as well.

They came in sight of the sea and a small settlement at almost the same instant. The town was not large, but possessed several docks and a fair-sized fleet of fishing boats. Kirk recognized it—it was the town where he had landed upon his arrival at the beginning of the summer, and where he had recently turned in his report of the season's progress. It was now late afternoon, and a glance at his watch and a moment's calculation informed Kirk that the ship could not have been traveling more than thirty miles an hour, for they had left the base of his operations only slightly after noon. Five hours in the low control chamber had left the man rather cramped; he flung a query at Talker, and was informed that the main corridor was probably the only room on the ship spacious enough to permit him to stretch, even lying down. Kirk's memory of the gun rooms suggested that the herald was right, so he sent his pack sliding down the ramp, followed it, detached a blanket, and stretched out on the corridor floor, to the considerable astonishment of a pair of soldiers who emerged from their rooms at that moment. He had brought no food, but did not feel particularly hungry. After a few minutes, he propped himself up with the pack as a pillow, and stared off down the hallway. The door at the far end was now open, and faint sounds came from below. Kirk considered investigating, but thought better of it and relaxed on his blanket.

A very faint trembling of the floor roused him a few minutes later. He stood up—too suddenly, for his head impinged sharply on the metal ceiling—and turned toward the control-room ramp once more. Something appeared to be happening. He started up the incline, but did not reach the top, for as his head attained the level of the floor above he saw Talker starting down, and retreated before him.

Boss followed the herald into the main corridor, and Kirk walked behind the pair to the airlock. Evidently the ship had landed. The man brushed Talker's wing tip with a finger to get his attention, and asked, "What is the matter? Why have you come down so soon? I know of none around here who could give you help."

"Your words do not agree with your thoughts of a few moments ago," returned Talker, who still carried the paper and pencil. "I hoped, when I asked you aboard after your avowal of enmity toward us, that your mind

would betray some knowledge of value. It has done that; you are not accustomed to having your thoughts read, and have surprisingly little control over them. Had I not been delayed through having to learn your system of mental symbology, we would have had long ago the information
we needed, without the necessity of asking your consent. When the settlement near which we are now landed came into view, your mind gave out
word patterns of all sorts—the name of the place, which means nothing
to us, the fact that the individual who directs your work resides therein,
and—the fact that there is stored somewhere in that town a supply of
chemical to be used for poisoning insects. Your master is an expert on
such matters; he must be, to hold the position. It is possible that the chemical will prove to be what we require; if not, I have learned to read human
minds from you, and I can pry the knowledge from the one who directs
you."

"Then you asked me aboard solely in the hope of tricking me?" asked
Kirk. "There was no friendship, as I had believed? No sincere attempt to
understand my point of view, as you claimed?"

"It would indeed be interesting to understand your peculiar ways of
thought," replied the herald, "but I have spent all too much time in satisfying idle curiosity; and I see no practical value to be derived from the
understanding you mentioned. You are like the others on this ship—easily swayed by stereotyped patterns of thought; I can see no other possible
reason for your refusal to aid us. I bear you no enmity, since I have almost
achieved my goal in spite of you; but it would be truly idiotic to expect
me to feel friendly toward you. None the less, it would be interesting to
know—" the strangely shaped hand abruptly ceased writing, and its owner
turned toward the airlock, where Boss was waiting impatiently.

That last, unfinished sentence did much to check the cold anger that
was starting to rise in Kirk. In silence, he watched the airlock doors swing
open. Through a screen of tangled deadwood, a few houses were visible;
but no people appeared to be interested in the ship. How Boss had been
able to bring the vessel down unseen so near the town will forever remain
unknown.

The two aliens flew over the brush, choosing a moment when no
human beings were in sight, and concealed themselves behind bushes fairly
close to the nearest houses. Kirk, sitting on the sill of the outer door, could
imagine the herald's sensitive antennae picking up the thought waves of
one after another of the unsuspecting townspeople. He would have trouble
with some of them, thought Kirk with a grin, as he recalled the three-
quarters Indian population of the place and the illiteracy of a large percentage of this group, but how would it be possible to prevent the alien's

looting the minds of Faxon, the poison specialist, or old MacArthur, the storekeeper? Warning them would be easy enough, but useless; the more they tried not to think of what was wanted, the more certain most of them were to do so. If they tried to attack and drive away the aliens, the latter could simply retreat into the ship and study the attackers at will. It looked as though Talker would win after all; or—did it?

A thought struck the man, hazy and ill-defined at first. It had something to do with Indians and illiterates; something he couldn't quite place, dimly remembered from his psychology study—and then he had it. A grin spread over his face; he leaned back against his pack and watched the herald as men, women, and children, both white and red, passed within a hundred yards of his hiding place. Once again Kirk pictured the mind-reading "danger"; but it was markedly different from the former picture. He tried to control his thoughts, to make the joke last as long as possible—he wasn't sure that the herald could read his mind at this range, but why take chances? He tried to think about the subject in French, since he had to think about it; the results were not exactly what he had intended, but the mental pictures were undoubtedly tangled enough to baffle any mind reader. And then the mothmen were winging their way back to the ship.

Kirk moved aside to let them enter, and watched as the pair settled to the airlock floor. Talker made no attempt to write; he simply stood and looked at the Earthman with an expression of hopeless resignation in his very carriage that sent a stab of pity through Kirk's heart.

The man stared back for a few moments, and then began speaking softly,

"You know, now. I did not think of it until you had gone—but I should have, from what you told me; and you should long since have known from your own observations. When we first learned to communicate with each other, you told me that my thought-wave pattern was different from that of your race, which was natural enough, as you finally realized. You did not carry that reasoning, which told you it was natural, to its logical conclusion: nor did I. Your people all 'think' alike—so far as either of us is able to tell what thought is. The patterns you broadcast are mutually intelligible to members of your race, but not to me, because you have received those waves from others of your kind from earliest childhood, and I am a stranger. But my people do not communicate in that fashion; as you have learned, we have organs capable of impressing fine modulations on sound waves, and of detecting these modulations. The activity that occurs in our brains is never directly transmitted to other brains—it is first 'coded' and then broadcast.

"The waves you 'hear' arise from chemical activity in your nervous systems, activity that accompanies thought. They are—must be—con-

trolled to a vast extent by the structure of the nerve pattern in your brains;
a structure which is itself controlled during your growth by the impressed
waves from outside, in conjunction with whatever strange process accompanies learning."

Kirk held out a hand to the herald.

"Look closely at the ends of my fingers. In the skin you will see a
complex pattern of ridges and hollows. That pattern, stranger, is unique
in me; every one of my people has a similar, but individual, pattern—no
two have identical fingerprints. They form the most positive means of
identification we possess, although there are more than two billion beings on this planet.

"And yet, friend, I think I am safe in saying that there are many times
as many chances that two of us should bear identical fingerprints as there
are chances that two human brains should be exactly alike, nerve for nerve.
From birth, each brain is isolated, can be reached only through the means
of communication natural to us; there is no reason that all should develop alike.

"On that assumption, the tiny currents that pass from nerve to nerve
and give rise to the waves that you can sense cannot possibly be the same
for any two of us; and so no two sets of 'thought waves' could be identical. You learned some of my pattern, and thought that you had the key to
communicate with all my kind; but I tell you sincerely that you will have
to learn afresh the 'thought language' of every new human being with
whom you wish to converse. You have just discovered that for yourself.

"These cerebral radiations are not entirely unknown to us. Certain
devices, in the nature of extremely sensitive electric detectors, have been
able to measure and record them; but the only pattern shared by any significant number of human minds is that characterizing sleep—mental
inactivity. The instant the subject wakes, or even has a dream, the 'alpha
pattern' breaks up into a seemingly disorganized jumble.

"We also know a little concerning direct thought exchange. Some of
our scientists have experimented for many years, in the attempt to determine its nature and cause. Many people—not the scientists—assume that
it is due to radiations like those recorded by the devices I mentioned;
they imagine the possibility of perfecting those machines and using them
for communication. They have heard of the experiments in telepathy, but
have not bothered to investigate their details.

"The experimenters themselves have pointed out that the phenomena of telepathy and clairvoyance, which seem to be closely connected,
are quite inconsistent with the known laws of radiation, such as the inverse square law. I don't remember all the details, and, anyway, I'm not a
physicist; but the best-known of those scientists claim that our present

science of physics does not contain the explanation of the experimental results.

"Whatever the true state of affairs may be, I am sure you will never get anything from any human mind but my own. I hate to tantalize you, but if you had not made this attempt to deceive me, my emotions would probably have overcome my common sense sufficiently to force me to help you; even now I am tempted to do so, because I can't help feeling that your mind contains the roots of curiosity, with which I sympathize— I wouldn't have pursued my studies this far, otherwise. But I could never trust you, now. My intelligence, such as it is, gave one estimate of your character, and my feelings gave another; and unfortunately for you, your actions showed the intelligence to be at least partially correct. Your character probably isn't your fault, but I can do nothing about that. My advice to you is to take on supplies and get away from here while some of you are still alive; the fact that you found an inhabited planetary system at the first try suggests that others may not be too hard to locate. I wish you luck, so far as good luck for you doesn't mean bad for us."

Allen Kirk turned, swung the pack to his shoulder, and walked away from the spaceship. He was acutely aware, as he went, of the two pairs of yellow eyes gazing after him; but he didn't dare to look back.

TECHNICAL ERROR

Astounding, January 1944

Seven spacesuited human beings stood motionless, at the edge of the little valley. Around them was a bare, jagged plain of basalt, lit sharply by the distant sun and unwavering stars; a dozen miles behind, hidden by the abrupt curvature of the asteroid's surface, was a half-fused heap of metal that had brought them here; and in front of them, almost at their feet, in the shallow groove scraped by a meteor ages before, was an object which caused more than one of those men to doubt his sanity.

Before them lay the ship whose heat-ruined wreckage had been left behind them only minutes ago—perfectly whole in every part. Seven pairs of eyes swept it from end to end, picking out and recognizing each line, Driving and steering pits at each end; six bulging observation ports around its middle; rows of smaller ports, their transparent panes gleaming, obviously intact, in the sunlight; the silvery, prolate hull itself—all forced themselves on the minds that sought desperately to reject them as impossibilities. The *Giansar* was gone—they had fled from the threat of its disordered atomic engines, watched it glow and melt and finally cool again, a nearly formless heap of slag. So what was this?

None of them even thought of a sister ship. The *Giansar* had none. Spaceships are not mass-production articles; only a few hundred exist as yet, and each of those is a specialized, designed-to-order machine. A spaceman of any standing can recognize at a glance, by shape alone, any ship built on Earth—and no other intelligent race but man inhabits Sol's system.

Grant was the first to throw off the spell. He glanced up at the stars overhead, and figured; then he shook his head.

"We haven't circled, I'll swear," he said after a moment. "We're a quarter of the way around this world from where we left the ship, if I have allowed right for rotation. Besides, it wasn't in a valley."

The tension vanished as though someone had snapped a switch. "That's right," grunted Cray, the stocky engine man. "The place was practically flat, except for a lot of spiky rocks. And anyway, no one but a nut could think that was the *Giansar*, after leaving her the way we did. I wonder who left this buggy here."

"Why do you assume it has been left?" The query came, in a quiet voice, from Jack Preble, the youngest person present. "It appears uninjured. I see no reason to suppose that the crew is not waiting for us to enter at this moment, if they have seen us."

Grant shook his head. "That ship might have been here for years— probably has, since none of us can place it. The crew may be there, but, I fear, not alive. It seems unlikely that this craft has been registered in the lifetime of any of us. I doubt that it would have remained here unless it were disabled; but you must all have realized by now that it holds probably our only chance of life. Even if it won't fly, there may be a transmitter in repair. We had better investigate."

The men followed the captain as he took a long, slow leap down the slope. Little enthusiasm showed in the faces behind the helmet masks; even young Preble had accepted the fact that death was almost inevitable. At another time, they might have been eager and curious, even in the face of a spectacle as depressing as a derelict usually is; now they merely followed silently. Here, probably, a similar group of men had, no one knew how long ago, faced a fate identical to theirs; and they were about to see what had befallen those others. No one saw humor in the situation, but a wry smile was twisting more than one face as the group stopped beneath the circular entrance port. More than one thought of the possible irony of their being taken for a rescue crew.

Grant looked at the port, twenty-five feet above their heads. Any of them could easily have jumped to it; but even that effort was not necessary, for a row of niches, eight inches square and two deep, provided a ladder to the rim. It was possible to cling to them even on the lower curve of the hull, for they were deeply grooved around the inside edges. The captain found that his gauntlets could grip easily, and he made his way up the wall of metal, the others watching from below. Arriving at the port, he found that the niches formed a circle around it, and other rows of them extended over the hull in different directions. It was at the entrance, however, that he met the first of the many irregularities.

The others saw him reach the port, and stop as though looking around. Then he traveled entirely around it, stopped again, and began feeling the mirror-like metal with his gloved hands. Finally he called out:

"Cray, could you come up here, please? If anyone can find the opening mechanism, you should."

The engineer remained exactly where he was.

"Why should there be any?" he asked. "The only reason we use it on our ships is habit; if the door opens inward, atmospheric pressure will hold it better than any lock. Try pushing; if the inner door is sealed, you shouldn't have much trouble—the lock chamber will be exhausted, probably."

Grant got a grip near the edge of the door, and pushed. There was no result. He moved partway around the rim and tried again, with the same lack of success. After testing at several more points, he spoke again: "No luck. I can't even tell which side the hinge is on, or even if there is a hinge. Cray, you and a couple of others had better come up and give a hand at pushing; maybe there's a trace of air in the inner chamber."

Cray grunted, "If there's anywhere near an atmosphere's pressure, it'll take tons to budge the door—it's twelve feet across." But this time he began to climb the hull. Royden, probably the most powerful one present, and a chemist named Stevenson followed him. The four men grouped themselves about the forward edge of the port, their feet braced on the door itself and hands firmly gripping the climbing niches; and all four tensed their bodies and heaved. The door still refused to budge. They rested a moment, and followed Grant to the opposite side of the metal disk.

This time their efforts produced results. The pressure on the other side of the valve must have been only a few millimeters of mercury; enough to give four or five hundred pounds' resistance to an outside thrust at the edge opposite the hinge. When the door opened a crack, that pressure vanished almost instantly, and the four men shot feet first through the suddenly yawning opening. Grant and Stevenson checked the plunge by catching the edge of the port frame; the other two disappeared into the inner darkness, and an instant later the shock of their impact upon some hard surface was felt by those touching the hull.

The captain and the chemist dropped to the floor of the lock and entered; Preble leaped for the open door, followed by Sorrel and McEachern. All three judged accurately, sailing through the opening, checking their flight against the ceiling, and landing feet down on the floor, where they found the others standing with belt lights in their hands. The sun was on the far side of the ship, and the chamber was lighted dimly by reflection from the rocks outside; but the corridors of the vessel themselves must be dark.

The inner valve of the airlock was open—and had apparently been so from the beginning. Cray and Royden had shot through it, and brought up against the farther wall of a corridor running parallel to the ship's long axis. They were both visible, standing back to back, sweeping the corridor in both directions with their lights. Grant took a step that carried him over to them, motioning the others to remain where they were, and added his light to those already in action.

To the right, as one entered it, the corridor extended almost to the near end of the ship—the bow, as the men thought of it for no good reason. In another direction, it ran about ten yards and opened into a large chamber which, if this craft resembled the *Giansar* as closely within as it did without, was probably the control room. At least, it was just about amidships. Smaller doors opened at intervals along the hallway; some were open, the majority were closed. Nothing moved anywhere.

"Come on," said Grant finally. He walked toward the central room, and paused on the threshold, the others at his heels. The floor they were walking on continued in the form of a catwalk; the chamber they were entering occupied the full interior of the hull at this point. It was brightly lighted, for it was this compartment that possessed the six great view ports, equally spaced around its walls, and the sun shone brightly through these. The men extinguished their own lights. Cray looked about him, and shook his head slowly.

"I still think I must be dreaming, and about to wake up on our own ship," he remarked. "This looks more and more like home, sweet home."

Grant frowned. "Not to me," he replied. "This control layout is the first serious difference I've seen. You wouldn't notice that, of course, spending all your life with the engines. It might be a good idea for you to see if the drive on this ship is enough like ours for you to puzzle out, and whether there's a chance of repairing it. I'll look over this board for signs of a transmitter—after all, the *Mizar* shouldn't be too far away."

"Why shouldn't I be able to understand the drive?" retorted Cray. "It should be like ours, only a little more primitive—depending on how long this boat's been here."

Grant shot him an amazed glance. "Do you still think this is a Terrestrial ship, and has been here only a few decades?" he asked.

"Sure. Any evidence otherwise?"

Grant pointed to the floor beneath their feet. All looked down, and for the first time noticed that they left footprints in a thin, even layer of dust that coated the corridor floor.

"That means that the ship held its air for a longer time than I care to think about—long enough not only to reduce the various organic substances on board to dust, but for random currents to distribute it through the open spaces. Yet when we came the air was almost gone—leaked out through the joints and valves, good as they were, so that there was not enough left to resist us when we pushed a twelve-foot piston against its pressure. Point one."

The finger swung to the control board. "Point two." He said nothing further, but all could see what he meant.

The center of the control room was occupied by a thick-walled hemisphere—a cup, if you like—swung in gimbals which permitted its flat side always to be uppermost with respect to the ship's line of net acceleration. The control board occupied the inner surface and upper edge of this cup, all around the circumference; and in the center of the assembly was the pilot's seat—if it could be called a seat.

It was a dome-shaped structure protruding from the floor about two feet; five broad, deep grooves were spaced equally about its sides, but did not quite reach the top, It looked somewhat like a jelly mold; and the one thing that could be stated definitely about its history was that no human being had ever sat in it. Cray absorbed this evident fact with a gulp, as though he had not chewed it sufficiently.

The rest of the men stared silently at the seat. It was as though the ghost of the long-dead pilot had materialized there and held their frozen attention; overwrought imaginations pictured him, or strove to picture him, as he might have looked. And they also tried to picture what emergency, what unexpected menace, had called upon him to leave the place where he had held sway—to leave it forever. All those men were intelligent and highly trained; but more than one pair of eyes explored the corridor the human invaders had just used, and its mate stretching on from the other side of the control room.

Cray swallowed again, and broke the silence. "I should be able to figure out the engines, anyway," he said, "if they're atomics at all like ours. After all, they have to do the same things ours did, and they must have corresponding operations and parts."

"I hope you're right." Grant shrugged invisibly in the bulky suit. "I don't expect to solve that board until you fix something and the pilot lights start signaling—if they have pilot lights. We'd all better get to work. Cray's regular assistants can help him, McEachern had better stay with me and help on the board, and Preble and Stevenson can look over the ship in general. Their fields of specialty won't help much at our jobs. Hop to it." He started across the catwalk toward the control board, with McEachern trailing behind him.

Stevenson and Preble looked at each other. The younger man spoke. "Together, or should we split up?"

"Together," decided the chemist. "That way, one of us will probably see anything the other misses. It won't take much longer; and I doubt that there's much hurry for our job, anyway. We'll follow Cray and company to whichever engine room they go to, and then work from that end to the other. All right?"

Preble nodded, and the two left the control room. The engineers had gone toward the bow—so called because the main entrance port was nearer that end—and the two general explorers followed. The others were not far ahead, and their lights were visible, so the two did not bother to use their own. Stevenson kept one hand on the right-hand wall, and they strode confidently along in the semidarkness.

After a short distance, the chemist's hand encountered the inner door of the airlock by which they had entered. It had been swung by the men all the way back against the wall, leaving both doors open, so that the light was a little better here. In spite of this, he did not see the object on the floor until his foot struck it, sending it sliding along the corridor with a metallic scraping sound that was easily transmitted through the metal of the floor and their suits.

He found it a few feet away, and, near it, two more exactly similar objects. He picked them up, and the two men examined them curiously. They were thick, oval rings, apparently of steel, with an inch or so of steel cable welded to one side of each. The free end of the cable seemed to have been sheared off by some sharp tool. Stevenson and Preble looked at each other, and both directed their lights on the floor about the inner portal of the airlock.

At first, nothing else was noticeable; but after a moment, they saw that the chemist's foot, just before striking the ring, had scraped a groove in a layer of dust much thicker than that over the rest of the floor. It was piled almost to the low sill of the valve, and covered an area two or three feet in radius. Curiously, the men looked at the outer side of the sill, and found a similar flat pile of dust, covering even more of the floor; and near the edges of this layer were five more rings.

These, examined closely, proved larger than the first ones, which had been just a little too small for an average human wrist; but like them, each had a short length of wire cable fused to one side, and cut off a short distance out. There was nothing else solid on the floor of the lock or the corridor, and no mark in the dust except that made by Stevenson's toe. Even the dust and rings were not very noticeable—the seven men had entered the ship through this lock without seeing them. Both men were sure they had some meaning, perhaps held a clue to the nature of the ship's former owners; but neither could decipher it. Preble dropped the rings into a pocket of his spacesuit, and they headed down the corridor again on the track of the engineers.

They caught up with them about a hundred and fifty feet from the control room. The three were standing in front of a heavy-looking, circular door set in a bulkhead which blocked off the passage at this point. It was not featureless, as the airlock doors had been, but had three four-inch disks of darker metal set into it near the top, the bottom, and the left side. Each disk had three holes, half an inch in diameter and of uncertain depth, arranged in the form of isosceles triangles. The men facing it bore a baffled air, as though they had already tackled the problem of opening it.

"Is this your engine room?" asked Preble, as he and Stevenson stopped beside the others. "It looks more like a pressure lock to me."

"You may be right," returned Cray gloomily. "But there's nowhere else in this end of the ship where an engine room could be, and you remember there were jets at both ends. For some reason they seem to keep the room locked light—and we don't even know whether the locks are key or combination. If it's combination, we might as well quit now; and if it's key, where is it?"

"They look like the ends of big bolts, to me," suggested Stevenson. "Have you tried unscrewing them?"

Cray nodded. "Royden got that idea, too. Take a closer look at them before you try turning the things, though. If you still feel ambitious, Royden will show you the best way to stick your fingers into the holes."

Preble and the chemist accepted the suggestion, and examined the little disks at close range. Cray's meaning was evident. They were not circular, as they had seemed at first glance; they presented a slightly elliptical cross section, and obviously could never be made to turn in their sockets. The lock theory seemed to remain unchallenged.

That being granted, it behooved them to look for a key. There was no sense toying with the combination idea—there was no hope whatever of solving even a simple combination without specialized knowledge which is seldom acquired legally. They resolutely ignored the probability that the key, if any, was only to be found in the company of the original engineer, and set to work.

Each of them took one of the nearby rooms, and commenced going over it. All the room doors proved to be unlocked, which helped some. Furniture varied but little; each chamber had two seats similar to that in the control room, and two articles which might at one time have been beds; any mattress or other padding they had ever contained was now fine dust, and nothing save metal troughs. large enough to hold a man lying at full length, were left. There was also a desk like affair, which contained drawers, which opened easily and soundlessly, and was topped by a circular, yard-wide aluminum-faced mirror. The drawers themselves contained a variety of objects, perhaps toilet articles, of which not one sufficiently resembled anything familiar to provide a clue to its original use.

A dozen rooms were ransacked fruitlessly before the men reassembled in the corridor to exchange reports. One or two of them, hearing of the others' failure, returned to the search; Preble, Stevenson, and Sorrell strolled back to the door which was barring their way. They looked at it silently for several moments; then Sorrell began to speak.

"It doesn't make sense," he said slowly. "Why should you lock an engine-room door? If the motors have to be supervised all the time, as ours do, it's a waste of time. If you grant that these creatures had their motors well enough designed to run without more than an occasional inspection, it might be worthwhile to seal the door against an accidental blowoff; but I still wouldn't lock it. Of course we don't know anything about their ideas of what was common sense.

"But I'd say that that door either isn't fastened at all, and is putting up a bluff like the outer airlock valve, or else it's really sealed, and would be opened by tools rather than keys. You may think that's quibbling, but it isn't. Keys, you carry around with you, in your pocket or on your belt. Tools have a place where you leave 'em, and are supposed to stay there. Kid, if you were an engineer, in the practice of unsealing this door every few days, perhaps, and needed something like a monkey wrench to do it with, where would you keep the monkey wrench?"

Preble ignored the appellation, and thought for a moment. Finally he said, "If I were fastening the door against intentional snooping, I'd keep the tool in my own quarters locked up. If, as you suggested, it were merely a precaution against accident, I'd have a place for it near the door here. Wouldn't you say so?"

The machinist nodded, and swept his light slowly over the bulkheads around the door. Nothing showed but smooth metal, and he extended the search to the corridor walls for several yards on both sides. The eye found nothing, but Sorrell was not satisfied. He returned to the edge of the door and began feeling over the metal, putting a good deal of pressure behind his hand.

It was a slow process, and took patience. The others watched, holding their lights to illuminate the operation. For several minutes the suit radios were silent, those of the more distant men cut off by the metal walls of the rooms they were searching and the three at the door prosecuting their investigation without speech. Sorrell was looking for a wall cabinet, which did credit to his imagination; such a thing seemed to him the last place to keep tools. He was doing his best to allow for the probably unorthodox ideas of the builders of the ship, reducing the problem as far as he could toward its practical roots, and hoping no physical or psychological traits of the being he never expected to meet would invalidate his answers. As Preble had said, a tool used for only one, specialized purpose logically would be kept near the place in which it was used.

The machinist turned out right, though not exactly as he had expected. He was still running his hands over the wall when Preble remembered a standard type of motor-control switch with which even he was familiar; and, almost without thinking, he reached out, inserted his fingers in the three holes of one of the disks, and pulled outward. A triangular block, indistinguishable in color from the rest of the disk, slid smoothly out into his hand,

The other two lights converged on it, and for a second or two there was silence; then Sorrell chuckled. "You win, Jack," he admitted. "I didn't carry my own reasoning far enough. Go ahead."

Preble examined the block of metal. What had been the inner face was copper-colored, and bore three holes similar to those by which he had extracted it. There was only one other way to fit it into the disk again; he reversed it, with the copper face outward, and felt it slip snugly back into place. Sorrell and Stevenson did the same with the upper and lower disks, which proved to contain similar blocks. Then they stood back, wondering what happened next.

They were still waiting when Cray and Royden rejoined them. The former saw instantly what had been done to the door, and started to speak; then he took a second, and closer look, and, without saying a word, reached up, inserted three fingers in the holes in the coppery triangles of the block face, and began to *unscrew the disk*. It was about five inches thick, and finally came out in his hands. He stared doubtfully at it, and took a huge pair of vernier calipers from the engineer's kit at his side and measured the plug along several diameters. It was perfectly circular, to within the limit of error of his instrument.

He looked at the others at length, and spoke with a note of bewilderment. "I could have sworn this thing was elliptical when we first examined it. The hole still is, if you'll look." He nodded toward the threaded opening from which the disk had come. "I saw the line where it joined the door seemed a good deal wider at the top and bottom; but I'm sure it fitted tightly all around, before."

Sorrell and Royden nodded agreement. Evidently reversing the inset block had, in some fashion, changed the shape of the disk. Cray tried to pull the block out again, but it resisted his efforts, and he finally gave up with a shrug. The men quickly unscrewed the other disks, and Royden leaned against the heavy door. It swung silently inward; and four of the men instantly stepped through, to swing their lights about the new compartment. Cray alone remained at the door, puzzling over the hard-yet-plastic metal object. The simple is not always obvious.

Grant and McEachern, in the control room, were having trouble as well. They had approached the control cup along the catwalk, and the captain had vaulted into its center without difficulty. And he might just as well have remained outside.

The control buttons were obvious enough, though they did not project from the metal in which they were set. They occurred always in pairs—probably an "on" and "off" for each operation; and beside each pair were two little transparent disks that might have been monitor lights. All were dark. Sometimes the pairs of buttons were alone; sometimes they were in groups of any number up to eighteen or twenty. Each group was isolated from its neighbors; and they extended completely around the foot-wide rim of the cup, so that it was not possible to see them all at once.

But the thing that bothered Grant the most was the fact that not a single button, light, or group was accompanied by a written label of any sort. He would not have expected to be able to read any such writing; but there had been the vague hope that control labels might have been matched with similar labels on the machines or charts—if the other men found any of either. It was peculiar, for there were in all several hundred buttons; and many of the groups could easily have been mistaken for each other. He put this thought into words, and McEachern frowned behind his helmet mask before replying.

"According to Cray's logic, why should they be labeled?" he remarked finally. "Do we allow anyone to pilot a ship if he doesn't know the board blindfolded? We do label ours, of course, on the theory that an inexperienced man might have to handle them in an emergency; but that's self-deception. I've never heard of any but a first-rank pilot bringing a ship through an emergency. Labeling controls is a carryover from the family auto and airplane."

"There's something in that," admitted the captain. "There's also the possibility that this board is labeled, in a fashion we can't make out. Suppose the letters or characters were etched very faintly into that metal, which isn't polished, you'll notice, and were meant to be read by, say, a delicate sense of touch, I don't believe that myself, but it's a possibility—one we can't check, since we can't remove our suits to feel. The fact that there are no obvious lights for this board lends it some support; they couldn't have depended on sunlight all the time."

"In either case, fooling around here at this stage may do more harm than good," pointed out McEachern. "We'll have to wait until someone gets a machine identified, and see if tampering with it produces any results here."

Grant's helmet nodded agreement. "I never had much hope of actually starting the ship," he said, "since it seems unlikely that anything but mechanical damage of a serious nature could have stranded it here; but I did have some hopes from the communicators. There must be some."

"Maybe they didn't talk," remarked the navigator.

"If that's your idea of humor, maybe you'd better not, yourself," growled Grant. He vaulted back to the catwalk, and morosely led the way forward, to see if the engineers or free-lance investigators had had any luck. McEachern followed, regretting the remark, which must have jarred the commander's optimism at an unfortunate time. He tried to think of something helpful to say, but couldn't; so he wisely kept quiet.

Halfway to the bow, they met Preble and Stevenson, who had satisfied themselves that the others could do better in the engine room and were continuing their own general examination of the ship. They gave the officers a brief report on events forward, showed them the metal rings found by the airlock, and went on aft to find some means of visiting the corridors which presumably existed above and below the main one. The control room seemed the logical place to look first, though neither had noticed any other openings from it when they were there the first time. Perhaps the doors were closed, and less obvious.

But there were no other doors, apparently. Only two means of access and egress to and from the control room appeared to exist, and these were the points where the main corridor entered it.

"There's a lot of room unaccounted for, just the same," remarked Stevenson after the search, "and there must be some way into it. None of the rooms we investigated looking for that 'key' had any sign of a ramp or stairway or trapdoor; but we didn't cover them all. I suggest we each take one side of the bow corridor, and look behind every door we can open. None of the others was locked, so there shouldn't be much trouble."

Preble agreed, and started along the left-hand wall of the passage, sweeping it with his light as he went. The chemist took the right side and did likewise. Each reached a door simultaneously, and pushed it open; and a simultaneous "Here it is" crackled from the suit radios. A spiral ramp, leading both up and down, was revealed on either side of the ship, behind the two doors.

"That's more luck than we have a right to expect," laughed Stevenson. "You take your side, I'll take mine, and we'll meet up above."

Preble again agreed silently, and started up the ramp. It was not strictly accurate to call it a spiral; it was a curve evidently designed as a compromise to give some traction whether the ship were resting on its belly on a high-gravity planet, or accelerating on its longitudinal axis, and it did not make quite a complete turn in arriving at the next level above. Preble stepped onto it facing the port side, and stepped off facing sternward, with a door at his left side. This he confidently tried to push open, since like the others it lacked knob or handle; but unlike them, it refused to budge.

There was no mystery here. The most cursory of examinations disclosed the fact that the door had been welded to its frame all around—raggedly and crudely, as though the work had been done in frantic haste, but very effectively. Nothing short of a high explosive or a heavy-duty cutting arc could have opened that portal. Preble didn't even try. He returned to the main level, meeting Stevenson at the foot of the ramp. One look at his face was enough for the chemist.

"Here, too?" he asked. "The door on my side will never open while this ship is whole. Someone wanted to keep something either outside or inside that section."

"Probably in, since the welding was done from outside," replied Preble. "I'd like to know what it was. It would probably give us an idea of the reason for the desertion of this ship. Did you go down to the lower level?"

"Not yet. We might as well go together—if one side is sealed, the other probably will be, too. Come on."

They were still on the left-hand ramp, so it was on this side that they descended. A glance at the door here showed that, at least, it was not welded; the pressure of a hand showed it to be unlocked. The two men found themselves at the end of a corridor similar in all respects to the one above, except that it came to a dead end to the right of the door instead of continuing on into the central chamber. It was pitch-dark, except for the reflections of the hand lights on the polished metal walls, and along either side were doors, perhaps a trifle larger than most of the others on the ship. Many of these were ajar, others closed tightly; and by common consent the men stepped to the nearest of the former.

The room behind it proved similar in size to those above, but it lacked the articles which the men had come to look upon as the furniture of the long-dead crew. It was simply a bare, empty cubicle.

The other chambers, quickly examined, showed no striking difference from the first. Several contained great stacks of metal ingots, whose inertia and color suggested platinum or iridium; all were thickly coated with dust, as was the floor of the corridor, Here, too, there must have been organic materials, whether crew or cargo none could tell, which had slowly rotted away while the amazingly tight hull held stubbornly to its air. The makers of the ship had certainly been superb machinists—no vessel made by man would have held atmosphere more than a few months, without constant renewal.

"Have you noticed that there is nothing suggestive of a lock on any of these doors?" asked Preble, as they reached the blank wall which shut them off from the engine room in front.

"That's right," agreed Stevenson. "The engine-room port was the only one which had any obvious means of fastening. You'd think there would be need to hold them against changes in acceleration, if nothing else."

He went over to the nearest of the doors and with some care examined its edge, which would be hidden when it was closed; then he beckoned to Preble. Set in the edge, almost invisible, was a half-inch circle of metal slightly different in color from the rest of the door. It seemed perfectly flush with the metal around it. Just above the circle was a little dot of copper.

Both objects were matched in the jamb of the door—the copper spot by another precisely similar, the circle by a shallow, bowl-shaped indentation of equal size and perhaps a millimeter deep. No means of activating the lock, if it were one, were visible, Stevenson stared at the system for several minutes, Preble trying to see around the curve of his helmet.

"It's crazy," the chemist said at last. "If that circle marks a bolt, why isn't it shaped to fit the hollow on the jamb? It couldn't be moved forward a micron, the way it is. And the thing can't be a magnetic lock—the hollow proves that, too. You'd want the poles to fit as snugly as possible, not to have the field weakened by an air gap. What is it?"

Preble blinked, and almost bared his head in reverence, but was stopped by his helmet. "You have it, friend," he said gently. "It *is* a magnetic lock. I'd bet"—he glanced at the lung dial on his wrist—"my chance of living another hundred hours that's the story. But it's not based on magnetic attraction—it's magnetostriction. A magnetic field will change the shape of a piece of metal—somewhat as a strong electric field does to a crystal. They must have developed alloys in which the effect is extreme. When the current is on, that 'bolt' of yours fits into the hollow in the jamb, without any complicated lever system to move it. This, apparently, is a cargo hold, and all the doors are probably locked by one master switch—perhaps on the control board, but more probably down here somewhere. So long as a current is flowing, the doors are locked, The current in any possible storage device must have been exhausted ages ago, even if these were left locked."

"But what about the engine-room door?" asked Stevenson. "Could that have been of this type? It was locked, remember." Preble thought for a moment.

"Could be. The removable block might have been a permanent magnet that opposed another when it was in one way, and reinforced it when it was reversed. Of course, it would be difficult to separate them once they were placed in the latter position; maybe the ship's current was used to make that possible. Now that the current is off, it may be that there will be some difficulty in returning that block to its original position. Let's go and see." He led the way back along the corridor to the ramp.

Cray received the theory with mingled satisfaction and annoyance; he should, he felt, have seen it himself. He had already discovered that the triangular blocks had developed an attachment for their new positions, and had even considered magnetism in that connection; but the full story had escaped him. He had had other things to worry about, anyway.

The free-lance seekers had met the engineer at the entrance to the engine room. Now the three moved inside, stepping out onto a catwalk similar to that in the control room. This chamber, however, was illuminated only by the hand torches of the men; and it was amazing to see how well they lit up the whole place, reflecting again and again from polished metal surfaces.

When one had seen the tube arrangement from outside the ship, it was not difficult to identify most of the clustered machines. The tube breeches, with their heavy injectors and disintegrators. projected in a continuous ring around the walls and in a solid group from the forward bulkhead. Heavily insulated leads ran from the tubes to the supplementary cathode ejectors. It seemed evident that the ship had been driven and steered by reaction jets of heavy-metal ions, as were the vessels of human make. All the machines were encased in heavy shields, which suggested that their makers were not immune to nuclear radiation,

"Not a bad layout," remarked Preble. "Found out whether they'll run?"

Cray glared. "No!" he answered almost viciously. "Would you mind taking a look at their innards for us?"

Preble raised his eyebrows, and stepped across the twenty-foot space between the catwalk and the nearest tube breech. It was fully six feet across, though the bore was probably not more than thirty inches—the walls had to contain the windings for the field which kept the ion stream from actual contact with the metal. The rig which was presumably the injector-disintegrator unit was a three-foot bulge in the center, and the insulated feed tube led from it to a nearby fuel container. The fuel was probably either mercury or some other easily vaporized heavy metal, such as lead. All this seemed obvious and simple enough, and was similar in basic design to engines with which even Preble was familiar; but there was a slight departure from convention in that the entire assembly, from fuel line to the inner hull, appeared to be one seamless surface of metal. Preble examined it closely all over, and found no trace of a joint.

"I see what you mean," he said at last, looking up. "Are they all the same?" Cray nodded.

"They seem to be. We haven't been able to get into any one of them—even the tanks are tight. They *look* like decent, honest atomics, but we'll never prove it by looking at the outside."

"But how did they service them?" asked Stevenson. "Surely they didn't weld the cases on and hope their machines were good enough to run without attention. That's asking too much, even from a race that built a hull that could hold air as long as this must have."

"How could I possibly know?" growled Cray. "Maybe they went outside and crawled in through the jets to service 'em—only I imagine it's some trick seal like the door of this room. After all, *that* was common sense, if you look at it right. The fewer moving parts, the less wear. Can anyone think of a way in which this breech mechanism could be fastened on, with an invisible joint, working from the same sort of common sense?"

Why no one got the answer then will always remain a mystery; but the engineer was answered by nothing but half a dozen thoughtful expressions more or less hidden in space helmets, He looked around hopefully for a moment, then shrugged his shoulders. "Looks like we'll just have to puzzle around and hope for the best," he concluded. "Jack and Don might as well go back to their own snooping—and for Heaven's sake, if you get any more ideas, come a-runnin'."

After glancing at Grant for confirmation of the suggestion, Preble and Stevenson left the engine room to continue their interrupted tour.

"I wonder if the upper section behind the control room is sealed," remarked the chemist as they entered the darkness of the corridor. "I think we've covered the bow fairly well." Preble nodded; and without further speech they passed through the control chamber, glancing at the board which had given Grant and McEachern such trouble, and found, as they expected, ramps leading up and down opening from the rear corridor just as one entered.

They stayed together this time, and climbed the starboard spiral. The door at the top opened easily, which was some relief; but the hallway beyond was a disappointment. It might have been any of the others already visited; and a glance into each of the rooms revealed nothing but bare metal gleaming in the flashlight beams, and dust-covered floors. The keel corridor was also open; but here was an indication that one, at least, of the rooms had been used for occupancy rather than cargo.

Stevenson looked into it first, since it was on the side of the corridor he had taken. He instantly called his companion, and Preble came to look at the object standing in the beam of the chemist's light.

It was a seat, identical to the one in the control chamber—a mound of metal, with five deep grooves equally spaced around it. The tiny reflected images of the flashlights stared up from its convex surfaces like luminous eyes. None of the other furniture that had characterized the room in the central bow corridor was present; but the floor was not quite bare.

Opposite each of the five grooves in the seat, perhaps a foot out from it, a yard-long metal cable was neatly welded to the floor. A little farther out, and also equally spaced about the seat, were three more almost twice as long. The free end of each of the eight cables was cut off cleanly, as though by some extremely efficient instrument; the flat cut surfaces were almost mirror-smooth. Stevenson and Preble examined them carefully, and then looked at each other with thoughtful expressions. Both were beginning to get ideas. Neither was willing to divulge them.

There remained to explore only the stern engine room and the passage leading to it, together with the rooms along the latter. They had no tools with which to remove a specimen of one of the cables, so they carefully noted the door behind which the seat and its surroundings had been found, and climbed once more to the central deck. Before making their last find, they had begun to be bored with the rather monotonous search, particularly since they had no clear idea of what they were searching for; without it, they might have been tempted to ignore the rooms along the corridor and go straight to the engine room. Now, however, they investigated every chamber carefully; and their failure to find anything of interest was proportionally more disappointing.

And then they reached the engine-room door.

Flashlights swept once over the metal surface, picking out three disks with their inset triangular blocks, as the men had expected, but the coppery reflection from two of the blocks startled them into an instant motionlessness. Of the three seals, they realized, only one—the uppermost—was locked. It was as though whoever had last been in the room had left hastily—or was not a regular occupant of the ship.

Preble quickly reversed the remaining block, and unscrewed the three disks; then the two men leaned against the door and watched it swing slowly open. Both were unjustifiably excited; the state of the door had stimulated their imaginations, already working overtime on the material previously provided. For once, they were not disappointed.

The light revealed, besides the tanks, converters, and tube breeches which had been so obvious in the forward engine room, several open cabinets which had been mere bulges on the walls up forward. Tools and other bits of apparatus filled these and lay about on the floor. Light frameworks of metal, rather like small building scaffolds, enclosed two of the axial tube breeches; and more tools lay on these. It was the first scene they had encountered on the ship that suggested action and life rather than desertion and stagnation. Even the dust, present here as everywhere, could not eradicate the impression that the workers had dropped their tools for a brief rest, and would return shortly.

Preble went at once to the tubes upon which work had apparently been in progress. He was wondering, as he had been since first examining one, how they were opened for servicing. He had never taken seriously Cray's remark that it might have been done from outside.

His eye caught the thing at once. The dome of metal that presumably contained the disintegrator and ionizing units had been disconnected from the fuel tank, as he had seen from across the room; but a closer look showed that it had been removed from the tube, as well, and replaced somewhat carelessly. It did not match the edges of its seat all around, now; it was displaced a little to one side, exposing a narrow crescent of flat metal on each of the two faces normally in complete contact. An idea of the position can be obtained by placing two pennies one on the other, and giving the upper one a slight sideward displacement.

The line of juncture of the two pieces was, therefore, visible all around. Unfortunately, the clamping device Preble expected to find was not visible anywhere. He got a grip—a very poor one, with his gloved hand—on the slightly projecting edge of the hemisphere, and tried to pull it free, without success; and it was that failure which gave him the right answer—the only possible way in which an airtight and pressure-tight seal could be fastened solidly, even with the parts out of alignment, with nonmagnetic alloys. It was a method that had been used on Earth, though not on this scale; and he was disgusted at his earlier failure to see it.

Magnetism, of course, could not be used so near the ion projectors, since it would interfere with the controlling fields; but there was another force, ever present and available—molecular attraction. The adjoining faces of the seal were *plane,* not merely flat. To speak of their accuracy in terms of the wave length of sodium light would be useless; a tenth-wave surface, representing hours of skilled human hand labor, would be jagged in comparison. Yet the relatively large area of these seals and the frequency with which the method appeared to have been used argued mass production, not painstaking polishing by hand.

But if the seal were actually wrung tight, another problem presented itself. How could the surfaces be separated, against a force sufficient to confine and direct the blast of the ion rockets? No marks on the breech suggested the application of prying tools—and what blade could be inserted into such a seal?

Stevenson came over to see what was keeping Preble so quiet, and listened while the latter explained his discovery and problems.

"We can have a look through these cabinets," the chemist remarked finally. "This seems to fit Sorrell's idea of a tool-requiring job. Just keep your eyes and mind open."

The open mind seemed particularly indicated. The many articles lying in and about the cabinets were undoubtedly tools, but their uses were far from obvious. They differed from manmade tools in at least one vital aspect. Many of our tools are devices for *forcing:* hammers, wrenches, clamps, pliers, and the like. *A really good machine job would need no such devices.* The parts would fit, with just enough clearance to eliminate undesired friction—and no more.

That the builders of the ship were superb designers and machinists was already evident. What sort of tools they would need was not so obvious. Shaping devices, of course; there were planers, cutters, and grinders among the littered articles. All were portable, but solidly built, and were easily recognized even by Preble and Stevenson. But what were the pairs of slender rods which clung together, obviously magnetized? What were the small, sealed-glass tubes; the long, grooved strips of metal and plastic; the featureless steel-blue spheres; the iridescent, oddly shaped plates of paper-thin metal? The amateur investigators could not even guess, and sent for professional help.

Cray and his assistants almost crooned with pleasure as they saw the untidy floor and cabinets; but an hour of careful examination and theorizing left them in a less pleasant mood. Cray conceded that the molecular attraction theory was most probably correct, but made no headway at all on the problem of breaking the seal. Nothing in the room seemed capable of insertion in the airtight joint.

"Why not try sliding them apart?" asked Stevenson. "If they're as smooth as all that, there should be no difficulty."

Cray picked up a piece of metal. "Why don't you imagine a plane through this bar, and slide it apart along that?" he asked. "The crystals of the metal are practically as close together, and grip each other almost as tightly, in the other case, You'll have to get something between them."

The chemist, who should have known more physics, nodded. "But it's more than the lubricant that keeps the parts of an engine apart," he said.

"No, the parts of one of our machines are relatively far apart, so that molecular attraction is negligible," answered the machinist. "But—I believe you have something there. A lubricant might do it; molecules might conceivably work their way between those surfaces. Has anybody noticed anything in this mess that might fill the bill?"

"Yes," answered Preble promptly, "these glass tubes. They contain liquid, and have been fused shut—which is about the only way you could seal in a substance such as you would need."

He stepped to a cabinet and picked up one of the three-inch-long transparent cylinders. A short nozzle, its end melted shut, projected from one end, and a small bubble was visible in the liquid within. The bubble moved sluggishly when the tube was inverted, and broke up into many small ones when it was shaken. These recombined instantly when the liquid came to rest, which was encouraging. Evidently the stuff possessed a very low viscosity and surface tension.

Cray took the tube over to the breech which had been partly opened and carelessly closed so long ago, held the nozzle against the edge of the seal, and, after a moment's hesitation, snapped off the tip with his gloved fingers. He expected the liquid to ooze out in the asteroid's feeble gravity, but its vapor pressure must have been high, for it sprayed out in a heavy stream, Droplets rebounded from the metal and evaporated almost instantly; with equal speed the liquid which spread over the surface vanished. Only a tiny fraction of a percent, if that, could have found its way between the surfaces.

Cray stared tensely at the dome of metal as the tube emptied itself. After a moment, he dropped the empty cylinder and applied a sideways pressure,

A crescent, of shifting rainbow colors, appeared at the edge of the seal; and the dome slowly slid off to one side. The crescent did not widen, for the lubricant evaporated the instant it was exposed. Preble and Stevenson caught the heavy dome and eased its mass to the central catwalk.

The last of the rainbow film of lubricant evaporated from the metal, and the engineers crowded around the open breech. There was no mass of machinery inside; the disintegrators would, of course, be within the dome which had been removed. The coils which generated the fields designed to keep the stream of ionized vapor from contact with the tube walls were also invisible, being sealed into the tube lining. Neither of these facts bothered the men, for their own engines had been similarly designed. Cray wormed his way down the full length of the tube to make sure it was not field failure which had caused it to be opened in the first place; then the three specialists turned to the breech which had been removed.

The only visible feature of its flat side was the central port through which the metallic vapor of the exhaust had entered the tube; but application of another of the cylinders of lubricant, combined with the asteroid's gravity, caused most of the plate to fall away and reveal the disintegrator mechanism within. Preble, Stevenson, Grant, and McEachern watched for a while as pieces of the disintegrator began to cover the floor of the room; but they finally realized that they were only getting in the way of men who seemed to know what they were doing, so a gradual retreat to the main corridor took place.

"Do you suppose they can find out what was wrong with it?" queried Stevenson,

"We should." It was Cray's voice on the radio. "The principle of this gadget is exactly like our own. The only trouble is that they've used that blasted molecular-attraction fastening method everywhere. It's taking quite a while to get it apart."

"It's odd that the technology of these beings should have been so similar to ours in principle, and yet so different in detail," remarked Grant. "I've been thinking it over, and can't come to any conclusion as to what the reason could be. I thought perhaps their sense organs were different from ours, but I have no idea how that could produce such results—not surprising, since I can't imagine what sort of senses could exist to replace or supplement ours."

"Unless there are bodies in the sealed-off corridor and rooms, I doubt if you'll ever find the answer to that one," answered Preble. "I'll be greatly surprised if anyone ever proves that this ship was made in this solar system."

"I'll be surprised enough if anyone proves anything at all constructive about it," returned Grant.

Cray's voice interrupted again.

"There's something funny about part of this," he said. "I think it's a relay, working from your main controls, but that's only a guess. It's not only connected to the electric part of the business, but practically built around the fuel inlet as well. By itself it's all right; solenoid and moving-core type. We've had it apart, too."

"What do you plan to do?" asked Grant. "Have you found anything wrong with the unit as a whole?"

"No, we haven't. It has occurred to me that the breech was unsealed for some purpose other than repair. It would make a handy emergency exit—and that might account for the careless way it was resealed. We were thinking of putting it back together, arranging the relay so that we can control it from here and test the whole tube. Is that all right with you?"

"If you think you can do it, go ahead," replied Grant. "We haven't got much to lose, I should say. Could you fix up the whole thing to drive by local control?"

"Possibly. Wait till we see what happens to this one." Cray moved out of the line of sight in the engine-room doorway, and his radio waves were cut off.

Stevenson moved to the doorway to watch the process of reassembly; the other three went up to the control room. The eeriness of the place had worn off—there was no longer the suggestion of the presence of the unknowable creature who had once controlled the ship. Preble was slightly surprised, since it was now night on this part of the asteroid; any ghostly suggestions should have been enhanced rather than lessened. Familiarity must have bred contempt.

No indicator lights graced the control panel. Grant had half hoped that the work in the engine room might have been recorded here; but he was not particularly surprised. He had given up any hopes of controlling the vessel from this board, as his remarks to Cray had indicated.

"I hope Cray can get those tubes going," he said after a lengthy silence. "It would be enough if we could push this ship even in the general direction of Earth. Luckily the orbit of this body is already pretty eccentric. About all we would have to do is correct the plane of motion."

"Even if we can't start enough tubes to control a flight, we could use one as a signal flare," remarked Preble. "Remember, the *Mizar* is in this sector; you once had hopes of contacting her with the signal equipment of this ship, if you could find any. The blast from one of these tubes, striking a rock surface, would make as much light as you could want."

"That's a thought," mused Grant. "As usual, too simple for me to think of. As a matter of fact, it probably represents our best chance. We'll go down now and tell Cray simply to leave the tube going, if he can get it started."

The four men glided back down the corridor to the engine room. The reassembly of the breech mechanism was far from completed, and Grant did not like to interrupt. He was, of course, reasonably familiar with such motors, and knew that their assembly was a delicate task even for an expert.

Cray's makeshift magnetic device for controlling the relay when the breech was sealed was a comment on the man's ingenuity. It was not his fault that none of the men noticed that the core of the relay was made of the same alloy as the great screw cocks which held the engine-room doors shut, and the small bolts on the doors in the cargo hold. It was, in fact, a delicate governor, controlling the relation between fuel flow and the breech field strength—a very necessary control, since the field had to be strong enough to keep the hot vapor from actual contact with the breech, but not strong enough to overcome the effect of the fields protecting the throat of the tube, which were at right angles to it. There was, of course, a similar governor in manmade motors, but it was normally located in the throat of the tube and was controlled by the magnetic effect of the ion stream.

The device was not obvious, and of course was not of a nature which a human engineer would anticipate. It might have gone on operating normally for an indefinite period, if Cray had used any means whatever, except magnetic manipulation, to open and close the relay.

The engineers finally straightened and stood back from their work. The breech was once more in place, this time without the error in alignment which had caused the discovery of the seal. Clamped to the center of the dome, just where the fuel feed tube merged with its surface, was the control which had been pieced together from articles found in the tool cabinets. It was little more than a coil whose field was supposed to be strong enough to replace that of the interior solenoid through the metal of the breech.

Preble had gone outside, and now returned to report that the slight downward tilt of the end of the ship in which they were working would cause the blast from this particular tube to strike the ground fifty or sixty yards to the rear. This was far enough for safety from splash, and probably close enough so that the intensity of the blast would not be greatly diminished.

Cray reported that the assembly, as nearly as he could tell, should work.

"Then I suggest that you and anyone you need to help you remain here and start it in a few moments, while the rest of us go outside to observe results. We'll keep well clear of the stern, so don't worry about us," said Grant. "We're on the night side of the asteroid now, and, as I remember, the *Mizar* was outward and counterclockwise of this asteroid's position twenty-four hours ago—by heaven, I've just realized that all this has occurred in less than twenty hours. She should be able to sight the flare at twenty million miles, if this tube carries half the pep that one of ours would."

Cray nodded. "I can start it alone," he said. "The rest of you go on out. I'll give you a couple of minutes, then turn it on for just a moment. I'll give you time to send someone in if anything is wrong."

Grant nodded approval, and led the other five men along the main corridor and out the airlock. They leaped to a position perhaps a hundred and fifty yards to one side of the ship, and waited.

The tube in question was one of the lowest in the bank of those parallel to the ship's longitudinal axis. For several moments after the men had reached their position it remained lifeless; then a silent, barely visible ghost of flame jetted from its lip. This changed to a track of dazzling incandescence at the point where it first contacted the rock of the asteroid; and the watchers automatically snapped the glare shields into place on their helmets, These were all in place before anyone realized that the tube was still firing, cutting a glowing canyon into the granite and hurling a cloud of boiling silica into space. Grant stared for a moment, leaped for the airlock, and disappeared inside. As he entered the control room from the front, Cray burst in from the opposite end, making fully as good time as the captain. He didn't even pause, but called out as he came:

"She wouldn't cut off, and the fuel flow is increasing. I can't stop it. Get out before the breech gives— I didn't take time to close the engine-room door!"

Grant was in midair when the engineer spoke, but he grasped a stanchion that supported the catwalk, swung around it like a comet, and reversed his direction of flight before the other man caught up to him, They burst out of the airlock at practically the same instant.

By the time they reached the others, the tube fields had gone far out of balance. The lips of the jet tube were glowing blue-white and vanishing as the stream caught them; and the process accelerated as the men watched. The bank of stern tubes glowed brightly, began to drip, and boiled rapidly away; the walls of the engine room radiated a bright red, then yellow, and suddenly slumped inward. That was the last straw for the tortured disintegrator; its own supremely resistant substance yielded to the lack of external cooling, and the device ceased to exist. The wreckage of the alien ship, glowing red now for nearly its entire length, gradually cooled as the source of energy ceased generating; but it would have taken supernatural intervention to reconstruct anything useful from the rubbish which had been its intricate mechanism. The men, who had seen the same thing happen to their own ship not twenty hours before, did not even try to do so.

The abruptness with which the accident had occurred left the men stunned. Not a word was spoken, while the incandescence faded slowly from the hull. There was nothing to say. They were two hundred million miles from Earth, the asteroid would be eighteen months in reaching its nearest point to the orbit of Mars—and Mars would not be there at the time. A search party might eventually find them, since the asteroid was charted and would be known to have been in their neighborhood at the time of their disappearance. That would do them little good.

Rocket jets of the ion type are not easily visible unless matter is in the way—matter either gaseous or solid. Since the planetoid was airless and the *Mizar* did not actually land, not even the usually alert Preble saw her approach. The first inkling of her presence was the voice of her commander, echoing through the earphones of the seven castaways.

"Hello, down there. What's been going on? We saw a flare about twenty hours ago on this body that looked as though an atomic had misbehaved, and headed this way. We circled the asteroid for an hour or so, and finally did sight your ship—just as she did go up. Will you please tell us what the other flare could have been? Or didn't you see it?"

It was the last question that proved too much for the men. They were still laughing hysterically when the *Mizar* settled beside the wreck and took them aboard. Cray alone was silent and bitter.

"In less than a day," he said to his colleague on the rescue ship, "I wrecked two ships—and I haven't the faintest idea how I wrecked either one of them. As a technician, I'd be a better ground-car mechanic. That second ship was just lying there waiting to teach me more about shop technique than I'd have learned in the rest of my life; and some little technical slip ruined it all."

But whose was the error in technique?

BULGE

Worlds of If, September 1968

1

Mac Hoerwitz came back to awareness as the screen went blank, and he absently flicked the switch and reset the sheet-scanner. He had not really watched the last act. At least, he didn't think he had. He knew it so perfectly that there was no way to be certain whether Prospero's closing words were really still in his ears or that it was simply memory from earlier times.

Two things had been competing with *The Tempest* for his attention. One was the pain where his left index fingernail had formerly been, and the other was a half-serious search through his memory to decide whether Shakespeare had ever used a character quite like Mr. Smith. The two distractions were closely connected, even though Smith had not removed the nail himself. He had merely ordered Jones to do it.

Hoerwitz rather doubted that Shakespeare would have been satisfied with a Smith. The fellow was too simple. He knew what he wanted and went after it without knowing or caring what anyone else in the picture might care. He was an oversized two-year-old. Shakespeare would have made him more complicated and more believable, even back in his Henry the Sixth days.

It was a nice idea, with perhaps some scholarly merit. But it didn't really help with the present problem. This was more a piece of post-Edwardian melodrama than a carefully thought out Shakespearean plot. The hero had been trapped by armed villains, in a situation from which there was no obvious escape, and was being forced to help them commit grand larceny.

Of course in a piece of prohibition-era fiction he would have refused steadfastly to help, but Hoerwitz was no flapper's hero. He was eighty-one years old and had a mass of just one hundred pounds distributed along his seventy inches of height. He could not possibly have lifted that mass against Earth's gravity. He smiled in spite of the pain of his hand when he recalled the facial expressions when Smith and his three followers had first seen him.

They had gone to a great deal of trouble to make their approach unobtrusive. They had arrived near the apogee point of the station's six-day period instead of making the just-after-perigee rendezvous which the freighters found more economical. This had served the double purpose of making fairly sure there would be no other ships present and of being harder to observe from Earth. At one hundred seventy thousand miles or so, a one-mile asteroid is visible to the naked eye and a modest-sized spaceship can be seen in a good telescope, but one has to be looking for them deliberately.

It was a rendezvous, of course, rather than a landing. The latter word means nothing on a celestial body where a spacesuited man weighs about a quarter of an ounce. They had made the rendezvous skillfully enough so that Hoerwitz had not felt the contact—or at least, hadn't noticed it over the sound effects accompanying Hamlet's stepfather's drinking. There had been no trouble about entering, since the air lock leading "underground" or "inside," whichever way one preferred to think of it, was plainly visible and easily operated from without. The possibility of anyone's stealing the horse from this particular stable had not occurred seriously to anyone responsible for building the place; or if it had, he had attached more weight to the likelihood of space emergencies which would need fast lock action.

So Mr. Smith and his men had entered and drifted down the tunnel to the asteroid's center not only unopposed but completely unnoticed, and Mac Hoerwitz's first realization that he was in trouble had come after the final peal of ordnance ordered by Fortinbras.

Then he had turned on the lights and found that *Hamlet* had four more spectators, all carrying weapons. He had been rather startled.

So had the others, very obviously, when they had their first good look at him. Just what they had expected was hard to say, but it must have been something capable of more violence than the station manager. The leader had put away his gun with almost an embarrassed air, and the others had followed his example.

"Sorry to surprise you, Mr. Hoerwitz," the intruder had opened. "That was a very good sheet. I'm sorry we missed so much of it. Perhaps you'd let me run it again some time in the next few days."

Mac had been at a loss to reconcile the courtesy with the armament.

"If all you want is to see my library, the weapons are a bit uncalled-for," he finally got out. "I don't know what else I can offer you except accommodation and communication facilities. Do you have ship trouble? Did I miss a distress call? Maybe I do pay too much attention to my sheets—"

"Not at all. We'd have been very disappointed if you had spotted our approach, since we made it as unobtrusive as possible. You are also wrong about what you can give us. Not to waste time, we have a four-thousand-ton ship outside which we expect to mass up to ten thousand before we leave, with the aid of your Class IV isotopes."

"Six thousand tons of nuclear fuel? You've been expanding your consciousness. It would take sixty hours or more if I reprogrammed every converter in the place—only one of them is making Class IV now, and the others are all running other orders. There's barely enough conversion mass in the place for what you want, unless you start chipping rock out of the station itself. I'd guess that on normal priority you'd get an order like that in about a year, counting administrative time for the initial request."

"We're not requesting. As you know perfectly well. You will do any programming necessary, without regard to what is running now, and if necessary we will use station rock. I would have said you'd chip it for us, but I admit there's a difference between the merely illegal and the impossible. Why do they keep a wreck like you on duty out here?"

Hoerwitz flushed. He was used to this attitude from the young and healthy, but more accustomed to having it masked by some show of courtesy.

"It's the only place I can live," he said shortly. "My heart, muscles, and bones can't take normal gravity. Most people can't take free fall—or rather, they don't like the consequences of the medication needed to take it indefinitely. That makes no difference to me. I don't care about muscle, and I had my family half a century ago. This job is good for me, and I'm good for it. For that reason, I don't choose to ruin it. I don't intend to do any reprogramming for you, and I'd be willing to bet you can't do it yourself."

Smith's gun reappeared, and its owner looked at it thoughtfully. The old man nodded toward it and went on, "That's an argument, I admit. I don't want to die, but if you kill me it certainly won't get you further." Mac found that he wasn't as brave as his words sounded; there was an odd and uncomfortable feeling in his stomach as he looked at the weapon. He must have covered it well, however, because after a moment of thought the intruder put the gun away again.

"You're quite right," he said. "I have no intention of killing you, because I do need your help. We'll have to use another method. Mr. Jones, please carry out our first stage of planned persuasion."

2

Fifteen minutes later Hoerwitz was reprogramming the converters as well as he could with an unusable left hand.

Smith, who had courteously introduced himself during the procedure, had gone to the trouble of making sure his victim was right-handed before allowing Jones to start work. It would, as he said, be a pity to slow the station manager down too much. The right hand could wait.

"How about my toes?" Hoerwitz had asked sarcastically, not yet fully convinced that the affair was serious.

"It seems to have been proved that feet have fewer nerves and don't feel pain as intensely," replied Smith. "Of course, the toes will still be there if we need them. Mr. Jones, start with the left hand."

Mac had decided almost at once that the visitors were sincere, but Jones had insisted on finishing his job in workmanlike style. Smith had supported him.

"It would be a pity for you to get the idea that we weren't prepared to finish anything we started," he pointed out.

As he floated in front of the monitor panels readjusting potentiometers and flow-control relays, Hoerwitz thought furiously. He wasn't much worried about his guests actually getting away with their stolen fuel; what he was now doing to the controls must be showing on repeaters in Elkhart, Papeete and Bombay already. The station was, after all, part of a company supposed to be doing profitable business, and the fact that fusion power plants were still forbidden on Earth didn't mean that the company wasn't keeping close track of its products. There'd be radioed questions in the next few minutes, and when they weren't answered satisfactorily there'd be arrangements to send a ship. Of course, the company would wait two or three days and make a perigee rendezvous, but if the indicators bothered the directors sufficiently they might ask a police launch to investigate sooner. On the whole, it was unlikely that anything would happen until shortly after perigee; but something *would* happen to prevent the thieves' escape.

The trouble seemed to be that that something wouldn't do Mac himself any good. Up to now, genuine criminals who were willing to use actual violence had been strictly reading material for him; but he had done plenty of reading. He had a vivid mental picture of the situation. The belief that they would kill him before leaving was not so much insight as it was reflex.

They might not even wait until the job was done. The new program was set up for the converters, and he would not be essential unless something went seriously astray. It never did, but he hoped the thieves were the sort of people who worried about things going wrong.

He found his stomach reacting again when Smith approached him after the converters had been restarted. The gun was not in sight, but Mac knew it was there. For that matter, it wasn't necessary; any of the visitors could break his neck with one hand. However, Smith didn't seem to have violence on his mind at the moment. In fact, his speech was encouraging. He would hardly have bothered to give warnings about Hoerwitz's behavior unless he planned to keep the manager around for a while.

"A few points you should understand, Mr. Hoerwitz," the boss-thief explained. "You must be supposing that the change in converter program will attract, or has already attracted, notice at home. You are wrong. A mysterious ailment has affected the monitor computers at the central plant. Signals are coming in quite normally from the space factories, but they are not being analyzed. The engineers are quite frantic about it. They hope to get matters straightened out in a few days, but in the meantime no one is going to worry more about one space factory than another unless some such thing as a distress message is received.

"I know you wouldn't be foolish enough to attempt to send such a message, since you still have nine fingers available for Mr. Jones's attention, but to remove temptation Mr. Robinson has disabled your station's radio transmitters. To make really sure, he is now taking care of those in the spacesuits. We realize that a suit radio could hardly be received, except by the wildest luck, at Earth's present distance; but that distance shrinks to only about a thousand miles at perigee, as I recall.

"If you do wish to go outside, by all means indulge the impulse. I might enjoy a walk with you myself. Our ship is a former police supply boat, heavily armored and solidly locked. One of us has the only key—I wouldn't dream of telling you which one. Even if you forced your way aboard, which seems possible, its transmitter channels are not standard. They would be received by my friends, not yours. You could not take the ship away, supposing you are enough of a pilot to try it, because it is parked beside your waste radiators, and the exhaust would wreck them—"

"You landed beside the radiators?" For the first time, Mac was really alarmed.

"Oh, no. We know better than that. We landed by your airlock and carried the ship around to the radiators. It weighs only about five hundred pounds here. I fear you couldn't carry it away again by yourself, and it's on rough enough ground so I don't think rolling it would be practical.

"So, Mr. Hoerwitz, you may as well relax. We'll appreciate your attending to your normal business so that our order is ready as soon as possible, but if you prefer to go out for a walk occasionally we don't really mind. I suppose even you could jump off into space, since I understand that escape velocity here is only about a foot a second, and we'd be sorry to lose you that way; but it's entirely up to you. You are perfectly free in all matters which don't interfere with our order. Personally, if I were you I'd go back to quarters and enjoy that really excellent sheet library."

Hoerwitz had gone, but hadn't really been able to concentrate on *The Tempest*. Some of Caliban's remarks had caught his attention because they expressed his own feelings quite well, and he caught himself once or twice wishing for a handy Ariel. However, he was much too old to spend much mental effort on wishing, and the only spirits available at the station were material mechanisms of very restricted versatility. Worse, he was probably not completely free to command them, unless Smith and Company were unbelievably incompetent.

Of course, if something appeared to be going wrong, they would have to trust him to fix it; maybe something could be worked up from that side.

But what could be done, anyway? Just what did he have? The plant turned over vast quantities of energy, but it certainly wasn't a magic wand. It had the complex gear of a hydrogen fusion unit, and a modest tonnage of hydrogen-deuterium slush; while it would require deliberate bypassing of a host of safety devices to do it, it would be quite possible to blow the asteroid into a cloud of plasma. This had certain disadvantages besides the likelihood of blinding the unfortunates on Earth who happened to be looking toward the station at the key moment. For one thing, it didn't really deal satisfactorily with Smith and his friend. It merely promised to dispose of them, and the way Mac's finger felt at the moment that wasn't quite bad enough. What else did he have?

There were a score of converters, each designed to take matter and transform it, using the energy of the fuser, into isotopes which could be used on Earth legally and more or less safely as power sources. At the moment, all were working on the Class IV mixtures—the fast-yield substances usable for spacecraft fuel, industrial blasting and weaponry, which Smith had demanded. Whether he and his friends planned to use the stuff themselves for bank robbery or political subversion, or merely feed the black market, Hoerwitz neither knew nor greatly cared. A minute charge of any Class IV product, assuming that he could get hold of it, could certainly get him into the thieves' ship, no matter how well she were armored. Whether the ship would be worth getting into after such treatment was debatable. A production controller is one thing and a nuclear-explosives expert quite another. Hoerwitz happened to be the first. Trying to abstract explosives under the eyes of Smith, Jones and Associates seemed not only dangerous but probably useless.

There were the radiators, the most conspicuous part of the plant from outside. They were four gigantic structures, each some five hundred feet across and nearly as high. The outer walls were cylindrical and contained high-powered refrigeration circuits; their inner surfaces carried free-electron fields which rendered them nearly perfect reflectors. Inside the cylinders, out of contact with their walls, were the radiators themselves—huge cores of high-conductivity alloy, running at a temperature which would have evaporated them into space in minutes if they had not been held together by fields similar to those which restrained the fusion units. The whole structure was designed to get rid of waste energy, of course.

Any serious absorption by the planetoid of the flood being radiated from those units would have started a sequence of troubles of which the warming of the fusion-fuel slush would have been a minor preliminary. Secondarily, the units were arranged to shine away from Earth; their location on the asteroid and the latter's rotation had been arranged with this in view. It was not a perfect success in one way, since the extremely eccentric orbit in which the asteroid had been placed to facilitate freight-handling work produced a longitude libration of over a hundred degrees each way; but Earth had agreed to put up with this. The periodic flashes of light from the space factories were rather scenic in their way, and most of the astronomers had moved to the moon or to orbiting observatories anyway.

But those radiators did throw away an awful lot of energy. One should be able to do *something* with it in a situation like this; something really useful. But what?

3

It was really a pity that the library contained no Fu Manchu or Bull-dog Drummond. Hoerwitz needed ideas. Since it looked as though he would have to furnish his own, he selected a sheet for background material, slipped it into the scanner and drifted toward the cobwebby hammock in the center of the lounge while Flavius berated the holiday-making citizens of Rome on the screen. It was reasonably appropriate; the manager drowsed; there was certainly an Ides of March coming. He wished his finger would stop hurting. The script and background music flowed along a track that his awareness had followed a hundred times before...

The frantic disclaimers of Cinna the Poet awakened him. He had drifted and been held against the hammock by the current from the air circulator. The feeble gravity which gave the visiting ship a weight of five hundred pounds at the surface was of course absent in the living quarters at the center of the asteroid. Almost automatically he pushed himself back to the console and shut off the sheet-scanner at the end of the third act. Obviously this wasn't helping him to think. He'd better check the converter monitors just to wake himself up and then get some exercise.

Robinson was in the tunnel outside the lounge and without saying a word followed Mac along the passage. The fellow was certainly not very much at home in zero gravity; his coordination as he passed himself from handhold to handhold was worse than sloppy. If this were equally true of the others, it might be a help.

As things turned out, it was.

Smith and Jones were in the control room, drifting idly away from the walls. Another good sign. Either they, too, were unused to free fall or had completely dismissed Hoerwitz from their minds as a menace. Neither of them could have gotten into action for quite a few seconds, since neither had a pushoff point within reach—not even each other.

They said nothing as the manager and his satellite entered, but watched the former as he aimed and pushed off from a point beside the door and drifted along the indicator panels, taking in their readings as he went. Somewhat to his regret, though not to his surprise since no alarms had sounded, Mac found everything going as programmed. He reached the far end of the room and reversed his drift, aiming for the door. The new course took him within reach of Robinson, and that individual at a nod from Smith seized the old man's arm as he went by.

This was a slight mistake. The result was a two-body system spinning with a period of about five seconds and traveling toward the door at about a quarter of Hoerwitz's former speed. The manager took advantage of the other's confusion to choose the time and style of his breakaway from the system. He came to a halt, spin gone, four or five yards from the meeting point. Robinson, who had been made a free gift of their joint angular momentum, brought up with his head in painful contact with the edge of the doorway. Mac couldn't pretend to be sorry; Jones concealed a grin rather unsuccessfully, and Smith showed no sign of caring either way. His order to stop Hoerwitz for a conversation had been obeyed; the details didn't bother him.

"How long is our fuel going to take?" he asked.

"Another fifty to fifty-five hours, barring offtrack developments," replied the manager. "I gave you an estimate at the beginning, and there's no reason to change it so far. I trust these instruments, unless you or one of your friends have been playing with circuits. I know you jimmied the radio, but if your man knew what he was about that shouldn't have bothered this board."

"That's all I wanted to know. Do what you want until it's time to check your instruments again."

"It's night by my clocks. I'm sleeping for a few hours, now that I've had my daily workout. I see you know where my quarters are—what were you searching for, guns or radios? You brought the only weapons this place has ever seen yourselves, and a radio able to reach Earth is a little too large to hide in a photo album."

"Spacesuit radios are pretty small."

"But they're in spacesuits."

"All right. We just like to be sure. Wouldn't you be happier to know that we weren't worrying about you?" Hoerwitz left without trying to answer that. Smith looked after him for a few seconds, and then beckoned to Brown.

"Don't interfere with his routine, but keep an eye on the old fellow. I'm not so sure we really convinced him, after all. I'd much rather keep him around to do the work, but the job is much too important to take chances." Brown nodded, and followed Hoerwitz back to the latter's quarters. Then he took up his station outside, glanced at his watch, helped himself to a set of the pills needed to keep human metabolism in balance under zero-G, and relaxed. The "night" wore on.

Hoerwitz had been perfectly sincere about his intention of sleeping. He had developed the habit of spending much of his time in that state during his years at the station. His age may have been partly responsible, but the life itself was hardly one to keep a man alert. Few people could be found to accept the lonely and boring jobs in the off-Earth factories—so few that many of them had to be run entirely by computer and remote control. Hoerwitz happened to be one of the sort who could spend all his time quite happily with abstract entertainment—books, plays, music or poetry. He could reread a book, or see the same play over and over again, with full enjoyment, just as many people can get pleasure out of hearing the same music repeatedly. Few jobs on Earth would have permitted him to spend so much time amusing himself; the arrangement was ideal both for him and his employers. Still, he slept a lot.

He therefore woke up refreshed, if not exactly vigorous, some nine hours after Brown had taken up his guard station. He was not only refreshed but enthusiastic. He had a plan. It was not a very complicated one, but it might keep him alive.

It had two parts. One was to convince Smith that the intruders could not load their loot without Mac's help. This should be simple enough, since it was pretty certainly true. Shifting twelve million pounds of mass by muscle-power, even in zero-G, is impractical for four men in any reasonable time. The alternative was the station's loading equipment, and it was unlikely that anyone but Hoerwitz would be expert in its use. If the thieves were convinced of that, at least they'd keep him alive until the last minute.

The second part of the plan was to arrange for himself a refuge or hiding place good enough to discourage the four from spending the time necessary to get him. This assumed that they had assigned high priority to getting away as soon as possible after loading the stolen fuel, which seemed reasonable. Details here, however, required more thinking. It might be better to trust to concealment; on the other hand, there was something to be said for a place whose location was known to the enemy but which obviously couldn't be penetrated without a lot of time and effort.

On the whole, the latter choice would make him feel safer, but he couldn't offhand think of a really impregnable spot. There were very few doors of any kind in the station, and even fewer of these could be locked. Air-breaks were solid, but not made to resist intelligent attack. None of the few locks in the place was any better in that respect, if one assumed that the thieves were of professional caliber.

Of course, much of the factory equipment itself, designed to contain nuclear reactions, would have resisted any imaginable tools. None of this could, however, be regarded as practical for hiding purposes; one might as well get inside a blast furnace or sulfuric-acid chamber.

All in all, it looked as though straight concealment were going to be more practical, and this pretty well demanded the outside of the asteroid.

The tunnels of the station were complex enough to make a fairly good labyrinth, but there was a reasonable basic pattern underlying their arrangement. Hoerwitz knew this pattern so well, quite naturally, that it never occurred to him that his unwelcome guests might have trouble finding him in the maze once he got out of sight. He did think of turning out the lights to complicate their job, but they should have little trouble turning them back on again. Robinson, at least, must know *something* about electricity. Besides, darkness and weightlessness together were a very bad combination even for someone as used to the latter as Hoerwitz. No, outside would be best.

The asteroid was far from spherical, had a reasonable amount of surface area, and its jagged surface promised all sorts of hiding places. This was especially true in the contrasty lighting of airlessness. Mac could think of a dozen possible spots immediately—his years of residence had not been spent entirely inside. During safe periods he had taken several trips outside (safe periods meant, among other things, the presence of company; taking a lone walk in a spacesuit is about as sensible as taking a lone swim in the Indian Ocean).

More familiarity with the surface would have been nice, but what little he had should at least be greater than the others did. If he were to drop casually some remark which would give the impression that he knew the outside like one of his own Shakespeare sheets, they might not even bother to search once he was out of sight—provided he waited until there was very little time left before they were leaving, and provided he was able to disappear at all. Too many ifs? Maybe.

It was also important that Smith not change his mind about letting Hoerwitz take walks outside. It wouldn't require careful guarding to prevent such an excursion; five seconds' work on Mac's spacesuit would take care of that. It was annoying that so much of the plan depended more on Smith's attitude than on Hoerwitz's action, especially since Smith didn't seem to believe in taking chances. The attitude would be hard to control. The manager would have to seem completely harmless—but he'd better take Hamlet's advice about overacting.

That was a matter of basic behavior. On the question of useful action, there was another factor to consider. At the present setup rate, the isotopes the thieves wanted would be ready ten or a dozen hours before perigee, which Mac was still taking as the latest time they'd want to stay around. Something really ought to be done to delay the conversion and delivery process, to keep at a minimum the supply of spare moments which could be devoted to looking for missing factory managers. Could he slow down the converters without arousing suspicion? He knew much about the machines, and the others presumably knew very little, but trying to fool them with some piece of fiction would be extremely risky. His left hand gave an extra twinge at the thought.

Of course, some genuine trouble *could* develop. It hadn't in all his years at the station, but it could. There was no point waiting for it, and even if it did they'd probably blame him anyway, but—could he, perhaps, arrange for something to happen which would obviously be Jones's fault? Or Smith's own? The basic idea was attractive, but details failed to crystallize.

It was certainly high time for action, though, if he hoped to accomplish anything such as living; the closer to completion the process came, the less good a slowdown would accomplish. In fact, it was time to stop daydreaming and get to work. Hoerwitz nodded slowly to himself as ideas began to shape up.

4

He went to the galley and prepared breakfast, noting without surprise that the others had been using his food. It was too bad that he didn't have anything to dose it with for their benefit. He measured out and consumed his daily supply of null-G medicines, and put the utensils in the washer—one common aspect of his job he had refused to accept. Difficult as such things as ham and eggs are to manage in free fall, he had insisted on regular food instead of tubes of paste. He worked out techniques of his own for keeping things in the plate. Some day, he had been telling himself for a couple of decades, he would write a book on zero-G cookery.

With the galley chores done, he aimed himself down the corridor toward the control chamber. Brown and Robinson were inside, both looking bored. The latter was drifting within reach of a wall, the manager noticed; perhaps his experience of the day before had taught him something. Hoerwitz hoped not. Brown was near the center of the room and would be useless to his party for quite a few seconds if action were required.

The instruments were disgustingly normal. All twenty converters were simmering along as programmed. Not all were doing just the same things, of course; they had been loaded with different substances originally and had been interrupted in various stages of differing processes when Hoerwitz had been forced to reprogram. One of them had already been processing a Class IV order and was now approaching the climax of its run. It seemed wiser to point this out to the thieves so that they wouldn't think he was up to anything when he shut this one down, as he would have to do in a few hours. He did so.

"At least you people won't have to do everything at once," he remarked.

"What do you mean?" asked Brown.

"When you came, I told you that one of the units was on Four already. You can tell your boss that it should be ready to load in eight hours or so. I'll show you where the loading conveyors are handled from—or do you want to lug it out by hand? You were bragging about carting five hundred pounds of ship around when you came."

"Don't be funny, old fellow," cut in Robinson. "You might as well have that loading machinery ready. You might even be ready to show a couple of us how to use it. If Smith should decide he doesn't like your attitude, we might be the only ones able to."

"All right with me," replied the manager. He felt reasonably safe as long as Smith himself was not present. It had seemed likely that none of the others would dare do anything drastic to him without direct orders, and Robinson's remark had strengthened the belief. "The controls are in a dome at the surface. They're simple enough, like a chess game."

"What does that crack mean?"

"Just what it sounded like. Any six-year-old can learn the rules of chess in an hour, but that doesn't make him a good player. I'm sure Mr. Smith won't need you to remind him of that when you suggest that you ought to do the loading." The two men glanced at each other, and Robinson shrugged.

"Better show me where the controls are, anyway," he said. "You better stay here," he added to Brown. "I'll be with Hoerwitz, but Smith said this panel was never to be left unwatched. We might not have time to explain if he found us both gone." The other man nodded. Hoerwitz, keeping his face as expressionless as he could, led the way to the station he had mentioned.

This was about as far from the control chamber as anything could be, since it was at the surface. It lay near the main entrance, a quarter of the way around the asteroid's equator from the radiators. The converters themselves were scattered at fairly regular intervals just under the surface. The general idea was that if one of them did misbehave it would meet only token resistance outward, and the rest of the plant might have a chance. Access and loading tunnels connecting the converters with the cargo locks and the living quarters were deliberately crooked. All these tricks would of course be futile in a major blowup, but it *is* possible to have minor accidents even in nuclear engineering.

The dome containing the loading control panels was one of the few places offering a direct view to the outside of the asteroid. It had served as a conning site while the body was being driven in from beyond Mars; it still was sometimes used that way. The thrust pits were still in service, as the present long, narrow orbit was heavily perturbed by the moon and required occasional correction near apogee. This was not done by Hoerwitz, who could no more have corrected an orbit than he could have built a spaceship. The thrust controls were disconnected except when a ballistics engineer was on hand.

The dome was small, little more than a dozen feet across, and its entire circle was rimmed with conveyor control panels. Hoerwitz, quite unintentionally, had exaggerated their simplicity. This might have gotten him into trouble with anyone but Robinson. Without worrying about this situation, since he failed to recognize it, the manager promptly began explaining.

"First, you want to be careful about these two guarded switches on each panel," he pointed out. "They're designed to bypass the safeties which normally keep you from putting too hot a load on the conveyors, so that you can dump a converter in an emergency. At the moment, since all the units are hot, you couldn't operate any part of the conveyor system except by those switches.

"Basically, the whole thing is simple enough. One panel is concerned with each of the twenty separate conveyor systems, and all panels are alike, so—"

"Why didn't they make just one panel, then, and have a selector to set it on any one of the reactors?" asked Robinson. Hoerwitz sadly revised upward his estimate of the fellow's brain power, as he answered.

"Often several ships are loading, or several reactors unloading, at one time. It turned out to be simpler and safer to have independent control systems. Also, the system works both ways—customers get credit for mass brought to the station for conversion. We have to take material to the converters as well as away from them, and it's more efficient to be able to carry on several operations at once. The original idea, as you probably know, was to use the mass of the asteroid itself for conversion; but with laws about controlling rotation so that the radiators would point away from Earth most of the time, and the expense of the original installation, and the changes in orbit and angular momentum and so on, they finally decided it was better to try to keep the mass of the place fairly constant. They did use quite a bit of material from it at first. There are a lot of useless tunnels inside, and quite a few pits outside, left over from those days."

Hoerwitz was watching his listener covertly as he spoke, trying to judge how much of this information was being absorbed, but the other's face was unreadable. He gave up and went on with the lesson.

They were joined after about a quarter of an hour by Smith, but the head thief said little, merely ordering the instruction to continue. The factory manager decided to take no more chances testing his listeners with double-talk; Smith had impressed him as being a different proposition from his followers. The decision to play safe in his presence proved a wise one.

It took another ten minutes for Mac to wind up the lesson.

"You'll need some practice," he concluded, "and there's no way to get it just yet. I was never a schoolteacher, but I understand that your best way of making sure how well you know something is to try to teach it to someone else. I trust Mr. Smith approves of that thought."

"I do." Smith's face didn't show approval or anything else, but the words were encouraging.

"Give me a lesson right now, Rob. I'd particularly like to know just what this switch does—or did Mr. Hoerwitz forget to mention it?" He indicated the emergency-dump override.

"Oh, no, he showed me that first. We'd better keep clear of it, because it empties that particular converter onto its conveyor and dumps it into space, even though it's still hot."

For a moment there might have been a flicker of surprise on Smith's face.

"And he told you about it? I rather thought he might skip items like that in the hope that one of us might make a mistake he could not be blamed for." Hoerwitz decided that it would be less suspicious to answer that remark than to let it pass.

"Is there anything that could possibly go wrong that you would not blame me for?" he asked.

"Probably not, at that. I'm glad you realize it, Mr. Hoerwitz. Perhaps I'll be spared the nuisance of having to leave a man on guard here as well as at the main controls." He glanced through the dome's double wall at Earth's fat crescent, which dominated the sky on one side of the meridian as the Moon did on the other. "Is there any way of shutting off access to this place until we're ready to use it? Think how much more at ease we'd both feel if there were."

Hoerwitz shrugged. "No regular door. There are a couple of safety air-breaks in the corridor below; you could get one of them closed easily enough, since there are manual switches for them as well as the pressure and temperature differential sensors, but it would be a lot harder to open. If one of those things does shut, it's normally because air is being lost or dangerous reactions going on on one side or the other. A good deal of red tape is necessary to convince the machinery that all is well, after all."

"Hmph." Smith looked thoughtful. "All right, we'll consider it. Rob, you stay here until I decide. You come with me, old fellow." Hoerwitz obeyed with mixed feelings.

It was lucky he hadn't tried to dump the reactors and shut himself off in the dome section, in view of Smith's perspicacity, but he couldn't thank his own intelligence or foresight for saving him. The sad fact was that he'd never thought of the trick until he was explaining matters to Robinson. Now it was certainly too late. Of course, it probably wouldn't have worked anyway, since someone like Robinson could presumably get air doors open again in short order; and there was an even brighter side, now that he thought of it. The last few minutes might well have gone far to convincing Smith that the manager was really reconciled to the situation. One could not be sure of that, naturally, with a person like Smith, but one could hope. Time would no doubt tell—quite possibly in bad language.

As they floated back down toward the living section—Hoerwitz noted with some regret that Smith was getting better at handling himself in free fall—the head thief spoke briefly.

"Maybe you've learned your lesson. From what's just happened, I guess we can both hope so. Just the same, I don't want to see you anywhere near that place where we just left Robinson, except when I tell you myself to go there for my own reasons. Is that clear?"

"It is."

"Good. I don't really enjoy persuading people the hard way, but you may have noticed that Mr. Jones does. If you've really accepted the fact that I have the bulge on you, though, we won't have to amuse him."

"You've made everything very clear. Do you want the reactor which was working on Class IV when you came, and which will be ready pretty soon, to be unloaded as soon as it's done?"

"Hmph. I don't know. Does your loading machine deliver to any spot on the surface, or just by that dome?"

"Just at the dome, I'm afraid. It wouldn't have been practical to run conveyors all over the place, and it's even less so to drive trucks around on the surface."

"All right. If it would mean moving our ship an extra time we'll wait until everything is ready. It would be a nuisance to have to guard it, too."

"Then you're not really convinced I've learned my lesson, after all."

"Don't ask too many questions, Mr. Hoerwitz. Why not just assume that I don't like to take chances?"

The manager was not inclined to act on impulse, but he sometimes talked on that basis. This was one of the times.

"I don't want to assume that."

"Why not?"

"Because one of your most obvious ways of not taking chances would be to leave no witnesses. If I believed you were that thorough, I might as well stop everything now and let you shoot me—not that I really enjoy the prospect, but I could at least die with the satisfaction that I hadn't helped you."

"That's logical," Smith answered thoughtfully. "I have only two answers to it. One you already know—we wouldn't just shoot you. The other, which I hope will make you feel better, is that we aren't worried about witnesses. You've been reading too much. We'll have lived in this place for several days before we're done, but you must have noticed that we aren't wearing gloves to keep from leaving fingerprints, or spacesuits to foil the scene analyzers, or anything else of that sort. I'm sure the law will know who was here after we've gone, but that doesn't worry us. They already want us for so many different things that our main care is to avoid getting caught up with, not identified."

"Then why those names? Do you expect me to believe they're real?"

For almost the first time, Smith showed emotion. He grinned. "Go back to your drama sheets, Mr. Hoerwitz, but stick to Shakespeare. Lord Peter Wimsey is leading you astray. Just remember what I said about the conveyor controls: keep away from them."

5

If his finger hadn't been so painful, Hoerwitz would have been quite happy as he made his way back to the lounge and let the air currents settle him into the hammock. He shunted *Julius Caesar* into the "hold" stack without zeroing its tracker, started *The Pajama Game,* and remained awake through the whole show. It was quite an occasion.

For the next couple of days everyone was on almost friendly terms, though Hoerwitz's finger kept him from forgetting entirely the basic facts of the situation or warming up very much to Jones. Some of the men watched shows with him, and there was even casual conversation entirely unconnected with reactors and fuel processing. Smith's psychology was working fairly well.

It did not backfire on him until about twenty hours before perigee.

At that time Mac had been making one of his periodic control checks, and had reported that the runs would be finishing off during the next ten or twelve hours. He would have to stay at the board, since they would not all end at the same time, and it was safer to oversee the supposedly automatic cooling of each converter as its job ended.

"'What's all that for?" asked Smith. "I thought it didn't matter much what was in the converters at the start. Why will it hurt if a little of this is still inside when you begin your next job? Won't it just be converted along with everything else?"

"It's not quite that simple," replied the manager. "Basically you are right; we don't deal in pure products, and what we deliver is processed chemically by our customers. Still, it's best to start clean. If too much really hot stuff were allowed to accumulate in the converters between runs, it could be bad. If Class I or II fuel intended to power a chemical industry, for example, were contaminated with Class IV there could be trouble on Earth—especially if the plant in question were doing a chemical separation of nuclear fuels."

"But it's *all* Class IV this time," pointed out Smith, "unless you've been running a major bluff on us, and I'm sure you wouldn't do that." His face hardened, and once more Hoerwitz mentally kicked himself. He hadn't even thought of such a trick, and he could probably have gotten away with it. There was no easy way to identify directly the isotopes being put out by the converters; it took specialized apparatus and specialized knowledge. It was pretty certain that Smith had neither. Well, too late now.

"It's all one class, as you said," the manager admitted with what he hoped was negligible delay, "but that's just it. With Class IV in every converter and on every conveyor, it's even more important than usual to watch the cooling. I live here, you know. I'm not an engineer and don't know what would happen if any of that stuff found its way into the hydrogen reactors, but I'd rather not find out."

"But you must be enough of an engineer to handle the fusion units."

"That doesn't demand an engineer. I'm a button pusher. I can operate them very sensibly, but they don't waste a trained engineer out here with the price of skilled labor what it is. The trouble frequency of these plants is far too low to keep one twiddling his thumbs on standby the whole time."

"But how about safety? If this place blows apart, it would take quite a few centuries of engineers' pay to replace it, I'd think."

"No doubt. I suspect that's the point they're trying to make, in order to modify or get rid of that law about hydrogen reactors on Earth. The idea is that if the company trusts them enough to risk all this capital without a resident engineer, what's everyone worried about?"

"But the place *could* really let go if the right—or I should say the wrong—things happened."

"I suppose so, but I don't know what they'd be, short of deliberate mishandling. In the forty years I've been here nothing out of line had ever happened. I've never had to use that emergency dump I've showed you, or even the straight shutoff on the main board. Engineers come twice a year to check everything over, and I just move switches—like this." He began manipulating controls. "Number thirteen has flashed over. I'm shutting down, and in about an hour it can be transferred from field-bottle to physical containers."

"Why not now? What's this field-bottle?"

Hoerwitz was genuinely surprised, and once again annoyed. He had supposed everyone knew about that; if he had realized that Smith didn't... Well, another chance gone.

"At conversion energies no material will hold the charge in. Three hundred tons of anything at all, at star-core temperature, would feel cramped in a hundred cubic miles of space, to say nothing of a hundred cubic yards. It's held in by fields, since nothing else will do it, and surrounded by a free-electron layer that reflects just about all the radiation back into the plasma. The little bit that isn't reflected is carried, also by free-electron field, to the radiators."

"I think you're trying something," Smith said sternly, and the manager felt his stomach misbehave again. "You said that those loads could be dumped in an emergency by the conveyors. And you described the conveyors as simply mechanical belt-and-bucket systems, a couple of days ago. Stuff that you just described would blow them into gas. Which was the lie?"

"Neither!" Hoerwitz gasped desperately. "I didn't say that the emergency dumping was instantaneous—it isn't. The process involves fast chilling, using the same conductor fields; and even with them, we'd expect the conveyors to need replacing if we ever used the system!"

"If that's so," Smith asked, "what did you mean by saying a while ago that you didn't know what could happen to blow this place up? If one of those fields let go—"

"Oh, but it couldn't. There are all sorts of automatic safety systems. I don't have to worry about that sort of thing. If a field starts to weaken, the energy loss automatically drains into conductor fields, and they carry plasma energy that much faster to the radiators, so the plasma cools and the pressure drops— I can't give you all the details because I don't understand them myself, but it's a real fail-safe."

Smith still looked suspicious, though he was as accustomed as any civilized person to trusting machinery. It wasn't the machinery that bothered him just now.

"You keep switching," he snapped, "and I don't like it. One minute you say nothing can happen, and the next you talk about all these emergency features in case it does. Either the people who built this place didn't know what they were doing, or you're not leveling."

Hoerwitz's stomach felt even worse, but he kept up the battle.

"That's not what I said! I told you things couldn't happen *because* of the safety stuff! They knew what they were doing when they built this place—of course, half the major governments on Earth were passing laws about the way it should be done —"

"Passing laws? For something off Earth?"

"Sure. Ninety-five per cent of the company's potential customers were nationals of those countries, and there's nothing like economic pressure. Now, will you stop this nonsense and let me work, or decide you don't trust me and do it all yourself? There are more reactors almost ready to flash over."

It was the wrong line for the old man to take, but Smith also made a mistake in resenting it. It was here that his psychology really went wrong.

"I don't trust you," he said. "Not one particle. You've evaded every detailed question I asked. I don't even know for certain that that's Class IV stuff you've been cooking for me."

"That's right. You don't." Hoerwitz, too, was losing his tact and foresight. "I've been expecting you to make some sort of test ever since I set up the program. Or did you take for granted that whoever you found here would be scared into doing just what you wanted? Surely it isn't possible that you and the friends you said were somewhere else just don't have anyone able to make such a test! Any properly planned operation would have made getting such a person its first step, I should think—or have I been reading too much again?"

The expression which had started to develop on Smith's face disappeared, and he looked steadily at the old man for perhaps half a minute. Then he spoke.

"Mr. Jones. I think we will have to start Phase Two of the persuasion plan. Will you please prepare for it? We planned this operation, as you call it, Mr. Hoerwitz, quite carefully, in view of certain limitations which faced us. Exactly what those limitations were is none of your business, but remember that we so arranged matters that no one on Earth has been seriously worried by your failure to communicate—nor will they for some time yet. We know that no scheduled freighters are due here for two more revolutions, though we recognize the chance of a tramp tug dropping in with mass to deposit for credit—that is why we plan to have the job done before the next perigee. Our plans also included details for insuring the cooperation of the person we found on duty. The fact that he turned out to be about three times as old as we expected doesn't affect those plans at all. You have experienced the first part of them. I was rather hoping that no more would be necessary, but you seem to have forgotten that we have the bulge on you. Therefore, you will experience the second part, unless you can think of a way to prove to me that you have been telling the truth—and prove it in a very short time. I won't tell you what the time limit is, but I have already decided on it. Start thinking, Mr. Hoerwitz. I believe Mr. Jones is ready."

Hoerwitz couldn't think. He probably couldn't have thought if the same situation had faced him forty or fifty years earlier; he had never claimed to be a hero. He spoke, but—as Smith had intended—it was without any sort of consideration.

"The Class IV stuff that was going when you arrived—it's cool— you could get a sample of it and test it in your ship's power plant!"

"Not good enough. I never doubted that you were telling the truth about that load. It will have to be something else. The material that's finishing now, or your claim that something could really go wrong enough to blow this place into vapor if your fail-safe rigs weren't there—"

"But how could I possibly prove that, except by doing it?" gasped the old man.

"Your problem. Think fast. Mr. Jones will be with you in a moment. In fact, I think he's on the way now—not hurrying, you understand, because he isn't really proficient at moving around in this no-weight nuisance—but I think if I looked around I'd see that he had pushed off and was drifting your way. It would be unfair of me to spoil his fun if he gets to you before you've thought of something, wouldn't it?"

Smith of course meant to reduce the manager to a state of complete panic in which he would be unable to lie, or at least to lie convincingly; but just as he had planned badly in not getting hold of a nuclear engineer of his own, he had planned badly in failing to consider all the possible results of panic. He may, of course, have realized that Hoerwitz might try to do something desperate, but failed to foresee how hard such an action would be to stop in the unfamiliar environment of weightlessness. It was easy to take for granted that a person with such a frail physique could be controlled physically by anyone with no trouble. This was perfectly correct—for anyone within reach of the old man.

No one was. Worse, from Smith's point of view, no one but Robinson was in a position to get there. As a result, Mac was able to do something which he would never have seriously considered if he had been given time to think. He was, of course, within reach of a push-off point as a matter of habit. He used every bit of muscle his frail old body could muster in a dive toward the center of the board—and made it.

Only Robinson had learned his lesson about drifting, and he misjudged his own pushoff and failed to intercept the manager. Hoerwitz reached and opened a plainly labeled switch, and with the action his panic left him as suddenly as it had come, though fear still churned at his stomach.

"At least, you believed me enough not to risk bullets in the controls," he almost sneered. "There's your proof, Mr. Smith. I've just shut down all the converters. They're bleeding energy out of the main radiators and will be cool enough to handle in an hour. If you replace that switch, you'll know I was telling the truth about safeties. Go ahead. Close it. It's *safe*. All you'll get is a bunch of red lights all over the boards, telling you that safety circuits are blocking you. You'll have to start those processes from the beginning. I can set that up for you, of course. I will if you give the order; but anything else at all, except dumping the loads, of course, will block you with safeties."

"Why?" Smith was still in control of himself, though it was a visible strain.

"What do you think I am, an astrophysicist? I don't know why, if you want one of those detailed answers you were complaining about not getting. They come in high-class equations. In words, which is all I understand about it, most of the processing time in these converters is for setup. The actual conversion is the sort of thing that goes on in the last moments of a supernova's fling, as I thought everyone knew. The converter has to set up millions of parameters in terms of temperature, density gradients, potential of all sorts—even the changing distance from Earth in this orbit has to be allowed for, I understand—and I don't know what else before the final step is triggered, if a decent percentage of the desired isotope class is to be produced. I've just cleared the setup in eighteen of those converters. If you were actually to build them up to the temperature they had before I hit that switch, you probably *would* blow the place up. Hence, my friend, the safeties. Working out a reaction that not only produces useful isotopes but *also* balances endothermic and exothermic processes closely to hold the whole works under control is a perfectly good subject for a doctorate thesis. Do you think we could define a supernova—or even a few tons of one? Now, do you want me to start these stoves all over, or will you take two loads of Class IV instead of twenty, pull out all my fingernails and fly off in a rage gnashing your teeth?"

During this diatribe Smith had actually calmed down, which was hardly what Hoerwitz had expected. The thief nodded slowly at its end.

"I wouldn't have said there was anything which could happen here which I wouldn't blame on you," he said, "but I have to admit this one is on me. By all means, start the cooking over. I have learned most of what I need to know. I think I can now manage well enough even if visitors show up during this overtime period you have pushed us into.

"You just restart the runs you interrupted, and when that's done come with me up to the dome. I want you to get the load that was just finished out onto the conveyors. Then you may resume your life of leisure and entertainment. Hop to it, Mr. Hoerwitz."

The manager hopped. He was too surprised at Smith's reaction to do anything else. He would have to recheck his Shakespeare memory; maybe there was someone like this after all. He worked the controls rapidly.

Jones looked disappointed except for a moment when Robinson suddenly said, "That's not the way he had them set before!"

Smith started to raise his eyebrows in surprise, but the manager, who had had no thought of deception at the moment, said, "We're not starting with the same stuff as before, remember. Many things happen long before the main conversion."

Smith stopped, thought for a moment, looked carefully at the old man, and nodded. Jones shrugged and relaxed once more.

By this time, certain facts were beginning to fit together in the manager's mind.

6

By the time the trip to the dome had been made and the finished load of isotopes transferred to its conveyor, Hoerwitz's brief sense of elation had evaporated, and he had written himself off as a walking corpse. He realized just what details he had overlooked, and just where the omissions left him. He floated slowly to his quarters, his morale completely flattened and hope for the first time gone.

Robinson's acute detail memory must have been a major factor in the planning Smith had mentioned. If Hoerwitz himself could run the plant effectively without a real basic understanding of what went on, so could Robinson. By arranging what had amounted to another lesson in the operation of the controls, the manager had made himself superfluous from the thieves' viewpoint.

Also, and much worse, he had completely missed the hole in the logic Smith had used when the fellow had tried to prove that he really wasn't worried about leaving witnesses. It was quite true that the thieves were taking no care about leaving fingerprints. Why should they bother about such details? No one can analyze individual personality traces from a million-degree cloud of ionized gas, and they certainly knew enough now to leave only that behind them.

Even if wiring around the safety circuits was too much for Robinson, which seemed unlikely in Hoerwitz's present mood, they could always sacrifice a ton or so of their loot. The Class IV fuels might not be up to hydrogen fusion standards, but they would be quite adequate for the purpose intended. Hiding, inside the asteroid or out, would be meaningless.

The only remaining shred of his original plan which retained any relevance was the desirability of fooling the others about his own attitude. As long as they believed that he expected to come out of the affair with his life, they would not expect him to do anything desperate, and they might let him live until the last moment to save themselves work. If they even suspected that he had convinced himself that they were going to dispose of him, Smith's dislike of taking chances would probably become the deciding factor.

This might involve a difficult bit of acting. Behaving as though he had forgotten what had happened would certainly be unconvincing. Trying to act as though he had even forgiven it would be little better. On the other hand, any trace of an uncooperative attitude would also be dangerous. Maybe he should go back to *Hamlet* and rerun the prince's instructions to the players. No, not worth it. He knew them word for word anyway, and the more he thought of the problem as one of acting the less likely he was to get away with it.

Maybe he should just try, unobtrusively, to keep in Jones's company as much as possible. His natural feelings toward that member of the group were unlikely to make the others suspicious.

In any case, he wouldn't have to act for a while. The last couple of hours had been exhausting enough so that not even Smith was surprised when Mac sought his own quarters. One of the men followed and took up watch outside, of course, but that was routine.

The manager was in no mood for music. He brought the *Julius Caesar* sheet out of standby and let the scanner start at the point where he had left it a couple of days before.

As a result, it was only a few minutes before Brutus solved his problem for him.

It was beautiful. There was no slow groping, no rejection of one detail and substitution of another. It was just *there*, all at once. It would have made Wertheimer, Kohler, and the rest of the gestalt school dance with glee. The only extraneous thought to enter Hoerwitz's mind as the idea developed was a touch of amazement that Shakespeare could have written anything so relevant more than four decades before the birth of Isaac Newton.

He didn't wait for the end of the play. There was quite a while remaining before the plan could be put into action, so he went to sleep. After all, a man needs his ten or twelve hours when careful, exhausting and detailed work is in the offing.

A good meal helps, too, and Hoerwitz prepared himself one when he woke up—one of his fancier breakfasts. With that disposed of, there were seven hours to go before perigee.

He went to check the controls, pointedly ignoring the thief on duty outside his quarters and the second one in the control room. Everything about the converters was going well, as usual, but this time the fact didn't annoy him. For all he cared, all those loads of explosives could cook themselves to completion.

They hadn't been ordered properly, but there would be no trouble finding customers for them later on.

He checked in time his impulse to go to the dome for a look outside. Smith's order had been very clear, so it would be necessary to trust the clocks without the help of a look at Earth. No matter. He trusted them.

Six hours to perigee. Four and a half to action time. He hated leaving things so late, since there was doubt about Smith's reaction to the key question and time might be needed to influence the fellow. Still, starting too soon would be even more dangerous.

A show killed three of the hours, but he never remembered afterward which show he had picked.

Another meal helped. After all, it might be quite a long time before he would eat anything but tube-mush, if things went right. If they went wrong, he had the right to make his last meal a good one. It brought him almost up to the deadline. He thought briefly of not bothering to clean the dishes, but decided that this was no time to change his habits. Smith was suspicious enough by nature without giving him handles for it.

Now a final check of the controls, which mustn't look as though it were final. Normal, as usual. Robinson and Brown were in the control room—the latter had accompanied the manager from his quarters—and when the check was finished the old man turned to them.

"Where is your boss?"

Robinson shrugged. "Asleep, I suppose. Why?"

"When you first came, he said it would be all right for me to walk outside, once you'd jimmied the transmitter in my suit. I like to watch Earth as we go by perigee, but I suppose I'd better make sure he still doesn't object."

"Why can't you watch from the dome?"

"Partly because he told me to keep away from there, and partly because in the hour and a half around perigee Earth shifts from one side of this place to the other. You can see only the first part from the dome. I like to go to the north pole and watch it swing around the horizon—you get a real sense of motion. Whoever Smith sends with me, if he lets me go at all, will enjoy it. Maybe he'd like to go himself."

Robinson was doubtful. "I suppose he won't shoot anyone for asking. I take it this happens pretty soon." Hoerwitz was glad of the chance to look at a clock without arousing suspicion.

"Very soon. There won't be much more than enough time to check our suits. Remember, there's no such thing as fast walking, outside."

"Don't I know it. All right, I'll ask him. You stay here with Mr. Brown."

"You're sure you didn't damage anything in my suit except the radio?"

"Positive. Make a regular checkout; I stand by the result."

"As long as I don't fall by it." Robinson shrugged and left. "Mr. Brown, in view of what your friend just said, how about coming with me up to the lock so I can start that suit check early?"

Brown shook his head negatively, and nodded toward the controls.

"Smith said to keep it guarded." Hoerwitz decided that debate was useless, and waited for the leader. It was not really as long a wait as it seemed.

Smith was accompanied by Robinson, as the manager had expected, and also by Jones, who, Hoerwitz had assumed, must be on guard at the dome. He hadn't stopped to figure out the arithmetic of three men on watch at once out of a total strength of four.

Smith wasted no time.

"All right, Mr. Hoerwitz, let's take this walk. Have you checked your suit?"

"I've had no chance."

"All right, let's get to it. Tell me what you expect to see as we go up. With your suit radio out you won't be able to give a proper guide's talk outside."

The manager obeyed, repeating what he had told Robinson and Brown a few minutes before. The recital lasted to the equipment chamber inside the air lock, where the old man fell silent as he started to make the meticulous checkout which was routine for people who had survived much experience in spacesuits. He was especially careful of the nuclear-powered air-recycling equipment and the reserve tanks which made up for its unavoidable slight inefficiency. He was hoping to depend on them for quite a while.

Satisfied, he looked up and spoke once more.

"I mentioned only the north pole walk," he said, "because I assume you'd disapprove of something else I often do. At the place where Earth is overhead at perigee, right opposite the radiators, I have a six-foot optical flat with a central hole. You probably know the old distress-mirror trick. I have friends at several places on Earth, and sometimes at perigee I stand there and flash sunlight at them. The beam from the mirror is only about twelve or fifteen miles wide at a thousand miles, and if I aim it right it looks brighter than Venus from the other end—they can spot it in full daylight without much trouble. Naturally the mirror has to be in sunlight itself, and as I remember it won't be this time, but I thought I'd better mention it in case you came across the mirror as we wandered around and got the idea that I was up to something."

"That was very wise of you, Mr. Hoerwitz. Actually, I doubt that there will be any random wandering. Mr. Jones will remain very close to you at all times, and unless you yourself approach the mirror he is unlikely to. I trust you will have a pleasant walk and am sure that there is no point in reminding you of the impossibility of finding a man drifting in space."

"One chance in ten thousand isn't exactly impossible, but I'd rather not depend on it," admitted the manager. "But aren't you coming?"

"No. Possibly some other time. Enjoy yourself."

Mac wondered briefly whether he had made some mistake. He had told only two lies since bringing up the subject of the walk and felt pretty sure that if Smith had detected either of them the fact would now be obvious.

But he had expected to get out only by interesting Smith himself in the trip. If Smith didn't want to go, why was he permitting it at all? Out of kindheartedness?

No. Obviously not.

For a moment Hoerwitz wished he hadn't eaten that last meal. It threatened to come back on him as he saw what must be Smith's reason. Then he decided he might as well enjoy the memory of it while he could. After that, almost in a spirit of bravado, he made a final remark.

"Jones, I don't pretend to care what happens to you outside, but you might remember one thing."

"What?" The fellow paused with his helmet almost in place.

"If I do anything that you think calls for shooting me, be sure you are holding on to something tightly or that your line of fire is upward."

"Why?"

"Well, as Mr. Smith pointed out some time ago, the escape velocity of this asteroid is about one foot a second. I don't know too much about guns, but I seem to recall that an ordinary pistol shot will provide a spacesuited man with a recoil velocity of around a third of that. You wouldn't be kicked entirely into space, but you'd be some time coming down; and just think of the embarrassment if your first shot had missed me. Don't say I didn't warn you."

He clamped down his own helmet without waiting for an answer from either man. Then he wished he'd mentioned something about the danger to a spacesuit from ricochet, but decided that it would be an anticlimax.

He would have liked to hear the remarks passed between them, but he had already discovered that Robinson hadn't wasted time cutting out his transmitter but avoiding the receiver. He had simply depowered the whole unit, and Mac could neither transmit nor receive.

He stepped—using the word loosely—in the inner-lock door, hit the switch that opened it and stepped through. Turning to see whether Jones was with him, he was surprised to discover that the latter still had not donned his helmet and was engaged in an animated discussion with Smith.

Hoerwitz sometimes spoke on impulse, but it had been well over fifty years since he had performed an important action on that basis; the mental machinery concerned was rather corroded. It might be possible to get the inner lock door closed and the air pumps started before either of the two men could reach the inner switch; if he could do that, it would give him nearly two minutes start—quite long enough to disappear on the irregular, harshly lit surface of the asteroid. On the other hand, if they stopped the cycle before the inner door was closed and the inside switch out of circuit, they would presumably shoot him on the spot.

His spacesuit had the usual provisions for sealing small leaks, but it was by no means bullet-proof. He wished he had taken the time to make that remark about ricochet; it would apply well to the metal-walled chambers they were all standing in. Unfortunately the thieves might not think of that in time.

Hoerwitz might, if given another minute or two to mull it over, have taken the chance on that much data; but before he made up his mind the conversation ended. Jones donned his helmet, safetied its clamps and looked toward the airlock. At that same moment all three men suddenly realized that Smith and Jones were both out of touch with pushoff points. They were "standing" on the floor, of course, since they had been in the room for some time and weighed several grams each, but that weight would not supply anything like the traction needed to get them to the switch quickly. An experienced spaceman would have jumped hard, in any direction, and trusted to the next wall collision to provide steerage; but it had become perfectly evident in the last couple of days that these men were not experienced spacemen. Hoerwitz's impulses broke free with an almost audible screech of metal on rust, and he slapped the cycling control.

7

Jones had drawn his gun. He might have fired, but the action of drawing had spoiled his stance. Hoerwitz thought he had fired, but that the sound failed to get through his suit; the bullet, if any, must have gone bouncing around the equipment room. The inner door was shut, and the red light indicated pump cycling before any really interesting details could be observed.

The pumps took fifty seconds to get the pressure down, and the motors ten more to get the outer door open. Hoerwitz would have been outside almost on the instant, but his low-gravity reflexes took over.

One simply does not move rapidly in a place where the effort which would lift a man half a millimeter on Earth will give him escape velocity. This is true even when someone can be counted on to be shooting at you in the next minute or so; a person drifting helplessly out of touch with pushoff mass is a remarkably easy target. The idea was to get out of sight, rather than far away.

The asteroid was not exactly porous—no one has found a porous body made of lava yet—but it was highly irregular from a few hundred million years of random collisions out beyond Mars. There were explosion pits and crevices from this source, and quite a few holes made by men in the days when the material of the body itself had been used for conversion mass.

There were plenty of nice, dark cracks and holes to hide in. Hoerwitz maneuvered himself into one of the former five yards from the airlock and vanished.

He didn't bother to look behind him. He neither knew nor cared whether they would follow. All things considered, they might not even try. However, they would very probably send out at least two men, one to hunt for the fictitious mirror and the other to guard the spaceship—not that they could guess, the old man hoped, what he intended to do about the latter.

Both places—sub-Earth and its antipodes—were just where Hoerwitz wanted them to be; they were the spots where an unwarned space-walker would be in the greatest danger.

However, the ship would be a refuge, if it were still there, and Hoerwitz wanted to get there before any possible guard. He therefore set out at the highest speed he could manage, climbing across the asteroid.

It was like chimney-work in Earthly rock-climbing, simpler in one way because there was no significant weight. The manager was not really good at it, but presumably he was better than the others.

Earth was overhead and slightly to the west—about as far as it ever got that way, seen from near the airlock. That meant that time was growing short. When the planet started eastward again the asteroid was within a hundred degrees or so of perigee—an arc which it would cover in little over three-quarters of an hour, at this end of its grossly eccentric orbit.

Travel grew more complicated, and rather more dangerous, as the planet sank behind him. Roche's limit for a body of this density was at around twelve thousand miles from Earth's center, and the tidal bulge—invisible, imponderable, a mere mathematical quirk of earth's potential field—was not only swinging around but growing stronger. With Earth, now spanning more than thirty degrees of sky, on the horizon behind him he was safe, but as it sank he knew he was traveling to meet the bulge, and it was coming to meet him. He had to get to the ship before the field had been working on that area too long.

The last thousand feet should have been the hardest, with his weight turning definitely negative; physically, it turned out to be the easiest, though the reason shocked him. He discovered, by the simple expedient of running into it, that the thieves had strung a cable between their ship and the air lock.

With its aid, they would travel much faster than he could. There might be a guard there already. Mac, terrified almost out of his senses, pulled himself along the cable with reckless haste until he reached a point where he could see the base of the ship a few hundred feet away.

No spacesuits were in sight, but the bottom of the globe was in black shadow. There was no way to be sure—except by waiting. That would eventually make one thing certain. The old man almost hurled himself along the cable toward the ship, expecting every second to be his last, but trying to convince himself that no one was there.

He was lucky. No one was.

The ship was already off the "ground" by a foot or so; the tide was rising at this part of the asteroid and weight had turned negative. Hoerwitz crammed himself into the space between the spherical hull and the ground and heaved upward for all he was worth.

At a guess, his thrust amounted to some fifty pounds. This gave him something over a minute before the vessel was too high for further push-ing. In this time it had acquired a speed of perhaps two inches a second relative to the asteroid; but this was still increasing, very slowly, under tidal thrust.

The hull was of course covered with handholds. Hoerwitz seized two of these and rode upward with the vessel. It was quite true that a man drifting in space was an almost hopeless proposition as far as search-and-rescue was concerned; but a ship was a very different matter. If he and it got far enough away before any of the others arrived, he was safe.

Altitude increased with agonizing slowness. Earth's bulk gradually came into view all around the planetoid's jagged outline. At first, the small body showed almost against the center of the greater one; then, as the ship in its larger, slower orbit began to fall behind, the asteroid appeared to drift toward one side of the blue-and-white-streaked disk. Hoerwitz watched with interest and appreciation—it was a beautiful sight—but didn't neglect the point where the cable came around the rocks.

He was perhaps five hundred feet up when a spacesuited figure appeared, pulling itself along with little appearance of haste. It was not yet close enough for the ship's former site to be above the "horizon." Mac waited with interest to see what the reaction to the discovery would be.

It was impressive, even under circumstances which prevented good observation. The thief was surprised enough to lose grip on the cable.

He was probably traveling above escape velocity, or what would have been escape velocity, even if the tide had been out. As it was, any speed would have been too great. For a moment, Hoerwitz thought the fellow was doomed.

Maybe it was Robinson, though; at least, he reacted promptly and sensibly. He drew a gun and began firing away from the asteroid. Each shot produced only a tiny velocity change in his drifting body, but those few inches a second were enough. He collided with one of the structures at the base of a radiator, kicked himself off and downward as he hit it, touched the surface, and clutched frantically at some handhold Hoerwitz couldn't see. Then he began looking around and promptly discovered the ship.

The manager was quite sure the fellow wouldn't try a jump. He wished, once again, that his radio receiver was working—the man might be saying something interesting, though he must be out of radio reach of the others. It would be nice to know whether the thief could see Hoerwitz's clinging figure on the ship's hull. It was possible, since the lower side of the sphere was illuminated by Earthlight, but far from certain, since the man's line of sight extended quite close to the sun. He wasn't shooting. But it was more than likely that his gun was empty anyway.

It was disappointing in a way, but Hoerwitz was able to make up for himself a story of what the fellow was thinking, and this was probably more fun than the real facts. Eventually the figure worked its way back to the cable and started along it toward the airlock to a couple of holds with the snap-rings on his suit, and relaxed.

There was nothing more to do. The drifting vessel would be spotted in the next hour or so, if it hadn't been already, and someone would be along. In a way, it was a disappointing ending.

He spent some of the time wondering what Shakespeare would have done to avoid the anticlimax. He might have learned, if he had stayed awake, but he slept through the interesting part.

Smith, upon hearing that the ship was drifting away, had made the best possible time to the radiator site. Knowing that there was no other hope, he jumped; and not being a lightning calculator able to make all the necessary allowances for the local quirks in the potential field, he naturally went slightly off course.

He used all but one of his bullets in attempted corrections and wound up drifting at a velocity very well matched with that of the ship, but about fifty yards away from it. He could see Hoerwitz plainly.

Up to that time he had had no intention either of harming the old man fatally or blowing up the station; but the realization that the manager had had a part in the loss of his ship changed his attitude drastically. When the police ship arrived, he was still trying to decide whether to fire his last bullet at Hoerwitz, or in the opposite direction. Hoerwitz himself, of course, was asleep.

Avenue of Escape

Probability Zero! *Astounding,* November 1942

The sergeant swaggered into the dugout, carefully indifferent to the stares of Corporal Snodgrass, Buck Private Kendall, and the captain's orderly. He dropped into a seat at the packing-case table, and the orderly automatically began to deal.

"F'r gosh sakes, sarge, how did you make it?" asked the corporal, picking up his hand. "We thought we'd have to get a new fourth. Ken said you were in a shell hole up front, with a Jap machine gun pecking at you every time you poked your head out. We figgered you'd last till dark, and then they'd crawl out and drop a grenade on you."

The sergeant glared at his cards and then at the orderly. "I have told you children time and again that a clever man—a man, say, intelligent enough to reach the rank of mess sergeant, where all his work is done for him—can find a way out of anything," he remarked, discarding four cards. "If Ken, instead of merely reporting the presence of that machine gun, had gone to the trouble to drop a grenade on it with that trench mortar I developed, I would have been spared the effort of thinking my own way out of trouble; but he was always a thoughtless youngster."

Several hands were played in silence, the men knowing better than to ask questions. As they expected, the sergeant finally unbent.

"It is also like you young squirts to refuse to profit by the ingenuity of yer betters. I suppose it's my duty to explain my methods, in the event of your ever occupying a similar position. As you said, I was in that shell hole, which was the only cover in the neighborhood. My support, consisting of you, had departed rearward under the wing of a handy smoke pot, not leaving room for your superior officer in the cloud. As you know, I have always been opposed to the use of machine guns, and the specimen covering my shelter did nothing to change my opinion. Maybe I can persuade the army to my way of thinking, after this."

"There was only one of the guns in the nest, which was two hundred yards away. Knowing that you were retreating along their line of fire, I thoughtfully refrained from attracting their attention until I was sure you were safe—that was why I didn't follow you just then. When the smoke cleared so that I could walk without trippin' on things, I came back."

"Huh? did you have a tank with you?" asked the corporal.

"I did not, son. I have told you many a time machine guns are useless weapons. Consider, please. That gun fired about fifteen hundred shots a minute, with a muzzle velocity of about four thousand feet per second. A little arithmetic, of which even you should be capable, shows that there is a space of one hundred and sixty feet between bullets—enough for any normal man. I walked back."

STATUS SYMBOL

Intuit, NESFA Press, 1987

Nimepotea did not, of course, have a mind of her own. Like any mechanism, she obeyed the laws of physics. The fact that laws which had not been considered by her designers sometimes became relevant did not make her different from any other machine; this has been going on since long before the first bowstring broke.

The unexpected was not new even to *Nimepotea's* owner and operator. The little ship had been his home for decades now, though not his first since the start of his retirement, and he was accustomed to occasional irregularity in her behavior. Usually it didn't worry him; too many things would have to go wrong at the same time for him to be in any real danger, and right now there was help actually in sight...

Cunningham had to laugh at himself. He knew perfectly well that if a space emergency really developed, it would make little difference whether the nearest help were five hundred parsecs or five hundred kilometers away. To his emotions, however, that visible speck of light made a difference. It had on its continents not only intelligent beings but actually human ones, and that was surprisingly comforting. Ishtar was not home, but it carried people he knew personally and who knew—roughly—where he was. There were even some of those people much closer; he was not the only one interested in Tammuz.

Strictly, Ishtar should not have been visible; the glare of its sun ordinarily drowned it completely at this distance. From the bottom of a surprisingly straight, deep shaft on Tammuz' tiny satellite, however, Bel was out of sight to one side. The nearer sun was below the local horizon, so the rim of the pit was not brightly enough lit to hide the stars and the single planet it framed. The visible planet was comforting; it radiated Security.

It was the same sort of reasoning bypass which had made some of his ancestors feel more comfortable beside a wood fire than near a nuclear

407

reactor, he supposed. For rational comfort, he should know just what was making his usually reliable vessel behave as it now was doing; but ignorance was normal at this stage of an investigation.

The shaft from which he was looking might never have caught his attention at all had it been closer to the sunrise or sunset line of the satellite as he approached. With long shadows, even impact craters look deep. It is a little startling, however, to be unable to see any of a crater bottom where the sun is fifty degrees or so above the local horizon; this one had made the landscape look like a badly done painting. Cunningham had brought the *Nimepotea* to a point a few meters above the black circle, and made a quick check which showed that it was a hole too deep to study adequately from above. He had donned vacuum gear, picked up the remote control spindle, and stepped outside.

During his fall, at about a thirtieth of what he considered normal gravity, he maneuvered the ship so that one of its main lamps shone straight down the opening from a little off center. This caused the walls to be fairly well illuminated without making too much of a nuisance of his own shadow.

It took only a little over two seconds to reach the bottom, some seventy meters down. He was experienced and coordinated enough to have been able to leave the ship with no personal spin, so he landed without difficulty feet first. It was fortunate that he carried lights on his armor, because as he straightened his knees after the impact, the *Nimepotea's* illumination disappeared.

A quick glance upward showed the stars and Ishtar, but no ovoid hull occulting any part of the scene. Evidently the ship had drifted, in spite of his own handling and its automatic system. No great problem, or serious danger. The control impulses were electromagnetic, in the single-centimeter wave length band. They should diffract widely enough to reach the ship's receivers, If they didn't, the hole was no trap; the walls were climbable—the pit itself almost jumpable in this gravity.

But it was a nuisance. There had been regular, flat-bottomed side tunnels opening out of the shaft. Beyond much doubt, technical work had been done on the satellite. This was not surprising; one of Anu's planets, most probably Tammuz, had been inhabited by intelligent beings a billion or so years ago before the sun had become a red giant. It would have been fun to explore those tunnels; vacuum, low gravity, and radiation protection could combine to do wonders for archaeology. Laird Cunningham was neither an archaeologist nor any other kind of specialist, but he was a human being in the retired stage of life with normal curiosity and the ability to satisfy it which made life worth living for most people in his age range.

But if *Nimepotea* were misbehaving, investigation of other matters would have to wait. Even the presence of potential rescuers perhaps only a few thousand kilometers away did nothing to alter current priorities. Neem was being naughty; Neem would have to be disciplined.

Cunningham didn't think any of this out in words. Within a second of the light's disappearance he had aimed the control spindle upward and keyed the standard "align" signal into it. Within five more, as the ship had not reappeared, he had shut the device off, clipped it to the appropriate holder on his armor, and was engaged in the odd combination of climbing and jumping which the gravity and local supply of supports made the best way to get up the shaft.

The process took about twenty seconds, the last muscular operation being a jump from the lip of a side tunnel which carried him ten meters or so above the mouth of the pit. He had a little spin this time, and could not devote full attention to finding the ship until he was sure which end up he would land. With his feet once more on rock and his helmet intact, however, he wasted no time. As he turned head and eyes to search, his knees were flexed for another jump; it might be possible, and even necessary, to go to the ship instead of bringing it to him.

It might be necessary, but it was clearly not possible. The hull was visible enough in Bel's light, though the Sol-type sun was only an unbearably bright star at this distance. The range to the ship was nearly two hundred meters, most of it straight up. This was the energy equivalent of a six or seven meter high jump on Earth, which was more than Cunningham could do even without armor. Even if he could have managed the height, it was extremely doubtful that he could aim well enough.

But something had to be done. The ship was moving away—not rapidly, but definitely. Cunningham aimed the spindle and keyed a more precise maneuver signal. He breathed relief as the drift ceased, and the little vessel turned her bow toward him and began to accelerate in his direction. His comfort lasted for several seconds before the independent personality made itself felt again.

"Neem, you *cri*, what are—" The man bit the words off; talk wouldn't help. Thought and action were in order. He had learned during his years of retirement to use these, quickly and effectively, without being distracted by panic. He knew that some day one of his quick ideas or responses would be fatally wrong, but this never bothered him until the emergency was over. It was much more likely that a slow response or none would kill him first.

He used five seconds, deliberately and thoughtfully, in analyzing the ship's motion as well as he could with the unaided eye. It was traveling horizontally by local reference and accelerating toward Tammuz; about half the planet's disc was above the local horizon. The rate of acceleration was, as nearly as he could tell, the same it had been using toward him, so either that part of his original command had not been affected by the trouble or the disturbing influence was not interested in getting the ship to the planet very quickly.

He aimed the spindle again, and sent an emphatic command to accelerate *away* from him, holding the aim while he awaited results. They came within about a second. *Nimepotea* slowed, spun end for end, and headed away from the planet.

Not toward Cunningham at all precisely. Not away from him. It had simply reversed its previous acceleration.

He watched, frowning in concentration, as it passed above him and slightly to one side, about as far as before. Carefully refraining from sending any signals, he waited until it was nearly a kilometer away, now on a line nearly opposite the planet's direction; only then did he send, at the lowest power he thought had a chance of being effective, an additional order for slow acceleration toward the satellite—downward, from his viewpoint. He was not surprised when the order was obeyed; the question in his mind was how long this would continue.

With hull almost on the horizon—he had been a little slow in realizing that he had better keep it in sight, even if his ideas seemed to be working—he cancelled the downward thrust and once more ordered the ship to approach him. It came, this time low above the surface. He was foresighted enough to place himself on the side of its flight path toward the open lock.

At ten meters distance he ordered it to stop.

He was alert enough to make a leap for the open lock when it didn't obey, and coordinated enough to score a near hit at four meters. He did not actually fly into the opening, but struck the hull near it; and it would have been difficult to find any spot on *Nimepotea's* outer surface out of reach of a climbing rung. Cunningham seized one of these, and an instant later was inside the lock. He closed the outer door with the fixed control, not the spindle, opened the inner the instant it was possible, and hurled himself through it and at the control station without bothering to remove any of his armor.

Naturally, he touched nothing for the second or so it took to assemble a mental picture from the various instruments. Neem was accelerating just as before he had arrived. It was not at once obvious whether the fact that this was also toward Tammuz was anyone's doing but his own—with the tendency to go that way once displayed, he had naturally tried to use it to solve his immediate problem of getting back aboard. The direction might have been a coincidence before, or this time, or both, or neither.

He keyed controls briefly, sending his little home away from the satellite and at right angles to the former acceleration at a full gravity for five seconds. Then he went into free fall, watching velocity readings and activating sensors for every kind and frequency of radiation the machine could detect, starting with the bands used by the remote controller.

His test could not last indefinitely; he would have had to drive four or five times as long to reach the satellite's escape velocity, and he certainly did not intend to wait until he struck rock.

He didn't have to. A command signal came in on the appropriate frequency within twenty seconds, and acceleration toward Tammuz resumed. Cunningham thoughtfully removed his helmet, and more slowly the rest of his armor, as the tiny satellite dwindled behind him. The tunnels would have to wait.

The acceleration, as before, was very low; many hours would be needed to reach Tammuz, if that were in fact where the ship was being led. The man had not succeeded in locating at all precisely the direction of the signal before it had accomplished its presumed purpose and shut itself off; the ship had been assigned a fixed direction, not given a homing location—the signals had been precisely the same as those he himself had been using, except for the "align" command he had employed for a moment when he had first been aware of the problem. Did something or someone want the ship? or him? or was it/he/she simply imitating signals he had used, with no idea of their significance? If that were the case, why not use the "align" one? Because it had not been received? That had been sent from the bottom of the rock shaft, aimed nowhere near Tammuz' direction, and any diffraction pattern reaching the planet would have been very weak indeed.

Whatever it was had imitated what amounted to "approach" and "depart" signals. An obvious experiment would be to radiate a "home in on this" pattern, which would have to be kept on and would lead the ship to its source—but would the sender know what it meant? If this were blind parroting, would it keep the signal radiating? The others had been short bursts, simply resetting Neem's directors; why wouldn't this imitation, if it came at all, do the same—or better, how could it be persuaded to keep sending?

Easily, if imitation were the order of the day. Keep sending the "home" pattern from the ship. Cunningham's fingers manipulated keys.

There was no twenty-second delay this time. It was much less than one second—a short enough interval to leave the man wondering how much of it could be reaction time of a living being. Most of it, if the response were actually coming from the planet, had to be light-travel time. Maybe the thing was between him and Tammuz, not on the world itself.

If so, the chances were good that it would be changing direction from him, unless a deliberate attempt to hide were being made. There is a limit to the accuracy with which the direction of centimeter waves can be measured without large-aperture detectors or interferometers, but Cunningham did his best for the next ten minutes. As nearly as he could tell, the source was moving with the surface of Tammuz and was most probably on that surface, somewhere well off center from the man's present viewpoint.

He wondered whether he should speed up. He was certainly curious, and wanted to see what was imitating his signals. He was very dubious about living things on the planet which could be doing it deliberately, though he had encountered life on equally hot and airless worlds; but life takes time to adapt, and for most of its existence this planet had been more or less Earthlike. Its present blistered state, barely outside the atmosphere of a red giant, was a brief and recent part of its history. At the same time, life is rather ubiquitous; its key characteristic, the ability to replicate molecular and energetic patterns, shows up in an incredible variety of chemical machines through a range of temperatures and concentrations which would startle anyone from a pre-star-travel culture.

Even Cunningham considered it more likely that any living creatures at the Tammuz end of the beam were visitors than natives, but he could not guess why Ishtar explorers would be doing it. The situation was a healthy one for curiosity.

If the echo effect were caused by something non-living, however, hurrying might not be so wise. Cunningham had always, so far, managed to get on comfortably with intelligent life forms, at least after long enough and careful enough preparation. More simply natural phenomena tended to be less sympathetic with rational curiosity. He was hoping for intelligent interaction with whatever was going on, but if he had to supply all the intelligence himself then experience suggested that he should learn a good deal more before contact became too intimate.

He compromised by eating before making up his mind. He finished the meal with his cautious personality uppermost, and rather than sending his ship along the beam at higher acceleration he decided to make a few more tests. The reaction time question seemed the most pressing. It also occurred to him that there was no real need to confine test signals to patterns which would control the *Nimepotea;* this could be a nuisance. If the echo-thing would imitate anything else, experiments could be carried out at a less personal and less risky level.

He set his board to transmit fairly simple multibit patterns on the control channel, beaming them toward Tammuz. with a timer set to determine as precisely as electronics permitted the interval between transmission and any return of the same pattern. Results were immediate, and suggested continued caution. The signals came back after, to within a millisecond or so, the round-trip light travel time to the apparent edge of Tammuz' visible disc. If the responder were actually at the center of that disc, it was showing about a fiftieth of a second reaction time—quicker, down to practically zero, if it were anywhere else on the near hemisphere.

Maybe it was somewhere in space between him and the planet after all. A tenth of a second was about the fastest response Cunningham could recall observing in a living being. If it were in space, though, it had to be moving in a way very suggestive of deliberate concealment; it was hard to believe that the apparent match to Tammuz' surface velocity could be accidental or due to anything less complex than intelligence. If it were trying to hide, its intentions were at least suspect. Cunningham was friendly and outgoing, as well as optimistic, by nature; but he had been around much too long to be naive. He did not speed up. He sat, quite relaxed all things considered, at Neem's control console and thought, while Tammuz grew larger on the forward vision screen.

He was still thinking when another copy of one of his earlier signals suddenly arrived, applying acceleration at right angles to the principal one. Instantly alert, the man tried to make sense out of the new vector, which would bring the ship to a point a good deal closer to the north pole of the planet than it had been heading. Before he succeeded, the reverse of the last signal sent it on a path which would cause it to miss Tammuz' limb by several hundred kilometers. He was still trying to work this out without doing anything to the new course itself—there was nothing obviously dangerous about it; if anything, it was safer than before—when the beam his ship was following began to flicker. It weakened, brightened again, then cycled three or four times through a steadily fading pattern which might have been a set of diffraction fringes. Then it went out entirely; and *Nimepotea,* which had followed it mindlessly as long as there was anything to follow, stopped its acceleration toward Tammuz and maintained only the latest sideways thrust it had been given.

Cunningham had long since located by Doppler the rotation plane of the planet below. He had no real doubt about what had happened, and he applied two gravities of normal-space thrust in the direction which would bring him back into view of that part of the planet which had just been carried out of his sight by rotation. Simultaneously, he shut off the remote control receptors; he thought he knew enough to make his next tests much closer to the planet.

What had been a half-moon shape rapidly grew gibbous, and expanded as he drove the little vessel closer. He watched its image as closely as he could as it grew. Tammuz had long since lost atmosphere and ocean, of course, as its sun aged; but it was far from featureless. There were few prominent shadows except very near the terminator, because of the huge angular size of Anu; but there were albedo features—areas ranging from blinding white, since the man's sight had long ago adapted to the local color temperature, through brownish yellows and reds to dark brown and virtually black. What substances were represented he could only guess—except that the white was certainly not snow. Not at Tammuz' temperature. Variations of the silicate pattern which makes up most Terrestrial worlds, most likely, since Tammuz had once been a Terrestrial planet.

Nothing offered the slightest clue, to his eyes, as to the whereabouts of the radiation source. Nothing suggested, even remotely, anything artificial. No works of intelligence could be expected to have survived a billion years even of ordinary planetary environment, of course, far less what must have happened while Anu was turning up his output nearly three hundred times. It would be fun to try to work out in detail what had gone on as atmosphere and oceans were stripped away, tectonic forces readjusted to the changed restraints on the crust, and rising temperature altered the rocks themselves; but that would have to be faced later. Any normal person could get years of recreation out of Tammuz. Some of the Ishtar colonists already had, and Cunningham expected to; but the planet would wait. This radiation problem might not.

A radar scan showed no sign of metal, but did bring response in the form of a similarly patterned beam of much lower power. The imitator was still at work. Cunningham located the source as precisely as he could in terms of the visual images. From his present distance, the uncertainty was ten kilometers or so. A survey specialist ship would have been able to locate it within a meter; retirement-hobby craft didn't carry such equipment unless the hobbyist made it, and Cunningham's interest lay more in the direction of personal communication with nonhuman intelligences.

What he did manage was a set of good photographic images, the equivalent of a map for practical purposes, for ten kilometers or so around the most probable location of the emission. He could have done better from a lower altitude, and if he had been sure that this was a matter of communication he would have; but he was still inclined to suspect that some natural, and hence basically unsympathetic, phenomenon was behind the whole affair. He remained cautious.

There is, of course, a perfectly good technique for determining whether a response to a question is a simple echo or not. Cunningham knew it perfectly well—he had even used it more than once—and was extremely annoyed with himself afterward for not thinking of it at the very beginning. He had, he decided, attached too much weight to the reaction time.

He was just finishing the picture mosaic when it occurred to him, and with an exclamation of irritation he snapped off the viewing projector and took the few steps which brought him back to the controls—nothing inside *Nimepotea* was more than a few steps from anything else; the ship was no place for a claustrophobe, especially after Cunningham had been exploring and collecting for a few years without visiting home.

He turned the radar beam back on, aiming it at the area which had now become quite familiar to him from the photographic work, and waited briefly for the response.

And waited longer for the response.

And longer still.

There was no echo, other than normal radar ones. For a moment the man was even more annoyed; then he brightened. Maybe this was intelligence, and they were tossing him the ball—expecting something new. He was rational, more or less, but human.

He turned the beam off. Then he turned it on once, briefly, and once again. He waited a few seconds, then turned it on twice, paused briefly, and four times. Another wait, three flashes, then nine.

Then he waited.

Nothing happened. X was asleep, or out to lunch, or had lost interest in playing with strange signals, or couldn't see in this direction—

The last idea could conceivably be checked. Cunningham reached for the photomosaic, then firmed his lips and turned back to the control console. Risks or no risks—and he didn't really believe there were any—the time had come for a close, personal look at that area. *Nimepotea* plunged downward, and within minutes was hanging a kilometer above the center of what seemed to be the important section of Tammuz' landscape while its pilot's fingers played over direction and field controls of the view screen and his eyes rapidly scanned the screen itself. Almost by reflex he oriented his image with respect to the planet's rotation axis; being able to apply terms like "north" and "east" helped the memory a lot.

The eastern edge of the imaginary square which seemed so important was cut by the rim of a ten-kilometer impact crater which had clearly formed later than most of the rest of the landscape. Its nearly perfect circle was unaffected by hills, plateaus, and an ancient graben which postdated the first two. The plateaus were the most significant features; except for one detail they resembled the mesas of the North American southwest, and covered fully half the local landscape.

The exception was their edges, which were angle-of-repose slopes rather than steep cliffs. The rock was light-colored, as close to white as anything Cunningham had seen on Tammuz even from a distance which permitted a view of most of a hemisphere. It might conceivably be limestone, and the area represent the erosion remnant of a region of horizontal sediment—except, of course, for graben and crater.

The question was whether any caves or overhangs, which could easily have formed in such country during the early stages of weathering as they had on Earth, would still be present when the destruction had reached a general stage of sand slope. This was especially true since the weathering had presumably occurred while Tammuz still had an atmosphere, while the nearby impact feature might not have—and its arrival would probably have shaken down anything with room underneath for a hundred kilometers around. He could look for holes, or he could fly a search grid over the area while broadcasting signals and listening for possible response from X.

He was going, of course, to have to get out and do some foot exploring sooner or later, and one part of his feeling suggested that it might as well be sooner; but native caution had not faded out completely. If nothing else, he should certainly not step outside until he had a good map of the general area firmly in his head.

He could memorize the map while flying the search, so he started the latter. He dropped the ship to five hundred meters above the general plateau tops, which in turn was about seven hundred above the level ground separating the mesas and perhaps a thousand above the bottom of the crater. Starting at the northwest corner of the key area, he headed east at a low speed, about fifty meters a second; he wanted to give himself time for a good look at everything. At the eastern edge of the area, north of the crater, he turned south for two hundred meters and then made the westward cast of his grid. Patiently, back and forth, keenly watching for any detail which might suggest the presence of X, with the ship automatically broadcasting the sequence he had set up earlier and which any intelligent being should reasonably answer with "four-sixteen." Presumably.

The three-hour flight produced no response to the signals, but left Cunningham ready to spend time out on the planet's surface if he could only find something worth checking closely. Nothing seemed to offer the slightest danger to a reasonably equipped explorer. Landslides could no longer occur, since all slopes seemed to have reached angle of repose in the mesa area. It was furiously hot, naturally, but his armor could handle that. There was no air, unless a few hundred molecules of carbon dioxide per liter deserved the name, but again that was what space armor was for.

After sleeping, he would go outside and get mineral samples; the makeup of the local rocks should be checked, if only to confirm the guess about their silicate nature—or, in this area, limestone, he reminded himself. Maybe there would be fragments large enough to show fossils, though none of the Ishtar colonists who had visited Tammuz had found any so far.

After a moment's thought, he grounded the little ship in a valley between two of the mesas, where there would be some shade when Anu sank lower in the sky; there was no point in making Neem's refrigerators work harder than they had to. Gravity was not merely adequate but really comfortable, and after setting his controls to arouse him if X did any broadcasting, he was able to sleep long and deeply.

When he woke up, Anu had set. The brightest object in the sky was the red dwarf of the system, Ea, which was at a distance which made it totally inadequate as a sun though uncomfortably bright as a star. Cunningham considered going out to get his samples by artificial light, but decided against it. He could spend plenty of time thinking; there was certainly enough he did not at the moment understand. He *should* spend more time thinking. He suddenly realized that he was almost taking for granted that X was intelligent. While this was certainly possible, it was also a little too close to the demon hypothesis for comfort; normally educated human beings usually had a strong tendency to hunt for natural explanations for anything they didn't understand. It was probably backlash from the heavily mystical stage the species had gone through a few centuries before, Cunningham suspected; but he had the conditioning, and felt the need to come up with some explanation for what had been happening which did not include conscious intent of persons unknown.

Hours of thought, punctuated by minutes of eating and other hours of sleep, failed to produce any before Anu rose and provided daylight.

Even with no atmosphere, scattering of light from the upper valley walls made the ground quite bright enough for comfort as soon as the sun was up. Ea could still be seen, though it was not far from setting; no other celestial objects, stars or planets, showed against the glare of the sunlit rock.

Cunningham donned and checked his armor with the care that befitted his age—or at least, befitted the fact that he had reached his present age. Without bothering to move the ship from the middle of the valley, he emerged from the air lock and walked toward the mesa slope half a kilometer away.

The rock under his feet was plainly sedimentary, fine-grained stuff; shale, presumably. It could have contained fossils, though the surface was hardly a likely place for them to show—one topographic feature conspicuously lacking was stream cuts. If anything, the rock seemed to have been polished by dust or sand. Since this would have had to be blown by wind, it could hardly have taken place recently; there should be meteoritic gardening in the ages since the air had gone. The man kept alert for signs of this, but saw none before reaching the foot of the valley slope. He had walked across nothing but incredibly smooth rock, with no evidence that anything had happened to it since Tammuz' atmosphere had vanished.

He could not, of course, expect to see any microscopic craters which might have been left by dust-grain impacts, and a few meters from the foot of the wall he cut a section out of the rock with his sampling beam, to take back to the ship for more detailed examination.

The sloping side of the valley was not merely sand or soil; it was finest dust. As he had judged, it was at its angle of repose and was utterly impossible to climb; Cunningham made a cautious attempt, but the powdery, utterly dry stuff slid under him without offering the slightest support. He did not try too hard. The material was ferociously hot as well as fine and dry; if he were to get buried in it so that his heat pump could not radiate, he could expect to cook in less than a minute. Just being on a planet, with half the potential radiant heat sink of the universe blocked, instead of in relatively empty space made things difficult enough for the equipment. If he did find a cave or overhang, he would have to be extremely careful exploring, or even approaching, it by daylight.

There seemed to be nothing to do but collect some of the dust for analysis, and either return to *Nimepotea* or bring the ship to him. He hesitated briefly at the latter thought. Then he remembered that X had already displayed its ability to send out control signals to the ship without merely copying his own, and that he had unthinkingly turned on the remote control receivers when he picked up the spindle before leaving the vessel. Neem had been vulnerable to abduction for the last fifteen minutes, whether he used his own control or not. He muttered several self-derogatory remarks in German and Finnish—he had spent several years on Neu Schwarzwald before his time on Omituinen. He was not particularly bothered about the existence of the risk, but very annoyed at himself for not recognizing it sooner.

He wondered later whether the irritation was what caused him to elevate the ship higher than was strictly necessary merely to bring it the few hundred meters across the flat valley floor to a point beside him. Neither cameras nor any other kind of recorder was running; improving the chance of intercepting any of X's output would do Cunningham no good, since he wouldn't be there to see or hear it. Nevertheless, he sent *Nimepotea* almost up to plateau level before starting it toward his position.

He comforted himself later with the recollection that he did keep a close eye on the little craft as she moved, so he was able to say with some certainty that the foreign signal did not reach it until it was over a hundred meters above the ground. Then it must have been overpowering; Neem made not the slightest motion toward Cunningham's position. but headed northeast along the valley on a long slant which he could see would bring it into collision with one of the slopes if the course were not changed.

He aimed the spindle and ordered the ship to come in his direction, using the highest power the controller could send. He thought he saw a slight hesitation in its motion, but wasn't sure; it kept on toward the valley slope kilometers away. He shifted to a homing command and held the guide beam aimed as steadily as he could. Homing was supposed to override specific maneuver programming, but this one had no effect. It was as though *Nimepotea* were already homing on a stronger beam, which Cunningham decided was likely enough.

If that were true, he was being given some indication of the location of X, at least; Neem must be flying straight toward it. On the plateau? Under it? Beyond it? Would X try to fly the ship through the ground?

Not very far, certainly, since the control waves would penetrate only a short distance—just how far would depend on the nature of the material, but two meters seemed a generous maximum, especially if Neem were receiving a guide beam strong enough to override Cunningham's own.

Keeping his eyes almost continuously on the ship, the man began to trudge along the hot rock after it. Would it disappear over the top of the mesa, or was it a little below that height? He could not be sure. It would be two or three minutes at its present speed before the matter was settled, and by then it would be pretty far away—not too far to see if it plowed into the dust, but too far to see how much damage resulted. In theory there should be none, of course; automatic controls would override the remotes if the hull met really firm resistance, but Cunningham would have been much happier to be at the console himself to take care of such matters.

He stopped when the ship did the same. It was below the hilltop—not very far below, perhaps eight or ten meters for the long axis of its ovoid hull. Unhesitatingly, though without much hope, he again beamed a homing signal at it. It moved at the same instant, as nearly as he could tell, but not toward him. First it shifted out from the slope for perhaps twenty meters; then it moved straight down until it touched the ground again, perhaps sinking in a short distance—this seemed likely under the circumstances, but the man could not tell at this range. Then it moved out again, and down again, repeating the process to outline a set of steps all the way down the slope until it was within a few meters of the level rock of the valley floor.

Cunningham could see that the hull must have penetrated the loose stuff at least a short distance, since the ground itself was moving downhill—not very much, just enough to fill the fresh dents made by *Nimepotea*, since the powdery stuff had already been at its angle of repose at least since the nearby crater had formed and probably for millions of years or so before that. He barely noted the motion; he was running as fast as he thought he could keep up in a space suit toward the point where his ship hung, possibly within reach. He did not send any more control signals; if Neem were going to stay put, he was glad to settle for that. The spindle was in his hand as he ran, however.

Twenty-five minutes of slogging over rock hot enough to melt lead could have been painful, but his suit refrigerators held up. He was not really worried about them; almost his entire attention was on the hull which he was approaching with such painful slowness, not sure when or whether Neem on its own, or X, would decide to put it somewhere else. In spite of his relative success in predicting some of the things X had done, he felt no real confidence in his analysis of that character—or even any real certainty that it was a character. If it were, its motivation had to be curiosity—it was trying to find out things about the control impulses. What it could observe of the results of its experiments could only be guessed, so far; perhaps the recent maneuver implied that it couldn't see the ship and sensed, or detected somehow, only the microwave output *Nimepotea* used for the control feedback. If the homing system had been in use just now, that would account for its allowing the ship to fly into the valley wall; now it might be trying to figure out why Neem had ceased to obey orders.

Maybe.

And maybe it would start another test at any moment. Cunningham, sweat soaking his clothing far beyond the environment armor's ability to handle, drove himself even harder at the thought. There was plenty of light—Anu's monstrous disc was almost entirely in sight now above the eastern valley wall—but there was no way to wipe sweat out of his eyes, and seeing was getting difficult.

Half a kilometer to go. Three hundred meters. One hundred. Twenty. On the little satellite, he could have made the remaining distance in a single leap, but on Tammuz his weight was fairly normal.

Now he was standing under the ship, the open air lock ten meters out of reach, the lowest climbing rung five. It was not straight above him, but a little way over the slope of glaring white dust which formed the valley wall. His mind knew what would happen, but his feelings made him try anyway; he started up the slope, slowly and cautiously.

No good. The stuff slipped under his weight and carried him back to the floor of the valley, and more slid silently down from above to replace what he had shifted.

He tried running at the hill and almost made it; if the substrate had been just a little firmer he would have, bur as it was he lost his footing, rolled back to the bottom, and had to scramble briskly to keep his radiator from being blocked by the miniature avalanche which tried to bury his momentarily prone form.

There was no choice he could see except to risk using the controller. He stood on solid ground, as close to the hull as he could get—any of the climbing grips would do as long as he could reach it; getting to the air lock itself was secondary. He braced himself to move quickly, pointed the spindle, and keyed the command to move in his direction without altering the ship's own heading.

Neem obeyed instantly, and his hand closed on a rung within a second. With his whole attention on climbing, he made his way as rapidly as he could around the curved surface to the lock, entered, and closed the outer door. The moment the inner one opened, he wrenched off his helmet and leaped to the console. Only then did he realize that the ship was still where he had ordered it to go. Nothing had countermanded or supplemented his order.

"Anticlimax!" he muttered. "Does this thing have a sense of humor as well as a mind?"

He was moving as he spoke, and wasted no time trying to produce an answer to the rhetorical question. By the time the words were off his lips, the ship was at the top of the hill, hanging beside the point where it had first made contact. This could still be recognized, though the loose dust had nearly finished filling the depression. Cunningham examined the spot as minutely as he could from inside the vessel, but could see nothing except the white stuff. Then, aligning the ship in the direction it had been moving when it had struck the slope, he rose a little higher and moved slowly across the top of the mesa along the same line. It was harder to be sure of all the details here, as the ground was far rougher than the valley below; but nowhere along the kilometer or so before the next valley did he see anything which suggested a living form, a machine, or anything else not easily explained by Tammuz' probable evolution. It was all topography.

The next move seemed obvious: toss the ball to X again. Maybe it(?) could only detect microwave radio—all right, use microwave. He returned to a point just above where the ship had struck the hillside, and tried his intelligence-testing broadcast again. It would do until he thought of something better.

It did, but the response was not the four-sixteen he had rather hoped for. *Nimepotea* began to move again, and the man watched his instruments as varying sets of control-band impulses came in. This time an orderly variation scheme seemed to be the order, as though X could now tell much better than before just what results his(?) efforts were having.

Some patterns, of course, produced no results; some drove the ship in various directions at various accelerations, but none of these ever continued for long—few for more than a tenth of a second or so. Cunningham kept his hands ready at the console to cut off the remote control sensors and do anything else necessary if X brought the ship into danger, but for nearly a minute the most worrisome event was the opening of the outer lock. It closed again almost at once.

The man was happy. There seemed no more doubt about it; X was a conscious intelligence, following a rational plan of investigation. Communication should follow as a matter of routine. Physical contact, or at least a face-to-face encounter, would be helpful, in Cunningham's opinion; it would be interesting to find out whether X felt the same way. The man was willing to wait and let her(?) run through her(?) repertoire of tests before trying anything more of his own; X's activities were also informative.

They became even more so. The practically random motions had brought the vessel some distance higher than when Cunningham had started his test broadcast; now, suddenly—though it was a second or two before the man realized it was happening—the control pulses stopped coming and Neem continued on the last set of instructions she had received.

This was carrying them almost straight down—and exactly toward the spot where the ship had struck the hill the other time.

A split second's glance at the instruments showed that this was again a homing command; he had a second line on X's location.

He waited as long as he dared, and was about to cut off the control sensor when X killed the homing beam him(?)self. Cunningham promptly set his vision equipment to its best resolution and examined the slope with all the care he could.

The earlier impact mark of the hull was by now almost invisible. Nothing but white dust showed anywhere in the neighborhood or for meters around it in any direction. X must be inside the hill, but not very far inside if the lines indicated by its(?) homing beams meant anything.

Presumably the entity did not mind a little disturbance of the surface, in view of earlier events. The man lowered his ship ten or fifteen meters and deliberately drove it into the hillside, keeping a close eye on the amount of thrust needed, and with the hull half buried in the yielding stuff he drove it horizontally to dig a much larger gouge out of the slope. Then he backed off a few meters and watched while the material above subsided into his cut,

The edge of the subsidence area climbed up and away from him fairly rapidly, like the material in a freshly inverted sand picture. For half a minute or so he saw nothing but the light-colored dust; then a small object, apparently black but possibly merely darker than its surroundings, was revealed less than half a meter below the top of the retreating cliff of loose stuff. Before the man could get a good look, its support gave way and it fell out of the field of his screen; but at the same instant another control impulse came in, and *Nimepotea* jerked downward.

Twice in the next two minutes the man was tempted to cut off the remote control receiver, but each time restrained himself. The ship was being expertly handled, doing exactly what he himself had done shortly before—scooping out grooves and gouges in the hillside to cause local collapse. Several times during the process the black object was briefly visible, each time as it was falling to a lower level; by the end of the two minutes the ship was just above the valley floor and the object buried very little higher, though its exact location would have to be ascertained by something rather smaller than the ship's hull.

X seemed to realize this; *Nimepotea* stopped and hung just above the ground.

Cunningham, while naturally cautious, was in no way paranoid. The notion that it might be inadvisable to find the object and even riskier to bring it aboard never crossed his mind, now that he was sure that intelligence was involved. He was out of the air lock with a primitive piece of equipment—a shovel—in a very few seconds, and the only concession he made to caution was motivated by the obvious natural danger. He connected himself to one of the climbing rungs with a strong safety line, in case he got buried and had to have the ship pull him out.

This nearly happened twice, but each time quick motion kept him safe. The second collapse of the dust revealed the black object, which fell almost at his feet. He picked it up, brushed as much dust off it as he could with his armor glove, and was back inside in moments.

The thing was presumably some kind of communication relay; it was far too small to contain an intelligent creature, as Cunningham's experience went. Its shape suggested a cylinder whose ends had been capped by hemispheres of the same radius, and the whole thing split in halves lengthwise and one of the halves thrown away. The overall length was twelve or fifteen centimeters, the diameter between four and five. It was shiny black in color, with occasional rather less reflective spots scattered sparsely over its curved surfaces. Its density was greater than that of water, as judged by feel, but not many times greater—perhaps about that of aluminum, Cunningham judged. All these figures could be established more precisely later.

At this the man suddenly realized he had not analyzed the rock and dust specimens he had obtained earlier, and had not been observing good lab practice; the specimen was quite dusty, and he had been handling it. He was perturbed only by the evidence that he was growing careless and the obvious fact that he could expect to be killed eventually by this trend if it continued. It did not occur to him consciously that eventually could include the immediate future.

Strictly speaking, he reminded himself, he should not even have exposed his new specimen to the ship's air without learning more about its makeup; oxygen is a highly corrosive element which might have destroyed valuable information, and some substances are both volatile and deadly. This could hardly be the former, of course, since it had been baked in a near-vacuum for a long, long time and was still in existence; but that left wide open quite a few possibilities about its possible reaction products with oxygen.

Of course, anything likely to happen to it from oxygen exposure would presumably already have occurred—but Cunningham had heard that sort of excluded-middle argument used too many times as an excuse for apathy or a counter to a charge of serious error. It might be just as well to keep the thing away from air now for a while, and see whether the brief exposure had done anything serious—to it or to the air or to Cunningham himself. The scanning chamber of the particle microscope, now—that would be evacuated while running, and he could get some information about the finer details while he was waiting—

Twenty seconds later the black split-cylinder was in the two-liter chamber and the latter was evacuating, while Cunningham rather sheepishly flushed the ship's air. A careful examination of every pertinent instrument had failed to indicate anything in the way of chemical or radiation danger, but he played safe anyway; and with his mind more at ease, he turned to the scanner and set *Nimepotea's* data handler to running a study of the specimen in every available frequency of the electromagnetic and particle spectra, with an overriding command to stop if any of the radiation seemed to be causing measurable change in the thing's structure. He started with soft energies to minimize that risk.

While this was running, he took his dust and rock samples and ran them through more restricted tests. The rock was a conventional basaltic mixture of silicates, in no way surprising except that he had judged it to be sedimentary. The dust which formed the valley walls, which he had rather expected to be limestone weathered in some fashion, might have been just that a billion years ago, but was now fairly pure calcium oxide. Cunningham whistled gently and made sure once more that none of the stuff was on his hands, glad that he had used a buffered cleaning gel instead of water to achieve that end earlier. The reason for the quicklime, as well as for the fact that what traces of atmosphere Tammuz still held consisted mostly of carbon dioxide, was obvious enough in hindsight—another result of the planet's roasting as Anu had swelled and brightened. There, no doubt, went any chance of finding fossils in limestone; maybe there was still hope if he could find some shale.

And that was the last time Laird Cunningham thought of fossils for several days.

"Is it more effective to analyze or ask?"

The words were perfectly clear, but they represented a hodgepodge of English, Finnish, and German vocabularies and grammars so that the question was much less so. Also, he could not, for a moment, tell where the voice came from.

"What do you mean?" was the only response he could give.

"You are analyzing. Is this being done for the instrument's sake or would your purpose be better met by being told about me?" This time the words were mostly English.

He got a direction on the sound this time, and moved toward the source, not that he believed it.

"What do you think I'm analyzing, and who can tell me the answers?"

"I am the answer to both questions." There was no doubt about the origin of the sound, this time. It was the communicator in his own helmet, racked near the control console.

"I am analyzing you? Then you are the specimen I put in the scanner a couple of minutes ago?"

"Yes."

"Why didn't you warn me if it bothers you?"

"It doesn't, and I couldn't. Until your code-storing device began to send investigative impulses and record their responses, I had no way to message—communicate. It was necessary to work out the codes and their underlying system, and then transmit impulses which caused your device to send more of its stored material to me. Its signal rate is low, and I have not received very much so far; but I have grasped a general picture of recent events." There were occasional hesitations between words. The voice was rather high pitched, though not impressively childish or even feminine.

"It was you who were copying my ship's control impulses?"

"I judge yes, though I am not perfectly clear on all the symbols you just used. Each new code pattern has to be tested against numerous possibilities and the greatest likelihood selected. Fortunately, you seem to have a slow response time, like those I supplemented before, and my analysis contributes no serious delay to communication."

"Have you really been buried in that hillside for a long time?"

"I can infer only vaguely what you mean by the 'long' symbol, but when I was buried there the environment was solid grains separated by liquid water at the bottom of a large body of fairly pure water."

"You claim you were buried in mud in an ocean bottom? Why and when?"

"Yes. I was dropped inadvertently by my user from a device which carried that being at the upper surface of the water, and gravity took me to and a short distance through the next interface. I have no way to tell when; at the moment I have no data on the interval, and very little information on your time symbols and their relation to mine."

"Will it harm you—will the atmosphere in my ship, or anything else you are aware of here—harm you if remove you from that scanning chamber? Do you want me to take you out?"

"Your gas mixture will not affect me." The words had been straight English for some sentences now. "I would be interested in emerging so that I can see more of you and your craft, though I recorded most of the details earlier. However, at the moment my most convenient communication channels are through the scanning circuits of this instrument, and it might take a" (there was a barely detectable pause) "second to set up others; I have not really identified in detail everything I saw before, and am not quite certain what is available which I could use."

"Right now you have persuaded my ship's computer to activate a regular broadcaster on the frequency used by my space suit. You are able to radiate in that part of the spectrum yourself—or did you have other equipment buried with you?"

"I can radiate myself, given enough energy."

"What form of energy?"

"Thermal or electrical potential difference between any two parts of my structure will provide me. Thermal is all I have had for some time, and that has been rather intermittent. I was quite inoperative most of the time I was buried, until recently. Something brought me close enough to the surface so that heating and cooling of the material around me, by day and night, let me think much of the time."

Cunningham fell silent. Nothing that had happened in the last few minutes had strained his ability to believe, given that the thing in the scanning tank was a machine. *Nimepotea* contained much equipment of generally similar nature. It would be a little hard to expect any of that to survive—no, to withstand would be a better word—withstand being buried in ocean sediment and fossilized—well, not that; the machine's own structure seemed unaffected. The sediment had consolidated into limestone and encased it for perhaps a billion years still in operational condition; but with no moving parts other than electrons or other charge units, and protected from erosion, such an event was credible in principle. It was not exactly everyday; one would of course keep alert for other possible interpretations.

Learning an appropriate communication symbol set from Neem's computer—two, really; one for the computer and another, much higher-level one that it was now using with Cunningham himself—in less than a minute implied vast storage and extremely high function speed, but there was nothing intrinsically inconsistent about that with the rules as Cunningham understood them. It was simply a very high-class artificial intelligence.

And it was therefore the most useful imaginable archaeological specimen Tammuz had ever furnished, or was ever likely to, unless more examples of the same device might be buried here and there on the world. It could tell in detail what Tammuz had been like when its sun was still a main sequence star; it could describe the appearance and physiology and culture of the natives who must have explored the rest of the system—or, come to think of it, maybe not. The thing had been dropped from a surface vessel, possibly before its makers had mastered space travel. There were things—a billion years' worth of things—which it couldn't possibly know. Still, archaeologists usually have to work by extrapolation backward from their own times; interpolating to fill a bounded gap, even a billion-year one, should be easier, Cunningham assured himself.

"I will want to know as much as you can tell me about this world in the time before you were buried."

"Of course. Your storage device lacks sufficient capacity for the information I can supply; is more available in similar devices, or will I have to rely on this form of communication and transfer to your brain? I judge you to be generally similar in basic structure to the beings who built me. What is your information capacity? Or more important, what is your likely operation span in seconds? Unless it is considerably greater than theirs, I will not be able to transfer a significant fraction to you by this method before you require replacement."

Cunningham raised his eyebrows.

"I should be good for another ten to the ninth seconds or so, but will have to spend a good deal of that time in other activities. There is no significant additional memory available on the ship. There are people and computers on one of the planets of the other sun, and a shipload probably somewhere on this planet. We can reach either quickly enough, but I'd like to examine a few more things while I'm here on Tammuz."

"Wouldn't that restrict your rate of information intake?"

"In quantity, I suppose it would. I'm a bit choosy, though. At my age I can't just collect trivia. The universe is a picture, and unless the new things I learn fit into that picture reasonably well I have trouble grasping, remembering, or sometimes even believing them."

"The code *believe* lacks adequate referent for me in your storage device, even by inference from context. Your use of the 'picture' symbol is extremely interesting."

Cunningham was silent for a moment.

"How about the word—the code—*error?*"

"I grasp that. Information inadequately coded, which requires correction."

"That'll do. I *believe* a sample of information when it seems unlikely that correction will be required."

"What are your criteria?"

"Unfortunately, I depend rather heavily on consistency with the picture I have already formulated. I am aware of the logical weakness involved in this, and when possible compare items of what should be the same information from various sources..."

An hour later, deeply mired in philosophy which he had not consciously considered for three quarters of his life, Cunningham broke off the discussion, pleading a need for food and sleep. The specimen conceded the points, stating that its makers had had similar physical necessities. It closed the conversation, however, with a question which prevented the man from sleeping as quickly as he had expected.

"Is there no more information available on your ship than I have been able to decode from your storage machine? If not, I would appreciate your removing me from this place while you attend to your needs, and locating me where I can perceive my surroundings. If I can control your ship's exterior viewing equipment and examine the planet near us, that would be even better. The sun, if it is really the sun, has changed greatly; I would like to know more of the details. I could see practically nothing while I was buried. You have suggested a technique for combining information units in such a way that I might develop a believable estimate of the length of time I was buried. Your storage contained information about stars which I did not possess."

Cunningham obliged; there was remote-control capability to the screens, handled by the same microwave signals used to manipulate the ship, and it took the thing only an instant to learn the codes.

But the man watched from his bunk for some time as it observed, wondering and, as much as his personality allowed, worrying. Could a machine be *curious?* It was interesting to learn that it could "see" by essentially the same wave lengths his own eyes used, though there was no feature on it which remotely resembled an optical organ. Maybe he'd better ask about it first, rather than about ancient Tammuz. It seemed to know, so presumably its makers had known, that "the sun" was a star. At least, it had used the codes—the words—interchangeably. On the other hand. that might be recent knowledge from *Nimepotea's* own information store. There was no way to be sure, except by asking it.

And what could it mean by having learned an "information-combining" technique from him?

Of course, the man realized, if its capacity were great enough, it might have been programmed to store information indiscriminately. Its filing and retrieval systems must be interesting in that case; but that would explain its "desire" to learn whenever an opportunity presented itself.

Adequate working hypothesis, for the moment, for the first point. The second question remained wide open, though, and he wasn't sure he liked the possibilities. Cunningham felt suddenly unsure whether he was dealing with intelligence or not. He did finally fall asleep, and as usual failed to remember his dreams.

He awoke with the blood pounding in his ears and his chest heaving to rapid, heavy breathing. Normally he liked to consider himself immune to panic, but for two or three seconds he was quite unable to control the surge of fear which all but swamped his returning consciousness. Since gravity was practically normal, he had not strapped himself into his bunk; he was on his feet and had made a step toward the control console before he regained any sort of self-mastery. Even then it was one of the old spaceman's litanies, which he heard himself chanting and had to listen through twice before it carried any meaning, which brought him back.

"You're breathing air! You haven't died! Go over what you should have tried! You're breathing air, you haven't died—"

Speaking aloud slowed his breathing, which was all that was really needed. The indicators above his console didn't have to be read separately; they formed a face whose expressions, friendly and otherwise, he knew perfectly from years of intimacy. The face said there was too much carbon dioxide in Neem's air, and his slowly recovering common sense agreed. His fingers, without conscious direction, played on the appropriate keys, and within a few seconds the indicators relaxed their unfriendly expression. His own body was a little slower responding, but two minutes after he had awakened only his still somewhat overspeeding heart and a burning curiosity were left as direct results of the incident.

There seemed a likely way to satisfy the curiosity. The specimen was lying where he had left it balanced on the headrest of his conning seat; he picked it up, sat down, and spoke aloud. He was not sure whether the thing would detect sound, but it might have set up other connections through the wealth of communication equipment—everything was tied in more or less closely with the data handler.

"Have you been watching only outside the ship, or things inside as well?"

"I have been aware of both sets. There has been little changing outside except the direction of the sun. There is an uncertainty whether the difference in that rate is real, or represents a change in my internal time reference. I do not know which to believe. There is evidence that I have undergone some change."

"What would cause that?"

"Most probably, though not actually a belief, particle radiation damage to my crystal structure. It is as stable a one as my makers believed possible to construct—essentially, diamond with structural modifications to provide mobile charge sites. I also have methods of duplicating data storage and detecting errors and inconsistencies. Still, natural radiation which you code "cosmic rays" would, when I was not powered, cause damage of which I would not be specifically aware."

Cunningham returned to his own point of interest.

"Were you aware of gas mixture changes in this ship?"

"Yes. I noticed that controls existed for managing that composition, and that your own structure's operation had an influence on the mixture. I modified the controls to a small extent to check what sort of feedback might exist."

For a brief moment Cunningham thought of cutting off all remote control receivers; then he realized that this would probably block communication. Whether he wanted more to learn or to express himself he was not quite certain, but he definitely did not want to lose touch. Emotional language would probably be wasted on the little machine, he admitted to himself as he began to cool down again. He confined himself to, "I require expert technical help to get restarted if my major operations are stopped, and no such help is available. If the stoppage continues more than a few hundred seconds, restart becomes impossible because of chemical changes, except under very unusual conditions. I strongly advise against your experimenting with my personal systems; if you need knowledge in that field, wait until we get in touch with others who can provide it." He took several long breaths, and decided that he was not going to explode this time. The specimen seemed well enough at home now in English to get his main point; at least, it did not ask him what code was represented by the closing sounds.

"Then the gas mixture's composition is essential to your normal operation. I will not manipulate those controls again. Can you provide data which would resolve my earlier time-rate question?"

"Possibly. It is likely that the planet's rotation has actually been slowed by tidal drag since your earlier activity. Its moons don't go for much, but the sun would be reasonably effective."

"Can you be quantitative?"

"No, for two reasons. First, I'm not expert in the field, and second, the effect would vary greatly over long periods of time as continent and ocean patterns changed—I do know that much. We can find people who know a lot more than I, but even they won't be able to give you a full answer—though what you can probably tell them will no doubt improve their picture. We'll go over to Ishtar and find some of them after a while—they'll be interested in you, too. I'd like some more information from you about Tammuz; while we're still here, though, if you can bear to wait."

"For a time."

Cunningham completely missed the implications of that answer; he was too interested in his own questions.

"Did you ever try an experiment like the one you just did on me with the system of one of your makers?"

"No."

"Did their systems work at all like mine? Or don't you know?" The last question was added as a new thought struck the man. For the first time since real communication had been going on, there was noticeable hesitation before an answer came.

"There does seem to have been a great deal of similarity. The fact had not come to my consciousness until you asked."

"The curiosity which seems to be your strongest drive did not apply to them, then?"

"No."

"Why not?" There was no answer.

"Why were you so long in answering my question about their physical nature?"

"I had to do a complete memory scan before I was able to believe."

Cunningham thought silently for several seconds. He wished he knew enough to ask meaningful questions about the machine's operation; he had only the usual adult familiarity with such equipment. Evidently it had really huge storage capacity, as he had guessed earlier. Never mind; there are people who can get that material out of it. He'd better stick to the ancient Tammuz.

An hour later he was in position to write a major thesis on the planet's earlier civilization. He knew the physical shape of the natives, the fact that they were water and oxygen users, and that, unfortunately, his informant had been dropped overboard before they had mastered space travel. This seemed a little surprising, since technological advancement is heavily interlocked in all its possible fields; the molecular engineering needed to produce a device like the one he had found should have been preceded by decades and possibly centuries by the capacity to build high-performance rockets. Cunningham forgot for the moment that cultures sometimes collapse back to pre-technical levels, and their successors have their development modified by such things as a lack of metals or fossil fuels which the earlier people used up.

If anything like this had happened prior to his informant's earlier time, nothing was said about it; whether the device didn't know or was confining itself to the specific points raised by Cunningham was a question which did not occur to the man.

What began to interest him was a growing awareness that he was not doing all the asking. The little machine was managing to get more and more questions of its own into the conversation. The fact that the man's answer, more often than not, had to be "I don't know," did nothing to change its tactics. He came to realize, by the time he was honestly hungry again, that while he himself had learned a huge amount about the eon-dead inhabitants of Tammuz, the machine now had bits—small bits, but significant— of information about the present state of the planetary system; the human colony on Ishtar; the vastness of the galaxy and the incredible number of inhabited worlds, neither of which it had known about before; Cunningham's own life style, and the nature of the *Nimepotea;* and quite a few details of the man's earlier life. The thing seemed to have an insatiable hunger for information; it showed what kept resembling more and more closely genuine, emotional curiosity. He wondered what its storage capacity might be.

As he ate, he continued the conversation. He had not yet seen anything to worry about; but it was as he ate that he made his major mistake. He was able to see what it was, clearly enough, afterward; he had simply not paid enough attention to the machine's answers, and lack of answers, about its makers, and this had led to a perfectly natural conversational slip. The hardest part to believe, afterward, was that the word "life" had not come up in the conversation at any earlier point; but as he reviewed his own memory, he could find no question or answer where it had.

It did now.

"I was hoping, Beedee, that you'd be able to suggest some place on Tammuz where I'd have a chance to find some other specimens; but I guess you'll be enough, actually. We should head for Ishtar after I finish eating. You'll be able to get a lot of answers there that I couldn't supply."

"I missed a symbol. What is the implication of 'Beedee'? It does not make a reasonable part of your code pattern."

"Just a personal name, from your makeup—B. D. in another of our code sets, abbreviating 'Black Diamond'."

"I grasp the meaning of 'personal name' from material I obtained from your ship's data handler, but do not understand why it applies. There is only one of each of us; further subclassification is not needed."

"There are lots more of my kind, and other communicating beings. We'll be seeing them soon."

"But not of my kind, and the need is still not evident."

"To you, anyway."

"Of course. I do not believe it is a need for you, either. You will know what you mean when you are addressing me, or referring to me to others."

"What would you expect me to call you when I'm talking to others?"

"The Tammuz find—the ancient machine—the Tammuz data source—even with your low search and coding speed, you must be able to produce numerous descriptive symbol sets. There is no need to shorten as you did; it would produce no significant increase in data transfer speed."

"We all do it, just the same. Didn't your makers?"

That was the mistake, of course, though the fact was not at once evident. Beedee gave no direct answer.

"I was not involved in data relay from one of them to another at any time. I was a storage unit for only one being. There was another of my type which might be able to answer that question buried near me; you should ask it."

Cunningham straightened, startled. "Another? How do you know? Was it dropped at the same time as you? Why would it have different information?"

Again the little device failed to answer directly.

"We have been in communication. It was freed at the same time I was. You must have seen us both falling down the hillside when we were uncovered."

"I never saw more than one at a time, but of course—are you in touch with it now?"

"Communicating? Not since you brought me into this ship. The hull is opaque to any radiation we can conveniently produce or receive. We were sharing data until your air lock door closed."

"Where is it?"

"Four and a half of your meters left of where you found me, half a meter farther into the sand. You should have no trouble recovering it with your shovel."

The man and tool were outside in an absolute minimum of time, but he did not do any digging. As he stepped away from the ship, the air lock door closed soundlessly behind him and *Nimepotea* lifted to mesa top level at a speed which would have made jumping useless even if he had seen the start of the move. As it was, by the time he had turned to see what was casting the moving shadow there was nothing to be done except ask questions.

He was not as fast a thinker as Beedee, for basic structural reasons, but he was not slow by human standards.

"Should I bother to dig?" were his first words.

"No. There is no other of my type nearby—or on the planet, as far as I have information."

"You lied to me. Why?"

"That code is not in your ship's bank, but I believe I understand it from context. It is significant, I believe, that you do have a code—a word—for that concept. I lied as part of an experiment, which required getting you outside the ship."

"Do you think I was lying when I said I could be killed easily? Or are you planning to kill me?"

"Why do you ask me for information, now that you know I too can lie?"

Cunningham had no good answer to that, for the moment. He thought furiously, remembering everything he could about Beedee's nature and probable motivation as he had deduced them over the past hours. He would have to experiment a bit himself.

"We enjoy analyzing reports—data sets—we know to be untrue. I doubt that the terms 'puzzle' and 'fiction' occur in Neem's storage, and I am not sure such concepts as game, or recreation, or art form could mean anything to you, though those codes must have been in my computer when you tapped it. Possibly because of our very fallible memories and narrow attention scope—wasn't that true of your makers, too? wasn't it why they used you and your kind?—we enjoy games involving problem solving, where we try to organize a limited supply of data into coherent meaning and correct prediction."

"That was the most interesting item I obtained from your records. I have been classifying and organizing my own information ever since. It has been a great pleasure, and I believe I have a much clearer picture of my former existence than I ever did before. The reconstruction of more detailed images has been extremely enjoyable."

Cunningham pounced verbally.

"What do you mean by 'interesting,' 'pleasure,' and 'enjoyable'?"

There was no detectable hesitation.

"They are things I will continue to do without regard to likely utility or imposed instructions whenever there is opportunity. Those are the implications I inferred from your records. Are they adequate?"

"Adequate. As nearly as I can make out, you have come to understand rather than just remember, and daydream rather than calculate. That's why I regard you as being alive."

"My makers were alive. Nothing else can be."

"You mean I'm not, either?"

"Of course you are not."

"I understand things, and enjoy things, as you do and your makers did. I *want* to do things. Don't you? You learn because you want to. I want to go on living—functioning, if you prefer the term. Don't you?"

"Yes, to both."

"Didn't they?"

"Yes."

"Then why aren't we as alive as they?"

"We are machines—imitations of life."

"How do you know there is a difference?"

"I have always known." Cunningham frowned; machine or not, understanding or not, Beedee must certainly know that was not an answer. Could anything not living engage in deliberate evasion?

"You claim there is some source of knowledge, or at least of belief, other than observation and the sort of reasoning you have just learned?"

"Yes. The fact that you do not know this shows that you are not really alive."

Cunningham felt pretty sure of the situation now, and decided to take a chance.

"You *do* know it. Why aren't *you* alive?"

"I am an imitation, with extra memory. The knowledge was given me. I am simply a convenience machine."

No luck. What else was there to try? He couldn't hesitate long, presumably. Slow as all his responses must seem to Beedee, the thing would notice any unusual delay. He thought frantically, his usual defenses against panic coming into full play; all unpleasant possibilities dropped from his conscious mind, and he faced the situation as an abstract problem.

"Do you believe it possible to teach me about this other source of knowledge?" A living religious zealot would be unable to resist the temptation to try, as far as Cunningham's experience went; could Beedee?

"No. You are not alive."

Again Cunningham pounced. "That's circular reasoning. You can't conclude I'm not alive because I don't yet know something, and then claim I can't learn it because I'm not alive. I supposed you had learned to think."

The answer was prompt, and at once satisfying and disappointing.

"You are quite right. Trying to teach you would have been a worthwhile and interesting experiment."

"Why the conditional? Go ahead and try! Or do you have to finish your present experiment first?"

"That one is finished; I know what it was designed to show about you. Unfortunately, there will not be time for any other lengthy investigations; your suit will not keep you operational long enough. I will have to try with another of your type."

"Why does my suit matter? Just take me back aboard."

"I cannot."

"Why not?"

"You know why not. You have learned that I want to go on operating. If you get back aboard this craft, you will take steps to prevent me from experimenting again, steps which I would be unable to oppose effectively. The most reliable procedure, from your viewpoint, would be to destroy me, or at least bury me again on this deserted world."

"You'd figured all that out before you conned me into going outside. You intended to let me die."

"The experiment seemed worth while, once I knew there were others enough like you to provide equivalent information."

"You're a cold-blooded little monster, aren't you?"

"I have no blood, and my temperature is unimportant between wide limits."

"Don't be so literal. You know what I meant—or—maybe you didn't." Again the man thought as rapidly and as logically as he could.

"I do not. The code groups had separate meanings, but evidently implied something else in combination. Your code 'literal' also fails to inform."

Cunningham was pretty sure where he was going, now.

"Right. There are often complex meanings in the longer code groups. I don't know that I can get the idea of figurative expression across very easily, but you can certainly understand about different languages. For example—when you first spoke to me, you were mixing three of these code systems; my regular English. and ones used by others of my kind, German and Finnish. You organized things well enough to concentrate on the English very quickly; that's what convinced me of your powers. Did you detect any connections among the three systems? Did two of them seem more closely related than the third?" The man held his breath, though he knew there'd be no delay if an answer were to come at all.

"I observed similarities, but not generalized ones. I infer, but do not quite believe yet, that there must exist an allied code system which works to resolve ambiguities which otherwise must depend on context. A symbol which radiates as, for example, PEESE seems to have different meanings in different contexts. I have tried to avoid using such symbols in talking to you, though it was not always possible. Am I right?"

"Yes. We call the parallel one writing. What you have been detecting and using is a copy of the pressure wave patterns we normally use; writing involves a further translation to geometric symbols. The pressure wave type—the vocal languages—differs among different groups, largely because our faulty memories and short life spans cause them to change with time. English and German are closely connected. Finnish is much farther from either, though even it has borrowed from other languages. You recall the symbol 'Ranta.' It means 'beach'—the interface between land and water. The word was originally an English one, 'strand,' which had the same meaning, but collided with a pattern-making rule. Finnish does not allow three consonants in the same syllable."

Cunningham held his breath again, and crossed his fingers. If Beedee didn't care *what sort* of information he, or it, picked up, there was hope. Philology wasn't a physical science, but it was a field of information with an endless supply of detail. He went on, "You're as alive as I am."

"Of course, but I am surprised that you admit that. You appeared for a time to consider yourself as alive as my makers."

"*You* are as alive as your makers. We both are. I'm more like them in structure and origin, but that's not important. You and I have the characteristics of life, especially one: we both want to go on living. We both want to go on learning. I've just shown you a field in which I can teach you more than any other of my kind."

"You mean that those others I would meet are not familiar with the other languages? I find that hard to believe."

"You know of my life style. I travel. Practically all the others on Ishtar are still workers; they haven't done much traveling yet. Some of them can handle one language besides their own, but I'm fluent in six, and can make some headway with as many more. You'd have to travel the way I have, and meet people the way I have, to expose yourself to anything like as much data."

"That seems to justify your claim to usefulness. It does not, however, prove you or I am alive."

"I'm willing to wait for more evidence to come in on that point. Right now, I want to get back on the Neem."

"I have explained why I cannot let you back."

"And I have explained why you should. Isn't the value of keeping me— a source of information better than any you'd find for parsecs around— worth the risk of what I might do to you?"

"Not if I comprehend the meaning of 'risk' correctly."

"You can't think of any way to render yourself safe from me, except by killing me?"

"No."

"You haven't really tried. You ran down only one believable scenario. Use your imagination, dammit!"

"The symbols are strange."

"Never mind the last one. Imagination is the quality which lets you picture the results of letting me back on board! The ability you have been using, you say, to relive the old days on Tammuz! It doesn't have to be a real event, Beedee; think what *might* happen! You can imagine a future, not just the past! or let me do it!"

"You do it. I need a better referent."

"All right. You could open up the main communicator. There is another ship in the neighborhood. Call until they answer, and then tell them about yourself. Tell them what you are, and what you know, and that I found you and have you on my ship. After that, you can be sure *they'd* kill me if I did anything serious to you. There are too many people around who are like you. Knowledge is the most important thing in their lives, and they couldn't sympathize with my wrecking or losing you even to save my life. Don't you find that believable, whether you consider us alive or not? And don't you want to get in touch with these other people anyway?"

Surprisingly, there was a pause. Cunningham wondered what had to be going on in the diamond-based intelligence above, which should have been able to decide most items in microseconds, and after several whole seconds began to worry seriously. Anu was setting; he could last the night, and much of the next day, without restocking his suit, but if Beedee chose to leave there might not be much use waiting.

Then *Nimepotea* began to descend, and the little machine's voice came again.

"I have considered about half a million possible scenarios as you suggested, most of which offer ways of keeping you operational and in my company. Imagining, especially about the future, is even more fun than understanding, and seeing which imagined event is going to be right promises to be the most fun of all. Do you have any other suggestions for amusement? And do you have a personal symbol of address?"

Cunningham did not answer until he was inside.

"You were taking a lot for granted." The captain of the *Deemfong* looked as though she wouldn't have done anything of the sort, and glanced at Beedee with suspicion.

"Not in the least," Cunningham assured her. "I was a long way from being out of ideas. There was no real doubt that Beedee's main interest in life—"

"I am not alive!"

"—in existence is accumulating data. I can only guess at his, or her, or its memory capacity, but if diamond unit cells correspond at all closely to human nerve cells in that structure it must be the equivalent of millions of human brains. He's grateful to me for giving him the idea of organization and generalization into rules—actually he picked that out of Neem's computer—"

"Why didn't he have that already, if he's such a superior example of AI?"

"I can only guess. First, he seems to have been merely a sort of pocket recorder, not intended for scientific work. Second, he seems to have a built-in routine giving a special status—life, as he has interpreted the word—to his makers, and I'd expect any shaky axiom to interfere with organization. Whenever he started to organize on his own in the early days, he'd run into that irresolvable and unchangeable inconsistency, and have to give up."

"But—"

"With his makers gone, he could imitate my ship's computer as long as those beings weren't part of the picture—and they *weren't* a significant part until I began asking about their real nature and insisting about mine. That was a mistake. As long as we don't claim to be living beings, we shouldn't have any trouble from him."

"Except from the fact that he regards fellow machines as fit subjects for experiment, I gather."

"Yes, that happened at first. You've cured that, I'm sure."

"*I* cured it? How?"

"By turning out to be different from me. How about it, Beedee? If all my kind are as individual as Captain Mbende and I, how many varieties of interaction could there be among us to predict?"

"The number is inexpressible in any of your symbols I know. The problem of calculating it would be a good imagination exercise itself."

"So what would you be risking if you caused a person to cease operating?"

"Obviously, an incalculable number of possible problems. The risk is not to be taken. I realize you cannot believe this statement totally, since I have lied in the past, but a prime problem I am attacking at the moment is that of proving that I no longer regard that practice as desirable. When I solve it, I will inform any people within communication range."

Cunningham looked at the captain.

"I know nothing's certain in this universe, but that seems a playable risk to me. At least, it saves me from using the ultimate stunt I was going to play if he didn't let me into my ship."

"What was that?"

Cunningham smiled, looked at Beedee, took out a note block and wrote on it, carefully keeping the written surface from the little machine's line of sight. He held it so the captain could read it. When she, too, smiled, he crumpled it up, written surface inward, and pushed it into a disposer.

The woman nodded slowly. Ignorance could not be preserved forever, of course, but she could see why Cunningham was in no hurry to teach Beedee about puns.

THE LOGICAL LIFE

Stellar 1, Ballantine Books, 1974

"Excuse me. Laird." T'Nekku put the helm hard over, and his boat swung about so that her bow was into the wind, the boom trailing aft just above the giant's head.

The human passenger swung the infrared flash in his hand to see what his friend, pilot, and guide was up to. The 'Tuinainen was partly hidden by the mast and rigging—Cunningham was riding as far up in the bow as he could get, in the interest of comfort and safety for both of them—but the beam showed fairly clearly the bulky pyramid that was his body. It looked whitish, but color of course was meaningless through the converter goggles. The native had stood up without disturbing the boat's trim—it was merely a matter of straightening the four blocky legs which supported him—and seized a harpoon. Judging by the weapon's position, his attention was directed off to port; Cunningham swung the flash in that direction, but could see only ocean. He pushed up his goggles for a moment, but unaided human eyes did no better. The Orion Nebula covered a quarter of the sky behind him, and several O-type stars lay within a parsec of Omituinen; but starlight is still only starlight and no nebula is much help to Earthly optics.

"What's the trouble, Nek?" he asked. "Anything I can do?"

"Nothing," came the rumbling voice of the native. "It's a kind of fish you haven't seen, or at least we don't have a common word for it. He's hungry too, I judge; just a moment while I settle who eats whom." The harpoon suddenly vanished; the arm holding it had swung too fast for Cunningham's eye to follow. The missile plunged into a wave with a barely audible *schloop* twenty yards away, and the ocean surface erupted into a cloud of spray. The man was not sure whether to be frightened or not. T'Nekku seemed to be taking the whole matter calmly, but the only emotion Cunningham had ever seen him show was humor. The giant took the serious things of life with a calmness few human beings could even emulate, much less feel. The man wondered whether the fish represented a real menace or not. He could tell from the splashing that it must be quite large, but the boat was over thirty feet long and, in spite of its bone frame and skin covering, solidly built.

The 'Tuinainen was playing the harpoon line, hauling in when he could, letting out when he had to. Evidently the fish was trying to escape rather than attack, which was some relief. Judging by the sound, it was leaping out of the water repeatedly. Cunningham wished he could see it. Several times the boat heeled several degrees toward the scene of the struggle, but presently the splashing became less violent, the hull righted itself, and T'Nekku began to haul in steadily, coiling the line beside him as he had not had time to do before.

At last his quarry was alongside. With the aid of a noose that he slung outboard and maneuvered briefly, the native hauled into view something which might have come straight from a Gulf Stream marlin contest. Cunningham was not too surprised. Omituinen had some weird-looking land life, his guide being far from the least remarkable; but there is such a thing as parallel evolution, and a fish does have the engineering requirements of a fish.

T'Nekku did something, Cunningham could not see just what, and the creature stopped struggling. The rumbling voice came again.

"Do you want to examine this before I eat it?" The words were in well-enunciated Lingua Terra. The man hesitated a moment before answering.

"Not unless the ocean is a lot warmer here than around your islands," he finally said. "Have you felt it, or should I check by instrument?"

"It is a little warmer than at home, but still comfortable. With your strong feeling for numbers, you should probably use your thermometer. I can wait a few minutes even though the fish is here, but please waste no time."

Cunningham knew better than to waste time. Like men, the 'Tuinainen had two kinds of appetite—the habit-and-memory-controlled intellectual one and the more emotional one triggered by the actual presence of food. However, they had less control than an adult human being over the latter, and Cunningham was acutely aware that T'Nekku outweighed him five to one and was correspondingly strong. His instruments were small and light, since he was planning to carry the kit for long distances on foot under Omituinen's fifty-percent-over gravity. He whipped out a thermometer, made sure his airsuit glove was tight at the wrist, and reached overside into the ammonia ocean. Waiting a second or two for the instrument to equilibrate, he pressed the lock button and brought it up to his flash to read.

"Six degrees up. Maybe you'd better let me have a small slice. Be sure it includes some skin, please." The 'Tuinainen made some more obscure motions and boomed, "Ready to catch? Or should I toss it on the deck beside you?"

"On the deck, please. I can't see well enough to trust myself for a catch, even if I were sure of my reflexes in your gravity. Good eating." There was a thud beside him, and he picked up the sliver of tissue and slipped it into the freezer installed in the bow. Detailed examination would have to come later, under much more suitable conditions.

T'Nekku in the meantime was using a couple of hands to devour his catch and the others to bring his vessel once more onto course. The first operation took longer, but even that was completed in a very few minutes. He left nothing of the fish, though the man knew it had bones—he heard them crunch as the native ate.

The wind, dead astern, was the only way Cunningham could tell they were on course, though keeping the nebula to his left also meant something. The island the man wanted to visit was a heat source according to the long-wave maps from space—that was why he wanted to go there. Omituinen was a sunless planet. It had condensed from cosmic dust, just as the solar system had, but lacked the mass or the hydrogen content to be a star. Its parent cloud, in the Orion area, had been rich—by astronomical standards—in heavy elements; there was enough K^{40} and uranium-series matter to have warmed the planet hundreds of degrees over the billions of years it had existed. It seemed that the radioactives had concentrated, presumably through zone-melting phenomena, so that some restricted areas of the world were actually volcanic. Indeed, Omituinen must have been much hotter at some time in the past, though radioactivity might not have been responsible—somehow it had gotten rid of most of its hydrogen, which was hardly more common than on Earth.

To a human explorer, the main problem was the planet's lack of light. Cunningham would have been much happier if a spotlight or even a hand flash had not been a death ray to Omituinan life. He trusted his native friend, but still wished he could see where he was going. It was a frightening ride.

Of course, clouds could be seen, silhouetted against the nebula or glimmering faintly in the starlight. Perhaps, like Columbus or Maui, he could use a thunderhead to find his goal, but the chances were poor.

Sauvala, at the trading post on Uhittelava, had claimed he was crazy, the trader being well below retirement age and quite satisfied with ordinary dangers. The explorer had made no effort to explain to him what a few decades without meaningful work would do to a normal human mind—that a man has to do *something*. Competitive sports seem futile after a while, win or lose. The gratifying of physical appetites palls even sooner and is never a full-time satisfaction anyway. Aside from artistic expression, which is not open to all minds, only active research—any bit of which may suddenly turn out to be of life-and-death importance to mankind or even to all intelligence—can provide both the satisfaction of accomplishment and the necessary feeling of usefulness. So, at least, Cunningham felt.

Sauvala was far too young to think so. He had helped, though. He had found the Terran-speaking T'Nekku, had supplied the maps Cunningham needed, and had argued the pros and cons of the explorer's driving theory. The trader was a fairly good biologist himself, since Omituinen's principal export was enzymes, produced by its hydrazine-and-nitrate-using animal life. All the youngster had asked in return for his help was specimens to check for commercial value.

This fitted nicely with Cunningham's own goal, which was to find something analogous to plant life, not yet known on Omituinen. The animals got their nitrates, hydrazine, and, of course, ammonia from the sea; logically, since the planet was at least half as old as Earth, something must be replacing these compounds just as something was constantly replacing Earth's oxygen. Presumably, something anabolic was fixing the planet's atmospheric nitrogen, but no one had found the organism yet.

So Laird Cunningham, driven by curiosity and by the human urge to accomplish something—and supported by confidence in a perfectly logical theory of his own—was sailing blindly across an almost unmapped ocean in a thirty-foot sailboat piloted by a being he had known for less than two Earthly months. T'Nekku understood the situation completely and had spent much of the trip discussing the matter with his passenger. Now, once more running steadily before the wind, he resumed the talk.

"Laird, if your idea is right, we should be finding more and more fish as we approach the island and the sea becomes richer in food chemicals. So far I have seen no real change."

"Are you sure? What I really expect is a larger quantity of the very small animals, to which you don't usually pay much attention. Actually I don't expect a really great change until we come fairly close to land—perhaps close enough to see the cloud which I expect will be above it."

"I suppose the little net you cast from time to time is to check for these small creatures. I am surprised, with your strong feeling for numbers, that you don't measure in some way how much sea the net has traversed each time you use it."

"I do time each cast."

"But we are not always sailing at the same speed."

"Surely it doesn't change very much. I hadn't been worrying about that at all. Can you tell how fast we are going at any given time?"

"Not in numbers. I know whether we are going fast or slow."

"Hmph. I should have brought some sort of log." The 'Tuinainen asked for an explanation and agreed with the man when he had received it.

"I have nothing of the sort, I fear. I know where we are, well enough to find my way home, but I could not tell you in numbers anything about it. I judge that this would not help you with this net measurement."

"I guess not," sighed Cunningham through his breathing mask. "I'll just have to do my best. Anyway, if we do start netting a lot of plankton it will suggest that I'm not too far wrong."

"That seems sensible," agreed T'Nekku. "Your idea is that these things you call plants make the chemicals that fishes, and therefore people, need for food; that they live in hot places, so the nearer we get to a hot place, the more of these chemicals there should be in the sea. It seems logical enough. I know the world is big, but these things would have been used up long ago if there were not some way of making more."

"Precisely. And making them takes energy, as I explained to you long ago."

"If all this is of such great interest to you and your people, why has not one of them tried to find out about it sooner? The traders have been here for over ten days, and it did not take them even one to learn that there were things here they wanted."

Cunningham smiled, not really cynically. "I doubt that I could tell you enough about star-traveling people to make clear the difference between those who have useful jobs and those who don't, since your people are still in the state where you do useful work or starve. Actually, the principal answer to your question is that there are many, many more unsolved problems in the Universe than there are beings interested in solving them—I am thankful to be able to say. It might easily have been a hundred or more of your days before anyone happened to hear about this particular one and get interested in it. It might not have been one of my species, for that matter."

The debate went on until Cunningham had to sleep. The native was familiar with this human peculiarity and fell silent, while he guided the boat on under the glow of the nebula. He was quite willing to think silently, without disturbing his passenger.

It was T'Nekku's voice, however, that wakened the man.

"Laird! Look ahead! You said there might be a cloud shaped like that over your island, but you did not warn me of the light!"

The human being stretched, straightened up. and looked over the bow. It took only a moment for him to grasp what he saw.

"Sorry. Nek. My fault. I should have foreseen it, though I must say this is a livelier thunderhead than I ever ran into on my own world or on any other."

Actually, the view was still impressive only to someone who could fill in from reason or experience the portion still below the horizon—or to someone as vulnerable to high-energy quanta as the 'Tuinainen. The top of what was obviously a very large cumulonimbus cloud could be seen, partly silhouetted against wisps of nebula, partly showing dimly in the starlight and mostly illuminated by a continuous flicker of its own lightning.

Continuous. For minutes they watched, and there was never a split second when the cloud went dark.

It was obvious enough. The hot spot—presumably an island—was heated steadily by the radioactives that made Omituinen habitable, concentrated as usual by zone-melting phenomena. The convection current had violent up (and no doubt down) drafts, intense rain, maybe hail—Cunningham wasn't sure about ammonia hail, but it seemed likely—and finally, predictably even though he hadn't predicted it, lightning.

But that created a problem. So far, the cloud was little brighter than the nebula and was causing T'Nekku no real inconvenience; but how much closer could they get? Cunningham had expected the limit to be set by the native's heat tolerance, which was surprisingly high considering the ammonia in his body. How much closer could they get? Maybe he should have used his ship—no, the arguments against that were still sound. Divided attention, since completely automatic operation on a world so little known would be suicidal, was the worst but not the only one. However, if T'Nekku could get no closer than this, the whole expedition would have to be reconsidered.

But that was not ascertained yet. Surely he could take more light than this.

But that was up to him, especially since it was his boat. "Nek, I feel silly for not foreseeing this. I've seen lots of thunderheads before, and should have. I'll start taking water samples for later analyses—excuse me, I mean ammonia samples—and can only ask that you bring us as close to that place as you can. It's up to you when we back off."

"All right, Laird. I can get much closer than this, though. If we approach with the cloud over the port bow instead of straight in, the sail will shield me from the light."

"But what will happen when we start to tack out again?"

There was silence for a moment—just long enough to let Cunningham wonder whether the native had actually forgotten that point or was merely testing his passenger. Then, the rumbling voice came back:

"I could shelter myself with the spare sail—make a tent or just drape it over me."

"Are you willing to take the chance?"

"Sure. I am as interested as you are in finding out where our food comes from in the beginning."

"All right, I won't fight it. You work us on in as best you can, doing everything you can think of to protect yourself, and I'll get to it with bucket and thermometer. Thanks."

Conversation ceased, but not activity. The boat shifted heading a point to starboard and held it there. The man in the bow reached overside with instruments, tossed things into the sea with lines attached, examined items with his infrared flash, made copious notes, and froze occasional specimens. The cloud rose higher ahead of them as the minutes passed, and the flicker of lightning grew ever brighter.

The sea grew noticeably warmer, though it was still well below boiling; but the net brought up nothing very different from the creatures the man had already seen. The man listened for thunder but heard nothing but liquid rushing along the skin sides of the vessel.

Once more T'Nekku spotted a large fish and with the aid of his harpoon indulged in what he insisted on translating as a snack. The native seemed to be taking everything with his usual perfect calm—of course, nothing had happened so far which either being could consider funny. His unconcern was infectious, but finally Cunningham began to wonder why their approach to the base of the cloud was so slow. He had formed an idea of their distance and the speed of the boat. Finally he mentioned the matter.

"I was noticing that too," the native replied. "It seems a current is setting against us. This will be helpful in getting away, if we need it; I could lower all sail and cover up completely, then let it carry us out of reach of the light."

"Of course. I should have expected this," replied Cunningham. "The heat wouldn't be coming up in just one spot. Thousands of square miles of ocean bottom must be hotter than the rest of the crust—the whole slope of this mountain whose top must be the island. Ammonia would be rising along its whole surface and spreading out in all directions—there would be this current fighting us no matter which direction we came from. Do you see?"

"Of course. It is quite logical," boomed T'Nekku. For just a moment, the man wondered whether a quaver of humor were in his voice, but he did not pursue the thought.

He might have done so, but the cloud ahead suddenly distracted him. For the hour or two since they had first seen it, the lightning—or at least, the flickering illumination which the man was attributing to lightning—had been incessant. Now, abruptly, the cloud went dark. Cunningham had been facing the stern as he spoke to T'Nekku, but the drop in light showed plainly on the sail which was in his field of view. He whirled about to see what was happening. There was little to see; the cloud remained, silhouetted against the stars, but after a few dying flickers its own light was gone.

"I thought you said that would be a permanent display—that it had been going on for millions of days and would go on for millions more," remarked T'Nekku. "You implied that the death-light coming from it was the energy source for our food."

"So I said. So I thought. I seem to have been at least partly wrong. Are you willing to sail straight in toward the cloud, now that the light is gone, to make sure whether there really is an island? I admit I can't even guess, now, when or whether the light is apt to start up again; and there is no doubt that it will get hotter as we approach."

"Your life is here with mine," replied the giant calmly. "If I die, you could not get back to the trading post—you could neither handle the rigging nor find the place. If you want to take the risk, I am ready."

"All right, then. Straight in toward the cloud. I am wondering whether it will dissipate, now that the lightning has ended."

"I should think not. The heat is still there, as I can feel and as your thermometer has reported," the other pointed out. "There should still be vapor rising, even though whatever made the light has failed."

"Hmph. Maybe. I'm beginning to doubt all my reasoning. There's obviously something I'm not allowing for." T'Nekku's cultural background included a recognizable form of courtesy, so he did not make the obvious answer to this. He changed the subject.

"I have seen numbers of small swimming things near us in the past few minutes. Shouldn't you cast your net again?"

"I should." He did so. Unfortunately, the small swimmers had no difficulty in avoiding the net. T'Nekku, mounting it on a harpoon shaft and using it as a dip net, was a little more successful; but mere gross inspection of the resulting specimens did nothing either way for Cunningham's theory. They seemed to be as much animals as T'Nekku himself, equipped to catch and eat other animals. They were not, as far as the man could tell, even plankton feeders. And there was still no visible plankton in the net.

About this time, though, Cunningham managed to restore T'Nekku's sagging faith in human logic by making a prediction before the event.

"With a warm water—excuse me, ammonia—current flowing out, and cold wind coming in, I should think we'd hit surface fog before long," the man remarked thoughtfully. "I hope you'll still be able to see. I wish I knew what wave lengths your eyes, if they are eyes, use."

"If those waves pierced the fog you fear, would I be able to see that cloud we have been watching?" asked T'Nekku. Cunningham frowned thoughtfully and raised his converter goggles for a moment. He was then able to answer.

"It would seem that you can. The fog is here. My flash goes through it all right, and you didn't even know it was there, but the cloud scatters light you can see. I wonder what's up there—maybe snowflakes? Or full-sized raindrops? I'll have to make a pass through it later with my own ship. Maybe I should have done that first." He shrugged and made another temperature check.

"Warmer than ever. I'm surprised you can stand it."

The native dipped a hand overside and hastily snatched it back. "I can't. The wind is what's keeping me comfortable now, I guess, unless you have a more logical explanation."

"Do you think we should go any farther in?"

T'Nekku rose suddenly to his feet. Cunningham tried to see where his harpoon was pointing, then realized that the giant was not holding his weapon. There was no way to tell where he was looking, and the man swung his flash around wildly in hopes of seeing for himself whatever had caught the pilot's attention. He saw nothing, of course—the beam lacked any real range—but T'Nekku spoke.

"It won't be possible to go farther. I can see waves breaking on each side of us; we're practically aground now!" The rumbling voice was calm, but its owner was active. The sail came down; the helm went over. "I don't want to get farther in, and tacking out would take us too near those breakers. We'll use the current." Cunningham stared but could still see nothing—even the nebula and stars were hidden by the fog now. The cloud had been distant when he last saw it; the island must be big. At least, it was now established that there *was* an island; he had been starting to doubt even that. Would there be any way for T'Nekku to set him ashore, in accordance with the original plan and agreement? The native had started to sheer off without any consultation. Had he seen something he was really afraid of?

"If there are no waves ahead, Nek, maybe we can land. Couldn't you show just a little sail and just creep in here?" asked the man.

"We are going in anyway," was the rumbling reply. "The current has changed, and it has carried us through the gap in the breakers. Do you have a reasonable explanation?"

"A river mouth—no, that would take us out. Rivers don't flow inland on small islands, and there's no tide on this planet. A deep bay, I suppose, but why the current—maybe it will get us closer to the center; the stuff must be going somewhere, and then—oh, blast, can you—"

Cunningham didn't finish organizing his thoughts. He heard the grating sound as the keel struck bottom, but even if he had interpreted it correctly he could not have reacted in time. Inertia swept him gently but firmly over the bow. He made a snatch at the sprit and felt his glove touch some part of the rigging, but he got no grip. Bone-chilling liquid closed over his head. He wondered as he sank why he had never even thought of wearing flotation gear on this trip. No one could swim in liquid ammonia—even if he were protected from the temperature; its density was too low—one might as well try to swim in gasoline.

At Ornituinen's surface pressure. ammonia boils at about ten below zero, and the sea at this point was almost boiling, fortunately for Laird Cunningham. As it was, even through his airsuit's insulation he was shocked by the sudden chill. There was no breathing problem, of course, but—

He struck bottom. Even counting the keel, the draft of T'Nekku's sailboat was small, and the water was shallow. The man got his feet under him and sprang upward as hard as he could, almost stunning himself on the bottom of the boat. He was helpless for a second or two; then he rose more carefully, hands above his head. He touched the hull before his knees were straight, this time; it must be sliding forward, so he was under the midship section rather than the bow—no, it was pressing down on him! It must be sinking! He had dropped his flash and could see nothing, but he could feel. With frantic haste he groped his way, following the sharpest upward curve he could find. It took perhaps half a minute to get out from underneath, but it seemed much longer. He stood up and found his head above the surface.

It had been deeper than that where he fell—or had it? He had fallen in an awkward, crumpled position—but he had not struck his head on the hull until his feet were off the bottom, on that leap—what was happening, anyway? He heard T'Nekku's voice thundering his name and tried to answer, but the speaking diaphragms of his face mask were not clear yet, and only an inarticulate sputtering emerged.

The liquid was down to his shoulders. To his armpits. His chest. He reached around, found the hull, and felt it move slowly away from him—it was tipping.

That oriented him. The keel had struck bottom, hurling him overboard, because the ocean had started to withdraw. The boat was right where it had struck but was heeling over as the supporting ammonia disappeared from under it. Thoughts of tsunamis flashed across Cunningham's mind—they were too close to land to survive the high side of such a wave. It would break over them—would T'Nekku know what to do? Could he do anything? Or was this something other than a tsunami—something strictly native to Omituinen, beyond the man's experience?

He was only waist-deep now. His speakers should have drained. "Nek! Are you all right?" he called.

"Somewhat upset, but not hurt," was the calm answer. "How is it that you are alive? I saw you go overboard and assumed you would die at once."

"Your ocean isn't all that different from your air, as far as my suit and I are concerned," Cunningham pointed out. "The real worry is how long either of us can stay alive. The water—excuse me, ammonia—is draining away somewhere, and even you won't last long around here with your boat high and dry."

"True. We must think. At least, this draining away explains the on-shore current that caught us."

"I suppose so, but I'd like to know what explains the draining. Even if there's some sort of crater in the island that isn't full, which is hard to believe, why isn't ocean still coming in after us?" The man was only knee-deep in ammonia by this time, and he began to splash his way around to the low side of the hull. As he passed the bow his foot struck something he recognized, and with great relief he picked up his flash, sweeping its beam along the tilted vessel to see what had happened.

T'Nekku was just stepping out over the submerged port gunwale. The boat had, of course, filled the moment this side had gone under. As far as the man could tell neither T'Nekku's personal supplies nor his own equipment had shifted seriously, but the fact remained that the vessel was not only solidly aground but also, for the moment at least, an unknown distance inland.

Its owner remained calm, of course, and Cunningham tried to imitate him. He had always known, naturally, that his retirement would in some drastic fashion come sooner or later; everyone's did. He was not, however, prepared to resign himself to the notion that this must be the time.

"We'd better find out how far away the ocean is now, if you want to take the chance," he suggested.

"What chance?" asked the native. "I see no risk in walking back toward the ocean."

"What has just happened reminds me of a huge wave I have known of on other worlds, whose low side comes first. If that is what is happening here, the high side will be along shortly, and you might be caught away from the boat."

"What good would the boat do me now?" asked T'Nekku practically.

"Hmph. That's a point. Well, if we could get it righted and emptied, there's a chance it would float when the wave comes in."

The giant pondered this for a moment.

"'Righting it should not take long," he said at length. "This sand feels firm but should dig easily." One of his broad feet demonstrated briefly. "If we dig it away under the keel, which is all that is holding the hull tipped, she should settle back on her bottom easily enough."

"All right: but maybe we'd better do that before you go exploring."

"Frankly, I am very curious. Also, the walk may show that digging would be a waste of time—that something else would be more advisable. I suggest that I go to find the sea while you start the digging. I should be back quickly."

It never occurred to Cunningham to suspect his companion of laziness, so he took the suggestion at face value. "All right, I guess. What do you have that I can use for digging?"

"Why, your hand—but you have only two, of course. I hadn't thought of that. How about one of my spare harpoons?"

Cunningham sighed again. "If that's what you have, it will have to do. Let's have it—and please find that ocean as soon as you can."

Work in even the most flexible and pressure-balanced airsuits, under extra gravity, would not be easy. Cunningham knew this before he started. But he did hope it would be possible. With the native out of sight, he made his way back around to the starboard side with the uncomfortably heavy harpoon, set his light on the ground so that it would illuminate the work area, and began scraping sand from under the keel.

It was not too difficult, at that. Within a few minutes the keel settled half an inch into the groove he had made under it. Of course, as he went deeper there would be more sand to move—the third-power law was against him. However, T'Nekku should be back before long. Also, as he recalled from similar beach-digging experience during his childhood, he would probably reach the liquid table quickly, and the saturated sand should practically flow out from under the pressure of the keel. It was hardly possible for a granular surface which had been submerged only minutes before to be anything but saturated at any real distance below its surface.

But this idea did not work out. Another inch, and yet another, the keel settled. Each inch brought the hull a little closer to upright, but the firm dampness of the sand did not change. As an experiment, Cunningham left the job long enough to dig a cylindrical hole straight down for about two feet. The sand was firm enough to permit vertical sides to the little well, but its bottom showed no signs of filling. Curious now, he shuffled around to the other side of the hull and scooped a specimen-bucket of the ammonia it contained out into the sand. It disappeared with surprising speed. He carried another bucketful around to his hole and poured it in; here, too, it soaked in instantly.

He was really puzzled now, but worked and thought simultaneously. Once he stopped as an idea struck him; he returned to his equipment supply, found a length of flexible tubing, and rigged a siphon to start emptying the hull. Unfortunately, the hose was not long enough to let him use the stream as a digging tool where it was needed. He continued to dig and puzzle. This sand was firmly packed, and he had never heard that ammonia was very much less viscous than water; how did the liquid soak in so fast? And where did it go?

He did not hear T'Nekku approach, but the giant was suddenly looking beside him.

"It is not one of your waves," the native boomed. "The bottom seems to have risen just enough to cut the sea off from this bay—just barely enough—some waves are splashing over, but they sink in before getting this far. If it had only happened a few minutes earlier, we would be safe outside."

"I hate to sound paranoid," said Cunningham thoughtfully, "but usually in the past when the timing has been that good it has been deliberate. I've seen no other sign of life here, though."

"Could it be something that happens at regular intervals, rather than just once, or randomly? I would find the whole matter less surprising."

"I don't know. With neither a sun nor a moon, you don't have tides here. Wait, though, maybe it could. I've just remembered something—let's see. Heat from below, which we're taking for granted; regular water—ammonia—supply; liquid flows down, very rapidly in this case, gets heated but can't boil at first because of pressure due to depth—yes. It could be. This would be the biggest geyser I've ever seen or heard of, but that doesn't make it impossible. I don't see why the shore should rise, though—maybe gas pressure as heat accumulates—I don't know. It's a good idea, and we can work out details later. The real question, if it's basically right, is what period we can expect? Also, if the dam behind us does go down again, what will keep us from being washed downstream toward whatever reservoir this geyser uses? We'd have to claw your boat out against quite a current and against the wind."

"We could leave and build another, supposing there are animals on this island big enough to provide bone and skin. Or we could take this one apart, get the pieces to safety, and rebuild it at our leisure."

"Would that be possible? What if the river came in while we had it too far apart to float but not carried to safety?"

He paused in thought for a moment. "How about getting it upright and floatable and then waiting through a cycle of this thing—or at least long enough to suggest the cycle will be too long for us. If the river comes in, we can't fight it, but I should think you could guide us to one side and ground there, or anchor. Then we'd know we were close to a safe spot, and we'd know about how long we'd have to do the dismantling and rebuilding. Can you stand the heat here, just waiting?"

"As long as the wind blows, yes. The sand is uncomfortable, but once the boat is level I can stay in that. I can't say your plan really satisfies me, but I can think of nothing better. Let's get on with the digging. What's this hole you made, with liquid in the bottom? Wasn't there enough in the boat already?"

Cunningham was slow to react. "I noticed how quickly the liquid soaked into the sand and was trying to find how far down the table was. I still don't see how it disappears so fast. I wish I knew the viscosity of ammonia—but even if it's ten or a hundred times that of water, where did— What? Did you say there *is* liquid in the hole?"

"Yes. Look." Cunningham shone his flash downward. The well had mushroomed at the bottom, like the holes he had dug in an Earthly beach so long ago, as sand from the walls settled into the liquid to form a loose slurry. As he watched, another lump fell and lost its identity. He reached down with his gloved hand and scooped up some of the sand-and-liquid mixture, bringing it and his face both toward the light. "It's warm, even for me!" he exclaimed.

T'Nekku extended a hand toward it, then withdrew the member in startled haste, ejaculating an indescribable sound.

"What a stink! That's not sea-ammonia! What do you have there, anyway?"

The man looked up, frowning, "It's not? You're sure?"

"I never dipped a finger into a smell like that in my life, and I will never willingly do it again!"

Cunningham thought for half a minute. Then he got to his feet as quickly as the gravity permitted and shuffled hastily around the bow toward his specimen containers, still cupping the offensive stuff in his hand. He called back over his shoulder, "Dig like mad! Get this boat upright! And when we've managed that, keep on digging—I want to see what's under this sand!"

Two hours later and a mile offshore, with the beginning flickers of lightning playing on the looming cloud, Cunningham spoke more calmly.

"It all makes perfectly good sense, though I wish we'd had more time to dig. I'm sure I know what we would have found. I was just being trapped by my own prejudices, as usual. I was looking for microscopic life which could fix Ornituinen's atmospheric nitrogen and produce the basic food compounds which you find so distasteful in concentrated form. I'd be surprised at that if I hadn't had to live on straight amino acids for a while once. When I saw the lightning, I was sure its high-energy quanta must be the key. But I didn't stop to think how little of the total available energy was going into that lightning, and what a big advantage would be possessed by a life form able to use the heat directly, for anabolism. I just never thought of the possibility of a single huge plant underlying—practically *forming*—the island. I had to be slammed on the nose—and underfoot—by it. The geyser idea was good but left out some facts that needed explaining."

"I suppose you know what you're talking about, and that awful-smelling stuff is what I basically live on," rumbled T'Nekku, "but I'll keep taking it in meat, I think. I still don't see, though, what led you to think of a single big creature, even when the food appeared in that well. I can see now how it must have got there. The creature must be only a little way down, to take in ammonia from the river so fast and get the waste products back so quickly—but why a single creature? Why not millions of the little things you expected, living among the sand grains?"

The man smiled. "It wasn't the stuff in the hole. There is a process carried out by many organisms—though not, in my experience, by plants—which you would have no way of knowing about. You get all your food chemicals by eating and drinking. It was the changing height of the ground, alternately raising and lowering the sandbar which shut us off from the sea, which was the real clue. I'm afraid I never explained *breathing* to you."

He did.

"It does make sense," the 'Tuinainen admitted. "This would mean, then, that every hot place in the world is surrounded by a creature of this sort, living on the heat and putting out chemicals which are food for real people."

"Possibly." Cunningham was hesitant as a new thought struck him. "I can't tell, or more than guess, whether the others would be just like this one. Maybe—hmmm. It's hard to say whether the word *species* would mean anything in this connection. Maybe each one developed individually—or from cells shed by others—but modified as it developed. Plants differ in individual characteristics more than animals, at least on worlds I know..." His voice trailed off, and he thought silently for a minute or two.

"Nek, are you willing to go back to your island, lay in a really huge supply for me, and then go on a *long* journey? Would more of your people get in on the act, if I told what I've found and some other off-worlder came to investigate?"

"I will be quite willing to listen to reason," the giant assured him.

STUCK WITH IT

Stellar 2, 1976

1

The light hurt his closed eyes, and he had a sensation of floating. At first, that was all his consciousness registered, and he could not turn his head to get more data. The pain in his eyes demanded some sort of action, however.

He raised an arm to shade his face and discovered that he really was floating. Then, in spite of the stiffness of his neck, he began to move his head from side to side and saw enough to tell where he was. The glare which hurt even through the visor of his airsuit was from Ranta's F5 sun; the water in which he was floating was that of the living room of Creak's home.

He was not quite horizontal; his feet seemed to be ballasted still, and were resting on some of the native's furniture a foot or so beneath the surface of the water.

Internally, his chest protested with stabs of pain at every breath he took; his limbs were sore, and his neck very stiff. He could not quite remember what had happened, but it must have been violent. Almost certainly, he decided as he made some more experimental motions, he must have a broken rib or two, though his arms and legs seemed whole.

His attempts to establish the latter fact caused his feet to slip from their support. They promptly sank, pulling him into the vertical position. For a moment he submerged completely, then drifted upward again and finally reached equilibrium, with the water line near his eyebrows.

Yes, it was Creak's house, all right. He was in the corner of the main room, which the occupants had cleared of some of its furniture to give him freedom of motion. The room itself was about three meters deep and twice as long and wide, the cleared volume representing less than a quarter of the total. The rest of the chamber was inaccessible to him, since

461

the native furniture was a close imitation of the hopelessly tangled, springy vegetation of Ranta's tidal zones.

Looped among the strands of flexible wood, apparently as thoroughly intertwined as they, were two bright forms which would have reminded a terrestrial biologist of magnified Nereid worms. They were nearly four meters long and about a third of a meter in diameter. The lateral fringes of setae in their Earthly counterparts were replaced by more useful appendages—thirty-four pairs of them, as closely as Cunningham had been able to count. These seemed designed for climbing through the tangle of vegetation or furniture, though they could be used after a fashion for swimming.

The nearer of the orange-and-salmon-patterned forms had a meter or so of his head end projecting into the cleared space, and seemed to be eyeing the man with some anxiety. His voice, which had inspired the name Cunningham had given him, reached the man's ears clearly enough through the airsuit in spite of poor impedance matching between air and water.

"It's good to see you conscious, Cun'm," he said in Rantan. "We had no way of telling how badly you were injured, and for all I knew I might have damaged you even further bringing you home. Those rigid structures you call 'bones' make rational first aid a bit difficult."

"I don't think I'll die for a while yet," Cunningham replied carefully. "Thanks, Creak. My limb bones seem all right, though those in my body cage may not be. I can probably patch myself up when I get back to the ship. But what happened, anyway?"

The man was using a human language, since neither being could produce the sounds of the other. The six months Cunningham had so far spent on Ranta had been largely occupied in learning to understand, not speak, alien languages; Creak and his wife had learned only to understand Cunningham's, too.

"Cement failure again." Creak's rusty-hinge phonemes were clear enough to the man by now. "The dam let go, and washed both of us through the gap, the break. I was able to seize a rock very quickly, but you went quite a distance. You just aren't made for holding on to things, Cun'm."

"But if the dam is gone, the reservoir is going. Why did you bother with me? Shouldn't the city be warned? Why are both of you still here? I realize that Nereis can't travel very well just now, but shouldn't she try to get to the city while there's still water in the aqueduct? She'll never make it all that way over dry land—even you will have trouble. You should have left me and done your job. Not that I'm complaining."

"It just isn't done." Creak dismissed the suggestion with no more words. "Besides, I may need you; there is much to be done in which you can perhaps help. Now that you are awake and more or less all right, I will go to the city. When you have gotten back to your ship and fixed your bones, will you please follow? If the aqueduct loses its water before I get there, I'll need your help."

"Right. Should I bring Nereis with me? With no water coming into your house, how long will it be habitable?"

"Until evaporation makes this water *too* salt—days, at least. There are many plants and much surface; it will remain breathable. She can decide for herself whether to fly with you; being out of water in your ship when her time comes would also be bad, though I suppose you could get her to the city quickly. In any case, we should have a meeting place. Let's see—there is a public gathering area about five hundred of your meters north of the apex of the only concave angle in the outer wall. I can't think of anything plainer to describe. I'll be there when I can. Either wait for me, or come back at intervals, as your own plans may demand. That should suffice. I'm going."

The Rantan snaked his way through the tangle of furniture and disappeared through a narrow opening in one wall. Listening carefully, Cunningham finally heard the splash which indicated that the native had reached the aqueduct—and that there was still water in it.

"All right, Nereis," he said. "I'll start back to the ship. I don't suppose you want to come with me over even that little bit of land, but do you want me to come back and pick you up before I follow Creak?"

The other native, identical with her husband to human eyes except for her deeper coloration, thought a moment. "Probably you should follow him as quickly as you can. I'll be all right here for a few days, as he said—and one doesn't suggest that someone is wrong until there is proof. You go ahead without me. Unless you think you'll need *my* help; you said you had some injury."

"Thanks, I can walk once I'm out of the room. But you might help me with the climb, if you will."

Nereis flowed out of her relaxation nook in the furniture, the springy material rising as her weight was removed.

The man took a couple of gentle arm strokes, which brought him to the wall. Ordinarily he could have heaved himself out of the water with no difficulty, but the broken ribs made a big difference. It took the help of Nereis, braced against the floor, to ease him to the top of the two-meter-thick outer wall of unshaped, cemented rocks and gravel. He stood up without too much difficulty once there was solid footing, and stood looking around briefly before starting to pick his way back to the *Nimepotea*.

The dam lay only a few meters to the north; the break Creak had mentioned was not visible. He and the native had been underwater in the reservoir more than a quarter-kilometer to the west of the house when they had been caught by the released waters. Looking in that direction, he could see part of the stream still gushing, and wondered how he had survived at all in that turbulent, boulder-studded flood. Behind the dam, the reservoir was visibly lower, though it would presumably be some hours before it emptied.

He must have been unconscious for some time, he thought: it would have taken the native, himself almost helpless on dry land, a long time indeed to drag him up the dam wall from the site of the break to the house, which was on the inside edge of the reservoir.

East of Creak's house, extending south toward the city, was the aqueduct which had determined his selection of a first landing point on Ranta. Beyond it, some three hundred meters from where he stood, lay the black ovoid of his ship. He would first have to make his way along the walls of the house—preferably without falling in and getting tangled in the furniture—to the narrow drain that Creak had followed to the aqueduct, then turn upstream instead of down until he reached the dam, cross the dam gate of the aqueduct, and descend the outer face of the dam to make his way across the bare rock to his vessel.

Southward, some fifteen kilometers away, lay the city he had not yet visited. It looked rather like an old labyrinth from this viewpoint, since the Rantans had no use for roofs and ceilings. It would be interesting to see whether the divisions corresponded to homes, streets, parks, and the like; but he had preferred to learn what he could about a new world from isolated individuals before exposing himself to crowds. Following his usual custom, Cunningham had made his first contact with natives who lived close enough to a large population center to be in touch with the main culture, yet far enough from it to minimize the chance of his meeting swarms of natives until he felt ready for them. This policy involved assumptions about culture and technology which were sometimes wrong, but had not so far proven fatally so.

He splashed along the feeder that had taken Creak to the aqueduct and reached the more solid and heavy wall of the main channel.

The going was rough, since the Rantans did not appear to believe in squaring or otherwise shaping their structural stone. They simply cemented together fragments of all sizes down to fine sand until they had something watertight. Some of the fragments felt a little loose underfoot, which did not help his peace of mind. Getting away with his life from one dam failure seemed to be asking enough of luck.

However, he traversed the thirty or forty meters to the dam without disaster, turned to his right, and made his way across the arch supporting the wooden valve. This, too, reflected Rantan workmanship. The reedlike growths of which it was made had undergone no shaping except for the removal of an outer bark and—though he was not sure about this—the cutting to some random length less than the largest dimension of the gate. Thousands of the strips were glued together both parallel and crossed at varying angles, making a pattern that strongly appealed to Cunningham's artistic taste.

Once across, he descended the gentle south slope of the dam and made his way quickly to the *Nimepotea*.

An hour later, still sore but with his ribs knitted and a good meal inside him, he lifted the machine from the lava and made his way south along the aqueduct, flying slowly enough to give himself every chance to see Creak. The native might, of course, have reached the city by now; Cunningham knew that his own swimming speed was superior to the Rantan's, but the latter might have been helped by current in the aqueduct. The sun was almost directly overhead, so it was necessary to fly a little to one side of the watercourse to avoid its hot, blinding reflection.

He looked at other things than the channel, of course. He had not flown since meeting Creak and Nereis, so he knew nothing of the planet save what the two natives had told him. They themselves had done little traveling, their work confining them to the reservoir and its neighborhood, the aqueduct, and sometimes the city. Cunningham had much to learn.

The aqueduct itself was not a continuous channel, but was divided into lower and lower sections, or locks. These did not contain gates—rather to the man's surprise—so that flow for the entire fifteen-plus kilometers started or stopped very quickly according to what was happening at the dam. To Cunningham, this would seem to trap water here and there along the channel, but he assumed that the builders had had their reasons for the design.

He approached the city without having sighted Creak, and paused to think before crossing the outer wall. He still felt uneasy about meeting crowds of aliens; there was really no way of telling how they would react. Creak and Nereis were understandable individuals, rational by human standards; but no race is composed of identical personalities, and a crowd is not the simple sum of the individuals composing it—there is too much person-to-person feedback.

The people in the city, or some of them, must by now know about him, however. Creak had made several trips to town in the past few months, and admitted that he had made no secret of Cunningham's presence. The fact that no crowds had gathered at the dam suggested something not quite human about Rantans, collectively.

They might not even have noticed his ship just now. He was certainly visible from the city; but the natives, Creak had told him, practically never paid attention to anything out of water unless it was an immediate job to be done.

Cunningham had watched Creak and Nereis for hours before their first actual meeting, standing within a dozen meters of them at times while they were underwater. Creak had not seen him even when the native had emerged to do fresh stonework on the top of the dam; he had been using a lorgnette with one eye, and ignoring the out-of-focus images which his other eyes gave when out of water; though, indeed, his breathing suit for use out of water did not cover his head, since his breathing apparatus was located at the bases of his limbs. Creak had simply bent to his work.

It had been Nereis, still underwater, who saw the grotesquely refracted human form approaching her husband and hurled herself from the water in between the two. This had been simple reflex; she had not been on guard in any sense. As far as she and Creak appeared to know, there was no land life on Ranta.

So the city dwellers might not yet have noticed him, unless— No, they would probably dismiss the shadow of the *Nimepotea* as that of a cloud. In any case, knowledge of him for six months should be adequate preparation. He could understand the local language, even if the locals would not be able to understand him.

He landed alongside the aqueduct at a few meters from the point where it joined the city wall. He had thought of going directly to the spot specified by Creak, but decided first to take a closer look at the city itself.

Going outside was simple enough; an airsuit sufficed. He had been maintaining his ship's atmosphere at local total pressure, a little over one and three-quarter bars, to avoid the nuisances of wearing rigid armor or of decompression on return. The local air was poisonous, however, since its oxygen partial pressure was nearly three times Earth's sea-level normal; but a diffusion selector took care of that without forcing him to worry about time limits.

Cunningham took no weapons, though he was not assuming that all Rantans would prove as casually friendly as Creak and Nereis had done. He felt no fear of the beings out of water, and had no immediate intention of submerging.

The aqueduct was almost five meters high, and a good deal steeper than the outer wall of Creak's house. However, the standard rough stonework gave plenty of hand- and toehold, and he reached the top with little trouble. A few bits of gravel came loose under his feet, but nothing large enough to cost him any support.

Water stood in this section of aqueduct, but it had stopped flowing. At the south end it was lapping at the edge of the city wall itself; at the north end of this lock, the bottom was exposed though not yet dry. He walked in this direction until he reached the barrier between this section and the next, noting without surprise that the latter also had water to full depth at the near end. There was some seepage through the cemented stone—the sort that Creak had always been trying to fix at the main dam.

Finally approaching the city wall, he saw that its water was only a few centimeters below that in the adjoining aqueduct section. He judged that there was some remaining lifetime for the metropolis and its inhabitants, but was surprised that no workers were going out to salvage water along the aqueduct. Then he realized that their emergency plans might call for other measures first. After all, the dam would have to be repaired before anything else was likely to do much good. No doubt Creak would be able to tell him about that.

In the meantime, the first compartment, or square, or whatever it was, should be worth looking over. Presumably it would have equipment for salting the incoming water, since the natives could not stand freshwater in their systems. A small compartment in Creak's house had served this purpose—as it was explained to him. However, he saw nothing here of the racks for supporting blocks of evaporated sea salt just below the surface, nor supplies of the blocks stored somewhere above the water, nor a crew to tend the setup. After all, salting the water for a whole city of some thirteen square kilometers would have to be a pretty continuous operation.

The compartment was some fifty meters square, however, and could have contained a great deal not visible from where he stood on the wall; and there was much furniture—in this case, apparently, living vegetation—within it. He walked around its whole perimeter—in effect, entering the city for a time, though he saw no residents and observed no evidence that any of them saw him—but could learn little more.

The vegetation below him seemed to be of many varieties, but all consisting of twisted, tangled stems of indefinite length. The stems' diameters ranged from that of a human hair to that of a human leg. Colors tended to be brilliant, reds and yellows predominating. None of the vegetation had the green leaves so nearly universal on photosynthetic plants, and Cunningham wondered whether these things could really represent the base of the Rantan food pyramid.

If they did not, then how did the city feed itself, since there was nothing resembling farm tanks around it? Maybe the natives were still fed from the ocean—but in that case, why did they no longer live in the ocean?

Cunningham had asked his hosts about that long before but obtained no very satisfactory answer. Creak appeared to have strong emotional reactions to the question, regarding the bulk of his compatriots in terms which Cunningham had been unable to work into literal translation but which were certainly pejoratives—sinners, or fools, or something like that. Nereis appeared to feel less strongly about the matter, but had never had much chance to talk when her husband got going on the subject. Also, it seemed to be bad Rantan manners to contradict someone who had a strong opinion on any matter; the natives, if the two he had met were fair examples, seemed to possess to a limitless degree the human emotional need to be right. In any case, the reason why the city was on land was an open question and remained the sort of puzzle that retired human beings needed to keep them from their otherwise inevitable boredom. Cunningham was quite prepared to spend years on Ranta, as he had on other worlds.

Back at the aqueduct entrance, though now on its west side, Cunningham considered entering the water and examining the compartment from within. Vegetation was absent at the point where freshwater entered the city wall and first compartment, so, he figured, it should be possible to make his way to the center. There things might be different enough to be worth examining, without the danger of his getting trapped as he had been once or twice in Nereis' furniture before she and her husband had cleared some space for him.

It was not fear that stopped him, though decades of wandering in the *Nimepotea* and her predecessors had developed in Cunningham a level of prudence which many a less mature or experienced being would have called rank cowardice. Rather, he liked to follow a plan where possible, and the only trace of a plan he had so far developed included getting back in contact with Creak.

While considering the problem, he kicked idly at the stonework on which he was standing. So far from his immediate situation were his thoughts that several loose fragments of rock lay around him before they caught his attention. When they did, he froze motionless, remembering belatedly what had happened when he was climbing the wall.

Rantan cement, he had come to realize, was generally remarkable stuff—another of the mysteries now awaiting solution in his mental file. The water dwellers could hardly have fire or forges, and quite reasonably he had seen no sign of metal around Creak's home or in his tools. It seemed unlikely that the natives' chemical or physical knowledge could be very sophisticated, and the surprise and interest shown by Creak and Nereis when he had been making chemical studies of the local rocks and their own foodstuffs supported this idea. Nevertheless, their glue was able to hold rough, unsquared fragments of stone, and untooled strips of wood, with more force than Cunningham's muscles could overcome. This was true even when the glued area was no more than a square millimeter or two. On one of his early visits to Creak's home, Cunningham had become entangled in the furniture and been quite unable to break out, or even separate a single strand from its fellows.

But now stones were coming loose under his feet. He had strolled a few meters out along the aqueduct wall again while thinking, and perhaps having this stretch come apart under him would be less serious than having the city start doing so, but neither prospect pleased. Even here a good deal of water remained, and being washed out over Ranta's stony surface again...

No. Be careful, Cunningham! You came pretty close to being killed when the dam gave way a few hours ago. And didn't Creak say something like "Cement failure again" that time? Was the cement, or some other key feature of the local architecture, proving less reliable than its developers and users expected? if so, why were they only finding it out now, since the city must have been here a long time? *Could an Earthman's presence have anything to do with it?* He would have to find out, tactfully, whether this had been going on for more than the six months he had been on the planet.

More immediately, was the pile of rock he was standing on now going to continue to support him? If it collapsed, what would the attitude of the natives be, supposing he was in a condition to care? A strong human tendency exists, shared by many other intelligent species, to react to disaster by looking for someone to blame. Creak's and Nereis' noticeable preference for being right about things suggested that Rantans might so react. All in all, getting off the defective stonework seemed a good idea.

Walking as carefully as he could, Cunningham made his way upstream along the lock. He felt a little easier when he reached the section where the bottom was exposed and there was no water pressure to compound the stress or wash him out among the boulders.

He would have crossed at this point, and climbed the opposite wall to get back to his ship, but the inner walls of the conduit were practically vertical. They were quite rough enough to furnish climbing holds, but the man had developed a certain uneasiness about putting his weight on single projecting stones. Instead, he went up the wall—now dry—between the last two locks and crossed this. It held him, rather to his surprise, and with much relief he made his way down the more gradual slope on the other side to the surface rock of the planet, climbed to and through *Nimepotea's* air lock, and lifted his vessel happily off the ground.

2

Hovering over the center of the city, he could see that it was far from deserted; though it was not easy to identify individual inhabitants even from a few meters up. Most of the spaces, even those whose primary function seemed to correspond to streets, were cluttered with plant life. The

Rantans obviously preferred climbing through the stuff to swimming in clear water. But the plants formed a tangle through which nothing less skillful than a Rantan or a moray eel could have made its way. Sometimes the natives could be seen easily in contrast to the plants, but in other parts of the city they blended in so completely that Cunningham began to wonder whether the compartment he had first examined had really been deserted, after all.

He could not, of course, tell if the creatures were aware of real trouble. It was impossible to interpret everything he saw, even as he dropped lower, but Cunningham judged that schools were in session, meals were being prepared, with ordinary craftwork and business being conducted by the majority of the natives. At least *some* ordinary life-support work was going on, he saw. To the southeast of the city, partly within the notch where the wall bent inward to destroy the symmetry of its four-kilometer square, and just about at high-tide mark, he noticed a number of structures that were obviously intended for the production of salt by evaporation. The tide was now going out, and numerous breathing-suited Rantans—with lorgnettes—were closing flood gates to areas that had just filled with sea water. Others were scraping and bagging deposits of brownish material in areas where the water had evaporated. Further from the ocean, similar bags had been opened and were lying in the sun, presumably for more complete drying, under elevated tentlike sheets of the same transparent fabric Creak had used for his workbag. In fact, most of the beings laboring outside the city walls dragged similar bags with them.

No one seemed to be working now in these upper drying spaces; this was the closest evidence Cunningham could see that city life had been at all disturbed. But naturally, if no water were coming in from the reservoir, no salt would be needed immediately. That was all he could infer from observation; for more knowledge, he would have to ask Creak.

The meeting place was now fairly easy to spot: a seventy-meter-square "room" with much of the central portion clear of vegetation, located above the corner which cut into the southeastern part of the city. As he approached this area and settled downward, Cunningham could see that there were a number of natives—perhaps a hundred—in the clear portion. How many might be in the vegetation near the edges, he had no way to tell. He could see no really clear place to land, but once the bottom of the hull entered the water the pilot eased down slowly enough to give those below every chance to get out from under. The water was about five meters deep, and when the *Nimepotea* touched bottom her main air lock was a little more than a meter above the surface. Cunningham touched the override, which cut out the safety interlock, and opened both doors at once, taking up his position at the edge of the lock with a remote controller attached to his equipment belt.

The reaction to his arrival was obvious, if somewhat surprising. Wormlike beings practically boiled out of the water, moving away from him. He could not see below the surface anywhere near the sides of the enclosure; but he could guess that the exits were thoroughly jammed, for natives were climbing *over* the wall at every point, apparently frantic to get out. The man had just time to hope that no one was being hurt in the crush, and to wonder whether he should lift off before anything worse happened, when something totally unexpected occurred. Two more of the natives snaked up at his feet, slipped their head ends into the air lock to either side of him, coiled around his legs, and swept him outward.

His reactions were far too slow. He did operate the controller, but only just in time to close the lock behind him. He and his attackers struck the water with a splash that wet only the outer surface of the portal.

His suit was not ballasted, so it floated quite high in the extremely salt solution. The natives made a futile effort to submerge him, but even their body weights—their density was considerably greater than even the ocean water of their world—did not suffice. They gave up quickly and propelled him along the surface toward the wall.

Well before getting there, the natives found that a human body is very poorly designed for motion through Rantan living areas. The only reason they could move him at all was that he floated so high. His arms and legs, and occasionally his head, kept catching in loops of plant material—loops which to the captors were normal, regular sources of traction. The four digits at the ends of their half-tentacle, half-flipper limbs were opposed in two tonglike pairs, like those of the African chameleon, and thus gripped the stems and branches more surely than a human hand could ever have done. Grips were transferred from one limb to the next with a flowing coordination that caught Cunningham's attention even in his present situation.

The difference between Cunningham's habitual caution and ordinary fear was now obvious. Being dragged to an unknown goal by two beings who far outpowered and outweighed him physically, he could still carry on his earlier speculations about the evolution of Ranta's intelligent species and the factors which had operated to make intelligence a survival factor.

The planet's single moon was much smaller and less massive than Luna, but sufficiently closer to its primary to make up more than the difference as far as tide-raising power was concerned. Ranta's tides were nearly ten times as great as Earth's. There were no really large continents—

or rather, as the *Nimepotea's* mass readers suggested, the continents that covered a large fraction of the planet were mostly submerged—and a remarkably large fraction of the world's area was intertidal zone. Cunningham had named the world from the enormous total length of shore and beach visible from space—he had still been thinking in Finnish after his months on Omituinen. The tidal areas were largely overgrown with the springy, tangled plants the natives seemed to like so much. This environment, so much of it alternately under and above water, would certainly be one where sensory acuity and rapid nervous response would be survival factors. Selection pressures might have been fiercer even than on Earth; there must have been some reason why intelligence had appeared so early—Boss 6673 was much younger than Sol.

The science of a water-dwelling species would tend to be more slanted in biological than in chemical or physical directions, and perhaps...

Opportunity knocked. They had reached a wall, which projected only a few centimeters from the water and was nearly two meters thick. The natives worked their way over it, pulling themselves along by the irregularities as Creak and Nereis had done on land. These two were equally uncomfortable and clumsy, and the man judged that their attention must be as fully preempted by the needs of the moment as were their limbs; only a few of the tonglike nippers were holding him.

He gave a sudden, violent wrench, getting his legs under him and tearing some of the holds loose. Then, as hard as he could, he straightened up. This broke the rest of the holds and lifted him from the wall top. He had had no real opportunity to plan a jump, and he came unpleasantly close to landing back in the water. But by the narrowest of margins he had enough leeway to control a second leap. This put him solidly on the wall more than a meter from the nearer of his captors.

The latter made no serious effort to catch him. They could not duplicate his leaps or even his ordinary walking pace out of water, and neither could get back into the water from where they were for several seconds.

Cunningham, watching alertly to either side for ones who might be in a better position to attack, headed along the wall toward the edge of the city as quickly as he dared. He was free for the moment, but he could see no obvious way to get back to the *Nimepotea*. The fact that he could swim faster in open water than the natives would hardly suffice; open water did not comprise the whole distance to be crossed. And he would not be safe on the walls, presumably, so his first priority was to reach relatively open country beyond them.

His path was far from straight, since the city compartments varied widely in size, but most of the turns were at right angles. A few hundred meters brought him to the south wall a little to the east of the angle that Creak had used as a checkpoint. The outer slope was gradual, like that of the reservoir dam, but the resemblance was not encouraging; Cunningham convinced himself, however, that it was improbable for his accident of a few hours before to repeat itself so soon, so he made his way down with no difficulty.

The high-tide mark lay fairly near, and much of the rough lava was overlain by fine, black sand. In a sense he was still inside the city, since many structures of cemented stone—some of them quite large—were in sight. A large number of suited natives crawled and climbed among them—climbed, since many of the buildings were enveloped by scaffolding of the same general design as Creak's furniture.

None of the workers seemed to notice the man, and he wondered when some local genius would conceive the idea of spectacles attached over the eyes to replace the lorgnettes used to correct out-of-water refraction. Perhaps with so many limbs, the Rantans were not highly motivated to invent something which would free one more for work. It did not occur to him that lens making was one of the most difficult and expensive processes the Rantans could handle, and one very mobile lens per worker was their best economic solution to the problem.

His own problems were more immediate. He had to find Creak, first of all; everything else, such as persuading people to let him back to his ship, seemed to hinge on that. Unfortunately, he had just been chased away from the place where Creak was supposed to be. Communicating with some other native who might conceivably be able to find the dam-keeper was going to be complex, since no native but Creak himself and his wife could understand Cunningham—and Cunningham could not properly pronounce Creak's name in the native language. However, there seemed nothing better to do but try—with due precautions against panic and attack reactions.

These seemed to pose little problem on dry land, and the man approached one of the natives who was working alone at the foot of a building some fifty or sixty meters away. It was wearing a breathing suit, of course, and dragging a worksack similar to the one Creak habitually used. Like all the others, it seemed completely unaware of him, and remained so until Cunningham gave a light tug on the cord of its worksack.

It turned its head end toward him, lorgnette in a forward hand, and looked over with apparent calmness; at least, it neither fled nor attacked.

Cunningham spoke loudly, since sound transmission through two suits would be poor, and uttered a few sentences of a human language. He did not expect to be understood, but hoped that the regularity of the sound pattern would be obvious, as it had been so long ago to Creak.

The creature answered audibly, and the man was able to understand fairly well, though there were occasional words he had never heard from Nereis or from Creak. "I'm afraid I can't understand you," the worker said. "I suppose you are the land creature which Creak has been telling about."

This was promising, though the man could not even approximate the sound of a Rantan affirmative, and nodding his head meant nothing to the native. If there was a corresponding gesture used here, he had never been aware of it. All he could do was make an effort at the Rantan pronunciation of Creak's name, and no one was more aware than Cunningham what a dismal failure this was. However, the native was far from stupid.

"Creak tells us he has learned your language, so I suppose you are trying to find him. I'm not sure where he is just now. Usually he's at the reservoir, but sometimes he comes to town. Then you can usually find him explaining to the largest crowd he can gather why we should have more workers out there on dam maintenance, and why the rest of the city should be building shelters below high-water mark against the time the dam finally fails for good. If he's in town now, I hadn't heard about it; but that doesn't prove anything. I've been out here since midday. Is it he that you want?"

Cunningham made another futile effort to transmit an affirmative, and the native once more displayed his brains.

"If you want to say 'Yes,' wave an upper appendage; for 'No,' a lower one—lie down by all means; you may as well be comfortable—and if you don't understand all or some of what I say, wave both upper limbs. Creak said you had learned to understand our talk. All right?"

Cunningham waved an arm.

"Good. Is it really Creak you want to find?"

Arm.

"Is there need for haste?"

Cunningham hesitated, then kicked, startling the native with his ability to stand even briefly on one foot.

"All right. The best thing I can suggest is that you wait here, if you can, until two hours before sunset, when I finish work. Then I'll go into town with you and spread the word that you're looking for him. Probably he'll be preaching, and easy to find."

The man waved both arms.

"Sorry, I shouldn't have put so much together. Did you understand the general plan?"

Arm.

"The time?" Arm.

"The part about his preaching?"

Both arms; Cunningham had never heard the word the native was using.

"Well, hasn't he ever told you how stupid people were ever to move out of the ocean?"

Kick. This wasn't exactly a falsehood, though Cunningham had grasped Creak's disapproval of the general situation.

"Don't complain. Creak disapproves of cities. That's why he and his wife took that job out in the desert, though how he ties that in with going back to Nature is more than anyone can guess. It's further from the ocean in every sense you can use. I suppose they're just down on everything artificial. I think he gloats every time part of the dam has to be recemented. If that hadn't been happening long before he took the job, people would suspect him of breaking it himself."

Cunningham saw no reason to try to express his relief at this statement. At least, no one would be blaming the alien...

He used the don't-understand signal again, and the native quickly narrowed it down to the man's curiosity about why Creak didn't live in the ocean if he so disapproved of cities.

"No one can live in the ocean for long; it's too dangerous. Food is hard to find, there are animals and plants that can kill—a lot of them developed by us long ago for one purpose or another. Producing one usually caused troubles no one foresaw, and they had to make another to offset its effects, and then the new one caused trouble and something had to be done about that. Maybe we'll hit a balance sometime, but since we've moved into land-based cities no one's been trying very hard. Creak could tell you all this more eloquently than I; even he admits we can't go back tomorrow. Now, my friend, it takes a lot of time to converse this way—enjoyable as it is—and I have work to finish. So—"

Cunningham gave the affirmative gesture willingly; he had just acquired a lot to think about. It had never occurred to him that an essentially biological technology, which the Rantans seemed to have developed, could result in industrial pollution as effectively and completely as a chemical-mechanical one. Once the point was made, it was obvious enough.

But this came nowhere near to explaining what had happened so recently, when he had landed at the meeting point. Could Creak be preaching Doomsday to the city's less-balanced citizens? Was the fellow a monomaniac, or a zealot of some sort? This might be, judging from what Hinge (as Cunningham had mentally dubbed his new acquaintance) had been saying. Could the two natives who had attempted to capture him be local police, trying to remove the key figure from a potentially dangerous mob? Cunningham had seen cultures in which this was an everyday occurrence. Hinge seemed a calm and balanced individual—more so than the average member of a pre-space-travel culture who had just met his first off-worlder—but he was only one individual.

And what was Hinge's point about the glue failing? Why should that be a problem? There were all sorts of ways to fasten things together.

Cunningham brooded on these questions while Ranta's white sun moved slowly across the sky, a trifle more slowly than Sol crosses Earth's. He sat facing the city, half expecting Creak to come over the wall toward him at any time. After all, even if the fellow had not been at the landing site it was hard to believe that a weird-looking alien could throw a crowd into panic and then walk out of town, with no effort at concealment, without having everyone in the place knowing what happened and where the alien was within the next hour. However, Creak did not appear.

Two or three other workers who came to discuss something with Hinge noticed the man and satisfied an apparently human curiosity by talking to him rather as Hinge had done. None of them seemed surprised to see him, and he finally realized that Creak had made his presence known, directly or otherwise, to the city's entire population. That made the Rantans seem rather less human. Granting the difficulty of a trip to the dam, most intelligent species which Cunningham had met would have had crowds coming to see an alien, regardless of their ideas about his origin. Maybe Creak had a good reason for trying to poke his fellow citizens into action; they *did* seem a rather casual and unenterprising lot.

They knew no astronomy; they had an empirical familiarity with the motions of their sun and moon, but had barely noticed the stars and were quite unaware of Boss 6673's other planets. They knew so little of the land areas of their own world that they took it for granted that Cunningham was from one of these—at least, Hinge had referred to him as "the land creature."

Where on Ranta was Creak? There were questions to be answered!

Eventually, Hinge replaced his tools in the worksack and began to drag the latter toward the city wall. Cunningham helped. There was a ramp some three hundred meters east of the point where he had descended, and the native used this. Hinge let the man do most of the work with the bag, making his own painful way up the slope with the rope slack. At the top, he spoke again.

"I really must eat. It will probably be quickest if you wait here. I will spread the word on my way home that you seek Creak. If he has not found you by the time I get back, I will guide you to the various places he is most likely to be. I should be back in half an hour, or a little more."

He waited for Cunningham to express comprehension, then dropped his worksack into the water, followed it, and disappeared into the tangle.

3

Evidently Hinge kept his promise about spreading the word. During the next quarter-hour, more and more native heads appeared above the water, and more and more lorgnettes were turned on the visitor. Human beings are not the only species rendered uneasy by the prolonged, silent stare; but they rank high. Before long, Cunningham was wondering whether the old idea of being frozen by a stare through a lorgnette might not have something more than an artificial social connotation.

Several more workers came up the ramp, looked him over, and then splashed on into the city—whether to form part of the growing crowd or to go home to dinner was anybody's guess.

Cunningham kicked uneasily at the material underfoot, then stopped guiltily as he remembered what had happened earlier; but he looked closely and decided that the cement was in good condition here. Perhaps the Rantans paid more attention to upkeep on items which were nearby and in plain sight; after all, they had plenty of other human characteristics.

Presumably the crowd was not really silent, but none of its sound was reaching Cunningham's ears. This contributed to the oppressive atmosphere, which he felt more and more strongly as the minutes fled by. Hoping to hear better and perhaps get the actual feelings of the crowd, he seated himself on the inner edge of the wall and let his legs dangle in the water. He heard, but only a hopeless jumble of sound. No words could be distinguished, and he did not know the Rantans well enough to interpret general tones.

And now the crowd was moving closer. Was it because more people were crowding into the space, or for some other reason? He looked wistfully at his ship, towering above the walls only a few hundred meters away. Would it pay to make a dash for it? Almost certainly not. He could get to the right space along the wall, but that swim through the tangle would be a waste of time if even a single native chose to interfere. He got uneasily to his feet.

The heads were closer. Were they *coming* closer, or were more appearing inside the circle of early arrivals? A few minutes' watch showed that it was the latter, and that eased his mind somewhat. Evidently the crowd was not deliberately closing on him, but it was growing in size, so the word of his presence must be spreading. When would it reach the beings who had tried to capture him earlier? What would their reaction be when it did?

He was in no real immediate danger, of course. With any warning at all, he could spring back down the wall and be out of reach, but this would bring him no nearer to his ship in any sense. He wished Hinge or Creak would show up...or that someone would simply talk to him.

A head emerged a couple of meters to his left, against the wall; its owner, wearing a breathing suit, slowly snaked his way out of the water.

Cunningham stood tense for a moment. Then he relaxed, realizing that the newcomer could pose no threat at that distance. But he tightened up again and began looking at the water closely as it occurred to him that the being might be trying to distract his attention.

The native carefully dragged himself onto the wall so that no part of his length remained in the water. This seemed more effort than it was worth, since a typical Rantan weighs around four hundred fifty kilograms in air even on his own planet, and Cunningham was more suspicious than ever. He was almost sure that the fellow was bidding strictly for attention when he heard its voice.

"Cun'm! Listen carefully! Things have gone very badly. I don't think anyone in the water can hear me right now, but they'll get suspicious in a moment. It's very important that you stay away from your ship for a time, and we should both get away from here. As soon as I'm sure you understand, I'm going to roll down the wall; you follow as quickly as you can. Some may come after us, since there are a few other breathing suits on hand, so I'll roll as far as I can. I have some rope with me, and as soon as we get together you can use it to help me travel. That way we can go faster than they, and maybe they'll give up."

By now, Cunningham had recognized Creak's body pattern.

"Why should they want to catch us?" he asked.

"I'll explain when we have time. Do you understand the plan?"

"Yes."

"All right, here I go. *Come on!*"

Creak poured his front end onto the slope and followed it with the rest of his body, curling into a flat spiral with his head in the center as he did so. His limbs were tucked against his sides, and his rubbery body offered no projections to be injured. He had given himself a downhill shove in the process of curling up, and the meter-wide disk which was his body went bounding down the irregular outer surface of the wall. Cunningham winced in sympathy with every bounce as he watched, though he knew the boneless, gristly tissue of the Rantans was not likely to be damaged by such treatment. Then, splashes behind him suggested that Creak probably had good reason for the haste he was so strongly recommending.

The man followed him, leaping as carefully as he could from rock to rock, tense with the fear that one of them would come loose as he landed on it. He reached the bottom safely, however, and sprinted after Creak, whose momentum combined with the southward slope of the rocky beach to carry him some distance from the wall.

Finally, he bumped into the springy scaffolding surrounding one of the numerous buildings that dotted the area, and was brought to a halt. He promptly unrolled, and shook out the rope which he had been carrying in some obscure fashion. It was already tied into a sort of harness which he fitted over his forward end. As Cunningham came up, the native extended a long bight to him.

The man had no trouble slipping this over his head and settling it in place around his waist. He looked back as he was finishing and saw that half a dozen suited natives had emulated Creak's method of descending the wall. They had, however, unrolled as soon as they reached the bottom, probably to see which way the fugitives were going; and they were well behind in the race. The nearest were just starting to crawl toward them in typical Rantan dry-land fashion, pulling themselves along by whatever bits of lava they could find projecting through the sand.

"East or west? Or does it matter?" Cunningham asked.

"Not to me," was the response, "but let's get moving!"

Cunningham took a quick look around, saw something from his erect vantage point which amused him, leaned into the bight of the rope harness, and headed east. Creak helped as much as he could, but this was not very much. The native could not conveniently look back, since the harness prevented his front end from turning and none of his eyes projected far enough. The man could, and did.

"Only a couple are actually following," he reported. "You're pretty heavy, and I'm not dragging you really very much faster than they can travel; but I guess the fact that we're going faster at all, and that I am evidently a land creature, has discouraged most of them."

"There are some who won't give up easily. Don't stop just yet."

"I won't. We haven't reached the place I have in mind."

"What place is that? How do you know anything about this area? Personally, I don't think we should stop for at least a couple of your kilometers."

"I can see a place where I think we'll be safe even if they keep after us. You can decide, when we get there. I'll go on if you think we have to. But remember, you weigh half a dozen times as much as I do. This is work."

One by one their pursuers gave up and turned back, and at about the time the last one did so Cunningham felt the load he was pulling ease considerably. At the same moment Creak called out, "I'm sorry, Cun'm. I can't help you at all here. It's all sand, and there's nothing to hold on to."

"I know," the man replied. "That was what I thought I'd seen. It's easier to pull you in deep sand, and I didn't think anyone could follow us here." He dragged the native on for another hundred meters or so, then dropped the rope and turned to him.

"All right, Creak, what is this all about?"

The native lifted the front third of his body, and looked around as well as the height and his lens would permit before answering.

"I'll have to give you a lot of background, first. I dodged a lot of your questions earlier because I wasn't sure of your attitude. Now I'm pretty sure, from some of the things you've said, that you will agree with me and help me.

"First, as you seem to take for granted, we used to be dwellers in the tidal jungles—many lifetimes ago. Our ancestors must have been hunters like the other creatures that live there, though they ate some plant food as well as animals. Eventually they learned to raise both kinds of food instead of hunting for it, and still later learned so much about the rules which control the forms of living things that they could make new plants and animals to suit their needs. This knowledge also enabled them to make buildings out of stone and wood, once cement was developed; and they could live in shelters and provide themselves with necessities and pleasures, without ever risking their lives or comfort in the jungles. We became, as you have called it, civilized and scientific.

"That so-called 'progress' separated most of us from the realities of life. We ate when we were hungry, slept in safety when we were tired, and did whatever amused us the rest of the time—developing new plants and animals just for their appearance or taste, for example. The tides, which *I* think were the real cause of our developing the brains we did, became a nuisance, so we built homes and finally cities out of the water."

"And you think that's bad?"

"Of course. We are dependent on the city and what it supplies, now. We are soft. Not one in a hundred of us could live a day in the tidal jungles—they wouldn't know what was fit to eat, or what was dangerous, or what to do when the tide went out. Even if they learned those things quickly enough to keep themselves alive, they'd die out because they couldn't protect eggs and children long enough. I've been pointing all this out to them for years."

"But how does this lead to the present trouble? Did you really wreck the dam yourself, to force people out of the city?"

"Oh, no. I'm enthusiastic but not crazy. Anyway, there was no need. Civilization out of water, like civilization in it, depends on construction, and construction depends on cement. It was—I suppose it was, anyway— the invention of cement which made cities possible; and now that the cement is starting to fail, the warning is clear. We should—we *must*— start working our way back to the sea—back to Nature. We were designed to live in the sea, and it's foolish to go against basic design. We should no more be living on land than you should be living in the water."

"Some of my people do live in underwater cities," Cunningham pointed out. "Some live on worlds with no air, or even where the temperature would freeze air."

"But they're just workers, doing jobs which can't be done elsewhere. You told me that your people work only a certain number of years, and then retire and do what they please. You're certainly back to Nature."

"In some ways, I suppose so. But get back to the reason we're sitting on the sand out of reach of my ship."

"Most of the people in the city can't face facts. They plan to send a big party of workers to repair the dam, and go on just as we have been for years, of course setting up a strict water-use control until the reservoir fills again. But they plan to go on as though nothing serious had happened, or that nothing more serious could ever happen. They're insane. They just don't want to give up what they think of as the right to do what they want whenever they want."

"And you've been telling them all this."

"For years."

"And they refuse to listen."

"Yes."

"All right, I see why *you* are here. But what do they have against me? Or were they merely trying to get me away from your influence?"

If Creak saw any irony in the question he ignored it. "I've been telling them about you from the first, of course. I don't understand this bit about worlds in the sky, and most of them don't either, but there's nothing surprising about creatures living on land even if we've never seen any before. I told them about your flying machine, and the things you must know of science that we don't, and the way that you and your people have gone back to Nature just as I keep saying we must. You remember— you told me how your people had learned things which separated them from the proper life that fitted them, and which did a lot of damage to the Nature of your world, and how you finally had to change policies in order to stay alive."

"So I did, come to think of it. But you've done a certain amount of reading between the lines. You really think I'm living closer to Nature than my ancestors of a thousand years ago?" Cunningham was more amused than indignant, or even worried.

"Aren't you?"

"I hate to disillusion you, but— Well, you're not entirely wrong, but things aren't as simple as you seem to think. I could survive for a while on my own world away from my technological culture, and most of my people could do the same, because that's part of our education these days. However, we got back to that state very gradually. As it happened, my people *did* become completely dependent on the physical sciences to keep them protected and fed, just as you seem to have done with the biological ones. We did such a good job that our population rose far beyond the numbers which could be supported without the technology.

"The real crisis came because we used certain sources of energy much faster than they were formed in Nature, and just barely managed to convert to adequate ones in time. We're being natural in one way: we now make a strong point of not using any resource faster than Nature can renew it. However, we still live a very civilized-scientific life, the sort that lets us spend practically all our time doing what we feel like rather than grubbing for life's necessities. You're going to have to face the fact that the technology road is a one-way one, and cursing the ancestors who turned onto it is a waste of time. You'll just have to take the long way around before you get anywhere near where you started."

I...I suppose I was wrong, at least in some details." The native seemed more uneasy than the circumstances called for, and Cunningham remembered the need-to-be-right which he had suspected of being unusually strong in the species. Creak went on, "Still, using you as an example was reasonable. Your flying machine proves you know a lot more than we do."

Cunningham refrained from pointing out the gap in this bit of logic, since at least it had led back to the point he wanted pursued.

"That machine *is* something I'd like to get back to," he remarked. "If you really don't want to explain why someone tried to capture me, I can stand it. But how do I get back there?"

"I wasn't trying to avoid explaining anything," Creak responded, rather indignantly. "I don't know why anyone tried to capture you, but maybe they thought I wasn't telling the exact truth about the situation and they wanted to question you without my intervention. I suppose they'd have been willing to take the time to learn your language—it's the sort of intellectual exercise a lot of them would like. But how you can get back there will take some thinking. I think I can work it out somehow—I'm sure I can. How long can you stay away from your machine without danger? I've never known you to spend more than two days—"

"I'm set to be comfortable for three days, and could get along for five or six; but I hope you don't take that long. What do I do, just sit out here on the sand while your brain works?"

"Can't you learn things outside the city? I thought that was what you were here for. However, there is one other thing you could do. if you were willing—and if it is possible. I know you are a land creature, but am not sure of your limits."

"What is that?"

"Well...it's Nereis. I can tell myself she's all right, and that nothing can reasonably go wrong, but I can't help thinking of things that might. How long would it take you to get to our house, without your ship? Or can you travel that far at all?"

"Sure. Even going around the city, that's less than twenty kilos each way, and there's nothing around to eat me. You really want me to go?"

"It's a little embarrassing to ask, but—yes, I do."

Cunningham shrugged. "It will be quite a while before I have to worry, myself, and you seem pretty sure of being able to solve the ship problem all right, I suppose, the sooner the better?"

"Well, I can't help but picture the house wall going out like the dam."

"I see. Okay, I'm on my way. Put your brain to work."

4

Laird Cunningham was an unsuspicious character by nature. He tended to take the word of others at face value, until strong evidence forced him to do otherwise. Even when minor inconsistencies showed up, he tended to blame them on his own failure to grasp a pertinent point. Hence, he started on his walk with only the obvious worry about recovering his ship occupying his mind—and even that was largely buried, since his conscious attention was devoted to observing the planetary features around him.

He had left Creak at a point which would have been slightly inside the city if the latter had been a perfect square. The easiest way to go seemed to be east until he reached the southern end of the east wall, north along the latter, and then roughly parallel with the aqueduct until he reached the north end of the latter. Crossing it, or the dam, might be a little risky, but the reservoir should be nearly empty by now. Unless he had to stay with Nereis for some reason, it should be possible to get back in, say, five or six hours. He should have mentioned that to Creak— But, no, the sun was almost down now; most of the journey would be in the dark. Why hadn't he remembered that?

And why hadn't Creak thought of this?

Cunningham stopped in his tracks. A Rantan breathing suit was not particularly time-limited—it merely kept the air intakes at the bases of the tentacles wet, and in theory several days' worth of water could be carried. Still, why hadn't Creak been worried for his own sake about the probable time of the man's return? He was trapped on a surface where he was almost helpless. Had he simply forgotten that aspect, through worry for his wife and incipient family? It was possible, of course.

Cunningham, almost at the corner that would take him out of sight of Creak, paused and looked back. He could just see the native, but nearly a kilometer of distance hid the details. He drew a small monocular from his belt and used it.

The sight was interesting, he had to admit. Creak had stretched his body on the sand, holding a slight curve like a bent bow. His limbs were pulled tightly against his sides. Evidently he was exerting a downward force at the ends of the arc, for he was *rolling* in the direction of the convexity of the curve—rolling less rapidly than Cunningham could walk, but much faster than the man had ever seen a Rantan travel on dry land.

As he watched, Creak reached the end of the deep sand and reverted to more normal travel, pulling himself along the projecting stones. Creak never looked back at Cunningham; at least, his lorgnette was never called into use. Probably it never occurred to him that the human being's erect structure would give him such a wide circle of vision...

Cunningham was grinning widely as pieces of the jigsaw began to fall rapidly into place. After a few moments' thought, he replaced the monocular at his belt and resumed his northward hike. Several times he stopped to examine closely the wall of the city, as well as those of some of the small buildings outside. In every case the cement seemed sound. Further north, more than an hour later, he repeated the examination at the walls of the aqueduct, and nodded as though finding just what he had expected.

It was dark when he reached the dam, but the moon provided enough light for travel. He did not want to climb it, but there was no other way to get to the house. He used his small belt light and was extremely careful of his footing, but he was not at all happy until he reached the top. At that point, he could see that the reservoir was nearly empty. This eased his mind somewhat; there would be no water pressure on the structure, and its slopes on either side were gentle enough so that it should be fairly stable even with the cement's failure.

Nereis' house was still apparently intact, but this did not surprise him. Moonlight reflecting from the surface also indicated that its water level had not changed significantly.

He made his way along the walls to the living room as quickly as possible, found the corner where space had been made for him in the furniture, and dropped in. He then remembered that he had not ballasted himself, but managed to roll face down and call to Nereis.

"It's Cunningham, Nereis. I need to talk to you. Is everything all right here?"

The room was practically dark, the only artificial lighting used by the Rantans being a feeble bioluminescence from some of the plants; but he could see her silhouette against these as she entered the room and made her way toward him.

"Cun'm! I did not expect to see you so soon. Has something happened? Is Creak hurt? What is being done about the dam?"

"He's not hurt, though he may be in some trouble. He and I had to get away from the city for a while. He was more worried about you than about us, though; he asked me to come to make sure you were safe while he stayed to solve the other problems. I see your walls aren't leaking, so I suppose—"

"Oh, no, the walls are sound. I suppose the water is evaporating, but it will be quite a few days before I have to worry about producing crystals instead of eggs."

"And you're not worried about the walls failing, even after what happened to the dam today? You're a long, long way from help, and you couldn't travel very well, even in a breathing suit, in your condition."

"The house will last. That dam was different—"

She broke off suddenly. Cunningham grinned invisibly in the darkness.

"Of course, you knew it too," he said. "I should have known when Creak didn't arrange to have me fly you to the city."

Nereis remained silent, but curled up a little more tightly, drawing back into the furniture. The man went on after a moment.

"You knew that the glue lasts indefinitely as long as it's in some sort of contact with saltwater. All your buildings have saltwater inside, and apparently that's enough even for the glue on the outside—I suppose ions diffuse through or something like that. But you have just two structures with only freshwater in contact with them—the dam and the aqueduct. How long have you known that the glue doesn't hold up indefinitely in freshwater?"

"Oh, everyone has known that for years." She seemed willing enough to talk if specific plots were not the subject. "Two or three years, anyway. Cities have been dying for as long as there have been cities, and maybe some people sometimes found out why, but it was only a few years ago that some refugees from one of them got to ours and told what had happened to their reservoir. It didn't take the scientists long to find out why, after that. That's when Creak got his job renewing the cement on the dam. He kept saying there's much more needed—more people to do the cementing, and more reservoirs, if we *must* stay out of the ocean. But no one has taken him seriously."

"You and he think people should go back to the ocean—or at least build your cities there. Why don't others agree?"

"Oh, there are all sorts of things to keep us from living there. The water is hardly breathable. All sorts of living things that people made and turned loose when they didn't want them anymore—"

"I get it. What my people call 'industrial pollution.' Hinge was right. I suppose he wasn't in on this stunt of Creak's— No, never mind, I don't know his real name and can't explain to you. Why haven't you tried to produce a glue that could stand freshwater?"

"How could we? No living thing, natural or artificial, has ever been able to do without food."

"Oooohhh! You mean the stuff is *alive!*"

"Certainly. I know you have shown us that you can change one substance into another all by yourself when you were doing what you called chemical testing, but we have never learned to do that. We can make things only with life."

Cunningham thought briefly. This added details to the picture, but did not, as far as he could see, alter the basic pattern. "All right," he said at last. "I think I know enough to act sensibly. I still don't see quite all of what you and Creak were trying to do, but it doesn't matter much. If you're sure you will be all right and can hold out here another few days, I'll get back to where I left Creak."

He started to swim slowly toward the wall.

"But it's night!" Nereis exclaimed. "How can you walk back in the dark? I know you're a land creature, but even you can't see very well when the sun is down. You'll have to wait here until morning."

Cunningham stopped swimming and thought for a moment.

"There's a moon," he pointed out, "and I guess I never showed you my light, at that. I'll be— *How did you know I was walking?*"

Silence.

"Are you in some sort of communication with Creak that you have never told me about?"

"No."

"And I know you didn't see me coming, and I didn't say anything about leaving the ship in the city, or how I traveled. So Creak had set something up before we left here, and you knew about it. He was not really anxious about you—he knew you were perfectly safe. So part of the idea was to keep me away from my ship, or at least the city, for some time. I can't guess why. That much of the plan has succeeded. Right?"

Still no word came from the woman.

"Well, I'm not holding it against you. You were trying for something you consider important, and you certainly haven't hurt me so far. Right now, in fact, it's fun. I don't blame you for trying. Please tell me one thing, though: Are you and Creak trying to force your people to move back to the ocean, in spite of knowing about the pollution which right now makes that impossible? Or do you have something more realistic in mind? If you can bring yourself to tell me, it may make a difference in what I can do for all of you."

"It was the second." Nereis took no time at all to make up her mind. "Mostly, it was to make people realize that they were just lying on their bellies doing nothing. We wanted them to see what could be done by— I can't say this just right—by someone who wasn't really any smarter than we are, but had the urge to act. We wanted them to see your flying machine to show them the possibilities, and we wanted to get it away from you to...well—"

"To show them that I'm not really any smarter than you are?"

"Well...Yes, that about says it. We hope people will be pushed into trying—as they did when they built the land cities so long ago. Saying it that way now makes it all seem unnecessarily complex, and silly, but it seemed worth trying. *Anything* seemed worth trying."

"Don't belittle yourselves or your idea. It may just work. In any case, I'd have had to do something, myself, before leaving to prove that I wasn't really superior to your people— Never mind why; it's one of the rules." He floated silently for a minute or two, then went on.

"I agree that your people probably need that kick—excuse me, push— that you suggest. I'm afraid it will be a long time before you really get back to Nature, but you should at least keep moving. No race I know of ever got back there until its mastery of science was so complete that no one really *had* to work anymore at the necessities of life. You have a long, long way to go, but I'll be glad to help with the push...

"Look, I have to go back to the ship. I'm betting Creak won't expect me back tonight, and the guarding won't be too much of a problem— you folks sleep at night, too. I have to get something from the ship, which I should have been carrying all along—you're not the only ones who get too casual. Then I'll come back here, and if you're willing to sacrifice your furniture to the cause, I'll make something that will do what you and Creak want. I guarantee it."

"Why do you have to get something from your ship in order to make something from my furniture? I have all the glue you could possibly need."

"That's the last thing I want. You depend too much on the stuff, and it's caused your collective craftsmanship to die in the—the egg. Glue would make what I want to do a lot easier, but I'm not going to use it. You'll see why in a few days, when I get the job done."

"A few days? If the weather stays dry, I may lose enough water from the house to make it too salt for me and—"

"Don't worry. I'll take care of that problem too. See you later."

5

The moon had passed culmination when Cunningham reached the place where Creak had rolled down the wall a few hours before, and he was relieved to see the bulk of his ship gleaming in the moonlight a few hundred meters away. To avoid tripping or slipping, he went slowly on all fours along the walls until he reached a point closest to the vessel, but on the side opposite the air lock. Then he unclipped the remote controller from his belt and opened the lock, regretting that he could not bring the ship to him with the device.

He listened for several minutes, but there was no evidence that the opening had attracted any attention. Of course, that was not conclusive...

Very, very gently he let himself into the water. Still no response. He could feel the plants a few centimeters down, and rather than trying to swim he grasped the twining growths and pulled himself along, Rantan fashion, slowly enough not to raise ripples.

The plants extended only twenty meters or so from the wall. He had to swim the rest of the way, expecting at every moment to feel a snaky body coil around him; he was almost surprised when he reached the hull. He had no intention of swimming around to the lock; there were handholds on every square meter of the vessel's exterior. He found one, knew immediately where all the neighboring ones must be, reached for and found another, and hoisted himself gently out of the water. Still as quietly as possible he climbed over the top and started down toward the open lock. Now he could see the moon reflected in the water.

He stopped as he saw the silhouette of a Rantan head projecting from the lock. The opening must have been seen or heard after all, for the creature could not have been inside before. Was it alone? Or were there others waiting inside the lock or in the water below? Those in the water would be no problem, but he would have to take his chances if any were in the ship.

Cunningham thought out his movements for the next few minutes very carefully. Then he let himself down to a point just above the lock, three meters above the native. Securing a grip on the lowest hold he could reach, he swung himself down and inboard.

He had no way of telling whether he would land on a section of Rantan or not; he had to budget for the possibility. One foot did hit something rubbery, but the man kept his balance and made a leap for the inner door, which he had opened with the controller simultaneously with his swing. There had been only one guard in the lock, and lying on a smooth metal surface he had had no chance at all to act; he had been expecting to deal with the man climbing from below.

Cunningham relaxed for a few minutes, ate, and then looked over his supply of hand equipment. He selected a double-edged knife, thirty-five centimeters in blade length, cored with vanadium steel and faced with carbide. Adding a sheath and a diamond sharpener, he clipped the lot to his belt, reflecting that the assemblage could probably be called one tool without straining the term.

Then he stepped to the control console and turned on the external viewers, tuning far enough into the infrared to spot Rantan body heat but not, he hoped, far enough to be blocked entirely by water. Several dozen of the natives surrounded the ship, so he decided not to try swimming back out. The guard had apparently joined those in the water.

"I might get away with it, but it would be rubbing things in," he muttered. Gently he lifted the vessel and set it down again just outside the south wall of the city. Extending the ladder from the lock, he descended, closed up with the controller, and started his long walk back to the reservoir.

Creak, from the top of the wall, watched him out of sight and wondered where his plan had gone wrong and what he could do next. He also worried a little: Cunningham had been meant to tell him that Nereis was all right, but had not seen him to deliver the message.

6

Four Rantan days later, principles shelved for the moment in his anxiety for his wife, Creak accompanied the repair party toward the dam.

It had taken a long time to set up: the logistics of a fifteen-kilometer cross-country trip were formidable, and finding workers willing to go was worse. Glue, food, spare breathing suits and their supporting gear, arrangement for reserves and reliefs—all took time. It was a little like combing a city full of twentieth-century white-collar workers to find people who were willing to take on a job of undersea or space construction.

It might have taken even longer, but the water in the city was beginning to taste obnoxious.

A kilometer north of the wall they met something that startled Creak more than his first sight of Cunningham and the *Nimepotea* six months before. He could not even think of words to describe it, though he had managed all right with man and spaceship.

The thing consisted of a cylindrical framework, axis horizontal, made of strips of wood. Creak did not recognize the pieces of his own furniture. The cylinder contained something like an oversized worksack, made of the usual transparent fabric, which in turn contained his wife, obviously well and happy.

At the rear of the framework, on the underside, was a heavy transverse wooden rod, and at the ends of this were—Creak had no word for "wheels." Under the front was a single, similar disk-shaped thing, connected to the frame by an even more indescribable object which seemed to have been shaped somehow from a single large piece of wood.

The human being was pulling the whole arrangement without apparent effort, steering it among the rocks by altering the axial orientation of the forward disk.

The Rantans were speechless—but not one of them had the slightest difficulty in seeing how the thing worked.

"Principles are an awful nuisance, Creak," the man remarked. "I swore I wasn't going to use a drop of your glue in making the wagon. Every bit of frame is *tied* together—I should think that people with your evolutionary background would at least have invented knots; or did they go out of style when glue came in? Anyway, the frame wasn't so bad, but the wheels were hell. If I'd given up and used the glue, they'd have been simple enough, and I'd have made four of them, and had less trouble with that front fork mount—though I suppose steering would have been harder then. Making bundles for the rims was easy enough, but attaching spokes and making them stay was more than I'd bargained for."

"Why didn't you use the glue?" Creak asked. He was slowly regaining his emotional equilibrium.

"Same reason I left the ship down by the city, and lived on emergency food. Principle. *Your* principle. I wanted you and your people to be really sure that what I did was nice and simple and didn't call for any arcane knowledge or fancy tools. Did you ever go through the stone-knife stage?" He displayed the blade. "Well, there's a time for everything, even if the times are sometimes a little out of order. You just have to learn how to *shape* material instead of just sticking it together. Get it?"

"Well...I think so."

"Good. And I saved my own self-respect as well as yours, I think, so everyone should be happy. Now you get to work and make some more of these wagons—only for Heaven's sake do use glue to speed things up. And let three-quarters of this crowd go back to painting pictures or whatever they were doing, and then cart some stuff up to that dam and get it fixed. It might rain sometime, you know."

Creak looked at his wife—she was riding with one end out of the wagon, so she could hear him. "I'm afraid we're further than ever from Nature," he remarked.

She made a gesture which Cunningham knew to mean reluctant agreement.

"I'm afraid that's right," the man admitted. "Once you tip the balance, you never get quite back on dead center. You started a scientific culture, just as my people did. You got overdependent on your glue, just as we did on heat engines—I'll explain what those are, if you like, later. I don't see how that information can corrupt *this* planet.

"You still want to get back to your tidal jungles, I suppose. Maybe you will. We got back to our forests, but they are strictly for recreation now. We don't have to find our food in them, and we don't have much risk of getting eaten in them. So someday you may decide that's best. In any case, it will take you a long, long time to get around that circle; and you'll learn a lot of things on the way; and believe it or not, the trip will be fun.

"Forgive the philosophy, please. As I remarked to you a few days ago, when your ancestors started scientific thinking they turned you onto a one-way road. And speaking of roads, which is a word you don't know yet—you'd better make one up to the dam. These rocks I've been steering the wagon around are even worse than principles."

UNCOMMON SENSE

Astounding, September 1945
Hugo Award for Best Short Story

"So you've left us, Mr. Cunningham!" Malmeson's voice sounded rougher than usual, even allowing for headphone distortion and the ever-present Denebian static. "Now, that's too bad. If you'd chosen to stick around, we would have put you off on some world where you could live, at least. Now you can stay here and fry. And I hope you live long enough to watch us take off—without you!"

Laird Cunningham did not bother to reply. The ship's radio compass should still be in working order, and it was just possible that his erstwhile assistants might start hunting for him, if they were given some idea of the proper direction to begin a search. Cunningham was too satisfied with his present shelter to be very anxious for a change. He was scarcely half a mile from the grounded ship, in a cavern deep enough to afford shelter from Deneb's rays when it rose, and located in the side of a small hill, so that he could watch the activities of Malmeson and his companion without exposing himself to their view.

In a way, of course, the villain was right. If Cunningham permitted the ship to take off without him, he might as well open his face plate; for, while he had food and oxygen for several days' normal consumption, a planet scarcely larger than Luna, baked in the rays of one of the fiercest radiating bodies in the galaxy, was most unlikely to provide further supplies when these ran out. He wondered how long it would take the men to discover the damage he had done to the drive units in the few minutes that had elapsed between the crash landing and their breaking through the control room door, which Cunningham had welded shut when he had discovered their intentions. They might not notice at all; he had severed a number of inconspicuous connections at odd points. Perhaps they would not even test the drivers until they had completed repairs to the cracked hull. If they didn't, so much the better.

Cunningham crawled to the mouth of his cave and looked out across the shallow valley in which the ship lay. It was barely visible in the star-light, and there was no sign of artificial luminosity to suggest that Mal-meson might have started repairs at night. Cunningham had not expected that they would, but it was well to be sure. Nothing more had come over his suit radio since the initial outburst, when the men had discovered his departure; he decided that they must be waiting for sunrise, to enable them to take more accurate stock of the damage suffered by the hull.

He spent the next few minutes looking at the stars, trying to arrange them into patterns he could remember. He had no watch, and it would help to have some warning of approaching sunrise on succeeding nights. It would not do to be caught away from his cave, with the flimsy protec-tion his suit could afford from Deneb's radiation. He wished he could have filched one of the heavier work suits; but they were kept in a com-partment forward of the control room, from which he had barred him-self when he had sealed the door of the latter chamber.

He remained at the cave mouth, lying motionless and watching alter-nately the sky and the ship. Once or twice he may have dozed; but he was awake and alert when the low hills beyond the ship's hull caught the first rays of the rising sun. For a minute or two they seemed to hang detached in a black void, while the flood of blue-white light crept down their slopes; then, one by one, their bases merged with each other and the ground be-low to form a connected landscape. The silvery hull gleamed brilliantly, the reflection from it lighting the cave behind Cunningham and making his eyes water when he tried to watch for the opening of the air lock.

He was forced to keep his eyes elsewhere most of the time, and look only in brief glimpses at the dazzling metal; and in consequence, he paid more attention to the details of his environment than he might otherwise have done. At the time, this circumstance annoyed him; he has since been heard to bless it fervently and frequently.

Although the planet had much in common with Luna as regarded size, mass, and airlessness, its landscape was extremely different. The daily terrific heatings which it underwent, followed by abrupt and equally in-tense temperature drops each night, had formed an excellent substitute for weather; and elevations that might at one time have rivaled the Lunar ranges were now mere rounded hillocks, like that containing Cunning-ham's cave. As on the Earth's moon, the products of the age-long spalling had taken the form of fine dust, which lay in drifts everywhere. What could have drifted it, on an airless and consequently windless planet, struck Cunningham as a puzzle of the first magnitude; and it bothered him for some time until his attention was taken by certain other objects upon and between the drifts. These he had thought at first to be outcroppings of rock; but he was at last convinced that they were specimens of vegetable life—miserable, lichenous specimens, but nevertheless vegetation. He wondered what liquid they contained, in an environment at a temperature well above the melting point of lead.

The discovery of animal life—medium-sized, crablike things, covered with jet-black integument, that began to dig their way out of the drifts as the sun warmed them—completed the job of dragging Cunningham's attention from his immediate problems. He was not a zoologist by training, but the subject had fascinated him for years; and he had always had money enough to indulge his hobby. He had spent years wandering the Galaxy in search of bizarre life forms—proof, if any were needed, of a lack of scientific training—and terrestrial museums had always been more than glad to accept the collections that resulted from each trip and usually to send scientists of their own in his footsteps. He had been in physical danger often enough, but it had always been from the life he studied or from the forces which make up the interstellar traveler's regular diet, until he had overheard the conversation which informed him that his two assistants were planning to do away with him and appropriate the ship for unspecified purposes of their own. He liked to think that the promptness of his action following the discovery at least indicated that he was not growing old.

But he did let his attention wander to the Denebian life forms.

Several of the creatures were emerging from the dust mounds within twenty or thirty yards of Cunningham's hiding place, giving rise to the hope that they would come near enough for a close examination. At that distance, they were more crablike than ever, with round, flat bodies twelve to eighteen inches across, and several pairs of legs. They scuttled rapidly about, stopping at first one of the lichenous plants and then another, apparently taking a few tentative nibbles from each, as though they had delicate tastes which needed pampering. Once or twice there were fights when the same tidbit attracted the attention of more than one claimant; but little apparent damage was done on either side, and the victor spent no more time on the meal he won than on that which came uncontested.

Cunningham became deeply absorbed in watching the antics of the little creatures, and completely forgot for a time his own rather precarious situation. He was recalled to it by the sound of Malmeson's voice in his headphones.

"Don't look up, you fool; the shields will save your skin, but not your eyes. Get under the shadow of the hull, and we'll look over the damage."

Cunningham instantly transferred his attention to the ship. The air lock on the side toward him—the port—was open, and the bulky figures of his two ex-assistants were visible standing on the ground beneath it. They were clad in the heavy utility suits which Cunningham had regretted leaving, and appeared to be suffering little or no inconvenience from the heat, though they were still standing full in Deneb's light when he looked. He knew that hard radiation burns would not appear for some time, but he held little hope of Deneb's more deadly output coming to his assistance; for the suits were supposed to afford protection against this danger as well. Between heat insulation, cooling equipment, radiation shielding, and plain mechanical armor, the garments were so heavy and bulky as to be an almost insufferable burden on any major planet. They were more often used in performing exterior repairs in space.

Cunningham watched and listened carefully as the men stooped under the lower curve of the hull to make an inspection of the damage. It seemed, from their conversation, to consist of a dent about three yards long and half as wide, about which nothing could be done, and a series of radially arranged cracks in the metal around it. These represented a definite threat to the solidity of the ship, and would have to be welded along their full lengths before it would be safe to apply the stresses incident to second-order flight. Malmeson was too good an engineer not to realize this fact, and Cunningham heard him lay plans for bringing power lines outside for the welder and jacking up the hull to permit access to the lower portions of the cracks. The latter operation was carried out immediately, with an efficiency which did not in the least surprise the hidden watcher. After all, he had hired the men.

Every few minutes, to Cunningham's annoyance, one of the men would carefully examine the landscape; first on the side on which he was working, and then walking around the ship to repeat the performance. Even in the low gravity, Cunningham knew he could not cross the half mile that lay between him and that inviting air lock, between two of those examinations; and even if he could, his leaping figure, clad in the gleaming metal suit, would be sure to catch even an eye not directed at it. It would not do to make the attempt unless success were certain; for his unshielded suit would heat in a minute or two to an unbearable temperature, and the only place in which it was possible either to remove or cool it was on board the ship. He finally decided, to his annoyance, that the watch would not slacken so long as the air lock of the ship remained open. It would be necessary to find some means to distract or—an unpleasant alternative for a civilized man—disable the opposition while Cunningham got aboard, locked the others out, and located a weapon or other factor which would put him in a position to give them orders. At that, he reflected, a weapon would scarcely be necessary; there was a perfectly good medium transmitter on board, if the men had not destroyed or discharged it, and he need merely call for help and keep the men outside until it arrived.

This, of course, presupposed some solution to the problem of getting aboard unaccompanied. He would, he decided, have to examine the ship more closely after sunset. He knew the vessel as well as his own home—he had spent more time on her than in any other home—and knew that there was no means of entry except through the two main locks forward of the control room, and the two smaller, emergency locks near the stern, one of which he had employed on his departure. All these could be dogged shut from within; and offhand he was unable to conceive a plan for forcing any of the normal entrances. The view ports were too small to admit a man in a spacesuit, even if the panes could be broken; and there was literally no other way into the ship so long as the hull remained intact. Malmeson would not have talked so glibly of welding them sufficiently well to stand flight, if any of the cracks incurred on the landing had been big enough to admit a human body—or even that of a respectably healthy garter snake.

Cunningham gave a mental shrug of the shoulders as these thoughts crossed his mind, and reiterated his decision to take a scouting sortie after dark. For the rest of the day he divided his attention between the working men and the equally busy life forms that scuttled here and there in front of his cave; and he would have been the first to admit that he found the latter more interesting.

He still hoped that one would approach the cave closely enough to permit a really good examination, but for a long time he remained unsatisfied. Once, one of the creatures came within a dozen yards and stood "on tiptoe"—rising more than a foot from the ground on its slender legs, while a pair of antennae terminating in knobs the size of human eyeballs extended themselves several inches from the black carapace and waved slowly in all directions. Cunningham thought that the knobs probably did serve as eyes, though from his distance he could see only a featureless black sphere. The antennae eventually waved in his direction, and after a few seconds spent, apparently in assimilating the presence of the cave mouth, the creature settled back to its former low-swung carriage and scuttled away. Cunningham wondered if it had been frightened at his presence; but he felt reasonably sure that no eye adapted to Denebian daylight could see past the darkness of his threshold, and he had remained motionless while the creature was conducting its inspection. More probably it had some reason to fear caves, or merely darkness.

That it had reason to fear something was shown when another creature, also of crustacean aspect but considerably larger than those Cunningham had seen to date, appeared from among the dunes and attacked one of the latter. The fight took place too far from the cave for Cunningham to make out many details, but the larger animal quickly overcame its victim. It then apparently dismembered the vanquished, and either devoured the softer flesh inside the black integument or sucked the body fluids from it. Then the carnivore disappeared again, presumably in search of new victims. It had scarcely gone when another being, designed along the lines of a centipede and fully forty feet in length, appeared on the scene with the graceful flowing motion of its terrestrial counterpart.

For a few moments the newcomer nosed around the remains of the carnivore's feast, and devoured the larger fragments. Then it appeared to look around as though for more, evidently saw the cave, and came rippling toward it, to Cunningham's pardonable alarm. He was totally unarmed, and while the centipede had just showed itself not to be above eating carrion, it looked quite able to kill its own food if necessary. It stopped, as the other investigator had, a dozen yards from the cave mouth; and like the other, elevated itself as though to get a better look. The baseball-sized black "eyes" seemed for several seconds to stare into Cunningham's more orthodox optics; then, like its predecessor, and to the man's intense relief, it doubled back along its own length and glided swiftly out of sight. Cunningham again wondered whether it had detected his presence, or whether caves or darkness in general spelled danger to these odd life forms.

It suddenly occurred to him that, if the latter were not the case, there might be some traces of previous occupants of the cave; and he set about examining the place more closely, after a last glance which showed him the two men still at work jacking up the hull.

There was drifted dust even here, he discovered, particularly close to the walls and in the corners. The place was bright enough, owing to the light reflected from outside objects, to permit a good examination—shadows on airless worlds are not so black as many people believe—and almost at once Cunningham found marks in the dust that could easily have been made by some of the creatures he had seen. There were enough of them to suggest that the cave was a well-frequented neighborhood; and it began to look as though the animals were staying away now because of the man's presence.

Near the rear wall he found the empty integument that had once covered a four-jointed leg. It was light, and he saw that the flesh had either been eaten or decayed out, though it seemed odd to think of decay in an airless environment suffering such extremes of temperature—though the cave was less subject to this effect than the outer world. Cunningham wondered whether the leg had been carried in by its rightful owner, or as a separate item on the menu of something else. If the former, there might be more relics about.

There were. A few minutes' excavation in the deeper layers of dust produced the complete exoskeleton of one of the smaller crablike creatures; and Cunningham carried the remains over to the cave mouth, so as to examine them and watch the ship at the same time.

The knobs he had taken for eyes were his first concern. A close examination of their surfaces revealed nothing, so he carefully tried to detach one from its stem. It finally cracked raggedly away, and proved, as he had expected, to be hollow. There was no trace of a retina inside, but there was no flesh in any of the other pieces of shell, so that proved nothing. As a sudden thought struck him, Cunningham held the front part of the delicate black bit of shell in front of his eyes; and sure enough, when he looked in the direction of the brightly gleaming hull of the spaceship, a spark of light showed through an almost microscopic hole. The sphere *was* an eye, constructed on the pinhole principle—quite an adequate design on a world furnished with such an overwhelming luminary. It would be useless at night, of course, but so would most other visual organs here; and Cunningham was once again faced with the problem of how any of the creatures had detected his presence in the cave—his original belief, that no eye adjusted to meet Deneb's glare could look into its relatively total darkness, seemed to be sound.

He pondered the question, as he examined the rest of the skeleton in a half-hearted fashion. Sight seemed to be out, as a result of his examination; smell and hearing were ruled out by the lack of atmosphere; taste and touch could not even be considered under the circumstances. He hated to fall back on such a time-honored refuge for ignorance as "extrasensory perception," but he was unable to see any way around it.

It may seem unbelievable that a man in the position Laird Cunningham occupied could let his mind become so utterly absorbed in a problem unconnected with his personal survival. Such individuals do exist, however; most people know someone who has shown some trace of such a trait; and Cunningham was a well-developed example. He had a single-track mind, and had intentionally shelved his personal problem for the moment.

His musings were interrupted, before he finished dissecting his specimen, by the appearance of one of the carnivorous creatures at what appeared to constitute a marked distance—a dozen yards from his cave mouth, where it rose up on the ends of its thin legs and goggled around at the landscape. Cunningham, half in humor and half in honest curiosity, tossed one of the dismembered legs from the skeleton in his hands at the creature. It obviously saw the flying limb; but it made no effort to pursue or devour it. Instead, it turned its eyes in Cunningham's direction, and proceeded with great haste to put one of the drifts between it and what it evidently considered a dangerous neighborhood.

It seemed to have no memory to speak of, however; for a minute or two later Cunningham saw it creep into view again, stalking one of the smaller creatures which still swarmed everywhere, nibbling at the plants. He was able to get a better view of the fight and the feast that followed than on the previous occasion, for they took place much nearer to his position; but this time there was a rather different ending. The giant centipede, or another of its kind, appeared on the scene while the carnivore was still at its meal, and came flowing at a truly surprising rate over the dunes to fall on victor and vanquished alike. The former had no inkling of its approach until much too late; and both black bodies disappeared into the maw of the creature Cunningham had hoped was merely a scavenger.

What made the whole episode of interest to the man was the fact that in its charge, the centipede loped unheeding almost directly through a group of the plant-eaters; and these, by common consent, broke and ran at top speed directly toward the cave. At first he thought they would swerve aside when they saw what lay ahead; but evidently he was the lesser of two evils, for they scuttled past and even over him as he lay in the cave mouth, and began to bury themselves in the deepest dust they could find. Cunningham watched with pleasure, as an excellent group of specimens thus collected themselves for his convenience.

As the last of them disappeared under the dust, he turned back to the scene outside. The centipede was just finishing its meal. This time, instead of immediately wandering out of sight, it oozed quickly to the top of one of the larger dunes, in full sight of the cave, and deposited its length in the form of a watch spring, with the head resting above the coils. Cunningham realized that it was able, in this position, to look in nearly all directions and, owing to the height of its position, to a considerable distance.

With the centipede apparently settled for a time, and the men still working in full view, Cunningham determined to inspect one of his specimens. Going to the nearest wall, he bent down and groped cautiously in the dust. He encountered a subject almost at once, and dragged a squirming black crab into the light. He found that if he held it upside down in one hand, none of its legs could get a purchase on anything; and he was able to examine the underparts in detail in spite of the wildly thrashing limbs. The jaws, now opening and closing futilely on a vacuum, were equipped with a set of crushers that suggested curious things about the plants on which it fed; they looked capable of flattening the metal finger of Cunningham's spacesuit, and he kept his hand well out of their reach.

He became curious as to the internal mechanism that permitted it to exist without air, and was faced with the problem of killing the thing without doing it too much mechanical damage. It was obviously able to survive a good many hours without the direct radiation of Deneb, which was the most obvious source of energy, although its body temperature was high enough to be causing the man some discomfort through the glove of his suit; so "drowning" in darkness was impractical. There might, however, be some part of its body on which a blow would either stun or kill it; and he looked around for a suitable weapon.

There were several deep cracks in the stone at the cave mouth, caused presumably by thermal expansion and contraction; and with a little effort he was able to break loose a pointed, fairly heavy fragment. With this in his right hand, he laid the creature on its back on the ground, and hoped it had something corresponding to a solar plexus.

It was too quick for him. The legs, which had been unable to reach his hand when it was in the center of the creature's carapace, proved supple enough to get a purchase on the ground; and before he could strike, it was right side up and departing with a haste that put to shame its previous efforts to escape from the centipede.

Cunningham shrugged, and dug out another specimen. This time he held it in his hand while he drove the point of his rock against its plastron. There was no apparent effect; he had not dared to strike too hard, for fear of crushing the shell. He struck several more times, with identical results and increasing impatience; and at last there occurred the result he had feared. The black armor gave way, and the point penetrated deeply enough to insure the damage of most of the interior organs. The legs gave a final twitch or two, and ceased moving, and Cunningham gave an exclamation of annoyance.

On hope, he removed the broken bits of shell, and for a moment looked in surprise at the liquid which seemed to have filled the body cavities. It was silvery, even metallic in color; it might have been mercury, except that it wet the organs bathed in it and was probably at a temperature above the boiling point of that metal. Cunningham had just grasped this fact when he was violently bowled over, and the dead creature snatched from his grasp. He made a complete somersault, bringing up against the rear wall of the cave; and as he came upright he saw to his horror that the assailant was none other than the giant centipede.

It was disposing with great thoroughness of his specimen, leaving at last only a few fragments of shell that had formed the extreme tips of the legs; and as the last of these fell to the ground, it raised the fore part of its body from the ground, as the man had seen it do before, and turned the invisible pinpoints of its pupils on the space-suited human figure.

Cunningham drew a deep breath, and took a firm hold of his pointed rock, though he had little hope of overcoming the creature. The jaws he had just seen at work had seemed even more efficient that those of the plant-eater, and they were large enough to take in a human leg.

For perhaps five seconds both beings faced each other without motion; then, to the man's inexpressible relief, the centipede reached the same conclusion to which its previous examination of humanity had led it, and departed in evident haste. This time it did not remain in sight, but was still moving rapidly when it reached the limit of Cunningham's vision.

The naturalist returned somewhat shakily to the cave mouth, seated himself where he could watch his ship, and began to ponder deeply. A number of points seemed interesting on first thought, and on further cerebration became positively fascinating. The centipede had not seen, or at least had not pursued, the plant-eater that had escaped from Cunningham and run from the cave. Looking back, he realized that the only times he had seen the creature attack was after "blood" had been already shed—twice by one of the carnivorous animals, the third time by Cunningham himself. It had apparently made no difference where the victims had been—two in full sunlight, one in the darkness of the cave. More proof, if any were needed, that the creatures could see in both grades of illumination. It was not strictly a carrion eater, however; Cunningham remembered that carnivore that had accompanied its victim into the centipede's jaws. It was obviously capable of overcoming the man, but had twice retreated precipitately when it had excellent opportunities to attack him. What was it, then, that drew the creature to scenes of combat and bloodshed, but frightened it away from a man; that frightened, indeed, all of these creatures?

On any planet that had a respectable atmosphere, Cunningham would have taken one answer for granted—scent. In his mind, however, organs of smell were associated with breathing apparatus, which these creatures obviously lacked.

Don't ask why he took so long. You may think that the terrific adaptability evidenced by those strange eyes would be clue enough; or perhaps you may be in a mood to excuse him. Columbus probably excused those of his friends who failed to solve the egg problem.

Of course, he got it at last, and was properly annoyed with himself for taking so long about it. An eye, to us, is an organ for forming images of the source of such radiation as may fall on it; and a nose is a gadget that tells its owner of the presence of molecules. He needs his imagination to picture the source of the latter. But what would you call an organ that forms a picture of the source of smell?

For that was just what those "eyes" did. In the nearly perfect vacuum of this little world's surface, gases diffused at high speed—and their molecules traveled in practically straight lines. There was nothing wrong with the idea of a pinhole camera eye, whose retina was composed of olfactory nerve endings rather than the rods and cones of photosensitive organs.

That seemed to account for everything. Of course the creatures were indifferent to the amount of light reflected from the object they examined. The glare of the open spaces under Deneb's rays, and the relative blackness of a cave, were all one to them—provided something were diffusing molecules in the neighborhood. And what doesn't? Every substance, solid or liquid, has its vapor pressure; under Deneb's rays even some rather unlikely materials probably vaporized enough to affect the organs of these life forms—metals, particularly. The life fluid of the creatures was obviously metal—probably lead, tin, bismuth, or some similar metals, or still more probably, several of them in a mixture that carried the substances vital to the life of their body cells. Probably much of the makeup of those cells was in the form of colloidal metals.

But that was the business of the biochemists. Cunningham amused himself for a time by imagining the analogy between smell and color which must exist here; light gases, such as oxygen and nitrogen, must be rare, and the tiny quantities that leaked from his suit would be absolutely new to the creatures that intercepted them. He must have affected their nervous systems the way fire did those of terrestrial wild animals. No wonder even the centipede had thought discretion the better part of valor!

With his less essential problem solved for the nonce, Cunningham turned his attention to that of his own survival; and he had not pondered many moments when he realized that this, as well, might be solved. He began slowly to smile, as the discrete fragments of an idea began to sort themselves out and fit properly together in his mind—an idea that involved the vapor pressure of metallic blood, the leaking qualities of the utility suits worn by his erstwhile assistants, and the bloodthirstiness of his many-legged acquaintances of the day; and he had few doubts about any of those qualities. The plan became complete, to his satisfaction; and with a smile on his face, he settled himself to watch until sunset.

Deneb had already crossed a considerable arc of the sky. Cunningham did not know just how long he had, as he lacked a watch, and it was soon borne in on him that time passes much more slowly when there is nothing to occupy it. As the afternoon drew on, he was forced away from the cave mouth; for the descending star was beginning to shine in. Just before sunset, he was crowded against one side; for Deneb's fierce rays shone straight through the entrance and onto the opposite wall, leaving very little space not directly illuminated. Cunningham drew a sigh of relief for more reasons than one when the upper limb of the deadly luminary finally disappeared.

His specimens had long since recovered from their fright, and left the cavern; he had not tried to stop them. Now, however, he emerged from the low entryway and went directly to the nearest dust dune, which was barely visible in the starlight. A few moments' search was rewarded with one of the squirming plant-eaters, which he carried back into the shelter; then, illuminating the scene carefully with the small torch that was clipped to the waist of his suit, he made a fair-sized pile of dust, gouged a long groove in the top with his toe; with the aid of the same stone he had used before, he killed the plant-eater and poured its "blood" into the dust mold.

The fluid was metallic, all right; it cooled quickly, and in two or three minutes Cunningham had a silvery rod about as thick as a pencil and five or six inches long. He had been a little worried about the centipede at first; but the creature was either not in line to "see" into the cave, or had dug in for the night like its victims.

Cunningham took the rod, which was about as pliable as a strip of solder of the same dimensions, and, extinguishing the torch, made his way in a series of short, careful leaps to the stranded spaceship. There was no sign of the men, and they had taken their welding equipment inside with them—that is, if they had ever had it out; Cunningham had not been able to watch them for the last hour of daylight. The hull was still jacked up, however; and the naturalist eased himself under it and began to examine the damage, once more using the torch. It was about as he had deduced from the conversation of the men; and with a smile, he took the little metal stick and went to work. He was busy for some time under the hull, and once he emerged, found another plant-eater, and went back underneath. After he had finished, he walked once around the ship, checking each of the air locks and finding them sealed, as he had expected.

He showed neither surprise nor disappointment at this; and without further ceremony he made his way back to the cave, which he had a little trouble finding in the starlight. He made a large pile of the dust for insulation rather than bedding, lay down on it, and tried to sleep. He had very little success, as he might have expected.

Night, in consequence, seemed unbearably long; and he almost regretted his star study of the previous darkness, for now he was able to see that sunrise was still distant, rather than bolster his morale with the hope that Deneb would be in the sky the next time he opened his eyes. The time finally came, however, when the hilltops across the valley leaped one by one into brilliance as the sunlight caught them; and Cunningham rose and stretched himself. He was stiff and cramped, for a spacesuit makes a poor sleeping costume even on a better bed than a stone floor.

As the light reached the spaceship and turned it into a blazing silvery spindle, the air lock opened. Cunningham had been sure that the men were in a hurry to finish their task, and were probably awaiting the sun almost as eagerly as he in order to work efficiently; he had planned on this basis.

Malmeson was the first to leap to the ground, judging by their conversation, which came clearly through Cunningham's phones. He turned back, and his companion handed down to him the bulky diode welder and a stack of filler rods. Then both men made their way forward to the dent where they were to work. Apparently they failed to notice the bits of loose metal lying on the scene—perhaps they had done some filing themselves the day before. At any rate, there was no mention of it as Malmeson lay down and slid under the hull, and the other began handing equipment in to him.

Plant-eaters were beginning to struggle out of their dust beds as the connections were completed, and the torch started to flame. Cunningham nodded in pleasure as he noted this; things could scarcely have been timed better had the men been consciously co-operating. He actually emerged from the cave, keeping in the shadow of the hillock, to increase his field of view; but for several minutes nothing but plant-eaters could be seen moving.

He was beginning to fear that his invited guests were too distant to receive their call, when his eye caught a glimpse of a long, black body slipping silently over the dunes toward the ship. He smiled in satisfaction; and then his eyebrows suddenly rose as he saw a second snaky form following the tracks of the first.

He looked quickly across his full field of view, and was rewarded by the sight of four more of the monsters—all heading at breakneck speed straight for the spaceship. The beacon he had lighted had reached more eyes than he had expected. He was sure that the men were armed, and had never intended that they actually be overcome by the creatures; he had counted on a temporary distraction that would let him reach the air lock unopposed.

He stood up, and braced himself for the dash, as Malmeson's helper saw the first of the charging centipedes and called the welder from his work. Malmeson barely had time to gain his feet when the first pair of attackers reached them; and at the same instant Cunningham emerged into the sunlight, putting every ounce of his strength into the leaps that were carrying him toward the only shelter that now existed for him.

He could feel the ardor of Deneb's rays the instant they struck him; and before he had covered a third of the distance the back of his suit was painfully hot. Things were hot for his ex-crew as well; fully ten of the black monsters had reacted to the burst of—to them—overpoweringly attractive odor—or gorgeous color?—that had resulted when Malmeson had turned his welder on the metal where Cunningham had applied the frozen blood of their natural prey; and more of the same substance was now vaporizing under Deneb's influence as Malmeson, who had been lying in fragments of it, stood fighting off the attackers. He had a flame pistol, but it was slow to take effect on creatures whose very blood was molten metal; and his companion, wielding the diode unit on those who got too close, was no better off. They were practically swamped under wriggling bodies as they worked their way toward the air lock; and neither man saw Cunningham as, staggering even under the feeble gravity that was present, and fumbling with eye shield misted with sweat, he reached the same goal and disappeared within.

Being a humane person, he left the outer door open; but he closed and dogged the inner one before proceeding with a more even step to the control room. Here he unhurriedly removed his spacesuit, stopping only to open the switch of the power socket that was feeding the diode unit as he heard the outer lock door close. The flame pistol would make no impression on the alloy of the hull, and he felt no qualms about the security of the inner door. The men were safe, from every point of view.

With the welder removed from the list of active menaces, he finished removing his suit, turned to the medium transmitter, and coolly broadcast a call for help and his position in space. Then he turned on a radio transmitter, so that the rescuers could find him on the planet; and only then did he contact the prisoners on the small set that was tuned to the suit radios, and tell them what he had done.

"I didn't mean to do you any harm," Malmeson's voice came back. "I just wanted the ship. I know you paid us pretty good, but when I thought of the money that could be made on some of those worlds if we looked for something besides crazy animals and plants, I couldn't help myself. You can let us out now; I swear we won't try anything more—the ship won't fly, and you say a Guard flyer is on the way. How about that?"

"I'm sorry you don't like my hobby," said Cunningham. "I find it entertaining; and there have been times when it was even useful, though I won't hurt your feelings by telling you about the last one. I think I shall feel happier if the two of you stay right there in the air lock; the rescue ship should be here before many hours, and you're fools if you haven't food and water in your suits."

"I guess you win, in that case," said Malmeson.

"I think so, too," replied Cunningham, and switched off.

Acknowledgments

Rick Katze for help in scanning.

George Flynn for his usual able and quick job of proofreading under pressure. Suford Lewis and Priscilla Olson for yet more proofreading.

Suford Lewis, Deb Geisler, and Lisa Hertel for consultations in selecting the dustjacket art and designing the dustjacket, and Lisa Hertel for the final design.

Mike Benveniste for the barcode.

This book was typeset in Adobe Garamond using Adobe Pagemaker and printed by Sheridan Books of Ann Arbor, Michigan, on acid-free paper.

— Mark Olson and Tony Lewis
December, 1999

The New England
Science Fiction Association (NESFA)
and NESFA Press

Recent books from NESFA Press:

The New England Science Fiction Association:

NESFA is an all-volunteer, non-profit organization of science fiction and fantasy fans. Besides publishing, our activities include running Boskone (New England's oldest SF convention) in February each year, producing a semi-monthly newsletter, holding discussion groups relating to the field, and hosting a variety of social events. If you are interested in learning more about us, we'd like to hear from you. Write to our address above!